Rave reader reviews for

CONFLUENCE ACADEMY, BOOK ONE

'Elemental powers, deadly tr
and the most chaotic ancie
★

'Like *Divergent, Harry Potter*
rolled into one. I literally cannot wait for the second book
★★★★★

'The world building, found family, magical animal companions
and slow-burn : . . I cannot recommend this book enough!'
★★★★★

'This book had me in a chokehold. Loved it all the way'
★★★★★

'This book deserves to go as viral as *Fourth Wing*! I loved it.
The characters, the plot . . . the yearning!'
★★★★★

'You will not want to put it down . . .
definitely the best read of the year for me'
★★★★★

'Full of tension, longing, and those irresistible
"touch her and die" vibes'
★★★★★

'This is going to be in my new top five romantasy novels'
★★★★★

UNBOUND

CONFLUENCE ACADEMY, BOOK ONE

PENELOPE BLOOM

MLP

First published in 2025 by Penelope Bloom

This paperback edition first published in 2025 by Mountain Leopard Press.
An imprint of Headline Publishing Group Limited.

1

Cataloguing in Publication Data is available from the British Library

Paperback ISBN 978 1 0354 4151 8

Typeset Garamond by CC Book Production

Printed and bound in Great Britain by Clays Ltd, Elcograf S.p.A.

Headline Publishing Group Limited
An Hachette UK Company
Carmelite House
50 Victoria Embankment
London EC4Y 0DZ

The authorised representative in the EEA is Hachette Ireland,
8 Castlecourt Centre, Dublin 15, D15 XTP3, Ireland
(email: info@hbgi.ie)

www.headline.co.uk
www.hachette.co.uk

Chapter 1

I volunteered to die four days ago. Now that the carriage finally stops rolling, I know the end is almost here.

Outside the padded carriage walls, voices shout orders, wagon wheels creak, and boots stomp through mud.

The selector snaps his fingers for my attention. 'We've arrived.'

'Where are we?'

'You'll see soon enough.' He produces a small badge with the letter 'V' from a pocket in his fancy robe. 'Pin this to your tunic.'

I take it, examining the metal. 'What's this for?'

'It marks you as a volunteer.'

I hesitantly pin the 'V' badge to my tunic, feeling like I've been branded. My fingers tremble slightly as I secure it, the metal cold against my skin. *Volunteer.* Technically, I suppose it's the truth, even if I felt like I had no choice in the matter. 'Why does it matter if I volunteered?'

'Confluence Academy keeps extensive records. It will be noted as you're processed and then you'll be free to discard the badge. The "why" beyond that is none of your concern.'

Confluence Academy? The words hit like a punch.

Confluence is the school where primals are trained. It is an even more well-kept secret than facts about the primals themselves. It's usually talked about with the same level of belief as vampires, siphons, and werewolves. Yet the selector just casually implied we're parked outside its doorstep.

'I thought Confluence Academy was just a story.'

'It's quite real, offering.' He sighs the words, as if this is a tiresome conversation he's had dozens of times – as if dragging people from their homes to a place they hardly believed existed was ordinary. 'Take her,' he says, nodding to the guards.

I'm hauled to my feet, my legs stiff and aching from days of travel. My heartbeat quickens, a desperate flutter against my ribs as reality crashes down. A stupid, hopeful part of me wants to believe that if this really is Confluence Academy, I might actually have a chance to live.

An academy. As in, a place where people are trained. It's not a sacrificial pit. There's not a fire dragon waiting to eat me outside the carriage like kids used to whisper about when I was little.

But it still feels wrong. Empire takes one person aged between eighteen and twenty-one from every town and city each year. Nobody ever sees them again. If the offerings collected by selectors were becoming primals, surely some would come back to tell their loved ones. The truth would get out.

The guard shoves open the carriage door, and I'm thrust into a world of pure chaos.

The damp, earthy smell of mud churned by hundreds of horses and boots hits me first. Then the pungent stench of fear and stale sweat. And something else – like the air after lightning strikes, but sharper. More alive.

My stomach knots so violently I nearly double over. I know that smell. It's the same smell that came with the storm three years ago. The smell that follows me into my nightmares. It's the smell of magic.

The phantom salt spray stings my eyes as the memory claws its way up my throat, threatening to drown me all over again. I push away the memories that threaten to surface – the screams, the water, the sickening sound of wood splitting beneath our feet. My fingers tremble, and I curl them into fists, using the bite of my nails against my palms to ground myself in the present.

Taking a deep breath, I force myself to focus on my surroundings instead of the past.

Hundreds, maybe thousands of carriages just like mine fill the massive courtyard spreading before me. Imperial guards herd dazed offerings from their vehicles toward a central location. The other offerings show just how far Empire's reach extends through their clothing – flowing silks from the eastern provinces, thick wools from the north, lightweight linens like mine from the coastal regions. I even spot a cluster of people who might be from the many islands that neighbor the main continent.

And all of them were selected, chosen out of a random lottery. Sentenced to die.

I idly trace the 'V' badge on my tunic. I thought I was ready to die, but I can't lie to myself. Ever since the Selector told us where we were . . . ever since that moment, I've felt the spark of hope threatening to ignite my insides.

Dragging my eyes from the crowd, I look up at the structure looming behind the sea of offerings and guards.

The sight steals my breath.

A castle rises before us, so vast it makes the defensive keep back home in Saltcrest look like a child's toy. Four colossal towers stand at each corner, each one distinctly different from the others.

The first looks more like a pillar of earth, as if carved from a single massive piece of granite, roots and vines climbing its surface like grasping fingers. I almost imagine I can see the stone itself breathing, expanding and contracting as if alive.

The second shimmers as currents of white air curl up its elegantly carved shape, swirling into clouds at its peak that seem to dance and shift. Occasionally, tiny lightning flashes illuminate the mist from within.

The third is constructed of dark, burnt stone covered in licking flames that send plumes of smoke skyward, yet the stone never burns or crumbles. The fire pulses with each gust of wind, almost like a heartbeat.

And the fourth is completely encased in a shimmering wall of water. Water that flows upward against the pull of the earth, against everything that makes sense.

My heart pounds against my ribs. These aren't just decorative elements. These are elemental manifestations of magic – real, tangible power on display as casually as other castles might display banners.

The central structure between these towers looks large enough to house thousands, its walls tall and imposing.

Confluence Academy. Just like the selector said. It has to be.

That tiny spark of hope turns to a flame – a flame I'm terrified to nurture but can't bring myself to extinguish. Could it really be true? That we've been brought here to train, not for slaughter? If they're going to make us into primals, it would mean far more than just surviving.

It would mean power. The kind of power that could make things right again. The kind that could have saved them.

Primals are the elite of the elite, and the magic they command is the stuff of legends. Rarely seen, often heard about, and completely surrounded in mystery and confusion. And now I'm standing in front of the academy that creates them. My eyes see it, and yet my mind still refuses to fully believe.

'Move it, offering!' A guard shoves me between my shoulder blades, and I stumble forward, nearly falling face-first into the mud.

I recover my balance and join the line of other offerings being marched through enormous doors, through a courtyard full of activity, and then into the castle's main hall. It's so much to take in I hardly even notice the pangs of hunger and thirst or the ache of being cramped in the carriage for days on end.

I catch glimpses of what must be students, most of whom are ignoring us. They're all too far to get a clear look at, though, and we're being marched through the building at a rough pace.

Looking around at the other offerings, I see badges like mine, except none bear the letter 'V.' The most common, by far, is an 'O.' There are a few 'R' badges scattered into the mix as well, but nobody else seems to have been crazy enough to volunteer like I did.

Several offerings nearby stare openly at my badge, whispering to their neighbors and pointing. Their gazes burn into me, making my skin itch. I fight the urge to rip the damn thing off and throw it away. I know it's irrational, but I almost feel like they can see my shame – see straight into my heart and know how ready I was to die for what I did.

One boy with hollow cheeks catches my eye. 'Why would you volunteer?' he asks, his voice barely audible over the commotion. 'Are you mad? They're going to kill us all, don't you realize that?'

Before I can respond, a guard shoves him forward, and his thin frame disappears into the crowd.

The great hall steals my attention. Soaring ceilings arch impossibly high above us, supported by columns carved to resemble various mythical creatures. Colored light streams through stained glass windows depicting epic battles between humans with glowing markings and elemental creatures. Some of the paintings look absolutely ancient, and they show humans fighting elementals – the wars that shattered civilization and brought us back to the beginning.

We're assembled into orderly rows facing a raised dais at the far end of the hall. I'm positioned beside a red-haired girl with mud-streaked cheeks and an oddly serene expression, despite our circumstances. A guard gives her a particularly rough shove, knocking her off balance.

I catch her arm before she falls, steadying her. 'You okay?'

She nods, offering a quick smile that brightens her whole face despite the grime. 'I'm Mireen. Thank you.'

'Nessa.'

'So . . .' her voice is low, quiet, and tinged with wry humor. 'Want to take bets on which of us is going to die first?'

'What would be . . .' I begin, trailing off as her smile widens.

'Sorry,' Mireen says. 'Where I'm from, we see a lot of death. I find joking about it makes the whole thing just a touch less terrifying.'

'In any case,' I say, keeping my voice to a whisper. 'Maybe death isn't so certain. Why would they mark us with badges and go through all this just to execute us? This is Confluence Academy. What if they brought us here to train us? To become primals?'

The words sound pathetic even to my own ears – the desperate bargaining of someone who's suddenly realized they're not ready to die after all. Minutes ago, I was ready to die. Now I find myself clinging so tight to the idea of survival it makes me sick.

'What if they brought us here as food for the students?' a boy beside us asks, his eyes wide with terror. 'Maybe primals eat people.'

'Primals don't eat people,' another voice responds.

'You sure about that? You ever seen a primal eat?'

'Never seen a primal. Period.'

Mireen offers me a sidelong glance that says she at least doesn't think we're about to be consumed. Then her eyes widen when they fall to my badge. 'A "V"? That means you volunteered, right?'

'It's a long story.' I can feel my expression shuttering, walls sliding into place like fortress gates before an attack.

To my surprise, Mireen nods instead of pressing me for answers. 'I didn't even think this place was real.' She looks around the large hall as more offerings are led in by guards.

A lanky boy with intelligent eyes sidles up beside me. Unlike the fear evident on most faces, he carries himself with quiet confidence.

'Ah! So there is another volunteer,' he says, nodding at my badge. 'Only two so far in the entire gathering. That's two out of about fifteen hundred offerings. Have you met him? The other "V"?'

'I haven't . . .'

'I'm Nolan, by the way.'

'Nessa.'

'In any case. Curious that so few would volunteer, isn't it? Or is it just that the tight age window means most loved ones aren't eligible to do it?' He has a rambling way of talking, almost as if he's thinking aloud.

I glance down at his badge and see an 'R'. 'What does yours mean?'

'Replacement. Somebody with no eligible next-of-kin ran once they were selected, and I was taken in their place.' He shrugs. 'It's okay though. My cousin is training to be a diviner, and she said she's picked up fire affinity markers in me.'

'Fire?' Mireen whispers, instinctively shifting away from him.

His smile falters. 'What, afraid I'm a Red Kingdom spy?' He wiggles his fingers, as if poking fun at the very idea.

'My uncle died fighting Red Kingdom. His unit was wiped out by one of their fire primals. Every last soldier burned so badly their armor was the only thing left on the field.' Her voice trembles with sudden, barely contained anger, all her easy-going nature evaporated in an instant.

I notice her slight accent then – a subtle drawl that marks her as a deep norther. Up that close to the border, tensions between Red Kingdom and Empire are on everyone's mind every day. The war is literally in their backyards. No wonder she said they see a lot of death where she's from.

Even for the relatively fortunate like those of us in Saltcrest, the war's reach is long. Supply blockages often cripple port trade, leading to shortages and starvation. The famine that claimed my best friend's life hit when I was just eight, and it was a direct result of the war.

'I'm Empire-born,' Nolan cuts in, voice tight. 'Last time I checked, Empire still accepts fire and earth primals. I'd be fighting right alongside people like your uncle if I became a primal.'

'And yet you don't have to look far to find stories of fires and earths betraying Empire. Turning coat to join Red Kingdom. They can't be trusted,' Mireen counters.

'Not every fire and earth elemental is loyal to Red Kingdom,' Nolan argues. 'Some of them choose to side with Empire, and Empire should be glad for it.' He stands straighter, back rigid with indignance.

'Come on,' I say, looking between them. 'We're all in the same boat now. The last thing we need is to make enemies of each other.'

Nolan shrugs, offering a hand to Mireen.

She swallows, then takes and shakes, even if she doesn't look particularly happy about it.

'Do you know what they're going to do with us?' I ask them both.

'You don't know?' Nolan says, leaning in and lowering his voice. 'It was a long journey from Marrow's Edge to here, which gave me quite some time to press my selector for answers. Tight-lipped fellow, but I did gather this much: they're going to test us for elemental affinity. Dangerous as all hells, of course. But people like me with affinities should survive.'

'Test us? How?' My pulse quickens, a bird's panicked flutter trapped beneath my skin.

'He wouldn't say. I did get the distinct impression it is a rather . . . deadly process, though. I'm afraid our numbers will thin dramatically before day's end.'

A thick lump forms in my throat as I look at Mireen. Her wide eyes say she's just as unhappy with the news.

'You never answered before. Did you meet the other "V" yet?' Nolan asks suddenly.

I shake my head.

'He's just coming into the room now. Right there,' he says, pointing through the crowd.

I follow his finger and feel the air rush from my lungs.

The other volunteer is tall, broader and more muscular than anyone else in our group, standing apart like a predator among prey. The space around him is conspicuously empty, as if everyone senses the danger rolling off him in waves.

He's beautiful in the way dangerous things often are – like the perfect stillness of a viper before it strikes. The moment of collapsed time when the danger is as clear as the impossibility of escape.

His features are carved perfection, sharp and soft in all the right places. He has a strong jaw, a mouth that looks made for both cruelty and pleasure, and those eyes – gods help me – they're the deepest shade of amber I've ever seen, almost molten gold in the fading light.

He turns to look straight at me, and everything else fades. The world narrows to a tunnel with him at the end of it, and my heart forgets to beat. Even across the distance, those eyes burn into me with an intensity that makes my chest tighten and my throat dry. Heat rushes through my body unbidden – a reaction I can neither control nor understand.

The left side of his face is twisted with burn scars that begin at his temple and disappear beneath his collar, yet somehow they only enhance his dangerous allure, like veins of fire frozen beneath his skin.

It's impossible not to hold my breath as his attention lingers on me.

Looking at him reminds me of how I used to feel back home on our fishing boat when a storm was about to roll in. Some instinctive part of me knew I needed to drop the oars and row for the docks – to save myself from the raw power coming my way. And yet all I ever wanted to do was stand there and stare. I wanted to watch the dark clouds gather and morph as the wind blew them straight for me, even when thunder shook the air itself.

Maybe that's why I can't look away. I've spent the last three years going out on our boat, secretly wishing those same storm clouds would roll in and wash me away, too. To urge the waters that took half my family to take me, too.

The scarred volunteer seems to offer the same kind of deadly promise – total annihilation by proximity, as if all it would take is to drift within his orbit to be torn to shreds.

I realize he's staring right back at me still, and I'm suddenly aware of just how fast I'm breathing and how hard my heart is beating. As his gaze drops to the 'V' on my chest, something in his expression shifts. His eyes narrow, and his jaw tightens. For a split second, I see his fingers curl into his palm, knuckles fading from a deep tanned color to pure white.

He stalks toward me with purposeful strides, his movements fluid like a predator's, and the crowd parts before him without hesitation.

Oh shit.

'Who is he?' I whisper, not taking my eyes off him.

'Not sure. Scary bastard though, isn't he?' Nolan murmurs. 'With burns like that, I'd bet he's from the border regions. Maybe even lived in Red Kingdom territory before Empire reclaimed it.'

Mireen's posture stiffens beside me. 'I heard the guards talking about a volunteer from the Red Kingdom border. If he's from there, you can't trust him, no matter which side he claims to be on.'

Before either of us can say more, the burned volunteer stops directly in front of me. He's even more imposing up close, towering at least a foot above me. The burn scars on his face tell a story of pain and survival, the tissue rippled and angry against his bronze skin. A muscle in his jaw ticks as he stares down at me.

'Volunteer,' he says, his voice deep and rough, like stones grinding together. 'Let me guess – here to serve the glorious Empire?'

The contempt in his voice when he says 'Empire' tells me everything I need to know about where his loyalties lie – or at least where they once did. Mireen might actually be right about him.

'I have my reasons,' I answer, lifting my chin to meet his gaze despite the way my heart hammers against my ribs.

'I'm sure you do,' he says. 'Someone probably fed you stories about honor and duty since you were a child. Made you believe sacrificing yourself meant something.'

His words sink into me like barbed hooks, drawing blood as they tear at wounds that haven't even begun to heal. They sting because they're a reminder that the only thing my sacrifice will have bought back home is relief. Relief that I'm gone and can't cause any more pain and suffering to the ones I love.

But I push the pain down, eyes hard as I stare up at him. 'You volunteered too. Are you speaking from experience?'

Something flashes in his eyes – surprise, maybe, that I'd challenge him. 'My reasons are my own.'

'What a coincidence. Mine too.' There's more ice in my voice than I expect, but I'm glad for it. This guy is beautiful, but he's a complete asshole.

He studies me for a moment, his amber eyes searching my face as if looking for something specific. 'So eager to die for a kingdom that sees you as nothing but a weapon.'

'You don't know a thing about me.'

He leans closer, and I can feel the unnatural heat radiating from his skin. 'You expect them to make a hero out of you. You'll be a weapon. An instrument of war. A scythe to reap the lives of thousands. Is that what you volunteered for?'

'I'm not here for Empire,' I say, the words coming out before I can stop them. 'I'm here because—' I snap my mouth shut.

No. He doesn't deserve an explanation. Nobody here does.

For a moment, the hostility in his eyes dims, replaced by something that looks almost like curiosity.

'Don't get in my way,' he finally says, his voice low. 'Whatever your reasons, this place will kill you soon enough.'

'Is that a threat?' I ask.

The ghost of a smile touches his lips. 'It's a fact.'

Before I can respond, a commotion at the front of the hall draws everyone's attention. The burned volunteer steps back, his expression closing off entirely.

He turns to leave.

'Wait,' I call after him. 'What's your name?'

He pauses, looking back at me over his shoulder. For a moment, I think he won't answer.

'Raith,' he finally says, the name landing like a challenge. Then he's gone, disappearing into the crowd as guards enter, followed by students in fitted black uniforms with silver trim.

'What was that about?' Mireen whispers, staring after him.

'I have no idea,' I say honestly. But the imprint of his gaze lingers on my skin like a brand, and I can still feel the unnatural heat radiating from him. Something about our exchange leaves me unsettled – and not just because of his hostility. There was something in his eyes when I said I wasn't here for Empire. It was almost calculating, and I wonder if I would've been better off letting him think he understood me. Do I really want a man like that feeling curious enough to keep an eye on me?

But there's no use because I suspect I already have his attention.

A hush falls over the hall as seven primals stride in, each accompanied by an elemental creature. The temperature shifts instantly, patches of cold sweeping through the gathered crowd.

I gawk at the creatures in their wake.

They come in all shapes and sizes. A wolf twice the size of a man made of pure water with sapphire eyes. A large eagle formed of swirling air currents. A thick serpent made of stone, flapping through the air on craggy wings as if it were weightless. There's even a fiery bird like a phoenix soaring above the group.

I've never seen anything so beautiful and terrifying – like watching destruction and creation dance together in perfect harmony.

Primals are something people whisper about – forces of death and destruction in the deepest, most dangerous battles of the endless war between Empire and Red Kingdom. Actually seeing them in the flesh makes me feel like I'm in a dream.

But are these even fully fledged primals ready for war? They don't look much older than us, making me wonder if they aren't even finished with their training yet. Whatever they are, they still seem terrifyingly powerful, and their elementals all look capable of shredding or crushing us if they wished it.

'Listen carefully,' a primal with a glowing white swirl of air marked on the back of his left hand says. He steps forward, his voice somehow amplified as a huge bear made of swirling winds prowls behind him. 'Legacies will proceed directly to the feast hall for dormitory assignments and orientation. Aspirants will report to Commander Starke for combat assessment.'

The 'legacies' and 'aspirants,' who seem to have already been given clean and well-made black uniforms, file out quietly. The legacies wear uniforms trimmed in silver and gold, while the aspirants have only the silver trim.

Among the group of legacies, one boy stands slightly apart. Unlike his peers who show off their elemental tricks, he observes with a measured stillness. He's tall, blond, and looks almost too pretty to be attractive. *Almost.*

When his nearly white eyes sweep across the mass of offerings, they linger briefly on me – not with disdain but with curiosity.

I feel myself blush, almost as if I'm worried he could hear my thoughts somehow. But then I realize he's just looking at the 'V' on my chest, and his attention makes more sense.

'Offerings,' the older student continues, his expression solemn. 'You stand at the threshold of a great honor – the test of elemental affinity. Those who pass will join the ranks of Empire's most elite. Those who do not . . .' he pauses, his gaze sweeping over us, 'will have given their lives in service to Empire. Remember, to be chosen as an offering is itself a profound distinction. This is not a punishment. This is the greatest opportunity you could ever hope to be granted. Remember that.'

The words sound noble, but the cold reality behind them isn't lost on any of us. Many, if not all of us, are sentenced to death, and our sentence is about to be carried out.

I can sense others around me shifting in fear, eyes wide with worry.

I don't feel fear, though. I only feel determination. All the pain I caused . . . maybe surviving here could somehow fix it. Maybe a primal could return home and make things right for Brissa and my mother. Maybe a primal could earn their forgiveness where I couldn't.

'What if we refuse testing?' someone calls out.

The boy shakes his head. 'You will all enter the testing chamber, whether on your feet or . . . otherwise.'

Another nervous murmur ripples through the crowd of offerings.

'Now,' he says, chin lifted, 'you'll all be taken to the Great Hall of Testing. Within, you'll either discover your affinity . . . or you'll meet your end. In either case, I suggest you face it with boldness.'

Before the guards can lead us away, a voice stops me.

'I wouldn't get too close to that one if I were you.'

I turn to see the legacy I'd noticed earlier standing beside me, his uniform pristine, his handsome face set in a friendly expression that doesn't quite reach his eyes. His wavy blonde hair is pushed back neatly from a broad forehead, revealing blue eyes so pale I'd taken them for white at a distance.

'Who?' I ask, instantly wary.

'The scarred volunteer. I'm Bastian,' he says, extending a hand. 'First-year, just like you.'

Except he's not just like me. Everything about him screams

privilege and good breeding – from his perfectly styled hair to his confident stance, as if the world has never once failed to deliver exactly what he wanted.

Coldness colors my smile. 'I'm Nessa. First-year who is apparently about to be forced to risk my life in a test I didn't consent to.'

Bastian offers a tight-lipped nod. 'It's frightening. I know.'

He doesn't. He can't know.

'Some of us legacies have been asked to help orient offerings these first few days. So, please, let me know if there's anything I can do to help.' He sticks his hand out.

'Sure. Get me out of having to take this test.' I take his offered hand reluctantly.

His handshake is firm, and as our hands touch, I feel a strange ripple of energy pass between us. He pulls back quickly, eyes sharpening slightly before his smile returns.

An uncomfortable moment passes before he speaks. 'My advice is to embrace the opportunity. It's like he said. We're all getting a chance to become something greater than we could have ever imagined. If we succeed here, we'll be critical pieces in the Empire's army, capable of defending thousands by ourselves.'

'Eager to become a pawn on somebody's chess board, are you?' I ask.

Bastian offers a surprised, half-cocked smile. 'We're all already on the board, Nessa. Better to turn yourself into a key piece instead of an expendable pawn, isn't it?'

I can't help smiling back. He has a point.

Bastian cuts his eyes toward the burned volunteer. 'By the way. I meant what I said earlier. Those from the border – even the ones technically on Empire's side . . . be careful trusting them. Those territories change hands often, and sometimes the ties to Empire are superficial.'

'What, do you think he's a spy or something?'

Bastian's expression is cryptic. 'I think anyone who volunteers for this place has secrets.' His gaze drops to my badge, then back to my face.

I wonder if I'm only a curiosity to him – something to watch with detached interest.

Before either of us can say more, guards shove me and the other offerings forward into the Hall of Testing. I give Bastian one last look, his tall form easily visible over the crowd, until I'm led down a long flight of stairs with the others.

We enter a cavernous chamber, easily large enough to hold all fifteen hundred offerings. Massive pillars carved to resemble intertwined elemental beasts support a ceiling so high it disappears into shadow. A pair of ornate double doors stand at the far end of the room. They're covered in glowing symbols that shift and change as I watch.

Smoke swirls and clings to the ground here. Colored light occasionally shifts from behind the doors, casting long streaks through the smoke that give the room an otherworldly atmosphere.

Beyond the doors, something growls, low and deep.

There's a collective shudder among the offerings, who are all being packed tightly into the room like cattle awaiting slaughter. It's only seconds before the air grows stale with our collective breath and fear.

A handful of guards stand in a semicircle before the doors, their faces impassive as they consult a long scroll.

'I bet I'm air,' a girl near me whispers excitedly to her neighbor. 'My grandmother could always predict storms before they came. That has to mean something, right?'

'My uncle says I've got water in my blood,' another boy responds. 'Says I swim better than fish.'

All around me, offerings whisper about their suspected affinities, clinging to family stories and coincidences like lifelines. Their words speak of confidence, but their voices betray them – a shakiness and frantic energy that reveals the terror they're trying so desperately to hide.

'They're all delusional,' Nolan mutters beside me. 'At best, one in six of us survives this.'

'Then why do you sound so confident?' I ask.

He gives me a thin smile. 'It's like I said. My cousin said I have fire affinity markers. Strong ones.'

'I hope you're right.' I mean it. Despite barely knowing him, I don't want any of these people to die. But I also don't want to die myself, and the realization sits like a stone in my gut – a selfish, heavy thing I can't quite dislodge.

A guard's voice suddenly cuts through the chamber, silencing all the voices. 'Eris Moraven.'

A girl near the front straightens her shoulders, looks around nervously, and then walks forward. 'Wish me luck,' she says.

A few nearby offerings mutter encouraging words.

The doors swing open just enough to admit her, then close with a heavy thud that reverberates through the stone floor.

The room falls silent. We all wait, barely breathing.

Ten seconds pass. Twenty.

Then we hear it – a scream so filled with terror and pain it doesn't sound human, cut short by a wet, tearing sound that turns my stomach. Blue light flashes beneath the doors, and the smell of ozone fills the air along with the coppery tang of blood.

Someone near me retches. A girl begins to sob quietly, the sound muffled by her hands pressed desperately against her mouth.

The playful whispers and hopeful chatter doesn't return. Silence reigns, because now we all understand what we're really waiting for.

Our turns to die.

Chapter 2

'Nessa Thorne.'

My name echoes through the antechamber, and my stomach drops like it's been cut loose from its moorings. The stench of burnt flesh still lingers from when Nolan entered that room thirty minutes ago. His screams had been mercifully brief.

The fire affinity markers he was so confident about hadn't saved him. And now it's my turn.

Mireen's hand finds my arm, her copper-red braid coiled like a crown around her head catching the dim, flickering torchlight. 'Good luck, Nessa.' She gives me a small, encouraging smile that crinkles the crescent-shaped scar at the corner of one eye. 'Remember, if you die in there I win the bet.'

I grin. 'I'll see you on the other side, Mireen.'

Just a few short days ago, I thought I already gave up my life when I volunteered. But now I feel soul-shaking terror, like I want nothing more than to run from this room and this claustrophobic place. It's as if some stubborn shred of hope has shone through thick clouds – a beam of yellow cutting across a gray landscape – and now it's the only thing I can see.

My legs feel weighted with lead as I force them forward, one reluctant step after another. My heart hammers against my ribs. I imagine the other offerings feel the same thing I felt as I watched others enter these doors. Relief it wasn't my turn yet. Guilt for feeling relief.

I take a deep breath and step through the doorway. The doors slam shut behind me with a sound like judgment, locking me inside with whatever horrors wait in this chamber.

The metallic taste of fear floods my mouth as I take in the circular room, far larger than I'd expected. The air crackles with power and smells of storms, burnt flesh, and the unmistakable tang of blood – so potent it makes my stomach heave. My heart thunders in my ears, drowning out everything but the screaming of my instincts to run, to hide, to escape. I force down the bile rising in my throat and scan the room, trying to steady my breathing.

That's when I see them. Bodies. Dozens – maybe hundreds – scattered across the floor in grotesque positions. People who stood where I'm standing not long ago, people who failed whatever test awaits me.

I swallow a scream of terror when I spot Nolan's wide, unblinking eyes staring from his charred corpse. His fingers are curled like claws, as if he'd tried to fight the fire that consumed him. A fire that couldn't have been natural – his clothes are barely singed while his flesh is blackened, like he burned from the inside out.

The scream building in my chest gets trapped behind clenched teeth, transforming into a strangled whimper that sounds pathetic even to my own ears. I force my eyes away from the carnage and look up at the chamber's vaulted ceiling, which disappears into shadow. With a shaky breath, I find some semblance of calm. I'm either going to die here, or I'm going to survive. Either way, I'd rather do it with my chin held high.

I walk up a series of steps, gradually bringing the 'test' into view, along with my first glimpse of . . . them. I avert my eyes at first, almost like looking away from the sun on a bright and clear day, focusing instead on the mundane.

I look at the four decorative stone pedestals, each supporting a vessel.

A bowl of black soil that smells of loam and decay. A silver brazier holding blue-white flames that dance and twist as if alive. A glass sphere filled with swirling air currents visible only through the dust they carry. A basin of water so still it resembles polished crystal, reflecting the room like a perfect mirror.

And behind each vessel stands an elemental of the corresponding element.

Elementals.

The power radiating from them presses down on my chest until my lungs strain for air. It's like being crushed by an invisible ocean, ancient and vast beyond comprehension. Their presence fills the chamber with an ancient, primal energy that makes my skin prickle and my bones ache. Every instinct screams at me to kneel, to bow, to show submission before creatures so much more powerful than myself.

But I don't. I take them in one by one, studying their strange features.

The earth elemental resembles a woman crafted of living stone and twisting roots, her eyes gleaming like a jungle cat's in the dim light. The fire elemental is barely humanoid, more a swirling column of flame with a face that forms and dissolves above the blaze. The air elemental is a shimmering distortion visible mainly through the way it bends light around its vaguely human shape.

And the water elemental . . . my breath catches at the sight of him. He takes the form of a warrior, tall and powerfully built, his body composed of crystal-clear water that occasionally reveals glimpses of stronger currents beneath, like rippling muscles. His face is strikingly handsome – strong-jawed with high cheekbones and eyes that are deeper than the most distant oceans.

Elementals in stories are always beasts – wolves, great sand worms, flying reptiles and sea serpents. I've never heard anything about elementals who can take the form of humans.

A pressure builds against my mind, making my temples throb.

'Approach.'

The word forms in my mind so clearly I think I can actually hear it. No – I do hear it, resonating through my skull like a physical vibration.

My knees almost buckle beneath me, my body rebelling against the sheer power behind that single command. My legs tremble as I force them to carry me forward, stopping at what I hope is a respectful distance. Their attention weighs on me until it nearly forces me to my knees, making me wish I could turn away as I might from the sun on a bright day with clear skies.

'*Purpose? Reason? Volunteer?*' The questions bubble up in my mind, clear and yet seeming to come from all directions at once.

I realize they're asking why I'm here, why I wear the volunteer's badge that marks me as someone who chose this path rather than being selected.

'It's complicated,' I say, my voice sounding thin and weak in the vast chamber.

'*Lie. Give us truth, or die.*'

The command slams into my mind with such force that my knees finally give, making me fall with my palms on the ground and head bowed. I feel the truth being dragged from me, as if their combined will is a hook in my soul.

'I volunteered because everyone was better off without me,' I admit, the words tasting bitter on my tongue. Some things feel more noble when they're never voiced – ideas rooted in logic so flawed it won't survive inspection.

'*Half-truth.*'

I sigh, fists clenching until my nails dig tiny crescents of blood from my palms. 'I got half my family killed, okay? Is that what you all want me to say?' My voice rises, cracking with emotion. 'They died because of me. They died because I couldn't control my emotions, and the storm came.'

My throat constricts around the words as they claw their way out, each syllable cutting like daggers dragged from my insides. I lower my voice, tears streaming down my cheeks.

'I don't know why it happened or how. I just know it happened because of me. I felt some part of me pulling the storm toward us, stoking it like a flame. It didn't matter how hard I tried to stop it.'

I swallow hard, the memory of black waves and screaming winds so vivid I can almost feel the spray on my face. The phantom roar of the tempest fills my ears, drowning out even the thundering of my heart. I think I can even taste the salt water on my tongue for a moment. I can smell that scent of ozone. *Magic.*

The elementals just stare down at me and the words keep pouring from my lips.

'Both my brothers and my dad died. For some reason . . . I didn't. My mom and sister never forgave me. I was a reminder to them. An unwelcome memory, and getting in that carriage was my way of making amends for what I did. Trying to, at least.'

I hang my head, throat thick with unshed tears. Every breath hurts like I'm inhaling shards of glass. I never talk about what happened – it's been locked inside me so long that speaking it aloud feels like tearing open a half-healed wound.

The elementals seem to confer amongst themselves, not with words but with pulses of energy that make the air shimmer and crack. The fire elemental flares suddenly, its form growing larger, tongues of flame reaching toward the ceiling. The earth elemental remains still, but the ground beneath my feet trembles like the beginning of an earthquake. The air elemental's form becomes more distinct, as if concentrating its essence. And the water elemental leans forward, his liquid features showing what almost looks like curiosity.

'*Begin the test.*'

That's it? I have to pour my fucking heart out and they just tell me to start the test? No words of comfort, no acknowledgment of my pain? Just a command, as if I were some kind of trained animal?

Anger flares hot in my chest, momentarily burning away the fear. The sheer audacity, the callousness – but anger won't keep me alive, and I swallow it down like bitter medicine.

The bodies surrounding me and the terrible smells are enough of a reminder. This isn't the time or place to be difficult. Heart thundering, I force myself to look back up at them. 'How do I begin?'

The water elemental gestures toward the four vessels.

'*Choose. Touch. Reveal.*'

I study each vessel in turn as I try to steady my breathing. The water vessel makes the most sense, of course. My home was on the coast. I spent half my life on the water, swimming before I could walk, helping my father and brothers with their fishing nets by the time I was six. And I'm almost certain I carry 'water affinity markers' as Nolan would have put it.

But those markers could go fuck themselves. They're the reason my father and brothers are dead – their bones long since picked away by fish in Deep Bay. If I might have an affinity for water, I'm not sure I want it. Every day would be a reminder of what I did and what I lost.

I turn away from the water vessel and approach the fire.

The heat intensifies with each step until it's nearly unbearable, like opening an oven door and leaning in. Sweat beads on my forehead and trickles down my back.

I stare into the flames, realizing they, more than any of the other elements, reflect how I feel inside. Fire, brimstone, ash. Those are the images in my mind – the flavor of my current state. I don't know how this test works. I don't even know if I'll only have one chance to prove an affinity before I'm obliterated like Nolan.

Frankly, I can't find it in me to care. Not right now. Not when everything feels so raw that I'm almost ready to embrace the idea of death.

I killed them. It was my fault.

Grief rises in a suffocating wave, threatening to pull me under completely. I don't fight it, letting it wash over me like the black waters that claimed my family.

I extend my hand, hovering it above the flames, close enough to feel my skin tighten and redden. I'm so tired of carrying this guilt, this burden. If the fire cleanses me, so be it.

I close my eyes, welcoming whatever might come.

But the fire has vanished, as if snuffed out. All that's left is the feeling of warmth inside my body, pleasant and powerful.

The fire elemental makes a sound like crackling embers, its form pulsing with what feels like alarm. Or maybe that's anger . . .

When none of them speak or move, I understand that I'm supposed to continue. I let out a long breath, then move to the next basin.

I approach the earth vessel, the scent of rich soil growing stronger. It reminds me of my family's small garden, of my mother teaching me to plant seeds when I was young. A memory from before everything went wrong. Back then, she was still able to look me in the eye without her hatred and disgust showing through.

As my fingers near the bowl of black soil, green vines sprout from the dirt, reaching up toward my palm and glowing as they touch, filling me with a sense of nature and connectedness. I frown, turning my hand over and finding it unmarked.

The earth elemental tilts her head, stone features grinding as she studies me with renewed intensity. I sense more communication firing between the elementals than before, almost giving me the impression of some kind of argument. Their energy pulses make my ears pop and my skin tingle uncomfortably.

The air sphere comes next.

As I present my palm, the winds collect and flow upward. I feel a lightness and nimble energy gathering inside my body.

The air elemental's form pulses and flickers, becoming less distinct as it retreats slightly.

That sense of raised voices and tempers increases even more. I feel it like a headache building behind my eyes, pressure growing until I'm sure my skull will crack.

Confusion and dread twist together in my gut like serpents. Something is wrong – terribly wrong – and I'm caught in the middle of it without understanding why. I may not understand what's happening, but I know I need to continue.

With a sense of inevitability, I move toward the final vessel. The water elemental looms above it, watching me with those bottomless eyes. My mouth goes dry as I approach, my pulse pounding so hard I can feel it in my fingertips.

I study the water, eyes cold and heart distant. I reach out toward it, my fingertips hovering just above the surface. For a breath, nothing happens. Then the water begins to float upward in droplets that gather in my palm before sinking into my skin. The sensation of cool calm and serenity fills me to join the other strange feelings.

A deep vibration fills the chamber as the wordless conversation continues. I focus on it, trying to hear the words through the pounding in my head.

Words roar in my mind, each so loud they seem to shake the air itself.

'Impossible.'

'Dangerous.'

'Potential.'

'Kill her.'

And then, more clearly and powerfully than any of the words before . . .

'Unbound.'

Movement catches my eye just as I feel heat flare against my left cheek. I whirl and see the huge fire elemental has raised a hand toward me. In that split-second, I know he plans to kill me.

This is it. This is how it ends.

My eyes lock with the fire elemental's molten gaze, and in that moment, I see only hatred – a burning need to erase me from existence. Time slows to a crawl.

Fire erupts from the elemental in a swirling vortex of flashing red and orange. The heat is so intense my skin blisters instantly, my hair crisping at the ends. I throw my arms up uselessly, a scream tearing from my throat.

But then the heat and the roar of fire is gone – replaced by the cool rush of water surrounding me in a perfect, shifting sphere. The water soothes my scorched skin, the pain ebbing away like a retreating tide.

The water elemental. He's saving me from the fire elemental. But why?

Steam rushes away from the outside of the sphere in a deafening hiss, even as the fire elemental roars in rage and blasts more magic toward me. Through the distorted wall of water, I see the water elemental standing between us, one arm extended toward me, the other toward the fire being.

'Do you truly fear a human so deeply, Pyraxis?' The water elemental's thoughts ripple through my mind like waves lapping at the shore.

'You dare call me a coward?' The fire elemental's response is more of a bestial roar than true words, burning through my thoughts.

'No. I ask you to seek understanding. Destruction will bring no answers, old friend. We need to exercise calm. Serenity. Patience.' The water elemental's mental voice is deep and steady, like the ocean depths.

'And if our patience allows her power to fester? To destroy balance? To kill more of our kind?' It's the Earth elemental speaking now, her thoughts heavy and slow like the movement of mountains.

'If the fates bring her now, then she IS balance.' The air elemental's voice is light and quick. *'We should let the winds of fate blow as they blow. It's not our job to stand in their way.'*

'We should kill her now and put an end to it,' Pyraxis hisses, flames licking at the edges of my water shield.

'Our destruction, or our salvation,' the water elemental says. *'We will not know which future she might create if we destroy her now. All we can know is to continue as we have . . . we've seen the folly in this.'*

'Our actions here may be of no consequence, in the end,' the air elemental adds. *'We should do nothing. We should let fate flow as it flows, as it will always flow.'*

When the water sphere finally thins, Pyraxis glares at me but doesn't raise his arm again. *'I still wish to kill her,'* he says in my mind, his voice scorching my thoughts.

I decide I'm officially not a fan of 'Pyraxis.' In fact, he can get fucked.

'She thinks insolent thoughts.' The fire elemental's flame-face contorts with rage. Heat blooms from his direction again and the air fills with the scent of embers and ash.

My eyes go wide in sudden terror. He can hear my thoughts?

The water elemental approaches me, those unfathomable eyes

studying me with new intensity. *'We all can. And you should not be able to understand us when we speak to one another. We must usually . . . shout . . . to be heard by those who haven't yet formed the primal tether.'*

The water elemental gestures, and a small pedestal rises from the floor with a grinding of stone, bearing what looks like a shallow bowl of silver liquid that shimmers with an inner light.

Understanding that I'm meant to place my hand in the liquid, I do so hesitantly. The silver substance is neither hot nor cold, but tingles against my skin as if alive. When I withdraw my hand, I see a mark has appeared – not the colored elemental symbols I've seen on primals or the other students, but a strange, silvery spiral that shifts and changes as I look at it, never quite the same from one moment to the next.

'Go,' comes an impression from all four elementals at once, the combined force of their minds making my ears ring.

'What does this mean?' I ask, staring at the mark on my hand. 'What am I supposed to do with this? What am I?'

My voice rises with each question, panic edging in as I realize they're about to send me away with nothing but cryptic warnings and a mark I don't understand.

Instead of answering, a door appears in the wall at the side of the room – one that wasn't visible before.

I hesitate, looking back at Nolan's still form. 'What about them?' I gesture to the bodies. 'They deserve better than to be left here like discarded trash. They had families, hopes, dreams—'

With a small nod, the water elemental gestures, and gentle waters flow from the ground itself, enveloping each body in a cocoon of liquid. The water of each cocoon swirls together, forms a perfect sphere, and then collapses on itself, leaving no sign of the dead.

A gust of wind pushes me toward the door. I struggle against it, feet sliding on the stone floor, but I'm inexorably moved through the doorway, which slides shut behind me with a sound like rumbling stone.

And then I'm alone and in near silence. It's only me and the strange, silvery spiral on the back of my hand.

I lean against the wall, gasping for breath, legs finally giving out as I slide to the floor. My entire body trembles uncontrollably, the delayed shock hitting me like a physical blow now that immediate danger has passed.

I breathe deeply, feeling a newfound appreciation for the sweetness of air filling my body. For the steady beat of my heart. For the simple miracle of still being alive.

In a way, I feel a strange relief. I offered up my sins for judgment, and . . . they let me walk away. They let me live.

I'm not ready to forgive myself, but maybe it all means there was a reason for me to keep going. Maybe there's some purpose to my life, and I need to keep fighting to find out why the gods didn't let me die back there.

The sound of nearby voices tells me I don't have long alone. I take one more look at the mark on the back of my hand and my stomach sinks. Based on the way the elementals reacted, I'm certain I won't find anyone else with a mark like this out there.

So how the hell am I going to explain it?

And more importantly – what exactly does 'unbound' mean?

Chapter 3

My entire body trembles as I stumble from the trial chamber. The stone hallway stretches before me – too bright, too loud, too everything.

First, I thought I would die when I volunteered myself for selection back in Saltcrest. Then I thought I would die when they told us of the trial we'd face and I began to hear the screams and the sounds of offerings dying in that chamber.

Death keeps staring me in the face and somehow I keep slipping through its grasp. But how much longer can my luck hold? How many more times can I dance with death before it finally claims me?

The dining hall looms ahead, voices spilling out in a chaotic symphony of relief and terror. I pause at the threshold, taking inventory of my own body like it's something alien. Legs, functioning but unsteady. Lungs, burning with each breath. And on the back of my left hand, that impossible silver spiral pulses against my skin, sending waves of pins and needles up my arm. I shove my hand deep into my pocket, fingers curling into a tight fist. Whatever happened in that testing chamber wasn't normal. Until I know more, this secret stays buried.

Inside the high-ceilinged dining hall, survivors cluster in small groups. It's tragically few compared to the hundreds who entered. Their faces bear the same stunned disbelief as mine must, that peculiar feeling of facing death only to find a new lease on life instead.

Many hold up their left hands, studying newly earned affinity marks with reverent awe. Air marks – spiraling white wind patterns that seem to shift and dance when viewed from different angles – dominate the room. Water marks follow close behind, stylized blue waves flowing across skin. I spot only a handful of earthy green mountain symbols, and even fewer fire marks – vibrant crimson flames that seem to pulse with a heartbeat of their own.

Affinity marks.

Everyone in the room now bears something we likely never thought to see on our own skin. The marks of a primal in training. Once we're done dealing with the shock of surviving and the dangers facing us, I imagine many will be exhilarant about our new circumstances.

The chance to become a primal is the chance to become more than just elite. Becoming a primal means securing status for yourself, your family, and your descendants for all of time. It's the highest honor and the greatest power imaginable, and now we're all seemingly on the path of earning it for ourselves.

I keep to the edges of the room, shoulder brushing against the cold stone wall. A few heads turn as I pass, eyes lingering on my pocket where my hand remains hidden. Do they know? Can they sense the wrongness of my mark? My skin crawls under their scrutiny, each glance feeling like an accusation.

It's clear how quickly the survivors are sorting themselves by affinity. My hidden hand is drawing more and more attention by the second.

'—supposed to report to the combat arena next,' a tall boy says nearby, his voice pitched high with barely contained panic.

'Combat? Today?' A stocky girl with cropped hair shakes her head, fingers unconsciously tracing the blue wave on the back of her hand. 'We just survived that nightmare, and now they want us fighting?'

'That's the point,' replies another boy with an edge of false bravado. 'They want to see who's worth training. If we want to be primals, we need to learn to be tough, right?' The words sound hollow, a lifeline he's clinging to.

I edge toward the corridor that leads deeper into the building, where a guard directs survivors, checking their marks before sending them along with instructions.

My throat goes tight, skin breaking out in a light sweat. There's no way out of this damn area without passing that guard. Without showing my mark – my impossible, unexplainable mark that had the elementals acting as if I was some sort of monster. The fire elemental even tried to kill me for it. So what the hells would the guards here do if they saw it?

Fingers close around my shoulder, making me jerk my head around.

I turn to see three students.

The first is a lean boy with platinum blonde hair and hard eyes. His green mountain mark – earth affinity – glows on the back of his hand.

Beside him stands a girl who is shockingly pretty and has a deadly edge to the way she holds herself. The sides of her black hair are clipped short and the top is braided down her back. The red fire mark blazes on her hand, seeming to draw light into itself rather than emit it.

The third towers behind them, broad-shouldered and scarred. I recognize him immediately – the volunteer from before the trial.

Raith.

His eyes are that impossible blend of yellows and oranges that seems to shift even as I stare up into them. He radiates intensity like a furnace radiates heat, commanding all of my attention despite the danger obvious in the other two.

My gaze drifts to his left hand where the red fire mark spreads across his scarred skin in unusual patterns, red tendrils snaking through the damaged tissue like molten metal.

'Yes?' I ask, driving my marked hand deeper into my pocket until my fingernails bite into my palm.

'Your mark,' the girl says. Even her voice is beautiful – sultry and soft – but she carries herself like someone who is anything but. There's something calculating in the way she watches me that I don't like in the slightest.

'What about it?' My voice comes out steadier than I feel.

'Show us your mark,' the earth affinity demands, nodding toward my concealed hand.

'She looks like a water,' the girl says, eyes narrowing. 'Or maybe it's just that she smells like a fish.' She crinkles her upturned nose, lips curling in a grimace.

The comment hits like a slap. I think of my family, of the sea that gave us sustenance before swallowing them whole. Of salt-crusted hands and the smell of home that I'll never know again. 'Fuck you,' I spit back. It's not clever, but patience and wit feel like far away memories at the moment.

I brace for her to hit me, but the cold fire in her eyes is somehow worse. It smolders there, deeper than simple anger. It's the quiet stare of someone who's killed before and wouldn't hesitate to do it again. It's the look of somebody who doesn't forget a slight – someone who won't stop until they've collected their due in blood.

She steps closer until I can feel her breath hot against my face and can count each perfectly curled eyelash. 'Show me. Your mark,' she says through her straight white teeth, the words barely above a whisper. 'If you're loyal to Empire, then you should have nothing to fear. Unless you're not?' her head tilts, the question lingering like a blade at my throat. 'Are you a traitor?'

I force myself not to flinch. Every instinct screams to back down, to submit, but I've seen enough of this place to know that weakness is a death sentence. My eyes shift to the scarred volunteer. He stares back, his expression unreadable.

'Show her,' he says, voice low and rough.

'Is she your leader?' I ask with a half-smile that feels more like a grimace. 'I didn't take you for the follower type.'

A muscle in his jaw tightens. Raith steps forward, one large muscled arm pushing the girl aside as if she weighs nothing. He towers over me, radiating heat like a furnace. 'Mark,' he repeats. 'Show it.'

I stare up at him, uncomfortably aware of how easily he could break me. With those huge arms and hands, I imagine he could snap my bones like kindling without breaking a sweat. Even the pretty girl could probably kill me without much effort. And I'm the short-tempered idiot who pissed them off.

But what choice do I have? Flash my silver mark and ask them to promise not to tell anyone? That feels even more suicidal than continuing to defy these three.

'I'd rather not,' I say, voice barely above a whisper.

The edge of his full lips twitches, almost imperceptibly. His eyes are all heat and dark promise. His right hand moves toward my pocket, and I'm suddenly, terribly certain that he's going to force my hand out and expose my secret to everyone.

A blur of gold hair flashes across my vision and suddenly a boy just as tall as the volunteer is standing between us. Bastian's legacy uniform gleams in the torchlight, the gold piping catching the light.

'Is there a problem, here?' he asks, voice carrying that casual authority that comes with generations of privilege. His eyes flick between me and the trio.

Only then do I realize we've drawn quite the crowd. Students have risen from their seats, eyes hungry for the first blood to be spilled. *Great. Trying to avoid attention and I end up center stage in whatever twisted drama is unfolding here.*

The girl and the earth affinity slink back, eyes lingering on Bastian's legacy uniform. None of us have the full picture of how the social hierarchy here will work yet, but something about the legacies feels clear, even without being told: legacies are not to be fucked with. Legacies are special. We are not.

If the volunteer knows he shouldn't mess with legacies, he shows no indication. That, or he just doesn't give a shit. He meets Bastian's gaze without flinching. 'Is there a reason you're here, legacy?'

Bastian's fists clench at his sides. The air around us shifts, as if pressure is building from nowhere and everywhere at once. The mark on my hand burns in response, and I have to bite my tongue to keep from gasping. I can feel air slowly shifting and flowing in toward Bastian. I can even see the dark, tangled locks of hair on the Volunteer's head beginning to stir in the unnatural breeze.

The deadly scent of magic builds in the air.

'Your name, offering?' Bastian's voice could freeze flames.

'Raith.' He doesn't blink, doesn't yield an inch.

'Family name?'

Raith's jaw tightens before he answers. 'Hollow.'

Recognition registers on Bastian's face, followed by that carefully measured look of sympathy the privileged always seem to have ready.

'Hollow . . . An orphan from the northern border, then. I—'

Raith moves so fast I barely register him shoving Bastian until the tall legacy is stumbling backward, nearly falling before he bumps into the stone wall. 'I don't need your fucking sympathy.' Raith spits on the ground, the saliva sizzling slightly where it lands. He turns to stalk away, the fire girl and earth boy falling in behind him like shadows.

A collective gasp rises from the students who were watching. Judging by their expressions, they seem to expect Bastian to strike Raith down where he stands.

But Bastian's face is a mask of calm as he brushes the spot on his uniform where Raith touched him. His eyes linger on Raith several moments before turning to me.

'Are you okay?' I ask, hardly daring to breathe for fear that the trio will come back.

'Fine,' Bastian says shortly. 'We should get you to the combat assessment.'

As we walk, I notice we're getting closer to the guards who are checking everyone's marks. My palms begin to sweat, and my breathing quickens. The silver spiral beneath my skin seems to writhe in response to my panic.

'Do they have to check our marks?' I ask, unable to keep the edge of hysteria from my voice.

'They're collecting the official count for Empire. Many die before Confluence Day and finally the Crucible, but Empire likes to keep statistics and have figures at every stage of development for its future primals,' Bastian explains. 'You'll be sent with others of your affinity for training, and after that, they'll send you to your affinity's tower.

That's where you'll get your room assignment.' His eyes drift to my hidden hand.

He must see the look of pure terror on my face, because he glances around, pulling me to the side for a moment of privacy in the busy corridor. 'I know fire and earth get a bad reputation, but it's not the end of the world. Here at Confluence, you'll mostly deal with your own affinity, anyway. What the others think of you is hardly going to matter.'

He thinks I'm embarrassed to bear one of the two elements most common in Red Kingdom. Fire or earth affinities. The marks of the enemy, to some. I wish it were only that.

The last thing I want to do is trust anyone here, but I can't see a way out. I either have to trust Bastian or the guard. The choice seems obvious.

Adrenaline pumps through me as I withdraw my hand from my pocket.

The silver spiral gleams with its own magical light, shifting and flowing like liquid metal across my skin. It moves with a life of its own, coiling and uncoiling in an endless dance.

Bastian's eyes widen, not with fear but with something else I can't place. His breath catches audibly.

'Extraordinary,' he whispers, reaching toward my hand before stopping himself. 'But . . . you're an offering. Your mother or father weren't primals?'

I shake my head, not understanding the question.

'Fascinating.' He scratches his chin, eyes sparkling with curiosity.

'You know what this means?' I ask, voice barely audible. 'Because I sure as hell don't, and I—'

'I think I do, yes. There's a book in my family library with this symbol on the cover. I'll send for it, but it may take some time. Weeks, possibly.'

Weeks. Will I even be alive weeks from now? The way this place seems to feed on fear and death, it's hard to imagine surviving until tomorrow, let alone for weeks. But I don't want to seem ungrateful, so I nod my head and smile. 'Thank you.'

Bastian hardly seems to hear me. He's still speaking, almost to himself. 'It should be possible for you to disguise it.'

'What?' I ask. 'How would I do that?' Does he really remember all of this from some old book, or is there more at play, here?

'Just . . .' he looks around again, then pulls me deeper into a private alcove. When his fingers brush my arm, I feel a jolt like lightning, stronger than when he touched me before the trial. The silver mark flares in response. Energy, cool and flowing like air seems to fill me.

Bastian pulls his hand back as if burned, eyes shifting to my mark warily, but the concern vanishes almost instantly. 'Close your eyes, clear your senses, and focus on the mark. Your life will be easier if you pick water or air. But whatever you choose, try to visualize the mark changing.'

I don't bother questioning if it's possible. I need it to be. I need some way to hide this, so I close my eyes and think about which mark to choose. Which affinity.

Earth and fire are historically dominant elements in Red Kingdom. Choosing them would mean a lifetime of reactions like the one Mireen gave Nolan before the trial. It would mean suspicion and increased scrutiny.

It's like Bastian said . . . my life will be easier if I pick water or air, even if neither element represents what I feel inside.

I still feel like fire, ready to lash out and burn everything around me to ash after the last few days. But that's not the normal me. It's not the girl who grew up loving her time on the waters in Saltcrest's bay. The girl who spent half her life reading currents and finding fish.

In the end, choosing anything but water would feel like running from my past. And maybe this place is going to claim my life before long, but I'm done running.

I squeeze my eyes shut, thinking about my father and brothers. I picture the flowing wave pattern I've seen on other hands. I reach for the memory of salt spray on my face, the rhythm of waves against our small boat, the peace I used to feel watching the tide roll in.

A sensation like icy fingers crawls across the back of my hand. My skin stretches and pulls as if being remolded by invisible hands. Heat flashes through my veins, followed by bone-deep cold, then both at once. I clench my teeth around a grunt of pain, brows furrowing as I focus through the discomfort until the sensations finally subside.

When I open my eyes, the mark has changed – appearing as a blue wave on the back of my left hand. Looking closely, I can still see threads of silver tracing through it like veins of quicksilver, but unless someone was specifically looking for them, they'd never notice.

'How did I—' I stare at my hand in disbelief.

Bastian flashes a half-smile, but the humor doesn't reach his eyes. 'Water. Okay. I guess you didn't want to be an air like me?'

I shake my head, still staring at the disguised mark. 'What does this all mean?'

His voice drops low. 'Just know this: if the wrong person finds out about your mark, it would be . . . trouble. You have to learn to keep it hidden. Tell no one.'

'Why do I feel like you know more than you're saying?' I search his face for answers.

His expression turns guarded. 'I've heard whispers. But I won't worry you with rumors because they may do just as much harm as good. I'll send for the book. Try to stay alive until then and keep this hidden. With luck, the book will give us some answers about what this means.'

I accept his explanation for now. It has the ring of truth, and frankly, I can only handle so many revelations in one day. Now that he knows my secret, he might be held complicit if it gets out. We're bound by this knowledge, whether I like it or not.

We rejoin the flow of survivors. With Bastian beside me, the guards barely glance at my now-blue mark before waving me toward the water corridor. My heart thumps so loudly I'm certain everyone can hear it as we pass. Did it work? Did they actually fall for it?

'Wait,' I say, pausing at the threshold. Something in Bastian's earlier words gnaws at me. 'What exactly happens in the combat assessment?'

A shadow crosses his face. 'A simple training match. Today, I think most offerings won't fully grasp what's going on here. Today, you should still be safe.'

'What the hell does that mean?' I ask, already growing tired of half-truths and cryptic warnings.

He steps closer, eyes scanning to make sure we're not overheard. 'You're an offering. Yes, you've all shown you have an affinity. But that's only the first step. You're not valuable to the Empire unless you earn an elemental tether on Confluence Day.' His voice drops even lower. 'Until you tether, you're expendable. They won't stop you from killing one another. *The strong weed out the weak,*' he says in a way that makes me think it's a common phrase around here.

Understanding hits me like ice water. 'So these combat assessments could turn deadly?' I ask, bile rising in my throat.

Bastian nods grimly. 'These two months before Confluence Day will be the most dangerous. They'll train you. They'll teach you about history and magic. But the real test? It's surviving until Confluence Day. Survive that, and the Academy will finally start treating you like the valuable resource you are. Until then, just about anything goes. Your peers won't realize it right away. But it won't be long before they do.'

My mouth goes dry, a cold dread settling in my bones. 'Who will I have to fight?'

Bastian's eyes dart over my shoulder, and his expression hardens. I turn to follow his gaze and find Raith standing with the other fire affinities, his eyes already watching me with an intensity that makes my skin prickle.

Though I can't say for certain, I think he is taking personal offense to the fact that I'm standing and talking to Bastian right now.

'Some days, the instructors will allow challenges,' Bastian says quietly. 'I expect they'll let us know we're able to issue them today as a way to set the tone. I would normally say not to worry, because you haven't had time to make enemies.'

My smile feels brittle on my face. He knows it, too.

Beside Raith, I see the beautiful, dark-haired girl with the braid. She's leaning with her arms crossed and her perfect lips are curved into a predatory smile. Like Raith, she's watching Bastian and me.

Already, I think both of them might just break me and leave me for dead if they're allowed to challenge me.

'Everyone,' a guard calls. 'Move along to the training arena. Sparring matches will begin soon.'

The girl meets my eyes, then drags a finger across her throat as she smiles sweetly.

My newly disguised water mark throbs on my hand, and somewhere deeper, the silver spiral pulses in rhythm with my racing heart – a heart I hope will still be beating in a few minutes.

Chapter 4

'Stance wider! Arms up! You're not dancing at a royal ball – you're fighting for your lives! For Empire! For your families and all those without the strength to fight for themselves!'

The instructor's voice echoes across the cavernous training arena, bouncing off ancient stone walls stained with centuries of sweat and blood. High arched windows frame the darkening mountains beyond, their jagged peaks tipped with snow.

I stand among nearly a hundred water affinities, muscles trembling with effort. The disguised mark on my hand tingles with a persistent itch I dare not scratch. More waters trickle into the room, their faces drawn and pale as they fall into formation beside me. I've lost track of time since stepping out of that carriage – has it been hours? Just minutes? My body can't tell the difference anymore, every moment seems to stretch on with agonizing slowness.

My body's survival instinct has been on high alert for so long I can finally feel it starting to dim, even though the threat clearly hasn't passed. Maybe it never will so long as I'm behind these walls.

My legs burn from holding the same defensive stance for so long, but I refuse to show weakness. Not here. Not when Bastian's words still ring in my mind.

Expendable.

Survive until Confluence Day.

A glint of deep copper catches my eye – Mireen's unmistakable red hair as she slides into formation beside me. Something loosens in my chest at the sight of her.

'What'd I miss?' she whispers, a wink softening her worried expression.

'Mireen!' I whisper-yell, relief flooding my voice. 'You survived the trial!'

'Focus!' the instructor snaps, his eyes finding me instantly in the crowd.

I straighten my spine and fix my gaze ahead, but the moment his attention shifts elsewhere, I'm smiling. Mireen lived. In this place of calculated cruelty, her presence feels like the first truly good thing since leaving Saltcrest.

The arena pulses with nervous energy as four distinct groups form around their respective instructors. The airs dominate with their superior numbers – nearly two hundred of them by my rough count. Waters are the second largest group with only a dozen or so fewer students than the airs. The earth affinities barely make thirty, and fires count only twenty-five among their ranks.

No black uniforms move among us. We all still wear the clothes of our homelands. It's a rowdy mixture of color, dirt, and styles.

I wonder what the aspirants and legacies are doing right now. From the way they were already given uniforms and allowed to bypass the trial, I imagine they're being fed grapes by beautiful men and women.

Lucky assholes.

My eyes drift inevitably to where Raith stands among the fires – tall, scarred, unmistakable. While nearly everyone in the room fumbles through basic forms, he moves with deadly precision, each strike and block executed with frightening efficiency. He looks like he was born to fight and bred to kill.

I'm not the only one watching Raith, I realize.

Every fire studies him with a mixture of respect and wariness, while girls from all affinities steal the occasional glance. His scars should make him grotesque, but instead, they only enhance the raw magnetism that emanates from him like heat from a forge. When his golden eyes catch the light, something deep and primal in my brain registers him as a predator – the most dangerous creature in a room full of prey.

I force my attention away, cheeks warming at my own foolish interest in the man.

Focus, Nessa.

'Waters, attention!' Our instructor – a lean man in his early thirties paces before us, intensity radiating from every inch of his body. His lilting accent hints of the Roselands in the deep south, soft syllables at odds with the hardness in his eyes. 'Assessment begins in five minutes. I strongly doubt any of you are capable yet, but no channeling your affinity. You need to be trained before you can use magic without accidentally killing someone.'

'What if we do kill someone by accident?' a boy calls out, his voice cracking midway through the question.

The instructor's eyes harden to chips of ice. 'Then you should hope their friends don't seek retribution.'

'That's it?' The words escape me before I can catch them, surprise overriding caution.

His gaze turns to me, measuring and dismissive in equal parts. I expect some kind of denial, even if I'll know it's false. His only response is to give the slightest nod.

'Does that mean you don't care if we kill people?' a small girl asks, her voice fracturing with barely contained terror.

'You're all training for war. If you graduate from this academy, you'll leave as a fully tethered primal ready to become the most lethal weapon in the Empire's army.' He says this as though reciting an old litany, words worn smooth with repetition. 'Earn the right to be valuable. Prove your worth. Survive. That's your role here, so embrace it, offerings.'

Murmurs ripple through our ranks, a wave of disbelief and fear that breaks our carefully maintained formation. He's not denying the question. Maybe my classmates will realize we're allowed to kill one another faster than Bastian thought.

'So other students can just . . . kill us?'

'They really don't care?'

'They just want the strongest to survive.'

'Then don't get killed, idiot.'

I keep my expression carefully neutral, even as my stomach flips and clenches in on itself.

Cull the weak. Strengthen the herd.

As part of the herd, I can't say I agree with the strategy at the moment.

Beside me, Mireen looks like she's balancing on the knife-edge of panic, her face drained of color as her hands fall limply to her sides.

'Hey,' I say quietly, angling my body to shield her from the instructor's view. 'We got this. I think most people are too worried about surviving to start trying to kill each other yet. I'm sure we'll be fine.'

Yet.

Even my flimsy attempt at reassurance falls flat. We both hear the unspoken truth hanging in the air between us.

She gives a shaky nod, tongue darting out to wet her chapped lips. 'Thanks,' she whispers, not looking convinced but offering a smile all the same.

The massive doors at the far end of the arena swing open with a groan that reverberates through the stone floor. Several figures in silver and gold enter – legacies, their presence commanding immediate attention despite their casual strides. Bastian is among them, his golden hair catching the light from the high windows. He scans the sea of offerings until his eyes find me. The subtle nod he gives is so quick I might be imagining it.

'Legacies,' our instructor says. 'Here to observe. Ignore them.'

Easier said than done when I can feel Bastian's gaze following my every move like a physical touch. What does he want from me? What does he see when he looks at me – a curiosity? A responsibility? Something else entirely?

The other legacies stroll about the room, hands clasped behind their backs with military efficiency. They observe us with clear disinterest and disdain. For that much, I can't say I blame them.

Other than Raith and a handful of standouts, we make a pretty pathetic picture as we resume stumbling through combat stances and practice drills.

The instructor of the fires approaches our group, expression grim. She's a severe-looking woman with black hair in a braid so tight it looks like it must hurt. She has lean muscles that speak of combat prowess.

She murmurs something to our instructor, who nods and then cuts his eyes directly to me. My heart skips.

'Waters. You'll each complete one sparring match,' he announces, voice carrying across our group. 'The match ends when your opponent yields or can no longer get up. You,' he says, beckoning me forward with one crooked finger. 'You've been challenged by one of the fires. Go with Instructor Kyreen. She'll show you to your opponent.'

'What?' Mireen gasps, her fingers briefly catching my sleeve.

'It's okay,' I lie, forcing a smile even as panic screams through every nerve ending.

My stomach is in my throat as I follow the fire instructor toward the smaller group of fires. Raith towers over them, walking at the front with his terrifying gaze fixed on me as he stalks forward. I feel like a mouse being watched by a hawk – each step bringing me closer to inevitable claws.

'Am I allowed to refuse the challenge?' I ask, voice smaller than I intend as we cross the vast space between groups. I can sense eyes from all corners of the room tracking my movement, wondering what I could have possibly done to attract this kind of attention so quickly.

She looks down at me, her eyes a deep, simmering orange that reveals no sympathy. 'No. Do you think you'll be able to politely decline when the Red Kingdom attacks an outpost you're defending? When they ambush your camp in the night?'

I swallow a sigh, steeling myself for what's coming. No escape, then. No mercy.

'Who challenged me? Her?' I ask, pointing at the beautiful fire girl with black hair who watches me with venomous contempt, her fists clenched at her sides so tightly I can see white knuckles even from this distance.

'Serena?' Kyreen asks, something like amusement flickering across her face. 'No. Though she wanted to. Raith Hollow seems to have beaten her to it.'

Fuck me.

Against Serena, I might have had a slim chance of surviving with only moderate injuries. Against Raith, though? There's no chance in any hell. No gods powerful enough to save me from this. I might as well have been asked to fight a dragon barehanded.

The pounding of my heart forms a desperate rhythm of fear. Blood roars in my ears until it's almost deafening.

It's only me and the giant, scarred volunteer with yellow-orange eyes.

Each step toward the raised platform sends jolts of nervous energy up my spine, skin prickling with gooseflesh beneath the weight of so many watching eyes. Some students are already sparring on other platforms, the dull sounds of impact punctuated by grunts and occasional cries of pain. Most, though, have stopped what they're doing to look our way.

Raith stands waiting at the edge of the mat, power radiating from him in almost visible waves. His expression remains carefully guarded, his gaze a wall I can't possibly see past.

Everything else fades to background noise as I desperately try to form a plan – try to figure out how I'm supposed to fight this mountain of man, muscle, and deadly intent standing across from me. My mind whirls through options, each more unlikely than the last.

The legacies have drifted closer, their silver and gold uniforms gleaming. Bastian stands among them, his expression inscrutable. Both fire and water instructors watch us intently, arms crossed in mirrored poses of assessment.

Raith settles into a fighting stance with the fluid grace of someone who has done this thousands of times before. I mirror him as best I can, trying to recall everything I've learned in the brief crash course on fighting we've all been given.

I quickly conclude that I'm royally fucked.

'Why me?' I demand as we begin to circle each other around the ring, my voice lower than I'd intended, betraying my nerves.

I expect some sort of asshole comment in response – something cutting and dismissive that confirms my expendability in his eyes. Instead, his gaze slides briefly to Serena, who is already fighting two rings over. She's on top of a muscular boy with a fire mark, relentlessly pounding her fists into his face as blood sprays across the stone in crimson arcs.

I swallow hard, my throat clicking with sudden dryness. 'You challenged me so she wouldn't?' I guess, keeping my voice low enough that our audience can't hear. Maybe there's some twisted chivalry at work here – choosing to defeat me himself rather than letting Serena torture me.

'No,' Raith says flatly, eyes snapping back to mine with predatory focus. 'Shut up and fight, Saltcrest.'

Saltcrest? How the hell does he know where I'm—

He catches me mid-thought, lunging forward and straight through my guard with a speed that seems impossible for someone his size.

His first strike comes fast – a testing jab that I barely manage to deflect, the impact vibrating up my forearm and sending shockwaves of pain to my shoulder. His second follows immediately, catching me in the ribs and sending me staggering back. The pain explodes like a bomb beneath my skin, air rushing from my lungs in a harsh gasp that echoes in the sudden silence around us.

Stars dance at the edges of my vision as I struggle to breathe through lungs that feel crushed. I force myself upright through sheer stubbornness, ignoring the spreading fire across my ribcage.

'That the best you can do?' I rasp, trying to sound confident rather than breathless and half-broken after just two punches.

A shadow of a smile plays across his lips, there and gone in an instant. That brief glimpse of amusement shouldn't make my stomach flutter, but it does – a treacherous warmth spreading beneath the pain of his strike.

He moves in again, this time with a combination I can't possibly counter. I take a hit to the shoulder that nearly spins me around, duck under another that would have connected with my jaw, but his leg sweeps mine and suddenly I'm falling, weightless for one terrifying moment before impact.

I brace for the hard slam of stone against bone, but he's there – grappling my body while somehow softening my fall. His body burns against mine, unnaturally warm in a way that can't be explained by physical exertion alone. Up close, his eyes reveal streaks of pure red and gold threading through amber, like cracks in the earth revealing bright yellow magma beneath.

Something stirs where we touch. A jolt of energy that feels the same as when I touched Bastian – almost as if something is being pulled from his body into mine. A current that flows between us, invisible but unmistakable.

He shifts, hooks a leg behind mine, pressing his hips against me with deliberate force. Hard.

The weight of him steals what little breath I've managed to recover. His body is solid heat and coiled strength, and for one disorienting second, I feel certain he's holding back.

A lot.

I groan, trying to fight free of him, twisting beneath his weight in a desperate bid for leverage that never comes. It's useless. He has me pinned completely, his larger body caging mine against the mat.

Raith turns his head, breath hot against my ear as a shiver races down my spine. 'I could break you in half right now,' he murmurs, voice dropping to a rough timbre that vibrates through my bones. 'You need to do better. Much better.'

As he grapples me, I still feel that strange draining sensation, stronger now with more points of contact between us. It's almost as if I'm pulling pure fire from his body, watching it flow through invisible channels and gather inside myself like water into a reservoir. Heat builds beneath my skin, seeking release.

'That's enough,' Bastian's voice cuts through the haze of pain and confusion. 'He clearly has her.'

'I'm not done, legacy,' Raith growls – actually growls – before he flips me to my back with sickening ease, his body pressed tight against mine as he secures an arm around my neck. The pressure is tight enough to be threatening, but I can still breathe – just barely. The message is clear: he could end this in seconds if he wanted to.

The fucking bastard is toying with me.

Sending a message.

'Submit,' he commands, his mouth so close I can feel the heat of the word on my skin. When I don't immediately obey, he tightens slightly. 'Submit,' he repeats, louder this time.

But surrendering isn't in my nature, even when logic screams that I should. Maybe I'm still hopeless in a fight, but I can at least prove I have the grit to keep trying. To keep fighting even when victory is impossible.

I make a few useless attempts to throw my elbows back, hoping to land at least one good hit before this is over. But he's too big and strong, and I'm completely pinned.

Raith's grip tightens incrementally, his legs splayed over my hips as he bends low over me, gradually restricting my airflow. The pressure against my throat builds until swallowing becomes a conscious effort, painful and strained.

'Fuck . . . you . . .' I gasp, each syllable a struggle as spots dance in my vision. I even manage something I hope looks like a smile, just to piss him off.

My lungs burn for air that won't come. Panic rises, sharp and primal, as my body recognizes the danger before my mind can process it.

'That's enough!' Bastian shouts again, his voice edged with genuine alarm now. I can hear him speaking hotly to the instructor, their words blurring together as my consciousness begins to fray at the edges.

'Yield,' Raith says against my ear, more quietly this time, and with a touch of urgency I wouldn't have expected from him. 'Just yield.' The last comes in a strained whisper.

And that's when it happens.

The strange warmth that's been building intensifies where our skin touches, like liquid fire seeping through my pores. It builds in my chest – a pressure that makes my ribs feel too small to contain it – then races through my veins, setting every nerve ending ablaze. My teeth ache with it, muscles spasming involuntarily as the energy surges through pathways I never knew existed in my body.

His body stiffens against mine. He feels it too.

At the same time, the instructors turn, locked in a heated argument with Bastian that's drawing more attention than our stalemate on the mat. No one is watching us closely anymore, their focus pulled to the more dramatic confrontation since I'm clearly outmatched.

'What are you—' Raith begins, voice tight with something between suspicion and disbelief.

The energy concentrates in my hands, drawn there by instinct rather than conscious thought. Tiny flames erupt from my skin, snaking around my body in intricate patterns and scorching Raith's clothing with ethereal tongues of orange and gold.

His element, not mine.

I feel heat in my eyes and my mouth, gathering and threatening to rush out of me like a volcanic eruption I can't contain.

Raith recoils as if struck, his hold loosening instantly. His expression flashes from shock to something I never expected – pure, primal fear mixed with . . . recognition? In an instant, it's gone, replaced by his usual mask of control. But I saw it. For one unguarded moment, the mighty Raith Hollow looked terrified.

Is he afraid of fire? No, that can't be right. He's a fire affinity himself.

Then what?

The flames vanish as quickly as they appeared, leaving behind a residual warmth and a lingering smell of scorched fabric. Around us, the assessment continues, no one having noticed the brief flare of magic. If they did, they must have assumed it was Raith's magic.

Raith recovers quickly, pinning me again with even more force than before, his body a rigid cage around mine. But something has changed. There's tension in him that wasn't there before – a wariness that borders on genuine caution.

'Yield. Do it, or I'll make you pass out this time. Your choice.'

I meet his eyes, seeing questions there that mirror my own. What just happened? How did I do that? Why did he react that way? The moment stretches between us, heavy with unspoken suspicions.

'I yield,' I finally gasp, the words scraping my raw throat.

His face returns to its usual mask of cold indifference, but his eyes still flare hot as they track my every movement.

I roll to my side, coughing and gasping for air that burns in my raw throat. My whole body trembles with exhaustion, muscles quivering like I've run for miles without stopping. Sweat drips from my hairline, running across my face in tickling paths and soaking my clothes.

All I want to do is curl up and fall asleep right there on the mat, but I force myself to stand, pulling up my body that desperately resists my every movement.

Don't let them see weakness. Not here.

'Winner, Raith,' announces the fire instructor, who claps him on the back like they're already friends, oblivious to whatever just transpired between us.

The water instructor has already moved his attention to other matches, my poor performance clearly not worth his time. Maybe I lost so badly he doesn't even see the purpose in giving me advice.

As we step off the platform, Raith leans close, his breath hot against my ear. 'Watch yourself, Saltcrest.'

I'm too exhausted to produce an elegant response. All I manage is a choked 'huh?'

His voice drops to a dangerous whisper that sends a chill down my spine despite his unnatural warmth. 'You channeled fire. I saw it. I felt it.'

I shake my head, heart racing anew. Admitting anything close to a vulnerability would be a mistake, so I say nothing.

'What are you?' he presses, one hand gripping my upper arm to keep me from escaping, his fingers burning against my skin.

'Sore, actually. From where you tried to choke me,' I deflect, lifting my chin to meet his gaze despite the trembling that's started in my legs.

Now the suspicion in his expression shifts, replaced by a fiery, dangerous kind of amusement that transforms his features. 'I could've done a hell of a lot more than make you sore, Thorne.'

'Like what? Kill me?'

He considers my suggestion casually. 'Maybe. If you give me a reason.'

'Like I said on the mat. Fuck. You.'

The way his full lips curve so slightly I could almost imagine it is . . . confusing. My brain says this man is a threat. His words say he's a threat. The fact that he just choked me out and probably internally bruised me says he's a threat.

But there's a heat pulsing just beneath his surface that makes me understand how moths can be drawn to flames, even though getting close will spell their doom.

'Hmm,' he says, voice little more than a low rumble.

And all he has to do is lift his eyes to mine.

Gods. That look feels like having his rough hands on my body – like something intimate in all the wrong ways. A promise and a threat wrapped together in burning amber.

Heat rushes to my face, and I hate my traitorous body for responding to him when I'm pretty sure he wouldn't think twice about killing me if it suited his purposes, no matter what he's trying to imply with that heated gaze. Frankly, my best guess is he just likes toying with his food before he delivers the death blow, and we're in the 'play' stage.

I force a glare, hoping he feels all the venom I try to put into the look.

Instead, his attention falls to my lips, lingering there before lifting back to study me with renewed interest. 'Angry. That's good. You'll need anger here if you plan to survive.'

Then he walks away, rejoining the fire affinity section as if our exchange never happened, leaving me standing alone with too many questions and not nearly enough answers.

Bastian grips my arm as soon as Raith is gone, his touch cool compared to the lingering heat of Raith's fingers. Again, I feel that strange sensation of energy passing from his body to mine.

I need to find out what the hell that sensation means. Am I draining elemental power? It certainly seemed like it on the mat.

'What was that?' Bastian asks. 'One minute, he had you pinned, then I looked away and you got out somehow. What happened?'

I shake my head, still struggling to process everything myself. 'I . . . don't know.'

He licks his lips, leaning closer and lowering his voice to ensure we're not overheard. 'Whatever is going on . . . you need to be careful until we have a better idea of what you are.'

We?

I can't decide if the way Bastian wants to take my problems on as his own is flattering or suspicious. He hardly knows me, yet speaks as though we're bound together in this. But I'm still trying to catch my breath, my thoughts scattered like leaves in a storm, so I just nod, even though I have no fucking clue how to be careful with something I can't control – something I don't even understand.

'I need to go,' Bastian says, his eyes darting to where the other legacies are watching us with undisguised curiosity. 'I won't be able to talk to you regularly. It'll draw too much attention. Remember, I'll bring the book when I can. Until then . . . be careful, Nessa. You have no idea how much danger you're in.'

He's already gone before I can respond, disappearing into the crowd without a backward glance. Before I can fully process what just happened – the fight, the strange fire, Raith's reaction, Bastian's concern – the sparring matches are declared over and we're being sorted into dormitory assignments.

The instructors talk about our schedule and lodgings while two older students drag a lifeless body from the room. I try not to look at it. Try not to think about it.

I do my best to focus on what I'm being told. Like how our schedule will include regular combat, weight training, and a full barrage of academic and magical training classes. Today, we're being shown a rare mercy and allowed to get settled in our rooms and rest for the remainder of the day.

Hoo fucking ray.

The instructors divide us by affinity, their voices cutting through the haze of exhaustion that's settled over us all. We're led from the training area through winding and confusing passages which are almost all lined with massive oil paintings depicting primals locked in battle – their elemental companions taking the forms of beasts from wolves all the way to fearsome dragons or great land worms large enough to swallow horse carriages.

I notice more than a few of us are limping, bleeding, or already swelling with bruises as we travel. The sounds of pained breathing and occasional whimpers echo off stone walls that I imagine have witnessed centuries of similar processions.

It must be settling in on everyone, just like it's settling on me. This is real. Hours ago, we may have expected to die. To be sacrificed. Executed. Maybe even something worse. None of us expected to be thrown into a military academy and trained.

The castle itself is magnificent, I have to admit – all polished stone halls lined with lush carpets and tapestries in empire gold, silver, and black. Magical lights illuminate our path, hovering in ornate sconces and pulsing gently with arcane energy colored to match one of the four affinities. We pass countless rooms, some of which are occupied by older students already taking classes. They glance as we pass with expressions ranging from pity to disdain, seeing in us what they once were – or perhaps what they're glad they never had to be.

With interest, I note that I only see the silver trimmed uniforms of aspirants or, far more rarely, the silver and gold of legacies. Where are the upper-year offerings?

My question remains unanswered as we move across a central courtyard and head toward a corner where I can see the blue water tower looming high above us, its upper reaches lost in the gathering evening mist. Magical water cascades down its exterior in perpetual, glimmering sheets that catch the last rays of sunlight in dazzling prisms.

With nearly two-hundred water affinities, we're broken into smaller groups and guided to the tower by older students.

'At least we're in far fewer pieces than I was expecting,' Mireen whispers as we climb the spiral staircase of the water tower, her voice muffled by the constant sound of flowing water. One of her eyes is swollen shut, and her once-neat braid is a tangled mess, as if somebody tried to pull it from her scalp. She's limping slightly, favoring her right leg.

'Common room is on the fourth floor landing,' explains the student assigned to walk us here, his tone bored as he recites what is clearly a rehearsed speech. 'First-year offerings can use the main common area. Aspirants and legacies get access to the private areas. And don't bother the older students. None of them will want anything to do with you, since most of you will be dead after Confluence Day, anyway.'

How encouraging. But there's a matter-of-factness in his delivery that says he's only stating a fact, not trying to scare us or show off.

'Surely not everyone here is an asshole?' a girl with deep brown skin asks.

'Assholes?' the older student replies. 'Call it what you want. You're all at the very bottom of the food chain. Stay alive long enough and you'll get better treatment. But survive a few years here and you'll learn it's not worth getting to know the first-years.'

On that cheerful note, we continue climbing.

The water tower has an odd, magical kind of beauty to it. The stones are a deep, oceanic blue that seems to shift with the play of light across their surface. Water trickles down the inside of the walls in carefully channeled paths, filling the space with a sound like fountains and burbling streams. The flowing water brings a pleasant humid quality to the air and a coolness that feels good on my overheated, sweaty body.

All the water reminds me of home – the good parts of home, at least. Of being on the water. Of the days before . . .

I jerk my thoughts away from the unwelcome memory, focusing instead on the now. On surviving. On finding a way through this madness, one day at a time.

We're allowed to claim our own rooms from the empty ones along a circular hallway, each with a single window view of the world beyond. Each has two beds, so Mireen and I naturally pair up, taking one of the first open ones we find. It's sparse, with nothing but the beds, a washbasin, and a view pointed toward the academy grounds – though our view is filtered through a flowing stream of water that surrounds the tower, making the scene look like a shifting watercolor painting.

After the day we've had, I'm too tired to care about the accommodations. My body aches everywhere, and I can already feel bruises blooming beneath my skin in the shape of Raith's hands.

'Rest while you can,' an older student warns as he passes our room. 'Classes and more training begin at first light tomorrow. You likely won't have this much time to recover again, so make use of it.'

Mireen collapses onto her bed with a groan that seems to come from her very soul. 'I'm going to die here, aren't I?'

I should reassure her. I should find some words of comfort or encouragement to offer. Instead, I find myself staring at my disguised mark and wondering what the hell I am.

'We'll find a way,' I say, my voice lacking real conviction even to my own ears.

A few quiet moments pass before she speaks again, thoughts apparently shifted to less morbid topics.

'What happened with that guy? The hot one with the scars?'

Mireen asks suddenly, her voice hushed as if afraid he might somehow hear us even here. 'I saw him talking to you quite a bit. Did he say why he challenged you?'

I open my mouth to deflect, but my mind is still full of his words. Full of the way it felt to have his hands around my neck. Full of the strange fire that came when I most needed it – and the fear that flashed across his face.

Part of me wants to tell Mireen everything, to share the burden of whatever the hell is happening to me. But another part suspects my secrets could have deadly consequences. Sharing them with Mireen would only put her in danger, and I won't take that risk.

'He didn't say much,' I say finally, staring at the ceiling where water-light dances in rippling patterns. 'But I think he's trouble.'

Mireen sighs as she adjusts herself in the small bed, wincing as she finds a particularly tender spot. 'I saw the way he was . . . mounting you. Maybe he just wanted an excuse to put his hands on you.'

I can still feel the places where he touched me, like burning shadows branded into my skin. I know I'll bear marks from that touch tomorrow once the bruises form fully. 'Somehow, I doubt that,' I say.

The vision of his face hovering over mine fills my mind as I clench my fist, feeling phantom flames lick across my knuckles. I've survived the offering ceremony, the elemental trial, and my first day at Confluence Academy.

But surviving isn't enough. I need to find out what the hell it means to be unbound – why I was able to call fire while touching Raith, and whether the strangeness of my abilities stop there.

This morning, part of me was ready to give up and die. Part of me still is, maybe.

But I want to see this thing through. I want to show all the assholes running this place that we're not fodder to discard. They expect us to die in droves before Confluence Day?

I'd love nothing more than to thrive. To shove their dismissal down their damn throats, if that's what it takes.

And not just them. There are the people like Serena and Raith who are stronger than me, and they think they can wield that power like clubs to keep me down.

Fuck that.

I'll make it to Confluence Day – whatever that is – and I'll even earn myself an elemental if that's the goal. And if, by some miracle, I survive to make it out of this place, I'll find a way to use my power to make it up to Brissa and my mother.

But for now, my reality revolves around one brutally simple truth.

This place and these people see me as expendable, and I intend to prove them wrong.

I'm going to live.

Chapter 5

There might only be one good thing about life at Confluence Academy, and it's a wonderful invention known as a 'shower.'

My body is a map of pain from my first two weeks at Confluence Academy. Every muscle screams in protest as I sink deeper into the steaming pool, hoping the hot water might erase the memory of Serena slamming me into a wall so hard this morning that I tasted blood. My tongue probes the inside of my cheek, still tender. I'm lucky I didn't chip a tooth.

All I did was look at her when I was leaving the dining room after breakfast. She's apparently still pissed she didn't get a chance to challenge me herself and beat me senseless that first day. Thankfully, Raith Hollow has kept his distance from me. He's apparently too busy excelling in every single subject and attracting followers like some kind of budding commander of the fire affinities.

I close my eyes and try to let these thoughts dissolve in the heat. It has become a daily ritual for me. I sink into the waters that remind me of home – of when home still felt like home – and I try to forget about the dangers and politics of this place for just a few moments.

The floating clouds overhead shift and churn with magic, releasing a gentle rainfall that patters against the surface of the pool. Steam rises in thick clouds around me, giving the illusion of privacy as other first-year waters strip off bloodied training clothes and descend into the communal bath. I got over undressing in front of other guys pretty quickly, because these showers feel like the only thing keeping me standing most days.

That, and it already seems like nearly everybody is sleeping around as much and as often as they can here. Prudishness is for those who don't face death every day, I guess.

We spar every morning, physically beating one another into submission after drilling forms with the instructors. On good days, nobody even ends up dead when the matches are over. After sparring, it's straight to weight training and endurance. Endless lifting, pulling, jumping, running, and sweating. There's a brief break to stuff food in our faces for breakfast in the grand dining hall, then it's on to academics.

We're taught field medicine, survival skills, battlefield tactics, history, and, most of all, information about the elemental plane and the magical creatures we're going to risk our lives to tether. I already know things like how to splint a broken bone with nothing but branches and weeds, edible and poisonous plants, and historical facts that never would've mattered to a girl like me from a fishing town – things like how the empire is ruled by three, two women and one man, based on a tradition that started with a set of triplets eight hundred years ago.

Our lessons on elementals are my favorite, though.

The other classes make my brain feel like it's aching from information overload, but I find I can't learn enough about elementals and the elemental plane to satisfy my curiosity. I already know, for example, how rare it is for second generation and older elementals to tether to humans. The young elementals, which are under a hundred years of age, can only take one form and tend to look like beasts from our world. Older elementals can take more forms. Some of the oldest, like the ones I saw during the elemental trial, can even take humanoid forms.

Last but not least, there's channeling class, where we're divided by affinity and taught how to harness the essence needed to craft magical spells. Unfortunately for me, none of the methods we're learning seem to work for me. Being 'unbound' must mean I channel magic differently, but I can't exactly ask someone for tips and tricks, so I've been utterly failing and drawing the anger of our channeling instructor every day.

If I wasn't so exhausted, I might just be giddy with excitement at the thought of learning to use magic. As it is, I'm too beaten and tired to really care. Survival has a way of pushing wonder to the back burner. Because beneath the classes, the new information, the sore muscles, and the daily grind, there's a constant heartbeat of violence here.

Eight students have already died during sparring, not counting the death on the first day. I've heard whispers of two more dying between classes, murdered by other first-year offerings, no doubt. So I've been doing my best to keep my eyes low and avoid notice, especially from people like Raith and Serena.

'Can't we just skip class?' Mireen groans from beside me, her copper hair plastered to her scalp.

'I wish,' I say, closing my eyes and sinking deeper until the water laps at my chin. But we both know missing classes or training sessions brings remedial assignments. From what I've heard, the remedial assignments are always many times worse than the original class.

'—another? Elements . . . At this rate, there won't be any of us left by Confluence Day.'

The surprise in the girl's voice catches my attention, and I strain my ears to hear the conversation. Through the shifting curtains of steam, I spot three figures – two girls and a guy who stand near the center of the pool, heads close as they speak in hushed voices. The girls aren't even bothering to sink low enough to cover their bare breasts.

Mireen follows my eyes, grinning conspiratorially. 'I heard the three of them sleep together every night.'

I raise an eyebrow. 'All three?'

Mireen shrugs. 'Sounds kind of fun, right?'

Part of me envies their confidence. Mostly, though, I just can't understand them. I'm too exhausted to even think about sex at the end of my days here. Maybe the release would be nice, but it's hardly on the top of my priority list. One thing is painfully clear already, though. The only thing the people in charge care about is that we show up to our classes and training on time. Between classes, first-year offerings are apparently free to fuck or kill amongst ourselves as much as we like.

'Yeah,' the guy says, his voice barely carrying over the patter of the magical rain. 'I think we should form some kind of team. I'm pretty sure I heard that Malakai guy and a few of his friends talking about something similar.'

'A team?' one of the girls asks. 'For what?'

'To protect ourselves,' the guy hisses, glancing around nervously. The steam is thick enough that we can only see them because of a few torches at the far end of the room, casting their figures in silhouettes. I don't think they realize we're in earshot.

'Malakai has killed the last two people he sparred with,' the guy continues. 'And today, one of his buddies did the same. They're obviously trying to thin us out. We need to watch each other's backs.'

My stomach turns. I'd witnessed one of those 'accidents' myself yesterday – a sparring match that ended with a first-year water offering on the ground, gurgling as blood filled his lungs. The instructors had simply shaken their heads and called for someone to remove the body, as if they were asking for someone to clean up a spilled drink.

I turn to Mireen and see the tight set of her jaw. She's listening now, too, her eyes sharp despite the languid posture she maintains.

'Am I crazy, or is that not a terrible idea?' I whisper, keeping my voice low enough that it won't carry across the water. 'Forming teams, I mean.'

'I don't know,' she admits, her voice equally quiet. A droplet of water slides down her temple. 'But I don't like where an idea like that leads.'

'I know. Forming teams sounds a lot like declaring war.'

Mireen chews her lip. 'We can at least watch each other's backs, even if we don't want to get involved, right?'

'Right.' The part I don't say is how it won't matter if the rest of us decide to treat this like a war. All that matters is if one group of people does. If this Malakai guy is forging alliances, then he already declared war. The only question for us is whether we want to become participants or victims.

Her fingers tighten around mine beneath the water, and I feel the familiar, terrifying pull starting deep in my core. I jerk my hand away like I've been burned, splashing water between us. Mireen gives me a confused look, but I make a show of wincing. 'Sorry. I think I may have tweaked something in my hand sparring yesterday. Still tender.'

The last thing I need is to draw power from the one person who might actually have my back in this place. I'm still waiting for Bastian to bring that book and maybe reveal some answers about what the hell being unbound means.

After our shower, I change into a fresh offering uniform. We were all given matching white uniforms that make us stand out like sore thumbs. The older students all wear black with gold bars on their shoulders – one for each year they've survived in the academy.

I check the back of my left hand discreetly as I button my sleeve, making sure the disguise is holding. The silver threads beneath the false blue wave pattern shift slightly, as if responding to my attention. Thankfully, nobody ever looks too closely at the mark, or they would probably suspect something was wrong with it.

Our academic classes rotate throughout the week, and today is Military Tactics.

I join a group of other first-year offerings heading from the showers. The other affinities have some kind of bathing facilities, too, but I've heard the water showers are the envy of every affinity. The annoyed looks we get from other affinities as we emerge with wet hair add credence to the rumors.

We walk in a loose group of white-uniformed offerings through the halls of Confluence. I feel like a sheep waiting for slaughter. I keep my eyes forward, focusing on where I'm going and not making eye contact with any passing upper-year students or even the first-year aspirants and legacies.

The corridors are wide and high-ceilinged, crafted from ancient stone that seems to absorb sound in a way that makes our footsteps echo ominously. Arcane symbols are carved into the walls at regular intervals, glowing faintly with stored power.

Most areas of the castle are, at least, well-lit and beautiful.

A beautiful place to die with the sunlight on my face. How wonderful.

The castle is large, but relatively simple to navigate. It's a three-story rectangle with one affinity tower at each corner and a large, central courtyard in the middle. Each section of the rectangle houses a different style of class or training. The northern section is for academics. The eastern section is dedicated to physical training, which is where we spar and exercise. The southern section is for channeling. The western section is the only one we haven't used yet, and my best guess is because it has to do with elemental tethers.

Every inch of this place is full of tapestries and relics that make it feel ancient, as if it has been standing since before time itself. The ghost of centuries of other primals in training feels like a thick presence everywhere I go, as if the screams of the dead and their blood lingers even now, reaching for us.

Military Tactics is the only class where first-year offerings, aspirants, and legacies all mix. It's a large lecture-hall style room and has more than enough space for every single first-year to sit at once.

Legacies sit at the very front of the room in comfortable, cushioned chairs.

Aspirants sit behind the legacies with a better view of the maps and chalkboards at the front of the class.

Offerings form a sea of white behind the smaller, black uniforms. A sea, maybe, but it's a thinning sea.

Only two weeks have passed and the room already feels noticeably less full. How many of us will be left by Confluence Day? How many of us will come back from the elemental plane at all?

I take a seat near the very back with Mireen, and we're joined by a dark-skinned boy with wire-framed glasses, intelligent eyes, and a freshly split lip.

'You okay, Ambrose?' I ask as he sits.

He idly touches his lip, then shrugs. 'You should see the other guy.'

'Should we?' Mireen asks, leaning past me to smirk at him.

'No, actually. He's completely untouched. I didn't even land a punch.' He adjusts his glasses, which sit slightly crooked across his nose. 'Just another day of getting my ass handed to me in sparring.'

'Join the club,' I say.

We all chuckle, but our laughter is cut short by the appearance of the fire offerings.

Raith walks at the front, and the others follow him in a tight group. The white offering uniform does absolutely nothing to hide the way his rows upon rows of muscles move beneath the fabric, fluid and powerful like some ancient predator. His scarred face and neck only add to the impression of barely contained danger. I force my eyes away, trying and failing to ignore the way my body reacts to him.

Skin flushed hot. A light sweat. Pounding heart. A pool of heat gathering in my lower belly.

He sits right behind the aspirants, and the other fires file in on either side of him, leaving an empty seat to his right and left, as if out of deference.

The dynamic within the water offerings is chaotic, with small packs of wolves and a larger group of – for lack of a better word – sheep.

The fires are a much smaller group, and they've already fallen into a military-like organization, with Raith as the apparent high commander.

The airs, as far as I can tell, get along better as a whole. If nothing else, fewer of them have died in training and I don't see as much open hostility.

The earths keep to themselves, but the aura of general suspicion around earths and fires means people generally don't make an effort to get to know them. Then again, everybody is too busy trying to stay alive to worry much about making friends.

'Can you believe that guy?' Ambrose asks. Like everybody else in white, he's watching Raith.

'Asshole,' I say, as if agreeing with Ambrose's unspoken assessment.

'Asshole,' Mireen agrees. She tucks a strand of copper hair behind her ear. 'Very, very hot. But yes, an asshole.'

I snort and shake my head, trying not to stare at the way Raith's broad shoulders taper to a narrow waist or how his hands — large enough to crush a throat without effort — are casually propped on the desk before him.

Looking at Raith has a way of bringing my mind straight to sex. To making me think that maybe a little nightly release wouldn't be the worst thing in the world, or how even if I'm sore as all hells, the right guy could still make it worth the effort. I'd blame my thoughts on the tension of knowing any of us could die at any moment, but that wouldn't explain why it's specifically him that triggers this response. In some ways, I think it's how he wears scars on the outside that feel like a reflection of my inner self. Scarred. Broken. Both of us volunteered for this, and I wonder if that means there's some kind of twisted kinship between us.

I tear my attention away, cheeks burning, and focus on the front of the classroom just as Instructor Pilton storms in, practically jogging down the steps until he's at the front, where he slams down a brief-case full of maps.

Instructor Pilton, like all in the north and eastern wings, isn't actually a primal. He's in his sixties with an explosion of gray hair and wild, tangled brows. His right arm is gone at the elbow, and the offering who asked about it on the first day got hit in the head with a piece of chalk.

In what I'm coming to see as 'the usual,' he spreads out his maps and begins going through historical battles and quizzing us on tactics and strategy. There's no introduction or preamble. He just launches straight into the topic.

Before he gets too deep, Mireen nudges me and points to something at the edge of the room. 'Look!' she whispers.

I follow her finger and see a small gray rat scurrying along the wall.

'He's a little survivor. Just like us,' Mireen says. 'So godsdamned cute. I wish we were allowed pets here . . .'

'You want a pet rat?' I ask with a sideways smile.

'I would take what I can get, Nessa.' Mireen's expression is wistful as she watches the rat slip between a crevice in the stones and disappear.

'Now,' Pilton says half an hour later as he whacks a large map with a thin, wooden pointing stick. 'Empire had intelligence reporting that Red Kingdom had already moved this deep.' He jabs a point several miles in from the border at the time. 'If you were given two primals and a thousand soldiers to handle the threat, where would you start?'

Questions are lobbed around the room.

'How many primals does Red Kingdom have?'

'Two,' Pilton answers, his voice carrying easily through the space. 'They have the same number of primals, but twice as many soldiers.'

A few students complain about the impossible task. Their voices rise in a chorus of protests about the unfair odds.

Bastian sits at the front, his golden hair making him visible even at this distance. He leans forward, his voice loud and clear. 'Attack their logistics,' he says. 'They're already miles into enemy territory. Cut off their supply lines and wait to engage until they're weakened from hunger.'

'Good,' Instructor Pilton says, tapping his pointing stick against his shoulder. 'Your enemy outnumbers you, so find a clever edge to gain an advantage. This is a wise line of thought.'

Raith's deep voice surprises me, rumbling through the classroom like distant thunder. 'Nerra River is a mile south of the enemy's position. Prepare an ambush. Destroy the bridge when the primals are on it. Use the element of surprise to slaughter them before they know what has hit them.'

Pilton raises his eyebrows, nodding. 'Ah. Good. The fifth element, if you will. Surprise. While Bastian's idea is less direct risk, we must also consider the enemy will steal and pillage whatever we deprive them of by destroying logistics. They'll take a toll in blood before they are weakened enough for the advantage to hold. Raith's plan has the advantage of nearly immediately dealing with the problem, rather than letting enemies continue to ravage our lands and claim lives. Very good.'

I roll my eyes at Mireen, who bites back a smile.

In every class I share with Raith, he excels. Even our instructors already seem to be favoring him. We haven't shared the sparring ring since the first day, but I can see him easily enough dominating his opponents. He's the most skilled first-year offering in the sparring ring, the strongest in the weight room, and when he decides to speak up in class, he always earns the approval of our instructors.

In truth, part of me is just annoyed I can't dare try to show him up in our academic classes. But trying to flex my brain and prove how smart I am would only draw attention. Attention, I've decided, is something I must avoid at all costs. Attention means questions. It means scrutiny. And scrutiny would likely mean exposing my unbound mark.

'What do you think Pilton would say if I suggested talking to them?' I whisper to Mireen and Ambrose. If the situation Pilton described was real, I'd honestly just want to know why they were in our territory. Chances are, it would be on orders from their leadership, and there could be a way to negotiate. Maybe they just need supplies or some information. Compared to thousands of lives, it seems like a much better option.

'Talking to them?' Ambrose asks, eyebrows raised high above the rims of his glasses.

'I think he might throw chalk at your head if you suggest that,' Mireen says, nudging me with her elbow.

Instructor Pilton is currently ripping apart Serena's idea about attacking them head on 'for the glory of Empire.'

'The enemy is not human!' Ambrose mocks in a whispered impression of Pilton. 'They're violent, bloodthirsty animals. Would you—'

A piece of chalk bounces off Ambrose's forehead, stopping him mid-sentence. He adjusts his glasses, blinking in surprise.

'If you have something to add to this discussion, offering,' Pilton says, his voice deadly calm, 'I invite you to stand and share it with the rest of us.'

Ambrose pales. 'No, sir. Sorry, sir.'

Pilton snorts and turns back to the map, but not before his eyes flicker briefly to me. I drop my gaze to my notes, suddenly very interested in the sketch I've made of troop formations.

I feel someone watching me and glance up to find Raith turned in his seat, eyes boring into mine. His expression is unreadable, but there's something assessing in his gaze that makes the hair on the back of my neck stand up. I hold his stare for a heartbeat, or two, before he turns back to the front, leaving me feeling undressed by his eyes, measured for a coffin, or both.

Charming.

When class is over, legacies rise first to leave. Aspirants follow, and then finally the offerings head out.

'Think Instructor Sestra is going to go any easier on you today?' Mireen asks as we head toward the southern wing of campus where channeling class is held.

'Doubt it.' The thought of channeling class makes my stomach clench with dread. Two weeks of trying and I still haven't been able to produce even a drop of water.

Ambrose nudges me from my other side. 'Have you tried . . . not being terrible at magic, Nessa? I imagine that would really work wonders with the woman.'

'Oh, yeah? That's a genius idea. I can't believe I didn't think of it.' I shove him back, but there's no real force behind it.

We're passing through the courtyard when I see Serena and a pair of fire affinities huddled in the shade of a tree with Malakai and what must be his 'team.'

I slow my pace and then stop to stare. 'What do you think that's about?'

Ambrose runs his tongue over his teeth. 'Well, Serena doesn't appear to be stabbing anyone. That rules out my best guesses.'

'You think Malakai is trying to make some kind of cross-affinity alliance? Is that a thing?' I ask.

Mireen shakes her head, blue eyes catching the mid-afternoon sun streaming into the courtyard. 'If it's not, I think they're trying to make it one.'

I study their body language, trying to pick up clues. Malakai is a mountain of muscle, carved like a statue meant to represent some hero from the stories. But the cruel turn of his features keeps him from being handsome. And his eyes . . . there's something missing in them. An emptiness, like there's nothing behind them but an empty pit of hatred dark enough to match his black hair.

He stands with his back straight, gesturing with controlled precision while Serena leans in, arms crossed but attentive. There's no friendly camaraderie between them – this is clearly transactional. One of Malakai's water allies keeps glancing nervously around the courtyard, as if worried they'll be seen.

'Why would waters care about teaming up with fires?' I ask. 'It's not going to help Serena if there are more water elementals to go around on Confluence Day, right? It's fucked up, but I at least understand why Malakai wants to . . .'

'Brutally murder fellow water offerings?' Ambrose offers. 'Yes. It's totally understandable. As long as you're a heartless psychopath, of course.'

'She's right,' Mireen says. 'Helping Malakai kill us shouldn't benefit her at all. It's suspicious as hell.'

'What is?' A deep voice asks from behind, making all three of us jump.

I'm surprised to see Raith, of all people, standing behind us. He somehow looks bigger every time I see him. I'm reminded once again how unfairly attractive he is despite the burn scars on the left side of his face and body. Being this close to him . . . it makes my lungs feel tighter, like I have to work for every breath. I do my best not to let it show, but I'm pretty sure I'm failing miserably.

'Nothing,' I say, acutely aware of the way my pulse has quickened.

'Right.' Raith's big hands are in his pockets, but the orange glow of his affinity mark is visible through the thin fabric. 'Nothing. That does sound very suspicious.'

Instead of walking around us, he walks right through our group, bumping me with his big, stupid shoulder. I stumble back, and my fingers instinctively grasp his forearm to steady myself.

The connection is immediate and terrifying. Power surges from him into me, hot and visceral, like liquid fire flowing up my arm. I snatch my hand back, but not before I see his eyes narrow in . . . is that suspicion, like he's confirming something?

He takes a step back, eyes darting to my left hand where my disguised water mark shifts and twists, faint threads of silver hidden within the blue.

I quickly tuck my hands behind my back, swallowing hard.

Mireen and Ambrose are looking at us both like we're crazy.

I brace for him to ask questions I don't want to answer, especially in front of Mireen and Ambrose. Instead, his expression settles back to a controlled neutral. He obviously felt what happened, and between me channeling fire during our sparring match two weeks ago, he has to suspect . . . something. But what?

I decide to change the subject. 'We were wondering what Serena's doing talking to Malakai.'

His attention thankfully shifts to where she's talking with him and his water affinities. 'That's a good fucking question.' His features harden and his fists clench before he turns from us, stalking toward the group.

I stifle a laugh when Serena sees Raith coming and practically runs away, disappearing into a hallway off the courtyard.

'Did you guys see that?' I ask, grateful for the distraction.

'The scary guy nearly knocking you to your face with a shoulder check and then you guys eye fucked for a few awkward seconds?' Ambrose asks. 'Definitely saw it.'

'No. Whatever Serena and Malakai were talking about, she didn't want to include Raith in it.'

'I thought he was their leader, or whatever?' Mireen asks.

'Me too. Maybe it's not as simple as it looks.'

We've already lingered too long in the courtyard, though, and I don't need to give Instructor Sestra more reasons to hate me, like showing up late to class. I give Serena's retreating form one last look, then shake my head and hurry toward the southern wing, trying to ignore the lingering warmth where the power I took from Raith still fills me.

Whatever is happening between Serena, Malakai, and the others, I'll have to figure it out later. Right now, I have to survive channeling class without revealing that I'm a fraud.

'You'll all need to do better than this,' Sestra's voice cuts through the dark and dusty classroom. I'm with a group of other first-year water offerings, and our task is to conjure a ball of water above our palms and hold it.

The room is filled with long tables and various containers of water. True water affinities are like vessels, apparently, constantly filling with water essence that allows them to channel water from nothing or interact with existing sources of water.

Most students can already manipulate water to produce floating balls of liquid that hover and shift above their hands. The more talented can even conjure water from thin air in smaller quantities. Everybody but me is progressing each day.

I still can't even get the containers of water to move, let alone draw it to my palm and shape it.

'It seems some of you likely needn't even worry about Confluence Day,' she says, lips curling down at the corners as she watches me struggle. 'As I seriously doubt you'll survive to see it. And if you do, your poor grasp of elemental magic will mean no elemental would even consider tethering you.'

Confluence Day. Everything here at school revolves around it, and we're told multiple times a day how fast approaching it is. We're told we'll be tested and assessed by the elementals of our affinity, but nothing more than that. Most often, we're reminded how many of us will die before the day even comes. Sometimes, on cheerful days, we're reminded that many of us will also die *during* Confluence day.

At some point, the constant threat of a horrible death loses a little bit of its sting. All I can do is wake up each day, struggle, and do my best to survive. The real challenge is not letting my fear for the people I've grown to care about petrify me. Mireen, and even Ambrose. I worry more about something happening to them, and most of my motivation to improve is driven by wanting to be able to protect them.

I stare at my palm where the disguised water mark ripples faintly beneath my skin. My fingers tremble with effort as I try to coax even the smallest drop of water to rise. Nothing happens. The silver threads hidden beneath the blue wave pattern seem to mock me – a constant reminder that I'm an impostor.

Sweat beads on my forehead with effort, but nothing I try seems to work. Sestra's instructions are all for true water affinities, not . . . whatever I am. Unbound. The word the elementals used still echoes in my mind at night. It's like trying to force a key into the wrong lock – I have power, I can feel it churning all around me like a storm-tossed sea, but I can't access it through the methods she teaches. I can't find out how to bring it into myself.

Every failed attempt is another risk. What if my mark shifts during class? What if the silver shows through while everyone is watching? I clench my fist, forcing the panic down. I can't afford to show weakness. Not here.

And I also can't afford to experiment with my powers for risk of showing what I really am. I'm stuck between two impossible choices, stagnating in a place where stagnation is as good as a death sentence.

Until we survive Confluence Day and tether an elemental, we're hardly more than trash here. Somehow, I've got to find a way to at least make it until then. How the hell I'm going to tether an elemental when I don't even have a normal affinity, though, is beyond me.

'Will channeling get easier once we tether an elemental?' a girl beside me asks, almost as if her own struggles have brought her mind to the same place as mine. Her forehead is beaded with sweat as a sphere of clear water above her palm shudders and finally collapses with a splash.

Sestra drifts through the room, severe features always making her seem to calculate and judge. She has skin so light it's nearly white, with shockingly blue eyes and markings that signal her status as a primal. Even though she's tethered to an elemental, I've never actually seen it. Apparently, that's rather common, as elementals can choose to reveal themselves or not to mortals.

'Will it be easier to perform a simple magical trick when you've tethered an elemental?' she asks, voice deceptively sweet. 'No. Because if you can't even do this, no elemental will deem you worthy of the primal tether.'

'What happens if we don't tether an elemental on Confluence Day?' Mireen asks.

Unlike me, Mireen has already shown a talent for channeling, which means Sestra hates her less than the rest of us. Otherwise, I doubt she'd even answer the question.

'You'll be trapped in the elemental plane. The rift between worlds opens briefly once each year. The only way back is with the tether of an elemental. To put it quite simply, tether or die.'

For just a moment, something seems to drift behind Sestra's eyes – a shadow of memory or perhaps grief – and her fingers absently trace one of the blue markings on her forearm. Then it's gone, replaced by her usual stern expression as her eyes sweep over the class. 'Which is one reason I push you all so hard. The elemental plane shows no mercy to the unprepared.'

'Tether or die, huh?' Mireen whispers. 'If I get stuck on the elemental plane, I'm going to find the cutest elemental and befriend it. We'll go on adventures together. It'll be great. Who says I have to die?'

'If there are any giant rat elementals, I'm sure you'll be in paradise.'

There's a sound of rushing water to my right. I look up suddenly, along with the rest of the class.

Malakai has conjured a long, twisting line of water that sprouts from his palm and has started whipping from side to side as it grows like some kind of tentacle.

'Cut off that spell,' Sestra commands, her voice sharp with warning. 'Spheres, Malakai. Spheres are the assignment, not—'

Malakai's eyes slide to the guy beside him – a burly East Coaster named Lorne. For a split second, I see the calculation and malice in Malakai's eyes.

Oh shit.

I'm standing before I know it, eyes wide and heart hammering in my chest.

Malakai is pretending he can't control the spell, even as I see the water sharpening into a blade-like shape.

I make it three long steps toward him, but I'm not fast enough.

One moment, the blade of water is whipping left and right. The next, Lorne is gripping his throat.

Blood trickles between his fingers as he stands, his chair scraping on stone and falling sideways. The sound echoes through the suddenly silent room.

There are gasps and a few screams as Lorne falls to his knees, eyes bulging. A gurgling sound escapes his throat as he tries to breathe through the blood. He reaches out, fingers grasping at the air, before collapsing face-first onto the stone floor.

A pool of crimson spreads beneath him, inching across the floor toward my boots. I freeze, unable to look away from the growing stain. My heart hammers in my ears, drowning out the chaos around me. I've seen death here, but the casual cruelty of this murder makes bile rise in my throat.

Malakai is barely attempting to look shocked or remorseful. He makes a few half-hearted excuses about how it was an accident, but his eyes scan the room, watching our reactions. When they land on me, I see a flicker of something predatory, and I quickly look away.

The whole ordeal only takes moments. Lorne is dead. The body is taken away, and class resumes, as if there isn't a pool of drying blood on the floor in the center of the room we're all supposed to pretend we don't notice.

Everyone is afraid to show fear here. Afraid to look weak. To look like a target.

An unpleasant blooming of shame rises up in me. Yes, I stood. Yes, I took steps toward the chaos. But what did I do after it was all said and done?

I looked away from Malakai, afraid of being next.

We all did, and I feel a sudden, burning hatred for this place and what it's turning us all into. I slowly take my seat again, eyes on my disguised mark.

The only indication Primal Sestra gives of noticing or caring about the 'accidental' murder is the slightest tightening around the corner of her mouth.

'Let this be a lesson,' Sestra says after a moment. 'In battle and war, you will be expected to continue performing your task, even when faced with horror. Show me how you can all press on in the face of adversity.'

My stomach churns as I stare at the dark stain spreading across the stone. Just minutes ago, Lorne was alive – breathing, thinking, hoping to survive this place like the rest of us. Now he's gone, hauled away like refuse, and we're all expected to continue practicing water manipulation as if nothing happened.

I look around at my classmates. Some are pale, hands trembling as they try to focus on their water spheres. Others have already adapted, eyes forward, determined to be among those who survive. But it's the third group that chills me – the ones watching Malakai with something like curiosity and even admiration in their eyes.

He's showing them another way to excel here. Why compete with your peers when you can simply eliminate them? Brutality and cold-blooded murder win out. Those who strike first have the advantage, and Malakai is putting together a team of killers just like himself.

People who will kill us, even if it only marginally increases their odds of becoming a primal or getting a better assignment after graduation.

I force my eyes back to my own hands, trying to ignore the metallic scent of blood still hanging in the air. Suddenly, my inability to channel seems like the least of my problems. The casual brutality makes me think of home – of my own guilt, my own bloody hands – and I push the memory away. I can't afford to drown in the past when death lurks so close in the present.

This place is a powder keg, and Malakai is already playing with fire.

But as I stare at the crusting blood that someone will eventually be ordered to clean, a darker thought takes root. If I can't learn to channel soon, I'll be next. Easy prey. A simple way for someone else to improve their chances.

And if I get myself killed, Mireen and Ambrose will be on their own. Alone in this place where allies are hard to come by and trust is a luxury few can afford.

I flex my hand, concentrating harder, desperation lending strength to my efforts. Still nothing.

Across the room, Malakai catches my eye and smiles. It's not a friendly smile – it's the kind of smile a predator gives its next meal.

I need to learn how to channel. I need to figure out what 'unbound' means. I need allies.

There's certainly no escaping Confluence Academy. Not alive, anyway. We've all been told the only way we leave here is as a full primal after five years of training or in a coffin. And despite everything, despite the danger and the horror and the lies I'm living . . . I'm not ready to die. Not yet.

Not here.

I close my eyes, pushing away all thoughts of Malakai, of blood, of failure. I reach down deep inside myself, searching for that well of power I know is there. And for just a moment – brief as a heartbeat – I feel something respond. I feel the latent water essence in the air drifting toward me, tentatively and slowly, but it's there.

A single drop of water rises from my palm, conjured from thin air.

Chapter 6

Ever since the elemental trial, the nightmares come almost every night. At first, they weren't so vivid. So terrifying. But night by night, they're getting stronger. More real. Dark water pressing in around me and the cold awareness of something vast moving beneath me, watching from the depths.

A deep, horrible voice whispers up to me from the darkness. 'Unbound . . . Nessa Thorne . . . Un . . . bound.'

I wake gasping, sheets twisted around my legs, the phantom sensation of drowning still tight in my throat. I bolt upright, gulping air and pressing a hand to my racing heart, my lungs burning as if they'd actually filled with water.

As if the challenge of daily life here at Confluence wasn't bad enough after nearly six weeks, my sleeping mind has decided to join in for the fun. Fucking wonderful.

'Another one?' Mireen's voice comes softly through the darkness. So much for not waking her.

'Sorry,' I whisper.

'Don't be sorry.' She sits up, then pauses, pointing to something near her bed. 'And promise you won't freak out, but I think we have a roommate.' She indicates tiny footprints in spilled powder by the wall. 'I've been leaving it crumbs. Figured if it's survived this long at Confluence, it deserves a medal. Or at least dinner.'

I notice the prints and shake my head ruefully. 'You're luring rats into our room. *On purpose?*'

'Singular. Not plural. And yes. Imagine how scary this place must be as a rat. He deserves someone who will love and look after him.'

I shake my head, smiling. 'If it bites me, I'm kicking him out.'

Mireen folds her arms. 'If he bites you twice. You've got to give him a chance to get his bearings.' I can already see how her body is growing more lean and muscular with our daily training regime through her thin night clothes. My own physique is changing, too. The soft places on my body are hardening every day, what fat I had melting away to reveal lean muscle. I'm even starting to gain some confidence in the sparring ring – a faint belief that I can stop someone from killing me if they try.

'So . . .' she leans forward, legs crossed on the bed. 'What do you see? In the dreams?'

I hesitate. Dreams are private things – especially here, where any weakness can be exploited. But this is Mireen. She even admitted when Malakai tried to 'recruit' her for his growing team of those he calls his elites. Mireen is far more talented than most when it comes to channeling, which is what earned her the invite.

Obviously, she turned him down, even though the temptation of not having to watch her back for him and his elites must have been immense. She also told me about it right away, confirming what I already knew. I can trust Mireen with my life.

'I see water,' I say, shivering at the memory that still burns vivid in my mind's eye. 'Darkness. Something . . . watching me.' I don't mention how that feeling of being watched persists even after I wake. I keep that to myself, not because I don't trust her, but because speaking it aloud would make it feel more real.

More terrifying.

She's quiet for a moment. 'My grandfather used to say dreams are messages. From the gods, maybe, or from parts of ourselves we don't understand.'

'Well, I wish this particular messenger would shut up,' I mutter, making her laugh softly.

There's more still I don't dare say aloud – like the voice I hear beneath the water, whispering words I'm beginning to understand. About how each night, I sink deeper, getting closer to whatever waits in those depths. How I'm beginning to think it's looking for me specifically.

Words have power, and I'm going to keep choosing not to give those particular ideas any more power than they already have.

'Today,' Instructor Blackstone announces to the exhausted water offerings assembled in the training room. The large, circular stone room in the eastern wing of Confluence. Morning sun pours in from every direction through high windows, cutting the space through with buttery shafts that highlight every speck of dust. 'You will select your primary combat weapon.'

Instructor Blackstone's scarred face surveys us with the detached interest of a butcher examining a particularly disappointing group of livestock. Racks upon racks of weapons have been brought in, and each instrument of death catches bits of light in a gleaming display.

I'm acutely aware of how many fewer of us there are now. Nearly every day, someone dies. Worst of all, the lion's share of deaths come within the first-year water affinities. We can all thank Malakai for that. I just wonder how much longer I can continue to exist beneath his notice. How much longer before he and his 'elites' decide to crush my skull on the training mat or a darkened hallway somewhere after hours.

Ambrose appears beside me, lips drawn in a tight line. 'Weapons! Yay. I was hoping they'd give us a more effective way to kill one another.'

'I don't think Malakai and his team need any help,' Mireen agrees.

Malakai stands at the edge, eyes hungry as he looks at the weapons. He was already big, but our continued training and hearty meals have him looking even more terrifying by the day. He's whispering with his two closest elites, Corpus and Titus. Corpus has deep, tanned skin and narrow eyes. He wears his platinum blonde hair in a long ponytail. He's lean and sharp where Malakai is thick and powerful.

His other companion is Titus, who keeps his head shaved, his fists permanently clenched, and always wears a scowl. Like Malakai, Titus is massive, and looks like he could tear me in half with his bare hands.

Malakai's makeshift army has grown over the weeks, but the most concerning is how the majority of its members don't make themselves known. There's no uniform. No official sign to tell us who might be following his orders.

Naturally, I haven't branched out and made new friends beyond Mireen and Ambrose, because doing so grows riskier by the day.

Blackstone gestures for us to approach the weapons. 'Choose wisely. This isn't about what looks impressive or feels powerful in your hand. It's about what will keep you alive in combat. You've been learning about your strengths and weaknesses these past weeks in sparring and training. Choose a weapon that compliments your strengths and avoids your weaknesses.'

I hang back, studying my options while others rush forward. Most gravitate toward longer swords or spears, weapons that keep enemies at a distance or look like they could cleave somebody in half. I'm not sure what would suit me – something light enough for my frame, but not so small that I'm forced within grappling range of larger opponents.

'Not those,' a voice says close to my ear.

I had been looking at the spears, wondering if I'd be strong enough to use something like that to keep people out of reach.

I turn to find Raith standing behind me. As always, his presence makes my body light up like an electric storm – nerves firing and skin flushing. I didn't even hear him approach. He shouldn't be here – this session is for water offerings only – but nobody challenges his presence.

Of course they don't. If one thing has become painfully obvious since our first day, it's that Raith is far and above the best of all the offerings. He's feared and respected in equal measure, even by some of the instructors.

'What?' I manage, startled by his proximity. He smells like campfire smoke and something else I can't name, something that makes my pulse quicken, something dangerous and intoxicating all at once.

I see Raith almost every day, but he generally doesn't seem to remember I exist. By all accounts, I'm average in most subjects and far below average in channeling. I can tell most instructors have already assumed I won't survive Confluence Day and are focusing their efforts on more promising students.

I've even heard students half-jokingly call him The Burned Prince, and I can hardly blame them. Common belief seems to be he'll be a top ranked primal in Empire's army by the time he graduates. I even overheard a pair of students speculating about how he might tether an older elemental on Confluence Day, which supposedly hasn't happened in decades. Young elementals tether us. Older elementals either have past tethers and scars from the deaths of their humans, or they've chosen not to get involved in the conflicts of men.

'Problem, Saltcrest?'

I flinch, realizing my mind had gone elsewhere as I stared at him. *Saltcrest.* He does remember me, then. And I still have no idea how or when he found out where I'm from.

Mireen and Ambrose have both taken what I assume are involuntary steps away from Raith. Even with the weapons on display, the other waters are also watching him with mixtures of wariness and awe.

I shake my head, heat creeping up my neck. 'Just trying not to imagine somebody skewering me with one of those.'

'Be the one doing the skewering, then,' Raith says simply.

Easy for him to say. I don't think Raith has even come close to losing a sparring match since he arrived. Even if someone did want to kill him, they'd have no chance. He's untouchable. Hardly even human.

And, for some reason, he's standing in the middle of us waters and talking to me.

He looks at the others, who are watching us openly. 'Fuck off,' he growls.

Eyes jerk away and people flinch back like he's a lion that just roared.

Except Malakai and his soldiers, I notice. They're watching Raith with calculated stares. Stares that don't make sense, unless they're really so bloodthirsty they'd go after people outside our affinity.

'It's okay,' I say to Mireen and Ambrose, who linger, even though they look like they want to scatter with the rest of the students.

At least I hope it's okay. Raith wouldn't kill me right here, would he?

But I see he's studying the weapons, then returning his focus to me. His eyes scan my body, and for a moment, I wonder if he's actually checking me out.

He reaches and gives my arm a squeeze, then frowns, as if not entirely pleased.

'What?' I demand.

'You need to take your training more seriously. You're still . . . squishy.'

'Excuse me?' My jaw drops in indignation.

I know I must be imagining it, but I almost think the corner of his mouth twitches upward at that. 'Short.' He's still staring at me – assessing me. 'Somewhat weak. But fast. Hmm.' He strokes his sculpted jaw with big, calloused fingers. 'Smart . . .'

Smart? I'm not sure how he knows enough about me to assume that, but—

Before I can respond, he moves past me, selecting a thin-bladed sword with a simple crossguard. It's shorter than a full-sized sword but longer than a dagger.

'This.' He offers it to me, handle first. 'Emphasis on speed and precision. Quick thrusts rather than hacking power. A thrust is faster than a slash. The blade is short enough that you should be able to strike first against anybody with a longer weapon. Against a shorter weapon, you'll use this to keep out of their reach,' he says, tapping my temple.

I take it hesitantly, testing its weight. The balance is perfect, the blade an extension of my arm rather than a burden. 'Why are you helping me?' I ask, suspicious of anything resembling kindness in this place.

'You intrigue me.' He steps closer, making my breath catch and filling my nose with that strange but intoxicating scent of his. 'And I don't think you're as weak as you let on.'

Before I can press further, he walks away, rejoining the fire offerings on the other side of the arena. They've already selected weapons, and they're training cooperatively, rather than trying to kill one another like the waters and airs do.

It's ironic, in a way. Before coming here, I was told fire and earth primals were all spies for Red Kingdom. Those who weren't spies, they said, just hadn't turned coat yet. They were painted as the animals and the ones to fear.

But here? The fires organize under Raith, and I only know of two who have died since we arrived. Meanwhile, more than thirty waters have died and half as many airs. The earths also have only had one or two deaths, and they've organized themselves under the leadership of a pair of twins named Otho and Vireena. I can see them with their glowing green marks training in the distance.

Both the earths and fires act more like a cooperative team than competitors. I'd be lying if I said I hadn't cursed Bastian a few times for not simply suggesting I disguise my mark and join the fires or earths. But then I wouldn't have Mireen or Ambrose.

'What was that about?' Mireen asks, joining me with a spear in her hands.

'I have no idea,' I admit, still fighting the urge not to stare and watch as Raith moves between the fires, correcting form and barking orders.

We spend the next hour working with our blunted practice weapons. The idea is apparently to reduce fatalities as we're training, but I have no doubts a determined student could still kill with these. I'm also pretty sure Malakai would have no problem using his giant, double-bladed axe to chop someone's head off, blunted or not. Thankfully, he's training with his people instead of trying to go for a kill at the moment.

Small victories.

My weapon – a rapier, as Blackstone calls it – suits me better than I expected. What I lack in strength, I make up for in speed and precision. By the end of the session, even Blackstone seems grudgingly impressed by my progress.

'Not entirely hopeless,' he concedes, which from him is practically a love letter.

As we leave the training yard, I catch the tail end of Raith's sparring match. He's using a two-handed sword that's bigger than my body, and he whirls through the air in a deadly dance of slashing training steel. It slices through the air with a thick whistle, and he shows perfect control, pulling his strikes against the guy he's fighting so he doesn't actually hurt him.

He freezes with the blade at his opponent's neck. They both pause a moment, then relax, clapping hands and patting shoulders. I can see Raith is giving him instruction now. The fire he's working with is thinner and more slight than the average offering, and I can see how he's looking up at Raith with unmasked adoration.

I shake my head as we leave for the showers. I may not understand the guy, but I can't deny he helped me pick what feels like the perfect weapon. In his own way, Raith may have just helped me survive.

After cleaning up and surviving another long day of classes, I say goodnight to Mireen and cross the star-lit courtyard toward the library. It's in the academic wing, and it has become my sanctuary in the endless nightmare that is Confluence Academy. While others use their rare free time to rest, fuck, or form alliances, I bury myself in ancient texts, searching for answers about what it means to be unbound while I wait for Bastian to come through on his promise to give me the book he mentioned that first day.

So far, I've found only fragments – old stories that may be nothing more than fiction meant to entertain small children. But the stories do talk about creatures known by many names that existed before the elemental plane merged with the human plane, creatures that lurked in the shadows of human history. Centuries ago. They were called vampires, essence drinkers, voids, and siphons. As far as I can tell, all the names point to the same creature – some sort of twisted version of a primal, like a human who feeds on living creatures to fuel its power.

But they're only stories, and none of them mention the word 'unbound' or talk about silver swirl marks. None of them explain why I draw people's power into myself if I touch them for too long. They don't explain why channeling doesn't work for me the way it works for everyone else here.

I sit at a secluded table in the back corner of the library, surrounded by stacks of dusty tomes. My eyes burn from hours of reading faded text in dim light, but I can't stop. Confluence Day grows closer, and with it, the reckoning I can't prepare for without understanding what I am.

'You won't find what you're looking for in those.'

I startle, nearly dropping the book in my hands. Ambrose stands at the end of the row, spectacles reflecting the late afternoon light streaming through high windows.

'What?' I close the book quickly, covering the illustration of a strange mark that looked tantalizingly close to my own, but apparently was unrelated.

He glances around, then steps closer. 'Secrets about the elementals. About what makes someone worthy of tethering. That's what everyone's after, right?'

I relax slightly. So he doesn't actually know what I'm looking for. It's not that I don't trust Ambrose. It's more that I don't want to tie either of my friends up in my mess.

Gods know I've hurt the people I care about enough already for one lifetime. I won't let them become victims of my collateral damage, either. As always, my thoughts even skimming across the memory of my brothers and father drowning in the storm I drew in blasts me with suffocating guilt.

I force the thoughts down, offering Ambrose an innocent smile instead. 'Just trying to survive until Confluence Day.'

'Aren't we all.' He drops into the chair across from me, lowering his voice. 'Did you hear the Rector's back?'

'Rector? That's what they call the headmaster here, right?' I keep my expression neutral, though my interest is piqued. 'I thought he was away on some assignment.'

'Rector Voss.' Ambrose pushes his glasses up with one finger. His eyes gleam with the excitement of sharing forbidden knowledge. 'He came back last night. Early.'

'What does that mean? Do you think he heard about Malakai's informal army? Maybe the amount of killing they're doing is excessive, even by academy standards?'

'No one knows for certain. I've heard a few rumors, of course. Probably nothing of substance.'

'What have you heard?'

Ambrose leans closer, voice low. 'Some say a rogue elemental was spotted near campus.'

I frown. 'A rogue elemental? I've never heard of something like that.'

Ambrose nods, as if my lack of knowledge on the subject isn't a surprise. 'They're completely mad. Driven wild by grief, and destructive as all hells.'

'And there's a rumor that one is near the academy?' I whisper, chest going cold.

'Just a rumor. Something like that slipping out of the elemental plane really shouldn't be possible. It's highly unlikely.'

I can't say why, but his mention of rogue elementals makes me think immediately of my dreams – of the dark shape I always sense just out of sight in the murky depths. 'What else do you know about them? Rogue elementals, I mean,' I ask, trying to sound merely curious rather than desperate for information.

Ambrose's eyes light up the way they always do when someone asks him about something he's studied. 'There are actually several categories of elementals. First, untethered elementals – those who have never formed a tether with a human. These are what students like us will typically tether on Confluence Day.' A second finger joins the first. 'Second, formerly tethered elementals whose primals died naturally. It's a less traumatic experience for them, and these generally

are the elementals willing to take on a new primal tether.' A third
finger rises. 'And third, rogue elementals – those whose tethers were
broken through trauma.'

'What kind of trauma?'

'According to the texts I've read, the tether between primal and
elemental is incredibly intimate – a joining of minds and energies.
When that tether is severed unnaturally, it leaves . . . scars. That can
mean a particularly traumatic death in combat. It can mean some
sort of betrayal – a primal who breaks the oath they make to their
elemental when they tether.'

'Oaths?'

Ambrose sighs dramatically. 'For someone who spends so much
time in this library, you really don't know much, do you? What are
you studying so much if not this kind of thing?'

'Nothing important.'

He tilts his head at me, then shrugs. 'A woman of mystery. I can
respect that. Anyway, yeah. Every elemental will ask its primal to
swear oaths. It varies based on the personality of your elemental. An
oath of truth. An oath of revenge. Whatever. But if you break that
oath?' He draws a finger across his throat.

He scoops up one of my books. 'What's got you so interested
in all this anyway?' He squints at the spine of the book, grinning.
'Fanciful Tales for Young Girls?'

I blush, snatching the book from his hands. 'Old stories sometimes hide truths others want to keep buried.'

That earns a raised brow from Ambrose. 'Now that, I can agree
with. You want hidden truths?' His voice drops even lower. 'I've
got one you don't need to go searching in books for. I heard more
whispers about Malakai seen scheming with Serena multiple times.
But you know what's weird?'

'What?'

'I heard both of them got called in to meet with Voss.'

I feel a faint blossoming of hope. 'You think he's shutting them
down?'

'Hard to say. Let's hope so, though. I frankly don't know if they're planning to keep any of us alive before Confluence Day.'

A chill creeps down my spine, because my friends and I have avoided his focus so far, but how much longer can that last? Especially now that he's working with Serena. How long before she whispers in his ear that he should kill me?

'Well,' Ambrose says, smiling out of one side of his mouth. 'There's someone I met last week. Someone who may have invited me to meet for a romantic stroll across the castle walls tonight. So if you don't mind . . .'

I chuckle. 'Alright. At least some of us are getting laid.'

'Not yet, but fingers are crossed,' Ambrose says over his shoulder as he leaves.

It's only a minute before movement makes me look up.

A tall figure slips into view, blonde hair and black uniform instantly marking him.

'Bastian?' I ask.

He approaches slowly, barely making a sound as his eyes fall to the books. 'I apologize for the delay. I know it must be difficult operating in the dark. How are you holding up?'

All I can do is stare as he sits down across from me, hand clutching something within his black uniform trimmed in silver and gold. His nearly-white eyes seem to see straight through me, but there's sympathy in his face. I think he might really feel bad for taking so long – that he might actually care how I've been doing.

'I'm alive,' I say with a shrug.

His smile is grim. 'That's most important. Yes.' When he pulls his hand from his uniform, he's clutching a small, leather-bound book. At a glance, it looks completely unassuming, but I lick my lips, fighting the urge to snatch it from his hands and start devouring it from cover to cover.

His eyes are heavy as he looks both ways, as if double checking we're not being watched. 'This is the book I told you about from my family's personal library. It took a few weeks for father to get it here. And . . . I spent the last few days reading it myself. Sorry. I wanted to make sure I knew more about what you were before I . . . trusted you with this.'

I frown. 'Trusted me? You're acting like I'm dangerous, or something.'

'You are. More than you realize. Oh, and the book is encrypted. Empire destroyed anything having to do with unbound centuries ago. The encryption is the only reason this one survived the purge. It's also part of the reason I didn't give it to you right away. I needed time to create a key you can use to decipher it. And Nessa? Don't write the actual text down anywhere. Guard that key with your life, and destroy it before you let anyone touch it. Understand?'

I nod my head as the gravity of what he's saying and what I am seems to settle in on me with new weight.

'Use the key. Read the book. You'll start to understand.'

He looks like he wants to say more, but he turns and disappears instead, leaving me with the strange book.

I run my fingertips over its surface, wishing it wasn't already so late. I doubt I'll have the energy to read much of it tonight before passing out, but I'm sure as hell going to try. Dread mingles with a desperate kind of hope as I stare at the book, wondering if I'm finally about to get some actual answers about what I am.

Chapter 7

I use the water tower common room to read Bastian's book because I don't want to wake Mireen with my candlelight. At this hour, it's empty – nobody is crazy enough to deprive themselves of sleep with the hell we endure every day.

Nobody except me, apparently. Or whoever is causing a girl in a nearby room to moan loud enough that I occasionally hear it.

My fingers tremble as I carefully open the book. I've spent weeks searching for answers about what the hell I am, and Bastian may have just handed me all of them. The leather cover is cool against my palms, the pages inside worn with age and heavy with secrets. The book even smells old, reeking of forgotten knowledge and buried truths.

It's just a book, but I can't seem to slow my breathing as I crack open the ancient cover and run my fingers down the first page.

It takes me a minute to get the hang of the key and the encoded text. It's not as simple as swapping letters for letters – there's a complex system based on sound patterns that makes my eyes burn with concentration. Every deciphered word feels like a small victory as I whisper them under my breath.

It's a full five minutes before I've decoded the first few lines.

'Unbound. The fifth affinity. Mender and the breaker. Dangerous, powerful, and essential.'

My breath catches in my throat. The fifth affinity. My affinity.

The small scrap of information is already more than I've managed to learn after poring through half the academy's library. And this is only the beginning. I already feel myself getting faster with the key

Bastian provided in neat, precise handwriting. But at this speed, it will take me days, if not weeks to decode the entire book.

It's half an hour before I've managed my way through the next passage.

'I mark these words in secret, for the tri-emperors have deemed the truth too dangerous to be known. I refuse to let the truth be destroyed. The real story is one of betrayal, love, destruction, and creation. It's a story that centers around the most powerful to ever claim the title of unbound: a story of Lorkan Grace. The truth they wish to hide is how a man seen as a hero single-handedly led to the death of thousands upon thousands, nearly breaking our world in two.'

A ball of ice forms in my stomach as I process the words, dread coiling through me like a serpent.

Destruction. Thousands dead. Is that what I'm capable of? Is that what waits inside me?

I push my burning eyes a little more, decoding the next two sentences to finish the first page.

'But that is where the story ends. This is where it begins . . .'

I sit back, closing the book as the excitement I felt mingles with a new feeling of dread. I thought this book would teach me how to excel. How to use the power I've been given. Now . . . Now I'm terrified it'll simply show me what nature of monster I can become.

A sudden yawn cracks my jaw. The candle flickers beside me, casting dancing shadows across the common room.

I don't remember falling asleep, but I jolt awake with a gasp, nearly knocking the unbound book and Bastian's written key from my lap.

Water. Everywhere. Filling my lungs. Something ancient watching from the depths. Waiting. Hunting.

Hunting for me.

I gulp for air that feels too thin, my uniform clinging to my sweat-soaked skin, heart hammering against my ribs like it's trying to punch its way out. The nightmare that woke me lingers, even as my brain switches itself back on. I can still see the dark water, the watching eyes, and feel the sensation of being hunted by something ancient and patient. The words that thing whispered still echo in my mind.

'Come to me. Find me. Free me.'

'Fuck,' I hiss, swiping at the cold sweat on my forehead. My hands are shaking.

The common room suddenly feels too exposed, too vulnerable.

I swear under my breath at how careless it was to fall asleep here with the book and key. Anybody could've stumbled in and taken them.

The thought sends a fresh wave of panic through my chest. I fold the key into a small square and tuck it into my bra, the paper scratchy against my skin. I clutch the unbound book in one white-knuckled hand and hurry back to my room, every shadow in the corridor making me jump in alarm.

I open the door quietly so I don't wake Mireen, whose gentle snores fill our small room. I slip the book under my mattress, checking twice to make sure it's completely hidden. I consider crawling into bed and getting much-needed sleep, but I know the nightmares will come back.

I'm not ready for them. My mind is too full of questions and fears, like a cauldron about to boil over.

Ambrose's warnings about Serena and Malakai echo in my mind alongside his revelations about rogue elementals. And I'm still thinking about the little I was able to decipher from the book.

If Lorkan Grace was so important, why have I never heard of him? But the answer seems obvious. It's like Bastian said. Somebody destroyed all records of whatever happened. Of people like me.

I already knew being unbound was dangerous, but now my understanding runs deeper. Far deeper. Whatever I am is dangerous enough that someone tried to wipe all memory of people like me from history itself.

In other words, I shouldn't exist. If the wrong person finds out I do, they'll make me disappear. I have no doubt of it.

My room suddenly feels too small, the walls pressing in, Mireen's soft breathing too loud in my ears. I need air. I need space.

I slip out and make my way down the stairs of the water tower, the stone steps cold beneath my bare feet. The chilly autumn night air hits me like a slap when I step outside, raising goosebumps across my arms. I pull them tight against my body, but I don't turn back for a coat. The cold is grounding, real – something to focus on besides the chaos in my head.

The castle is different at night – hushed and watchful, shadows pooling in corners where torchlight can't reach. Every creak of ancient wood, every whisper of wind through stone corridors makes me flinch. I have no destination in mind, just the desperate need to move, as if I can outrun all the things that seem to be chasing me. All the dangers closing in from every possible angle.

My feet carry me upward, through rarely used passages and narrow staircases, until I find myself at the top of the western wall. The air here is crisp with the last gasp of summer, warm days giving way to cold nights.

I give that a moment's thought, because the idea of seasons continuing to change and the world going on, even while I'm trapped in these murderous walls is strange and alien. It was the peak of summer when I volunteered for selection. I was sweating that day, the sun beating on my exposed neck as I stood in the town square, wondering if I would actually do it this year.

And now I'm here. The leaves will fall soon, and life outside these walls carries on, oblivious to our struggles here. On the outside, passing weeks meant shifting where we looked for fish and what we could catch. It meant summer festivals, fall ceremonies, the harbor games that came every spring. Here, though?

Each new day only means I've survived a little while longer. Each new day brings the threat of approaching danger, like Confluence Day, which keeps creeping toward us like a prowling beast.

I pull my arms tighter around myself, suppressing a sudden shiver that has nothing to do with the bite in the air, the reality of it all sinking into my bones.

From here, I can see all four elemental towers glowing in the darkness. They're all as beautiful as they are strange. With enough power, primals can apparently imbue objects with magic, which is how they were constructed centuries ago.

I'm halfway along the raised castle wall, hand trailing idly on the waist-high wall that's the only thing standing between myself and a hundred-foot drop, when I notice I'm not alone.

Raith stands at the edge, his scarred profile outlined against the night sky. He doesn't turn at my approach, though I know he hears me. His hands rest on the stone, shoulders rigid with tension, muscles coiled tight beneath his thin shirt.

For a moment, I consider retreating. Whatever brought him here in the middle of the night is his business, not mine. But something stops me – maybe the way his knuckles have gone white where they grip the wall, or the haunted set of his jaw.

I see something of how I feel in his posture. Sense some connection.

'Couldn't sleep?' I ask, my voice barely carrying over the soft night breeze.

He doesn't answer immediately. With Raith, the silence seems to be a kind of language in its own right. It carries weight and meaning.

His profile is sharp in the moonlight, the scarred side of his face catching the light in a way that makes my chest ache.

'No,' he finally says, the single word rough around the edges.

I move to stand beside him, not too close, leaving space between us. We both stare out at the academy grounds, the green field where we were all unloaded from Empire carriages as offerings. It was only five weeks ago, but it already feels like I was another person then – naive, terrified, unaware of the power building beneath my skin. Unaware of what terrible potential might lurk within me.

Beyond the fields, I see the forest and finally a ridge of mountains rising like black teeth against the star-filled sky.

'Bad dreams?' I ask, the words feeling inadequate for the weight they carry.

His jaw tightens, the scarred side of his face catching moonlight in a way that makes the damaged tissue look almost silver. 'Always.'

I nod, understanding more than he probably realizes. Even before I began dreaming of the beast in the dark waters, I was haunted by dreams about a storm so massive and powerful it destroyed everything in its path. Three years ago, the nightmares of the storm included horrific glimpses of tanned, familiar hands rising above churning waters – the last glimpses I ever had of my father and brothers.

Compared to these new dreams haunting me, those all feel quaint and gentle by comparison. 'Mine are getting worse. More real,' I admit, the words raw in my throat. 'Like something's trying to claw its way into my head.'

'What do you dream about?' he asks, surprising me with the question. He seems different tonight. More approachable, somehow. Maybe it's the simple fact that he's not glaring like he wants to kill me. Or fuck me. With Raith, it's honestly hard to tell. Or maybe it's my own confusing attraction to the man clouding the picture, making me see what I want to see.

I hesitate, unsure how much to reveal. My fingers absently trace the disguised mark on my hand. 'Water. Darkness. Something watching me, hunting me. It feels ancient, hungry.' I swallow hard. 'It feels like it's waiting for something.'

His eyes shift to me then and my breath catches in my throat, an electric current racing down my spine. 'Since when?' he asks.

'They started maybe three weeks ago, I think, maybe before. But it's every night now. The same dream, but . . . more. Clearer.' I wrap my arms tighter around myself. 'What about yours?'

I don't actually expect an answer, but I'm surprised when he exhales slowly, a sound so weighted with pain it makes my chest ache. 'Fire,' he says simply.

The word hangs between us, heavy with everything he isn't saying. *Fire.*

My memory flashes with the image of his fear when fire sprouted from my fingertips during our training match that first day. The way his eyes widened, the way his body went rigid.

It makes sense. How else would he have those twisted scars running up half of his face and the right side of his arm and hand?

I almost ask him how he's managing to not just survive but thrive as a fire affinity – how he could stand to be bound to the thing he must fear. My fingers itch to reach out and touch his scars, to trace their jagged paths.

And yet I don't need to ask, because I feel I understand completely.

Fire took something from him. What, exactly, I can't say. But he's learning to use the thing that hurt him – to control what he fears.

Isn't that exactly what I tried to do by choosing to join the water affinities? Only I'm hardly learning to channel. It feels more like I'm fumbling in the dark with my unbound power. The book Bastian gave me will hopefully hold some information I can use to improve, but I'll have to keep finding time to work through the complex code, and spare time isn't something we have a lot of here at Confluence.

'Do you always come here when you have bad dreams?' I ask, my voice softer than I intended.

'Ever since my first night here.' His gaze remains fixed on the distant mountains.

'It's peaceful,' I say, my eyes drawn again to the vast expanse of darkness before us.

'It's quiet,' he corrects, but there's no edge to his words.

He's right in his own way to correct my wording, I realize. Peace is an illusion here. There is quiet, yes. There is sometimes even the semblance of calm. But there's always danger nearby, isn't there? Always a threat hanging over our heads, ready to strike us down when we least expect it.

We stand in silence that gradually shifts from awkward to something almost comfortable, the space between us charged with something I can't quite name. I don't know how long we remain there, side by side without speaking, before voices drift up from below.

'Who the hells told him?' a woman's voice asks, low and urgent.

'He wasn't supposed to be back for months yet. Perhaps not even until the Crucible.'

'That remains to be seen,' a man responds. 'But the Rector obviously heard about the body with the burned-out mark. Why else would he be here?'

Raith and I both go still, listening. His body tenses beside mine, still as the night itself.

Both voices sound older. Instructors, I think, though I can't see them because they're walking in the open third-floor hallway directly beneath the wall we're standing on. Their whispers are drifting up from the many windows below.

'Elements. What a fucking mess. If anyone asks, we assumed it was a prank by one of the fires. Scorch marks to imitate a siphon, not the real thing.'

'If anyone asks, I'm claiming I never saw a thing. Do you have any idea—'

The voices are silenced suddenly as a door snaps shut below.

Siphons? Goosebumps rise all over my skin, a chill that has nothing to do with the night air settling deep in my bones.

I glance at Raith to find him already watching me, his expression unknowable but his eyes burning with intensity.

'Siphons?' I ask, my voice barely above a whisper. 'Did I hear them right? And what would that have to do with dead people's marks?'

Part of me wants to laugh the idea away, but I can't ignore the amount of fear in their voices as they spoke. I can't ignore the way my own mark seems to burn beneath my skin, as if responding to the words. Siphons are supposed to be monsters from children's tales. Pure fantasy.

Raith's expression hardens. In an instant, the vulnerability and openness brought on by his nightmares is gone. He's all hard lines and intensity again. Unreachable and unreadable. 'You should go back to your room. It's not safe to wander at night.'

'And yet you told me you've been wandering the castle at night since day one.' I raise my eyebrows, surprised by my own boldness.

His full lips come the closest to a smile I've ever seen on him, and the sight is breathtaking – transforming his face into something almost unbearably beautiful. I forget to breathe for a moment, but the near-smile is gone as quickly as it came. 'Nobody else here has the balls to tease me, let alone provoke me,' he says.

'If you think you'd find balls between my legs, you'd be sorely disappointed.' The words leave my mouth before I can stop them.

Smooth, Nessa.

His eyes flick to mine, something dangerous flaring in them as he steps closer. 'Trust me,' he says, his voice dropping to a tone that slides over my skin like velvet, 'disappointment is the last thing I'd feel.'

The air between us charges with electricity, and I'm suddenly aware of how close we're standing, how the moonlight cuts across the sharp angles of his face. His gaze drops briefly to my lips before returning to my eyes, the intensity in them making my heart stutter.

Holy. Shit.

Fire explodes in my lower belly, unwelcome but not quite unpleasant. It spreads through my veins like wildfire, leaving me dizzy with a hunger I've never felt before. I'm hyperaware of him – his height, the breadth of his shoulders, the way his fingers curl around the stone railing. When did breathing become so difficult?

My brain scrambles, all thoughts of mysterious deaths and fairy-tale beasts forgotten. My mouth opens, and I can't seem to form a coherent thought in response. And the way my name sounded in his rough, deep voice? Gods. I could get used to that, even if I know Raith and everything he represents is not a good idea for me.

It's worse than 'not a good idea.' It's suicidal.

He's a fire. He's probably somebody Serena either wants, or, for all I know, already has. If he showed the slightest interest in me where she could see, I'd probably be dead before dawn.

Getting involved with Raith could literally get me killed in more ways than one, which is a fact I very much need my body to understand. Why, then, does every nerve ending in my body feel like it's been set alight at the mere suggestion of his touch?

'Go back to your room, Nessa,' Raith says suddenly, his voice deeper than before, rough like he's fighting for control. 'Try to sleep.'

'Will you?' I ask, reluctant to leave despite every rational thought screaming at me to run, my traitorous feet refusing to move.

He turns back to the view. 'Eventually.'

I know a dismissal when I hear one, but I linger a moment longer. It is taking time and effort for the arousal he sparked with those few words to fade – for common sense to wrestle control of my thoughts and body again. 'If I have the dream again tomorrow night . . . will you be here?'

Raith doesn't look at me, but I see his shoulders tense, then relax on an exhale. 'I don't make promises.'

It's not a yes, but it's not a no either. I'll take it.

'Goodnight, Raith.'

As I turn to go, his voice stops me. 'What we heard . . . I wouldn't speak of it to anyone. If the Rector is involved, then the information is extremely dangerous. You don't want to be called into his office for questioning. Trust me.' For some reason, his eyes fall to my left hand when he says that – to my disguised mark.

I slip it in my pocket, nodding, a chill running down my spine at his warning.

Trust him. Yeah. That hardly seems like a good idea. And yet . . . part of me wants to. Part of me already does, whether I like it or not.

He's facing away, his broad silhouette a solitary shape against the vast night sky.

His words follow me all the way back to my room, settling into my mind like heavy stones in the churning current of my thoughts.

When I finally sleep again, the nightmares don't return. Instead, I dream of amber eyes and scars that look like rivers of gold in moonlight – and of strong hands touching places that make me wake with a gasp, my body aching for someone I know I can never have.

But the most dangerous things are always the ones we want the most, aren't they?

Chapter 8

'The elemental trial will claim some of your lives,' Instructor Sestra announces, her voice slicing through the classroom like an executioner's blade.

My stomach twists, sending my breakfast churning in a nauseating swirl. Not because of the 'some of you will die' part – that's been hammered into our skulls since day one at Confluence Academy. Death is our constant companion here, trailing us between classes, during training, and hovering at the foot of our beds each night.

No, it's the brand new bit of information. A fucking water trial? Isn't daily life here enough of a damn trial?

My pathetic excuse for water channeling is barely enough to form a wobbly sphere when I'm secretly dipping my fingers into a smuggled waterskin. The trick has been the only thing keeping me from lectures and remedial classes with Sestra, but I know it won't be enough for long. It's already not enough.

The others are advancing so much faster than me that I know it doesn't even matter how I do in my combat training. By now, most of them could kill me with water magic and I'd be virtually powerless to defend myself. So much for the world-shattering dangerous potential of an unbound.

I'm so completely screwed.

Around me, worried whispers ripple through the classroom of white-uniformed first-year offerings. At least I'm not alone in my panic, though I doubt anyone else has quite as much to fear as I do.

'Before any of you ask—' Sestra's voice cuts through the murmurs, causing Mireen to lower her hand sheepishly beside me. 'No. You will not be allowed to know the nature of the trial beforehand, just as you won't be able to know how you'll be tested on Confluence Day or what you'll face in the Crucible. Learning to prepare for the unknown is part of your training here, so get used to it.'

Sestra paces the front of the classroom like a predator sizing up which of us to devour first, her silver-streaked black hair pulled into a severe bun that seems to yank her facial features into an eternal scowl. Her deep blue eyes – the mark of water affinity – scan us with cold calculation.

'A true primal adapts. They overcome. They improvise,' she continues, fingers laced behind her back as she prowls. 'Our job is to make sure we don't insult the elementals by sending unworthy students into their realm. And make no mistake. If you're not worthy, the elementals will hunt and kill you for sport on Confluence Day.'

From two rows ahead, Beck leans forward, his broad shoulders making him stand out among the class. With his shaggy, sandy blonde hair and easy-going attitude that seem at odds with this place, he tends to draw the wrong kind of attention in class.

'Hold on,' he says, not bothering to hide his skepticism. 'I heard the real reason you let us kill each other is because there aren't enough elementals to go around. Now we're worried about insulting them, too?'

The temperature in the room seems to drop ten degrees as Sestra's gaze fills with venom. She detests questions almost as much as she despises Beck himself.

'Perhaps you should try using your brain, Beck,' she says, each word dripping with icy disdain as she glides toward his desk. 'Why would the academy care if there aren't enough elementals to tether the number of students we send?'

'Uh,' Beck says, clearly struggling as Sestra plants her palms on his desk, leaning into his space until he shrinks back. 'Maybe Empire likes a high success rate? With tethering . . . or something?'

Sestra's nostrils flare as she inhales deeply, then releases a long-suffering sigh that makes Beck wince. 'What difference would it make to us if you died here or in the elemental plane? The tri-emperors only concern is that we provide them with fully trained primals each year. They don't care in the slightest what happens to you here or how we produce the human weapons for their war.' Her voice drops dangerously. 'Have you ever wondered what would happen if the elementals decided we aren't capable of sending them worthy students fit for elemental tethers?'

Beck swallows hard enough that I can see his throat bob from where I'm sitting. He shakes his head, leaning back so far in his seat that he might topple over any second.

I have a strict policy of never speaking unless directly called on in classes – being noticed here is rarely a good thing – but I can't stand watching Beck squirm any longer. I clear my throat, my voice sounding foreign to my own ears as the words tumble out.

'They might start going to Red Kingdom's side, instead?'

The words hang in the air long enough for me to regret them.

Sestra whirls, surprise etched across her face. I've been here five weeks, and this might be the first time I've said more than absolutely necessary in front of the class. Just as I feared, the unwanted attention ripples outward – including to the back edge of the room where Malakai watches me with narrowed eyes, his head tilted in assessment. Both of his student soldiers flank him, still as statues but equally attentive now.

My skin crawls under their scrutiny. Stupid, stupid, stupid. I should have kept my mouth shut.

'Nessa Thorne . . .' Sestra glides from Beck's desk – which prompts him to finally breathe again and slump forward with visible relief – and approaches me with measured steps. 'You are . . . correct. Surprisingly,' she adds under her breath.

Her eyes hold mine for a terrifyingly long moment, dissecting me like a specimen under glass.

'If only your skills in channeling weren't so dismal, I would say your flash of insight shows some actual potential.'

The barb stings, but I keep my face carefully blank. She's not wrong. Next to my classmates, my abilities are pathetically underdeveloped. I've learned I have to physically touch water or somebody full of water essence to channel it. Considering I can't participate in channeling class while submerged in water, it has hardly been an advantage.

Sestra finally turns her attention back to the class, freeing me from her scrutiny. 'As Miss Thorne helpfully pointed out, we're not interested in encouraging you to kill one another. Our job is to shape you into weapons. Your job is to be worthy if you survive to Confluence Day. It's to avoid bringing shame on the academy and all the history that has preceded you. It's to become worthy of the incredible power of a primal.'

I exhale slowly, trying to steady my racing pulse.

After class, Mireen grips my shoulders and bulges her eyes dramatically, the crescent scar under her left eye crinkling as she smirks. 'Since when are you the one calling out answers?' she asks, her eyes dancing with amusement. 'Decided it's finally time for people to realize how clever you are?'

Ambrose slides up beside her, pushing his wire-rimmed glasses up with one finger and crossing his arms. His dark hair is cut so precisely it might have been measured with a ruler.

'Not to take away from your little moment,' he says, his voice carrying that blend of arrogance and affection I've come to expect from him, 'but was it really that genius of an insight? I was like . . . two seconds away from coming to the same conclusion myself.'

'Of course you were,' I mutter, rolling my eyes, but not without a small smile.

'Hey,' a deep voice says, and I turn to see Beck's blue eyes – the same shade that all water affinities eventually develop, though mine were this color from birth. 'Thanks for saving my ass back there.'

'Oh,' I say, suddenly awkward under his grateful gaze. 'It was nothing. I couldn't watch her pick on you like that.'

'Yeah, well,' Beck shrugs with a stack of books clutched in one hand. 'I appreciate it all the same. There's enough distrust and

scheming going on amongst ourselves as it is. It's nice to see somebody showing a little fucking camaraderie for once.'

I share a quick look with Ambrose and Mireen, a silent conversation passing between us.

Can we trust him?

I sense uncertainty from both of them. Lately, we don't know
who is working with Malakai and maybe even Serena. There's a dark
alliance growing within our affinity and possibly between them.
Anybody could be part of it.

And yet . . . I hate the way fear is making us turn on each other.
The fear has been isolating us, driving people into smaller and smaller
groups that are easier for Malakai to target. What we need is to show
strength and prove we'll still band together despite their reign of fear.

'You could sit with us at the dining hall tonight. If you wanted,'
I offer, ignoring the slight widening of Ambrose's eyes.

Beck's eyebrow flicks upward. 'You're sure?'

'Yeah.' I lift my chin slightly. 'If you're with Malakai, you can tell
him we're not scared.'

Ambrose raises a finger. 'Uh, on my behalf, please tell Malakai
I'm scared shitless and don't want to die. I just want to survive to
Confluence Day, tether a badass elemental, and become a primal.
We're not all as crazy as Nessa.'

'Fuck Malakai,' Mireen agrees, planting a hand on my shoulder
and squeezing. 'But . . . don't directly tell him I said that. Just . . .
that's how I feel. Privately.'

Beck's face splits into a grin. 'I like it. And I'm not with that
asshole. I was friends with Tucker and Volsa.'

His expression darkens as he continues. 'I'm pretty sure they
shoved Tucker off the cliffs the second week here. He liked to go
out there to clear his head, and he turned up dead at the bottom
of the rocks.'

Beck's voice drops lower. 'And Malakai just plain murdered Volsa
in the sparring ring last week. *Accidentally* edged his training weapon
with razor-sharp water and practically cut her in two.' By the time

he's finished talking, the amusement is completely gone from his face, replaced by a haunted look I recognize too well. His thick jaw ticks in tune with his anger. 'So, yeah. Fuck him.'

The words hang between us, heavy with the shared knowledge that surviving in Confluence isn't just about mastering our affinities – it's trying not to join those whose names are now whispered about in past tense.

'We should head to the dining hall,' Mireen says, her voice dropping as she notices something over my shoulder. 'Before we miss the good food.'

The sudden tension in her posture makes my skin prickle.

Beck, who seems oblivious, smiles wide. 'I think we're going to get along *really* well, Mireen. Getting to the dining room first is . . .' he trails off as he sees the look on my face.

Malakai has appeared at the end of the corridor, his perfect posture and immaculate uniform making him look like a recruitment poster for Confluence. His blue eyes – already darker than most water affinities – seem to absorb light rather than reflect it. Four of his followers flank him, spreading out to block the hallway.

'Nessa Thorne,' he says, voice deep and ominous.

I keep my face carefully blank. 'Is there something you needed, Malakai?'

'Hm. I don't know. Maybe you can tell me. From where I'm standing, it looks a hell of a lot like you're trying to collect strays.' His gaze slides to Beck, who stiffens beside me. 'People might start thinking you're trying to form your own little coalition.'

My pulse accelerates, but I force my breathing to remain steady. 'People can think whatever they want.'

'Your channeling is . . . interesting, Thorne,' Malakai says, smiling in a way that doesn't reach his dark eyes. 'Wouldn't you agree, Serena?'

I hadn't even seen her until now. Serena emerges from behind one of Malakai's followers, her raven-black hair gleaming in the late afternoon light that is streaming through the high windows. Unlike Malakai's cold demeanor, Serena radiates heat and barely contained violence – a fire through and through. She even has the deep yellow-red eyes of a fire, now.

Serena steps closer, trailing a finger along the wall that leaves smoke in its wake. 'Something is certainly wrong with her. I have no idea what he sees in you,' she adds in a whisper only I can hear.

He? Who is she talking about?

'I'm still learning,' I say, fighting to keep my voice steady. 'We all have different methods.'

'Different,' Serena repeats, stopping just a few feet away. 'Yes, you certainly are different, aren't you? Maybe we should find out exactly how different. We could open her up. Just a little bit. Find out if the answers are under her skin?'

She extends her hand. The smoke drifting up from her fingers intensifies and the air begins to shimmer with heat. Behind me, I hear Mireen's sharp intake of breath and Ambrose's panicked whisper: 'Nessa, let's—'

'You should all step away from her. Now.'

The voice slides through the tension like a sharpened blade. Bastian steps into the corridor from a classroom doorway, his movement so casual it might have been coincidental if not for the perfect timing. His legacy black, silver, and gold stand out amid our whites.

'In your positions, I would be wary of someone you don't understand,' he continues, walking toward us with unhurried confidence. 'Not every student is foolish enough to show what they can do. Some are clever enough to keep tricks hidden. To invite underestimation.'

I stare at him in disbelief. What is he doing? He's trying to convince them I'm secretly dangerous?

Malakai's eyes narrow. 'This isn't your concern, legacy.'

'Isn't it?' Bastian stops beside me, close enough that I can feel the slight current of air that seems to perpetually surround him. I can see it whipping the fabric of Malakai's uniform against his muscular body.

An ominous whistle of gathering energy fills the hall as the currents of air pick up. It rushes past all of us, buffeting Malakai and his people until they have to squint and raise a hand, covering their faces.

And then the magical wind stops suddenly, the stillness feeling unnatural and dangerous in its wake.

'I've been tasked with observing first-year progress for my father. All first-years.' Bastian's emphasis is subtle but unmistakable.

Serena's hand drops and the shimmer of heat fades, but smoke still curls from her long, elegant fingertips. 'Are we supposed to know who your father is, legacy?'

'Someone like you? I imagine you wouldn't. He sits on the tri-emperor's inner council. One of their many tasks is monitoring operations here at Confluence Academy. They have the power to intervene in cases that threaten the integrity of the academy. I've been asked to keep an inside eye on proceedings here. To monitor.'

Malakai's group takes a collective step backward, expressions going pale.

Bastian's smile is pleasant, as if he's simply sharing information and not stepping between a possibly violent encounter. 'Apparently, the tri-emperors have been displeased with some of the more recent graduating classes of primals. They're seeing increasing amounts of brutality and a lack of cooperation. It's causing issues on the war front. It's difficult to say, but they may be considering less ideal assignments for students who are reported to be excessively violent.' He shrugs as if none of it is too deeply important, but the implication hangs between them.

Malakai and Bastian stare at each other for several heartbeats. Something unspoken passes between them – a history or under-standing I'm not privy to. Finally, Malakai inclines his head slightly.

'Nothing here should warrant the attention of the Council,' he says, voice soft but edged. 'Come, Serena. We'll continue this discussion another time.'

As they retreat down the hallway, I notice movement in the shadows of an adjacent corridor. Raith stands there, watching the entire exchange, one hand resting on the hilt of the sword he's been wearing at his hip since we selected our weapons yesterday. Our eyes meet for a moment, and I realize with absolute certainty that had Bastian not intervened, Raith's solution would have involved that blade and significantly more blood.

But also . . . what the fuck?

One minute, I think he wants to kill me. The next? I'm certain down to my bones that he would've stepped in and slaughtered everyone in this hall to keep me from getting harmed.

Raith gives me an almost imperceptible nod before melting back into the shadows.

'You should be more careful,' Bastian says quietly, once Malakai and his followers are out of earshot. 'They're looking for weaknesses, and you've given them reason to look harder.'

'I didn't ask for your help,' I say, though the words lack heat.

'No, you didn't.' Something flickers in his eyes – concern, maybe, or calculation. 'But I gave it anyway. Don't waste it by being careless. Do you mind giving us a moment?' he asks Ambrose, Beck, and Mireen.

The three of them practically fall over themselves in such a way that it's comical. Mireen's bulged eyes in my direction promise she's planning to ask if I'm sleeping with Bastian later. Ambrose looks like he wants to vomit out of fear from even being spoken to by a legacy. Beck looks like a loyal dog trying to decide if it should bite the much larger animal potentially threatening its friend.

I smile at them. 'It's fine. He's not going to hurt me.'

I hope.

'We'll wait right over here,' Mireen says, taking the others down the hall far enough to give me privacy.

Bastian shows no sign of even noticing the effect he has on people. Instead, he fixes his nearly white eyes on me, face serious. 'Were you able to figure out the key?'

'Yes,' I said. 'I only have a little spare time each day, so it's slow going, but—'

'Good,' he says. 'And you've hidden it somewhere safe? Separate from the key?'

I nod. 'The book is in my room. The key is here,' I say, touching my left breast before I think how odd that must look. The key is folded small and tucked into my bra, but Bastian doesn't know that.

He squints.

'Sorry,' I say quickly. 'It's just . . . It's on me. I'm keeping it with me at all times.'

'Okay. And Nessa? About the trials this weekend.'

This weekend? That's already more information than Sestra gave us. That means I only have three or four days to prepare.

His jaw flexes as if he's trying to decide whether he wants to say something. Finally, he gives my arm a soft squeeze. 'Be careful. It's going to be dangerous. There are rumors of a rogue elemental near campus. If you see or sense anything of the sort, you run. Don't try to fight it. Don't try to reason with it. Just run.'

With that, he walks away, leaving me with more questions than answers.

Beck lets out a low whistle as he comes back with the others. 'What the hells was that about? And how the hells did you get in the pants of a legacy? I tried that the first week and nearly got myself turned into lava. Totally worth it, but still.'

'You tried to fuck a fire? And a legacy, at that?' Mireen asks, mouth hanging open in shock at the sheer stupidity of it.

Beck rubs the back of his neck, grinning crookedly. 'I only made my willingness apparent. She . . . didn't seem to appreciate my interest.'

'Beck is suicidal. Good to know,' Ambrose mutters. 'Can we please go eat now, before someone else decides to threaten us in the hallway?'

There's no place in Confluence where the social divides are more obvious than the dining hall. The large space is full of long, wooden tables with bench-style seating, the polished oak surfaces reflecting the golden light from dozens of lanterns hanging from iron chains.

The Academy sets out food of all kinds at regular times. Roasted duck, carved chicken, steaming potatoes, delicious sweets, soft bread with salted butter, and just about anything else I could imagine out for the taking. The abundance still makes me dizzy sometimes.

Across all years and social groups, the students always cluster together by affinity. The colored marks on their hands showing clusters of blue, white, green, or red. Legacies sit with legacies, aspirants with aspirants, and offerings with offerings. Affinity, social status, and class year divide us as clearly as the border markings on a map between warring countries.

I glance upward at the upper-years, noting how much less rowdy they seem. How much more hardened. Some are only a year older than us, but the way they carry themselves is a testament to what it takes to survive this place. To how much we'll all change if we make it through our first year alive.

I look around at my slowly growing group of friends and hope beyond hope that we'll all make it together. I can't stand the thought of losing any of them, even our new addition of Beck. I guess the last three years were so fucking lonely in Saltcrest that I'm desperate for connections, now. Hungry for friends. For meaning.

Beck slathers honey and butter on a piece of bread and takes a large bite, closing his eyes in momentary bliss. Mireen, Ambrose, and Beck have been making increasingly outlandish guesses about what the water trial will be as we eat. For my part, I'm shoveling down food as quickly as I can because I want to have as much time as possible to look over the unbound book Bastian gave me last night.

That book feels like my best hope of surviving the trial, especially if anything in there talks about how to make better use of my powers. My marked palm burns slightly beneath its disguise, a constant reminder of how I don't truly belong with any affinity group here. I'm something else. Something different.

And if last night's brief reading of the book is any indication, I'm something dangerous.

It would be the ultimate irony if I sacrificed myself to the selector because I thought Saltcrest and my family would be better off without me, only to wind up unlocking an even more poisonous and dangerous potential by coming here.

The thoughts are sour, and I set down what's left of my food, appetite suddenly vanishing.

But I can't feel sorry for myself. There's no room for that here. I'm too far behind, and I desperately need to learn to improve my channeling skills before the water trial and Confluence Day.

The other students are already beginning to specialize – finding unique magical talents beyond the simple things we practice like creating water orbs. Some can already make intricate shapes or move their magic through the air with speed and velocity.

And me?

I'm not making any progress, and the gap between me and the others is growing by the day. It's only a matter of time before someone notices just how different I am.

'What do you think, Nessa?'

I jerk my eyes up, realizing I'd been staring at my disguised mark as the others talked, my thumb unconsciously rubbing over the altered skin. 'Hm?' I say.

Mireen frowns, her red brows drawing together. 'About the water trial. What do you think it's going to be?'

'Oh. I don't know. Maybe they'll see which of us can swim fastest.' I try to keep my voice light, as though I haven't been calculating my odds of survival and finding them dismally low.

'Yeah, I wish,' Beck says, wiping honey from his chin with the back of his hand. 'I swim like a fish.'

'And fuck like a bear, from what I hear,' Mireen adds with a wiggle of her brows.

They all laugh as the conversation drifts to who is sleeping with who – a regular topic here at Confluence. From what I can gather, most of the first-years here are sleeping around like every day could be their last day on this Earth. Even the occasional story of someone getting killed when they agreed to meet somewhere private for sex hasn't seemed to slow the practice.

Put people in life-or-death situations often enough, and I guess they have to blow off steam somehow.

I find my eyes scanning the room for Raith. He's not hard to find. He's at least half a head taller than the next tallest first-year, his broad back stretching the white uniform across shoulders that seem carved from stone. The other fires all eat quietly with him in the center, occasionally shooting him admiring glances.

My gaze drifts further, and I notice Bastian at the legacy table with the handful of other legacy airs. The legacies make up the smallest number of us, and there are only three other legacy airs in the first-years. Unlike the animated chatter at our table, his face is serious as he barely touches his food. Suddenly, his eyes lift and point straight at me across the large room with unsettling precision. I quickly look back at my plate, a shiver crawling up my spine.

Bastian knows more about me than anyone here, and yet I know next to nothing about him. And if the unbound book says I'm something so dangerous I shouldn't be allowed to exist, what does it say about Bastian if he's trying to protect me? Trying to help me?

I make excuses to go straight back to my room after dinner. Ambrose, Beck, and Mireen all insist on walking me to my room because it's not safe to be around campus by ourselves anymore.

As soon as I'm alone again, I pull the unbound book from beneath my bed and decide on a different tactic tonight. I'll decode the first few words of each chapter until I think I've found one that might give me some clues on how to use this affinity to channel better. History lessons and deeper truths can wait until after I survive the water trial.

I pull the folded paper key Bastian gave me from my bra, frowning when I notice it has smeared slightly after a day of sweating and training with it tucked so close. I may have to find a better place to hide it from now on.

I honestly don't know how Bastian had time to decipher the book and create the key from scratch in such a short period. The intelligence required for such a thing is frankly terrifying. On one hand, it's reassuring to know someone so capable is in my corner. On the other? It's worrying. Someone that sharp could easily manipulate me. Use me for their own goals.

But there's nothing to be done about it for now. All I can do is focus on learning more about what I am. Until I know that, I can't begin to guess what the right path is.

My fingers are clumsy with anticipation as I work through the cipher. It takes nearly half an hour, but I finally spot the word 'channeling' in the first sentence of a page about halfway into the book. I spend the next hour lost in the work of decoding the pages, my eyes burning and back aching from hunching over the book.

Finally, the words begin to assemble into something coherent, revealing secrets that just might mean I'll finally be able to make some progress. The relief is like water after a full day in the sun pulling heavy nets of fish.

Progress.

A slow smile spreads over my face as I let that idea sink in.

The pages talk about something I've sensed but haven't known how to do yet. To not just absorb the elemental essence of objects or people I touch, but to draw it inward from the world around me through the air itself. If possible, it could completely change my fortunes here.

I set down the book and start practicing the new techniques until I'm too tired to keep my eyes open.

For the first time since arriving at Confluence, I fall asleep with something that feels dangerously close to hope.

Chapter 9

Passages from the book Bastian gave me have run through my mind on repeat all morning like a desperate prayer I can't stop reciting. The book is currently hidden beneath my mattress, leaving me to poke and prod the ideas in my mind instead.

Even my increasingly terrifying nightmares of a beast in dark waters hunting me can't dim my excitement. Not today.

'Unbound are vessels. Empty chalices waiting to be filled. The paradox of flesh – to be nothing and everything at once. In their emptiness, they promise both creation and destruction.'

After weeks of being left to probe in the dark for answers about what I am, I'm finally getting scraps of truth. Even if most of the passages are vague and often unclear, they're starting to stitch together to form a fuzzy picture about what it means to be unbound.

Last night's reading did provide one clear, undeniable insight, though. An insight I should be able to use. All this time, I've been trying to pull water from within myself. It's how our instructors teach us to channel, and it's the way I hear everyone else talking about what it feels like. But that's not how my affinity works. The unbound don't generate power; they borrow it. They take it.

'Draw from the world around you,' the book had said. *'Elements exist in all things – the moisture in air, the heat in stone, the gust of wind, and the spark in friction. The unbound can coerce these elements where others command. The unbound can pull them, shape them like a conductor shapes music from instruments.'*

Which explains why I've been failing so spectacularly. I've been trying to play the damn instrument when I should have been directing the orchestra.

'Nessa!' Mireen's voice snaps me back to reality as she not-so-discreetly breaks apart stale bread and sprinkles the crumbs beneath her bed. 'We're going to be late for weapons training. Again. I could pretend to be you, but my ass isn't nearly big enough to pull off the disguise.'

I'm braiding my hair, so I toss her an amused glare over my shoulder. 'I'm almost ready. And your boobs are too small, too. You forgot that part.'

She tosses a dirty training top at my head in response, and we both laugh. If nothing else, Mireen is an expert in finding ways to make me smile or laugh, even when my thoughts are at their darkest.

I make sure my braid is tight and my training weapon is strapped to my belt before I get up to leave.

If I rule out the ever-present possibility of death, then weapons training has already become my favorite part of the day. I'm neither the strongest, biggest, or even the fastest of students here. Fighting unarmed puts all those deficiencies on full display. Without a weapon, I'm hopeless.

My only talent there is an ability to endure pain and punishment, meaning I tend to tap out and yield much later than other students. But I've taken to the rapier right away.

Sure, I still take blunted weapons to the face, arms, and stomach more times than I'd like, but it's all in the name of training. And so far, I've been able to avoid getting matched against any of Malakai's people.

But today is open for challenge matches, which means the danger level is amplified. A lot.

We reach the eastern training room just as Instructor Blackstone is pairing students for sparring. As usual, the training room smells like sweat with the faint scent of copper – no doubt from recently cleaned blood.

Blackstone's eyes sweep over us, narrowing when they land on me.

'Thorne. You've been challenged by Davrin today.'

I freeze, my blood turning to ice. My heart slams against my ribs so hard I swear I can hear the echo.

Davrin. One of Malakai's soldiers. Built like a mountain with eyes as dead as a shark's.

Our instructors are careful not to show anything resembling mercy most of the time, but I think I sense a flicker of something from Blackstone. Maybe it's the knowledge that Davrin is almost certainly planning to use this challenge match to kill me.

I look at Mireen, Ambrose, and Beck. All of them have gone shades of white. But then Blackstone continues pairing up the challenge matches, revealing that we've all been challenged by Malakai's people today.

Shit, shit, shit.

We share a wide-eyed panicked look, and then we're ushered into our training rings. Each of us faces death, and I already know my heart will break if any one of us doesn't make it.

This isn't random. Malakai's been watching me since yesterday's hallway confrontation. This is his answer – a not-so-subtle attempt to remove me from the equation. Worse, he's targeting my friends because of me, too. The guilt crushes down on my chest like a physical weight, making it hard to breathe.

This is exactly why I've stopped myself every time I'm tempted to confide in them about my unbound affinity. All my precautions and one moment of carelessness in class yesterday put our lives in danger.

Beneath the fear and worry, I feel something else. Something hot and prickly. Something like rage.

Fuck Malakai. Fuck the people who want to turn this place into more of a horror show than it has to be. Fuck them for *wanting* to kill. For targeting us because I had the nerve to speak up in class.

A cold calm settles over me. A strange confidence. A sense of determination that I will not let this be the day that anybody I care about dies. Not today.

Davrin collects his practice sword – a heavy, two-handed affair that could crush my skull with a single blow, blunted edge or not. His lips curve in a smile that doesn't touch his eyes as he takes his position across from me. I draw my practice rapier, feeling its familiar weight settle in my palm.

I scan my eyes around the large training room. Nobody is paying the waters any attention. The airs are sparring and dealing with challenge matches, too. The fires are fighting in organized pairs, with Raith's large form easily visible from this distance. The earths are fighting as well.

Nobody is coming to save you, Nessa. Nobody is going to save your friends.

And nobody is watching . . . the realization makes me smile, just slightly. No audience means that maybe – just maybe – there's something I can do.

I only have moments, so I work quickly. I reach my senses into the room around me, searching for elemental essence the unbound book said I should find. I feel only traces, but I desperately urge them inward, *pull* them inward by force. And it works.

It's not the sudden rush of power I feel when touching other affinities, but it's something. It's a candle flame instead of an inferno, but it's better than nothing.

I draw in as much as I can of each element, slowly building a reserve of magical energy in my core.

'Begin!' Blackstone calls, and Davrin charges, throwing himself into a deadly horizontal swing that will cleave me in half if I don't move.

I dance to the side. The practice blade whistles past my ear, disturbing the air enough to ruffle my hair. I dart forward, landing a quick thrust against his shoulder before retreating out of range.

'Lucky,' he growls.

Maybe it was. But if I'm going to survive this, I need more than luck.

I also don't have the luxury of only worrying about myself. I glance to my left and see Mireen using her matched daggers to deflect heavy blows from Kira, another of Malakai's student soldiers.

Desperately, I use the air essence to command a small column of air to blow into Kira's face. To my shock, it actually works.

Kira squints, flinching in surprise as a gust ruffles her hair. Mireen takes the opportunity to dart inside Kira's guard and press a dagger to her neck, earning a yield.

I hear the whistle of steel slicing through the air, but it's too late.

I turn, eyes wide as Davrin's greatsword slams straight down into the place between my shoulder and my neck.

The blow crumples me to the ground, rapier clattering from my hands. Pain explodes through my body like shattered glass, every nerve screaming in protest as darkness edges my vision.

Fuck. I need to survive my own match if I want to help. Survive, Nessa.

But even as Davrin readies for another strike, I hear Ambrose grunt with pain.

I clench my teeth, reach for my rapier, and roll away from Davrin's next strike at the last second. My fresh injury burns with agony at the movement, but I ignore it.

I get to my feet, desperately looking for a way to buy enough time to try to help Beck and Ambrose, but Davrin is advancing again. He's driving me back with measured swings that leave no opening to get inside his reach and use my smaller rapier. I'm losing ground, my back inching closer to the outer edge of the training ring. Once I'm cornered, his superior strength will end this quickly.

The unbound book's passages flash through my mind. *'Elements exist in all things. Elements draw magical essence. Essence that waits to be commanded, to be controlled.'*

I drop low, dodging another swing, and press my free hand against the stone of the training yard floor. *Concentrate. Feel.*

There's earth energy here – cool, solid, steady. I inhale, drawing it up through my fingertips, feeling it flow into me like water soaking into parched earth. The sensation is intoxicating – like the first gulp of air after being underwater too long, like finding something I never knew I was missing.

Strength seeps into my muscles. Not much – just a trickle – but I feel suddenly more grounded, more stable. When Davrin's next blow comes, I parry it aside instead of dodging, the impact vibrating up my arm but not overwhelming me.

His eyes widen in surprise, and I use that moment to strike.

My rapier is a blur, darting in faster than before, landing three swift touches to his chest and arm. Now it's Davrin being driven back, his face twisted in confusion and growing anger.

'What the fuck?' he snarls, swinging wildly.

I duck and turn just in time to see Ambrose using the quarterstaff he chose to parry blow after blow from Krete, a greasy-haired water who wears a permanent scowl and worships the ground Malakai walks on. I try to reach into the air like I did to help Mireen, but there's none left inside me. The small gust I used to help Mireen must have exhausted my reserves.

Ambrose lands a crushing strike to Krete's outer knee, sending the bigger man to the ground without my help.

I spot Beck easily overwhelming his opponent, landing two-handed strikes with the axe he uses. The blows are so hard that his opponent's swords are knocked from his hands.

And then Davrin is on me again, aiming a diagonal slash that will crack my neck if it lands.

I slip under the blow, touching the ground again as I roll. This time, I deliberately pull more energy – not just strength, but something else.

The stone beneath my fingers seems to ripple for a heartbeat.

Davrin steps forward, ready to bring his blade down on me as I come out of the roll, but his foot catches on a suddenly uneven paving stone. He stumbles, balance lost for a crucial moment.

My rapier finds his throat before he can recover.

For a moment, I think how easy it would be to press it deeper and punch through his throat. To end him. That might send a message to Malakai and his soldiers to leave us the hell alone. The dark thought slithers through my mind like poison, tempting and terrifying all at once.

But it's only a thought. That's not who I am.

That's the line I can't cross. The difference between his people and me.

'Yield,' I say, voice steady despite my racing heart.

For a terrible moment, I think he'll continue fighting anyway. His eyes burn with murderous intent, and the muscles in his thick neck cord beneath my blade.

'Yield,' Blackstone repeats from the sidelines as he drifts toward our match, his tone making it clear this isn't a suggestion.

'I yield,' Davrin finally spits.

I lower my weapon, taking a step back. The borrowed energy drains from me quickly, leaving me light-headed and slightly nauseated. Not free, I realize. I've taken something that must be returned. The balance must be maintained.

I release the excess energy back into the stone. I release the warmth I gathered from the torches and the water saturating the air, feeling it flow from me like water finding its level.

Even with the energy gone, I'm tired down to my bones. Whatever I did took something from me. Something that will take time to recover, I imagine. And it's something I'm going to have to avoid using at all costs moving forward.

If anyone ever sees I can manipulate elements other than water, I'll be exposed. If Bastian's first warning hadn't made the danger of exposure clear, the book has. People used to know and fear what I am. They used to hunt us down because they were terrified of what we could do if allowed to live.

Mireen is at my side a moment later, fingers probing the place where Davrin's blow landed. She produces a small vial from her pocket, uncorking it. 'Found some juniper leaf growing just outside the castle walls. We used it back home for pain.' The salve smells of mint and something sharper as she dabs it on my skin. The pain eases immediately.

I lift a brow. 'We're not supposed to leave the castle walls.'

Mireen leans closer, smile conspiratorial. 'Tell that to the cute guy who insisted on "ravaging my perfect body in nature."' She shrugs. 'In any case, he knew when we could sneak out. The sex wasn't anything special, but now I can stretch my legs from time to time.'

'You'll have to tell me more about this mysterious guy later.' I give my shoulder an experimental rotation and find the balm works amazingly well. 'And thank him for me.'

'Impressive footwork, Thorne,' Blackstone says, interrupting us. There's a hint of surprise on his face. 'Perhaps you've been paying attention after all.'

From across the training area, I feel Malakai's eyes boring into me, cold and calculating. He's standing over the dead body of a girl who is bleeding from a horrible wound to her neck, eyes wide and unseeing.

'By the four elements, Malakai . . . Again?' Blackstone grumbles as he notices, leaving us to head toward the dead body.

'Got carried away. My mistake,' Malakai says, voice devoid of all emotion.

I watch Blackstone dragging the body from the room, hating how I can already feel myself normalizing all the death. Maybe that's the most horrifying part of life at Confluence. I can look at a corpse and feel sadness, but not shock. I can feel the selfish relief of knowing I'm not one of the dead. Neither are my friends. Four of us lived when Malakai wanted us dead. It's harder than it should be to feel the appropriate emotions for the ones who didn't live.

But if I gave every death here its proper respect, I'd never come up for air. That's what this place is doing to us. It's teaching us to keep moving forward, no matter what surrounds us. No matter what hells we've just passed through.

The dead girl will join the pile of corpses in the back of my mind – the ones that drift into my thoughts every night and linger like haunting ghosts, a grim backdrop to the recurring nightmares of being trapped in the water with the thing that hunts me.

Davrin and Malakai's other soldiers join together in a small group, several of them glaring occasionally in my direction.

Mireen looks at Malakai's people and then back at me as she

gives me a shoulder to lean on. 'You know this means trouble, right? Malakai is probably going to dream of playing jump rope with your intestines tonight.'

I shoot her a look.

She smirks, then lowers her eyes. 'Sorry. But you know I'm right. In spirit at least.'

All I can do is nod my head, because she is right. I've just painted an even bigger target on my back. And now the bull's-eye is bright red.

'That was quite the display,' a familiar voice comments.

Bastian stands nearby, observing the training session with arms casually folded across his chest. His legacy uniform is immaculate as always, making our sweat-stained training clothes look even more pitiful by comparison.

'What are you doing here?' I ask, immediately suspicious. Other than the instructors, he's the only non-offering in the whole room.

'Observing,' he replies smoothly. 'As I told you. It's one of my assignments here.'

His eyes drop briefly to my left hand, then back to my face. 'I see you've been doing your reading. That's good.'

With that cryptic note, he walks away.

'Okay,' Mireen says, tilting her head. 'What was that about?'

I shrug, aiming for nonchalance and probably missing by a mile. 'Legacy business, I guess?'

The rest of the training session passes in a blur of sparring matches and drills. With the challenge matches over, the immediate threat of death is gone.

Still, I can feel Malakai's attention never wavering, his gaze a constant pressure between my shoulder blades. More than once, I catch Serena watching from the fire affinities, her fire-marked hands clenching and unclenching like she's imagining them around my throat.

By the time we're dismissed, my nerves are raw, stretched thin by the constant vigilance. The brief victory against Davrin feels hollow now, overwhelmed by the knowledge that I've only made my situation more precarious. Malakai will see our survival as a personal insult. If we weren't already at the top of his hit list, we will be now.

'Weapons away, first-year waters,' Blackstone calls. 'And for those who haven't yet heard, the water trial begins at dawn two days from now. Report to the eastern shore of Mirror Lake. Wear something suitable for swimming. No weapons will be necessary.'

A chorus of nervous whispers erupts around us. Mirror Lake is the vast body of water at the edge of campus, its depths rumored to be bottomless in places. What kind of trial awaits us there?

I see other combat instructors relaying similar messages to the other affinities. The airs burst into nervous whispers. The fires look to Raith, who only nods and seems to calm them. The earths take the news with stoic acceptance.

'Mirror Lake?' Beck joins us as we exit the room, his sandy hair plastered to his forehead with sweat. 'That can't be good.'

'Why not?' I ask, though I'm already certain I won't like the answer.

'Tucker talked about it once before they—' Beck says, lowering his voice. 'Apparently, there's some kind of beast that lives in it. He said students get eaten every year by the thing. Swallowed whole.'

'If the monster eats me, I hope I give it indigestion. I've been told I'm very spicy,' Mireen says with a too-bright smile that earns a confused stare from Beck. I'm starting to get used to her macabre sense of humor – maybe to even appreciate the touch of lightness it brings in otherwise dark moments.

I can see why people who are surrounded by death would make a habit of it.

Ambrose appears on my other side, still sweaty from exertion.

'Tell Beck he's full of it, please,' I say to Ambrose. 'He says there's a monster in the lake that eats students. Swallows them whole.'

'She's right, Beck,' Ambrose says. 'It doesn't swallow them whole. It drags them to its lair in the deepest section of the lake. At least that's what I heard.'

'Thank you both for that incredibly comforting information,' I mutter. My insides go tight at the thought of the lake. At the question of what could be waiting in its depths. The similarity to my recurring nightmare isn't lost on me, either, but I try my best not to think on it.

We part ways to clean up before classes, but as I turn toward the water tower, a hand grips my arm, pulling me into the shadow of a stone archway. I whirl, ready to fight, only to find myself face to face with Raith.

In the darkness, his eyes catch what little light remains, reflecting it with an unnerving focus that makes me wonder if he can see straight into my thoughts. 'What did you do in there?' he demands, voice low and rough. Even from the brief touch, I feel a hint of the fire essence I pulled from him, dancing and twisting within me with the promise of power.

'In where?' I ask, hoping the innocent act might work.

His grip tightens slightly. 'Don't. I saw what happened with Davrin. The stone moved.'

Fear grips my heart. It claws up my throat like a living thing, threatening to choke me. If Raith noticed, who else might have? 'I don't know what you're talking about.'

'Bullshit.' His eyes search mine, looking for lies. 'You pulled energy from the stone. I felt it. Just like you pulled fire from me that first day. You need to be far more cautious. Anybody could've seen.'

The revelation hits me like a punch to the gut. He felt it? How? And why does he care if people see?

Before I can respond, his expression shifts, something like reluctant concern flashing across his features. 'Malakai has friends among the third-years who help with the trial. They'll likely tell him where everybody enters the lake. That means he'll know where to find you.'

I blink, thrown by the warning. 'Why tell me this? How do you even know for that matter?'

He turns to leave, but I catch his wrist, the contact sending another surge of warmth into my body. 'Why are you helping me?' I press.

His jaw tightens, eyes dropping to where my fingers circle his wrist. 'Maybe I'm just saving you for later,' he says finally, the words held together by tension and something unspoken. The electricity between us is practically visible, crackling in the air like static.

I don't believe him for a moment, but he pulls free and strides away before I can push him for more.

All I'm left with is the warm memory of where our skin touched. That, and the knowledge that Malakai is probably going to use the trial to hunt me down and kill me. Unfortunately for him, I'm starting to see I'm not nearly as defenseless as he thinks.

And if he wants to come after me when I'm literally surrounded by water? Well . . . I might actually have a chance to make him regret it. A dangerous smile forms on my face – for once, I don't feel like prey waiting to be slaughtered. I might finally have teeth of my own.

Chapter 10

'You look like shit,' Mireen observes helpfully as we trudge down to Mirror Lake in the predawn chill. Over my shoulder, I see Confluence Academy's four elemental towers punching through a cloud of mist.

My heart sinks like a stone in deep water. Part of me wonders if this will be my last time seeing the academy – if I'll die out here in these murky depths.

We walk with the other water offerings in our best attempt at 'swimwear.' Since they don't provide us with anything except uniforms and underwear, most of us have simply stripped down to nearly nothing. Some of the guys have just removed their tops and wear the long white slacks we're given for bottoms.

Weeks of hard training and being fed well is already shaping us into something new. Muscles ripple where they didn't before and stores of fat have melted away, long since burned for energy or survival.

'I look like shit? Thanks,' I mutter, stifling another yawn. After Raith's warning, sleep had been impossible. I'd spent half the night trying to decode more of the unbound book, searching for anything that might help me survive whatever waited in the lake. I'd even foolishly crept out of the room and looked for him at the wall, but I haven't seen him again since that first night. When I finally did lie down to sleep, the nightmares came more vividly than ever before.

Worse, when I *did* finally drift to sleep, Mireen's 'pets' managed to wake me several times. Her single rat has either multiplied or told friends about easy access to food. Our room is now shared by several chittering, scurrying little rats who sometimes climb my bed to sniff my face in my sleep.

Mireen calls it cute. I call it difficult to sleep through.

The eastern sky is just beginning to lighten as we reach the lakeshore, where Primal Sestra waits with several other instructors and groups of older students in black uniforms, either trimmed in aspirant silver or the silver and gold marking them as legacies. Behind them, the lake stretches like black glass, mist curling across its surface in ghostly patterns.

The remaining first-year water offerings gather in nervous clusters, their breath fogging in the cold air. Malakai and his people cluster together, eyes hard and violent as they look at us. Shirtless, I can see just how terrifyingly racked with muscle and power his body is. He looks like he could punch a hole straight through stone, and I know he's no slouch when it comes to channeling, either.

A ball of worry and anger forms in my chest at his attention. Half of me wants to lift my middle finger and the other half wants to shrink away in fear.

'Waters,' Sestra's voice carries across the shore without effort. 'Today you face the element that calls to you. Those who pass will continue their journey toward Confluence Day. Those who fail . . .' She leaves the sentence unfinished, but we all know what failure means here.

'The trial is simple,' she continues. 'I have placed elemental echoes at varying depths throughout the lake. Each of you must retrieve at least one echo to pass. There are enough echoes for all of you, but some will be harder to find than others.'

She gestures, and an aide brings forward a shallow bowl filled with what looks like clear marbles. 'These are minor water echoes – impressions left by water elementals. Finding one will require you to sense its resonance with your own affinity. Channeling will be necessary both to locate them and to survive the depths.'

At this, my stomach drops like I've swallowed a handful of stones. *Channel to survive the depths. Channel to find the echoes.*

Of course.

Am I going to have any chance of this when I'm not a real water affinity?

Maybe. Being submerged in water will give me a unique advantage here. I'll be surrounded by a nearly unlimited supply of water essence. For once, I might actually be positioned to excel at something.

'Instructors and third-years will take you to various locations around the lake. On their signal, you will enter the waters and begin the trial. You will have until sunset.'

'Please tell me that brilliant brain of yours has a plan,' Mireen whispers, her teeth chattering as she eyes the black water.

I stare at the mist curling off the lake's surface. 'Get in, grab the first echo I find, get out before anything eats me.'

She bumps her shoulder against mine. 'Simple. Elegant. Probably won't work. See you on the other side anyway.'

We're separated and led to various points around the lake. I'm not happy to see a third-year with a dangerous glint in her eye is the one leading me. I'm reminded of Raith's warning. Malakai has friends in the upper years. Friends who told him where certain people will be entering the lake. For all I know, he'll be making a line directly for me as soon as the trial begins.

But I can't hide forever.

Staying scared is only going to mean staying weak. And I'm fucking tired of being scared.

So if he wants to come hunting for me during the trial? Let him. Let Malakai think he's going to ambush me. Let him think he'll have the advantage if he finds me.

My body feels electric with newfound resolve. Davrin couldn't handle me two days ago during challenge matches. Let's see Malakai do better.

They're brave thoughts from a shivering, half-naked girl pretending to be a water affinity – a girl whose knowledge about her affinity is coming a few paragraphs a night from an old book.

'Go,' the third-year says from behind me. I don't miss the half smile she wears. Why the hells does a third-year want to help first-year waters kill one another?

It makes me wonder if there's actually something more to Malakai's murderous intent. What if it's not just simple bloodthirst or ambition? What if there's some other angle I'm not seeing?

But now is hardly the time to dwell on mysteries.

I wade through the slimy shallows of the lake, my breath fleeing the moment the icy water touches my bare skin. Goosebumps erupt across my body, but I force myself to keep walking deeper, feet slipping on submerged rocks slick with algae.

Eventually, I'm deep enough to swim and submerge myself beneath the waters. We've trained with Sestra to form bubbles of air around our mouths beneath the water.

Before now, I've never succeeded. This knowledge wasn't exactly helping me sleep once Raith told me about the trial. I decided I could, at worst, swim on the surface and just hold my breath as much as possible.

I fumble in the freezing cold and dark waters for several minutes, bobbing to the surface to gulp air and then diving down again as I try to draw water and air together to make a bubble around my mouth.

It's slow work, but I eventually succeed.

Sort of.

Instead of a small bubble around my mouth and nose, I end up creating a huge one around my entire head. It stretches and threatens to break if I swim too fast, but it provides me with air and a surprisingly clear view of the lake's depths.

I see vegetation rising from below, swaying eerily in unseen currents. If I squint, I think I even see a few distant dark shapes moving through the water. Other students, maybe?

I glance behind my back, suddenly sure I'll see Malakai himself coming at me. But it's just more water and more vegetation.

With the bubble in place, I find my thoughts drifting to Beck and Ambrose's stupid story about some kind of sea monster as I swim.

It would be easier to dismiss if their stories and this lake didn't seem to match what I've been seeing in my nightmares for weeks.

Pushing it all from my mind, I focus on the task at hand. I need to find an echo to pass the trial, and I need to pass the trial to make it to Confluence Day.

So how the hell am I going to do that?

According to the book, the unbound can sense the elements differently – not by creating, but by feeling what already exists. I let myself sink slightly, trailing my fingers through the water, trying to sense . . . something.

At first, there's nothing. Just cold, dark water. Then, gradually, I become aware of currents – little eddies and flows that seem to carry whispers of . . . intention? Memory? I can't quite grasp it, but I know it's there.

I dive deeper, following one such current. The light fades quickly, leaving me in greenish twilight. My ears pop and pressure builds around me, but I push on, drawn by something I can't name.

There – a flicker of blue light perhaps twenty feet below. An echo?

I swim toward it, my head feeling like it might cave in as the pressure continues to mount.

Once I'm closer, I can see it's indeed one of the marble-like echoes, nestled in a crevice between rocks. I reach for it, fingertips closing around the smooth sphere.

I sense something coming toward me.

I swirl so fast the bubble around my head nearly pops. And then I see him. Malakai is swimming toward me with a bubble around his eyes, nose, and mouth and a shifting, shimmering kind of water dagger in one hand.

Panic clutches at me, threatening to keep me stuck in place – motionless and helpless.

And then he's on me.

I kick off the ground, dodging his first stab in what feels like slow motion. He comes again, and I see he's moving faster than he should be able to – using the water to propel himself, somehow.

I barely twist out of the way of another attack as his big body flows past, yanking me to the side with the force of his movement.

A cold reality settles over me.

Do something, or you're going to die down here.

Malakai turns, dagger in his hand as his muscular body ripples in the dark depths of the water. Something about the muffled silence of fighting for my life beneath the water – with nothing but my ragged breath echoing within my own bubble – feels wrong. Claustrophobic.

I reach into the water, struggling to even think of what I would do with my powers if I had complete command. Form a weapon of my own? Try to push him down with heavy currents? Pop his bubbles?

Before I can even start to try, he's on me again, rushing through the water like a human arrow, dagger extended toward me.

I jerk to the side, but I'm not fast enough this time. The cold bite of his weapon shocks me, pain exploding through my nerves like lightning, my screams piercing inside the solitude of my air bubble.

He stabbed me in the left shoulder. Blood so dark it almost looks black clouds out from the wound, gushing from between my clasping fingers.

Distantly, I sense something else in the water with us. Another student, maybe? Or are more of his soldiers on their way to take turns stabbing me?

No. I'm not going to die like this. Not this easily.

I don't think. I let instinct take over. My mind reaches into the water until I feel like I can make it move at my command. Using an invisible tendril of lake water, I press in on Malakai's face, watching with satisfaction as his eyes open wide and the bubbles providing him air smear and pop, scattering into thousands of tiny bubbles that rush upward.

While he's distracted, I kick toward the echo I dropped, scoop it up, and then realize my situation has gone from bad to worse.

I see three shapes coming from behind Malakai, soldiers of his, by my guess. All three are holding magical weapons.

But there's something else. Something much more dangerous.

It wasn't them I sensed in the waters. The thing I sensed is far, far larger than them. And it's moving fast. At first, I think a cloud is passing over the lake far ahead that casts a deep shadow behind the three approaching student soldiers. But then it twists and moves in a way that shadows don't.

Two deep blue eyes suddenly appear behind the three figures, and the eyes make sudden sense of the shadow. It's a serpent with massive wings, and it's coiled and waiting behind the three students, its massive mouth opening slowly.

Malakai manages to get his bubbles back in place over his face. He looks triumphant for a moment, and then he must see the look on my face.

He turns, and a cluster of bubbles bursts up from his head. A scream, I hope.

Maybe I'm about to die, but at least I got the chance to see Malakai become so scared he screamed and broke his spell.

My smile fades when the creature – which looks like it's at least seventy or eighty feet long with wings at least that wide – explodes forward. The first student disappears, seemingly swallowed by the massive shadow of the beast.

It slithers out of view, leaving only a dark stain slowly spreading in the otherwise deep blue water. The other two students turn, see the blood, and begin frantically swimming for the surface.

Malakai turns from them and comes toward me, knife still raised.

Is he serious? Killing me is still his fucking priority?

Even as I see the shadow rush up from the depths again and aim for one of the remaining two student soldiers, I turn my attention to Malakai. I grip the water again with a power that feels like it's already running thin. I form a rope of thickened water and wrap it around his ankle, anchoring him to the ground.

I flinch as he flies toward me, then watch with surprise as the rope of water actually holds. He's jerked back just inches before he reaches me with his knife.

I make the rope extend, wrapping it around his legs and ankles, squeezing them together and pulling him down until he's stuck on the lake's floor.

My ragged breaths and my pounding heart roar inside the bubble of air I'm channeling around my head.

There's only one of Malakai's allies left, and they've almost reached the lake's surface. I see them pass through a shaft of sunlight, temporarily revealing enough detail to make out it's a girl swimming in the white offering underwear. Whatever weapon she had is long since dismissed as she focuses on escape.

And then I see the creature swirl and twist up from the darkness below. Its body is elegant and lethal – sinuous lines covered in thick scales that catch the sunlight in glittering patterns. The navy blue serpent keeps its wings tucked tight to its side as it gives a swish of its long, finned tail. It explodes upward, jaws snapping shut around the girl just before the beast's momentum carries it above the lake's surface.

For a moment, it's completely gone, leaving only the disturbed ripples of water from its ascent.

And then it crashes back down, those deep blue eyes pointed straight for Malakai as it pumps its tail, rocketing toward him.

Fuck.

I see him struggling to escape, but he can't. He's still anchored by the magical rope of water I'm channeling.

Maybe he's screwed either way – maybe we both are – but I don't want to be part of his death. Maybe he deserves to die, but I'm not going to stain myself by being the one to do it. I don't have time to think about whether that's the right or wrong decision.

I release the spell, and even from twenty feet up, I can see the relief and confusion in Malakai's face.

I wince, eyes closed because I don't want to see the beast eat him. I wait three heartbeats, then I can't keep them closed anymore. I open my eyes and scream.

Two blue eyes, the size of dinner plates, hover directly in front of me. White steam curls from reptilian nostrils and rows of teeth like blue crystals are slowly revealed as it opens a mouth large enough to swallow me whole.

Behind the dragon-like head, its serpentine body drifts back, so long that the finned tail is shrouded in shadow. Dread creeps into my bones as I see dark wings spreading slowly in the waters. The sheer size of the monster settles on me, making the blood drain from my head until I think I might pass out.

It's huge.

Ancient.

Fucking impossible.

To lose consciousness would be a mercy. There's no surviving this thing.

It has to be an elemental, but something so huge and powerful defies all explanation.

It twists suddenly, curling in on itself as Malakai stabs it from below. A small burst of blue blood drifts from the wound as it turns to look at its attacker. With a movement I can only describe as dismissive, it slaps its tail through the water, slamming into Malakai so hard his air bubbles explode again and his body goes limp to float in the water.

It turns its attention back to me.

I can't say what the hell I'm thinking, but I know there's no point in attacking it. And it's close enough to touch, so I reach a hand out and place it on the beast's snout, even as my lungs burn for air.

As soon as I touch it, I feel a rush of power, but it's nothing like when I touched Raith or Bastian or anyone else. This power feels . . . dirty. Messy. Chaotic.

It surges into me almost greedily, filling me like a waterskin until the pressure seems like it might burst me from the inside.

My body becomes a lightning rod in a storm, every nerve ending screaming as the raw, untamed energy floods through me. I think I scream, but I lose all sense of time as the energy floods me. The only thing I remember is a faint, ethereal voice and the sensation of being lifted.

'Thank you, unbound. If you see me during Confluence Day, you must run. I can't keep it from hurting you. So run.'

I blink several times, frown in confusion, and then wonder why I'm not dead. I can sense that time has passed. Seconds or minutes, I'm not sure. But I must have lost consciousness.

I cough, spitting up water and wincing at the memory of my shoulder. I was stabbed.

I sit up, and shout in fear.

Malakai is lying beside me on a rectangle of magical water. The rectangle is keeping us above the water and slowly drifting toward shore, where I see students climbing from the water with glowing echoes in hand. I spot some other affinities and first-years waiting on the shore as well.

I touch the place where Malakai stabbed me and feel only smooth skin. When I look at my bare shoulder, I see a magical blue mark like a scar, but oddly beautiful.

What the hell happened?

I try to remember. I saw Malakai's allies being eaten. I let Malakai go so he would have some chance of escape, but then the creature was right in front of me. And then . . . it spoke to me.

So it was an elemental, then. But gods. It must have been a truly ancient elemental to take a form so large and powerful. And it must have healed me and put us on this water platform.

It . . . saved us? But why would it save us and then warn me to run if I saw it on Confluence Day?

Malakai coughs and sits up, his muscular body already showing hints of an ugly purple bruise forming from his armpit to his hip. He sees me and his eyes harden.

I hold my palms up, then realize I'm still holding an echo.

His eyes fall to it, too. He doesn't have an echo.

'I could have let you die back there,' I say, scooting back on the platform and reaching for water essence. But I find I'm completely exhausted. The power slips through my fingers like sand.

Malakai's features harden. 'You should have let me die.'

'Malakai . . . come on,' I say, scooting back more, though there's not much room to escape on the small magical rectangle of water. 'For once, just be a decent human being.'

He snorts through his nose. 'You've got no godsdamned idea what kind of human being I am. Keep the echo. And don't think this changes a fucking thing between us, Thorne.' Without another word, he pushes off the water platform and disappears beneath the depths of the lake.

I let out a long breath and collapse, body shivering as I clutch the pearl-like echo as if my life depends on it.

Alive. I'm alive, and with any luck, my friends will be too when the trial is over.

For the first time in weeks, I think maybe we actually have a chance of making it to Confluence Day. I showed down there I'm finally getting some grasp of my powers.

No. More than some. I fought Malakai off by myself. I survived coming face to face with whatever that thing was.

I lie on my back, eyes closed as the sun warms my nearly-frozen body. A small smile spreads across my lips.

I can do this. It's never going to be easy. It's never going to be pretty. But I can fucking do this.

Chapter 11

I'm barefoot as I pad my way to the spot on top of the castle walls. I hug my arms close, wishing I'd had the foresight to put on more clothes before stepping out here. It seems like winter decided to offer a preview tonight, with bitter cold wind blowing in from the snow-capped mountains to the west of campus.

But I stubbornly keep climbing the steps to the highest wall. I may not want to admit it, but I know the reason I've left my room isn't for fresh air tonight. It's because I'm hoping I'll find him again.

Raith.

I may have survived the water trial and faced whatever the hell that creature was, but the nightmares are only getting worse. I still see it . . . him . . . her . . . hells if I know – in my dreams, and they're more vivid every single night. Each time I close my eyes, those glowing blue depths are waiting, pulling me under. Memories of dark red clouds of blood that had been Malakai's allies stain the waters, their deaths feeling somehow like my fault.

I suppress a full-body shudder as I round the corner and freeze, pulse immediately racing.

In the center of the wall, silhouetted against the stars, stands Raith.

He turns his head as soon as I'm in view and gives the slightest nod.

Maybe I hoped to find him here, but it doesn't stop the instinctive fear he triggers in me. I might as well approach a wolf in the forest. Something about him screams danger, yet I'm still drawn forward, danger be damned.

With one deep, calming breath, I head toward him.

'You're going to freeze,' he growls.

'Does that bother you?'

Raith looks annoyed and concerned as he kneels and actually places his big hands on my bare feet. Steam rises from his skin, making the air shimmer and glow faintly orange.

'What are – oh.'

I sigh with relief as heat doesn't just pass between our skin, but it also envelops my chilled feet and legs. The stone beneath me even seems to warm as the scent of smoke and campfires fills the air. That wonderful cocoon of heat spreads from my toes and creeps up my body, almost like a lover's caress, warming me to the bone. It feels like being wrapped in the world's most perfect blanket, banishing the chill in an instant.

And part of me wonders if those invisible hands of fire are Raith's – if he can feel the perfect touch sliding up my body, whispering along my curves and most sensitive places.

It's done in seconds, and Raith stands, assessing me with those molten gold eyes. 'Better?'

'Much . . . thank you.'

He rests his forearms on the half-height wall and leans out, surveying the darkened landscape beyond.

'I haven't seen you here since the first time,' I say after a while. 'Does that mean your bad dreams stopped?'

Raith doesn't answer immediately. 'No . . .'

'So you've been avoiding me?'

I study his profile, watching the way the twisted and burned flesh beside his mouth moves slightly as his lips curve down at the edges. 'The less you know about me, the better.'

I frown. 'I don't think that's for you to decide. You act like you want me to think you're my enemy, but then you keep showing up and helping me when it matters. You warned me about Malakai yesterday, and it might have saved me this morning.'

Raith suddenly looks up. 'During the trial? What did he do?'

'He . . . attacked me.'

His eyes scan my body, leaving no inch unturned as if he's searching for injuries. The intensity of his gaze makes my skin prickle with awareness. With . . . pleasure. He frowns as his gaze falls to my shoulder. I can't say how he knows, but he half-raises his fingertip, almost like he wants to touch the place Malakai stabbed me. The place the water dragon mysteriously healed.

'He hurt you. Didn't he?' There's rage in the simple words. Barely concealed. I can sense it running red hot within him.

I open my mouth to deny it, but shake my head instead, shrugging. 'He got me. But it's nothing.' I turn away, hugging my arms to myself again as if cold, even though Raith's magic is keeping me perfectly warm. The memories of what happened beneath those dark waters . . . somehow, I know it's not over. I know that thing isn't done with me.

I sense Raith watching me.

'What?' I ask.

'You're not telling me everything. I heard things. One of the third-years told me that—'

'You're friends with third-years?'

Raith's blank expression says it all. Of course he is. Ambitious older students can probably tell he's destined for great things. They want to become friends now and garner favor to benefit themselves when we're all part of Empire's army. Those of us who survive, anyway.

'Tell me what happened in the lake, Nessa.'

I glare at him. 'No.'

His lips twitch, giving the faintest hint of amusement. And gods, it almost hurts to look at the damn man because he's so gorgeous. Even with the scars, or maybe because of them, his face draws my eyes like a work of art I can't stop studying. 'I heard Malakai and three of his people went after you. I heard only Malakai survived. And I heard you two were seen floating together on some kind of water magic atop the lake.'

'Okay.'

'Tell me you're not working with Malakai.'

I scowl, leaning forward in disbelief. 'Wait, really? That's what you're worried about? For a minute, I thought you were actually concerned about my safety, but I see how this works, now. Serena and Malakai are plotting something and cutting you out of the equation. Now you hear some rumor that I was seen with Malakai and you're ready to assume the worst? Well, fuck you. That's my answer. Fuck. You.' My hands curl into fists at my sides, and I can feel Raith's borrowed heat boiling under my skin.

Raith's silence is somehow louder than words, his gaze fixed on me with an intensity that charges the air between us. I sense danger there. What would he do if I had told him I was working with Malakai? Kill me right here? Torture me for information?

I push off the wall, feeling my temper flaring as the fire I borrowed from him swirls inside my body. 'Sweet dreams, Raith.'

'That's . . . actually not bad, Nessa,' Primal Sestra notes before gliding away from where I'm sitting in channeling class. With a smirk, I release the sphere of water I've been holding over my palm. The droplets scatter with a satisfying splash.

One benefit of the terrible nightmares is I don't spend much time sleeping. That means I have more time to read through the unbound book, and I'm also getting faster at working through the code. I've even memorized a few specific sound patterns, which lets me read the occasional word without referencing Bastian's key.

Mireen looks over at me and wiggles her eyebrows after Sestra walks away. 'Look at you. Passing the water trial and now you're earning praise from Sestra?'

I bite back a smile. 'She's only impressed because I was so terrible to start.'

Beck leans in from my other side. 'You really were. After our first few days, I thought Sestra was going to kill you herself.'

Ambrose, who sits beside Beck, leans his head forward, voice low. 'When are you going to tell us what happened in the Lake, Nessa?

I'm hearing wild rumors, and as your friend, I should be the one spreading wild rumors.'

'Later,' I say, glancing toward Malakai. Even with three of his soldiers dead, Malakai's 'army' is still intimidating, but I think others are starting to wonder if his group is as untouchable as they thought. Malakai's lowered eyes as he focuses on his channeling tells me he feels it too. The confident swagger he normally carries is dimmed, though so slightly I could be imagining it. 'Common room after Military Tactics?'

'We'll be there,' Beck says, rubbing his hands together. 'This is going to be juicy, isn't it? I heard you punched an instructor in the face and grabbed a handful of echoes from the bowl itself.'

Ambrose leans in closer. 'I heard she wrestled a water serpent by its horns, then rode it back to shore.'

I can't help laughing softly, which earns me a stern look from Sestra. We all sit back in place and resume working on our spells, but my mind is spinning with a thousand thoughts, making it hard to concentrate.

Confluence Day is only three days away. I still have no idea why those instructors were talking about siphons. I don't know if Malakai is planning to get revenge for what happened, or if he's going to avoid me now that he knows what I'm capable of.

And it doesn't even end there.

The more I read of the unbound book, the more it dawns on me that Bastian read all of this too. He knows all of this about me and more. Considering he's supposed to be reporting back to his father in some kind of important council, I have to wonder if he has mentioned me.

From what I'm reading, I know enough to say that would mean deadly consequences for me.

And Raith . . . I'm still pissed from our encounter in the middle of the night. I know he doesn't owe me anything, but it stings to think he could even imagine I'd be working with Malakai – that I'd be helping to murder people. The accusation burns like acid in my chest, all the more painful because part of me had started to trust him. An even smaller part of me had started to think he cared about me. Worried about me.

Stupid. I see that much now.

The rest of the classes pass in a blur as my thoughts twist and turn over everything that has happened and is yet to come. I'm the first one to the common room in the water tower after Military Tactics because I can't find an appetite tonight.

I take a spot on a large, comfortable couch by a window lined with decorative silver filigree. A magically blue-tinged fire burns in the hearth beside me, warming me even as the night's chill seeps through the castle walls. By some miracle of magic, the water that always runs down the walls here has started to get warmer, and now it gives off wisps of steam as it runs down the walls, heating the tower slightly.

I itch to read my unbound book as I wait for the others to show, but I know it would be insanity to pull it out here. I only read the book at night when Mireen is asleep or on nights when she's out sharing someone else's bed. Thankfully, she doesn't ever bring her partners to our room.

Older students come in and disappear up the side stairs that lead to the private sections of the common room. I see a few aspirants and legacies also passing through the general common room to their private areas as well. There are only a handful of other first-year water offerings in the room, and they're clustered together on the far side with books spread out, studying for one of many upcoming tests.

It's half an hour before Mireen, Beck, and Ambrose have all joined me. Mireen sits beside me, offering to fix my braid – which was nearly pulled out of my head during sparring this morning. Beck and Ambrose take the single seats opposite our couch, leaning in, eyes and faces intent.

'Okay,' Beck says. He glances to his side, seeming to confirm the others in the common room aren't close enough to listen in. 'Spill it.'

And I do, though I omit a few choice details. I tell them about Malakai's attack and the giant creature. I even tell them how it healed my wound and saved us with a raft of water magic. I don't talk about the powers I used, admit I sort of saved Malakai's life, or tell them the creature had already been visiting me in my nightmares for weeks.

But the story is sensational enough that they don't seem to sense I've left anything out.

Ambrose sits back, a crease forming between his brows as he taps his chin in thought.

Beck lets out a low whistle, giving me a look like he's seeing me for the first time.

Mireen's pace as she braids my hair slows and eventually stops as the story hits the most dangerous parts.

'Gods, Nessa,' Mireen says. 'I thought all the stories I was hearing were bullshit. People were even talking about it in the dining hall. Someone said you gave Rector Voss the finger as you rode away on a water dragon.'

I grin. 'I've never even seen the Rector, let alone made vulgar gestures at him.'

'So Malakai was just . . . on the raft with you when you woke up?' Beck asks. 'Did he try to come at you again?'

I consider lying, but I think my friends deserve to at least know what we're dealing with when Malakai is concerned. 'He . . . seemed to think I saved him, somehow.'

Beck tilts his head. 'But you didn't.'

'No,' I say quickly. 'Not exactly, at least.' I sigh as their faces darken. 'I managed to kind of snare him to the lake floor during the fight. When I saw the creature coming for him, I just couldn't bring myself to keep him trapped. I know he has done terrible things. I know he's a terrible person. But . . . there wasn't time to think. Some part of me just didn't want to be involved, so I let the spell go. I honestly thought we were both dead anyway, and maybe I didn't want my last act to be helping somebody die a terrible death, I—' my voice cracks and I realize how fast I've been talking. My hands are trembling in my lap and my throat feels raw with guilt. Of all the secrets I'm holding from my friends for their own safety, this isn't one of them. Even as shame threatens to overwhelm me, it feels good to let it out.

Mireen gives my arm a soft squeeze. 'Hey. This place brings out the worst in us. I think Malakai deserved whatever he was about to get, but you can't blame yourself for wanting to be a bit of light in all this darkness. And we certainly don't blame you for it. Right?' She looks at Beck and Ambrose, who bulge their eyes and shake their heads quickly.

'No,' Beck says. 'Don't blame you one bit. So you're not a murderer. Big deal. We still like you.'

'I think it's admirable,' Ambrose agrees. 'Maybe your mercy will make Malakai reconsider the way he's been acting.'

'I don't think so,' I admit. 'The last thing he said was how nothing between us changed.'

'Asshole,' Mireen mutters. She looks like she wants to hunt him down and drown him herself, and I love her just a little more for it.

There's a lull in the conversation before Ambrose leans in closer, eyes lit with interest. 'The creature you saw . . . what did it look like, exactly?'

'Kind of like a giant sea serpent mixed with a dragon, maybe? It was dark, though. I only saw bits and pieces. And it was huge, with blue eyes.'

'Fuck,' Ambrose whispers.

'What?' Beck says.

'It's just that not many elementals could fit a description like that. To be so large and take such a powerful shape . . . It sounds like one of the ancients, but it also sounds like it has gone rogue.'

'You told me about that,' I say. 'Elementals driven mad by broken tethers or the death of their tethered humans, right?'

He nods. 'But I've never heard of one of the ancients tethering a human. Something that powerful going rogue is . . . dire. And how the hell is it here? How is it in our world swimming around Mirror Lake?'

I think about the dreams I've been having – the sense that I'm being hunted and the predator has been drawing closer with each dream. And then, for the first time in weeks, I think about the storm I called back in Saltcrest three years ago. The storm that I accidentally drew in. The storm that killed my brothers and my father. The memory hits me like a physical blow, making my chest constrict painfully.

Did I survive only to draw in an even bigger storm here? A storm in the form of an ancient rogue elemental? The death of the three I'd seen eaten beneath the waters suddenly rushes in to pile on my back, heavy with the weight of guilt.

'I'm not sure,' I say quietly.

The others shift the topic of conversation to Confluence Day, but my mind lingers on the rogue elemental.

An instinct I can't describe tells me I haven't seen it for the last time. There's a kind of connection between us. With a sudden certainty that turns my insides to ice, I know when I'm going to see it next. A shiver runs down my spine as my gut twists with dread.

The beast is going to be waiting for me on Confluence Day, but this time, I'll be ready for it.

Chapter 12

Nothing went according to plan.

I clutch my side, wincing at the pain in my ribs. I landed hard. So fucking hard that it takes me a moment to clear my head and remember what the hells is going on.

My eyes are blurry and full of stars as I blink, climbing to my feet and shaking off the disorientation. The last few minutes were a maelstrom of chaos, but they come back to me like snapshots of madness.

First-years assembling in the courtyard as reality itself seemed to split at the seams, opening a portal.

Instructors shouting about instability.

Odd tendrils of magic lashing out from the portal, snatching students and dragging us inside.

I must have been grabbed and dragged here, but I can't remember it.

It all clicks into place piece by piece. Where I am. What this is.

The air is charged and feels . . . wrong. The colors are too vivid – like someone cranking up the saturation until my eyes burn. And the sky . . . it's not the sky I've spent my life living beneath.

I'm in the elemental plane.

My heart thunders against my ribs. Confluence Day is finally here. I either tether an elemental today, or I die.

I sweep my eyes around, taking in my surroundings. This place isn't what I expected. I imagined shattered ground seeping magma and torrents of water or unbearable winds. Instead . . . I see a forest to my left that's a brighter green than anything I ever imagined. More distant still, I see it's all ringed by a wall that must be two hundred feet high. The wall looks like it's made of the elements themselves, shifting in ways that my eyes can't quite focus on.

Did the elementals build this?

I know from classes that elementals live in cities like us with rulers, politics, and wars. But somehow it didn't seem . . . real. It makes me wonder what this place is to them. The area where humans appear once a year hoping to tether with them. And what would stop elementals with a grudge from coming here to hunt for sport?

As if in response to my thought, a scream cuts through the silence, high and terrified, ending in a wet gurgle.

I spin toward the sound, automatically drawing my training rapier. It's not much, but having a weapon in hand makes me feel slightly better, silly as it may be.

About fifty yards down the treeline, a group of students has emerged from another point in the rift. They're scattered and disoriented, just as I was moments ago.

But they're not alone.

A massive creature prowls among them, its body a living flame in the rough shape of a wolf. It's at least three times the size of any natural wolf, its paws leaving scorched prints on the black stones. As I watch, it lunges forward, jaws closing around a screaming air affinity. His body ignites instantly, becoming nothing but ash in seconds.

Another pulls back a long spear and jabs at the wolf. His weapon dissolves in his hand.

His body follows a moment later.

We're not meant to fight these things. We never were. If they are hunting us . . . *Gods.* We'll stand no chance.

The remaining students scatter, some running toward the twisted forest, others plunging into the still waters of a nearby lake. The fire wolf – elemental – chooses another target, a girl. She doesn't even have time to scream.

My stomach heaves as panic, disgust, and anger war for first place. Bile burns the back of my throat, but there's no time for weakness.

They sent us into a fucking slaughter, but I'm not going to join the dead. Not today.

If I want to stay among the living – if I want a chance of finding and helping my friends through this – I need to move. Now.

I scan my surroundings, looking for any sign of Mireen, Beck, or Ambrose. Nothing. I'm completely alone, and the fire elemental is working its way methodically along the shoreline, hunting down students one by one.

How long before more elementals show up?

Something in the water yanks one of them down suddenly, cutting off their scream before it has time to begin.

I need to run.

But which way? The twisted forest offers cover but no clear path. The water might provide safety from a fire elemental, but even worse things likely lurk below its surface.

The memory of the massive water serpent flashes through my mind – those intelligent eyes, the way it spoke to me. *'If you see me during Confluence Day, you must run.'*

Is it here? Is it hunting in these waters? I decide to follow the lake's shore toward the huge wall in the distance. It will keep me close enough to the trees to run for them if something else comes, and close enough to the water to dive in if the wolf spots me.

I've only taken a few steps when I feel it – a change in the air, a sudden chill across my skin. I freeze, instinct screaming at me to remain absolutely still.

The water beside me shifts, a gentle ripple marring its perfect surface. Someone else screams in the distance as the wolf continues its hunt.

I hold my breath, certain that the water serpent has found me. I can feel the twisted signature of its presence. I know it's close, and it fucking terrifies me.

But what emerges isn't the dragon-like creature from the lake. It's something smaller, more human-sized – a perfect sphere of water rising from the surface, hovering at eye level. Inside the sphere, colors shift and change, almost forming an image before dissolving again.

I take a step back, unsure if this is a threat or something else.

The sphere follows, drifting closer.

'Stay back,' I warn, though I have no idea if it can understand me. Stupidly, I point my rapier at it.

The sphere stops, hanging in the air between us. Then it begins to change, elongating, taking shape. Water flows and reshapes until I'm staring at a mirror image of myself, perfectly formed in living water.

'What are you?' I whisper.

The water-me tilts its head, examining me with curiosity. Then it speaks, its voice like the distant sound of waves.

'What are you?' it echoes, though the inflection makes me think it's a genuine question, not simply mimicry.

Before I can answer, a roar echoes from behind me. The fire wolf has finished with the other students and is now turning its attention toward me, its flaming body rippling with heat.

The water entity looks toward the approaching predator, then back at me.

'Run,' it says simply. 'Do not enter the water. It waits for you there.' The elemental dissolves back into the stillness of the lake.

I don't need to be told twice. I'm terrified of the wolf, but the thought of diving into those depths and facing the ancient rogue elemental again . . . no. I simply can't make myself do it.

I turn, sprinting away from the wolf and toward the twisted forest.

I duck between forms that only vaguely resemble trees. They're like sculptures of wood frozen in the act of melting, their surfaces smooth and flowing. Some have what look like fruits hanging from their branches – perfect spheres that pulse with inner light.

I glimpse strange shapes between the trees – green entities drifting like spirits and a massive caterpillar with claws and horns slithering up one of the tree things.

I hear distant screams, the metallic clash of weapons, and triumphant shouts from all around.

Behind, the fire wolf's paws striking the ground with percussive thumps as it gallops, each impact like a small explosion. It's hunting me now, and there's no way I can outrun it.

I need to hide.

I weave into a thicker section of trees, jumping down small ledges, turning, and skidding to a stop behind a tree. I press my back against its smooth surface and have no way of knowing if the wolf lost sight of me or not. My breathing sounds impossibly loud in my ears, and my heart feels like it might burst.

The footfalls slow, growing more deliberate. *Hunting. Tracking.*

I close my eyes, trying to control my breathing. Every exhale feels like a betrayal, revealing my hiding spot like a fucking spotlight. This isn't how it ends. I refuse to die here, alone in this alien place, without even trying to tether an elemental.

This *can't* be how it ends.

A low growl rumbles through the forest, so close I can feel the heat of it on my skin.

I open my eyes and find myself staring directly into the blazing gaze of the fire wolf. Its eyes are rubies of anger and fire, intelligent and savage. It regards me with what almost looks like curiosity, its head tilted slightly to one side.

For a moment, neither of us moves.

The heat of its body so close is unbearable. As it draws closer, the hairs on my arm turn black at the edges and curl.

Its jaws part, flames licking between dagger-like teeth, and it lunges.

I throw myself sideways. Heat sears an excruciating line across my back as I roll across the ground. Pain tears through me, but I force myself back to my feet, running deeper into the forest.

The fire wolf is right behind me, so close I can feel its heat on my heels. I zigzag between tree-sculptures, ducking low branches, leaping over twisted roots. But it's no use. The creature is faster, stronger, built for the hunt.

I burst into a clearing and come to a stop. There's nowhere left to run. The trees end at a sheer cliff that drops away into nothingness – a void where reality simply ceases to exist.

I turn, panting, to face my pursuer.

The fire wolf pads into the clearing, its movements slow and deliberate again.

It knows I'm trapped.

Heat waves ripple through the air between us, scorching my lungs with each breath.

This is it, then. After everything – surviving the selections, the challenge matches, daily life at Confluence, and even a rogue elemental and Malakai during the trial – I'm going to die here, alone, without even understanding what I truly am.

The thought ignites something in me.

Not fear.

Fury.

My hands ball into fists, nails cutting half-moons into my palms. No. I refuse to die like this. Others have died so I could make it here. To this moment. To today.

Failing isn't an option.

I stand straighter, facing the elemental directly. My breathing comes in ragged gasps, but my voice comes out steady enough to get the point across.

'Come on, then,' I snarl, forcing steel into my voice. 'An elemental asshole ten times your size tried to eat me once. It didn't work out for him, so let's see if you can do better.'

The fire wolf hesitates. Something like surprise dances in its molten eyes.

Then it growls – the sound like a furnace roaring to life – and lunges for my throat.

I don't run. I don't flinch. Instead, I prepare to try to grab it with my bare hands. I'll likely burn myself to a crisp, but I'm sure as hell going to try to suck whatever power I can from it and make it regret testing me.

Then something changes.

A sound like the ocean crashing against cliffs fills the clearing. The temperature plummets. The wolf hesitates, head tilting as one fiery ear cocks toward the sound.

A blur of deep blue flashes across my vision – so fast I almost miss it. The massive form crashes into the fire wolf mid-leap, sending it tumbling across the clearing in a spray of embers and ash.

Where nothing had been a moment before, there now stands an enormous serpentine creature, its scales the dark blue of the deepest ocean depths, wings spread wide like sails catching a storm.

The water dragon from the lake. The ancient elemental.

Steam hisses violently where the creatures touch, water threatening to quench the flames of the wolf with every contact. With one swipe of its forepaw, it sends the wolf tumbling backward to slam into a tree. Flames leap up around the impact, consuming the tree as the wolf stands again and shakes his head, eyes fixed on the other elemental.

The water dragon roars, the sound vibrating through the soles of my feet and into my bones, rattling my teeth. The very air trembles as it positions itself between me and the fire wolf.

I get my first clear look at it and my jaw drops. In this world, the blues are sharper and deeper – eye-watering in their intensity. It stands on two powerful hind legs, long serpentine body erect with forelegs that end in three deadly curved claws. The tail winds behind its hind legs, curled and tipped in a barb of scales that gleam wicked and pure black like obsidian.

Its head is as large as my whole body and dragon-like, with two elegant horns that sweep back with a single twist. The wings are veined and tipped in those same obsidian colored spikes, nearly translucent as the beast spreads them wide and lets out a terrible roar that shakes my insides.

The fire wolf snarls, the sound seeming impotent compared to the roar.

The water dragon lets out a low, clicking snarl as it prowls to the side, its size dwarfing even the big wolf.

Fire and water. Ancient enemies.

With a howl of fury, the fire wolf attacks, leaping high, as if hoping to catch the dragon by the throat.

The water dragon moves with impossible speed for its size, snapping at the smaller elemental with teeth like icicles. They clash in another burst of steam and energy, their battle shaking the clearing.

I stumble back, watching in awe as these primal forces wage war. The fire wolf is fast and vicious, but the water dragon is ancient and powerful. For every burning bite the wolf manages to land, the dragon counters with crushing force. Water rises from the ground in thundering pillars that slam into the wolf's flaming body.

It yelps. Not in anger, but in pain.

Eventually, the fire wolf realizes it's outmatched. With one final snarl of defiance, it turns and flees back into the forest, its flame dimming as it retreats.

The clearing falls silent. Too silent.

Relief at being saved quickly fades away as I realize how screwed I am.

It only fought off the wolf so it could have me for itself. Now I'm going to die. My death is just going to be watery instead of fiery.

Considering how my brothers and father died, I guess it's fitting that the water should take me too in the end.

Slowly, the water dragon turns to face me. Up close, I can see the corruption eating away at its magnificent form – patches of scales that seem to dissolve into mist, eyes clouded with madness.

'You,' it rumbles, its voice like waves crashing against rock in my mind. *'I told you to run.'*

I'm surprised to sense some of the same intelligence from when it spoke to me during the trial. 'I'll happily run if you step out of my way,' I reply, surprised at my own boldness. The words tumble out before I can stop them – apparently near-death experiences make me mouthy.

The dragon studies me, its massive head lowering until we're eye to eye. Despite its size and power, I sense no immediate threat. But that doesn't make sense. I've come to know this beast through my nightmares. It has been hunting me. It wanted me dead. There's no doubt in my mind about that.

'Why aren't you killing me?'

There's a long pause. I sense it struggling somehow, as if each word comes with a cost. *'You . . . weakened it in the lake. For a time.'*

'Weakened what?'

Instead of speaking, it turns slowly so I can see the largest patch of that mist-like . . . nothingness. The thick serpentine shape of its body seems to fade and drift up in smoke all along its right side.

The dragon's eyes close briefly, as though in pain. When they open again, I see the madness swirling deeper, threatening to consume what lucidity remains. *'You can run, angry human. I can hold it off for a time. Only a time.'*

Angry human? Seriously? I want to laugh at the ridiculousness of the nickname, but the danger is still too real.

I study the creature before me, seeing beyond its terrifying appearance to the ancient intelligence trapped within. Something about its suffering calls to me, resonates with a part of myself I'm only beginning to understand.

I know I should run. I should take its offer and not think twice. Except . . .

'Can I help you? Somehow?'

'You must run,' it roars in my mind, and now I feel as though I hear two voices. One is wise and old and the other is deep and bestial, twisted and terrible.

'And what happens to you if I run? Why did this . . . other thing inside you want me dead? Was it because I can hurt it?' I desperately flip through my mental catalog of everything I've read so far in the unbound book. Countless passages talk about how unbound have the power to unmake. They also talk of a power to draw in. To absorb and consume. It still doesn't make complete sense to me, but I know what I've already seen.

In the lake, I pulled something from this creature. Whatever I did let an intelligence shine through. So maybe I could . . . do more.

The deep blue eyes flash, and ink-like blackness swirls within. Its body shifts, head lowering as it begins to pace and circle me, long body stretching out as it walls me in.

'Run . . . little one, before you are destroyed.'

'No.' Pulse racing, I push down my terror and reach a hand up for its large snout. With one snap of its massive jaws, it could destroy me. I brace for the pain, but only feel my palm land softly on the scaled surface between nostrils that trail steam.

A rush of sensation and power passes into my hand. My body wants to draw it in, to try to absorb it like I did in the lake.

The dragon breathes out heavily, as if my touch is both a relief and something to struggle against. The heat of its breath and the scent of salt water and sea life washes over me, but I don't pull my hand away. I drive my focus deeper.

And then I feel it. There's an inky film coating everything within the dragon. I could draw the power and maybe some of that stain with it, or I could try to draw only the stain itself.

I close my eyes, struggling to grapple with forces I barely understand as I reach for the corruption within the dragon. And I pull.

Nausea rocks me as the first waves of it enter my body.

Fuzzy images and memories that aren't my own flash through my mind. Ancient battles. Elementals fighting elementals. Then the first tethered primals. A powerful woman and a smaller version of the serpent I see now. The two of them fighting side by side for centuries. And then . . .

Betrayal.

Broken tethers. Broken oaths.

Everything after that is twisted by the black film, and I sense the tragic awareness of an ancient intelligence confined in its own mind – unable to reach out and stop its own body from wreaking havoc for centuries . . . I feel the pain of how it watched its friends slowly succumb to the same fate.

But that corruption is reaching into me, now. It's trying to slither under my own skin and coat me. Claim me.

'*Unbound,*' the voice comes into my head more clearly than before. '*You will destroy yourself if you don't release it. Use your gift. Channel it away from yourself as I cannot.*'

My mind is already slipping, but his words register. I try to not just draw in the sickness like poison from a wound. I try to push it outward. To vent it.

Tendrils of black drift out of my body, curling like snakes.

They try to slither back into my body, to drive themselves under my skin. But the dragon closes its eyes and breathes out. Cool, refreshing magic washes over me and the black tendrils flake away as they flow from me.

I lose all sense of time as I keep pulling from the beast and it keeps washing me in that refreshing magic. Minute by minute, I sense the water dragon diminishing in size, but I also feel the corruption fading both from it and from me.

I can't say how long passes before I realize I'm no longer looking at a massive, corrupted dragon. Before me stands a sleek, powerful water elemental, perhaps a third of its former size but whole again, its scales gleaming like polished sapphires in the strange light. Its eyes are clear now, revealing an intelligence and wisdom that takes my breath away.

It lets out a deep breath filled with so much relief it nearly breaks my heart.

'*Unbound . . . You have freed me from my prison. I was once known as Typhon, first heir to the water throne and ruler of the tides. I owe you a debt, and you may name your price.*'

I hear metal clashing nearby as if people are fighting.

Then a deep shout of pain and desperation. It's close, and it's unmistakable.

Raith.

'We have to help,' I say. 'Help me save him. The one who just shouted.'

Another voice echoes through the forest, this one weaker than before. Raith is running out of time.

'He needs our help,' I say urgently.

'The fire-touched. Yes.' Typhon's head tilts slightly. *'I can sense him. He's strong. You wish to save him for mating purposes. Very well. Get on my back.'*

I stare. *Mating purposes?*

I don't have time to think about the odd comment. I'm too busy trying to figure out how the hell I'm supposed to get on his back. He's not as huge as he once was, but his hind legs are still nearly the height of my whole body.

As if sensing my hesitation, he extends a wing, offering it like a leathery ramp. I don't have time to waste, so I run up his wing then stare at his scale-covered back. Just as I'm about to wonder how the hell I'm supposed to hang on, blue light shimmers on his back as a saddle materializes beneath me. Glimmering blue straps that look made from pure sapphires slide over my thighs and waist, securing me into place.

The wings behind me flap in a powerful burst, and wind rushes against my face, forcing my eyes into narrow slits. We explode upwards and it feels like my stomach stays where it was back on the ground hundreds of feet behind us.

Each beat of his wings makes us lurch forward at such incredible speeds it makes my eyes water.

The flight is over before I know it. Typhon lands with shocking grace for his size at the edge of a clearing. A clearing where I can see Raith covered in blood, his powerful body hacked and bloody in several places. But he's still standing, even as blood drips freely from him.

And there's a panther made of pure flames fighting beside him. With him.

Thank the gods. He tethered an elemental. But Raith and his new elemental are badly outmatched. Five students are creeping closer to him, weapons drawn.

I see Malakai and Serena among the still-living, and both have tethered elementals of their own.

Even as I watch, Malakai's elemental – a shark-like creature that slices through the air as if it's water – flashes past Raith and tears a chunk from his leg with a vicious bite. The panther slashes at the shark, landing a heavy blow that wounds but doesn't stop the creature from slipping away.

Typhon flaps his wings again, yanking us forward so fast it threatens to make me sick. We land with a crash in the center of the conflict, putting us between Raith and the stunned semi-circle of attackers.

Raith is wounded. Badly. His elemental is also dripping fire from a gash that hisses steam on its side and it walks with a limp as it circles him protectively.

Even if his wounds look mortal, the defiance and fire is still blazing in Raith's eyes. He's planning to fight until he drops dead. But the thought of him dying is . . . it's not something I can handle. We're going to find a way to save him. I don't care how. We're going to fucking do it.

From Typhon's back, I take in the scene of the battle.

Raith and his elemental killed three attackers, but there are still five standing, plus Malakai and Serena's new elementals.

Malakai bleeds from a deep slash that runs from his scalp to his cheek, and one of his eyes looks completely ruined. Serena seems untouched, and she's flanked by a snake made of flames. It's nearly ten feet long, and it coils around her ankles.

Malakai's elemental swims through the air behind him, teeth glinting.

But they're all staring at me now, and the look of dumbfounded shock as they see the water dragon I'm riding almost makes everything I've gone through to get here worth it. Their expressions almost make me want to laugh – a hysterical, giddy kind of triumph surges through me despite the danger, despite everything.

Serena steps forward. 'What the fuck . . . How?' she breathes.

'Get rid of them,' I command, not caring in the slightest how Typhon chooses to interpret my words. They all deserve to die for what they've done, and if Raith is going to have any chance of surviving, we can't afford to be gentle or take our time here.

There's a moment of building power, like the feeling of water pulling away before a huge wave forms in the ocean. The others feel it, too. The two elementals react first, the shark and fire snake retreating slightly.

Malakai takes a stumbling step backward, brows furrowing. 'What are you doing? Is that a godsdamned fucking dragon? That's not—'

And then there's a sound of rushing water. Massive pillars of blue punch up from the soil and smash down with enough force to shake the ground. There are dozens of them. Hundreds. Each is as wide as five men standing side by side, and I see one smash down on one of Malakai's soldiers who isn't fast enough. When the water clears, the man lies motionless, body crushed and lifeless.

My stomach lurches. Even if they deserve it . . . Gods.

But I sense that Typhon could have crushed every single attacker if he wanted. It's almost as if he's showing mercy – letting them flee rather than slaughter them where they stand.

Malakai and Serena sprint away with their people, disappearing over a far hill before Typhon's magic can destroy them.

The flood of power fades, leaving the clearing drenched and deep craters in the ground all around Raith, like a protective ring.

I slide off Typhon's back, running to Raith's side as I kneel and try to hold him upright before he can wobble and fall where he stands. Up close, the severity of his wounds is even worse than I thought. I don't know how he's even breathing. He blinks, one eye crusted shut from a wound that's bleeding heavily on his scalp.

There's a soft thud as he releases his heavy sword.

'Saltcrest . . .' he says, voice weak. 'Looks like you tethered some kind of . . . fish.'

'Shut up,' I say, throat thick with emotion. The ache in my chest is unbearable as I watch him struggle to stay conscious. Maybe things have been complicated between us, but Raith has only ever helped me . . . even if it's in his own, strange way. I don't want to see him die. I can't watch him die.

The fire panther limps to his side and settles down low with a pathetic whimper, resting its head on his thigh. Somehow, the flames licking the creature don't even seem to singe Raith's clothing.

'What can we do?' I ask Typhon, throwing the question over my shoulder, voice tinged with desperation.

'There is a way . . .'

'What is it? I'll do it. Whatever it is.'

'Swear my oath. Take my tether. Do this, and . . .'

'And what?' My voice borders on hysteria. I can feel Raith slumping in my arms. I can sense the life leaking out of him with each heartbeat. He practically burns in my hands, and there's so little of him left I can't even feel his energy trying to flow into me. 'What do we do?' I shout.

'Tether me, and I . . . may be able to help him. But you must tether. Swear my oath.'

I look over my shoulder at him. There's a distant itch, like maybe I should be careful with freely swearing my oath, especially to whatever Typhon is. But that's why we're here, isn't it?

Confluence Day is about swearing oaths, tethering primals.

'Okay. Yes. Whatever we need to do, just do it.'

Typhon's gaze seems to pierce through me, seeing every hidden corner of my soul. *'A tether is not something to be taken lightly.'*

I force a breath, trying to find a calm I don't feel. 'Sorry. You're right. I'm ready.'

Typhon studies me, ancient blue eyes seeming to delve into the depths of what I am. Finally, he nods his head. His voice thunders in my head, booming and loud with ethereal power. *'Swear to seek truth where there is deception, to bring balance where there is chaos, and to remember what others have forgotten. I ask that you use the unbound gift to mend the wounds your kind have wrought, not to drive them deeper.'*

'I swear it,' I say, the words feeling right on my tongue. They feel like more than words as something deep, deep within me resonates and snaps into place. That resonation extends toward Typhon, and I can . . . feel it. A tether forming, like a bundle of magical strings connecting us. Binding us.

'I swear it as well,' Typhon responds. 'I am yours as you are mine, until the stars fade and the waters still.'

A current of power flows from Typhon to me. It enters through my palm, racing up my arm to the silver mark on the back of my hand. The mark burns suddenly, painfully, and I gasp as it transforms – the silver spiral now threaded with deep, glowing blue like water caught in moonlight.

The tether settles into place, and suddenly I can feel Typhon's presence in my mind – not invasive, but there, like the awareness of another person in a room.

But there's no time to revel and bask in the awe I feel. Raith is running out of time.

'Now what?' I ask.

His voice comes more clear now, gentle and directly into my thoughts. Before, it was the sound of a beast shouting from several rooms away. Now it's as if we're in the same room. 'Place your hand on the wound.'

I put my hand on the worst wound – the gash across his stomach. His eyes snap open and he sucks in a sharp breath, clutching my wrist.

'Raith,' I say carefully. 'It's okay. I'm going to try to help you.'

I see the reluctance in his face. Trust isn't easy for him, even now. Even here. But finally, slowly, he nods his head and relaxes ever so slightly.

The panther of flames resting on his thigh growls low and fierce at me.

'I'm just trying to help,' I say to the panther.

'Trust her, young one,' Typhon's voice extends to Raith's elemental. It lays its head down again, eyes still watching me with distrust.

'What do I do?' I ask Typhon.

'I can channel through you, but it will greatly diminish me for a *time. Now that we're tethered, you are the vessel through which my magic flows. But you are a narrow straw through which I am trying to pass oceans.'*

I glare. 'Okay, I get it. I'm weak, you're strong. Just do it.'

I can feel Typhon's annoyance in my mind as he shifts closer. And then there's a rushing sensation passing through the tether. Blue light flashes around my hand, lighting Raith's bloodied skin from within.

Slowly, the wound inches together. Raith's face draws tight, teeth bared as he grimaces.

'Sorry,' I whisper.

'Don't apologize to him. You are saving his life,' Typhon growls.

'Doesn't mean I can't be sorry it hurts.'

I sense a feeling almost like Typhon rolling his eyes. Ancient, probably immortal, immensely powerful . . . but I think he has a lot of learning to do about humans.

My skin burns as Typhon continues pushing power into me. I can feel his strain. I can even feel how he's running low on energy as the lesser wounds on Raith's body start to heal.

'That's all. Any more, and I won't be able to get us back through the rift when it opens.'

'Raith?' I ask, touching his cheek.

His eyes flicker open and he smirks, teeth still stained red with blood. 'Saltcrest . . . tell your fish I owe him.'

'Save your strength, Raith.' I turn my attention to his fire panther. 'I'm Nessa and this is Typhon. Do you have a name?'

The fire elemental stands, orange eyes distrustful as its thick tail bats from side to side, leaving a trail of flames and smoke.

'He is called Pyrin,' Typhon says.

'Okay, Pyrin. Are you strong enough to carry him?'

But I see the fire still leaking from the creature's side. It's wounded too, though that doesn't stop it from trying to duck its head under Raith and take his weight.

But Pyrin can't lift him. Not wounded as he is.

'Typhon, can I put him on your back?'

Typhon lets out a low, audible growl that's not in my mind. *'It would disgrace me to let another human ride me.'*

'Will you do it for me? Please?' I ask.

'My gratitude is still fresh, human. But you wear it thin.'

'Please.'

He sighs, steam curling from his nostrils. But then he's using his wing to carefully lift Raith. A thin rope of water wraps around Raith's waist and pulls him into place on Typhon's back, where the dragon secures him in place.

Raith groans and his blood slicks Typhon's back, but he hooks one powerful arm around Typhon's neck and holds tight.

'Your human is trying to choke me,' Typhon notes.

'He's trying not to fall off.'

The sound of crunching branches makes me turn my head. Serena and Malakai are circling back, their elementals drifting behind them. Typhon doesn't need to tell me he's too weak to fight again. Raith is half conscious, Pyrin is wounded, Typhon's down to his last drops of power, and I'm not going to fight off Serena, Malakai, and both their elementals by myself.

'We need to get out of here,' I say, looking around desperately for an escape route.

Raith stirs, his eyes opening as he shifts on Typhon's back. I see him looking at me. There's a questioning glint in his eyes, as if he's wondering why I'm risking so much to save him.

He wants to know why?

Well, he can join the fucking club.

'Later,' I promise. 'Right now, we need to—'

'Run,' Typhon interrupts, a single, magical blue strap slipping around my waist and pulling me to sit on Typhon's back. I guess his magic is too thin right now for fancy saddles. *'The rift is this way.'*

Together, the four of us move through the forest, Typhon leading the way with us on his back while Raith's fire panther, Pyrin, trots behind us with a slight limp.

Behind us, I hear Serena's furious scream. 'Catch them! Don't let them leave.'

We break through the treeline onto an expanse of round black stones. The air around the stones shimmers with heat. In the distance, I can see a glittering light in the air – the rift, beginning to stabilize.

'*There,*' Typhon says, nudging us toward it. '*Quickly.*'

We run. Even in his diminished state, Typhon has to slow to avoid outpacing Pyrin.

Just as we reach the rift, Serena and Malakai burst from the trees not far behind.

Shit. They're too close. There's no way we'll make it to the rift before—

A gust of air whips across the beach, flaring flames to life between the dark rocks and making Malakai and Serena shield themselves.

Bastian rides in on a horse made of pure wind, his gold hair blowing behind him as he dismounts and unstraps a spear from his back. He looks over his shoulder, expression unreadable as he takes in the sight of Typhon, Raith, and Pyrin with me.

I can't help the surge of relief I feel at seeing him. Bastian. Always showing up when I need him most, but never revealing the slightest about who he is or why he cares about helping me.

'Go, Nessa,' Bastian shouts, voice carrying over the growing rush of wind.

'But you—'

'I'll be fine,' Bastian says. 'Go.'

I hesitate for only a moment – wondering if maybe there's some way I could find Mireen, Ambrose, or Beck and offer them help here. But I know the only way to return is to tether. And there's no way I can even get to them without abandoning Raith for dead and drawing Malakai and his people to them.

'Can you find Mireen, Beck, and Ambrose? Make sure they're safe?' I shout.

'I'll do what I can. Now go!' Bastian shouts. He's already parrying a strike from Malakai as his elemental clashes with both the shark and the fire snake.

I bounce on my feet, wishing I could do more to help. But he's likely only waiting for me to be gone so he can flee. With that horse, there's no way they would catch him.

'Let's go,' I say, turning and running for the rift with the others.

We plunge into the rift, the elemental plane dissolving around us as we're pulled back toward our own world. Toward Confluence Academy.

Chapter 13

I sit beside Raith in the healer's room, studying him as he lies with his eyes closed and his body covered in thick bandages.

I lift my shirt to expose the burns on my back, wincing as the academy healer applies a salve and then wraps my torso in clean linens. 'You're lucky,' she says. 'These aren't too deep. I don't think you'll scar.'

'Thank you,' I say, smiling as she nods and drifts to join the other healers tending to dozens of wounded students who are being carried in every few minutes as more and more return from the rifts.

Beck, Ambrose, and Mireen all sit beside the bed with me.

There's an air of tense anticipation between all of us. For now, students are still fighting to tether elementals as the window to return to campus remains open. In a few hours, the rift will close, and anyone who hasn't returned will be assumed dead.

After that, we'll all be forced to participate in a celebratory ceremony, as if our victory isn't shadowed by the ghosts of hundreds and even thousands of dead going back to that first day when we arrived in our carriages. The thought makes my stomach turn.

Mireen's hair is still soaked and she has a gash on the side of her neck that the healer bandaged when we arrived. Her braid has come loose in several places, leaving her copper hair to stand up and catch the fading evening light that streams through the windows. 'So . . .' she says softly. 'Are you going to tell us what is going on with your mark, Nessa?'

I instinctively twitch to put my hand in my pocket, but force it to still. My pulse skyrockets. The silver threads running through the blue and the patterns are different than everyone else who tethered. Even the blue is a deeper shade than their marks, as if some of that unnatural color saturation from the elemental plane is showing straight through my skin.

Typhon already told me it would draw attention. He said it was because he's an ancient, and the depth of his tether is many times more powerful than the types my classmates will have. It explains the deep, vibrant blue, but not the threads of silver. I've managed to work on disguising them more, but not before my friends saw.

'Um,' I say, scratching the back of my neck. 'It's complicated.' Gods, how do I even begin to explain this? The most obvious answer is to admit the truth about Typhon to my friends. Admit I tethered a fucking ancient and blame him on the strangely intense water mark on my hand. 'I think it has something to do with the elemental I tethered, though. At least that's what he says.'

For now, they can't see him. Elementals can choose to remain hidden from all but their tethered human, and I haven't seen any other elementals showing themselves as students return from the rifts.

I can see Typhon lurking in the corner of the room like a dragon twice the size of a horse. They can't. Not unless he chooses to let them.

'Caution will prevail when tethers are fresh,' Typhon notes, casually reading my thoughts and responding, as if it's the most normal thing in the world. That's going to take some adjustment.

'Hey,' Ambrose cuts in. 'We've all known there was something different about you since the start. And if you don't want to talk about it, then you don't have to.'

Mireen nods quickly. 'He's right. I just wasn't sure if the mark was connected, or if . . .'

'Did I tell you guys Uther is a fucking water bear?' Beck asks, eyebrows wiggling. I'm not sure if he's interrupting because he's just that excited, or if he's trying to divert the conversation to save me from having to share.

Either way, I appreciate it.

'About fifty times,' Ambrose says, though there's some amusement in his voice. 'And Mireen's elemental is an adorably deadly otter thing, which . . . frankly I am having trouble imagining.'

Mireen sits up straighter, glaring at Ambrose. 'Ollie is deadly. He has these claws. He's cute, yes, but he does have claws. And he's fast.'

We all grin.

'And,' Ambrose continues a little smugly. 'I completely understand you're all just a touch jealous of Akaron. Water hawks are, after all, quite rare.'

'I'll take my cute but deadly otter.'

'A bear, Ambrose,' Beck says. 'Uther is a fucking bear. Who wins in a fight, a bear, or a little flimsy hawk?'

Ambrose waves them both off, eyes fixing on me. 'Do we get to hear what form your elemental takes?'

The healer on duty is fussing with bandages of a girl a few beds over, so I wait until she heads back to her office and leaves us in relative isolation. Raith still seems to be sleeping, but I guess there's no use hiding it from him. He saw Typhon with his own eyes.

I have to take a few deep breaths, building up the willpower to tell the truth.

'Well . . . you guys remember that story about the terrifying water monster in Mirror Lake? And the huge dragon thing I told you about that nearly killed me during the Water Trial?' My pulse skyrockets, dread about their reactions crashing on me like a wave.

Ambrose leans forward so slowly I almost don't see it. Mireen's eyes start to widen. Beck scratches his nose, still oblivious to where I'm going with this.

'*Is it okay if I tell them?*' I ask Typhon. I'm still getting used to the fact that he can hear my thoughts.

His answer comes into my mind. '*I am Typhon, first of his name. Tamer of oceans. Tidefather. Do you think I fear being known by fragile creatures made of meat and bone? Hah!*'

I grin as my friends watch me, waiting for my answer. 'People are tougher than you think. Stick around and you'll get a chance to see that.'

'*Once again, you forget I was among your kind for centuries. I know and understand humans, perhaps better than you do, angry human.*'

'Sure you do.' I mentally roll my eyes.

I take a breath, trying to decide the best, most gentle way to explain this to my friends. How exactly do you tell someone your elemental is essentially a giant, ancient dragon?

Mireen grins slightly. 'It's okay, Nessa. You don't have to be embarrassed if it's like . . . a goldfish or something. Ollie told me he'll get bigger and more fierce as we train. So even a goldfish would eventually be something to reckon with if you train right.'

I bite my lip. 'Typhon isn't a goldfish . . . He's kind of like . . . a water dragon?'

Beck narrows his eyes, his attention finally locked in. 'When you say dragon . . . do you mean like a bat? Because wings are cool, but I'd hardly call a bat a dragon.'

'Young elementals can't take a form like a dragon, Nessa,' Ambrose says softly, as if explaining something gently so he doesn't hurt my feelings. 'They have to tether several humans and gather strength over centuries to . . .' he trails off, gaze falling to the floor. Maybe he's recalling my mention of the lake monster.

Mireen's mouth hangs open. 'A dragon?' she whispers. 'Can we see it?'

'*Typhon, are you willing to show them?*' My stomach flutters with nervous energy.

I sense a world-weary sigh from my elemental, but the widened eyes and audible gasp from Mireen tell me he has revealed himself.

'Holy. Shit,' Beck whispers. 'You tethered a fucking dragon? Malakai is never going to mess with you again.'

'Impossible . . .' Ambrose breathes.

'He's so cute!' Mireen says, standing and taking a step toward him.

'*Tell her if she calls me cute again, I'll eat her and her damned otter.*'

'Um,' I say, taking Mireen's arm. 'It might be best to give him some space. He hasn't been around humans in a long time.'

'*This is untrue. I have been eating them for the past few centuries.*'

I'm suddenly thankful my friends can't hear him. His manners need a lot of work.

After a barrage of questions, most of which I answer truthfully, I've caught them up to speed on the 'what the hells' and the 'how the hells.' The only part I haven't mentioned is about my unbound affinity. It was easy enough to claim the silver threads in my mark were just a side-effect of Typhon's ancient power.

Part of me does want to tell them, but I also know even more than I did before. I know what I am is dangerous, even if I don't fully understand *why* I'm dangerous yet. Bringing them in will put them at risk, and we've all got more than enough threats against our life as it is. The guilt of keeping secrets from them weighs on me like heavy stones, but I can't risk their lives. This unbound burden is mine to carry, and I won't put it on their shoulders unless I absolutely have to.

Beck's elemental shows itself first. It's a bear that is about half as tall as Beck when on its four legs, and probably taller if it stood on its hind legs.

'Meet Uther,' he says, patting the bear on the head. Uther snaps at him, and Beck pulls his hand back with a sheepish smile. 'He's grouchy, but we're already becoming fast friends.'

His bear looks like he's made of living water of the deepest blue. In most ways, it looks like a bear, except for the peculiar long eyebrows and dangling beard of water on its face.

I don't dare say as much aloud, but I honestly think it's kind of cute.

Mireen's 'Ollie' shows himself next. He's the size of a dog and swims through the air with a sleek body that seems made the same way of most water elementals – as if he's a living formation of water. Though the eyes and a few parts, such as its teeth and claws, do seem somewhat more solid. Ollie's 'claws' that Mireen bragged about look about as deadly as a cat's.

'You know,' Ambrose says. 'I have heard that the smaller elementals are often a sign that the primal commands more powerful channeling skills. Maybe Ollie is a little less of a front-line fighter, but he'll bolster your magic as you guys train together.'

Mireen scratches his head as Ollie continues to swirl around her. She talks to him in a baby voice. 'You could fight on the front lines if you wanted, couldn't you?'

Instead of snapping at her or seeming annoyed, Ollie just curls tighter into her, making me smile. They say elementals are drawn to people who match their own nature. I think it's true for my friends, but I don't know if Typhon was exactly a natural pairing for me. At least I hope not, based on his personality.

I feel him growling inside my mind and grin.

Ambrose shows his water hawk, Akaron. The water hawk is perched on Ambrose's shoulders. Despite being smaller than the bear, his claws look substantial enough to do some serious damage, and there's no playfulness in the hawk's deep blue eyes. He actually gives me the slightest nod as I take him in.

I nod back, because I don't want to be rude.

We take a while swapping questions and stories from our time in the elemental plane. I learn that Mireen and Ambrose were able to stick together for the most part, and they didn't face any trouble from fellow students. Both felt called to their elementals, and they had to dive into some deep waters to find them. In a way, it sounds like their experiences were almost identical to what we faced during the water trials as we searched for echoes.

Beck, on the other hand, supposedly had to wrestle Uther because they were both fighting over the same fish. Beck claims he was hungry, and the two reached a stalemate and agreed to share the fish in the end. I'm highly skeptical of the story, but that's not a shock when it comes to Beck. He has a new story about his conquests with girls across campus almost daily, and all of them are 'older students we wouldn't know.'

After a while, Mireen's smile fades and she seems to remember Raith who lies between all of us, still motionless and radiating heat.

'So . . .' Mireen says. 'You saved the terrifying guy who basically runs the first-year fire offerings . . . because?'

'Malakai and Serena were trying to kill him. It was five on one when I got there, and Raith had already downed a few of them.' I resist the urge to get defensive – Raith's life was worth saving, period.

Beck kicks a foot up on the bed, leaning back so the wooden chair beneath him groans like it might snap in two. 'Okay. Sure. But if I walked into a forest and saw a bunch of wolves trying to kill each other, I don't know if I'd pick one and try to save it. You know?'

'He has . . . helped me a few times.' The words sound pathetic even to my own ears.

That earns raised brows from everyone.

'Helped you how?' Mireen asks. 'I seem to recall him nearly choking you to death your first day here. And other than that, he's always glaring at you like he wants to eat you for dinner.'

'Yeah, well, I don't think trust comes easy for him. And I won't pretend I know why, but he has been helping me. He kind of . . . looks for me. In his own way.' Even I can hear how weak that sounds.

Ambrose gives Mireen a sideways look.

Beck nods knowingly, snapping his fingers. 'So you two are fucking? That's all you had to say. It does make sense. I mean, no offense, obviously, but you're gorgeous, Nessa. I never made a pass at you because I assumed you were taken. It was the only explanation for you not hooking up with anyone. But you've got it all going on. Face? Check. Body? Double check. And your ass is—'

'Beck,' Mireen says, turning his name into a sigh and a curse at the same time.

'What?' Beck says. 'Look at her.' He gestures. 'Of course I wouldn't sleep with you. I mean, I would. But I won't because I respect you. And you guys brought me in, probably saving me from Malakai. Even if being your friend now sort of makes me more of a target . . .'

When nobody says anything for a few seconds, Beck's eyes narrow to slits. 'Or . . . I will sleep with you? If that's what I'm supposed to say? Fuck, guys. I'm lost here. Uther is no help, either. He's just saying how hungry he is.'

'Keep your fucking hands to yourself,' Raith groans, surprising all of us. He coughs and sits up slightly, wincing as he probably aggravates his dozens of wounds.

'Hey, easy,' I say, thinking twice before I reach out to touch his bare skin. The blanket has fallen down to reveal his ripped and muscular torso. My breath catches despite my best efforts.

And his scars.

There's a collective intake of breath as everyone else sees, too.

The entire left side of his body from his belly button to his pec and all around the side is twisted with more burn scars.

'Hands off,' Beck says, holding both palms up toward Raith, who is glaring at him. 'You got it, big guy.'

Raith might be the only first-year Beck could actually call 'big guy,' considering Beck already towers over most students with his size.

'How do you feel?' I ask Raith.

'Fine. Where is Serena? Where's Malakai?'

'I'm not sure. Last I saw them was in the elemental plane on our way out. But I assume they'll be back on campus by now. Unless . . . maybe Bastian could have killed them. But that doesn't seem like something he'd do if he could avoid it.'

He nods, pulling the blanket back over his body as if he's ashamed of the scars. It's a simple gesture, but it breaks my heart. A tightness seizes my chest that has nothing to do with my own injuries. Scarred or not, there's an unnatural beauty to Raith. And by now, all of us at Confluence bear our own scar tissue on the inside. The fact that he has to wear his for everyone to see isn't fair, and I hate it for him.

'You are soft for him,' Typhon notes. *'Perhaps you should mate with him. It would relieve some of the emotion I sense clouding your mind.'*

'Typhon . . . do me a favor and shut up.' I feel heat rush to my face.

'Such a small, angry, insolent human. You are worse than Korthan. He at least respected my power and authority. He knew how highly esteemed I was among the elementals, and he would never dare speak to me so. Unless, of course, I interrupted his meals. Korthan was passionate about meal times.'

I bite back a smile. For all Typhon's talk, I can feel something of his real emotions through the tether connecting us. I feel the bottomless well of his gratitude for saving him from the madness that trapped him for so long. Even if both of us are too stubborn to admit it aloud, I know he can feel my gratitude, too. Typhon is the reason Raith is alive. He's the reason I'm alive.

At my thoughts, I feel a slight warm glow through the tether, and it widens my smile.

'Is your elemental okay?' I ask suddenly. 'Pyrin, right? Last I saw, he was wounded.'

Raith nods, eyes closing as if the exhaustion of his wounds is making it hard for him to stay awake. 'He is healing. He'll be fine. Tell your elemental thank you. He saved us. Pyrin is grateful, too.'

'He is welcome,' Typhon says. *'I approve if you wish to mount him, angry human. He is a strong mate, and he shows an acceptable level of respect toward me.'*

I don't dignify that with a response, but I sense a flicker of amusement through the tether. Maybe Typhon isn't as thick as he lets on.

'Leave us,' Raith says suddenly.

'Uh,' Ambrose says. 'No offense meant, Raith, but the four of us watch each other's backs. We're not about to leave her alone with a fire.'

'Even if you're more cut up than a holiday ham,' Beck adds with a severe nod.

'Unless you want privacy to . . . you know,' Mireen asks, brows raised as she looks at me.

'You can trust him. *I trust him,*' I add, realizing that I really do. 'Malakai and Serena were trying to kill him. Raith could have let Serena challenge me the first day here and had me out of his hair. If he wanted me dead, I'm pretty sure I'd be dead already.' Though the fact that my friends had the guts to stand up to him makes something warm and fierce surge in my chest.

Raith says nothing, which feels slightly unhelpful, but I give him a pass since he just nearly died.

My friends exchange wary looks, but after a little more convincing, they finally agree to wait out of earshot. They won't leave the room, but they'll at least give us the privacy to talk alone.

Once they're huddled at the edge of the room watching us with distrustful eyes, Raith speaks again. 'You healed me.'

'Technically, Typhon did it through me. I don't think I can take credit.'

Raith nods. 'Typhon. The beast from Mirror Lake. Before Confluence Day, he was a rogue elemental. Pyrin can confirm that much. Mad for centuries, exiled by his kind and feared.' He lets the words hang, the implied question clear.

'Well . . .' I say slowly. 'People change.' I try to sound more confident than I feel.

That earns the faintest smile from Raith. 'Rogue elementals don't. You're unbound, aren't you?' His voice is so low I know none of the nearby patients a few beds over can hear. I'm grateful for that much, at least, but his accusation makes my breath catch all the same.

Instinctively, I shake my head. 'I don't know what that means.' My heart thuds so loudly I'm shocked he can't hear it.

'It's good that you are keeping it quiet. Your secret is safe with me. I'll be honest . . . I thought you were . . . something else. When you drew my power in, I was almost sure of it. But it makes more sense now. *Unbound*,' he says it again, as if testing how it feels on his tongue.

'What did you think I was?'

'Not important. But what you are . . . does anyone else know?'

I think about Bastian, and even if I don't know why he's helping me yet or even if what he's doing is helping, I feel like I shouldn't admit he knows.

I shake my head.

'What about them?' Raith gives a slight jerk of his head toward my friends at the corner of the room.

The three of them huddled there with their new water elementals are honestly kind of adorable. They look like they're expecting to have to come in and wrestle a half-dead Raith off me at a moment's notice. I feel another swell of gratitude for them. My throat tightens with emotion I refuse to show.

Even in a place like this. Even when trust feels like it might be a deadly mistake, I know all three of them are ready to lay their lives down for me. For all of Confluence Academy's faults, I have to admit the daily threat of death here does help us form tethers not just with elementals, but with some of the other students.

'No,' I say. 'I didn't want to put them in danger.'

'Good. That's good.'

There's a short pause, so I decide to ask the question that has been on my mind. 'Why were Serena and Malakai trying to kill you?'

Raith's eyes flash with secrets. 'You haven't told your friends what you are because it puts them in danger. That's why I won't answer your question.'

I let out a breath, annoyed at his secrecy but also unable to argue. Frustration may twist at my insides to admit it, but he is right. It's like he said. I'm doing the exact same thing with the others.

'You should go. They'll be having the tethering ceremony soon. You should ask your elemental if he can take any less conspicuous forms. He's an ancient, right? It's the only way he could take such a powerful form.'

'I am Typhon. Known and feared among my kind as ancient, wise, and powerful.'

'Something like that,' I say in answer to Raith's question.

'Can you take other forms?'

'My dignity would prevent me from diminishing myself. Let them see my power. Let them tremble in fear. Why should I hide?'

'He . . . wants to know why he should hide. He's got a bit of an ego.' I resist adding that his ego may be larger than the entire elemental plane.

'Does he care about keeping you alive?' Raith asks. 'Because rogue elementals don't return from madness. That's not supposed to be possible. Even for an unbound. But finding out he's yours will draw attention. Even if it's just because people will know tethering an ancient means you're going to be the most powerful primal in both kingdoms by the time you graduate. If you graduate. There are people . . . things . . . that would do anything to stop you from gaining that kind of power.'

'Is he right?' I mentally ask Typhon.

'On some counts . . . on the others, I have been blinded by madness for too long to know. Perhaps the fire-touched is right. I will suffer the indignity of diminishing myself only because your death would . . . be unfortunate.'

I turn and smile at him as he looms in the corner, looking somewhat ridiculous in the small room with his head hunched to fit. 'Did you just admit you don't want me to die, Typhon? Does that mean you like me?'

He lets out a low growl as steam hisses from his snout. 'I find you acceptable. And my gratitude runs deep, angry human. In time, I suspect we will come to find our pairing was a fortunate one. Perhaps.'

'He says he'll do it,' I say, turning back to Raith.

'Good. Now go. And keep them close,' he says. 'Serena, Malakai, and the others saw your elemental. Keep that in mind. But Serena knows she can't admit she tried to kill me without turning all the fires on her. Most of the earths are loyal to me, too.'

'They are?' I ask. 'Why?'

'It's not important. But Malakai knows how powerful you'll become. If he's smart, he's probably going to try to come after you sooner, rather than later. So keep your friends by your side at all times. We can't know if they'll try to get the truth about Typhon out or not. But we should be ready for anything.'

'Okay.'

Raith surprises me by reaching out and touching my hand. I feel some of his fire flowing into me, swirling in my lower belly in a way that's not entirely unpleasant. 'You saved me back there. I don't take a debt like that lightly, Saltcrest.'

I shake my head. 'You don't owe me. It's fine.'

'I do. So don't get yourself killed while I'm healing.'

'Got it. Once you're done healing, I'm free to die?' I can't stop the playfulness that slips into my voice.

'Once I'm done healing, I'll see to it myself that nobody lays a fucking hand on you.'

I want to laugh, but the sudden intensity and severity of his words makes electricity prickle across my skin instead. The fierce determination on his face steals my breath. He means it. *Gods, he means it.*

'They will have to get through me, too,' Typhon says.

I don't just have an ancient water dragon swearing to protect me from danger. Now Raith Hollow, the most terrifying and deadly student at Confluence Academy, just said he's going to become my glorified bodyguard.

Chapter 14

'Today, we mourn those who passed and celebrate those who did not,' Rector Voss announces from a high balcony overlooking the courtyard of Confluence. His voice echoes across the stone as rain patters softly down on all of us. Somewhere in the distance, thunder rumbles, deep and low. 'To stand here today alive and tethered to an elemental is a testament to your value, students. Know this. Find pride in this.'

The entire school is gathered, with first-years at the front as we're 'celebrated' for our elemental tethers.

For our success.

For the luck of living where so many others died violently.

I can still see the empty spaces where students once stood. Students whose names I hardly dared to learn because I knew it would only make their likely deaths harder. The girl with the crooked smile from channeling class who once sent her summoned water sphere to my palm to save me a day of Sestra's lectures. The tall boy who I used to see doing extra push ups and training in the courtyard every evening. The pair of twins who always had smiles on their faces.

Gone.

My chest throbs with a familiar ache – that hollow, gnawing feeling that comes with surviving when others didn't. I swallow hard against the lump in my throat.

But I know I'm lucky to have an intact group of friends who survived with me.

Mireen and Beck are to my left, while Ambrose is to my right.

'He's handsome,' Mireen whispers from beside me. She still bears scrapes and a few bandages, like everyone who made it out of the elemental plane alive.

'Shh,' I say, giving her arm a subtle whack. She's not wrong, though. Rector Voss stands well over six feet tall with black hair streaked in gray at the temples. He has elegant features with a long, pleasant-to-look-at face, and his skin is tanned and unmarked, which I find odd. I would've thought the leader of a school for primals would be a primal himself.

Rector Voss is dressed in an immaculate black robe with a circular sigil I've seen around the campus. It bears four marks, one for each of the affinities. Each of the *known* affinities, at least.

My fingertips idly trace the disguised mark on the back of my left hand.

Voss stands with hands folded behind his back, eyes scanning over us with an intensity that makes my skin crawl – like he's searching for something specific among the survivors. He doesn't even seem to notice the rain, though most of us are already shivering by now.

All the instructors, both primal and otherwise, are lined up beneath the wall where Voss stands. There are also Empire guards present and selectors, which is the first time I've seen anybody who wasn't immediate staff of the academy since the day we arrived.

'First-years . . .' Voss continues after a long pause. 'You've survived against all odds. Legacies. This was expected of you, but your journey to earning a primal tether was no less impressive. Aspirants. You took a risk coming here, and now you can see the fruits of your labor.'

He gives another long pause, and I sense people shifting behind me. There are well over a hundred surviving first-years spread out to my right and left. All tethered, now, or else they wouldn't have had a way to return through the rift.

I suppress a shiver for any who were unlucky enough to survive until the rift closed. I can't imagine the suffocating horror of realizing you had run out of time – of knowing you were untethered, and the only doorway back to your world was about to close.

The thought alone sends ice through my veins. To be trapped there, abandoned and alone, watching your only escape vanish while darkness closed in around you . . .

It makes me think the students I saw get turned to ash by the fire wolf may have been the lucky ones.

Behind me, there's a row of students representing each year, up to the fifth-years. The entire school is gathered here, assembled in the courtyard. With everyone lined up and organized, it's frighteningly clear how each class is smaller than the one before it. Fifth-years seem to have less than a hundred surviving students.

The attrition never stops. Every year here is a trial to survive. A life-and-death struggle with no end in sight.

'Offerings,' Voss finally says, lips spreading to reveal straight teeth with sharp canines. 'Congratulations to you, especially. Confluence Academy is not a kind place, and offerings know this better than anyone. I'm happy to announce that your survival means you are offerings no longer. Today, you all become aspirants in every sense. You'll find new uniforms in your rooms, and student officers will help show you to your new quarters. You'll now have access to more areas in the library, you will not have to share your rooms, and you'll find your class schedule has been reduced to give you more time to pursue areas of interest and recover.'

I look at my friends, eyes wide with excitement, a strange flush of heat spreading through my chest. We all assumed something like this was coming, but nobody was certain. All we knew was the second-years didn't seem to have a single offering in their ranks.

'Also, I should note that aspirants and legacies are highly discouraged from killing fellow classmates. Yes, deaths will still occur in the course of your training, but we expect the number to be far smaller than what those of you in the offerings quarters will have grown used to. Our fragile alliance with the elemental plane and Empire's orders mean you have all just become far more valuable assets to us. Indispensable, even. So, again, wanton murder of classmates will not be overlooked any longer. I advise you all to set aside any grudges or ill-feelings you may harbor from your first two months here on campus.'

I can't tell if I'm imagining it, but I think I see Voss's gaze lingering on Malakai. Something passes between them – an understanding, perhaps, or a warning. My muscles tense.

No matter his words, I don't feel any of the lingering tension between my shoulders lighten. Killing each other may be discouraged, but I imagine some will still find a way. The only difference is they'll have to be more discreet and creative, now.

'Today, you have all formed the beginnings of a tether with your elemental companions. You'll spend the next five years learning to strengthen that tether, growing your personal power and the abilities of your elemental in the process. By the time you graduate, you'll cease simply being a tethered and you will become primals, the deadliest weapons in Empire's army.'

There's a sudden cheer from the courtyard that drowns out the falling rain. I look around, wondering how anyone could cheer right now when it still feels like we're prisoners. I notice just a few others who aren't cheering, Bastian included.

It warms me to him slightly to see he's not celebrating. If Raith wasn't still recovering in the healer's room, I imagine he would be stony-faced now, too.

So many died for us to get here. If this is a victory, it's one that was built on a pile of corpses so large it makes my stomach turn. And becoming weapons? The thought certainly doesn't make me want to cheer.

'You are wise for your thoughts, angry human,' Typhon rumbles in my mind. Even when he's hiding himself from others, I can always see him. I can sense him, too, even if he's not in view. It feels like an internal compass, always pointing toward Typhon.

'You know you can just call me Nessa, right?' I think back, fingers curling into my palms as the small round of cheers and clapping continues.

'I will call you by your name when you earn the distinction.'

'Is that how it is? Maybe I'll start calling you little boy blue. How would you like that?'

'You wouldn't dare.' A flash of heat travels down our tether, mixing anger and something almost like amusement.

I smile to myself. I've already come to understand that Typhon is uptight and a little grumpy at the best of times. But he knows he's going to have to take one of his lesser forms soon, and he is clearly upset about it. He wants to spread his wings and maybe "roast a student or two" to assert our dominance. I told him that wasn't going to happen.

'Now,' Voss says, 'as is custom, newly tethered first-years will approach the selectors and present your elementals for categorization. You will be required to share your elemental's name and age. And . . .' Voss hesitates, smiling slightly. 'In the highly unlikely case any of you have bonded an elemental old enough, you will present any other forms it's capable of assuming.'

A few older students chuckle, as if the suggestion is ridiculous.

'So we need to lie about your age. Do we need to make up a name for you, too?' My throat tightens at the thought of revealing even a fraction of what Typhon truly is.

'The indignity doesn't cease . . .' His mental voice reverberates with disdain.

'Please, Typhon. Raith was right. If we come out and show how powerful you are, I'll probably be dead by the end of the week. I don't care if the Rector is trying to say we're safer now than we were before. I'll believe it when I see it.' I remember Malakai's cold eyes watching me, calculating.

'They would have to get through me first, angry human.'

'And I'd still rather avoid that. So can we please just be discreet, even if it's apparently against your nature?'

'You may claim my name is . . . Typhonus.'

I blink, then slowly drag my eyes to where he's sitting straight-backed and proud in front of the students.

'Typhonus? So subtlety and deception aren't in your nature either,

are they? What other forms can you take? Maybe I can try to think of a name that seems like it fits your shape.'

'I can take many forms, angry human. My earliest was a type of flying fish known as a kuratokken. They are native to—'

'Flying fish. Good. That sounds really unimpressive. We'll call you Pondus. Flying fish. Aged . . . thirty? Is that too young?'

Typhon turns his dragon-like head toward me in outrage as the first students begin approaching and presenting their elementals to the selectors.

Most elementals take the forms of animals I recognize, but crafted out of pure elemental energy. I note with interest that the younger elementals other students bonded seem more insubstantial, somehow. They're generally more transparent and seem less solid, unlike Typhon who just . . . looks like an actual blue dragon for the most part. Most elementals are also roughly the same size, maybe that of a regular sized dog or slightly larger. Voss watches from high up on the balcony, eyes sharp and full of interest, as if he's still searching for something – or someone. His gaze fixes on me for a moment, lingering just long enough to send a chill down my spine.

'Pondus is not a fitting name for someone of my status and power. A pond? You really wish to name me after such a small and insignificant body of water?'

'Oceanus?' I suggest. *'And I doubt we'll need to use the name much beyond today. It's just for official records to keep who you are hidden.'*

Typhon sighs, making steam rush from his dragon-like snout. He turns his face away from me. *'Very well. Only because it will ensure your safety.'*

'Thank you, Typhon.'

There's a slight blossoming of warmth through the tether. *'The kuratokken is only one of my other forms, you know. I could choose something slightly more impressive. My second tether granted me the ability to keep the wings of the kuratokken and elongate my body to resemble an ancient sea serpent known as a markoth. It is not as grand as my current form, of course, but it's rather impressive.'*

'*The less impressive, the better. Let people underestimate us. If anyone ever tries to come for me, we'll have the element of surprise when you show them what a badass you truly are.*'

That earns another pulse of appreciation through the tether.

'*Very well. Should we consider eliminating the one-eyed water-touched and the fire-touched girl from the planes? They know my true form, along with their allies. If we're going to such lengths to conceal it, I imagine they represent liabilities in the plan.*'

'*No.*' I fire the thought back without even giving it real consideration. '*They are killers. We're not.*'

'*And if we must become killers to survive?*'

'*We'll be protectors. If we're cornered and there's no other choice . . . then we'll go from there. But I still think it matters to draw the line somewhere. To not let this place turn us into something else. Surviving here won't mean shit if I have to become a monster to do it.*'

'*Hmm . . . Noble,*' Typhon muses. '*But what will we do if they tell others about my form?*'

'*Who would believe them?*' I counter. '*Is anyone seriously going to think Nessa Thorne tethered Typhon, first heir to the water throne and ruler of the tides? Ancient, badass water dragon and formerly rogue elemental?*'

I sense his pleasure. '*You remembered my titles.*'

I grin. '*You've reminded me of them a few times.*'

'*Your point is taken. I believe the other flesh bags underestimate you. We shall let your enemies live for now to preserve our own morality, as you say. If the time for consuming your enemies comes, I will eat them with joy and righteous justice in my heart.*'

'*We'll cross that bridge if it comes.*'

'*Bridges? Hah! I have wings, angry human. No body of water is an obstacle to me. It is simply an opportunity to crush my—*'

'*It's an expression, Typhon. Lighten up.*'

He makes a low growling sound and sits a little lower, blue eyes deep and fierce as he watches the ceremony.

The legacies and aspirants – or at least those who were aspirants before Confluence Day – finish presenting. Some of the legacies, like

Bastian, present elementals quite a bit larger than the dog-sized that seems standard. Bastian's horse is the size of a real horse, and one legacy girl with an earth marking has a golem made of stones that's almost twice her height.

But now the former offerings are approaching, and it won't be long before it's my turn.

Beck eventually has his name called. He presents Uther and earns a few impressed noises from the gathered students. After Mireen's turn, I approach the selectors and wait.

'Present your elemental,' the selector says. Compared to the way the selectors treated us that first day, I feel a twinge of satisfaction to see a hint of fear on the man's face. We're not helpless offerings anymore, and he knows it.

'Ready?'

Typhon walks beside me in his water dragon form, and then closes his eyes. His body swirls, losing form as the water currents twist and reshape him. A moment later, he's significantly smaller and looks like an ordinary fish, but with butterfly-like wings and a strange formation of whiskers on his head that almost looks like a crown.

I have to try not to smile. Seeing him contained in such an unassuming form makes me picture a great lion in the body of a kitten.

'Are you wearing a crown?'

'I am heir to the water throne. And . . . this being has a formation of sensory glands that do resemble a crown. Yes.'

The selector's eyes narrow slightly. 'What is that?'

'Uh,' I say.

'Kuratokken,' Typhon reminds me. *'They were known as king fish by the original humans nearly fifteen hundred years ago. Celebrated for their regal—'*

'Some kind of flying fish,' I say.

Anger passes through the tether.

'Inconspicuous, remember?'

Typhon floats beside me, his annoyance obvious even in his small fish eyes.

'I see. Age?'

'Old enough to make his eyes water.'

'He's thirty.'

'Quite young. Hm. Very well. Name?'

I glance over my shoulder and see students whispering and a few smiles behind me. The flying fish is admittedly one of the least impressive forms any elemental has taken. Except, of course, the poor earth affinity who tethered some kind of large mosquito thing.

'Oceanus.'

The selector's eyebrow twitches up, but he nods and scribbles the information down on his parchment. 'Congratulations, and thank you for your service.'

Before the selector has even finished his sentence, Typhon turns himself invisible to other eyes and shifts back into his dragon form. He growls low and angry in my mind. *'You owe me a great debt for that, angry human.'*

As I walk back to my place, I catch Serena staring at me, her brow furrowed. She leans over to whisper something to Malakai, whose single eye narrows, jaw tensing as he watches me pass.

A problem for another day.

The dining hall buzzes with an unfamiliar energy as students settle in after the ceremony. Some gather around the warm fires, trying to dry off and warm up after standing in the downpour for over an hour.

Soaked hair and uniforms or not, the atmosphere in the dining room among first-years feels almost like relief.

Maybe I didn't want to cheer during the ceremony, but I have to admit I feel what everyone else feels. For the first time in two months, it feels like we've earned at least a moment to kick back and relish in how much we've overcome.

Typhon refused to leave my side to go check on Raith, so I had to rely on second-hand information that students in the healer's room were visited afterward by the selectors and allowed to present their elementals in private.

I'm surprised to find myself already itching to go check on him.

My fingers tap against the wooden table as I think about his tightly regulated, so-rare-they're-almost-nonexistent smiles and the intensity in his eyes. The memory of his warmth beside me in the elemental plane sends a flush of heat to my cheeks.

Just thinking about the way he looked at me then – like I mattered, like I was worth protecting – makes my heart do this stupid fluttering thing I can't seem to control.

I settle for keeping an eye on Malakai, Serena, and the students I know for sure are part of his unofficial little army. So long as they're here in the dining hall, Raith should be safe from any sort of assassination attempt.

'You can relax, angry human,' Typhon says. *'I know the fire-touched and his safety are important to you. I've established a line of communication with his elemental, Pyrin. I will alert you if there's any cause for concern. Pyrin says the fire-touched is currently resting and safe.'*

'Oh. You can do that?'

'The things I can do would make your fragile meat brain explode with wonder.'

'Right. Well, thank you.'

Typhon has decided to sit directly on a table of food, invisible to all but me, as students reach through him to grab heaping helpings.

'Doesn't that bother you?' I ask him. 'That girl literally just reached through your belly to grab a slice of pie.'

'They are insignificant to me. This spot gives me the best vantage point to watch for danger.'

I grin around a mouthful of warm, buttery mashed potatoes. 'This is super weird, right?' I ask Mireen who sits across from me. She nods.

'Yeah. Definitely. Ollie is . . . talkative. He wants to know what everything tastes like in exhausting detail. I'm still trying to get used to having another being in my head.'

'Uther has a lot of opinions,' Beck says. 'Good ones, though. And he's actually kind of hilarious. You guys should've heard him during the ceremony. He had so many priceless one-liners. He kept telling me how many bites he could eat everyone's elemental in. One. Half of one. A nibble. The guy is stone cold,' Beck says wistfully, shaking his head at the memory.

'Akaron doesn't talk much,' Ambrose says as he slices into a steak. 'But he's really intelligent. Having him in my head is like having a clone of myself in a way. Like another, extra brilliant mind.'

'Is he humble like you, too?' I ask, barely holding back a smile.

Ambrose smirks. 'Yes. We're both extremely humble, actually.'

'So . . . care to explain why your elemental looked like a flying fish and you called it Oceanus?' Mireen asks. 'People were laughing about it.'

'Yeah,' I say. 'We thought it was better to be discreet.'

Ambrose leans closer, eyes scanning the nearby students to make sure nobody is listening in. 'So he can take two forms?'

'More than that, supposedly. He . . . really didn't like having to be a fish. He wanted to show them what he is.'

'I bet,' Ambrose says. 'I still can't believe he's . . . well,' Ambrose glances to his side again and settles for raising his eyebrows significantly.

'Yeah,' I agree.

'What's he like?' Mireen asks.

'Um . . .' I look up at Typhon, who is sitting with his serpentine body coiled around the table, his back straight, head held high, and his wings spread as if he's trying to sun himself from the high dining room windows. 'Proud? But he really cares about keeping me safe, too. I feel like I already trust him with my life.'

As you should,' Typhon growls with a satisfied undercurrent.

Mireen's right. It's hard to get used to having another voice constantly interjecting in my own head. But there's also something oddly comforting about it. I've felt so crushingly alone at times, especially since the storm three years ago. Even when surrounded by people, it often feels like I'm on an island.

Like I'm swimming against a current that keeps pushing me farther and farther from shore, with no one to throw me a rope.

'So,' Beck says, not bothering to finish chewing. 'I hear the classes in the western wing are particularly dangerous. All about strength-ening our tethers and learning to fight side by side with an elemental.'

Ambrose nods. 'Heard the same.'

'I'm just happy they aren't going to let us openly kill each other anymore,' Mireen says.

'Yeah that's all well and good, but did you hear Rector Voss? New uniforms,' Beck says. 'I can't wait. Maybe the aspirant ones won't chafe so much.'

'I think that's a personal problem,' Ambrose says. 'Mine are perfectly comfortable.'

Beck claps Ambrose on the back. 'That's because you're not muscular enough, yet, brother. How are you so slight with what they feed us and all the training they put us through, anyway? Is your brain stealing all the nutrition, maybe?'

Ambrose cuts him a look. 'I was very thin when I came here. This is actually the largest I've ever been.'

Beck nods. 'What did you do before this, anyway? It certainly wasn't any kind of manual labor.'

'My parents owned a book shop. I was hoping to become an author. Historical studies. Things like that.'

Until today, none of us have ever talked much about our lives before Confluence. I can't say why, exactly, except to guess that it's too painful to dwell on what was. Maybe we all decided it's easier to pretend our past lives are like the dead – they're behind us, and talking about or thinking of them will only cause more suffering.

There's a slight pause as everyone else must be having similar thoughts.

Beck speaks, all the humor and bravado gone from his voice. His eyes are distant, but a faint smile touches his lips as he talks. 'I was a farmer. We grew all sorts of things. Had the best corn you've ever tasted, too. It had this sweetness you couldn't match anywhere south of the divide.'

Mireen chews her lip. 'I helped with the wounded. We were so close to the fighting with Red Kingdom that pretty much every girl in my town either helped with the injured from the front lines or worked on supplies – clothing, food, weapons, and things like that. I spent most of my life seeing the kind of damage primals do to people. Especially fires,' she adds with a look in my direction.

Is she trying to warn me about Raith?

But my thought cuts short when I realize they're all watching me now – waiting for me to share about my past.

'I'm from a place called Saltcrest,' I say eventually. The name of my home feels strange on my lips already. My throat tightens. 'I used to fish with my brothers and my father most days. I was always good on the water, so I mostly guided the boat and helped lead us to where the catches were. My oldest brother, Rodrick, used to joke that I was half fish.' My smile fades when the memory of crashing waves and the sight of a hand vanishing beneath the water fills my mind. The phantom sensation of water filling my lungs and the burn of salt in my nostrils makes me shudder.

The memory seems to have physical weight – the weight of the water pressing down, the screams swallowed by howling wind, the desperate, frantic reaching for something, someone to hold onto as the current pulled us apart. I blink hard and force the images away before they can consume me.

If the others sense I'm not saying more, they don't push me on it. Instead, Beck thankfully changes the subject, even if it's not to a particularly cheerful topic. 'So what are we going to do about Malakai?'

'We should keep an eye on him,' I say. 'For now, I don't care what Rector Voss said. We should still assume he's coming for us.'

Ambrose, Mireen, and Beck all nod seriously.

'I'm just going to ask the uncomfortable question,' Ambrose says slowly, leaning close and keeping his voice low. 'Wouldn't we be doing ourselves and the rest of the first-years a favor if we struck first? Why wait for them to catch us by surprise. Why not make a plan to . . .'

I shake my head. 'I don't want us to become the things this place is trying to make us. Weapons. That's what they want us to be. They put our backs to a corner and hope we'll turn into killers to get out. But I want us to be better than that. Trying to kill Malakai for what he did would be the Confluence way. It would be the easy way. But I still want to be *me* when I'm done with this place. Killing Malakai would kill part of me, and I'm not willing to give that up. Not for him.'

There's a pause around the table and then Beck breaks it by raising his mug toward us. 'To being the good guys, then.'

Mireen's smile is crooked. 'To being the good guys. And all the people who died, giving us far more rooms to choose from and ample closet space.'

Ambrose nods seriously and sticks his cup out. 'To being the good guys. Not what Mireen said.'

'Rude,' Mireen mutters.

I clank mine with the other cups. 'To being the good guys.'

After we've all taken a sip, Ambrose frowns. 'So we'll wait and see with Malakai. Where do we stand with Raith and Bastian, though, Nessa? Can we count them as allies?'

They heard the part about Bastian saving me and Raith in the elemental plane, but this is the first time they've asked about him beyond the usual teasing when he has gone out of his way to say something to me in public.

'I think we can trust Raith.' My voice wavers just slightly, and I feel my cheeks warm again. I seriously need to get whatever that reaction is under control.

'And Bastian . . . I'm still not sure. I'm not sure I fully trust any of the legacies.'

'But you trust a fire?' Mireen asks. Her tone is sharp, and she lets out a soft sigh. 'Sorry. I know the two of you went through something together in there. I just . . . have trouble believing we can trust him.'

'I get that. But he has had so many chances to kill me, now. I can't see what his game could be if he really is an enemy. Why leave me alive for so long only to come after me later?'

'I don't know,' Mireen says. 'But I still think we should all keep our guard up. Anybody except the four of us is a question mark. And here? Question marks can kill you.'

Beck raises his cup with a goofy smile. 'Another toast!'

Ambrose groans, but grips his cup.

'To surviving,' Beck says. 'Even when death tried really, really hard to get us. And to our new friends. Uther, Akaron, Ollie, and . . . what did you call him again? Oceanus?'

'He will use my proper name, or I will show him the price of his disrespect.'

'He knows it's not your real name, Typhon. He's just trying to keep us safe. Remember?'

Typhon says nothing, but I sense resignation through the tether.

'Right,' I say. 'Oceanus.'

'To them,' Beck says.

We all clatter our glasses together. And though the mood is celebratory all around us, I worry the relief we all feel is only temporary. Tomorrow, I'll still be unbound. I'll still have to figure out how to navigate my time here without revealing that deadly secret to anyone. I'll still know Bastian and Raith know exactly what I am and Malakai wants me dead.

Across the dining hall, I catch a glimpse of Rector Voss watching our table, his expression unreadable. As our eyes meet, he gives me a slight nod, his lips curving into a smile that doesn't reach his eyes.

Something about his attention makes the hair on my arms stand up.

'Your heart rate has increased,' Typhon observes. *'What troubles you?'*

'I don't know. Just a feeling.' I shake my head and turn my attention back to my food. Soon, I'll need to figure out how I'm going to keep myself and the people I care about alive.

But for today? For one brief moment, I can allow myself a moment to feel relief.

We all did it. We all fucking survived.

Chapter 15

Two months after Confluence Day, and I still sometimes do a double take when I see myself in the black aspirant uniform trimmed in silver. My hair is getting longer, but I keep it braided close and tight. Otherwise, opponents will use it against me in the sparring ring.

The tanned skin I had my whole life from days on the waters has faded to be more pale. My lean, wiry frame has filled out, too. Now, when I look at myself, I can actually see . . . a warrior. Someone strong. Someone who might have handled the way things happened in Saltcrest differently. Would the person I'm becoming just hang her head and let my sister and mother ignore me? Would she accept all the blame for something she couldn't control?

I'm still not sure, but I can feel I'm changing. Hardening.

I lean closer, inspecting my eyes. They're a deep blue like most water affinities, but they've always been. The change is when I look close enough, there are flecks of silver, like the reflection of stars across the sea at night. I have no doubt the silver is from my unbound affinity. Nobody has mentioned them, and I hope it stays that way.

I move away from the mirror and snatch up my practice rapier, strapping it to my hip for easy access. I train with it every day, and unlike my first few weeks here at Confluence, I rarely go to sleep aching or bruised anymore. I might even go as far as to say I'm getting pretty damn good with the thing.

'Better than good,' Typhon notes.

I smile at him. When he's not being stuffy and cranky, he's actually pretty supportive. He's currently sunning himself by the morning light coming through my window in one of his many forms – this one a thick salamander the size of a large dog.

My new aspirant room is three times the size of the one I shared with Mireen, with a private bathroom that has actual hot water on demand. I have my own desk, a small window overlooking the central courtyard, and enough space that Typhon can stretch out in his dragon form without knocking things over – though he seems to prefer showing off how many forms he can take.

My uniform is sleeveless, letting my arms – which are now more toned than they've ever been in my life – show. Aspirants and legacies get the privilege of a little more wardrobe flexibility than we had as offerings. We have dress uniforms, thicker padded uniforms for cold days, and light, sleeveless uniforms for heavy training days or heat. Even the quality of the underwear we're given is significantly improved, and thank the fucking gods for that.

The last significant change of the past months has been my unbound mark. When I'm alone in my room and relax the slight focus needed to keep it disguised, I can see how it has grown. Threads of silver like constellations have grown outward from the back of my hand. They reach halfway up my fingers and curl around my wrist like an intricate tattoo.

'A growing mark is a sign of a strengthening tether,' Typhon reminds me. *'It should be a source of pride. It's a visible indication of how impressive we are.'*

'Yeah, well . . . *unlike some ancient water dragons, I try my best not to seem impressive.'*

'I do not try to be impressive. I simply am.'

I smile as I lace up my boots and pour a trickle of focus into my mark. I watch as the silver swirl shifts and changes, turning blue and taking the shape of a wave like a normal water affinity. *'Coming to tether class today?'*

'I would sooner bathe in fire than spend another day pretending to be a fish while you toss blobs of water at targets. But yes. I will come, because I still do not trust Malakai or his small fish companion.'

'It's more like a terrifying flying shark that looks like it wants to eat everybody.'

'To me, it is insignificant. If that creature came within a foot of you, I would bite it in half and bathe in its blood.'

I turn, narrowing my eyes. 'We don't want to do anything to draw his attention again.'

'I do not like the fear you feel when you're around Malakai. You are my tethered, angry human. I will not let any harm come to you, and you should be able to relax and focus on your studies with this truth.'

'Thank you, Typhon. I know . . . it's just hard to ever really let my guard down here. The deaths did drop way off like Voss said, but I can see it in Malakai's eyes. It's like he's just waiting for the right moment.'

'I believe your fire-touched lover will also dissuade him from trying to harm you. The other students here seem to fear the fire-touched. I must admit I admire his power. For a nearly worthless human, he's rather less unimpressive than usual.'

'Did you just compliment another human, Typhon?'

'No,' Typhon's response carries such regal indignation that I laugh aloud.

'And he's not my lover. He helps me with training from time to time. And he's keeping an eye on Serena for me while I keep an eye on Malakai. It's a mutually beneficial relationship. That's it.'

'Relationship. Yes. This is what humans call it when they perform intercourse.'

I put my hands on my hips and stare at him. To his credit, he keeps his dragony face pointed toward the window, refusing to acknowledge me. 'For somebody who is in my head twenty-four hours a day, I shouldn't have to tell you nothing has ever happened between us.'

'As someone who is always in your head, I sometimes find myself confusing your dreams and reality. So, you'll excuse me if the numerous fantasy encounters where you two are very naked and very entwined are clouding my memories.'

'Typhon . . . I swear to the gods. I will—'

He transforms suddenly into his flying fish form, rounded eyes regarding me coolly. *'We should leave. You will be late for class if you don't begin walking soon.'*

With a sigh, I head out into the hall with my rapier feeling like a comfort at my hip. We're still not allowed to carry sharpened weapons around campus, but they do let us take our practice weapons anywhere we go, now. Raith offered to start privately training me a few weeks ago. To my mild frustration, he treats the lessons with complete professionality.

He's a patient, skilled, and highly effective teacher. And absolutely nothing else. No mentions of the things we went through together. No implication that he sees me as anything except someone else to protect. It has felt like the emotional equivalent of having a door slammed in my face.

But if nothing else, the training is useful, and it's helping me become one of the most capable duelists in our affinity.

I also finished reading the entire unbound book weeks ago, but now I've been spending my nights re-reading passages to be sure I haven't missed anything. But the contents of the book have made it hard for me to look Bastian in the face. He knows what I am. What I really am. He knows what I'm capable of becoming, and the harm I could bring not just to myself but to all of the combined kingdoms and even the elemental plane.

At times, I feel like a monster, and I hate that Bastian knows. Except I can't figure out why he's keeping it quiet. If he had even the slightest doubt about my character, he would go to the nearest authority and make a case to have me executed.

'No one will execute you, angry human. I would bite their heads off and drink the marrow from their bones if they tried.'

I grin to myself. *'Thanks, Typhon. That's . . . sweet?'*

By the time I reach tether class, I'm running late. The massive blue doors swing shut behind me as I slip into the cavernous, circular room. Students are already working on their magic as our instructor, Primal Ryke, paces the room with his muscular arms tucked behind his back, hands clasped around his wrists.

'Late again, Thorne,' he notes, deep blue eyes regarding me.

'Sorry,' I say, slipping into the room.

Mireen spots me from across the room and waves. Her braid whips around as she directs Ollie, her water otter, in a synchronized attack with her own water daggers. The elemental's form has grown more substantial over the months – less transparent, more defined, with deeper blue coloring. He zips through the air, slashing at training dummies that crumble under the water's pressure.

Primal Ryke prowls between pairs, occasionally demonstrating forms with his own elemental – a graceful water crane that towers over him when it stretches its wings.

Training with our elementals takes several forms. Some classes are theoretical, and some school us on the little bits of elemental history humans are privy to. This class is about learning to fight along with our elementals in combat. Some students hack at training dummies while others fight in sparring matches, combining what we know of weapons training with elemental combat.

'Nessa,' Primal Ryke says as he approaches me. 'Where is Oceanus?'

'He's . . . going to appear soon,' I say, earning a few smirks from nearby students. The 'flying fish' story has become something of a running joke among first-years.

Ryke nods toward the far side of the room where Beck and Ambrose are teaming up to obliterate a pair of wooden training dummies. Uther is clawing chunks out of one while Akaron uses watery talons to slash out where the eyes would be. 'Join your friends for combat practice.'

I maneuver through the pairs of students, dodging streams of water and the occasional errant elemental. The room smells of clean stone and the faint ozone scent that accompanies channeled magic. High windows let in shafts of winter sunlight that catch on the droplets of water hanging in the air, turning them to prisms.

'Someone's late,' Beck teases as I approach. Uther, his water bear, rears up on hind legs beside him. The elemental has grown in size since Confluence Day, now standing slightly taller than Beck even when he's standing on all fours.

'Typhon was being difficult,' I mutter.

Ambrose adjusts his glasses, which he somehow manages to keep dry despite the water flying everywhere. 'Fascinating. The connection between elemental mood and tether strength is still understudied, but my theory is—'

'Save the lecture,' Beck interrupts. 'Let's see if Nessa can finally best me.'

I draw my rapier, feeling its familiar weight. Two months of constant training have built muscle memory I never thought possible. 'Didn't I win last week? And like six times before that?'

Beck grins and channels water into a swirling shield before him. 'Hm. I don't seem to recall ever losing to you.'

'It's Beck's secret weapon,' Ambrose says. 'Weaponized stupidity.'

'He's right,' Beck says. 'I am a weapon. Just like Ambrose said.'

'That's . . . not at all what I meant. I was saying—'

'Blah blah,' Beck says. 'We got it. I'm a living weapon. Deadly as I am handsome. Now come on, Nessa. Let's see if you can finally beat me.'

I center myself, focusing on the moisture in the air. Drawing from the environment rather than from myself has become easier with practice. Bits and pieces from the unbound book along with Typhon's knowledge of unbound status have massively accelerated my progress.

Normal water affinities push the water from within themselves.

For me, it's the opposite. I extend my awareness outward, drawing from sources beyond myself. Moisture in the air, gusts of wind, the stored potential in the stone beneath my feet, and the bits of heat in human bodies or torches all work. Except I only ever channel water when others are watching for obvious reasons. My biggest advantage is versatility, but while I'm posing as a water affinity, I'm forced to stick to only water.

In other words, everybody else in this room has a reservoir of power the size of a lake and I'm drawing from something more like a bathtub. But the limitations have made me more precise. More strategic. The others waste power while I make use of every drop of essence I can grab.

We circle each other as Ambrose and Mireen back away to give us room. Beck moves first, sending a wave of water rushing toward me like a battering ram. I sidestep, using a pulse of energy from my palm to disperse it. The water falls to the ground in harmless drops.

Drawing more moisture from the air, I form three spinning discs of water and launch them in quick succession. Beck blocks the first two with his shield, but the third catches him in the shoulder, knocking him back and sending him twisting through the air like a ragdoll.

Uther slips under him, cushioning his fall with his watery back.

'Not bad,' Beck admits, sliding off Uther with a grateful pat on the beast's head. He shakes water from his sandy blonde hair.

I'm about to respond when I feel a familiar prickle at the back of my neck. I turn slightly, just enough to confirm my suspicion.

Raith stands in the doorway, leaning against the frame with his arms crossed over his chest. Even from across the room, I can feel the heat of his attention on me as he tracks my movements. His affinity mark has grown more than anyone in the first-years. Lines of red-orange trail up his thick forearm and reach the bottom of his left bicep in a way that's admittedly . . . nice.

Our eyes meet briefly, and a ghost of a smile touches his lips before his expression returns to its usual stoic mask. It's been like this for weeks now – him appearing at the edges of wherever I am, watching, assessing. Keeping his promise to protect me, but maintaining a careful distance in public.

The private training sessions are different. Twice a week, we meet in an abandoned training room in the eastern wing. There, he's been teaching me how to use my size and speed to my advantage, how to fight opponents twice my strength, how to survive. His hands adjust my stance, his voice low and rough as he corrects my form, his body close enough that I can feel his unnatural heat.

But it's always professional. Always clinical. There's never idle conversation, and as far as I can tell, his one and only purpose is to make sure I can defend myself better.

I force my attention back to Beck just in time to dodge a water whip aimed at my legs. 'Too busy drooling to defend, huh?'

'Shut up,' I say, glaring as I pull my attention from Raith.

My momentary distraction costs me. Beck's next attack catches me in the chest, drenching me from neck to waist.

We're all able to put force behind our attacks, but being a water carries the advantage of letting us practice with relatively harmless spells when we want. In a real fight, Ryke has been teaching us how to sharpen each droplet of water, turning an otherwise harmless splash into a deadly blade that can cleave through flesh and bone.

But Beck's attack is nothing more than cold water splashing and soaking me as it connects.

I pull the water from my clothing. Droplets magically wick from the fabric, my skin, and my hair, drifting in front of my body in a wall of droplets. With a thought, I reach into each droplet and reshape them into inch-long needles.

'Hey now, that's—' Beck starts, but I gesture, and the needles fly toward him.

They form an outline, punching pinprick holes in the loose points of his clothing but not even scratching him. He looks behind and sees the needles stuck in the stone wall, then looks down at his clothes and pulls his sleeve out. Dozens of little holes let the light through.

'Gods, Nessa,' Beck says, grinning. 'You're scary as hell.'

As I release the water needles, letting them splash to the ground, I feel another presence behind me. Not Raith this time.

'Impressive control, Thorne,' Primal Ryke says, his voice cool but not unkind. 'For someone who could barely form a sphere two months ago, your progress is . . . noteworthy.'

Coming from Ryke, this is practically effusive praise. I duck my head, unused to compliments from instructors. 'Thank you.'

He studies me for a moment, head tilted. 'Your channeling has a unique signature. Almost as if . . .' He trails off, then straightens. 'The Rector mentioned . . . well, never mind. Just report to his office tomorrow at sunset. And don't be late for once.'

Report to the fucking Rector's office? Holy shit . . . Ryke gives the order almost casually, but there's nothing casual about the command.

The Rector doesn't interact with students or our daily life here. So what the hells did I just do to get put on his notice? I can already feel my palms sweating and my breath coming quick at the idea, but I try to pretend I'm calm as I nod to Ryke.

'*I do not like this,*' Typhon notes.

'*Agreed.*'

I catch Beck and Ambrose exchanging a look as Primal Ryke walks away.

'Private meeting with Rector Voss,' Beck whispers, wiggling his eyebrows. 'Sounds . . . intense.'

'Stop it,' Mireen says, shoving him. 'It's probably nothing. And Nessa is getting really good. Better than most of us. They're probably just wanting to help along a student with so much potential. Maybe he wants to talk about putting her in a more advanced class, or something.'

I smile, but there's a tight ball of worry in my chest.

Attention. This is exactly what I've been trying to avoid for so long. A one on one with the Rector himself is . . . concerning to say the least. I think about slipping out of class to tell Raith and ask his opinion, but when I look toward the doorway where he stood, I see he's gone.

All that's left is the lingering heat of where I felt his gaze on my skin and the tendrils of fear spreading through my insides.

Tomorrow, I'll meet with Rector Voss, and I'll hope like hells he's not about to interrogate me about Typhon or my affinity. If he so much as suspects what I am, the 'meeting' could be more like an execution.

Chapter 16

The western wing library has become my sanctuary. Unlike the main library where many still study for more generic topics, this one is reserved for aspirants and above. It's older, with towering shelves that reach to vaulted ceilings and narrow windows that let in shafts of colored light. Ancient tomes are chained to the shelves, their spines cracked with age and use. The air smells of dust, parchment, and aged leather.

The only sounds are the occasional rustle of a page being turned or the scratch of a quill.

I've claimed a table in the furthest corner, hidden behind a shelf of texts on elemental taxonomy. It's late evening, and most students have already left for dinner. Perfect for reading more of my unbound book away from prying eyes. I've long since memorized and destroyed the key Bastian made for me, meaning it's safe to read the book in slightly more public places.

Typhon lounges beside me in his dragon form, tail curled around the table's legs, wings tucked tight against his serpentine body. He lifts his head occasionally to scan for threats before returning to what I can only describe as a draconic nap.

'You should eat,' he grumbles as my stomach makes an embarrassingly loud noise. *'Human bodies are inconveniently fragile. Without food, you grow weak quickly.'*

'I will. After this section.'

I'm close to a breakthrough with the book. The text is often impossibly dense, and I'm catching things on my second and third readthrough that I didn't on the first. Mostly, though, I read it every chance I can get because it's my only source of information about what being unbound means. About what I am and the history of people like me.

Tonight, I'm reading about 'manifestations' for the hundredth time. Supposedly, unbound can develop a unique, one-off kind of power independent of the affinities. Things like enhanced strength, making plants grow from nothing, matter manipulation, and even terrible things like the ability to pull the blood from people's bodies with their mind.

These manifestations seem to be the reason humans eventually hunted down and exterminated unbound people. Apparently, Lorkan Grace manifested a power so terrible that people saw the existence of unbound as an existential threat. Worse, unbound can also tether people somehow, just like primals tether elementals. Lorkan was also said to have used the human tether for some nefarious purpose, but the book is vague on the specifics, so I'm rereading again for hopes of finding something I've missed.

After half an hour, I'm left with the same uncomfortable conclusion. No matter how many times I try to read it a different way, I can't see another explanation. Unbound can tether people. Lorkan used this ability to make some kind of monstrous army that threatened civilization itself.

'I smell your fear,' Typhon observes, rising to full alertness. *'What troubles you?'*

I hesitate. Typhon can always feel my thoughts, but I've learned it only happens if he's trying to pay attention. At times, he seems to tune me out, like when I'm focusing on the book. He finds the subject upsetting for some reason and prefers not to talk with me about it. But maybe tonight he'll be willing to help shed some light on it for me.

'The book. Can unbound tether themselves to other humans?'

Typhon's eyes narrow to slits. It's a few moments before he responds. *'Yes. Lorkan Grace was the first to discover a quirk of this ability. Somehow, he was able to twist what had been a typical tether into something more like slavery. To pass fragments of his own manifestation* to those he tethered, changing them into monstrosities and beasts he could command.'

'Monstrosities? What do you mean?'

'Creatures who walked the world as humans, but they fed on the life essence of human or elementals. I believe Lorkan used this essence to grant himself eternal life of some sort. As far as I know, he was never found or killed. It's very possible he still lives, along with his creatures.'

'You didn't think this would be worth telling me?' I demand.

'You already think yourself a monster, angry human. I did not want to add fuel to the flames. The past of what people like you have done does not change you. I wanted you to have time to think on this before you knew more. Perhaps, with time, you can use your abilities for others as you did for me. To free them from madness.'

'Wait . . . you think I could do that for other rogue elementals?'

'Yes. Not now, but when you're stronger. The elemental world suffers greatly from the rogue elementals. Especially the ancients, like me. You met the royal council on the day of your affinity trial. The leaders of elemental kind toil to find a way to stop the destruction of these rogues – to fight the madness slowly corrupting our strongest. You could be the key. I suspect it's why they allowed you to live, even though unbound have the ability to cause true death to elementals.'

'Wait . . . true death?'

'Yes. With enough strength, unbound can draw an elemental completely dry. It's the only way to truly kill us. To erase us from existence. Humans hunted your kind because they feared Lorkan's creatures and his influence. My kind joined the fight because we feared the true death. But we paid deeply for our mistake. Without unbound, none can cleanse the madness slowly taking us.'

Before I can answer, a shadow falls across my table. I close the book and slip it out of view by instinct, hiding it in my lap.

'Late night reading?' Raith asks, voice low and rough. The fire markings of his affinity glow in the dim library light.

He carries a smell of woodsmoke on his body – a scent I've come to crave and enjoy.

I slip the unbound book into my bag, tucking it between more innocent texts. 'Just research.'

Raith's eyes follow my movement, but he doesn't comment. Instead, he slides onto the chair opposite me, his large frame making the wooden seat creak. 'You missed dinner.'

'I lost track of time.'

His gaze flicks to Typhon, who has shifted to alert watchfulness. Raith is one of the few people Typhon regularly shows himself to, rather than remain invisible.

'Your dragon doesn't remind you to eat?'

'I have been telling her for hours that humans require regular sustenance,' Typhon complains, forgetting Raith can't hear him.

'He tried,' I admit. 'But I was focused.'

Raith reaches into his pocket and pulls out a small bundle wrapped in cloth. He unwraps it to reveal several thick slices of bread, cheese, and an apple. 'Eat.'

The simple command should irritate me, but my stomach growls loudly in response. 'Thanks,' I mutter, taking a slice of bread. I try to convince myself he just happened to be carrying food – that he didn't specifically go to the dining room and put together a meal for me.

I want to believe it, because the way my heart softens to think of him worrying and caring about me so much feels dangerous. There's still so much I don't know about Raith. And there's the obvious divide between our affinities. He's a fire. Even if the first-year fires feel like far less of a threat than my own affinity, I can't ignore the things students whisper about the fires and earths.

There are always rumors of traitors among them. Students simply biding their time as they wait for commands from Red Kingdom. Commands to turn on us and sabotage our efforts.

Mostly, I think it's all paranoia. But I have to admit the doubt lurks inside my own mind, too. And what would be more valuable to Red Kingdom than an unbound tethered to an ancient water dragon? If Raith was a spy for them, he'd likely be rewarded handsomely for delivering me on a silver platter.

But I don't want to believe any of that. I admire Raith, whether I like it or not. And . . . I like how it feels when he's with me.

We sit in companionable silence while I eat. This is how it often is between us – words unnecessary, the quiet somehow comfortable rather than awkward. I've learned more about Raith through his silences than his sparse conversation.

'Rector Voss wants to meet with you. I heard Primal Ryke say it.'

I swallow a bite of bread. 'Yeah . . .'

Raith's jaw tightens almost imperceptibly. 'When?'

'Tomorrow at sunset.'

He nods slowly, as if confirming something to himself. 'I'll be nearby. During your meeting. Make a loud enough noise, and I'll come for you.'

I stare. 'I'm meeting with the Rector, Raith. What is it you think you'll do if I'm in trouble?'

Raith says nothing, but the fire in his eyes speaks volumes. He'll burn this place down if he has to. If that's what it takes to keep me safe. And gods, I hate how my stomach flips from the knowledge.

'*Someone approaches. The air child,*' Typhon's head swivels toward the library entrance.

I've grown used to Typhon's peculiar ways of referring to people. The 'air child' can only be Bastian. Sure enough, moments later, Bastian's tall form appears between the shelves, moving directly toward us with purpose.

He looks as pristine as ever in his legacy uniform, golden hair pushed away from his broad forehead. But there's tension in his shoulders, a tightness around his eyes I haven't seen before.

'Ah. How convenient,' Raith mutters, just loud enough for me to hear. 'Your legacy admirer has impeccable timing.'

I shoot him a warning look as Bastian reaches our table. The two have maintained an uneasy truce since Confluence Day, bound by their shared knowledge of my secret but clearly distrustful of each other's motives.

'Nessa,' Bastian says with a nod. 'Hollow.' He acknowledges Raith with cool formality.

'Strathmore,' Raith responds, equally frigid.

I resist the urge to roll my eyes. 'What brings you to the library this late, Bastian?'

'I was looking for you, actually.' He glances at Raith, then back to me. 'I heard you've been selected for private instruction with Rector Voss.'

'News travels fast,' I say.

Bastian shifts, uncharacteristically hesitant. 'May I speak with you? Privately?'

Raith doesn't move, his eyes fixed on Bastian with quiet challenge.

'Anything you have to say to her can be said in front of me,' Raith states, voice deadly calm.

'Is that because you're too dense to comprehend it, or because you fancy yourself as some sort of guard dog?'

'Maybe come closer. Find out if I bite.'

An unseen breeze drifts through the library, subtle but the threat is clear enough to make goosebumps rise on my arms. Bastian's eyes seem to go whiter, unseeing as he stares at Raith.

The air around Raith shimmers and turns blurry with heat. His eyes darken, the gold catching with flecks of red as if they're growing hotter.

'It's fine,' I interject before they can go further than aggressively glaring. 'Raith knows everything anyway.'

Bastian's pale eyes widen slightly, then narrow. 'Everything?'

'Enough,' I confirm.

The choice of words earns a sharpening of the eyes from Raith, but he doesn't comment.

Bastian hesitates, then sits beside me, creating a triangle between us. His voice drops to barely above a whisper. 'Very well. Then I suppose it won't hurt if he knows my father has been making inquiries about Voss. The Council is . . . concerned.'

Raith's expression darkens. 'About?'

'Disappearances. The number of deaths are closely monitored and reported at the academy, despite how it may have seemed when you were offerings. Deaths of aspirants and legacies are not something the academy or Empire takes lightly. Training accidents have to be explained. Consequences exist if too many are lost.'

'And?' Raith presses.

Bastian carefully avoids looking at Raith, as if he's just speaking to me. 'And there have been an unusual amount of deaths among students this year. Deaths of aspirants. Deaths of a few legacies. Older students. And the Rector has been . . . uncooperative when it comes to reporting the circumstances. Details aren't adding up.'

Raith's eyes meet mine, and I know what he's thinking without him needing to say a word. Months ago, we overheard instructors talking about strange deaths. Deaths that had them talking about siphons, which seemed like pure fantasy to me at the time.

The bread in my stomach feels like lead. 'And you're telling me this because . . . ?'

'Because my father doesn't trust Voss. And neither should you.' Bastian's eyes drop to the swirling patterns of my mark. 'Especially you.'

'He threatens us,' Typhon growls, smoke curling from his nostrils. *'Say the word, and I will remove this threat.'*

'No one is removing anyone,' I respond silently. *'Bastian is trying to warn us to be careful. He's looking out for us.'*

'Why? Why does the air child care about your welfare? I don't trust him. I'll eat him and his horse. Simply give me the word, angry human.'

'What do you suggest I do?' I ask Bastian. 'Refuse the summons? That would only draw more attention.'

'Go,' Bastian says. 'But be careful what you reveal. Voss is . . . persuasive. People tend to tell him more than they intend.'

'He's being deliberately vague,' Raith says, his voice edged with frustration. 'Either tell us what you know or stop wasting our time with cryptic warnings.'

Bastian's composure cracks slightly. 'I'm trying to help, Hollow.

My father doesn't cast suspicion lightly. This meeting with the Rector could be incredibly dangerous for Nessa.'

'I'll be careful,' I promise Bastian. 'Thank you for the warning.'

He nods, rising to his feet. 'Just . . . remember appearances can be deceiving. Voss is charming, intelligent, and utterly ruthless when it comes to achieving his goals.' He hesitates, then adds, 'If anything unusual happens, find me immediately.'

After Bastian leaves, Raith and I sit in silence, the weight of his warning hanging between us.

'Do you trust him?' Raith finally asks.

'I don't know. But he's only telling me to be careful. I think I was going to do that either way.'

Raith considers this, his scarred face thoughtful in the torchlight. 'You're smart. Forget what Bastian says. Just follow your instincts. They've gotten you this far.'

I smile at the compliments. Raith doesn't try, but he has a way of making me appreciate myself more. There's a no-nonsense way about him and a tendency to acknowledge strengths in others. He makes me believe his compliments when they come, and he never makes me question their intention. It's easy to see why the fires practically worship him.

Serena is the only fire who seems to want him out of the way, but she knows she'll be torn to shreds if she makes a move against him and anyone discovers it. Like Malakai, I'm worried she's only waiting quietly for a rare moment of weakness – that she'll never stop watching and waiting.

I start gathering my books. 'Thanks, Raith. I'll be careful. And I'll trust my instincts.'

As I rise to leave, Raith catches my wrist. The contact sends a familiar rush of heat through me – partly his natural fire, partly something else entirely. My breath catches as his thumb traces a small circle on my pulse point.

'Be careful,' he says, voice lower and rougher than before. 'If anything feels wrong – anything at all – you get out of there. Promise me.'

The power in his eyes makes my heart stutter. For all his gruffness, all his careful distance, there's something in the way he's looking at me now that makes my skin flush and my pulse race.

'I promise.'

He releases my wrist slowly, his fingers trailing along my skin. 'Remember. I'll be waiting somewhere nearby tomorrow. Just in case.'

'I don't need a bodyguard, Raith.'

His lips curve in a rare half-smile that transforms his face. 'Not your call, Saltcrest. I'll be there.'

The simple words send warmth spreading through me that has nothing to do with elemental magic. Before I can respond, he stands and collects his things.

'Tomorrow at sunset, then,' he says.

I nod, suddenly unable to find words.

As we part ways at the library door, I glance back to see him watching me go, his expression impossible to read in the shadows. Something has shifted between us tonight – something subtle but undeniable. And as I make my way back to my room, I can still feel the phantom heat of his fingers against my skin, like a promise or a warning.

Chapter 17

I know the Rector himself isn't likely about to murder me as soon as I step into his office. The knowledge doesn't stop dread from coiling around my spine like a serpent, tightening with every step I take toward the meeting.

'If he is a fool, he can try to harm you. I will simply eat him,' Typhon notes as he glides through the air beside me in his ridiculous fish form, butterfly-like wings flapping rapidly. He didn't even make me beg him to take the form this time, and I'm grateful for it, even if I know he's hiding himself from others.

The Rector's office lies atop a winding spiral staircase in a seldom used section of the castle. As I climb, I notice the paintings lining the stairwell – frame after frame depicting former Rectors of Confluence, I assume. They're all sitting in the same office, even if the furniture changes from painting to painting.

By the time I reach the top of the stairs, my heart is pounding, and it's not from exertion. Daily training here has me fit enough to jog up these stairs without losing my breath.

I drum a nervous pattern on my thighs as I walk the simple hallway lined with stained glass windows. A single door waits. The door to his office, just where I was told I'd find it.

No guards. No staff. No sign of Raith, either, even though I know that doesn't mean he isn't close. For such a large man, he can draw less notice than a shadow when he wants.

Somewhere nearby, he'll be watching. Waiting. I haven't caught so much as a glimpse of him since I left my room, but the thought of him standing vigil calms my racing heart. It's a whispered promise from the darkness I shouldn't need or want, but it's there all the same.

The stone hallway feels too narrow, the air too thin, and every step brings me closer to what I'm starting to think might be a death sentence.

'This human has power,' Typhon warns as we reach the ornate double doors leading to the Rector's chambers. *'I sensed it during the ceremony. I sense it now, even through these walls. Be on your guard, angry human.'*

'He's not a primal, though.'

'And yet I sense his power.'

Wonderful. Even more reason to be scared shitless.

I close my eyes outside his office and say a silent prayer to whatever gods might be listening.

I lift my hand to knock, but the doors swing open before my knuckles make contact.

'Miss Thorne,' Rector Voss says, standing in the doorway with a pleasant smile that doesn't quite reach his eyes. 'Right on time. Please, come in.'

I step into his office, immediately struck by how different it is from what I'd expected. No oppressive darkness, no instruments of torture, no intimidating displays of power. Instead, the circular room is filled with warm light from dozens of candles. Bookshelves line the walls, interspersed with maps of Empire and curious artifacts displayed in glass cases. A massive desk of polished wood dominates the center, its surface neat and organized.

Voss himself looks just as he did during the tethering ceremony – tall, imposing, yet somehow approachable in his perfectly tailored black robes. His hair is still that striking black with distinctive silver streaks framing his face, and his eyes – a light, nearly colorless gray – study me with unsettling intensity.

'Please, sit,' he says, gesturing to a chair across from his desk.

I take the admittedly comfortable chair, lowering myself slowly in case there are hidden spikes or spears in the cushions.

There aren't.

His lips flick to the side with the faintest smile. 'You're right to be cautious. Caution is good here. And I know your survival as an offering depended on it. But I assure you, you're safe here.'

The simple words feel surprisingly true to me. It helps to know Typhon is right beside me – to know he would do anything to protect me. 'Okay,' I say.

'Good,' Voss threads his fingers together, leaning toward me on the desk. 'Now . . . I think the best way to handle this is to come out and say it. You're unbound—' he raises a hand, eyes calm and unthreatening. 'No need to run. No need to panic. I meant it when I said you're safe here. I only intend to help you.'

My mouth has gone dry and my heartbeat thunders in my ears like a thousand tiny needles pricking at my consciousness. My fingertips dig into the armrests of the chair so hard I hear the leather creak.

'For one who knows the signs, it's quite obvious, Nessa. Nobody betrayed you. Nobody shared your secret with me, assuming some knew.'

I blink. 'Signs?' It's the only word I manage as my words crystallize into frost on my tongue.

'If he tries anything, I will end him,' Typhon promises.

'People and elementals aren't so different, you know . . .'

'How so?' I ask when it's clear he's waiting for me to continue – gently forcing me to participate in whatever this is.

'Paranoia. Fear. Distrust. It runs deep in both races. They both feared what your kind could become. See . . . there was once a powerful unbound who discovered the true potential of your affinity. When they saw what he was capable of, they lashed out. They hunted your kind down to the last. Elementals and humans worked together to exterminate the unbound. There was no mercy. No quarter. And as far as we know, they succeeded. But I've been searching for your kind for quite some time now. Fruitlessly, until today.'

I wet my lips tasting fear and curiosity in equal measure. 'Why would you still be looking for unbound if they were supposed to be gone?'

'Because the proven bloodlines were destroyed, yes. But the nature of affinity is a natural thing. An evolution, if you like. It was only a matter of time before it manifested again. A phoenix from the ashes.' He gestures with both hands toward me, his smile warm. 'And look how you rise, Nessa Thorne.'

'I'm not sure I understand . . .'

'That's alright. I only wanted you to come today to introduce myself and establish a line of trust. I know what you are, and I have no intentions of speaking with anyone about it. There are, as you've clearly intuited on your own, many who would see you dead if they knew. I don't want you dead. I want you to flourish, Nessa. I have access to texts that Empire itself doesn't know still exist. Call it a perk of my position. Since I was a young boy, I've taken a special interest in unbound. You could even say my fascination with your kind led me to taking this position at Confluence. And now, I'm happy to offer you all the help you could want in understanding your powers.'

My breath hitches at his words. I try not to let it show, but I feel hunger. Longing. The answers he's promising. I want them so badly it hurts. Not just for my own survival, but to become strong enough to protect myself and the people I care about. 'What can you tell me?' I ask, tone carefully neutral. I'm still not sure if this is some kind of trap. Some elaborate scheme to get me to admit more than I should.

He smiles, pleased to hear me asking questions, I assume. 'Your manifestation. I could help you unlock it. I'm guessing you don't know what that means.'

Thanks to Bastian's book, I actually do, but I shake my head all the same. I'm not going to offer up more information than necessary. I'm also not going to implicate Bastian if this is all a trick.

'Unbound develop one or more special, unique abilities. These powers came in so many varieties it was truly remarkable. One of my favorite subjects was simply reading and learning about the special powers they held. Prophetic visions. Minor time reversal. Levitation, flight, the ability to shapeshift. And, of course . . . there were even some quite special powers that drew more than their fair share of misunderstanding. I dare say a few unbound are responsible for many of our myths and legends.'

After a moment, he stands suddenly, gesturing for me to do the same.

'In any case, I deeply appreciate your time, Nessa. I know your schedule here is unforgiving. If you haven't gathered as much already, I am extending a formal offer to mentor you,' Voss says, his voice somehow closer though he hasn't moved. 'To help you discover your unique gift safely, where others can't witness and misconstrue.'

'Why would you help me?' I ask.

'Because talent should be nurtured, not feared.' His eyes catch the candlelight, reflecting it back like twin flames. 'Because I believe you could become something extraordinary.'

I want to believe him, with a yearning that hollows me from the inside out. He's offering me power and understanding. Here at Confluence, both of those things mean survival.

'I'll make one suggestion,' Voss adds, leaning closer. 'Tell no one what you are. Not your friends, and especially not the fire affinity who watches you so closely.'

Raith's face flashes in my mind, eyes burning with that intensity that makes my pulse flutter, and something inside me rebels against the command. He already knows. And some part of me also knows out of everybody here at Confluence, Raith might be the one I trust most – the one I'm most likely to confide in. 'I—'

'For your safety,' Voss interrupts smoothly. 'There are those who would destroy you simply for existing, Nessa. Your secret must remain between us until you're strong enough to protect yourself.'

I find myself nodding. What he says does make sense. There's no reason to risk trusting others now. Not when I still have so much to learn. Not when it would be safer to wait until I can protect myself from those who would betray me. And it's what I've already been doing for months, even if I've been getting closer to wanting to tell Mireen and the others. 'I understand.'

'Excellent.' Voss smiles. 'We'll begin your private training soon. For now, you should rest.'

He gestures suddenly toward the door, signaling the end of our meeting. As I move to exit, my legs feel unsteady beneath me like my bones have turned to water.

'Remember,' he says as he guides me toward the door with a hand on my shoulder, 'not a word to anyone about what you are. About what we discussed. It's for your protection.'

I nod again. Distantly, I recognize he's touching me and none of his power is flowing into me. If nothing else, it's a confirmation he's not a primal or the carrier of an affinity. It makes trusting him a little easier.

The moment I step into the hallway, the door closes behind me with a soft click.

I lean against the wall, drawing in deep breaths. My thoughts feel sluggish and syrupy, like the Rector just stuffed so much unexpected information in my head that I'm still struggling to process it. And after months of hiding what I am, the burden of secrecy has been partially lifted. Someone else knows – someone who wants to help, not hurt me.

'That was . . . unexpected,' Typhon says carefully. 'Are you well, angry human?'

'I'm fine,' I murmur. 'Just . . . surprised. I can't believe he wants to help me.'

Before I can collect my scattered thoughts, movement in the shadows catches my eye. It's Raith. He's leaning against the wall about twenty feet down the hallway, arms crossed over his chest, golden glowing eyes a predator's in the dim light.

For a split second, I see something shockingly close to concern on his face.

Is that concern for me?

The emotion evaporates so quickly I think I might have imagined it. Anger takes its place, along with his usual distrustful scowl. 'What happened in there?'

I shake my head. Raith knows I'm an unbound. He knows parts, even if he doesn't know the whole story. Especially the parts about how dangerous I could become and how many would kill me for what I am. And yet . . .

The Rector's words ring in my mind. Tell no one.

'Nessa?' Raith steps closer, close enough that I can feel the warmth radiating from him like standing beside a hearth – comforting and warm at a distance, but dangerous or even deadly if I drift too close. 'What's wrong?'

'Nothing,' I manage to say. 'He just . . . wanted to talk about my progress.'

Raith's eyes narrow, clearly sensing there's more. 'And?'

'And . . . he's offering to mentor me. Private sessions.'

Raith's jaw tightens, a muscle ticking beneath the scarred skin. 'You're not telling me everything.'

'I am,' I insist. 'That's all it was.'

He studies me for a long moment, those amber eyes seeming to look right through me. 'I don't trust him.'

'You don't trust anyone,' I counter, trying for lightness I don't feel.

'Not true.' His voice drops lower, rougher. 'I trust you.'

Something twists in my chest at his words, a feeling so sharp and sudden it steals my breath leaving a hollow space beneath my breastbone that aches with possibility. I want to tell him everything – about Voss, about the reason I volunteered months ago in Saltcrest, about the fear that's been my constant companion since discovering what I am. I try to form the words, but they catch in my throat like fish bones. Nothing comes.

'I should go,' I say instead, confused and suddenly exhausted. 'It's been a long day.'

Raith catches my wrist as I turn to leave, his touch sending a familiar current of heat up my arm awakening every dormant nerve ending in its path. Not just the natural warmth of his fire affinity, but something deeper, more unsettling. For a moment, I feel the pull of his power, the instinctive urge to draw it into myself.

'Nessa.' His voice is barely above a whisper. 'If you're in trouble, tell me.'

I meet his eyes, seeing real concern there, and something else – something that makes my heart race for entirely different reasons.

'I'm fine,' I say, genuinely believing it. 'Just tired.'

He releases me reluctantly, his fingers trailing along my skin. 'Tell me when you're meeting him next. I'll be here. Just in case.'

'You don't have to do that.'

'You can tell me when you'll be here, or I'll simply make a point of following you around at all hours. One way or another, I'll be here.'

My lips curve up. 'You're threatening to stalk me?'

'If that's what it takes.'

'Why? Why have you been trying so hard to keep me alive? And don't tell me it's because I helped you in the elemental plane. You were protecting me before that.'

Raith's face is an unreadable mask. It's several long seconds before he finally answers. 'There was somebody I used to know. Somebody who was a far better person than me. I failed to keep him alive when the time came, and I swore I would find a way to make it up to him.'

I frown. 'What do you mean?'

'You remind me of him. In a way. There's a . . . light in you. Something that seems like it would go on burning even in a fucking rainstorm. That's how he was. Too good for this world, maybe. And I let it take him.'

His eyes blaze with the memory, and my heart aches for him, his grief becoming mine for a moment, sharp as broken glass and twice as cutting.

'What was his name?' I ask, voice soft.

'Gareth.'

He doesn't say more, but the silence seems to have a voice of its own with Raith. I feel a sudden certainty that Gareth and his death had something to do with the scars on Raith's body. Maybe Gareth is even the reason he's here at Confluence.

'I'll let you know before I come back here.'

'Good. Now get back to your room, Nessa. I'm going to hang back and make sure he doesn't have you followed.'

I nod, not trusting myself to speak again. It's not because I'm worried I'll talk about what Voss told me, either. I'm afraid to speak because Raith finally let down his walls, even if it was only for an instant. And gods. I didn't realize how badly I wanted to be let inside his guard – to be closer to him.

Ever since that first day, I felt a confusing kind of connection to him. A pull.

And until recently, all I've ever sensed was him pushing me away from that force.

Tonight, he let me drift just a little bit closer, and I'm terrified by how much I want more of that feeling – that closeness.

I head down the stairs, noting Typhon's unusual quietness but figuring he's just grumpy after a day of posing as a flying fish.

Despite the confusion lingering at the edges of my mind, one thought remains clear in the swirl of emotions the last half hour brought: I've found an ally in the most unexpected place. Someone who understands what I am. Someone who can help me control my powers.

And all I have to do is keep it to myself.

Chapter 18

'You're outnumbered three-to-one. The enemy has the high ground on this ridgeline here with established fortifications. What's your plan?' Instructor Pilton's voice cuts through the Military Tactics classroom, his single arm gesturing emphatically at the large map pinned to the front wall.

Two days have passed since my meeting with Voss, and I still can't shake the unusual lightness in my chest. The knowledge that the Rector of Confluence knows what I am, understands it, and doesn't want me dead . . . to call it a relief would be an understatement. Tomorrow evening, I'll meet with him again for my first official mentoring session. With any luck, I might even manifest my power during our meeting.

Considering my unbound manifestation could be absolutely anything, my mind has been constantly wandering with possibilities. Mostly, though, I just hope it's not something terrible – something like what Lorkan Grace manifested.

I drag my attention back to the map, studying the scenario Pilton has laid out. The classroom is arranged in tiers, with legacies at the front in comfortable chairs, aspirants behind them in decent seating, and until recently, offerings crammed at the back on hard benches. Now that we're all aspirants, the class feels less stratified, though old habits die hard. Most former offerings still cluster toward the back, myself included. Little by little, we've mingled with those who started as aspirants, but it's slow progress. For the most part, cliques and groups of trust already formed before Confluence Day, and we're still seen as outsiders.

A legacy in the front row – a tall, thin air with white-blonde hair – suggests sacrificing a portion of his forces for a distraction so the rest of the squadron can get behind the enemy for a surprise attack. Pilton immediately launches into a critique of the approach, his bushy eyebrows drawing together as he paces.

'You could solve this tactical problem easily,' Typhon notes dryly in my mind. *'One ancient water dragon could eliminate their entire force without complex maneuvering.'*

'Not helpful,' I mutter under my breath.

'Miss Thorne,' Pilton calls suddenly, making me straighten. The damn man misses nothing. 'You seem to have strong opinions on this matter. Care to share your approach with the class?'

All eyes turn to me, and heat floods my face like I've stuck my head in an oven.

Mireen covers a smile beside me. She knows I hate being called on in class. Ambrose just looks jealous as he lowers his raised hand. Beck is picking something out of his teeth, feet kicked up on the chair in front of him.

After a moment of hesitation, I say what I was already thinking in response to his question. 'There's a river to the south. Water primals could use it to create enough fog to get earth and fire primals on top of the enemy before they knew what was coming. Earths could use the cover to raise a wall behind the enemy, then airs could blast away the fog, letting the fires come in with clear view to destroy the enemy in close range.'

Pilton's eyebrows rise slightly, his perpetual scowl easing. 'Utilizing elemental strengths in combination. Not entirely without merit.' From him, the gruff words are quite the compliment.

As attention shifts back to the front, I sense eyes still on me. I glance sideways to find Bastian watching from his seat among the legacies, his nearly white eyes thoughtful. He offers the slightest nod of approval before turning back to the lesson.

Malakai is watching me, too. Despite warnings that we're not supposed to openly kill one another, he hasn't stopped acting like the commander of a small force of elites within the water first-years. He sits surrounded by a small group of eight muscular, intimidating waters.

So far, he hasn't spoken to anyone about Typhon's true form that I know of, but I can feel the threat of his knowledge hanging over me daily. That, and the obvious possibility that he's going to find a moment when I least suspect it to come for me again. Or Raith.

As stupid and irrational as it is, the idea of him or Serena trying to hurt Raith again scares me more than them coming for myself.

'Foolish,' Typhon notes, as if my private thoughts are an open book meant for his commentary.

'Didn't ask,' I bite back.

When class ends, I gather my notes, watching as Beck and Ambrose argue animatedly about which of them was first to sleep with a fellow water affinity named Kali. Beck doesn't believe Ambrose even slept with her, but Ambrose is adamant he had her first.

Mireen rolls her eyes at me as she passes them, motioning that she'll meet me later at dinner.

'Interesting solution,' a voice says at my shoulder.

I turn to find Bastian standing closer than I expected, his tall frame blocking the view of anyone behind us. Up close, he looks tired – fine lines at the corners of his eyes that weren't there before, a slight pallor beneath his tan.

'Just common sense,' I reply, tucking my notes into my bag. 'Use the tools you have.'

'Like the book?' he asks, voice dropping so low I almost miss it.

I freeze. We haven't spoken in what feels like ages, let alone about the book. 'It's been . . . educational.'

His eyes search mine. 'Found what you were looking for?'

'Not entirely.' I glance around to ensure no one is within earshot. 'I never properly thanked you. For the book, and for what you did during Confluence Day.'

He gives a slight nod. 'No thanks needed. We both got what we wanted.'

'And what did you want, exactly?'

Bastian's smile doesn't reach his eyes. 'To help, of course.'

'Why?' I press. 'Why go to such lengths for me?'

He's silent for a long moment. 'What you are . . . dangerous or not, there are people who would value what you can become. And there are people who would see you destroyed before they took the risk of letting you grow. I've seen enough destruction for one lifetime.'

I frown. 'What does that mean?'

His gaze shifts, focusing on something over my shoulder. 'You never did listen about him.'

I don't need to turn to know who he's looking at. 'Raith has been nothing but helpful.'

'Has he?' Bastian's voice cools. 'Almost every year, there are those who slip into Confluence under false pretenses. Those with dangerous intentions. Intentions that could harm Empire.'

'And you think Raith is one of them?'

'I think there's more to him than meets the eye.' He taps my notebook with one finger. 'Just as there's more to you. Be careful who you trust with your secrets, Nessa.'

'Including you?' I challenge.

His smile is almost sad. 'Especially me.'

Before I can respond, he moves past me, rejoining the stream of students leaving the classroom. I watch him go, puzzled by the warning – or was it a confession?

As I turn to leave, I catch sight of Raith standing near the door. As usual, he stands apart by his size and the dangerous aura that seems to cling to him like smoke.

Our eyes meet across the room, and electricity arcs between us, sharp and undeniable as lightning splitting the sky. His gaze drops briefly to my lips, then returns to my eyes with an intensity that sends pure fire coursing through my veins. One side of his mouth lifts in the barest hint of a smile before he tilts his head slightly toward the east wing – a silent confirmation of our training session later.

I give the smallest nod in return, and he's gone, disappearing into the corridor with lethal grace.

I exhale slowly, unsettled by how every fucking time our eyes meet I feel like I'm falling apart. Or is it the complete opposite? That the pieces of me are trying to snap back together when he's around? Whatever this thing is between us, it's getting stronger, harder to ignore.

'Quite the pair of admirers you've collected,' Beck says, appearing at my side with a grin. 'The legacy prince and the scarred warrior. If this were a bard's tale, there'd be a duel by sunset.'

'Don't be ridiculous,' I mutter, shoving him lightly. 'Bastian was just asking about classwork. And I'm pretty sure he's not a prince.'

'Right. And I'm secretly tethered to a dragon instead of a bear.' Beck winks, falling into step beside me as we leave the classroom. 'Come on, admit it. The two hottest guys at Confluence can't keep their eyes off you. And you know there are plenty of other guys who would love to get into your bed, but they're too terrified of those guys to make a move.'

'You're delusional.'

'Am I? Serena looks ready to flay you alive every time Raith so much as glances your way.'

The mention of Serena, as always, sends a spike of annoyance and rage through me. 'If she wants Raith, she has an odd way of showing it. Remember what she tried during Confluence Day?'

'Some women would rather kill a man than see him shared with another. Just ask Brunhild.'

'Who?'

Beck grins. 'This girl I met. She's . . . something,' he says with a wistful smile. 'Speaking of, I'm going to pay her a visit before elemental combat. Wish me luck.'

Beck leaves me at the east wing entrance, heading away with a spring in his step as he dodges a pair of fourth-year earths with hard eyes and absolutely massive muscles. I watch him go, noting how he moves differently now – a new confidence in his stride, strength in the set of his shoulders.

We're all changing, becoming something more than what we were.

'You spend half your day thinking of the fire-touched, angry human,' Typhon rumbles. *'You have much to learn. Sexual penetration will not improve your odds of survival. Training will.'*

I smile. *'Jealousy doesn't suit you, Typhon. And it's training with him I'm thinking about. I learn more sparring with Raith than I do in a week of Weapons class.'*

'I am not jealous of a human,' he sniffs indignantly. *'I simply question the wisdom of spending time alone with one who radiates such dangerous heat.'*

'The heat's not so bad,' I reply, feeling my cheeks warm at the admission.

The truth is, I've been thinking about Raith almost constantly since the night outside Voss's office. The concern in his eyes, the roughness in his voice when he said he trusted me, the lingering heat of his fingers on my wrist – all of it repeats in my mind like a song I can't stop humming. And beneath it all runs a current of curiosity about the person he mentioned, this Gareth who mattered so much to him.

I wonder if Gareth is connected to those nightmares that brought him to the top of the academy walls. To the fire that haunts him.

I've seen fleeting glimpses of Raith in the dining hall and during regular training, but except for that moment in tactics class today, he's been surprisingly scarce.

Reaching the training room door, I pause, drawing in a deep breath to steady my racing heart. It's just training, I tell myself. Nothing more.

We've done this dozens of times already, and Raith is always clinical and serious. He's all business, and that's exactly how this session will go, too. And yet my breath still hitches and warmth floods me as I push open the door and step into the familiar empty training room we've used so many times now.

Torches flicker in iron brackets along the walls, casting long shadows across the stone floor. Raith used a trick of his fire affinity to light these, and they seem to burn for days without needing to be lit, even when he's not in the room.

Training equipment lines the edges of the room – wooden dummies, racks of practice weapons, targets for projectile practice.

But I'm the only one in the room.

Disappointment crashes through me like a wave breaking against rocks. Has Raith decided not to come? Or maybe our agreement for this evening wasn't as clear as I thought. I move to the weapons rack, selecting one of the heavier rapiers Raith likes me to train with to improve my strength. I guess I can still work through some forms, even if he doesn't show.

And I can pretend I don't feel a lurching sense of disappointment.

'You're early.'

I whirl at the sound of Raith's voice, nearly dropping my rapier. He stands in the doorway, leaning against the frame with casual grace that belies the power in his body. In the torchlight, half of his features lie in shadow, making it hard to read his expression.

'Maybe you're just late,' I reply, pleased with how steady my voice sounds despite the sudden swarm of butterflies taking flight in my stomach.

He steps into the room, closing the door behind him.

Closing it between us and everyone else, which is exactly how it feels when I'm alone with him – as if it's only us, even when I know Pyrin is likely hidden nearby and I can sense Typhon's presence.

Raith's eyes never leave mine as he crosses to the weapons rack, selecting his preferred training sword. The fire markings that thread through his scars seem more vivid today, the red lines pulsing slightly like the beating of a heart.

'You've been avoiding me,' I say, the words escaping before I can stop them.

This isn't the kind of thing we usually talk about here. I tend to stay quiet and let him lead. I trust him to keep things professional and clinical. But today . . . Today I'm having trouble holding back.

Raith's brow rises, the unburned side of his mouth curving slightly. 'Have I?'

'Two days. Not even a word about when you'd want to train next.'

'I didn't realize you were keeping count, Saltcrest.' There's something in his voice – a warmth, a hint of amusement – that sends a delicious shiver cascading down my spine. And even if it's a silly nickname, I feel my belly do flips every time he calls me 'Saltcrest.'

I shrug, aiming for nonchalance. 'Just an observation.'

He tests the weight of his training sword, the muscles in his arm shifting beneath tanned skin. 'I've been busy. They had the fire affinities working with some of the upper-years this week. Patrols and inspections of fortifications.'

'Fortifications . . . walls . . . actually, yeah, I can see why you would know a lot about those.'

Raith turns, one eyebrow cocked. He's giving me a look like he's not quite sure I'm actually saying the words he's hearing. 'Meaning?'

'You're good at putting up walls around yourself. I can see why they wanted an expert like you along for inspections.'

He walks with a slow, deadly grace through the darkness between torches, sword held low and steady in his hand. Many of the waters in my year like to perform flourishes and practice trying to look like experts. Raith has never bothered with any of that.

The way he moves and holds that sword might as well be a whispered threat in the ear of any who lay eyes on him.

Danger, says the voice.

Anyone with functioning instincts knows down to their bones that the word hardly captures the reality of it. Raith is lethal. Barely caged violence. And yet . . .

'Walls aren't always meant to defend those inside,' Raith says as he begins to circle me. He's not yet in a fighting stance, but I feel the electric potential – the near certainty that he'll strike soon.

I sink into my knees like he taught me, imagining my feet as both heavy and fluid, ready to sink in and absorb in a block or flow into an attack at a moment's notice. I relax my wrist, letting my rapier rest with a relaxed wrist, parallel to the ground and pointed straight toward Raith, tracking his movements as he continues to circle me.

'So you'd have me believe your walls are protecting me? Is that it? You've caged yourself in because you're so dangerous?'

Without warning, he lunges, his blade a blur as it arcs toward my shoulder. I react on instinct, parrying the strike and using his momentum to slip past his guard, my own blade stopping inches from his ribs.

'Better,' he acknowledges, genuine approval warming his voice. 'You're learning.'

'My teacher is . . . decent.'

I hold his eyes for a moment, waiting for him to pick up the conversation where we left it. But he steps back, his body language making it clear.

Conversation over. It's time to train.

We settle into the familiar rhythm of training – attack, parry, riposte, retreat. With each session, the dance becomes more fluid, my body learning to anticipate his movements, to sense the shift in weight that precedes a strike, to recognize the subtle signs that telegraph his next attack.

But something is different tonight. There's a tension in the air between us that wasn't there before – or perhaps it was, and I'm only now allowing myself to acknowledge it. Raith moves closer than necessary when correcting my form, his fingers lingering when he adjusts my grip, his eyes holding mine a heartbeat longer than they should.

'You've been practicing,' he observes after disarming me for the third time, though it took him twice as long as usual.

I retrieve my rapier, watching him carefully. 'When I can.'

'With your friends?'

'Sometimes. Usually alone.' I settle back into my stance, blade raised. 'Beck, Ambrose, and Mireen stay busy. They're all caught up in relationships. Having fun when they can. Not exactly itching to spend every spare moment training like us.'

Raith's sword lowers slightly, interest flickering in his amber eyes. 'Relationships . . . something you're not spending time on?'

I put a fist on my hip, raising my eyebrows. 'I'm with you or in the library every spare moment I have. When would I squeeze in sex?'

'Good,' he says.

I bite my lip, smirking. 'Good? Why does it matter to you if I'm having sex with people, Raith?'

'Because you're in a great deal of danger. It means you're keeping your priorities straight. It's good.' He raises his sword again. 'Does your little fish have any guesses on what aspect you'll manifest? Stories about unbound always talked about unique powers.'

The question catches me off guard. I only know about the aspect because of the book and Voss. How the hells does Raith know to ask? 'I . . . no. He hasn't said anything.'

'Disappointing. If you're lucky, maybe you'll get a weird crown like him. You two could match.'

The deadpan delivery makes me laugh, the sound echoing in the stone room. Raith's expression softens at the sound, something warmer than amusement flickering in his eyes.

'You know, for someone so terrifying, you can be surprisingly funny sometimes.'

'Don't tell anyone,' he says, mock-serious. 'I have a reputation to maintain.'

'Tell the fire-touched if he mocks me again, I will eat him, starting with his feet. I will chew thoroughly.'

'I'm not telling him that.'

Typhon glares at me, but says no more.

We resume our sparring, but the atmosphere has shifted, the earlier tension giving way to something almost playful. Raith even offers occasional corrections without his usual brusque efficiency, explaining the reasoning behind certain movements, showing me how to use my smaller size to my advantage.

'You're thinking too much,' he says after a particularly complex sequence leaves me winded and frustrated. 'You're trying to match my strength instead of using your speed.'

'Easy for you to say,' I grumble, pushing sweat-dampened hair from my forehead. 'You're built like a wall.'

'Alright. If I'm a wall, then what chance of winning do you have if you try to be a smaller wall?'

My sour look is all the answer he gets.

'You're quick, Nessa. And clever. Use that. Don't smash a wall into a wall. Climb it. Find a way around it.'

I attack again, trying to follow his advice. Instead of meeting his powerful strikes directly, I redirect them, using his momentum against him. For several exchanges, we're evenly matched – until my foot slips on a patch of damp stone, throwing me off balance.

Raith's training sword halts a breath from my throat. In the same instant, my rapier stops just short of his ribs, a lucky reflex that saved me from total defeat.

'Draw?' I suggest, breathing hard.

His eyes drop to my blade, then back to my face. 'Impressive recovery.'

We're standing close – too close, with my back nearly against the wall and his larger frame blocking any escape. I can feel the heat pouring off him in waves, sense the barely restrained power in his body. His eyes hold mine, and it feels like there's something there . . . something more than just a casual training session.

Almost as if I'm not the only one who is battling to keep things clinical.

'Raith,' I begin, not sure what I'm going to say.

He steps back, lowering his sword. 'Again.'

But when we resume, Raith's movements are more aggressive, his strikes coming faster and with more force. It's as if he's suddenly trying to put me through my paces, pushing me harder than ever before.

I match him as best I can, frustration building with each failed attack. He's deliberately keeping me at a distance now, physically and otherwise, and I can't understand what changed.

When he disarms me yet again, my patience snaps. 'What is your problem?'

Raith stares at me, breathing hard, a muscle ticking in his jaw. 'What?'

'One minute you're actually being decent, almost friendly, and the next you're treating me like I'm just another training dummy for you to beat on.' I retrieve my rapier, pointing it at him accusingly. 'So what is it? What changed?'

'Nothing changed.' He turns away, moving to replace his sword on the rack.

'Bullshit.' I step between him and the rack, blocking his path. 'Tell me.'

'Move, Nessa.'

'No.'

His eyes narrow dangerously. 'You're playing with fire.'

'You're more than just a fire, Raith. You're a person. A person I happen to respect and appreciate. So stop acting like you're going to burn me if I get too close.'

The words hang between us, loaded with more meaning than I intended. For a heartbeat, I think he'll simply brush past me, end the session, retreat behind his walls again. Instead, he studies me with those burning eyes, something shifting in his expression.

'The only thing you'll get from me is pain, Nessa. I know you think otherwise, but believe me when I tell you that I'll hurt you. I won't want to. I won't try to, but I can promise you that much.'

'After everything we've been through here . . . you really think I'm afraid of a little pain?'

'You should be.' His breath is a whisper, eyes lowered to my lips, now. I can sense the resistance in his body language starting to fade.

We're standing close again, close enough that I have to tilt my head back to hold his gaze.

'No,' he says suddenly, moving like he's about to walk away from me. 'You don't know what you're asking for.'

I catch his wrist, feeling the familiar surge of power flow between us. 'Raith, wait—'

He turns back so suddenly that I stumble against him, my free hand landing on his chest to steady myself. I feel the rapid beat of his heart beneath my palm, the unnatural heat of his skin even through his sweat-soaked tunic. His eyes drop to my mouth again, and everything else – the training room, the academy, the whole world – seems to fall away.

I don't know which of us moves first. All I know is one moment we're standing there, balanced on the knife's edge of something dangerous, and the next his mouth is on mine.

The kiss is nothing like I imagined – and gods help me, I have imagined it. It's not gentle, not tentative. It's fire and hunger and need, raw and consuming. His hands frame my face, surprisingly gentle despite the fierce press of his lips against mine. I respond with equal fervor, my fingers curling into the fabric of his tunic, pulling him closer.

He tastes like smoke and cinnamon, heat and danger. When he deepens the kiss, a small sound escapes me – half sigh, half moan – and something in him seems to break loose. His arms slide around me, lifting me slightly until I'm pressed fully against him, feeling every hard plane of his body.

Power surges between us, stronger than ever before. I can feel his fire affinity flowing into me, warming me from the inside out. But unlike previous times, it doesn't seem to scare him – if anything, the sensation seems to drive him wilder. His kiss grows more urgent, his hands more possessive.

And then, abruptly, he pulls away.

For a moment, we just stare at each other, both breathing hard. His eyes are dark, pupils blown wide, the amber irises thin rings of gold around black.

'We can't do this,' he says, voice raw.

'We just did.'

His jaw tightens. 'And it was a mistake.'

The words hit like a slap. I step back, putting distance between us, grateful for the wall at my back to keep me upright when my legs feel suddenly unsteady.

'Why? What is it you're not telling me?'

He runs a hand through his hair, frustration evident in every line of his body. 'There are things about me you don't know. Things that would put you in danger.'

'So tell me.'

'I can't.' He shakes his head. 'The less you know, the safer you are.'

'That's not your decision to make.'

'It is when my choices could get you killed.' Raith turns away, pacing the length of the room. 'This – whatever this is between us – it can't happen. Not now. Maybe not ever.'

'Is this about Gareth?' I ask, gentler now. 'About what happened to him?'

He stops, shoulders tensing. For a long moment, he doesn't speak. When he finally turns back to me, his expression is carefully controlled again, but I can see cracks in the mask.

'Partly,' he admits, 'but it's more complicated than that.'

'Then help me understand.'

'I'm here for a reason, Nessa. A purpose. Getting . . . distracted . . . isn't part of the plan.'

'So I'm a distraction?'

'You're a complication.'

I cross my arms, trying to ignore the lingering heat of his kiss. 'And what exactly is this great purpose that I'm complicating?'

Raith sighs, running a hand over his face. 'I don't want to hurt you.'

'Then don't.'

'It's not that simple.'

'It could be.' I take a step toward him. 'Whatever you're hiding, whatever you're here for – I'm stronger than you think. And I'm already involved, whether you like it or not.'

'You think I don't know you're strong, Nessa? You fucking flew in on an ancient water dragon and saved my ass when Serena and Malakai were about to kill me. You're the strongest person I know here. But that doesn't mean I'm going to drag you into my mess.'

'Maybe I can help you. Maybe I want to be able to help you. You shouldn't have to face whatever it is all by yourself, Raith. You have to let someone in.'

Something in my words seems to harden his resolve, wiping any hesitation from his face. 'I did once. And now they're dead. I should go, Nessa.' He moves toward the door, pausing with his hand on the handle.

'Raith—'

'Goodnight, Nessa.'

The door closes behind him with quiet finality, leaving me alone in the suddenly too-large room. I touch my fingers to my lips, still warm from his kiss, and fight the urge to scream in frustration.

'That was . . . unexpected,' Typhon observes, making me feel suddenly awkward. It was so easy to forget he was there, watching and observing everything.

I glare at him. *'Were you watching the whole time?'*

'Of course. Did you think I would leave you alone with him?'

'Maybe I wanted privacy.'

'Clearly,' Typhon sniffs. *'Though I fail to see what you find so appealing about mating with the fire-touched.'*

'We weren't—' I break off, cheeks burning. *'We just kissed.'*

'A prelude to mating.'

'Can you stop saying "mating"?'

'Would you prefer "copulation"? "Reproduction"? "Sexual congress"?'

I grab my practice rapier from where I dropped it and storm toward the door. *'I'm going back to my room now. Feel free to not follow me.'*

'As if I would leave you to wander alone.' Typhon slips into his fish form, wings fluttering as he swims through the air beside me. Despite his many complaints about the form, he has begun shifting into it on his own more often now. Part of me wonders if he secretly likes being

so small for a change. *'The fire-touched is hiding something significant, angry human. I sense conflict in him – divided loyalties, perhaps.'*

I slow my pace, curiosity overriding my irritation. *'What do you mean?'*

'His pain runs deeper than those scars. Something drives him beyond simple survival or ambition. Something that frightens him more than death.'

'You got all that from watching us train?'

'I gathered it from watching him look at you.' Typhon's fish-eye swivels to regard me. *'He fears for you more than himself. An unusual trait in humans, I've observed.'*

'So he's protecting me. But from what?'

'That,' Typhon says, *'is the interesting question.'*

We exit the eastern wing into the main courtyard, where evening has already settled. Stars glitter above the towers, and a fresh blanket of snow has fallen. The courtyard is mostly empty at this hour, with only a few students hurrying to their final classes or back to their dormitories, arms clutched tight against the snow, except for a pair of fires who walk with the air shimmering around them like personal heaters.

Lucky them.

I spot Serena across the open space, standing with several other fires. Her gaze finds mine, and the hatred in her eyes is so pure, so undiluted, it pins me in place like a butterfly to a board.

Beside her stands Malakai, his ruined eye covered with a black patch, his remaining one fixed on me with calculating intensity.

I expect them to approach, to threaten or taunt me as they've done before. Instead, Serena simply smiles – a slow, vicious curving of her perfect lips – before turning away, drawing Malakai with her.

'They plot against you,' Typhon observes unnecessarily.

'Tell me something I don't know.'

'I could eat them both. It would solve many problems.'

I shake my head, continuing across the courtyard. *'As tempting as that sounds, I don't think consuming students would exactly help us stay under the radar.'*

'You humans and your tedious moral considerations.'

My mind drifts back to Raith, to the kiss, to the walls he keeps rebuilding between us. Whatever secret he's keeping, it's clearly eating him alive.

I touch my lips again, remembering the heat of his mouth on mine, the desperate hunger in his kiss. For a moment, everything was perfect – for one brief, shining instant, there were no secrets between us, no barriers. Just pure connection, raw and real.

And then he pulled away.

Whatever Raith is hiding, whatever danger he thinks he's protecting me from, I'm going to find out. Because now that I know what it feels like to be close to him, I'm not sure I can go back to keeping my distance.

Even if it burns me in the end.

Chapter 19

Rector Voss paces his office with hands clasped behind his back as he watches me. He has four devices that remind me of the vessels used during the elemental trial. Each, he says, holds a great deal of elemental energy I should be able to draw from.

I pull water and fire at the same time as he instructed, try to sort of 'twist' them together, and then I watch with satisfaction as steam hisses up from my fingertip. The power swirls within me, hot and cold battling for dominance until I force them to coexist like sworn enemies forced into a lover's dance.

Voss smiles in a way instructors here rarely do. It's open approval.

The feeling is addictive, especially when I spent the last three years before coming to Confluence learning that absolutely nothing I ever did could win back the approval of my mother and sister.

The thought brings a fresh torrent of sadness to my mind I know could drown me if I let it. I hesitate a moment, then lift my eyes to Voss in a break between exercises. 'Three years ago, I think I called a storm.' I'm not sure why I'm admitting it, except that he might be one of the few people who could help me better understand what happened.

He pauses his pacing, then turns to face me, nodding. 'Ah, yes. The four affinities often experience signs before they're marked. Stories say unbound experienced far stronger events. Was this storm the first trace of power you felt before coming to Confluence?'

'No,' I admit. I think back on a childhood full of unexplainable, odd moments that I tried my best to keep hidden.

Fires flaring. Sudden gusts of wind. Rumblings beneath the earth. And, of course, the storms . . .

When I could, I explained it all away, even to myself. Outside Confluence Academy, power and hints of magic were dangerous. Even a whisper of someone with power could mean masked Empire soldiers arriving at your door after dark. People with powers went missing, just like the offerings taken every year.

As far as any of us knew, they were all being taken for execution.

Now I know they were probably just brought here. And I suppose the truth wasn't so different from what we believed. How many of those taken would have actually survived? Nearly two thousand students between offerings, aspirants, and legacies arrived on the first day. By the time students reach fifth year, the class size apparently has shrunk to less than a hundred. The losses are mind-numbing.

'I imagine this storm came with a great deal of emotion. Yes?' Voss's eyes hold mine, keen with interest.

I nod my head. 'We were all arguing. There was a festival that day. A stupid, silly thing, but it was a chance to dress up, dance, and just be normal for a change. To forget for a moment that I was going to grow old on fishing boats pulling nets. That morning, my father said we would be back in time for me to go. But the fishing was too good that day to pass up. He said we needed to stay as long as the nets were coming up full. And . . . I got mad.'

Voss presses his lips together in sympathy. 'And then the storm came?'

'And then it came . . . I was the only one who lived. It's why I volunteered to come here. My sister and mother apparently suspected I had powers all along. They blamed me for keeping it a secret. Called me selfish. Said if I just admitted I was a freak, Empire would've taken me away before I could've got them killed. Nothing I ever did fixed it, either. So that third year, I volunteered.' My words catch in my throat.

'Brave,' Voss says softly.

'No . . . I did it because I was a coward. I couldn't bear the idea of facing them one more day. I always saw the same thing in their faces. They thought I was a monster. Then I came here and found out I really am. Unbound. If people knew, they'd look at me just like my mother and sister did. Like a monster.' The words pour out of me. They've been building ever since I finished the unbound book for the first time.

'Only because they don't grasp what you can become.'

'Isn't that the problem? Unbound can do so much harm. It's too much power for any one person. So they're right to see me as a monster.'

'No, Nessa. This world of ours is . . . flawed.' Voss's voice softens, taking on a quality I've never heard in it before. 'Great individuals with the power to make change are exactly what we need. People like you. Unbound.'

All I can do is shake my head. 'I just want to survive this school. I want to help my friends survive. And maybe if I do that, I want to go back to Saltcrest and see if there's a way to use my influence and position to help my mother and sister. Maybe it won't mean earning their forgiveness, but I can at least try to ease their burdens.'

'I understand, Nessa. You still don't grasp what you are. What you will become. So you're still thinking small. But that's fine. There will be time, yet.' His lips curve into a smile I can't quite read.

'Rector Voss?' I ask, fingertip idly running across the smooth surface of the clear sphere filled with swirling air. 'Could you do anything to make sure more of us survive? Tighten the restrictions? Add Empire guards to patrol the halls? Remind students we're not supposed to kill one another anymore? Anything?' I add, hating how small my voice sounds. 'It's just that I sense something building here. Another storm.'

His smile is sad. 'Whether you realize it or not, Empire guards are already not powerful enough to stop even you first-years. It would take ten or more ordinary men to bring one of you down. And primals capable of controlling you are too busy being deployed in the war effort. No, Nessa, I'm afraid you're all quite dangerous. Too dangerous to truly control. And even if I could, these methods have been proven over many many centuries. The primals who graduate after their fifth year are sharpened blades. Absolutely deadly and nearly perfect weapons. Empire knows this, and they won't change the way we run things for fear of weakening their strongest tools.'

Weapons. Tools. Deadly. None of those words are things I want to become, but what choice do I have?

'There's really nothing you can do?'

'I'm doing what I can. Right here,' he says, gesturing to the vessels and then to me. 'With the proper training, you'll be more than capable of protecting yourself and the ones you care about, Nessa. And whether you see it yet or not, you'll eventually be powerful enough to change things, if you wish. All things.'

I frown at the odd tone in his words, but his quick smile convinces me I'm just being paranoid. And protecting the people I care about . . . That's at least something I actually want. Something that matters.

'Oh, Nessa, there's something I wanted to tell you . . .' Rector Voss says, moving to sit and lean on his desk as he watches me continue to practice pulling multiple elements at once. 'You've perhaps heard mention of the Crucible – your final test for the first year, if you will. But you won't have heard any details about what this test entails. That will change in a few days when your instructors will be told to share.'

I swallow hard. *Another fucking test.*

Voss offers a sympathetic pursing of his lips. 'I can give you a bit of forward warning, Nessa. It's not much, but it might help. This year, you'll be sent outside the castle walls with groups no larger than five per team. I can't share the details until the moment before the Crucible begins, but I can tell you that the winning team will all earn promotion to legacy status. I don't think I need to tell you a prize like that will likely create fierce, bloody competition.'

My breath catches. Promoted to legacy status? Other than Bastian, the legacies might as well be untouchable to us. They seem to exist in their own, privileged bubble on campus with the best perks and the best training. It's already an open secret that they're being groomed for positions of leadership after Confluence, even among the primals. They'll be the generals. The commanders and captains.

The idea of being promoted to their ranks . . . it's enough that even regular students without Malakai's bloodthirsty streak would be driven to do just about anything.

'I'm afraid the legacies will be competing in the Crucible as well,' Voss continues. 'Most years, they win. They're often given a task in opposition to yours, but it varies. There's one final thing your instructors may not share.' He pauses, elegant fingers folded as he regards me. 'Every year, we lose quite a few students during the Crucible. Empire sees it as a way of making sure the primals who survive have what it takes to come out of a war-like situation alive.'

'I thought becoming aspirants meant the academy didn't want our lives being thrown away?' A bitter taste like ash fills my mouth. More deaths. More conflict.

'And that's true. We don't want senseless murders in the halls. Pointless training accidents. But you should see the real truth of it, Nessa. We don't want these things because they eventually only reveal the bullies and the ruthless. A superior soldier can be killed when his guard is down by an inferior one. Now that we've culled the weakest, your lives will only be risked in ways that select for better soldiers. The Crucible is exactly that. It's a war game, and there will be deaths, but these deaths will serve a purpose. They will sharpen you. Hone you.'

I lower my eyes, unsure what the hell I'm even supposed to say to that.

'They treat you like blades, not humans,' Typhon growls.

'Then they had better hope one of those blades never decides to turn on its master.'

'Angry human . . .' Typhon says, but I sense a note of pride in his tone.

Rector Voss saves me with a quick clap of his hands and a smile. 'In any case. I've kept you here too long. Please,' he gestures toward the door, helping me pull my chair out as I stand. 'As before, I would ask that you still keep what we do here between us. For your safety, of course. But feel free to warn your friends about the Crucible.

The legacies will already know it's coming, but it may be a helpful advantage for your fellow aspirants to know a few days before the announcement. You'll have some time to gather your team in peace.'

'Thank you,' I say as I leave his office and step into the narrow hallway that leads back to the stairs.

As soon as the door closes, Raith seems to unfold from the shadows at the far end of the corridor. I notice the hard angles of his face and the tension in his jaw, the careful way his eyes scan me as if checking for injuries.

'You came,' I whisper.

Raith waits for me to approach before he speaks. I find myself noticing how his breath slightly quickens when I move closer.

'Surprised?' His voice rumbles low in his chest.

'After last night . . . I guess I thought—'

'That was a mistake,' Raith says quickly.

I give a jerky nod of my head, even as a stab of pain punches through my chest at his words like a blade between my ribs, sharp and precise. 'Yeah. I know.'

'Good.'

We head down the stairs single file with Raith in front because the stairs aren't wide enough for us to walk side by side. At the bottom, a few students pass in either direction, but nobody pays me much attention. Raith, on the other hand, is already known as the most deadly first-year aspirant across all affinities. Girls look at him with open lust. Guys look at him with envy and respect.

At best, they look at me with anger, because rumors about his 'interest' in me have been spreading since the first week on campus. Some look to laugh because my elemental is a flying fish. Others occasionally ask me about the events at Mirror Lake, but those rumors are mostly old news, now, replaced with more recent events.

'Nessa . . .'

I wet my lips, heart suddenly racing just to hear my name from his mouth like a spell that only he knows how to cast. I feel like I'm leaning into him, drawn toward his warmth. Toward his heat. For a heartbeat, Raith's eyes drop to my lips, and the corridor seems to narrow until there's nothing but us. Then footsteps echo as another pair of students approaches. Raith steps back abruptly, expression shuttering closed.

'I told you it would be dangerous to know . . . certain things about me,' Raith says. 'But there is something I can tell you. Something that might be more dangerous to keep a secret.'

I try to hide the disappointment I feel as I lean back, dragging my eyes up from his mouth. Right. Truths and secrets. These things are more important than talking about the kiss.

The fucking kiss that feels like it tipped my entire world sideways.

No big deal.

'Humans,' Typhon mutters in my mind.

'Okay.' I tell myself I shouldn't be watching the way his hands move as he speaks, shouldn't be remembering the sensation of his fingers against my skin. But my body doesn't seem to care what I should or shouldn't do.

'Do you remember that night on the castle walls? You had a nightmare. We heard instructors talking about deaths. They mentioned siphons.'

'Rings a bell . . .' I say, as if I haven't thought about every single encounter with Raith on near repeat like a favorite song I can't stop coming back to.

'Siphons are real.'

Words from the unbound book float into my memory unbidden: *'Many common pieces of folklore and stories told to small children can be traced back to unbound and their unique manifestations. Old tales of vampires, for instance, are believed to be an unbound who could feed on blood for strength. Some say stories of siphons can be traced back to Lorkan Grace and his wife Milena.'*

'How would you know that?' I whisper. Even seeing mentions of siphons in the book and hearing the instructors whisper about them hadn't quite convinced me. Somehow, the words coming from Raith finally make it hit home with an uncomfortable chill like a breeze carrying the stench of graves and rot on an otherwise clear and sunny day.

Siphons.

They're the things of children's tales. Stories to scare kids who try to sneak out of their house at night. Shapeshifting beasts who could suck their soul out through their ears, twisting it up and slurping it down like strands of spaghetti.

Surely the truth is less . . . that.

'Did you already know about this?' I ask Typhon.

'I know many things. Things you need not concern yourself with as you focus on your studies here in school. If relevant, I shall share them when the time is right.'

I decide that is a conversation I'll dig into with my prickly water dragon later, letting it drop for now.

Raith has been hesitating. Before he speaks, I can tell he's not going to tell me how he knows about Siphons. 'Look . . . I just need you to know they're real. Okay? And most importantly, I need you to know there's at least one of them on campus right now. It's likely posing as a student or a member of the faculty. And it has already started killing. So I want you to make sure Typhon is always ready to protect you.'

Typhon lets out a low, audible growl I know only I can hear. Right now he's pacing in circles around Raith, his long, serpentine body dragging as he forms a ring around us. He's either not showing himself to Raith, or Raith is doing an inhuman job of not looking frightened.

'I think Typhon is ready to protect me at all times, whether I tell him to be or not.'

'Good,' Raith says. He seems to relax slightly, broad muscular shoulders slumping slightly as if he's letting out a great deal of tension. 'Good,' he says again more softly.

'I'd ask how you're so sure, but I already know you won't tell me. So can you at least teach me how to spot one of these siphons?'

'They'll look and sound like normal people. In most ways, they are. But they're almost like . . . anti-primals. They can't channel their own magic, but they can feed on it. And their appetite is bottomless. A siphon can drain people and elementals down to nothing. You won't know you're looking at one until it's too late.'

The only time I've ever seen Raith come close to looking scared was that first day when I made fire grow from my fingertips. But there's fear in his eyes as he talks about siphons. A deeper, more animal fear than anything I've seen on his face before.

It makes my blood run cold.

'What do they want?'

He shakes his head. 'I don't know. They strike against both Empire and Red Kingdom. Whoever or whatever they're loyal to, it doesn't seem to follow political lines. But whatever it is they want, it leaves corpses in its wake. If the instructors were talking about bodies and siphons, it means they found a drained body. The affinity mark on the body would be burned out. Anyone who knew what they were looking for would know for certain. That means they're here, Nessa. So promise me you'll be careful.'

'Why are you only telling me now?'

His expression hardens. 'Because I had to do some digging to confirm it. And . . . now I'm sure. There's one here at Confluence. So fucking promise you'll be careful.'

'I will. But if these things are striking Empire and Red Kingdom, why doesn't everybody know they're real? I grew up thinking they were just children's stories.'

'Better to let people think they're just fanciful things. Then those in power don't have to admit there's an enemy they can't control. An enemy they can't stop. Sometimes, the best way to maintain power is to create an illusion that it's untouchable. They're not. And the siphons are very real. So be careful, and trust no one.'

'What if I trust you?'

He licks his lips, eyes falling for a moment. 'Then I've failed at keeping as much distance as I should.'

He looks like he's about to turn to leave, so I reach instinctively and touch his arm. That familiar tendril of flame flows from him and into my fingertips, swirling inside me like a pleasant summer breeze.

'Raith . . . there's something Voss told me. We're all going to have to participate in some kind of Crucible. Like a final test before we graduate the year.'

He says nothing, but something in his expression makes me think he already knows. Once again, it's another layer of mystery. Another secret.

Everything about him screams danger, yet somehow that only makes the pull toward him stronger like a moth to flame, knowing it will burn but unable to resist the light.

'You knew?' I ask.

His eyes fall. 'The Crucible is a poorly kept secret in some circles. But yes. Groups of five. That means you, Mireen, Beck, and Ambrose will probably talk about recruiting a fifth. But don't do it.'

'Why, because of the siphon? Don't you think that's a little paranoid? If this siphon has been on campus all year, they could've killed me a dozen times over by now.'

'We can't pretend to understand why they're here. Unless we know the "why", we can't assume you're safe from them.'

I tilt my head. 'All of this . . . following me around campus and lurking in the shadows. Helping me train weapons . . . Telling me about the siphon . . . is it all just because of what happened on Confluence Day? Am I really supposed to believe that?'

If eyes are windows to the soul, Raith's are blacked out and covered by thick curtains. He blinks, then grips my arm softly. 'I would tell you more if I knew it wouldn't put you in danger. I mean that,' Raith says, his tone hard. 'Malakai will come for your team during the Crucible. You can be sure of that.' He speaks like it's a simple warning, but I can feel the concern beneath it.

And then he's gone, fading into the dark shadows of the corridor ahead and leaving me with the warmth of his power still swirling inside my body like embers nestled beneath my skin. That, and about a thousand questions.

Raith speaks with absolute certainty about things no former offering should know. Each revelation only deepens the questions of who he really is – and why he's chosen to share these secrets with me.

I should be terrified of all the things he won't tell me.

Instead, as I watch his shadow disappear around the corner, I realize something that scares me far more than siphons or the coming Crucible.

I'm falling for him. I'm falling for someone who is desperately trying to tell me not to – to warn me that he's dangerous. I can try to grip tightly to those warnings like handholds, clinging to them like lifelines. But I'm still slipping toward the edge and toward the point of no return little by little.

Gods help me. Every instinct I have is telling me not to. Even Raith himself seems to be telling me not to. But I'm still falling for Raith fucking Hollow.

Chapter 20

Titus circles me with a huge two-handed sword held at the ready. Like all our training weapons, it's blunted, but given that it's at least three pounds of steel, I doubt it matters. Titus is one of Malakai's elites, and I'm sure he would be willing to suffer any punishment for 'accidentally' killing or maiming me.

Surviving Confluence Day earned us some protections, but the threat of death only dropped to a low, haunting whisper instead of a deafening scream. It never really leaves, and with the Crucible coming, everybody feels it more now. It's the warm, rancid breath of a predator breathing down our necks.

This is basic weapons training, and we're not supposed to channel. I still keep my mind on high alert, just in case Titus decides to cheat. If he does, I'll be ready.

For now, I keep circling him on the raised stone platform, rapier pointed at his throat. Raith taught me to watch the feet and the hips of my opponent, so that's where my eyes stay.

Titus coils slightly on his back leg and my instincts tingle with warning before my brain can even process what's happening. I'm already shifting to my side, ducking the overhead strike that's about to come.

His sword whistles past me, clattering against stone hard enough to fire off sparks.

I move to step inside his guard and press my blade to his throat, but he savagely yanks his elbow backward, smashing into my temple and sending me toppling sideways.

The blow makes sparks fly across my vision and my head spin. An immediate, sharp throbbing erupts in my head.

Shit.

He's fast. We all are now, but he's also twice my size.

I roll, dodging another strike, then another. I barely get back to my feet, breaths coming in raw gasps already. I'm starting to become numb to danger, but I can feel a sudden jab of terror leaking up through my walls like ice water flooding into a sinking ship.

Come on, Nessa.

Distantly, I can sense others finishing their matches and gathering to watch us. Most weapons fights are over quickly. The other affinities are finishing up, too, along with Raith, who was first to win his match and is already on his way toward us. Even with Raith coming, I force myself to refocus on Titus. Distraction now could be fatal.

'Come on, Nessa,' Beck calls. 'Go for his balls. Small targets, I know, but you can—'

Beck's voice fades to background noise as I barely lean back, dodging the tip of Titus' sword before it can split my face horizontally.

Gods. He's definitely going for the kill.

'Allow me to bite him,' Typhon suggests, and there's a slight note of urgency in his tone. *'I could leave him alive and only remove a few pieces of his meat sack.'*

'No biting. But if he kills me, I give you permission to kill him back.'

I feel a pang of reluctance and irritation through the tether, but also acceptance.

I dodge two more strikes, try to get in range to land a blow with my rapier, and earn a vicious kick to my stomach that sends me crumpling to the ground.

I clench tight as waves of sudden nausea roll through my body twisting my insides like a wet rag being wrung out.

Okay. New plan.

I reach into the water saturating the air, drawing scraps of power into my body. Yes, I'm going to cheat, but only a little. And only in a way that nobody will notice.

Sweat runs down Titus' scalp, so I reach out and direct as much of it as I can into his eyes as I get back to my feet, weapon drawn.

He flinches, blinking through the stinging salt and nearly dropping his guard to wipe his eyes.

I don't wait.

I'm already dashing toward him, spinning as he tries to strike, and then I'm behind Titus. My blade is pressed to the side of his neck. 'Yield,' I say, breath still coming in hard gasps.

Titus tenses, and I think he's about to push his luck and fight on. But finally, he relaxes. 'I yield.'

My victory earns a few secret smiles from Beck, Ambrose, and Mireen, but nobody else visibly reacts. Well, unless I can count the way Raith is looking at Titus as a reaction. It almost looks like Raith is thinking about dismembering Titus limb by limb. The orange on his mark flares suddenly, pulsing quickly. I've learned from our training sessions that it pulses when his emotions are running high.

The other first-year fires, including those who were offerings before Confluence Day, gather around Raith and drag his attention away with something that looks relatively urgent. They're all speaking quickly to him as he listens, nodding his head. Serena is the only notable absence.

Word spread about what she tried on Confluence Day, and now she's more or less exiled to spend time with Malakai and the other waters who follow him. Nobody else wants anything to do with her.

But other than Raith and my friends, nobody dares to show a reaction to the outcome of our match. The official announcement of the Crucible completely erased any of the relaxed tension of the past few months. Surviving Confluence Day is in the past, now, and surviving the Crucible is on everyone's minds. Worse, many already seem driven to do whatever it may take to win. Even if it means murder.

In just a few weeks, we'll all divide into groups of five and fight for a chance to earn legacy status for our team. And, of course, we'll be isolated outside castle walls where it seems like anything will go.

People are going to die, and we all know it.

As I step down from the platform, I notice an odd tingling in my hands. I feel a blend of elements suddenly bend toward me like metal shavings to a magnet.

The ache in my stomach from where Titus kicked me turns warm, then the pain eases slightly. Power flares. Before I can even stop to wonder what's happening, the sensation is gone.

'Hmm,' Typhon rumbles. '*What was that, angry human?*'

'*I was hoping you could tell me.*'

I lower a hand to my stomach and touch it, finding the skin is still tender, but maybe less than before?

My friends approach me once I'm off the sparring ring.

Ambrose is covered in sweat and sporting a raised welt along his cheek, like he caught a blade there. 'Gods, Nessa. From here, it looked like he was going for killing blows.'

'He was,' I say, still distracted by whatever that sudden power was.

Mireen is sweaty but seems uninjured, her red hair still intact in a tight and intricate braid that keeps it close to her scalp. 'You'd think they would want us learning to work together.' There's an edge to her tone – the same edge I've learned always comes when she's talking about Empire and Red Kingdom. 'Instead they keep structuring this place so we're at each other's throats. What good does that do any of us?'

'Well,' Beck says as we all head toward the showers. 'Pilton makes it seem like primals tend to fight in small groups on the outside. It's not like we're going to be deployed together as a large group at any point. Maybe it makes more sense for us to form strong loyalties with just a few.'

'Don't defend them,' Mireen snaps. 'Titus could've killed Nessa back there.'

'He was certainly trying. I guess the announcement of the Crucible means attempted murder is back on the menu.'

'Nah. Titus couldn't have killed you,' Beck says. 'I had Uther standing up there, hidden from sight. If I thought she was in trouble, I would've had him rip Titus' arms off and beat him over the head with them.'

'Like Nessa needs the help of your bear,' Ambrose says. 'In case you've forgotten. She's got a—'

'Flying fish,' I cut in with a meaningful smile.

'Right,' Ambrose says. 'That.'

'Speaking of the Crucible,' Mireen says, lowering her voice as we pass a group of legacies on our way to the showers. 'I heard it's going to be in the wilderness beyond the academy walls. They'll drop us somewhere in the forest, and we'll have to navigate to a specific point while other teams try to stop us.'

'And find a relic,' Beck adds. 'That's what one of the third-years told me. We have to find a specific relic and bring it back, all while surviving other teams and whatever nasty surprises they've hidden out there.'

'Great,' I mutter. Though I know from Voss's advice that whatever the third-years say will happen can't be fully trusted. They change the Crucible each year to keep us on our toes. 'Sounds like a fun weekend trip.'

We split off after weapons training, get showered, dressed in fresh uniforms, and then I sit with my friends in Military Tactics, struggling to focus the whole time and not simply stare at Raith's back, puzzling over what's going on in his mind.

My lips still tingle with the memory of our kiss, followed by his immediate withdrawal. Ever since that kiss, he has been impossible to reach. We trained once together, but he kept it completely professional again. When I did try to talk about what happened, he changed the subject.

I keep replaying his warnings about siphons, about the danger lurking on campus. As much as I try to push it away, part of me wonders if Raith himself could be the danger he's warning me about. The thought makes my stomach lurch with a knotted ball of emotions like thorny vines.

What if Raith *is* the siphon? It wouldn't be impossible. He did volunteer to come here. He does know things he shouldn't. And he seems adamant that I need to keep my distance from him to stay safe.

'*Shall I eat him?*' Typhon asks.

Without anywhere good to sit, Typhon is curled up on the stage near professor Pilton. His head lifts at his question, deep blue eyes glinting as his thoughts reach me easily from across the room.

'*How about we agree that if I ever actually want you to eat someone, I'll ask? You don't need to keep asking if I want you to eat people.*'

'*Hmm,*' Typhon grumbles. '*And if the option of me consuming your foes doesn't occur to you? Am I permitted to remind you of the option?*'

I grin to myself. '*Yes. Sure.*'

Pilton is deep in argument with two legacies over an interpretation of a historical battle. Pilton thinks the primals in the story were reckless, and the two legacies are trying to argue they had no choice.

Mireen leans over, voice low. 'So who can we trust for our fifth? For the Crucible?'

I shake my head as Raith's words come back to me. He told me not to trust anyone.

And yet his reasons feel like they're far too ridiculous to say aloud. I can't tell Mireen we can't add a fifth because they might secretly be the siphon hiding on campus. But if Raith was the siphon, he wouldn't have been so worried about us trusting a fifth. Unless he's not the only siphon . . .

Ugh. It's a confusing mess and I wish the damn man would just give me a straight answer for once.

'I'm not sure,' I whisper back. 'Maybe we're better off just keeping four? We know we can trust each other, and we work really well as a team.'

She narrows her eyes, making the crescent scar on her cheek crinkle. 'Yeah, but going into the Crucible down a person seems like a bad move, right? Especially if Malakai's team targets us. We'll need every advantage we can get.'

'I know a few girls,' Beck says, leaning forward so I can see him past Mireen. 'What are we prioritizing? Body or face? Because if we need both a good face and body, the list is a little smaller, but I could still come up with a couple options.'

'Beck, just shut up,' Mireen says, shaking her head and smiling slightly.

'There's Lysander,' Ambrose suggests, nodding his head to a serious water affinity with black hair parted down the middle. 'He's not with Malakai.'

'Yeah,' Beck says. 'Because he's with nobody. Because he's creepy.'

'Don't be mean,' I say, even though deep down, I find it hard to completely disagree. Lysander has always kept to himself. While that means he's likely not one of Malakai's people, it also makes it hard to trust him.

'Tamarin?' Mireen suggests. 'If nothing else, she has good judgment.'

'How do you figure that?' Beck asks.

'Because she hasn't ever slept with you.'

Beck places a hand over his heart in mock outrage. 'How dare you.'

We're all smiling when a piece of chalk flies across the room and bounces off Ambrose's forehead.

'Are we boring you, Ambrose?' Pilton asks.

Ambrose claps both hands over his head, wincing. 'Why the hells is it always me?'

'I'm starving,' Beck says half an hour later once we're let out of class. The other aspirants with black uniforms and silver piping are filing out as we linger. 'I hope they have that honey butter again in the dining hall.'

'I think you may have eaten the entire year's supply last night,' Ambrose says.

'You joining us?' Mireen asks me.

'Um, not yet. I wanted to squeeze in a little studying,' I say.

My excuse earns skeptical looks from all three friends.

'Studying. Right,' Beck says. 'You know, if I wasn't so offended that you are obviously hiding a ravenous sex life with Raith, Bastian, or both from us, I'd almost be impressed. You really do sneak around well.'

Red colors my cheeks. 'It's nothing like that,' I protest, though the memory of Raith's lips on mine sends a completely different message through my body. Except that I think it really may be nothing for Raith. I'm the only fool who can't seem to stop making more of it than I should.

'I think it's Bastian,' Ambrose says matter-of-factly. 'The mysterious, handsome legacy who occasionally finds excuses to be around Nessa at just the right time? And if I was a woman—'

'Thank gods you're not,' Beck mutters.

'I would choose Bastian,' Ambrose continues.

'Agreed,' Mireen says. 'And that's speaking as an actual woman. I know you trust Raith, Nessa, but I don't. There's something off about him. And I still haven't forgotten he's a volunteer from so close to the border. I know his family is dead, but there's a chance they were all Red Kingdom before—'

'Mireen,' I say sharply.

She lowers her eyes. 'Sorry. I'm just worried about you. I know you two spend time alone together. In . . . some capacity. What if he tries to hurt you? What if he's not being honest about his loyalties?'

'Then I'm pretty sure I'd be dead already. You guys don't have to trust him, but I do. Okay? So if you trust me, can you at least just believe in me enough to stop worrying?'

Ambrose shrugs. 'She does have a flying fish following her around. I don't think even Raith Hollow stands a chance if he pisses that thing off. Maybe Nessa's right. We shouldn't be worried about her.'

'But she hasn't said which one she's fucking,' Beck says. 'Can you at least tell us that much? Is it Raith? Or is it really both?'

I put my hands on my hips. 'I'm not sleeping with either of them. Bastian has helped me a time or two, but we've hardly even talked much. I know almost nothing about him.'

'Ah,' Ambrose nods wisely. 'But you have talked to Raith a lot? Pillow talk, perhaps?'

'All of you. Go!' I say, one side of my mouth curving in amusement. 'Terrible detectives. Every last one of you.'

'So she says,' Beck jokes as he throws his arms around Mireen and Ambrose, leading them down the hall toward the dining room.

Almost as soon as they're gone, a girl steps in front of me, eyes orange and blazing.

Serena.

For a split second, I consider shouting for them to come back, but Typhon walks behind Serena, looming at nearly three times her size so he barely fits in the corridor. I may not want to reveal his real form, but I at least know he's here, ready to protect me.

'Nessa,' Serena says. She wears her raven black hair in two long braids with the rest falling free to spill around her shoulders. It's a show of confidence. Loose hair is a liability in combat, and she's not-so-subtly projecting her confidence.

'What do you want?' I ask.

'To warn you.'

I frown. 'Not necessary. I already know you and Malakai are ruthless assholes. Let me guess . . . you'll all be coming for us during the Crucible? Already figured that out myself. Titus tried to take my head off in weapons training today.'

'No. I heard your friends. You should listen to them. Raith has you fooled, just like everybody else. Why did you think I risked everything to go after him on Confluence Day?'

'Because you're jealous of him?'

'Because he's not what he says he is. Hollow isn't his real last name. At least it wasn't.'

The words hit me with unexpected force like a physical blow to the chest. I try to keep my expression neutral, but my mind races. Not his real name? What else has he lied about?

'Would this be an appropriate moment to remind you that I am willing to eat this girl if you wish?' Typhon asks.

'I might actually give you permission to eat this one. So keep on your toes.'

'Mmm . . . Very good,' he rumbles.

'This is sad, even for you,' I say, trying to sound dismissive while my thoughts spin with possibilities. 'You couldn't backstab us on Confluence Day, so now you're trying to spread rumors and lies to get back at him?'

Her cat-like eyes tighten. 'Ignore my warnings if you like, Nessa. But Raith is dangerous. I don't know exactly who he was before he came here, but I've seen enough to know he isn't loyal to Empire. He's a traitor, and he's gathering all the fires to his cause. Someone has to put a stop to it. We're prepared to offer you and your group protection during the Crucible if you help us take him down.'

That is a surprise. I open my mouth to laugh, but I'm too stunned to speak at first.

'You really think we'd help you?'

'It's your choice.'

'I'm not a bloodthirsty killer. So, no. I'm never going to be part of Malakai's little group.'

'Is that what you think we are doing?' She tilts her head, and her full lips curve into a smile. 'We're sons and daughters of soldiers. All of us. Soldiers of Empire. We've been weeding out anyone we suspect could be Red Kingdom sympathizers. You do know who Malakai's father was, right?'

'Why would I know that?'

She taps her lower lip with a manicured nail. I notice tendrils from her fire mark have curled in elegant, flame-like lines up her long finger. 'He was a commander in Empire's army. Entire unit wiped out when a supposed Empire Earth primal collapsed a ravine on them. Thousands dead. All because Confluence Academy failed to discover someone's true loyalties before graduating them and putting them in position to cripple our forces. We can't count on the academy to do the work for us. We need to get our hands dirty for the good of Empire.'

I fold my arms. 'Right. So you're sanctimonious murderers? Got it.'

'Your elemental, Nessa . . .' Her eyes flicker momentarily to where Typhon hovers invisibly to her. 'It's strong enough to make a real difference. With you on our side, we could really make change. We could go after full primals who we suspect. Nothing could stop us.'

A chill runs down my center and settles like a block of ice in my gut. Nothing could stop them? From what, exactly, I wonder. Murdering everybody who shows even a hint of individuality or fails to completely bow to Empire?

'I'm not joining you. I have no interest in pretending to be judge, jury, and executioner. How many innocent students have you all already killed? How many times have you been wrong?'

'Does it matter? One primal slipping through to graduation could kill thousands of innocents. If we have to kill hundreds to stop that, it's worth the risk. Isn't it?'

'No,' I say.

'Do you know why I really wanted to kill you that first day?'

'I'm guessing you're going to tell me?'

'Because you volunteered. The statistics aren't hard to find, Nessa. Over the decades, volunteers are the most likely to be traitors. Why do you think Raith even pays attention to you? He's hoping you're like him. Turncloak. Traitor. Scum.'

'So you've wanted me dead since the first day and I'm still alive? Empire may want to look for some better servants if you're the best it has, then.'

Her nostrils flare as she eyes me. I can feel the potential of violence in the air. There's a subtle heat gathering behind me, too, and I wonder if her elemental snake is coiling around me, preparing to reveal itself and strike.

'They'll be dead before a hair on your body gets touched,' Typhon warns.

'Don't get it confused, Nessa,' Serena says. 'I still don't trust your intentions. But I saw the elemental you tethered, even if I don't understand why an insignificant weakling like you would be granted such a beast . . . I'm only making you this offer because of your elemental.'

'Fuck you. That's my choice.' I give her a sickly sweet smile, and then bump her shoulder as I move to pass her.

'Wait,' Serena says.

I pause, but don't turn to look at her.

'Remember something, Nessa. As an ally, you could be incredibly valuable to us. As an enemy? You're dangerous. And you might threaten everything we're trying to do. So choose wisely. We won't wait forever.'

I look around and see it's only the two of us in the hall now.

'Typhon, show yourself so she gets the message.'

'With pleasure.'

Typhon, who is at least twenty feet high from paw to shoulder, stands to his full height, wings spread and teeth bared as he leans into Serena's face. To my eyes, nothing changes, but Serena suddenly flinches back, screams, and tries to push herself away until her back bumps hard into the wall.

Her snake appears, but it looks insignificant next to Typhon.

'Just in case you forgot,' I say. 'So keep that in mind if you get ideas about fucking with me or my friends. That includes Raith.'

Typhon transforms suddenly into his flying fish form and gives her a small slap on the cheek with his tail.

The little pop sound is almost comical.

Serena flinches back like she has been stabbed and her elemental snake hisses, fires flaring across its coiled body.

Apparently satisfied, Typhon drifts toward me and hovers over my shoulder.

'What was that?' I ask him, barely holding back a smile from the look on Serena's face as we leave her behind.

'You never let me eat people, so I improvised. If I can't eat them, I will settle for humiliation.'

Even if it feels good to put Serena in Her place, I know the victory is only temporary. Malakai and his people aren't the type to be scared off so easily. They'll still come for us, maybe even harder, now. We'll be lucky if there aren't several groups hunting us during the Crucible.

But my thoughts return to everything Serena said as I cross the courtyard, giving a group of third-year fires a wide berth as they sit comfortably in a cocoon of warmth that melts the falling snow and keeps them warm despite the winter chill.

Raith not being who he claims to be. Malakai and Serena with what could be considered a noble cause, even if their methods are monstrous. And somewhere on campus, a siphon hunts, perhaps for me specifically.

The Crucible suddenly feels like the least of my worries.

As I round the corner, I nearly collide with a tall figure in a black robe.

'Nessa,' Bastian says, surprise clear in his voice. He looks left and right, then jerks his head for me to follow him to a small, more private alcove off the main hall.

'What is it?' I ask.

'I shouldn't be telling you this . . . but my father and some of the Council are coming to watch this year's Crucible.'

A cold fist of fear reaches for my insides and squeezes. Empire officials watching the Crucible means . . .

Bastian nods, as if seeing I've already figured it out. 'Your powers. You need to be discreet. Even there. If any of them suspect what you are, I don't think even the academy could protect you.'

'Why do you keep helping me?' I blurt suddenly. 'Does your father know about me?'

Bastian's regal features show no sign of emotion or surprise at the questions. 'No. He doesn't. But I read enough to suspect one of your kind would appear again. So far, I believe you're worthy of the power you hold.'

So far?

Again, it's as if Bastian reads my thoughts. 'Whether I like it or not, Nessa, I have an obligation to Empire. If I thought you couldn't be trusted any longer with your power, I'd end you myself.'

'He could try,' Typhon growls, shifting instantly from his fish form back to the massive dragon.

I decide not to acknowledge the threat as a question occurs to me. 'How will they watch us during the Crucible? Won't we be in the wilderness?'

'There are forms of air magic. With enough power, vision can be carried long distances and bent at will. Just know there will be eyes on you, Nessa.'

'Okay. So if you decide I'm a threat, you'll kill me yourself. But until then, I had better be careful so your father and his friends don't? Am I missing any important details here?' The sarcastic bite is clear in my tone.

Bastian lets out a slow breath, then rakes a hand through his blonde hair. It's a rare moment of vulnerability from a man who hardly ever shows anything but complete control. The glowing white cloud and wind markings on his left arm glow bright enough to show through his black sleeve. 'I'm doing my best here, Nessa. This isn't the sort of thing I was trained for, if you can imagine that.'

I give him a slight smile. 'Sorry. Maybe they can add a pesky unbound awareness section for the next generation of legacies, then.'

He licks his lips, glances up and down the hall, then lowers his voice more. 'Look . . . even the Council isn't without ambition. If you survive the Crucible, you'll have a chance to make allies. Make strong allies, Nessa. It's your best chance of surviving. Help them see you can be trusted with this power, and they may start to view you as a potential weapon to wield instead of a weed to destroy.'

I fold my arms. 'Ever since coming here, all I ever hear about is how deadly we can become. How great a tool we can be for somebody else to wield. What if I don't want to be somebody's tool?'

His eyes darken. 'Then you would be walking a very dangerous path. An unbound without loyalty is an existential threat. Not just to humanity, but to elementals. You want my advice? Learn your place. Embrace it. Because if you refuse to be wielded, they'll just break you instead.'

He looks like he's about to say more, but a trio of girls approaches. 'Remember,' he says quietly. 'There will be eyes on you during the Crucible.'

And with that, Bastian disappears down the hallway.

I hug my arms to myself, suddenly cold and feeling more alone than ever.

Chapter 21

'That's not good enough,' Raith says. His face is plastered with sweat, handsome features twisted with frustration. 'You know they're all coming for you during the Crucible, right? You've got to do better, Nessa.'

I let my rapier fall by my side. It's late, and only starlight shines through the abandoned training room window. I mop sweat from my own forehead. My arms feel like they're made of lead, and my lungs burn with each breath. 'Oh. Right. Now that you've reminded me my life is on the line, maybe I'll just magically be better. That's a great suggestion.'

He has been pushing me even harder than usual all night, and my temper is admittedly running thin.

I've heard humans often press their meat sacks together in mating rituals to relieve tension. I could close an eye, if you wished.

'An eye? Don't you mean both eyes?'

I won't let your enemies sneak up on you just because you've shed your clothing and put your disgusting, fleshy body on display.

Raith raises his one-handed sword, then flicks it toward my legs. 'Stance wider, Nessa. You know better.'

Clenching my jaw, I widen my stance and raise the rapier. Sometimes, having Typhon interjecting in my head makes me feel a little like I'm going mad. But I put his prodding from my mind and focus on Raith.

Even when we're just training, Raith requires my full attention. He's the most skilled opponent I've faced by far. Every time I get better, he seems to ratchet up his own skill, proving he's still holding back against me.

'*Mating rituals are nothing to be ashamed of,*' Typhon continues, despite my attempts to block him out. '*Though the elemental mating ritual is far more beautiful than the human ritual. I've seen what you humans do. My last primal was quite fond of the ritual, and she would perform it most nights. Disgusting. She sometimes even performed a solo variant that was quite pathetic to witness.*'

'Typhon? Would you please shut up?'

'*Insolent, small, insignificant—*'

I tune out his indignant words as Raith advances.

He performs a series of attacks like a whirlwind of death. I dodge what I can and block only as a last resort. Each block requires me to grip the tip of my rapier and the handle together. I have to brace my whole body against the attack, and the vibration sends a shock through my arms that makes them go numb and tingly.

It's like trying to stop a horse charging at full speed with nothing but a narrow sliver of steel. Each blow makes me think the rapier is going to snap in half, but by some miracle, it holds.

Part of me wants to ask him to take it easy. To ask why tonight of all nights, it seems like he has ramped his usual intensity up several dozen notches. But I don't say anything. I keep on training.

It's nearly an hour before he finally makes a loose gesture with his sword. 'Take a rest. If you need one.'

'I'm good,' I say, though my gasping breaths betray me. My arms are dead weights hanging from my torso. My toes, hamstrings, and calves are aching from being in a fighting stance for so long.

Raith studies me. His eyes rake over me, assessing every weakness. 'You're still too small. The things I'm teaching you may help you survive a duel. One on one when you can focus on one opponent. But what the hells are you going to do when it's more than one opponent? When they're all bigger and stronger than you?'

'So we're listing deficiencies? Is it my turn, then? Because you're an asshole when you're mad. And you are about as transparent as a fucking brick, so I have no idea why you're pissed and taking it out on me.'

His jaw ticks several times before he responds. 'I'm trying to keep you from winding up dead.'

'And the only way to do that is to insult me and beat me senseless all night?'

'I'm training you. Preparing you.' His voice roughens with intensity. 'I won't always be around, Nessa. What happens if your enemies come for you when I'm not able to help?'

'I was thinking I'd ask my giant water dragon to join the fight in that case,' I say, even though Bastian's words from the other day ring clearly in my mind.

'There will be eyes on you.'

Revealing Typhon won't necessarily reveal I'm unbound, so it'll still be an option in case of emergency. But he's an ancient.

'That is correct. Ancient. Powerful. Feared and revered.'

'Don't go throwing yourself a party yet, Typhon. Ancients like you are all supposed to be mad. If people connect the dots, they're going to wonder why you're not entirely crazy.'

'Entirely crazy? I'm not crazy at all.'

'Debatable,' I reply with a small grin to myself. 'But even if they don't realize you're actually an ancient, they'll figure out you're powerful. And I imagine those people from Empire will feel the same way Serena did – that my tether to you makes me a valuable weapon they'll want to manipulate. And gods, Typhon . . . I'm tired as hell of people trying to use me.'

'Then continue your training with the fire-touched. Become strong. Make yourself worthy of my tether.'

Raith is watching me with arms crossed. Ever since we tethered elementals, it's not entirely uncommon to see someone's eyes get a distant look. Usually, it means they're locked in conversation with their elemental.

'How do you two fight together?' Raith asks. 'You and Typhon.'

'What do you mean?'

He lifts the bottom of his shirt to wipe his face, giving me a glimpse of rows and rows of stomach muscles. So many that my breath catches and I forget for a moment what we were even talking about.

'I don't see why those lumps of muscle make your heart rate rise so much, angry human. They are like dragon scales, but worse and less functional in every way. Why do they only cover the stomach? What protective purpose do they serve?'

I decide to ignore Typhon. He's talkative tonight, which I've learned is something that happens when he's worried about me. He can talk a big talk, but sensing his emotions through the tether in addition to his words makes it hard for him to hide his true motivations. He's worried about me. Just like Raith is. And he rambles when he's worried. Raith apparently turns into a cold asshole.

'An ancient does not worry. We prepare. I am simply preparing a battle plan to dismember your enemies and perhaps snack on their corpses if time permits.'

I send a quick pulse of gratitude through the tether.

Raith is staring at me. 'Hasn't he been training with you? What the hells is he thinking?'

I can tell from the way Raith's eyes move over my shoulder and then go up, up, and still more up that Typhon just revealed himself. He doesn't like when people question him. And he does like getting to show people his dragon form, even though there's only a handful he's allowed to show.

I can feel the cool moisture of his water magic behind me as he looms closer to Raith, teeth bared.

'Tell him I do not need a partner in combat. I am more than a match for any human or elemental. I am ancient. I am Typhon.'

'Typhon doesn't seem to think we need to train together. He's . . . pretty confident in himself. We also can only train with him in his flying fish form in class. So it's not like we aren't practicing at all.'

'That was not the message I told you to convey, angry human.'

Raith shakes his head. 'No. That's not good enough. You two need to learn to fight together. That's half of being a primal. You should be practicing fighting from his back.' His voice grows more intense with each word. 'Hells, I saw him fly on Confluence Day. Have you two at least been practicing flight? Can he still fly in our world, or was that only when he was larger?'

'Did he just call me small?' Typhon takes a step forward, his teeth bared as mist rolls from his mouth in waves that quickly chill the room.

Raith's fire panther, Pyrin, appears behind him. He's growing faster than most elementals, and he already stands taller than Raith, with his shoulders just above Raith's head. His fiery body is growing more solid, too – less like a shifting cluster of flames that takes the shape of an animal. I still don't think he'd stand a chance against Typhon, but it would be less of a mismatch than I'd expected.

'False. I could eat him in two bites. However, I happen to like Pyrin's company. He and I like to joke about our foolish humans together. I would prefer not to eat Pyrin.'

'We're not eating either of them.'

'I know. I would do the eating. You would do the watching.'

'Typhon . . .'

With resignation, he takes a small step back. Raith never flinched, but Pyrin seems to relax slightly as Typhon backs off.

'You need to find time to practice with him in his dragon form,' Raith says.

I glance at Typhon. Despite all his large and scary dragony features, I see an almost comical shifting of his eyes from Raith to me.

'You would demean me with practice exercises?' Typhon rumbles through my mind.

'You want to keep me from dying, don't you?'

Resignation thunders through the tether as Typhon sulks to the corner of the room and sits with straight-backed posture so he looks like an indignant statue.

If only. Statues don't constantly shove their opinions in your mind.

'Careful, angry human.'

'Typhon might be willing to do some training exercises with me.'

Raith looks past me to the dragon, then nods. 'Good.'

There's a moment as Raith checks the edge of his sword. The blunted weapons won't cut, but after enough blocks and parries, they can gain chips in their edges that can cause some serious damage. He's always making sure his sword doesn't have any before he'll fight me.

For all his deadly intensity, he's always strangely careful about that sort of thing with me.

'There's something I wanted to ask you,' I say suddenly. I wasn't sure if I'd get the nerve to ask him to his face, but now I can tell I won't be able to keep this in. It's not my way. 'Serena cornered me after Military Tactics the other day. She said Hollow isn't your real last name, and . . . I know that. Everyone does. Hollow is a name given to orphans, so why would she tell me it's not your real name? She said it like your original last name was some sort of secret. Something that would reveal who you really are?'

The mention of Serena's threat makes him lift his eyes to me. They're like golden torches partially obscured by the dangling threads of his hair. 'I wasn't always a Hollow. Yes. But like you say, it's hardly a revelation. When my family was murdered, my name changed.'

There's a cold matter-of-fact quality to his words that makes my chest tighten painfully. 'Murdered?'

He hesitates. 'Most people who die where I'm from are murdered. War is hell.'

'Right,' I say.

He hides something. Press him for answers. Put your blade to his throat and demand them.

'We're not doing that, Typhon. But yes. Raith is always hiding things. He doesn't even deny it.'

'When was your last meal?' he asks suddenly. 'I know you've been skipping them. You've got to keep your strength up, Nessa.'

He's changing the subject. It's what he always does when the topic drifts too close to the truth. 'Raith . . . You know everything about me. You know . . . what I am. You know about Typhon.' My heart rate quickens as I force myself to continue. 'I mean, gods, we kissed, Raith. Even if you're trying very hard to pretend it never happened. It did. And do you really think I'd do that if I was planning to betray you?'

His eyes are hard. 'You don't know who I am.'

'So fucking tell me!' I don't mean to shout, but my voice echoes in the small room.

'I'm someone you shouldn't get close to. Somebody you shouldn't care about. That's all you need to know.'

'Except it's not. I need to know why you're helping me. Why you care about me. Every fucking person in this academy makes me feel like I'm going mad. They bend over backwards to save my life but nobody will give me a straight answer about *why*. I need more than half-answers, Raith. I need the full truth for once.'

'Then you're going to be disappointed, Nessa.' His voice strains with barely-contained emotion. 'I'll keep training you. I'll help you survive the Crucible, and when you're eventually strong enough to watch your own back, we can pretend we never met.'

'But that's not what I want, Raith. Don't you get that?'

A touch of something finally seems to ignite behind his hard eyes. 'Nessa . . . you don't know what you're dealing with.'

'Then. Tell. Me.'

'I can't.' He hangs his head, shakes it, then looks back up at me. I can see pain in his eyes. Despite all his hard edges, I realize it's actually hurting him to keep these secrets. He wants to tell me, but he really thinks he can't. 'It's not that I don't trust you. Okay? Can you at least take that for now and be content? I do trust you. With my fucking life. And even if it makes me a fool, I can't stand the thought of something happening to you. If telling you the truth about me means there's a chance of you getting hurt, then I'm not doing it. Even if you hate me for it.'

'Raith . . .'

He straightens, and I can see a shift in his expression. Topic closed. Conversation over.

'During the Crucible,' he says, as if we'd been talking about it all along. 'I'll do my best to keep an eye on you and your group. I know Serena and Malakai will have at least a few groups coming after you.'

I think about forcing the topic back to his secrets, but I saw the pain in his eyes. Maybe it makes me a fool, but I believe him. I don't think he's keeping secrets to hurt me. I think it's the opposite. Even if it frustrates me to no end, I can at least respect that. For now.

'You'll keep an eye on us? Won't that stop you from having a chance at winning?'

'Fuck the legacies. I don't want their privilege. I have no interest in winning.'

I raise an eyebrow. 'I heard they get comfier beds, though.'

'Comfy beds. Lighter class schedules. Favoritism from Empire.' His lip curls slightly. 'Yes, they get it all. And the only cost is being a dog on someone's fucking leash. I'll pass.'

'That, at least, is something we can both agree on.'

'I want you to try to win the Crucible.'

I squint at him. 'You just said fuck the privileges of being a legacy.'

'For me. Malakai wouldn't be able to touch you if you were a legacy. Not even he would dare.' Raith's voice drops lower, more intense. 'They won't admit it aloud, but Confluence protects legacies like they're royalty. Nobody here wants their primal parents and grandparents showing up asking why their child was killed. Honorary legacy or not, you'd be safe if you were one of them.'

I fold my arms. 'So I'm just some fragile princess you want to protect? Put me in the gilded tower where all the privileges and connections in the world can keep me safe?'

My comment earns a rare smile from Raith. 'Fragile princess? Fuck, no. You're deadly, Nessa. You've proven that several times over. But you don't realize what you're up against. This is bigger than Confluence. It's bigger than Malakai and Serena. Becoming a legacy would dramatically improve your chances of surviving to graduate your fifth year.'

'Will a siphon care if I'm a legacy or not before it tries to drain me?'

Something dark passes over his eyes. 'No. But the training we're doing. That might help you against one of them.'

'Typhon could handle one, right?'

'Honestly? I'm not sure. Siphons are extremely powerful. They can summon a kind of void elemental. Its bite can be deadly to elementals, just like a siphon's touch can drain the life of a human. If you find yourself against a siphon, all I want you to think about is running. Do whatever you can to get away.'

'And what will you do if you find one?' I hate that part of me is watching and listening to his reaction so closely – that some part of me is actually wondering if Raith is a siphon himself. Even if it feels like a stretch, it would at least explain why he's so adamant that I can't know the truth about him.

'I'll fucking kill it.'

The pure venom and hatred in his voice almost convinces me there's no way he's a siphon. That, and his tether with Pyrin. I can't say for certain, but I've never heard of siphons being able to tether elementals in any old stories.

'I've got to get back to the fire tower,' Raith says suddenly. 'I'm trying to train them up as much as I can before the Crucible.'

'Why do they all treat you like some kind of leader? Even the original aspirants seem to look up to you.'

He shrugs. 'I'm good in a fight. They recognize they can learn from me. It's just survival instincts.'

'Then what's in it for you?'

'Maybe I'm not the monster you like to assume. Maybe I just want to help them.'

I put a fist on my hip as he heads for the door. 'I never said you were a monster. I don't think—'

He turns, half a smile on his mouth. 'I know. You've never looked at me like I'm a monster. It's . . . one of a few things I like about you.'

And then he's gone, leaving me alone in the training room, blushing like a complete fool.

'I shall follow the fire-touched. If he reveals he is a siphon, I will destroy him. This is a sound plan.'

'I need you with me, Typhon. What if somebody looks at me wrong? Who will threaten to eat them?'

'Hmmm . . . Perhaps you speak truth.'

'Was what he said about siphons true? They can summon void elementals?'

'This is not what we would call them. But in a sense, yes.'

'You didn't think this would be helpful to tell me sooner?'

'My knowledge runs more deeply than a well. If I allowed you to jump into those depths, you would surely drown.'

'On knowledge?' I hope he can hear the dry annoyance in my response. Conveying emotion into thought conversations is a skill I'm trying to learn.

'If I believe my knowledge will aid in your survival, I will share it, as I've already said. If I believe it is a distraction, I will withhold it.'

I pause, waiting for him to share something. When nothing comes, I turn to face him as he lies calmly in the corner of the room. 'Well? Do you have any knowledge that will aid my survival?'

'Yes.'

'Which is?' I prompt, biting back annoyance even though I'm sure he feels it through the tether.

'The fire-touched is correct. If you see siphons, you should run. And I trust him. My suggestion would still be to perform the mating ritual. Humans are highly emotional creatures. Letting him enter you would improve his dedication to keeping you safe. This would be a sound strategic decision.'

'I hereby ban you from speaking about mating rituals or me being entered, Typhon.'

'The angry human thinks she has the power to ban me from sharing my wisdom. This amuses me greatly.'

He's not kidding. A strong pang of amusement passes through the tether. Despite my annoyance with him, I can't help shaking my head and smiling.

'I'm going to my room. To sleep. Maybe you need to go find an elemental to mate so you can get your mind out of the gutters.'

I am a skilled mate, and performing the ritual with another elemental would require several days. When you are less likely to get yourself killed in my absence, I may do exactly that. For now, I must remain watchful and vigilant.

I know I don't have to tell him I'm glad he's here. He'll feel it through the tether.

I'm especially grateful as I walk through the chilly halls on my way back to the water tower. Every time I learn more about siphons, I feel more terrified by the idea that one of them is lurking on campus, searching for something.

But what the hell is it they're looking for?

Chapter 22

'Um . . . Beck? What exactly is this?'

Beck smiles wide as he gestures to a group of five first-year waters he has paraded into the common room. It's late, but our promotion to aspirant privileges means we have a light day of classes on weekends, so we're all less exhausted than usual. At least most of us are. Some seem to be using the extra time to sleep with everyone they can.

The fear that every day could be our last has a lot of students acting without reserve. Who is sleeping with whom doesn't even qualify as an interesting rumor at this point. If anything, my lack of sexual activity is more rumor worthy than someone bedding a different partner every night.

I eye Beck and his small parade of pretty girls. A prickle of foreboding crawls up my spine – whatever he's doing, I'm sure it's going to be stupid.

'Agreed,' Typhon says. *'His elemental, Uther, also lacks deep intelligence. And he's rather promiscuous, from what I hear.'*

'Elementals gossip about sex, too?'

'We do not gossip. We simply exchange facts, suspicions, and bits of news.'

'So you gossip.'

Typhon blows out a puff of steam from his nostrils and turns his head slightly from me, his reptilian pride clearly wounded. *'In any case. It seems the yellow-haired human is displaying his mating conquests. Impressive. I can deduce he has a preference for large milk glands in sexual partners. Curious. Would those not prove a hindrance in combat?'*

'These,' Beck says, sweeping his arm with a flourish, 'are my suggestions for our fifth Crucible member. Each woman here was carefully vetted.'

One of the girls – a redhead with a curvy figure and, as Typhon noted, large 'milk glands,' cocks her head. 'You said you had a surprise for me.'

'Right, Misti!' Beck says, moving to touch both her arms and bend down to her height. 'You've got a one in five chance of being added to our group. That's the surprise.'

'But who are these other girls?' she asks, pointing at the others, who all look equally confused. 'You told me you didn't talk to Havi anymore.'

'Excuse me?' Havi asks. She's a dark-skinned girl with upturned eyes and cat-like features. 'You said Misti was "old news."'

'Old news?' Misti asks, stepping out of line to face off with Havi. A dagger of water forms in her hand and the temperature in the room drops like a stone. 'You want to see old news? Because I can show you—'

'Ladies, ladies,' Beck says, stepping between them. 'We can all be friends here. But . . . only one of you can be our fifth. So who is it going to be?'

'In a way, it's almost impressive,' Mireen says out of the side of her mouth. We're both sitting on the safety of a comfortable couch as we watch the tensions rise among Beck's girls. 'How does someone so dumb manage to string along so many people?'

'Hold on,' a black-haired girl named Poltrice cuts in. 'Are you still sleeping with all these whores, too?'

'Hah,' Brunhild says. She's taller than all the other girls by at least a head and nearly Beck's size with broad shoulders and muscular arms. 'She admits she is whore. This is funny.'

'What did you say?' Misti says, raising her water dagger, her eyes flashing dangerously.

'Real man sleeps with who he likes. Just like real woman does. Weak woman calls names.' Brunhild spreads her wide arms. 'We should fight for him.'

I raise my eyebrows and look to Ambrose. He has a small handful of nuts he smuggled from the dining room and he's snacking on them eagerly, eyes wide as he watches the unfolding chaos.

'We don't need to fight,' Beck says. 'I was hoping we'd just—'

But all hells break loose.

Misti gets disarmed and pinned to the ground by Poltrice, who is tackled by Brunhild.

There's some hair pulling, a lot of shouting, a little bit of unsanctioned channeling, and then the elementals appear.

I pull my feet up to keep my distance from the melee as water elementals clash amid the wrestling and screaming girls. Despite the tensions, nobody is going for fatal attacks, thankfully. It looks more like a training session on overdrive.

Somehow, it's all over in less than a minute. Beck is slapped no less than four times as disheveled and pissed girls storm out of the room.

Once the dust has settled, Brunhild is the last one standing and she wears a satisfied grin.

Beck clears his throat and brushes some dust from his uniform. 'Well,' he says. 'That's basically how I planned for things to go. More or less. Winner, Brunhild!'

'This was good plan,' Brunhild notes, arms folded as she nods with satisfaction.

'Meet Brunhild,' Beck says, gesturing with both hands. 'Her elemental was that giant crab doing the hair pulling. The crab is called Dora.'

Mireen eyes me. 'Is he serious?'

'I think he has no idea how ridiculous he is,' Ambrose adds. 'It's both his greatest strength and greatest weakness.'

'I thought we agreed to stick with four,' I say carefully. 'No offense, Brunhild.'

'Offense taken,' she says seriously. Her blue eyes regard me coldly, sending an involuntary shiver down my spine.

'If she kills you, can I let some of my rats crash in your former room?' Mireen asks. 'Mine is getting kind of crowded.'

I squint. 'How many rats have you adopted, exactly?'

'Not important,' Mireen sits back, hands folded as she whistles innocently.

Beck puts an arm around Brunhild's shoulder. He's big enough that even she looks small beside him, but she's nearly a head taller than me and looks like she could snap me in half. 'Don't mind Nessa. She's just a little paranoid. Thinks everybody wants to kill us. But that's only because a lot of people here have tried to kill her. You could argue it even makes sense, from her point of view.'

'She makes offense. That's what she makes,' Brunhild says.

'Okay, I'm just going to say it,' Mireen says. 'Brunhild already looks like she wants to smash Nessa into little pieces. I don't know if that's the best quality in a fifth member of our group.'

'Or,' Beck says, eyebrows high. 'Hear me out . . . the fact that she's not trying to hide wanting to crush Nessa a little bit is exactly why we can trust her. If she was with Malakai, she'd be sneakier than that, right? She'd be playing nice right now and trying to weasel her way onto our team. Then during the Crucible, she'd spring her trap.'

'I hate to say this,' Ambrose says. 'But that actually does make some sense.'

'Maybe we make group of four,' Brunhild says, her deep voice heavily accented, though I can't place where it's from. I wonder if it's from somewhere distant, maybe even off the main continent. 'We take the small one with big ass, drop her out window, and then we find stronger replacement?'

'Big ass?' I blurt. The only thing keeping me from laughing is the fear that Brunhild might actually try to throw me out a window.

'She's not wrong,' Mireen says with a shrug.

'Uh,' Beck says. 'I love the enthusiasm and creative problem solving Brunhild, that's one of my favorite things about you. But Nessa stays. We like her.'

'Hm,' Brunhild says, blue eyes assessing me. 'If sexy bear likes her, then Brunhild will like her. It is settled.'

Ambrose sputters with laughter. I look his way, biting back my own smile as I see him mouth the words 'sexy bear'?

'Alright, sexy bear,' Mireen says, barely keeping a straight face. 'Why don't you take Brunhild back to where you found her for now. We'll keep her in mind as a potential fifth.'

Beck gives a thumbs up and leads Brunhild out of the common room. Before they're out of view, Brunhild takes a generous handful of Beck's left butt-cheek.

Classy.

'Are we sure we can trust Beck's intelligence?' Ambrose asks once he's gone. 'I'm starting to worry he's getting dumber by the day.'

'The scarier question is how he's convincing all these girls to sleep with him,' Mireen says. 'He's not *that* cute.'

'So, what do we think about the scary blonde girl?' Ambrose asks. He pulls his rounded glasses from his face and gives them a wipe on his black aspirant uniform. 'I actually am leaning toward trusting her. And we saw she can handle herself in a fight. Akaron didn't sense anything off about her, either.'

'I still think five is better than four,' Mireen says. 'Brunhild seems loyal to Beck, at least. I think we can trust her.'

'And what happens when Beck moves on and sleeps with a few other girls before the Crucible? Can we trust Brunhild not to go on a violent rampage and rip us all limb from limb?'

'Hmm,' Ambrose says. 'We just need to get Beck to promise to keep his dick in his pants. Or at least only release it for Brunhild.'

I chuckle. 'Yeah. Good luck with that.'

'Good luck with what?' Beck asks as he returns to the room.

'We can't use her as a fifth,' I say. 'The moment you get bored and sleep with another girl, she'll turn on us.'

'Brunhild is very open-minded about that sort of thing. On our way out, she asked how you were in bed, Nessa. I think she has come around on you. Honestly, I think she's planning to make a move on you. Or maybe she wants me to make a move on you? I wasn't sure which it was.'

Mireen nudges me. 'You could be Brunhild's big-assed girl toy on the side.'

'First of all, my ass isn't that big.'

Beck pulls a face.

'What?'

'I mean . . . it's impressive. I'll leave it there.'

Ambrose looks like he's trying very hard to stay out of the conversation.

'Believe it or not,' I say, annoyance touching my voice. 'I'm a lot more worried about surviving the Crucible than what you and Brunhild think about my body, Beck. So I need to know if you think we can actually trust her not to try to get us killed.'

'Brunhild could have killed me already if she wanted. I let her tie my hands to the bedpost all the time. I'm completely defenseless. Naked. A little scared. Very aroused. But—'

'That's plenty of input, Beck,' I say, holding up a hand to stop him before he mentally scars me. 'Thanks.'

Beck shrugs. 'I'll just say this. She's got the strongest grip I've ever seen. And not just in her hands.'

'Ugh,' Mireen says, holding up both hands. 'Didn't ask, Beck.'

'I'd rather know I can trust everyone in our group,' I say. 'Even if she's strong.'

'Very strong. Full body,' Beck adds.

'Even if she's strong,' I repeat, trying to pretend I didn't hear him. 'She's a question mark. I'm not sure it's worth the risk.'

'Does this have something to do with Voss?' Mireen asks slowly.

'I don't know,' I say. Whenever they ask about my meetings with Voss, I feel a sudden and almost uncontrollable need to change the subject. My skin prickles with anxiety. The entire focus of my relationship with Voss revolves around being unbound – around the secret I'm still keeping from my closest friends. 'I just know Raith said he'll look out for us. He's not interested in winning to earn a spot as a legacy, so he's going to just keep an eye out for us.'

'Wait, what?' Ambrose leans forward, eyebrows high. 'Who

wouldn't want to be a legacy? You know there's an entire section of the library they only give legacies access to?'

'He had . . . strong words about legacies. Just trust me. He's not interested in winning. So with Raith and his group protecting us and Typhon, I don't really see why we need a fifth.'

'And you think nobody in Raith's group will actually want to be legacies?' Beck asks. 'They'll just agree to follow him for babysitter duty?'

'You've seen them. They're all loyal to him. Except Serena.'

'What if she's had enough time to change some of their minds since Confluence Day?' Ambrose asks. 'She's a terrible person, but I have to admit I can imagine her . . . charming her way into a few hearts.'

Beck nods. 'Serena is fucking hot. He's right. I could imagine a hypothetical situation where getting into her pants could convince me to do some stupid things.'

'Beck . . .' Mireen warns.

'Hypothetical. I said hypothetical.'

I chew my nail. I honestly hadn't thought about Serena winning over allies. A sudden itch to talk to Raith and try to warn him rises up in me. My pulse doubles at the thought of something happening to him.

'What about Bastian?' Ambrose asks. 'Is he going to look out for us during the Crucible, too? He's got nothing to win, so that would at least make more sense since I know he wants to get in your pants.'

'I've tried to tell you guys a thousand times,' I sigh.

'Just like you've told us there's nothing between you and Raith?' Mireen asks, wiggling her eyebrows. 'And yet you guys are constantly sneaking off together?'

'It's not constantly. I've told you he just helps me train.'

'Convenient,' Beck says, leaning against the wall and folding his muscular arms over his chest. 'They disappear to train. An activity that leaves people looking a lot like they just vigorously fucked.'

'Nessa has been getting good with that rapier really fast,' Ambrose notes. 'If he's not actually training her, how do you explain that?'

'Easy,' Beck says. 'Raith lets her practice with his "rapier" every night. Two hands. One hand. *No hands.*'

Mireen covers her mouth so I don't see her smile, but I whack her on the arm anyway.

'You're all ridiculous. Except Ambrose. Thank you, Ambrose.'

'Just to be clear, I still think you guys are having sex,' Ambrose says. 'I just also think you're finding time to train. And I definitely think something's going on with you and Bastian, too.'

'Wow,' I say, shaking my head. 'I've only spoken to Bastian a handful of times since we got here. I hardly even know him.' It feels mostly true, at least. His gift of the unbound book and his knowledge about what I am seems like a level of intimacy that adds weight to our few meetings.

But at least the essence of what I'm saying feels true: I don't think Bastian has any particular feelings for me. If anything, he's just another person who is trying to decide how he can best use my abilities. The only difference is I have no idea what use he thinks he can have for me. All I know is they don't involve me being dead, which lets me trust him to an extent.

'You have to admit,' Mireen says. 'It's suspicious that both men just happen to be around you so often. Not that you don't have a great personality, but . . .'

'I've got to go,' I say, standing suddenly. I'm still thinking about Raith. About Ambrose's point. If Raith doesn't know Serena could be raising allies, he might be in far more danger than he realizes. My chest tightens at the thought.

'Nessa,' Mireen says. 'We're just kidding around. The Crucible is looming over all of us like an executioner's blade. Talking about dumb stuff like this makes things feel a little more normal. It's nice to at least act like we're not fighting for our lives once in a while.'

I shake my head. 'It's okay. I get it. I'm not upset, I just . . . need to talk to someone.'

Beck and Ambrose share a look. Beck loops his thumb and

forefinger into a circle and slides his other index finger into the circle meaningfully while mouthing the word 'talk.'

Ignoring him, I rush to leave the aspirant's section of the water's common room and head down the spiral staircase.

'Ahhh,' Typhon says. *'I now understand what the circle and finger gesture means. It's a depiction of sexual activity. They believe you're going to look for the fire-touched to mate.'*

'Raith doesn't want me like that, Typhon. I just want to make sure he has thought about the possibility of Serena secretly gathering allies.' Even as I say the words, I feel the flutter in my belly that seems to accompany thoughts of Raith these days.

'And yet I feel the truth through the tether, angry human. You know he has likely thought of this. You just crave his . . . scent?'

'Is there a way to just . . . shut the door on you for a little?'

'I would still be able to sense you through doors and communicate with you. I am Typhon. Ancient, immensely powerful, and blessed with the form of a water dragon. I could simply break the door.'

With a sigh, I try not to focus on his continued rambling in my mind as I head for the fire tower. I've never gone there before, but I figure it's where I'll find Raith.

There are no strict rules about entering the towers of other affinities. In fact, I know plenty of students sleep around between affinities, even if the fires and earths are slightly more taboo partners for waters and airs. For some, that seems to be half the fun.

Even if there's no rule against it, I find myself hesitating at the entrance of the fire tower. I tell myself I'm being silly, then push through the wide double doors at the base of the structure. Considering the outside of the fire tower is bathed in constant, swirling flames and smoke, I assumed it would be unbearably hot inside. Instead, it's only pleasant and warm. The walls glow a soft yellow-red, providing plenty of light as I climb a spiraling staircase that's similar to the one in the water tower.

I reach the first landing, which would have been where the offerings were housed if the layout was the same as the water tower. I pass it, heading higher up the tower toward where the aspirant rooms should be.

I find a long hallway lined with the same glowing yellow-red bricks. There's a pair of girls with orange eyes and glowing fire marks a little ways down the hall. Both wear uniforms marking them as first-years, which seems like a good thing. The upper-years often act like we don't exist, so I doubt any of them would be able to tell me where to find Raith.

'Um, hi,' I say, stopping a few steps away from the girls.

Their eyes fall immediately to my affinity mark, then lift to my eyes. I see recognition there.

'You're Nessa,' one says. 'The one who nearly got eaten by a rogue elemental during your trial.'

'And then she tethered a flying fish on Confluence Day,' the other adds with a cruel smile. 'To think, people thought you surviving that elemental during the trial meant you were bound for big things.'

Typhon prowls into my view, teeth bared as his long, serpentine body coils around the girls, wings slowly unfolding.

'You told me to stop asking if I could eat people. So I shall not ask.'

'Telling me you're not asking is pretty similar to asking, Typhon.'

'Noted.'

'I was wondering if either of you know where I could find Raith.'

They share a knowing look. One folds her arms and eyes me up and down again. This time, it's more of a feminine appraisal and has nothing to do with my affinity. 'So the rumors about you two are true?'

'No,' I sigh. I've already had my fill of talk about rumors and silliness for one day. It's taking effort to keep my temper from flaring now. 'I just need to talk to him.'

The girls share another look, as if deciding whether they want to tell me.

'Okay,' one says. 'We're actually on our way to meet him right now. You can tag along. Just promise to keep your little flying fish away from us.'

I force a smile as they laugh at my expense and start walking.

'I am not asking to eat them, but I am sending you awareness of my hunger through the tether. Do you feel it, angry human?'

I grin. *'Quit trying to circumvent the no eating people rule, Typhon. I get it. You want to eat them.'*

'If I were permitted to speak about my desires to eat humans, I would start with the one on the left. And I would do it in my prestigious kura-tokken form. The "flying fish" as she so dismissively puts it.'

I continue following the girls as we leave the fire tower and pass through the courtyard. *'I think your kuratokken form might be too small for eating people.'*

'I am Typhon. I would find a way.'

We enter the eastern wing of campus, pass through halls that are mostly empty at this hour on a weekend, and stop outside a pair of doors. 'This is it,' one of the girls says.

I hear muffled voices inside and nod.

The girls push open the doors and I follow them inside.

And then they slide in behind me, closing the doors tightly and throwing the latch over the lock.

I frown, then squint against the brightness of torches in the empty classroom. There are nearly a dozen figures approaching me.

'Raith?' I ask, my voice coming out as little more than a whisper.

'Oh . . . what did you bring us?' asks a familiar voice.

And then Malakai steps in front of the torches, flanked by Serena and several very large and angry-looking students.

Fuck.

Chapter 23

'Careful,' Serena says, hips swaying as she walks into view, her figure outlined against torchlight like a predator stalking prey. 'Her water dragon will be here, too. Nobody try anything stupid.'

'At least someone recognizes my power,' Typhon mutters in my mind.

A sharp pulse hits through our tether – hunger, raw and demanding. He's asking, again, if he can eat them.

'Let's be smart, Typhon. Even you probably couldn't fight off fifteen students and elementals.'

'It would be a glorious death.'

'Right. Death. So we're going to be smart. I have no interest in dying tonight, no matter how gloriously.'

'Shall I alert the fire-touched about your situation?'

I go rigid, eyes darting between the students slowly circling me like wolves. My heart hammers so hard I wonder if they can hear it.

'You can do that?'

'I can communicate with his elemental. I suppose I could also reach out to the air-touched you are rumored to vigorously mate with.'

'Bastian?'

'Yes. I should also admit I am only asking to give you the illusion of choice. I already reached out to them several minutes ago when I suspected the humans who led you here of treachery.'

'And you didn't think to warn me?'

Rage explodes in my chest, hot and vicious. Typhon is supposed to protect me, and he just let me walk straight into this?

'Yes. Better to face our enemies than hide in the shadows from them. I will admit I didn't expect . . . quite so many of them, however.'

The slight throb of apology through the tether softens my anger. We're still screwed, though.

Serena slides inside my space and plucks my rapier from my waist. Blunted or not, I still feel naked once she takes it.

'Just to be safe,' she says, eyes holding mine as she steps back, her smile cutting like a blade.

'Are they close?' I ask Typhon through our tether.

'Yes.'

'I didn't see anything,' I say, trying to keep my voice steady despite the situation. 'Just let me walk out of here, and I won't talk about this. Whatever it is.'

'Hmm,' Malakai says, lips curving into a smile that doesn't reach his eyes. 'Serena mentioned she gave you the opportunity to work with us. Said you weren't particularly receptive, though. We could use your dragon, Nessa. Maybe there's bad blood between us, but we're willing to leave it in the past.'

'You tried to kill me during the water trial. And you had your goons try to kill us in the training arena. And you've murdered dozens of innocent students.' I lift my chin, refusing to cower even as my insides quiver with dread. 'So fuck leaving anything in the past. I want nothing to do with you bastards.'

Malakai's smile widens, teeth flashing white in the torchlight. 'I'll admit I like your spunk, Nessa. Almost as much as I like the idea of having that water dragon on our side.'

'It's never going to happen.'

He nods, eyes falling to the floor for a moment as if he's considering something. 'I believe you. That's too bad. Because it means you're also too dangerous to keep alive.' His gaze flicks to the two first-years. 'Veeni and Jira, you did good bringing her here. Titus, it's your turn to get rid of the body. It has been a while since we threw one over the cliffs. That should do for her.'

My stomach clenches and bile rises in my throat as I take a step back, only to bump against the doors. If Veeni and Jira turned to Serena's side, how many other fires can't be trusted? My pulse hammers in my throat, but I start preparing to fight. If they're really going to try to kill me, I'm taking some of these fuckers down with me.

Typhon moves in front of me, spreading his wings wide, his long body rippling with power.

Malakai, Serena, and the gathered students all take a huge step backward, eyes suddenly wide with fear.

'Let them see what they threaten. Let them see Typhon. First of his name!'

He throws his head back and lets out a roar that rumbles through my chest, shaking dust from the ceiling and rattling my bones. The sound vibrates through every inch of my body, making my teeth ache and my ears ring.

Elementals flash into view around the room as the students draw weapons and prepare for a fight. Three fire elementals and twelve water elementals bathe the room in magical light, red and blue.

Veeni and Jira, the first-year fires who led me to the room, make the first move. Just as Typhon engages with four elementals, biting into one and throwing it hard enough to shatter stone, the girls rush me.

They're both holding daggers, and I'm unarmed. Unarmed, maybe. But not defenseless. Fucking far from it.

I reach into the stone beneath their feet, shifting the earth upward. A stone rises in front of Veeni's feet, tripping her and sending her flying forward.

I step back, pull water from the air, and form a small buckler of water over my right wrist. I barely raise it in time to knock away Jira's dagger, the impact sending shockwaves up my arm that make my teeth rattle.

There's a chaos of movement around me as Typhon creates a deadly barrier between me and most of the students. He's biting, clawing, and spraying magical torrents of water at elementals and students alike, but there are too many of them. He's only able to keep them back. To buy time. And it's not without cost.

His body is already slashed with several wounds that leak blue energy, each gash making my own skin tingle with sympathetic pain.

'Stop worrying over me, angry human. Defend yourself.'

He roars, slamming his claws down on a dog-like beast of water that explodes in a cloud of mist. He blasts away Titus and several other waters with a column of water that sends them flying back as if from an explosion.

Malakai's shark, which has grown quite a bit larger since Confluence Day, slices through the air and bites hard on Typhon's shoulder.

I grip Veeni, who is trying to overpower me and plunge a dagger into my chest as we battle our way back into the corner of the room. I feel other students working their way around Typhon to get closer.

There's no chance. Death is coming. It's only a question of when.

I clap both hands to Veeni's face. Instead of letting her energy pass into me, I actively try to pull it from her.

Water magic rushes out of her body into my hands, faster and faster as her eyes widen and her mouth hangs open in a silent scream. The power fills me, electric and cold, coursing through my veins like liquid ice. It rushes through me in a torrent, drowning out everything but the sensation of raw power.

Her dagger clatters to the stone beside her as she slumps, but I don't let go. I keep draining her, filling myself with magic, feeling the power leak from her body as it floods mine.

She finally wrenches free, but it's too late. I'm full of water magic, brimming with it, power crackling beneath my skin. Jira is back on her feet and rushing me with three other students. I throw my left hand out in a swiping motion. Almost without effort, a crescent of thick water rushes out, catching all of them in the stomach and sending them flying away.

I could sharpen the water. I feel the possibility – know with little more than a thought, my magic could slice through flesh instead of bruise. But even now, even here . . . I still don't want to be like them. I want to be better.

'Get her!' Serena shouts, rushing toward me with a pair of daggers.

I gesture, blasting away a dog made of fire and a watery lizard with one hand and slick the ground beneath Serena's feet with the other. Without missing a step, she floods the area with fire, turning the water to steam, and keeps coming.

And then the scent of smoke reaches my nose.

Smoke?

I risk turning my head halfway and see the locked double doors are consumed by flame. A moment later, a blast of thick air blows them inward, shattering the doors into splinters of sparks and ash that knock away several more students.

Serena skids to a stop, turning to raise a wall of flames that incinerates debris before they can hit her.

Raith and Bastian stand in the doorway along with several other first-year fires.

'Stop,' Bastian says, voice clear and full of authority, even in the middle of the chaos.

To my surprise, everything does stop. Well, almost everything. As soon as the students and elementals stop moving, Typhon casually lowers his head and bites Veeni's arm off.

My eyes go wide as I stare at the gushing blood and screaming girl. My stomach heaves, and I swallow hard against the rising nausea.

'Apologies,' Typhon says calmly through our tether. *'But I do not allow humans to trick or try to kill my angry human. We can say the arm was eaten during the heat of battle, if anyone asks.'*

Veeni falls to her knees clutching the wounded remains of her arm as Jira slides to her side and tries to help. The rest of the students only watch warily as their wounded elementals nurse wounds and limp back to their sides.

Raith strides into the center of the room as his fire panther stalks behind him. He comes right for me, eyes searching me from head to toe with an intensity that makes my skin heat. 'Are you hurt?' he asks, voice rough with concern.

I shake my head, unable to look away from the fierce worry in his eyes. 'I'm okay.'

He holds my gaze a few more moments, and I can see just how worried he was. It's practically boiling off him. As the relief of seeing me unhurt settles in, though, I see rage slowly taking its place, his eyes darkening to near-black.

'Veeni . . . Jira . . . There's no coming back from this.'

Jira lowers her eyes, as if ashamed. Veeni is too busy clutching the stump where her arm was, eyes still wide in shock. She's whimpering softly.

'And *you*. Serena,' Raith says, voice cold as the edge of a blade.

She straightens, eyes hard. 'It looks like an even fight, now. Is this how we're going to do it, Raith Hollow? Should we just have it out right here? You, the legacy, and your loyal first-year fires against us?'

Raith says nothing, but he unsheathes his sword with a whisper of steel that sends a shiver down my spine. At his cue, the first-year fires behind him begin drawing weapons, too. Their fire elementals wink into view like blazing stars in the night sky, casting a wall of orange light over half of the room.

Bastian steps between both groups of students and elementals, his majestic horse made of pure air behind him. He looks between both groups. 'No,' he says. 'You're all Empire property. Valuable Empire property. I won't stand by and watch you slaughter one another. Disperse and return to your rooms now.'

'And if we don't, pretty boy?' Malakai asks.

'There are systems for dealing with this kind of infraction. Systems that aren't public knowledge. If you carry on here and fight, you'll find yourselves envious of those who died. They, at least, won't survive to endure the punishment.'

There's an uneasy silence.

Raith looks my way, and I can tell he's asking what I want him to do. He'll still fight them if I ask.

Gods. He really will. It's written in every line of his body, in the coiled tension of his shoulders and the fire flickering at his fingertips. The realization steals my breath for a moment.

But I shake my head.

At my signal, Raith slides his sword back into its sheath. He stands tall and proud in front of Malakai and his people. 'Let me make something perfectly fucking clear.' His voice is heavy, powerful, and feels more like the growl of a beast than something human. 'She's under my protection.' He points my way. 'If any of you think you're going to hunt her down during the Crucible, you'll find us there to stop you. If you come for her on campus, it will be your blood on the stone. That's a fucking promise. Am I clear?'

Serena smirks and tilts her head. 'Is she really so good in bed, Raith?'

He walks closer to her until he towers over her smaller form. I notice with satisfaction how she tenses in his presence, like she's already regretting her words.

'Am. I. Fucking. Clear?' he asks, words barely a whisper.

There's a long, tense silence before she lowers her eyes.

'Good.' Raith steps back. 'Malakai?'

Malakai gives a casual shrug. 'Got it. We'll have to kill you and your little soldiers before we can kill Nessa. Did I miss anything?'

'Enough,' Bastian says. 'Nessa. With me. The rest of you get back to your rooms. Oh, and one more thing . . . The only people who know about him are in this room,' Bastian points to Typhon, who is still chewing on Veeni's arm in a way that makes my stomach twist with nausea.

A twinge of panic rises in me. Even if the people in this room keep quiet about Typhon, I can see the truth will get out eventually. Now all the fires know. Any of Malakai's people who might not have believed what they heard from Confluence Day have seen Typhon for themselves now, too.

Problems for another day.

Can you even digest that?' I ask through the tether.

'I am chewing as an intimidation tactic. And for my enjoyment.'

Bastian's finger is still aimed at Typhon. 'If word about him spreads beyond the people here, I'll know it was one of you. That water dragon is an official academy secret. Speak about it, and I'll find you.'

There are some murmurs and shared looks of confusion as Bastian gestures for me to join him.

'Come on, Typhon. Let's get the hells out of here.'

'One thing before I go,' he says.

Typhon transforms into a flying fish and swims right up to Malakai's face. I think he's about to actually say something to him, but instead, he spits a small jet of water in Malakai's only remaining eye.

Malakai flinches in shocked surprise, reeling back and clutching his face. A moment later, he roars in anger and reaches for Typhon, but the flying fish slips out of the way and weaves back to me.

'Direct hit,' Typhon says with smug satisfaction.

Malakai, his shark, and his people try to come after me, but I hear Raith draw his weapon again. 'Back the fuck off. I'll cut every last one of you to ribbons. Whatever mysterious punishment the legacy promised or not. Fucking try me.'

I spare a glance behind and see Raith and the fires are forming a protective wall to stop Malakai and his people from coming after me.

Once we're in the hall, Bastian sighs. 'You alright?'

I nod, though my hands are still trembling with leftover adrenaline. 'Thanks. I think. Were you telling the truth back there? About the punishment?'

'No. If there was a bloodbath in that room, it wouldn't have made Empire happy, but the winners would simply go on with a slap on the wrist, assuming they were caught and held accountable.'

I frown as we enter the courtyard again, and the wide-open fresh air makes me feel like I can finally catch my breath. I nearly died back there. A few more moments and I almost certainly would have.

And even if she deserved it, I still keep replaying the way Veeni screamed when Typhon bit her arm off. Gods . . .

'To be what you are will require violence, angry human. You must be willing to show your enemies the price of crossing you. If we don't, they will only grow more bold. She should consider herself lucky if an arm was the only price for delivering you to your enemies.'

'You're sure it had nothing to do with all her flying fish comments?'

'The comments are why I bit the arm off at the shoulder instead of the elbow. Words carry a price. She learned that tonight.'

Bastian stops and gestures to a bench at the edge of the courtyard. 'Let's sit a moment before you go back to your room.'

I hesitate. 'What about Raith? We just left him back there with Malakai and Serena.'

'I'm pretty sure Raith can handle himself. Nothing is going to happen. Not tonight, at least.' He gestures for me to sit.

'Word about Typhon may spread after tonight, regardless of what I said.'

I nod. 'Maybe it's for the best.'

'I doubt that. Within these walls, sure. Students knowing how powerful you are will be good for your safety to a certain extent. But outside Confluence? You tethered an ancient, Nessa. The ancient elementals are known. There are only nine of them, and they're all mad by broken bonds and dead primals. There will be questions. People will want to know how you tethered an ancient. How you cleansed its madness.'

'What do I tell them?'

He lets out a long sigh, shaking his head. 'Eventually, people are going to find out you're unbound, Nessa. It's simply too big a secret to keep. It might not be this year, but I think by next year, it will certainly start to become known. We need to shift our focus. We can't hide you forever, so we need to gather allies we can trust. Powerful allies who can shield you from those who would rather see you destroyed.'

'We?'

'I gave you that book because I believe in the good you can do. I won't be the only one who thinks having an unbound on our side could be the key.'

'The key to what?'

'You've finished the book, which means you know about Lorkan Grace. Something the book doesn't say for certain has to do with siphons. Lorkan Grace and Milena Grace created the siphons. We don't know how, precisely, but we know it was them. We don't believe the siphons could still exist if Lorkan and Milena were dead. And we have strong evidence that several siphons are still active.'

'So they're still alive?'

'That's the logical conclusion. We believe he's still alive. Still fueling the siphons somehow. Still using them to keep the war between Empire and Red Kingdom raging.'

I shake my head. 'What could I possibly do about that?'

'Frankly, I don't know. But I do know what we did in the past didn't work. We hunted down the unbound and tried to exterminate them. We killed the good and the bad, and now we have nobody left to oppose Lorkan and Milena. Maybe there's nothing you'll be able to do. But maybe there is. I intend to keep you alive so we can find out.'

His words settle on me like weights until I feel like bending beneath their pressure. 'I'm nobody.'

'Whether you like it or not, that's not true. Not in the slightest.'

Agreed. You are the angry human. Loyal follower and distinguished side-kick of Typhon, first of his name. You have stopped me from eating several humans, despite my great hunger. You have only allowed me to eat one single arm. This, in itself, is a great feat.

'I didn't allow you to eat that arm. That was all on you.'

I sense amusement through the tether, and I feel a wave of appreciation toward him. It may not have always been clear to me, but behind all his bluster and arrogance, Typhon is a little less dense than he comes off. He knows how to cheer me up, even after a disaster like the confrontation back in that empty classroom.

'Bastian?' I say.

'Yes?'

'Raith thinks there might be a siphon at Confluence. Is that possible?'

His elegant features twist. 'It's quite likely. Yes. But how would he know?'

I open my mouth to say something, then worry I've already said too much. The last thing I want is to get Raith in trouble with Bastian or the people he's connected to. I may trust Bastian to an extent, but I have no idea if I can trust him to protect Raith. 'Raith has helped me. A lot.'

Bastian's eyebrows draw together. 'I'm aware.'

'So you won't . . . turn him in, or something, right?'

'I want to keep you alive, Nessa. Raith serves as a formidable guard dog, as far as I'm concerned. I should caution you, though . . . I suspect you may feel some emotional connection to him. I would strongly advise against it. As long as he thinks there's a chance of you sleeping with him, he may remain trustworthy. But giving him what he wants may cause him to grow bored, and—'

'I'm not choosing when and where to spread my legs as a negotiation tactic, Bastian.' My voice comes out sharp as glass.

He flinches at my tone, then nods. 'I'm only suggesting caution. Raith volunteered to be here. We have no records of where he lived going back more than a year before he volunteered. It's highly likely he has ties to Red Kingdom. A spy for the enemy who wants to sleep with you is at least predictable. If you give him what he wants, it's harder to predict what he'll do. That's all I'm saying.'

'And it's none of your godsdamned business,' I snap.

Bastian smiles slightly. 'Understood. I said my piece. The rest is up to you.' He stands. 'Speaking of guard dogs. It looks like yours wants a word. Stay safe, Nessa. And remember to use discretion during the Crucible. As I said, Empire will have plenty of eyes watching.'

He walks off, quickly disappearing into a corridor.

And then I see Raith lingering at the edge of the courtyard. Once Bastian is gone, he approaches.

'Fuck him,' he says simply.

I laugh at the unexpected words, the tension in my chest easing slightly. 'He has saved me a few times.'

Raith shrugs. 'It's the only reason I don't kill him.'

'You would kill a legacy? For what, exactly?'

There's a flicker of something in Raith's eyes. Something I'm almost tempted to read as jealousy. 'I don't trust him with you.'

'That's funny, because one of his favorite topics is how I shouldn't trust you with me.'

Raith sits beside me, his body giving off that addictive scent of woodsmoke and something deeper – something that always makes my stomach flutter with warmth and my skin prickle with awareness.

'He wants you in his bed,' Raith says bluntly.

'No. Definitely not. I'm not even sure Bastian is interested in women.'

That earns a sharp look from Raith. 'You think he's interested in men?'

'I think he's too busy . . . scheming to worry about things like that. I know the rumors, but—'

'So you two haven't ever . . .'

I tilt my head at Raith, smiling despite all the tension still twisted up inside me from the last half hour. 'Are you asking if I've slept with Bastian? Because if you're going to ask me that, I'm going to ask how many dozens of girls you've been with since we arrived here.'

'None,' he says simply.

The simple admission takes my breath away. I'd assumed . . .

'You haven't been with anyone here? You really expect me to believe that?'

'You can believe what you want. Have you slept with him?'

'No. And nobody else,' I add after a moment.

'Good,' Raith says.

That draws a chuckle from me. 'Good? Why is that good, Raith?'

'It's just good.' He stands suddenly. 'Come on. I'm walking you back to your room.'

'You are?'

'I just had to rush to a random classroom, burn down a door, and nearly fight a small-scale battle to stop Malakai and Serena from murdering you after learning two fires I thought I could trust had turned on me. So, yes, I'm walking you to your fucking room.'

I try to ignore the swirl of pleasant, but confusing emotions his words trigger and the way my heart flutters wildly in my chest. 'Okay,' I say.

We walk in silence for a few moments before I blurt a question that has been on my mind for weeks. 'Were you born in Red Kingdom?'

Raith pauses in the shadows of a corridor. It's several seconds before he answers. 'Yes.'

My throat goes dry, pulse quickening. The admission would be enough to get him thrown behind bars or worse. I know that much. Despite my pounding heart, I push for more. 'Are you here to . . . hurt Empire somehow?'

'No.'

I swallow hard. 'Then why?'

His eyes are dark as he stares at nothing, memories seeming to swirl just behind his vision. 'The less you know, the safer you are. But I can at least say I'm not . . . here to hurt Empire. My loyalty isn't to Red Kingdom, either.'

'Then why would it be dangerous for me to know more? I don't understand.'

There's another long pause, as if it goes against everything in his nature to answer my question.

'Because I'm supposed to be dead. Only a handful of people know I'm not, and if they found out I was alive. Hells, if they knew I was here? They'd burn this whole fucking place down if they could. Anybody and everybody I cared about would be ash, too. So I can't tell you more. I can't . . . I can't care about you, because then it would be my fault if they found me. It would be my fault that they'd come after you. Hurt you because of me. And I won't have that.'

The barely controlled emotion in his voice breaks my heart. I open my mouth to say something, but no words seem to capture what I'm feeling. All this time, I don't know what I thought, but now I can at least see enough to understand.

He didn't try to shut me out after the kiss because he didn't want me.

He has been trying to shut me out because he *does* want me. And he thinks letting himself want me would get me killed.

'Raith . . .' I finally say, voice barely a whisper. 'I'm already in danger from more things than I can count. Malakai and Serena want me dead. Everybody who was just in that room knows about Typhon now, and if they think I'm a threat to them, they'll probably want to kill me when my guard is down. Bastian knows, and he says Empire is coming to watch the Crucible, so if I have to reveal Typhon to save myself, they'll know too. And I'm fucking unbound, whatever that even means. I don't think you could put me in more danger than I'm already in if you tried. So can't we at least just . . . be whatever it is our hearts want us to be?'

His hand lifts as if he's about to cup my face, but he frowns and pulls it away, shaking his head. 'Yes, you're in danger already. But I'm doing everything I can to protect you from it. If Empire's going to be watching during the Crucible, then we'll just have to make sure you don't need to reveal what you are. We'll stop anybody who comes for you. Simple as that.'

'I don't know how I'm going to survive, Raith. Even with your help. Even with Bastian's help . . . It feels like death is coming at me from so many angles I can't keep track of it all. I'm scared. I know I shouldn't admit it, but I am.' My voice breaks on the last words. 'And if I'm going to die, can't I at least have one thing I want before I do?' My eyes hold his, and I see the conflict there. The hunger. The need.

He licks his lips, eyes falling to my mouth. 'And what is it . . . What do you want so badly?'

'You,' I breathe. 'Gods, Raith. Isn't it fucking obvious already? Can't you see how—'

He's kissing me before I can take another breath. It's a desperate kiss, all heat and hunger. His big hands are on my body, squeezing and gripping me greedily as he pushes himself against me and lifting me like I weigh nothing – pressing my back against a stone pillar and spreading my legs around his waist.

The thin fabric of our uniforms does nothing to hide the perfect shape of him against me or the heat of his friction as our bodies press together. Every point of contact sends sparks of fire magic through my skin – his essence burning into me, tasting of smoke and cinnamon and raw power.

The red-hot magic flowing from his body swirls in a delicious mixture that rushes beneath my skin and fills me in a way that has me moaning against his lips. 'Oh, gods,' I gasp.

His lips are perfect and soft against mine, but the kiss is hard and his hands are so strong, gripping my thighs with a possession that makes me dizzy. His tongue teases mine as it slides into my mouth, swirling and claiming with a need that makes my entire body tremble.

I thread my fingers into his hair, pulling him closer, desperate to erase any space between us. He growls against my mouth, the sound vibrating through my chest and igniting a fire low in my belly. His hips rock against mine, and I can feel exactly how much he wants me as it presses hard between my legs.

'Nessa,' he groans against my mouth, one hand sliding up to cup my face. His thumb strokes my cheek, surprisingly gentle for how tightly his other hand grips my hip. The contrast sends shivers down my spine.

I break the kiss, gasping for air, and his mouth immediately finds my neck, teeth grazing the sensitive skin beneath my ear before trailing hot, open-mouthed kisses down to my collarbone. Every touch brands me, makes my skin prickle with heat.

'Raith,' I manage, my voice a breathy moan as his hand slides under the hem of my shirt, fingers splaying across the bare skin of my back.

'I know,' he says, voice rough with desire. 'We need to stop.'

But he doesn't stop. His mouth finds mine again, and I meet him with equal hunger, our bodies moving together in perfect rhythm. His hands slide lower, cupping my ass and pressing me harder against him as my legs tighten around his waist.

The friction is delicious torture, making heat spiral between my legs. I roll my hips, desperate for more, and he breaks the kiss with a hiss.

'Fuck, Nessa,' he breathes, forehead pressed to mine. 'If we don't stop now—'

But I don't want to stop. I want to feel him everywhere. Want to drown in the fire of his magic and the heat of his body until everything else falls away.

He closes his eyes, jaw clenched tight as he battles for control. With obvious reluctance, he slowly lowers me to my feet, but keeps me caged between his body and the pillar.

'You have no idea what you do to me,' he says, voice rough. 'No fucking idea.'

I look up at him, still breathing hard as a wicked smile plays at my lips. 'I think I have some idea.'

His mouth quirks in a half-smile, but his eyes remain dark, hungry. 'I'll walk you to your room.' He steps back, putting space between us, but his hand finds mine, fingers lacing together. 'And I'll stay outside your door tonight. Make sure no one bothers you.'

The simple gesture makes my heart ache more than the kiss. This connection between us, whatever it is, runs deeper than just physical attraction. And I know, no matter what dangers are coming for me, having Raith at my side means I won't face them alone.

'Okay,' I say, squeezing his hand.

'I'm not going anywhere,' he promises, and for the first time since arriving at Confluence, I almost believe I might survive this.

Chapter 24

'Good,' Rector Voss says. 'Very good.'

I exhale, the magic hovering above my hands dispersing into the air like morning mist over water.

Every time I channel, I'm reminded of the storm three years ago. The image of my father's hand briefly rising above the churning, black waters – reaching for a life that was already gone.

The guilt comes fresh and hot, burning like acid under my skin.

But this same power that stole everything from me is now my only path to redemption. As the energy flows through me, I feel the chains of fear falling away. For years, I've been terrified of what lurks within me – the destructive force that turned my mother and sister against me. I try to focus on the future instead of the past. A future where I might master this power, make amends, and maybe even protect others instead of destroying them.

The possibilities feel endless.

'Limitless except for keeping your quarters in reasonable order,' Typhon grumbles through our bond. *'With the meager possessions they allow you students, your ability to create absolute chaos is truly remarkable. Undergarments were hanging from above your window this morning. How does something such as this happen?'*

'I don't recall asking for commentary from grumpy dragon grandpa,' I shoot back silently.

'There are humans who would prostrate themselves before me. Who would sacrifice limbs for the chance to tether me. And you call me a "grumpy dragon grandpa?" Insufferable, ungrateful . . .'

Despite his complaints, a current of warmth flows through our tether. Typhon may grumble, but he can't hide the emotions that pass between the tether. It makes his constant complaints and chiding feel amusing rather than obnoxious.

Thank the gods for that.

'Your control is improving,' Typhon concedes. *'For a fragile, insignificant human, at least.'*

Voss scribbles furiously on his parchment, leaving me in one of those painfully long silences that Typhon typically fills with unsolicited wisdom.

'The fact that you're too foolish to solicit my guidance doesn't diminish its value, angry human.'

My lips twitch into a smile. I've grown accustomed to having him respond to every stray thought that crosses my mind. *'My control may be improving like you say, but I'm still miles behind everyone else at Confluence.'*

'The power of an unbound is different.'

'Different,' I repeat. *'So far, the difference seems to be that I have far less capacity to channel than my peers, but I can touch every element. Maybe it would feel useful if I could openly show my powers instead of searching for subtle uses that won't be noticed.'*

'In time, you will reveal yourself.'

'And then be hunted.' I know from reading the book that unbound weren't just hunted for the potential to manifest unique and deadly powers. There was something else. Something else I have tried desperately not to think too much about because . . .

'Because it makes you feel like a monster,' Typhon says softly in my mind, finishing the thought.

I tense, eyes falling to the floor while Voss still scratches down notes on his parchment. *'It's just a book, Typhon. I can't believe everything it says. Maybe I can't really . . . do that.'*

'Then allow me to confirm the contents, because I witnessed unbound myself. As the book says, unbound have the ability to tether not just elementals, but humans as well. Just as it was with me, you can require your oaths to be sworn by a human and accept their tether. This joining

will also increase your power and grant them a shadow of your own. This was the secret Lorkan Grace and Milena Grace discovered. It was the secret that ignited everything and led to the destruction of your kind.'

'I'm not going to tether people,' I bite back. From the moment I read it in the book, I tried to forget I'd seen it. The idea felt . . . wrong. Twisted. Dark.

'Whether you use your full potential or not is of no consequence. They will call you dangerous because they will fear what you could become, should you choose. With the desire, you could reshape this world of yours as you see fit.'

'I don't want to reshape the world, Typhon. I just want to fix my own little corner of it. I want my mom and sister to forgive me. I want to survive this place.'

There's a heavy shock of protective instinct through the tether. I feel it flood into me so strongly that it takes my breath away. *'And you shall survive, because I will protect you. No matter the cost.'*

I spare a small smile for Typhon who lies in the corner, his serpentine body coiled around as his head rests on his scaled torso. His deep blue eyes gleam, somehow seeming as bottomless as oceans.

I glance at Voss's paper and see he has drawn four sectors – one for each element. He's taking notes in each, as if keeping separate track of my progression with each discipline.

'In any case, even if you refuse to use your full potential by tethering others,' Typhon continues. *'You demonstrated a unique gift when you stripped away my madness. If you could restore me to my senses, then you could free the other ancients as well. You could also free the elder elementals who have lost themselves. This alone would send shockwaves through both your world and mine. If those elementals chose to tether to your people, it would dramatically increase the power at your kind's disposal. If not . . . it would make my kind far more powerful in our own right.'*

'Do you really think I should do that? Try to free more elementals from madness?' The weight of the possibility settles heavy on my shoulders.

'The answer isn't simple. The other ancients . . . they are not perfect.'

'Unlike you?' I tease.

'Precisely,' he replies, completely missing my sarcasm. *'We must consider carefully before deciding if healing them is wise. And we need you significantly stronger first. I could have easily destroyed you in the lake or on the elemental plane. We can't risk exposing you again until you're properly prepared.'*

'How have you been feeling?' Voss asks abruptly, yanking me from my internal conversation with Typhon.

'Fine, I guess?' The words come out more a question than a statement.

'Your powers. Do you feel they're progressing?'

My fingers flex unconsciously. 'I'm improving some, but it doesn't feel like enough.' A heaviness settles in my chest as I think about my limitations. 'Sure, I can manipulate small amounts of elemental energy without drawing power directly from someone. A stone rising from the floor. A sudden gust of wind. A needle of water materializing from nothing. A flare of heat dancing across my palm. But my classmates—' My eyebrows draw together. 'My classmates are becoming devastating now that they've tethered. Malakai crafts shapeshifting weapons from water. Mireen can summon entire waves of water from nothing. I can barely—'

'You can do far more than them,' Voss interrupts, his half-smile knowing. 'Your powers are different, Nessa. Subtle. You're discounting that when you draw from someone, you can temporarily surpass their abilities. And you have access to all four elements, even if in limited quantities.'

Memories from last night flash through my mind – draining enough water magic to blast people away like dust in a hurricane. But it required physical contact, and my enemies won't always stand still while I reach for them. It also exposes me.

The memory of last night also includes what happened with Raith afterwards. It's not an unpleasant thought, but it feels too private to have here with Voss staring at me. Heat rises to my cheeks as I recall Raith's touch, his intensity, the way he made me feel . . .

*'And me subjected to your mating-obsessed brain. Let the scarred
human dock with you, place a baby inside your body, and be done with
it. All this time spent imagining the act is time wasted. You could be
thinking of your training, of—'*

'Typhon?'

'Yes?'

'Shut up.'

Voss perches on the edge of his desk, long legs crossed and arms
folded as he watches me. His silver hair is swept back from his face,
revealing shrewd eyes that see too much.

'I should mention I heard about yesterday's confrontation,' Voss
says slowly, his gaze never leaving mine. 'Veeni arrived at the healers
missing an arm. She won't identify her attacker, of course. The stories
we've gathered make at least one thing clear. It was Serena, two fires,
and the waters against you and Raith Hollow with the rest of the fires.
And Bastian, of all people, showed up in time to stop the fighting
from getting worse, from what I understand.'

I shift uncomfortably. 'Something like that.'

'Am I to assume . . . you bit Veeni's arm off? Or was it your flying
fish, which seems rather small for such a significant wound.'

My chest constricts, pulse hammering against my ribs. Does Voss
know about Typhon? I've had no choice but to trust him with my
unbound status, but I've managed to conceal the fact that I tethered a fucking ancient water dragon on Confluence Day. At least, I
thought I had.

'I . . . don't know what happened to her,' I manage. 'There was
nearly a fight, and then there wasn't. Bastian got there in time to
stop it from happening.'

Voss cocks his head, amusement playing at the corners of his
mouth. 'Nessa. I'm not a fool, so don't treat me like one. What
happened to Veeni's arm? What really happened?'

His tone sends ice crawling up my spine. Shit. Has he seen
through my 'Oceanus' the flying fish lie? Does he actually know
about Typhon?

'*Should I prepare to strike, angry human?*' Typhon's voice reverberates with dangerous potential.

'*No. He hasn't given us reason not to trust him yet. Everything he's done has been to help. Let's . . . wait and see.*'

I straighten my spine, forcing calm into my voice that I definitely don't feel. 'I would rather not say, Rector Voss.'

He studies me for several excruciating seconds before shrugging. 'Veeni will survive, naturally. With sufficient practice, she may even learn to conjure a relatively functional fire-based arm for short durations. Such things are possible with adequate skill.'

'Oh.' I inwardly curse myself for the relief I feel. Despite knowing she deserved every bit of what happened, guilt has gnawed at me since last night.

'*I should have removed her head instead. Let her magically replace that!*'

'Typhon, don't be a dick.'

'*Elementals do not possess dicks. We have a far more sophisticated organ known as—*'

I quickly block him out, refocusing on Voss who's watching me with undisguised curiosity.

'Have you and your friends secured a fifth member for the Crucible? I assume my early warning allowed you first selection.'

'We're . . . working on it.' I shift my weight on the chair. 'But there's something else I hoped to ask about. Something related to finding our fifth.'

'Oh?' Voss lifts his chin slightly, eyes sharpening.

'I heard a rumor. About . . . siphons.'

Voss's expression remains perfectly neutral, and I find myself rambling to fill the uncomfortable silence.

'Here at Confluence. Is that even possible? Could there be a siphon on campus? I know they are just supposed to be monsters from children's stories, but I thought if anyone would know it would be—'

Voss rises and circles his desk to sink into his chair. He leans forward, fingers forming a steeple. 'It is possible. Yes.'

His straightforward admission knocks the air from my lungs. 'Where exactly did you hear this rumor?'

'I don't recall.' The lie seems to hang in the air, bright and obvious as it waits for him to strike it away and demand the truth.

But his only reaction is the smallest tick at the corner of his mouth. 'I see. Little is known about siphons. Even among the powerful. Though encountering a siphon and living to tell of it is virtually unheard of, we know they exist. Would you like to know how, Nessa?'

My throat works against a sudden dryness, but I nod.

'It's the condition of the victim afterward. If they had no affinity, the eyes become empty sockets of shadow. The veins blacken, and every drop of liquid in the body evaporates, leaving a shriveled, horrific corpse. For those with an affinity, the mark is completely blackened, as if burned away. The sight is . . . deeply disturbing.'

I think back to the hushed conversation I overheard with Raith months ago on the castle walls. 'Has a body like that been found here? On campus?'

A troubled shadow crosses his features, like storm clouds momentarily blotting out the sun. 'That would be extremely concerning. It would mean our protections have failed and the siphons are far more powerful than we anticipated – that they can move freely among us even in a place where the average student possesses enough power to overwhelm several trained soldiers.'

'So . . . it wouldn't be possible?'

Voss interlaces his fingers, eyes never leaving mine. 'I didn't say that. I merely said it would be concerning.'

'Does anyone know what they look like? Siphons, I mean.'

'Just like you and me. Identical, if they wished it. We believe they can adopt the forms of those they observe. Or perhaps physical contact is required to steal another's appearance. We don't know. But it's the only explanation we've conceived for how they evade detection so thoroughly.' Voss sighs. 'Centuries of confronting them and our knowledge remains pitifully limited.'

'So what *do* we know?'

'Good,' he says with a half-smile. 'You're asking the right questions. We know they can kill elementals. Truly kill them.'

A pulse of raw anger passes through the tether from Typhon. I know elementals can 'die' in a fight in our world, but Typhon has assured me they're just energy. Under normal circumstances, they can't truly die. They can just be dispersed and need time to gather themselves back into being. But siphons can absorb them into nothingness. Real death.

I gnaw my lower lip, considering. 'Elementals must despise siphons even more than humans do.'

'Astute observation. Yes. And now you've discovered the root of conflict between elementals and humans. The histories claim siphons were created by an exceptionally powerful unbound with a unique manifestation. The specifics are murky, naturally. These events transpired over a thousand years ago. Ancient times.'

'Do the histories explain why an unbound created siphons? Why do something so terrible?'

'No. It's not recorded. All we know is the elementals disagreed on how to address the threat. This division led to fires and earths primarily allying with the Red Kingdom while waters and airs mostly sided with Empire.'

'So everything – our entire conflict – really began because of one unbound?'

Voss nods. 'Thus the need for discretion regarding your status. Both elementals and humans fear what your kind can become. We need only examine our history to see the devastation wrought by a . . . single unbound individual.'

His words carry weight. Nauseating weight. They drive home the point I've already been feeling poised at my throat since finishing the unbound book. They make me feel like the monster I fear I could be – the monster my mother and sister thought but worse in every way.

'Why help me, then?' My voice emerges smaller than intended. 'Why not throw me over the castle wall and be done with it?'

'*He could try,*' Typhon roars in my mind.

'Because I believe you can help us. How, specifically, is a matter for another time. For now, concentrate solely on improvement. You must survive to be useful to anyone, and I cannot personally shield you during the Crucible.'

Voss suddenly claps his hands and offers a friendly smile as he stands. 'In any case, these matters needn't concern you today. Focus on what you can control. Your training. Maintaining your academic standing. Finding a fifth for the Crucible. Surviving. Because you're useless to everyone dead. That is one certainty you can cling to.'

My fingers twist into the fabric of my clothes. 'But you said siphons might assume any form. How can I trust anyone knowing that?'

His eyes lock with mine with an intensity that sends shivers cascading down my spine. Then he smiles again and the moment evaporates. 'Trust is a luxury of the powerful. There's your answer. Continue developing your strength and you will earn the luxury of trust. You will trust because you will fear no one. Now, return to your room before darkness falls completely. There are monsters in the shadows, after all.' He says this with a playful twist of his lips, but his words feel like ice-cold fingers on my neck all the same.

As I make my way back to my quarters, I can't shake the feeling that Voss is testing me. That behind his wisdom and apparent honesty, he's measuring my reactions, determining whether I'm capable of something more.

What that something might be, I have no idea.

Chapter 25

Blood streaks my training blade and drips from my fingertips, spattering against the stone floor in bright red drops.

'Shit, Nessa. I'm so sorry.' Beck's face looms over me, his brow furrowed with concern as he offers his hand. 'I didn't mean to actually cut you.'

I cradle my arm where his blunted practice sword has somehow managed to carve a bloody gash across my upper arm. The wound stings like acid as blood wells up between my fingers.

'I'm just impressed you managed to finally land a hit on me,' I say through clenched teeth before accepting his outstretched hand. My sleeve soaks with crimson as I get to my feet.

Mireen moves closer to inspect my wound. 'If you die from this, I'm taking your good boots,' she says with a straight face. When Beck looks appalled, she rolls her eyes. 'Relax. It's a compliment – her boots are the only thing worth inheriting.'

We've claimed one of the many hidden training areas scattered across campus. Technically, I think they're meant as spare classrooms. Confluence used to house far more students each year, but the numbers have dwindled over the centuries, meaning the castle is full of unused spaces that collect dust. Or rather, spaces that would collect dust if students weren't taking advantage.

Our walk to this place from the water tower had us passing dozens of closed doors and the muffled sounds of students clashing in training matches. That, and the distinctive scent of ozone permeating the air signaling the heavy use of magic across campus.

The Crucible is coming fast, and everybody knows it.

Beck and Ambrose are leaning in, staring at the wound. We've all seen plenty of wounds by now, and we're relatively desensitized. But this cut is bleeding heavily, and it looks pretty deep. I may need stitches and be forced to chew the horrible herbs they give at the healers to prevent infection. If I'm truly unlucky, they'll make me chew up the herbs and stuff them into the wound.

'We're going to have to start making you practice with Uther instead, Beck,' Mireen says, moving closer to inspect my wound. As she bends down, something small and gray peeks out from her pocket, whiskers twitching. She casually tucks it back in with practiced ease, not missing a beat. 'I think you've drawn enough blood for one day.'

Ollie dips closer to my wound, his liquid body rippling with concern.

Beck looks genuinely distraught, his sandy hair falling across his eyes as he shakes his head. His massive bear elemental Uther materializes behind him, mimicking Beck's posture of contrition. 'Fucking hell, I'm sorry, Nessa. You're so damn slippery and fast. I think I was swinging harder than I realized just trying to catch you before you could dodge, and—'

'It's not as bad as it looks,' I lie. The pain screams otherwise.

Ambrose adjusts his glasses with a professorial air. 'Technically, practice blades can develop burrs if they're used enough. You probably caught her with a worn edge.'

His water hawk Akaron perches on his shoulder, head tilted as if examining my wound from a distance. Like many of the elementals, Akaron has grown more substantial over the months, his watery form more detailed, more predatory. The temperament matches Ambrose's increasingly analytical approach to everything around him.

'Hmm,' Ambrose continues, suddenly intrigued. He takes my arm gently, turning it to examine the cut. 'The blade created a perfect bisection of the dermal layer, but the subdermal tissues remain largely intact. That's good.'

I pull my arm back. 'Glad my pain is academically stimulating.'

'Sorry,' he mumbles. 'I've been doing some extra studying on anatomy and your wound is more informative than the sketches in my books.' He takes a step back, but his eyes don't leave my wound.

A burning sensation spreads through my arm. Not just pain – something else. Heat flowing beneath my skin, gathering at the injury site.

'Interesting, angry human,' Typhon's voice rumbles through my mind.

'What?' I wince as the burning intensifies. It feels like someone is holding dozens of candle flames just beneath my arm and they're inching closer. It's nearly unbearable, but . . .

'Look at your arm.'

I pull my hand away from the cut. Instead of a gaping wound, I see the edges of my skin knitting together before my eyes. The blood flow slows, then stops. Within seconds, the only evidence of the injury is a thin white line and the blood already spilled.

'What the . . .' My voice trails off as I stare at my arm in disbelief.

My friends fall silent, all eyes locked on the miracle happening before them. Even their elementals freeze, sensing the significance of what they're witnessing.

'Did you just . . .' Mireen's voice is barely above a whisper. 'Did Typhon do that? You said he healed Raith during Confluence Day, right?'

I touch the newly healed skin, the phantom pain already fading. 'I don't know.'

'She is bound to an ancient,' Ambrose notes. 'I guess it would be disappointing if that didn't come with some perks.'

'Typhon can heal her?' Beck whispers, voice laced with awe.

'Was that you, Typhon?' I ask him, even though I already feel like I know the answer.

'No. That was you. It means your unbound power has finally manifested,' Typhon's mental voice carries a weight of significance. *'The ability to mend. To heal. This is rare and valuable beyond measure. I suppose it is no surprise, as the four-eyed one states. I, too, have some ability to heal, as you saw on Confluence Day.'*

'How rare?' I ask in my mind, unable to tear my eyes from the seamless skin where a bleeding wound had been seconds before.

'Among the four base affinities? It is unheard of. True healing – not just accelerating natural processes but actually remaking that which is broken – it is a power that even kings would kill to possess. It is sought after more than the ability to call down pillars of fire or raise mountains.'

My mouth goes dry. Just what I need – one more reason for people to come after me. One more target painted on my back.

Beck leans closer. 'So . . . can Typhon heal me, too? Because I've got this thing on my back I think might be infected. Maybe he could take a look.'

'Shut up, Beck,' Mireen says.

My heart races with anxiety. This is dangerous – too many people seeing something they shouldn't, asking questions I can't answer. They are all my friends, but ever since my conversation with Voss, I can't ever fully shake the fear that anybody could be a siphon in disguise.

'Typhon, what do I do? They can't know what I am.'

'Tell them it was me. They want to believe you are one of them. It is the simplest explanation, and humans love simple explanations for complex truths.'

'It's like nothing ever happened,' Beck says, reaching for my arm to examine it. His fingers are surprisingly gentle for someone so large. 'No scar. Just . . . nothing.'

I put on a smile. 'Typhon said it was him. He just thought the wound looked bad enough to justify it. I guess he doesn't mind letting me suffer small scrapes and bruises, though.'

Mireen shakes her head slowly, as if still in awe. 'That's . . . incredible, Nessa. Do you think he could heal others, or just yourself?'

'Could I heal others?' I ask Typhon through the tether.

'In time, with practice,' Typhon confirms. *'Even now, perhaps, though it would cost you more. You do not just command the flesh to mend – you reforge it with your own essence. It is not without price.'*

'What price?'

'*Energy. Life force. The same power that flows through your veins. Healing yourself is like moving water from one part of a lake to another. Healing others is like transferring water from your lake to theirs. It can be replenished, but not instantly.*'

'I'm not sure,' I admit to Mireen. 'He healed Raith, but it cost him. He was even larger before that, and he's still not back to his original size.'

Ambrose's eyes haven't left my arm. 'You should document this. Keep records of whenever it happens. Note the circumstances, the sensations, everything.'

'Why does everything have to be a research project with you?' Beck asks, rolling his eyes. 'Is this why Noraveen broke up with you? Did you try to document the circumstances and situations when you blew your load too early?'

'She broke up with me because her ex got killed in a training accident and she realized she loved him,' Ambrose says flatly.

Beck rubs the back of his neck, wincing. 'Sheesh. Way to make it awkward.'

'And I document and study because knowledge is power,' Ambrose snaps. 'And power is survival.'

Beck claps his hands together, his earlier distress evaporating. 'Well, bummers aside . . . We're going to crush the Crucible now. Nessa already has a fucking water dragon that can eat our enemies. And now we know it can heal our wounds in a pinch. We're going to be unstoppable.'

'Speaking of our team,' Ambrose interjects, 'we still need to decide on our fifth. The Crucible is only a week away now. Is Brunhild really our only option?'

'Is your arm okay?' Mireen asks quietly as the boys begin to debate, her concern cutting through her usual veneer of toughness. The rat in her pocket scurries up her uniform to perch on her shoulder. This time, she doesn't seem to even notice.

I flex my fingers, rotate my wrist. 'It feels fine. Better than fine, actually.' And it does – there's a strange vitality flowing through me, as if the healing had not just fixed the wound but somehow improved me. Despite that, I also feel a kind of small part of me is hollowed out. I wonder if it's the life force Typhon talked about that needs to recover.

'Is this normal? I feel . . . different.'

'Your power grows, angry human. With each use, each manifestation, you become more of what you truly are.'

'And what is that, exactly?'

'Something this world has not seen in a very long time. Something both wondrous and terrifying.'

His cryptic answer does nothing to calm my nerves.

Beck points at Mireen. 'Gods, Mireen. You told me you were done keeping the fucking rats.'

'That's not what I said. You just chose not to listen properly, Beck.'

'So what *did* you say?' Ambrose asks slowly, eyes distrustful as he studies the rat, whose whiskers twitch from Mireen's shoulder.

'I said I was finding new homes for them. I just . . . slip them under doors at night. Legacies have the best rooms, so I usually start there. And they all know they can come back to their momma if they're ever hungry or need something. This rat,' she says, reaching up to scratch its belly, 'was my first. He still gets to stay in my room, don't you Bartemus?'

I smile, watching as she nuzzles her nose toward the rat, who leans in and lets her. 'So you've been filling the legacy rooms with rats, Mireen?'

'Usually just one per room.' She sounds a touch defensive. 'Unless they were sibling rats or particularly good friends, then I send them in small groups.'

'And what about my room, Mireen?' Beck asks, sounding like he's on the verge of hysterics.

Mireen shrugs in a way that says she definitely rat bombed him.

After the two of them finish bickering, we set aside our weapons and sit to revisit the topic of Brunhild and whether we should add her to our group.

'She's strong as hell,' Beck says, slapping the mat to emphasize his point. 'And her elemental is a fucking giant crab with claws that could snap a man in half.'

'She also threatened to throw me out a window,' I remind him.

'That was before she got to know you,' Beck argues. 'And anyway, she didn't actually do it, which shows restraint.'

'Setting the bar pretty low there, Beck,' Mireen says dryly.

'Her combat performance is apparently top-tier,' Ambrose adds, ever the practical one. 'Physically, she's nearly as strong as Beck. Having two powerhouses on our team provides a tactical advantage.'

'Is that all that matters?' I ask.

Ambrose frowns. 'What else should matter in a life-or-death scenario like the Crucible?'

'I don't know. Maybe trust? Loyalty? Knowing someone has your back because they actually care if you live or die, not just because it benefits them?'

The room goes quiet. We've all seen enough death at Confluence to know exactly how fragile life is here, how quickly someone can go from friend to memory.

'I trust her,' Beck says, his voice softer than usual. 'I know that might not mean much coming from me, but . . . she's not what she seems at first. There's more to her than just muscles and threats.'

'My intuition is telling me she's trustworthy,' Ambrose says, touching his temple. 'Despite the window-throwing threat.'

I sigh, studying my newly healed arm. The weight of the coming Crucible presses down on me, along with all the other dangers circling ever closer. Can we really trust someone we barely know?

Your friends are right to be concerned about numbers, angry human. In battle, a single ally can tip the balance between life and death.

'Even if that ally might be the one to stab us in the back?'

'Do you not think me capable of destroying any threat to your person? If she is foolish enough to betray you, she'll meet my teeth.'

'Meet your teeth?'

'You asked me to stop talking about eating people. I chose to speak figuratively to avoid breaking your rule.'

I snort at Typhon's words, drawing curious glances from my friends.

'Sorry,' I say. 'Just thinking about when Brunhild called Beck her "sexy bear."'

Beck's smile is wistful. 'She has a way with words, doesn't she?'

'We want someone we can trust, too, Nessa,' Mireen says, suddenly serious. 'After everything we've been through, our team is the only family I've got left in this place.' She doesn't say it, but I know she's thinking of the people we've all lost since arriving at Confluence — dead in training, dead in their beds, just . . . gone.

'Mine too,' I admit.

'And mine,' Ambrose adds quietly.

Beck nods, his usual jovial expression subdued. 'Same here. That's why I'm pushing for her. I really do think she'd fight for us.'

After another half hour of debate, I finally relent. 'Fine. Let's add Brunhild. But Beck, if she betrays us, I'm feeding you to Typhon.'

'Deal.' Beck's face splits into a wide grin.

'So it's agreed upon, then,' Ambrose says, rubbing his hands together. 'The five of us against whatever the Crucible throws at us.'

'And against Malakai and Serena,' Mireen adds grimly.

'Don't remind me,' I say with a sour smile.

We're gathering our gear to leave when the heavy wooden door to the training room swings open. A breathless first-year water – Lissa, I think her name is – stumbles in, her eyes wide with urgency.

'Sorry to interrupt,' she pants, 'but I heard your team was training here. I'm trying to find any teams I can that aren't with Malakai and Serena.'

I frown. 'What do you mean?'

'Sorry. I'm Lissa. I'm teamed with Jorvan, Markus, Toreena, and Vas. All of us have lost somebody to Malakai and his fucking "soldiers". But we thought he gave up trying to grow his little army after Confluence Day. Turns out he didn't. He was only doing it more quietly.'

'How do you know this?' Ambrose asks.

'Because he tried to recruit Jorvan. Forgot he killed Jorvan's best friend, I guess. He told him he's already got nearly half the waters on his side. Five full teams ready to go. Jorvan played along to learn as much as he could. Malakai wants to kill everyone who isn't on his team. He's promising to use his legacy privileges to help anyone who sides with him.'

I frown. 'Thanks, but that's hardly new information.'

She shakes her head. 'You don't get it. There are the people obviously allied with him, but he's recruiting people to lay low, too. People to turn at the last second. And he's not just recruiting waters. He has allies across all affinities already.'

'Why are you telling us this?' Mireen asks. 'Before Confluence Day, you told me to fuck off when I asked about Malakai and who he was coming for.'

Lissa sighs. 'Yeah, I remember. But I also didn't know who the hell to trust at that point. Malakai has made it pretty clear he wants to kill you guys the most. Especially Nessa. So I'm pretty sure you're not with him. Anyway, I wanted to know if we can trust you during the Crucible. We're not going to try to win. We're just going to form a protective group and try like hell to stay alive. Maybe if Malakai and Serena see we're not a threat to the prize, they'll leave us alone.'

'Nothing like death and the threat of dismemberment to bring former enemies together, huh?' Mireen muses.

'Cowards,' Typhon notes.

'You don't have to worry about us,' I say. 'I can't promise we'll go along with your plan. But we're not with them. If there's a chance to help you and your team, we will.'

I'm relieved when my friends all nod their heads without hesitation.

'Thanks for letting us know, Lissa,' I say. She nods and leaves, the door closing behind her with an ominous thud.

'We need more allies,' Ambrose says immediately. 'More than just Brunhild.'

'There's Raith,' I suggest, and immediately regret it when three pairs of eyes lock onto me with varying degrees of suspicion and amusement.

'Your scarred fire boyfriend?' Beck teases, but there's seriousness underneath it. 'You're really sure he's trustworthy?'

'He's not my boyfriend,' I mutter, ignoring the heat that rises to my cheeks. 'And yes, I trust him.'

'Why?' Mireen asks, and it's not an accusation, just a genuine question. 'He's from the border, Nessa. A volunteer. And he's a fire.' She lets out a breath. 'I know they aren't all as bad as I thought at first, okay? It's just . . . hard for me to believe we can trust someone like that with our lives.'

'I'm inclined to agree with Mireen,' Ambrose says. 'I know he's been helping you train, but beyond that – why do you trust him?'

I think of Raith's hands, strong and sure as he corrects my stance. The way he pushes me harder than anyone else because he seems to believe I'm capable of far more than I would ever dare. The tenderness that sometimes flashes through when he thinks I'm not looking.

'He's had plenty of chances to hurt me,' I say finally. 'He chose to help instead. That counts for something in this place. And he was the first one to show up when I walked into the trap with Malakai and Serena last week.'

Ambrose nods slowly. 'Logical. Though emotional attachments can cloud judgment.'

'I'm not—' I begin, but Beck cuts me off with a snort.

'Please. Every time you look at him, it's like watching a starving person stare at a feast. The real question is whether he's with us or just with you.'

Before I can respond, Mireen steps in. 'Whether or not we can trust Raith, at least we know we have Typhon on our side.' A small smile plays across her lips as she watches the small flying fish that now hovers near my shoulder. 'Even if he is . . . modest in size, assuming he won't risk showing his true form during the Crucible.'

'I will show her modest when I consume a small village in front of her eyes.'

'*You will not.*'

'*No, I will not. But I could, and that is the point.*'

'I'm not sure yet,' I say to Mireen's point about whether Typhon will be able to show his true form. 'But I know I'm not going to let any of you die just to preserve the secret about him.'

'This is all great,' Beck says. 'But I'm starving, and the dining hall is going to fill up if we don't get our asses moving soon. So . . . can we continue this conversation over food?'

We make our way through the tower's winding stone staircase, our earlier lightness now tempered by the news of Malakai's expanding coalition. The dining hall will be packed this time of evening, but none of us have the luxury of skipping meals with the Crucible so close.

'What do we actually know about the Crucible itself?' I ask as we descend. 'Beyond the whole "teams of five" thing?'

'It's a test of survival and combat skills in unknown terrain,' Ambrose replies. 'From what I've gathered, they drop us somewhere remote and we have to navigate to a specific location while other teams try to eliminate us. I've spoken with upper-year students and consulted texts. The details change every year, but these generalities do seem to stay the same.'

'Eliminate as in . . . ?'

'Kill, incapacitate, whatever gets the job done,' Ambrose says bluntly.

Beck shrugs as we walk through a long hall lined with tapestries painted in faded oils. Each shows famous battles and primals with huge, impossibly large elementals locked in combat. 'I heard there's more at stake than just the winning team getting promoted to legacy status. They apparently use our performance to help decide our assignments and positions after graduation. Fuck up too badly, and you'll wind up getting sent behind enemy lines on a suicide mission or something.'

'I doubt that,' I say.

'Doubt all you want,' Beck says with upturned palms. 'I'm only saying what I've heard.'

'What you heard from some girl you were sleeping with?' Mireen asks.

'Hey,' Beck snaps. 'The words spoken over pillows are often the most true.'

As we cross the courtyard, snowflakes drift lazily from a steel-gray sky. The cold bites through my uniform, but I barely notice. My attention is fixed on a tall, scarred figure standing at the edge of the training yard, watching me with eyes like torches in the darkness.

Raith.

Even from this distance, his gaze burns into me, igniting a heat that washes away the cold evening air. My body remembers the feel of his hands, the press of his mouth against mine, the solid weight of him pinning me against the wall.

Behind him stands his fire panther, Pyrin, its flaming form more substantial than before, more detailed. The elemental's fiery eyes seem to track me as well, its head tilted in what almost looks like curiosity.

Mireen follows my gaze and sighs. 'Just go already.'

'What?' I tear my eyes away from Raith to look at her.

'We all know you want to talk to him,' she says, a knowing smirk on her face. 'I'll just bring you something to eat later.'

'I don't—' I start to protest, but Beck cuts me off.

'Come on, Nessa. It's painfully obvious.' He gestures vaguely at my face. 'You get all . . . glowy when you see him.'

'Glowy?' I sputter.

'It's an accurate assessment,' Ambrose confirms. 'Your pupils dilate, your respiration increases, and your cheeks flush. Classic signals of sexual arousal and attraction.'

'Have you been studying me?'

He shrugs. 'The signs are rather obvious, Nessa.'

I want to argue, but Raith is already moving away, heading toward the eastern section of campus. If I'm going to catch him, it has to be now.

'Fine,' I concede. 'I'll meet you all later.'

'You know,' Mireen says, her voice dropping so only I can hear, 'you don't have to be ashamed of wanting him. I know I've made it hard for you to feel okay about it, and I'm sorry for that. I just . . . want to make sure you're careful. Okay? I care about you, and I know you trust him, but . . .'

'But what?'

Her eyes are serious, the crescent scar beneath one eye catching the dim light. 'But I've watched people I care about die because they trusted the wrong person. I couldn't bear it if that happened to you, too.'

The sincerity in her voice catches me off guard.

'I'll be careful,' I promise. 'I'm not as reckless as you think.'

She raises an eyebrow, clearly unconvinced. 'Use protection,' she teases.

I roll my eyes and break away from the group, my heart racing as I follow Raith's retreating form. He doesn't look back, but somehow I know he's aware of me following him. It's in the deliberate pace of his steps, the slight tension in his broad shoulders.

'He intends for you to follow,' Typhon observes. *'This is a human mating ritual, yes? The male leads, the female pursues. Very primitive.'*

'It's not a mating ritual, Typhon.'

'The elevated cortisol and pheromones your body is producing suggest otherwise.'

'Can you please not monitor my bodily functions? It's creepy.'

'I am tethered to you, angry human. I sense what you sense, whether I wish to or not. And right now, you are very . . . sensory.'

I ignore him, focusing instead on not losing sight of Raith as he weaves through the less traveled paths of the campus. Pyrin has disappeared again, as elementals often do when not needed, but I can still feel Typhon's presence hovering close by.

He leads me to a small, sheltered alcove beneath one of the stone archways connecting the buildings. It's secluded but not completely private – anyone could pass by, though few do in the dinner rush. When he finally turns to face me, his expression is unreadable as always.

'You're avoiding me,' I say, immediately regretting how accusatory it sounds.

One corner of his mouth quirks up. 'I'm literally standing in front of you.'

'You know what I mean. Since . . .' I trail off, unsure how to finish. Since he kissed me like the world was ending? Since he made me feel things I'd never felt before?

He takes a step closer, and I have to force myself not to back away – not out of fear, but because the magnetic pull between us is almost overwhelming. Up close, I can see the fine details of his scars, the way they twist across his skin like rivers of frozen fire. The flecks of orange floating in golden eyes.

'I shouldn't have done that,' he says, voice rough. 'Put my hands on you. It was . . . reckless.'

'I wanted you to,' I counter, refusing to let him dismiss what happened between us. 'I still do.'

His jaw tightens, eyes darkening as they drop to my lips. 'You don't know what you're saying.'

'Pretty sure I do.' I step closer, close enough to feel the heat radiating from his body. It's always there, that unnatural warmth – like standing near a banked fire. 'Did you not want to?'

His laugh is harsh, disbelieving. 'Is that what you think? That I didn't want to?'

'How would I know? You kissed me again. And you started avoiding me. Again.'

'I've been busy.'

'Busy avoiding me.'

'Busy trying not to think about you,' he growls, and the raw honesty in his voice makes my heart stutter. 'Busy trying not to imagine what would have happened if we hadn't stopped that night.'

The words hang between us, charged with possibilities. I can't help the way my breath catches, the way my body responds to the images his words conjure – his hands on my skin, his mouth trailing down my neck, my body pressed against his with nothing between us.

'Nessa—' He breaks off, takes a breath. 'There are things happening. Dangerous things. I need to stay focused, and you . . .' He shakes his head. 'You're a fucking distraction I can't afford right now.'

'A distraction?' I step closer, close enough that I can feel his heat beckoning me like a siren's call. 'Is that all I am to you?'

He growls – actually growls – and suddenly his hand is at the back of my neck, fingers tangling in my hair. He doesn't pull me closer, doesn't push me away, just holds me there in that exquisite tension.

'You know damn well that's not all you are,' he says, his voice a dangerous rumble that I feel more than hear.

His eyes lock with mine, and I see conflict raging there – desire and restraint, need and fear, all battling for dominance. His thumb brushes the sensitive skin behind my ear, sending shivers down my spine.

'Then what am I to you, Raith?' I challenge, my voice barely above a whisper.

'A risk,' he answers, his grip tightening slightly. 'A beautiful, tempting risk that I shouldn't be taking. For your sake and mine. I've told you I'm dangerous for you. More than you can understand.'

'I'm not afraid.'

'You should be.' His gaze drops to my mouth again, hungry and hot. 'You have no idea what I'm capable of – what you'd be walking into if you got tied up with me.'

'Then show me,' I breathe, leaning in, closing the distance between us until our lips are almost touching. 'Because I don't think vague threats are going to be enough to stop me from wanting this. From wanting you.'

For one breathless moment, I think he's going to kiss me again. I can feel his resistance crumbling, sense the moment he's about to give in.

Before he can respond, his eyes shift to something over my shoulder, his entire body tensing. His hand drops from my neck as he puts himself between me and whatever he's seen.

'What is it?' I whisper, my hand automatically falling to the practice rapier at my hip.

'I don't know,' he mutters. 'Something . . . wrong.'

I follow his gaze but see nothing – just shadows gathering as twilight deepens across the courtyard. Yet I feel it too, a creeping coldness that has nothing to do with the winter air. A presence that raises the hair on my arms and sends a shiver down my spine.

'Typhon?'

'I sense it, angry human. Something that does not belong. Something . . . hungry.'

'Is it what I think it is?'

'Perhaps. There is a void where there should be presence. A darkness that consumes light. I have felt such things before, long ago.'

Raith's hand goes to his sword, the metal whispering against the scabbard as he draws it partially. 'Stay behind me.'

'I can fight,' I remind him.

'I know.' His voice softens slightly, even as his body remains tense and ready.

We stand frozen, watching the shadows, the moment of passion between us now replaced with shared vigilance. The presence feels like it's circling us, assessing, calculating.

'If it attacks, I will reveal myself,' Typhon warns. 'The consequences be damned.'

'You can't. People will know.'

'I will not let you die to protect a secret, angry human. That is not the oath I swore.'

After a long, tense moment, the strange sensation fades, leaving only an echo of dread in its wake.

'What was that?' I ask, my voice barely audible.

Raith's jaw works as he slowly sheaths his sword. 'Don't know.'

He studies me for a moment longer, then nods once. 'I'm walking you back to your tower.'

I should protest. Should remind him I can take care of myself. But the memory of that cold, watching presence is still too fresh, and the warmth of him beside me too comforting to refuse.

'Alright,' I agree.

As we walk, our shoulders occasionally brush, sending jolts of electricity through my skin. Neither of us speaks for a while, but the silence isn't uncomfortable. It's charged, full of all the things we're not saying.

'He does not mate with you, yet he acts as though you belong to him. As if you are his charge to protect,' Typhon observes. *'Humans are strange creatures.'*

'It's complicated.'

'It seems very simple to me. You desire him. He desires you. I fail to see what complicates this natural process.'

'Everything else in the whole damn world complicates it, Typhon. He's keeping secrets. I'm keeping secrets. We're surrounded by people who want to kill us. There's possibly a siphon hunting on campus. And that's not even counting the Crucible.'

'Ah, yes. The human tendency to overthink simple matters. In the elemental realm, desire is acted upon or it is not. There is no . . . what is the word? Angst.'

'Well, I'm sorry we're not as evolved as you are.'

'Apology accepted. Though I must note that even with all these complications, your body still responds to his proximity.'

I can't argue with that, so I don't try.

'So,' Raith says suddenly, breaking the silence. 'You can heal now.'

I stumble slightly, caught off guard. 'How did you—'

'Pyrin told me.'

I stare. 'I only just figured it out. How the hell would he know?'

'Typhon told him.'

There's a trickle of embarrassment and guilt through the tether.

'Perhaps I mentioned it in passing. I am proud of your power and wished to share with someone who would understand its importance. Nothing more.'

I can't make myself feel mad, though. I only smile and shake my head. 'An ancient and a fucking gossip,' I mutter under my breath.

'Such disrespect,' Typhon scoffs.

'The healing is a good thing, Nessa. It's incredible.' There's a kind of sadness in his eyes I can't figure out as he speaks.

'He thinks of someone who could have used your ability. Someone he lost.'

'How do you know that?'

Raith stops walking, turning to face me. 'You know how many people die here from injuries that could have been healed with the right skills? How many lives could be saved in battle with a single person who can do what you did?'

'I'm still figuring it out,' I admit. 'I don't even know if I can heal others, or just myself.'

His eyes hold mine, intense and searching. 'Just be careful who knows about it. There are people here who would kill for that kind of power.'

'Bad news for them. Killing me isn't going to grant them the power.'

'No, but it might convince them to go to desperate lengths to coerce you.'

'People like Malakai?'

'Among others.'

At the entrance to the water tower, Raith stops. His fingers graze mine – brief, barely there, but deliberate, sending a trickle of fire into my body.

'I'm not going to let anything happen to you, Nessa. Or your friends. Not even during the Crucible,' he tells me. 'The fires are with me on this. You know we're not what the others think of us. We're good people. Honorable, loyal. They know what Malakai and Serena are doing and they think it's fucked up. Veeni and Jirai excluded, of course. The rest of us will be there and we'll be ready to watch your backs.'

Gratitude and appreciation swells within me. 'Thank you. And . . . thank them for me, too.'

'And I also meant what I said about you being a distraction.' His eyes soften, just for a moment. 'A fucking beautiful distraction, Nessa.'

My heart swells at the words, at the tenderness in his voice that so few ever get to hear.

'You don't have to protect me, you know,' I tell him. 'I'm stronger than I look.'

'Trust me, I know exactly how strong you are.' His hand reaches up, thumb brushing across my cheek in a touch so gentle it makes my breath catch. 'That doesn't mean I don't want to keep you safe anyway.'

For a moment, we're suspended in perfect stillness, the world narrowing to just the two of us. His eyes drop to my lips again, and I feel myself leaning in, drawn by that invisible current that always seems to pull us together.

'This place changes people,' Raith says. 'Hardens them. Strips away the things that make us human and only leaves hard, sharp edges. But not you. You're still in there. Still alive. Still you. And that . . . that's fucking worth protecting.'

I feel myself leaning closer to him, eyes falling to his lips as my heart feels like it's flipping over itself.

'Raith . . .'

He steps back suddenly, the moment broken. 'I should go.'

Before I can respond, he turns and walks away, back straight, posture alert. Even now, he's scanning for threats, always the protector.

I watch until he disappears into the growing darkness, trying to ignore the ache in my chest that has nothing to do with fear and everything to do with wanting something I'm not sure I can have.

'You could have had it just now,' Typhon observes. *'If you had claimed his lips with yours, he would not have resisted. Pyrin agrees that you two are making an elaborate dance out of what could be done in a few simple thrusts.'*

'First of all, I'd appreciate it if you and Pyrin stopped gossiping behind our backs.'

'We are elementals. We do not gossip. We simply share observations.'

'You're just a big, ancient, powerful gossip and I won't be convinced otherwise. And it's not as simple as you make it out to be. Raith is hiding something big and he's warning me not to get involved. He thinks I'll be

*in even more danger if I do, and more danger is probably the last thing
I need right now.'*

*'Blah, blah, as you humans say. It is only you humans who insist on
making it complicated.'*

Maybe he's right. Maybe I'm overthinking everything. But as I
climb the tower stairs toward my room, I can't shake the feeling of
cold, hungry eyes watching from the shadows. Waiting. Patient.
Inevitable.

Chapter 26

I'm on my way to channeling class when I see something that slows my pace. A group of second-year fires passes with their elementals on full display. Though I haven't heard anything direct, it seems clear that the older students are preparing for some kind of test as well. The Crucible might only be for first-years, but it seems like the challenges don't stop if we survive this year.

One of the upper-year fires bumps me and doesn't apologize as his huge fire lion glares down at me. They both appear oblivious to Typhon's threats.

'I could suck the marrow from their bones if you'd permit it,' Typhon growls.

'Not worth it, Typhon.'

Another fire catches my attention, but this one is a first-year. I've seen him practicing with Raith several times. I'm pretty sure his name is Cade. He's more narrow in the shoulders and shorter than the average first-year, and there's an innocence in his expression that feels out of place on campus. It's as if, somehow, the cruelty here hasn't touched him yet.

Cade spares a glance over his shoulder before pausing with his hand on the door of a random classroom. Something about his furtive movements triggers an alarm in my mind – his shoulders hunched, his steps too careful, like he's afraid of making noise.

The corridor is quickly emptying as students head to afternoon classes after lunch. I've been wandering the halls, taking what Ambrose calls 'the scenic route' to channeling class, trying to clear my head of the thousands of thoughts swirling through it. The Crucible. My new healing abilities. Raith's hot-and-cold behavior.

And I've come to enjoy watching the flow of students across campus. Noticing the differences in older students compared to ourselves. Paying attention to the way the lines between affinities seem to have blurred ever-so-slightly with each year of survival here at Confluence. In a way, it's encouraging. It makes me think that things could get better with time.

I know I should hurry to class, but something tugs at me as Cade pulls open the door. He's slender with close-cropped dark hair and the red-gold eyes common among fire affinities, probably around my age but with a smaller build that makes him appear younger.

I'm about to move on when I hear a loud crash from inside the room, followed by a cry of pain that makes me freeze. I look around to see if anyone else has reacted, but nobody is stopping. Nobody else cares.

'Perhaps we should continue on our way,' Typhon suggests, his tone disinterested. 'The affairs of small fire humans are of no consequence to us.'

'What if he's hurt? Or in trouble?'

'Then that is the natural order of things. The weak perish. The strong survive. This is the way of all worlds, angry human.'

I roll my eyes. 'The strong should protect, not just survive. I know you believe that too, deep down.'

Typhon says nothing, but I do feel a faint pulsing of approval through the tether as I approach the door, pressing my ear against it. There's another crash, followed by muffled voices. I ease the door open just enough to peer inside.

It's a smaller room with a few pieces of equipment lying around as if students have been using it as a makeshift training arena. There are blunted weapons lying haphazardly and a fighting ring marked out by chalk on the stone floor.

Cade is on his knees, surrounded by three earth students who tower over him. All of them are large and racked with muscles, the green mountain marks glowing on their hands. Their expressions are hard and unforgiving. The largest of them – a thick-shouldered student with a shaved head and a cruel smile – holds a thick warhammer in two hands as if he's thinking about slamming it down on the fire affinity.

'Please,' Cade gasps, 'I was only coming to practice. I didn't know you all were here.'

'Practice what?' the earth student sneers, pressing the blade closer. 'How to be a Red Kingdom spy?'

'I'm not. I've never even been near Red Kingdom—'

'Liar,' another earth student hisses, kicking over a weapon rack with a thunderous crash. A boar that looks like it's made of pure stone materializes behind him, eyes like emeralds as it prowls a circle around the kneeling fire. 'Fuckers like you are the reason nobody trusts us. Malakai says he can help us weed out the traitors. And that if we don't, you turncoats will stab us in the back during the Crucible at the first chance you get.'

'I'm not a turncoat. I swear it.'

Fucking Malakai again. His reach extends beyond just the waters. I'd heard rumors, but now I can see it plain as day.

'Yes. Evidence of your water enemy expanding his influence,' Typhon observes. *'This is useful intelligence. Let us leave the weak one to his fate.'*

Cade's eyes meet mine through the crack in the door. Instead of looking to me for help, it almost seems like he is worried about *me*. Worried I'll intervene and get hurt?

Godsdammit . . .

'I feel a foolish idea forming in your mind, angry human.'

'Want to know what I think?' The earth with the hammer leans closer. 'You're one of Raith Hollow's little pets. Everyone sees him collecting his little band of fire freaks. Training them in secret.' He spits on the floor. 'Probably getting ready to slit our throats while we sleep.'

Cade straightens, eyes growing defiant. 'Raith isn't a traitor. He's one of the few good people at this fucking school.'

'The weak one has some backbone after all.'

The third earth catches the fire student by the hair, yanking his head back. 'Malakai says Hollow's recruiting for Red Kingdom. Says he's building an army right under our noses.'

My fingers tighten around the door handle. This is escalating, and fast.

One of the earths produces a knife, pressing it against the fire's throat until a thin line of blood dribbles free.

'Fuck it,' I mutter, pushing the door open.

Three heads snap toward me. Cade's eyes widen further with both hope and horror.

'Three on one? Hardly seems fair,' I say as I step inside, forcing a calm I don't feel into my voice. My fingers drift to the rapier at my hip. I keep my posture loose, ready to move.

'Mind your own business, water,' the leader says, not taking the blade from Cade's throat. 'This is between us and the fire traitor.'

'That's Nessa Thorne,' one of the earths says. 'She's fucking Raith and that legacy with the blonde hair.'

'Ah,' the one with the hammer says. 'That's why you're here. Does he ask you to watch over his pets in exchange for orgasms? Not a bad deal, I guess. For him at least.'

I step fully into the room, letting the door close behind me.

'Should I show myself?' Typhon asks.

'Flying fish only.'

The earths face me as the fire takes the opportunity to move away and come toward me. All three earth elementals are in plain view now – a stone wolf and a serpent made of vines have joined the rock boar.

I let Typhon materialize in his flying fish form, knowing he appears small and harmless to them. No need to reveal our true strength unless absolutely necessary.

'I'm not here to fight,' I say, holding up my hands. 'Just looked like three people picking an unfair fight.'

The earth with the shaved head comes closer. 'All we wanted to do was send a message. But maybe you can save us the trouble. Tell your fire boyfriend that we know what he's planning. Malakai knows, too. You think you can trust those Red Kingdom sympathizers? They'll cut your throat the second they get the chance.'

Cade edges closer to me, his elemental – a small fire fox – materializing at his feet.

I assess the three earths carefully. They're big, but size isn't everything in a fight. Especially not against someone trained by Raith.

'We're going to walk out of here. I'd suggest none of you follow,' I say, sliding my feet into a ready stance that looks casual but isn't. 'Okay?'

'She suggests we don't follow,' one of the earths says. 'Sounds like a threat, doesn't it?'

'Sounds a lot like a threat,' the earth with the hammer agrees.

'It's not a threat. We're just going to walk away, and you're all going to let us.'

'Or what? Your flying fish will slap us?'

The leader laughs, a harsh sound that bounces off the high walls. 'Your boyfriends aren't here to protect you, Thorne. Malakai and Serena both want you dead, so maybe we could do them a quick favor. Wonder how long it'd be before someone found your bodies in here. Maybe a week? Maybe—'

The training room door flies open with enough force to slam against the wall, making all of us jump. Framed in the doorway stands Raith, his face cast in shadow, eyes burning with cold fury. His fire panther, Pyrin, slinks in beside him, flames rippling across his muscular form with every step.

The atmosphere in the room changes instantly, like the air before a lightning strike.

'Hollow,' the earth leader acknowledges, his bravado faltering slightly.

Raith's gaze sweeps the room, taking in the fallen weapons, the fire student's bloodied neck, and me standing between them all. Something dangerous flashes in his eyes, and I feel a chill despite the heat that rolls off him in waves.

'Cade,' he says to the fire student, his voice deceptively calm. 'Outside. Now.'

The student – Cade – doesn't hesitate. He scurries past Raith and disappears into the corridor.

'You three,' Raith continues, his attention fixing on the earths. 'What part of "leave my people alone" was unclear?'

The leader straightens, though I notice his hand has a slight tremor. 'We were just—'

'I know exactly what you were "just" doing,' Raith cuts him off. 'And I know who put you up to it. Tell Malakai that if he has a problem with me, he can face me himself instead of sending you to do his dirty work.'

'You calling us his fucking lackeys?' the second earth demands, hands clenching into fists as his stone bear grows larger behind him.

Raith doesn't even blink. 'I'm calling you stupid. There's a difference.' His voice drops even lower. 'Fucking with my people when I warned you. That is very stupid. Now get out while you still can.'

For a moment, I think they might be foolish enough to challenge him. The leader's eyes dart between Raith and me, calculating odds. But then Pyrin growls – a sound like wood cracking in a bonfire – and the decision is made.

'This isn't over,' the leader mutters as they file past Raith.

'It never is,' Raith replies, his tone flat.

Once they're gone, Raith turns his attention to me. He doesn't look pleased.

'What the hells were you thinking?' he demands, closing the door and stalking toward me. 'Three earths? Alone?'

'I was thinking Cade looked like he needed help,' I reply, bristling at his tone. 'And how the hells are you always showing up when I'm in danger?'

'Typhon told Pyrin what was happening. I left channeling class as soon as I heard.'

'Typhon . . .'

What use are allies if you don't call upon them in times of need? Of course, I could have ripped them all to ribbons, even in my kuratokken form. But I imagined the sight of the fire-touched would send them scattering. My assessment was correct, as usual.'

'So you can show up when Typhon calls for you, but you stand me up for weapons training?' I ask.

Raith runs a hand through his dark hair, leaving strands standing on end. 'I was busy. But I had one of my people stand watch while you trained. I always do when I can't be there.'

'Seriously?'

'Yes.'

As much as I want to be mad that he's assigning people to stand watch over me without even running the idea by me . . . I find I'm both flattered and even a little bit charmed. 'Well,' I say, trying to stoke the anger I know I should feel. 'I don't need you treating me like some damsel in distress, because I'm not.'

'I know exactly how capable you are. But I don't expect my enemies or yours to fight fair. That means I want to be ready to punch back if they come for you.'

'Let me guess, even if I ask you to stop, it won't matter?'

'Correct.'

I sigh, shaking my head.

'Look. I haven't been trying to avoid you. I've just been dealing with . . . complications.'

'What complications?'

'It doesn't matter.' He gestures to the door. 'We should check on Cade.'

'You mean the guy you just dismissed like he was a nuisance?' I ask, refusing to let him change the subject.

His jaw clenches. 'That's not what happened. Cade knows I don't see him that way.'

'Isn't it? You barely looked at him.'

'Because I was more focused on making sure you didn't get yourself killed,' he retorts. 'And for the record, Cade knows the drill. Safety first, questions later.'

I frown. 'What drill? Do you make a habit of rescuing him?'

Raith's hard features momentarily soften. 'Let's just say it's not his first run-in with trouble.'

Before I can press further, Raith opens the door. Cade stands in the corridor, his back pressed against the opposite wall. He straightens immediately when he sees Raith, brushing self-consciously at the small bloodstain on his collar.

'I'm sorry,' he blurts out. 'I was trying to keep a low profile like you said. But they—'

'It's not your fault,' Raith interrupts, his voice gentler than I've heard it before. He approaches Cade and examines the cut on his neck. 'It's shallow. You'll be fine.'

To my surprise, Raith produces a small cloth from his pocket and carefully cleans away the blood. The tender care in the gesture makes something twist in my chest. I'm instantly reminded of his mention of a brother he lost. *Gareth.*

'Did you at least remember what I taught you?' Raith asks.

Cade's face falls. 'I froze up. Couldn't remember any of the moves.'

'That's normal,' Raith says. 'It happens to everyone the first few times.'

'Not to you,' Cade mutters.

'Even me.' Raith glances at me, then back to Cade. 'This is Nessa Thorne, by the way. She was trying to help you, which was brave but reckless.'

'Yeah . . . I know who she is. Everyone does. Thanks, Nessa,' Cade says to me, his eyes still downcast. 'But you shouldn't have risked it. They're looking for any excuse to hurt fires right now.'

'Why?' I ask. 'What's happening?'

Cade and Raith exchange a look, and I get the distinct impression they're deciding how much to tell me.

'Malakai has been spreading rumors,' Raith finally says. 'Telling people that the fires are working with Red Kingdom. That we're planning to sabotage the Crucible with outside help.'

'That's ridiculous,' I say. 'Everyone has to see he's lying.'

'Do they?' Raith raises an eyebrow, the scarred side of his face pulling taut. 'Look at history, Nessa. Every time there's conflict, the fires get blamed. We're the outsiders, the ones who don't fit neatly into Empire society. Even the earths don't get quite the same blame as us since they're more often used defensively in combat. Fires are easiest to blame. Simple as that.'

'But that's—' I begin, then stop, the words lodging in my throat as I realize he's right. Even someone who seems as sweet and kind as Mireen carries her prejudices deeply. Even I can't pretend I don't have some of my own.

'He speaks truth,' Typhon observes. *'Humans do love their tribalism.'*

Cade shifts nervously from foot to foot. 'I should go. I'll be late for elemental conditioning.'

Raith nods. 'Take the west corridor. Fewer people.'

Cade hesitates, looking between us again. 'Are we still on for our training tomorrow?'

'Same time, same place,' Raith confirms. 'And Cade? Next time, don't go anywhere alone. Stay with Tifa and Jenner like I told you.'

Once Cade disappears around the corner, I turn to Raith. 'Why are you helping him?'

'I'm teaching him to survive,' Raith says. 'Just like I'm teaching you.'

'Considering we've kissed twice, I hope you're not teaching him *just* like me,' I say with a half smile.

Raith's face is hard, but his eyes fall. I want to say more, to ask him why he withdraws every time we get closer, but there's something in his expression that stops me – a weariness that goes bone-deep.

'How many others are you protecting?' I ask instead.

He shrugs, avoiding my gaze. 'A few.'

'Why?'

'Because someone has to. Because I can.'

We start walking, falling into step beside each other. I'm already late for channeling class, but suddenly that doesn't seem to matter much.

'Is your work training all these other people the reason you've been too busy to make time for me?' I ask after a moment of silence.

'That, and other things.'

'What other things?'

He shoots me a sidelong glance. 'Has anyone ever told you that you ask a lot of questions?'

'It's been mentioned.'

A reluctant smile tugs at the corner of his mouth, and my heart does that stupid flutter thing it always does when he lets his guard down, even for a moment.

'So?' I press. 'What's kept you so busy that you couldn't spare an hour for training the other night?'

He sighs, slowing his pace. 'Malakai is recruiting across affinities, building alliances. The earths you just met? They're just foot soldiers. He's got at least fifteen teams aligned with him now, maybe more.'

'Fifteen?' My throat tightens. 'That's—'

'A small army,' Raith finishes. 'More than half the surviving first-years. And they're all coming for anyone who isn't with them.'

'Including us.' It's not a question.

'Especially us.' He runs a hand over his face, the scars stark against his skin in the corridor's harsh light. 'I've been trying to build alliances of our own. Talking to other fires, some airs who are on the fence. Even a few earths who haven't bought into Malakai's bullshit.'

'That's why you've been missing training? You're building your own army?'

'Not an army. A safety net. People who will watch each other's backs during the Crucible.' He gives me a pointed look. 'People who will watch your back.'

Something warm unfurls in my chest at his words. Despite all his talk about keeping me at a distance, he's still been working to protect me. He almost makes it sound as if all of his efforts are just to keep me safe. But the thought is ridiculous, and I dismiss it before it can take root.

'I can take care of myself, you know,' I remind him, though there's no real heat in it.

'I know you can,' he says, surprisingly serious. 'But nobody survives Confluence alone, Nessa. Not even you. Especially not this year.'

We've reached a junction in the corridor – left leads to the channeling classrooms, right to the fire tower. We both stop, hovering in that space between parting and staying.

'Cade reminds you of someone,' I say. 'That's why you're helping him, right?'

Raith goes very still. 'What makes you say that?'

'The way you looked at him. Like you were seeing someone else. And what you told me about your brother. Gareth. It just seemed like maybe there was something there . . .'

He's silent for so long I think he won't answer. When he finally speaks, his voice is rough, like he has to force the words out.

'He's a lot like Gareth. Yeah.' The admission seems to cost him something.

I wait, not pushing, giving him space to continue or not.

'Gareth was a fire, like me,' Raith says, his eyes fixed on some distant point. 'My younger brother, but still smaller than other kids his age. Easy target.'

I hear what he doesn't say – that Gareth isn't alive anymore. That something happened to the brother he speaks of in past tense.

'Is that why you came to Confluence?' I ask softly. 'Because of Gareth?'

His eyes snap back to mine, suddenly guarded again. 'He's one of the reasons. Yes.'

It's not the whole truth. I can see it in the way his shoulders tense, the way his elemental, Pyrin, paces restlessly at his feet, flames flickering with agitation. But it's more than he's shared before, and I know better than to push my luck.

He takes the brief pause as an opportunity to change the subject. 'Have you and your fish started practicing together yet?'

Tell the scarred fire human I am not a fish. I am a dragon who chooses, out of generosity, to appear as a fish to avoid terrifying the lesser

beings around me. As one who has seen my true form, I expect him to
acknowledge the grandeur and splendor and not make foolish fish jokes.'

'Not yet. But I'll make sure we do soon.'

'Good,' Raith says, but there's warmth in his voice. His eyes meet
mine, and for a moment, there's no impending Crucible, no danger,
no complications – just the two of us standing too close in an empty
corridor, drawn together by something neither of us fully understands.

'I should let you get to class,' he says, breaking the spell.

'Right. Yeah. Sestra is going to pop a blood vessel with how late
I am. Gods know she already hates me for being a failure of a water
channeler.'

'You didn't tell me you were struggling in classes.'

'Just channeling . . .' I look around, making sure we're alone.
'What I am . . . it doesn't work the same way as a normal affinity.
Nothing she teaches works for me. And I can't keep up with the
other waters. But I can't show Sestra I'm progressing in other areas.
Obviously. So . . . she just thinks I'm terrible and despises me for it.'

'Fuck her.'

I laugh. 'I don't see how that would help.'

Amusement touches his expression. 'You know what I mean.'

'Yeah, well . . . I should get going.'

His expression turns serious again. 'Be careful, Nessa. These next
few weeks before the Crucible – they're going to be dangerous.
Malakai's making moves, and he's not the only threat out there.'

'The siphon,' I say quietly. Cold, icy terror slips under my skin at
the memory of that feeling the other night – like something hungry
was lurking just out of view and waiting to strike.

He nods. 'Just . . . watch your back.'

'I thought that was your job,' I say, trying for levity.

'It is.' His voice drops, sending a shiver down my spine that has
nothing to do with fear. 'But I can't be everywhere.'

'Can't you?' I tease. 'Because lately it seems like whenever I turn
around, you're there. Lurking in shadows, swooping in to save the day.'

'I don't lurk,' he protests.

'You absolutely lurk. It's very mysterious and brooding.'

A student passes by, glancing curiously at us before hurrying on.

'Go,' Raith says again, taking a step back. 'Before someone sees us together and adds more fuel to Malakai's rumors.'

We part ways at the junction, each heading toward our respective classes. I can feel his eyes on my back as I walk away, watchful, protective.

My guard dog, as some have started calling him. But there's more to it than that – more to him than the dangerous exterior he shows the world. The gentleness with Cade had revealed that much. The mention of Gareth had shown even more.

'He carries much pain,' Typhon observes, uncharacteristically somber. *'Pain and purpose intertwined.'*

'I know.' And I do know, somehow. I can see it in the way he moves, the way he keeps a barrier between himself and others, the way he tries to hold himself apart from me. Raith Hollow is a man with ghosts, with burdens I can only begin to guess at.

But for all his warnings about danger – about himself being dangerous for me – I can't bring myself to stay away. Something about him calls to me, draws me in despite every rational thought telling me to keep my distance.

Maybe we're both a little reckless, a little broken. Maybe that's why we keep circling each other, unable to fully connect, unable to fully let go.

As I slip into channeling class, murmuring apologies for my tardiness, I can still see the fierce protectiveness in his eyes when he faced down those earths. Still hear the rough edge in his voice when he spoke his brother's name.

Gareth. A piece of the puzzle that is Raith Hollow. Not the whole picture, not by far, but a start.

Tomorrow, I decide. Tomorrow I'll push a little harder, dig a little deeper. Tomorrow I'll try to understand the man who seems determined to protect me while keeping me at arm's length.

I just hope we have enough tomorrows left.

Chapter 27

'We need to talk.'

Raith's voice startles me as he materializes from the shadows just outside the water tower. I nearly drop my flask, glancing around to make sure no one has noticed us. Some fourth-years are arguing in low voices nearby – a pair of fires and earths, their elementals on display as tempers seem to run high.

'About what?' I ask, keeping my voice low, though I don't know why, exactly. Everybody's attention is on the arguing fourth-years.

'Not here.' His eyes – amber in the morning light – scan the tower stairs behind me. 'Meet me at the eastern gate in an hour. Wear something you can move in.'

I arch an eyebrow. It is a weekend, so our class schedule is light. I had been planning to find an empty room to practice pretending to be a water affinity. Sestra has been threatening some kind of exam, and I want to be ready when it comes.

'Something I can move in? Are we training again?'

'Better than training.' For a moment, something almost playful flashes across his face. 'I want to show you something.'

Before I can ask more questions, he slips away, footsteps silent against the stone floor. I watch him go, curiosity piqued despite my better judgment.

An hour later, I'm waiting by the eastern gate, dressed in my training leathers with my practice rapier secured at my hip. The guard station beside the main gates leading outside the castle stands empty – unusual for midday – but I don't question the stroke of luck.

'They rotate guards at this hour.' Raith appears beside me,

seemingly from nowhere. 'Usually, they stop for a game of dice before returning to their posts, meaning we've still got a bit.'

'How do you know these things?' I ask. It's far from the first time Raith has known something he should have no way to know.

He offers a cryptic smile. 'I pay attention.'

He looks . . . amazing. He wears the black aspirant uniform trimmed in silver like the majority of students at Confluence, but he wears it so damn well. Broad shoulders. Narrow waist. Thick arms corded with muscle. And his face. Gods. Even with the majority of the left side twisted by scars, he's beautiful.

He wears his training sword across his back. By now, every last first-year knows he's the deadliest of all of us with that blade.

'So . . . we're leaving the grounds?' I can't keep the surprise from my voice. Students rarely leave Confluence except under very specific circumstances. We're prisoners here in all but name.

'If you're afraid, we could skip it.' There's a challenge in his eyes, and something else – an invitation.

'Lead the way,' I answer, refusing to be baited.

We slip through the gate, cross the grassy field that still bears faint signs of the divots driven by hundreds of carts arriving to drop us off after Selection Day. Beyond the field is what looks like endless forest. I expect Raith to immediately set a punishing pace, as he does in our training sessions, but instead he matches his stride to mine, our shoulders occasionally brushing as we navigate the uneven terrain.

The trees are all bare by now, providing soft footing under our feet. The air carries a cold bite as winter starts taking hold.

'Where are we going?' I finally ask after several minutes of companionable silence.

'The quarry.' He pushes a low-hanging branch aside for me. 'It's the most likely location for this year's Crucible.'

'How can you be sure?'

'I'm not. But I've been making trips outside the walls since we arrived. Staff has been coming out this way occasionally. I've followed their tracks, but I haven't caught any of them in the act yet.'

The casual admission shocks me. Most students wouldn't dare sneak out once, and Raith has been doing it regularly? Following the tracks of instructors and gathering information? I'm suddenly struck by how much more well-suited he is for this whole experience than I am – how of all people, I feel like the worst to be gifted with the burden and blessing of being unbound.

'*You are worthy, angry human,*' Typhon notes. '*Unrelated topic . . . if we find wild game, I humbly request to eat it.*'

'*Fine. But don't make it suffer.*'

I sense Typhon take off, flying high overhead as he begins his hunt.

We follow a narrow game trail that winds through ancient trees, their massive trunks covered in emerald moss.

'You really think we have a chance in the Crucible? Every day, it seems like our odds get worse,' I ask, voicing the fear that's been growing since my disastrous water channeling exam.

Raith stops so suddenly I nearly collide with him. When he turns, his expression is unexpectedly earnest.

'I wouldn't be training you if I didn't.' His voice lacks its usual edge. 'You're stronger than you think, Nessa. Stronger than any of them think.'

'I failed a basic water channeling exercise yesterday,' I remind him.

'Water channeling isn't everything.' He resumes walking, slower now. 'The Crucible is likely going to test more than just affinity strength. It will test survival instinct, adaptability, clear thinking under pressure.' His gaze slides to me. 'You excel at all of those.'

The unexpected praise warms me. 'You've been watching me that closely?'

'I watch everyone,' he says, but there's a softness in his tone that contradicts his words. 'You're just . . . more pleasant to watch than the rest.'

A giddy, girlish smile threatens to split my face, but I try to contain it as much as I can.

We walk in silence for a while, the forest growing denser around us. Sunlight filters through the bare canopy in dappled patterns, dancing across the forest floor with each breeze.

'You never talk about yourself,' I say, breaking the quiet. 'Not really.'

'What's there to talk about?' His voice is carefully neutral.

'Your family, where you grew up, how you came to Confluence . . .' I study his profile. 'You know practically everything about me, but you're still a mystery.'

He's quiet for so long I think he won't answer. When he finally speaks, his voice is low, almost distant.

'I had two siblings. An older sister and the brother I told you about.' Past tense. The loss evident in those simple words. 'My brother, Gareth, was the youngest. Serious kid, always had his nose in a book.' A ghost of a smile crosses his face. 'He wanted to be a scholar, not a warrior.'

'Were you close?' I navigate around a fallen log, noting how Raith automatically extends his hand to steady me, then lets go the moment I'm secure.

'As close as brothers can be when one is destined to lead and the other to follow.' Something dark flickers in his eyes. 'I tried to protect him. Failed.'

Uttering the words seems to physically pain him, and part of me is sorry for asking. I can see it in the tight line of his jaw, the way his fingers briefly clench at his side. 'Destined to lead?' I ask carefully.

His jaw ticks. 'This is why I try not to talk about myself. Too easy to say things I shouldn't. I'm going to ask you not to press the issue, Nessa. Forget I said it.'

I start to smile, but then realize he's serious. The earnestness in his expression and . . . fear there wipes the amusement from my face. I nod instead. 'Okay . . .'

He looks relieved. 'Good.'

'What happened to Gareth? To your siblings?'

He's quiet for a moment, clearly picking through the truth and deciding which scraps he can share. 'Fire.' His hand rises unconsciously to the scarred side of his face. 'Betrayal.'

I choose my next words carefully, hyper aware that the wrong question or statement could have his armor back up in the blink of an eye. 'Is that why you're here? Did the person who betrayed you and your family come here? Or . . .'

'Have you told your friends about being unbound, yet?' he counters.

I flinch. The question feels like a punch of guilt. Unexpected and unpleasant. 'I haven't . . .'

'Because you care about them. Because the knowledge could put them in danger.'

I feel another stupid smile crossing my mouth. 'Are you saying you care about me?'

Raith almost rolls his eyes. 'No. I just dedicate the majority of my waking hours to worrying about your safety. I spend hours training you, keeping an eye on you, and thinking about you because I don't give a shit about you.'

I lower my eyes, but Raith crooks his index finger and lifts my chin, forcing me to meet his eyes. 'Of course I fucking care about you, Nessa. If that wasn't clear to you by now, I'm going to be worried about your observation skills. But we need to keep moving if we're going to get you back in time for classes.'

I don't trust myself to speak, so I swallow my words and hope the way my heart flutters isn't as obvious as it feels.

We emerge from the tree line to find ourselves at the edge of a massive quarry – a vast bowl carved from the mountainside, its steep walls plunging to a relatively flat center. Ancient mining equipment lies abandoned around the perimeter, and at the quarry's deepest point, a dark pool of water glimmers in the sunlight.

'This is it?' I ask, momentarily distracted by the sheer scale of the place.

Raith nods, surveying the terrain with a critical eye. 'Perfect for an elemental battleground. Earth affinities have raw material to work with, water has the pool, air has open space, and fire . . .' He gestures to the dry brush that dots the quarry floor. 'Plenty of fuel.'

I walk to the edge, peering down at the drop. At least sixty feet to the quarry floor, with few obvious paths for descent.

'All we can really do is guess, but I think this place is where it will happen,' Raith continues, coming to stand beside me. 'Could be that we'll start here in the quarry itself. Like a bloodbath. Or it could be that this is the final battleground. Maybe we'll be out in the woods and have to work our way here. I'm not sure yet . . .'

The wind shifts, carrying his scent. I find myself greedily breathing it in, drinking in the automatic comfort it brings.

We kneel at the top of the quarry's edge in silence for a few moments before I speak. I know my mind should be on the Crucible, but I find myself picking over every word he's said since we left campus. 'Does Cade remind you of Gareth? I noticed the way you were with him. It reminded me of a big brother. I thought maybe . . .'

He meets my gaze, and pain flashes across his face, so raw and sudden it makes my chest ache. 'I see some of Gareth in Cade. Yes,' His voice drops. 'The kind of person that's too good for such a shitty world. And Kiera would've liked you. A lot.'

I frown, surprised. 'Why do you say that?'

'Because you're strong. Compassionate. You find a way to live in the filth of a place like this without letting it touch who you are. It's how she was. It's one of the things I admired so much about her.'

I bite my lip. 'Thank you.'

Raith gives the slightest nod of his head, eyes shifting back to the quarry as sadness seems to take hold of him. 'After they died . . . I swore I'd make surviving mean something. Whether I needed to be a shield or a sword, I didn't care. I just knew I'd make absolutely fucking sure nobody I cared about could be taken from me again. *Nobody.*'

In that moment, I see past the walls he's built – glimpse the depth of guilt and grief he carries. I see how the way he keeps himself aloof isn't emotional detachment or coldness. It's to protect himself from how deeply he cares. He can't bear the thought of losing anyone else, and he's terrified of opening himself to more hurt.

Before I can stop myself, I reach for his hand, my fingers sliding between his.

His skin burns against mine, the unnatural heat of a fire affinity, but he doesn't pull away. He doesn't even pull away when some of his fire starts to flow into me. With practice, I've learned to slow it substantially when I want, making the flow a trickle instead of a torrent.

The faint passage of power feels oddly intimate, like part of him is becoming part of me, temporarily joining with my essence in a quiet, private dance.

His fingers tighten around mine, just for a moment, before he gently disengages.

'There's more to see,' he says, but his voice has lost some of its hardness. 'There's a path down on the eastern side.'

As we pick our way along the quarry's edge, I find myself watching him more closely than the terrain. There's a grace to his movements, an awareness of his surroundings that speaks of years spent looking over his shoulder. Whatever shaped him into the man he is now left scars deeper than the visible ones on his face.

'What about you?' he asks unexpectedly. 'Your family. You never mention them either.'

'There's not much to tell,' I say reflexively. Protecting myself from the tragedy has become an instinct already – so automatic I hardly give it a moment's thought. I slow my pace, shaking my head. 'Sorry. No. That's not true. Around the time I turned sixteen, I started to notice strange things would happen when my emotions ran high.'

Raith gives a knowing nod. 'Early signs of elemental affinity are strange like that. Sometimes the unmarked can briefly demonstrate power to rival a primal, even if they can't control it.'

'I called a storm,' I say as we walk. 'I was mad over something stupid. My brothers and my dad were on the boat with me and I was fuming all morning. And then by the time I saw the storm coming, I couldn't stop it. Our boat got thrown against rocks and we were all flung into the waves. I tried to get to them, but everything happened so fast. I nearly drowned waiting out there on the waves hoping they'd come back up – diving as long as my breath would hold and trying to search for them.

'When I finally floated back to shore on a piece of wreckage, I was dumb enough to tell my mom and sister the truth about what happened. I guess I thought they'd understand and forgive me. They . . . didn't. They hated me for it. So I spent three years doing everything I could to make it right. I worked to get a new boat. I spent every day fishing to earn money like we would have if my dad and brothers were still around. I tried so fucking hard, and it never mattered.'

I wipe at my stinging eyes, shaking my head and laughing at myself. 'And I shouldn't feel sorry for myself.'

'Fuck that. You couldn't control it. You didn't know.'

'If I hadn't been mad that day, they would—'

'People get mad, Nessa. Fuck the Empire for making people think powers are something they need to hide. Maybe if you weren't worried about being captured in the night for showing your abilities, you could've learned to control it. It's not your fault.'

I look away from him, nodding even though I know I'm not letting his words through my walls. 'Yeah. I know.'

Raith cups my face, turning me toward him. His touch sends another wave of fire passing into my skin that pools and curls inside me until it feels like he's touching me all over. I know my cheeks are burning, but I can't stop the transfer of energy this time. 'It's not. Your. Fault, Nessa.'

I hold his eyes, and somehow I feel his sincerity passing through his touch, too, almost like a shadow of the way emotions move through my tether with Typhon. I know he means the words down to his bones.

'I think . . . I'm worried if I believe that, it'll mean I'm not paying for what I did. That I'm letting myself off the hook.'

'You volunteered,' he says softly, and I can see the realization dawning on him. 'That's why. You were punishing yourself.'

I can't meet his eyes anymore. Hearing it aloud makes me feel silly and foolish for it. 'They were happy to see me go.'

'They don't know what they lost,' Raith says quietly.

The simple statement catches me off guard. Before I can respond, he stops, raising a hand in warning. His entire demeanor shifts, tension radiating from every line of his body.

'What—' I begin, but he places a finger against his lips, then points toward a clearing ahead.

Two figures are approaching – one tall and imposing. The other is a familiar silhouette that makes my throat tighten. Bastian and . . . I don't recognize the older man, but I do recognize his ornamental uniform. He's an air primal, and a high ranking one at that. There's also an uncanny resemblance between him and Bastian.

The primal has blonde, nearly white hair and regal features. He's similar height to Bastian and a similar build. I can't be certain, but I would be shocked if I wasn't looking at Bastian's father.

Raith pulls me behind a massive fallen tree, his movements silent as shadow. We crouch together, hidden from view but close enough to hear their conversation. His arm wraps around me, protective and strong as he pulls me against his body. I do my best not to get distracted by the pleasant contact, focusing on the faint conversation I can barely make out.

'—wasting my time with these reports,' the primal says, his aristocratic voice sharp with impatience. 'I need something concrete, Bastian. Something worth reporting.'

'I told you, there's nothing definitive yet.' Bastian's voice lacks its usual arrogance, sounding almost defensive. 'But the instructors found another body last week. That's three this month.'

'Another burned-out mark?'

'Yes,' Bastian says.

Beside me, Raith goes utterly still. His hand finds mine in the shadows, squeezing in silent warning.

'The implications of a siphon on campus are dire,' the primal says with a disappointed sigh. 'But it may ultimately serve our purposes all the same.'

'Father, there's something else.' Bastian's voice takes on an urgency I've never heard from him before. 'You need to use your influence to call off this year's Crucible.'

The man folds his arms, scowling. 'Call off the Crucible? It has never been done.'

'Malakai and Serena are forming a small army. They're making alliances across affinities. I'm worried it's going to be a bloodbath this year.'

'It typically is, Bastian. You know this better than most.'

'How do you think the tri-emperors will react if half the first-year class ends up dead before graduation? Possibly more?'

His father scoffs. 'That won't happen. The majority of students will rush for the objective. Only a few small skirmishes will play out. There will be ten dead. Maybe twenty at most. This has gone on for centuries, Bastian. It's almost always the same.'

'Something's different this year. I can feel it. You have to call off the Crucible. With the Council's influence, you could—'

'Absolutely not.' His father's voice turns glacial. 'The Crucible proceeds as planned. The sponsors have paid, the observers will arrive soon, and you will perform as expected. I've already arranged to have your performance observed more closely to ensure you will be on the right track after you graduate your fifth year. This is critical, Bastian. Not just for you, but for me as well. You will disgrace me if you fail to—'

'People will die.' Bastian's voice rises slightly. 'Far more than usual. Malakai has almost all the earth affinities allied to him. He's got half the waters or more and as many airs. And Raith Hollow has almost the entire first-year class of fire affinities following him like he's some kind of commander. It's not going to be a chaotic series of skirmishes, father. It's going to be a full-out war. One side against the other. It'll be a bloodbath.'

'Then ensure you're not among the casualties.' His father's tone allows for no argument. 'Alliances form and break every year. This is no different. And if it is a disaster, the Council will simply use it as an opportunity to remove Rector Voss ahead of schedule.'

'Malakai isn't just looking to win. He's hunting. And whatever he's after—'

'Enough.' His father cuts him off. 'Malakai's actions serve a purpose, just as the siphon does. War is never comfortable, son. It's never pretty. It's about making the best of the situations you're given, and we can use this. We can use all of it.'

'What do you mean his actions serve a purpose? Surely the—'

Their voices fade as they move deeper into the forest, leaving a heavy silence in their wake. Raith and I remain frozen in our hiding place, his hand still wrapped around mine.

'That was . . .' I struggle to find words.

'Dangerous,' Raith finishes for me, his expression grim. 'I don't think he would have let us live if he knew we overheard.'

'Why would they want Voss removed?'

'Not sure. But I wouldn't repeat that to anyone if you value your life. He admitted to knowing a siphon is here and is planning to let it continue killing. Same with Malakai. Whatever he wants, it's not in our best fucking interest. We can be sure of that much.'

We rise slowly from our hiding place, both of us scanning the surrounding forest for any sign of Bastian or his father.

'Do you think Malakai or Serena could be the siphon?' I ask suddenly.

'I'm not sure. It's why I'm watching everyone.'

'Bastian seemed genuinely concerned,' I say, still processing what we've heard. 'I'm so used to seeing him calm, collected, and in control.'

'People wear many faces here.' Raith's expression darkens. 'Trust none of them.'

'I trust you . . .' the words slip out of me like an admission, even though it's not the first time I've told him.

There's something like pain in Raith's face, but he nods. 'You shouldn't. But we need to head back. We've been gone too long already.'

As we make our way through the forest, a new awareness crackles between us – shared knowledge, shared danger. Raith walks closer to me than before, his eyes constantly scanning our surroundings, one hand never far from his blade.

We reach the eastern gate just as the sun begins its descent, slipping back onto Confluence grounds unseen. The castle rises before us, its spires gleaming in the late afternoon light. From this distance, it looks beautiful, majestic – impossible to imagine it harbors a predator hunting students from within.

Raith pauses before we return to the main grounds, his hand catching my wrist. 'Be careful, Nessa.'

'I will.' I meet his gaze directly. 'You be careful too.'

There's a softening around his eyes, a tension in his jaw that wasn't there before. For a breathless moment, I think he might say more, might finally stop holding himself back so much around me.

Instead, his fingers brush lightly against my cheek, a touch so brief I might have imagined it. 'Meet me tomorrow. Same time, training room. We have work to do.'

Then he's gone, melting into the shadows of the castle as if he were born from them, leaving me alone with questions I'm not sure I want answered and a growing certainty that surviving the next week might be the greatest challenge I've faced yet.

'Not a single worthy prey in the entire damned forest. Squirrels and lizards. Pah! I demand a true hunt!'

'Typhon, not right now.'

I feel resignation through the tether as I sense him soaring through the air high above. He rarely flies, so I feel a sense of awe as I look up and see his wings spread wide and his serpentine body twisting through the air as if he's swimming. Soon, I'll need to train with him like Raith said. I'll need to learn to ride on his back and fight while mounted. Anything less would be a terrible waste of the potential we share.

The blue of his body catches the light like reflections on the water so he sparkles high above, wings nearly translucent as he passes across the sun.

A swell of pride and comfort fills me.

Maybe the dangers are many here, but so are my allies. Typhon, Raith, Mireen, Beck, Ambrose, and maybe even Bastian. They're all ready to fight with me against whatever comes, and I can't imagine anyone else I'd rather have on my side.

Chapter 28

The water channeling exam is every bit the disaster I anticipated. Twenty students stand in a circle around a large basin filled with water. Sestra watches us with her perpetually disappointed expression, making notes on a parchment as we take turns attempting to manipulate the water.

Exams at Confluence supposedly contribute to some kind of evaluation score we're not allowed to see. If we survive to graduation, our evaluation score will be a large factor in deciding where we wind up in the hierarchy of primals.

The channeling classroom smells wet and musky from repeated spells splashing and misting water in every direction. Morning sunlight cuts through the arched windows, lighting faces that are both eager and nervous. I count myself among the nervous.

'An unbound with an ancient elemental does not get nervous. She gets ready. She prepares for battle. To prove herself. To excel,' Typhon growls.

'Yeah, well, tough shit, Typhon. This unbound gets nervous. Especially when she's about to take a test she knows she's going to fail.'

We've known some kind of test was coming for days now, but we weren't told any details about what we'd be asked to do or when it would take place. Not that extra time would have helped me much. The other water affinities are naturally growing in power as their tethers strengthen.

Mireen, predictably, excels. Channeling has always been a strength of hers, even before tethering Ollie. But the relatively small water otter also seems to have a gift for channeling, making Mireen one of the strongest channelers in our affinity. She forms perfect, complex shapes from the water when it's her turn – spirals, cubes, even a miniature version of Confluence's castle that earns approving nods from the other students.

Beck does well enough, managing to create a decently sized wave that splashes several students, earning him a sharp reprimand from Sestra but appreciative laughs from others.

Ambrose performs exactly as Sestra instructs without the extra flair of Mireen.

Even Brunhild manages to complete the task successfully.

Then it's my turn.

I step forward, aware of every eye on me. The whispers have already started – they always do when I'm called to demonstrate my abilities. Malakai's supporters watch with barely concealed contempt.

'Thorne,' Sestra says, her voice clipped. 'Show us a basic water control exercise. Level three.'

Level three. The instructors rate elemental control exercises on a scale of one to ten – one being the simplest manipulation, ten being mastery-level complexity. Level three is considered basic for most first-years by this point in the term, but it's already beyond what I've managed to convincingly fake.

'I suggest cheating,' Typhon says through our tether. *'Touch one of your classmates, steal their power, and perform a level ten water spell just to close their fleshy, flat-toothed mouths.'*

'I'm not going to cheat. I'm just . . . going to give it a shot.'

'Bah. It's only cheating if you get caught.'

'That's . . . not true. And I thought you were supposed to be some kind of elemental nobility of impeccable ethics?'

'I am effective. There's a difference. If morals or ethics got in the way of what I needed to do, I would simply eat them.'

With a sigh, I close my eyes and reach for the water with my senses. There's essence in the bowl of water, in the moisture in the air, and even . . . I can feel a kind of mental expanding as I strain to find more water essence to pull inward. For the first time, I feel it in my classmates and Sestra, too. I feel the water in their bodies.

That's new.

I gently draw it all in toward myself, watching everyone carefully for reaction. I don't want them to be hurt, but I know what I'm doing isn't sucking the water from their bodies. I'm just . . . collecting the magical counterpart water attracts over time.

Each drop fills me with potential. Too much potential. The realization slams into me too late. I need to vent this energy before it comes rushing out of me on its own and out of control.

I try to focus on the task, creating and shaping a modest quantity of water as Sestra expects. But it's hopeless. I'm filled with overwhelming power, not control.

There are no delicate designs or details to prove I'm the master of the water. Instead, the entire basin surges upward in a massive wave that hovers precariously for a split second before crashing down, soaking half the class – including Sestra.

I let out a gasping breath and wipe water from my face. 'Sorry,' I wince as students sputter and curse all around the room. 'I . . . lost concentration.'

Sestra's expression could curdle milk. With a flick of her wrist, she draws the water from every student in the room at once, except for me. She snaps her fingers and the collected water seems to vanish, splitting in a million tiny droplets to rejoin the air in the room. 'Pathetic.'

'I know, I'm sorry—' I press my soaked hair out of my face and wipe water from my eyes.

'This is the third time you've failed a basic channeling exercise in the last week, Thorne. Your elemental must be questioning its choice.' She makes a harsh note on her parchment. 'Another failure.'

Humiliation burns through me as I step back into the circle. Mireen squeezes my shoulder sympathetically, while Beck offers a supportive grimace. Across the circle, Malakai watches with a satisfied smirk that makes me wish I had left him back in Mirror Lake for Typhon to devour when he was still mad.

'*I could still eat him,*' Typhon notes from the corner of the room. '*It's not too late.*'

'We talked about eating people.'

Typhon sighs. *'You were the one who brought it up this time.'*

'Just because you listen to all my thoughts, it doesn't mean each one is intended for you.'

Typhon's annoyance is plain through the tether. Steam billows out of his large nostrils as he coils his body in a circle and lies down, blue eyes glaring up at me.

'Don't let them see they get to you,' Ambrose whispers, his eyes knowing behind his glasses as he watches Malakai and his allies. 'That's what they want.'

He's right, of course. I force my expression into neutrality as the next student takes their turn. But inside, frustration simmers. If only I could show what I'm truly capable of – summon Typhon in his true form, bend all four elements to my will. The looks on their faces would be worth it.

Almost worth it, anyway. I'd have a few moments of satisfaction before Empire higher-ups were breathing down my neck. Some might want to steal me away and turn me into their personal weapons. More likely, I'd wind up dead before any of that happened.

By the time the class ends, my mood has plummeted to new depths.

'Sestra's blind,' Mireen mutters as we leave the classroom. 'She acts like you're not improving.'

'Am I?' I ask, guilt gnawing at me. My friends don't understand the real reason I'm 'struggling.' They don't realize I may not be able to form pretty pillars of water, but I can already weave water and fire together to make jets of steam thanks to what I learned from Bastian's unbound book and Voss's lessons. But none of those talents are going to get me through Sestra's class, so I'm stuck letting my friends think I'm falling behind.

Another lie in a growing collection.

'Of course you're getting better.' She links her arm through mine as we walk down the corridor. Ahead of us, Beck and Ambrose argue good-naturedly about lunch options. 'Everyone progresses at different rates. And honestly, who cares about perfect water columns when the Crucible is all about survival? And you've got Oceanus the flying fish,' she adds with a wink. 'And the most deadly first-year promising to watch your back, along with a legacy I'm pretty sure has a massive crush on you. And us.'

'Sestra cares,' I mutter, even though I know she's right. I also don't even bother arguing with her about Raith and Bastian because I know it's a lost cause. My continued failure in channeling class is getting to me. 'She's determined to make me look like I don't belong here. If there wasn't already a target on my back, she's painting one herself. It's like she's trying to make sure people think I'm weak. Easy prey.'

'Sestra is a bitter old woman,' Mireen says with surprising venom. 'Don't let her get to you.'

I grin, because I know Sestra lavishes Mireen with praise and the two of them seem to get along better than most. I still appreciate Mireen trying to cheer me up, though, so I don't make a point of mentioning it.

We enter the dining hall, its soaring ceiling a masterpiece of architectural wonder. Massive crystal chandeliers hover without visible support, casting rainbow-flecked light across the stone floors polished to a mirror shine. Around us, students from all years take seats and dig into heaping plates of steaming food, their colored markings denoting their affinities – the blue spirals of water, the amber flames of fire, the emerald mountain patterns of earth, and the silvery wisps of air.

I find my eyes lingering on the first-year legacies, who sit in small groups, divided by affinity. Most days, I hardly even see the legacies except at meal times. They're all busy with special classes and assignments, some of which even take them beyond the walls of Confluence. Since they've been training their whole lives for this, first-year legacies are already far beyond the rest of us. Most of them will wind up being our generals and commanders if we survive to graduation.

It's hard to believe five of us might get promoted to legacies if we win the Crucible. But I'm hardly worried about that. I just want the people I care about to survive it.

Despite my mood, I still marvel at the beauty of Confluence sometimes. For all its dangers, the castle itself is breathtaking. And even if I hate to admit it, I've come to find a kind of happiness here in my daily routines. The endless weapons training leaves me bruised and sore, the exercises only make it worse, and then it's hours of academic classes, channeling practice, and working with our elementals to strengthen our tethers and learning to fight together with them.

I enjoy the education and the challenge. I've learned so much in such a short period of time. I love the friends I've made, the feeling of getting stronger every day, and the sense that I'm capable of protecting the people I care about more and more with each step I take. And . . . well, it's hardly worth pretending I don't enjoy thinking about what might happen with Raith. Gods know I dream about it constantly.

We join Beck and Ambrose at our usual table, where platters of steaming food already wait.

'So,' Beck says around a mouthful of roasted meat, 'I saw you royally fail, but I didn't get to hear what Sestra's said to you when she chewed you out before class ended.'

'Beck!' Mireen hisses, kicking him under the table.

'What? We all saw it.' He shrugs unapologetically. 'I'm just asking for details.'

'Nothing new, really,' I reply, tearing my bread into small pieces. 'Just how I'm a total failure, an embarrassment to the academy, and probably going to wind up as a bloodstain during the Crucible.'

'Harsh,' Beck says, biting a huge piece out of his bread, hardly chewing, then swallowing. 'Did you suggest she go fuck herself? What do you have to lose at this point, right? It's not like she could be even more shitty to you. And I doubt she could fail you any harder than she already has.'

'That's terrible advice,' Ambrose interjects, adjusting his glasses. 'Antagonizing instructors before the Crucible is strategically unsound.'

'Everything is "strategically unsound" with you,' Beck complains. 'Using the restroom without making sure there's enough wiping tissue would be strategically unsound.'

Mireen narrows her eyes. 'Yes . . . it would, Beck.'

He shrugs. 'I'm just saying. Sometimes you've got to live your life. See what happens.'

Ambrose ignores him, turning to me instead. 'Speaking of strategically unsound . . . we should start practicing with Brunhild. If she's going to be our fifth, we need to make sure we work well together.'

I nod, even though my mind swims with responsibilities already. Training sessions with Raith. Time I want to devote to still pouring over the Unbound book, looking for anything I might have missed. Finding a way to slip outside the castle and practice flying with Typhon. All this on top of our usual duties here.

'I'll let her know,' Beck says. 'You guys free tonight? I could see if she can meet us.'

'Not tonight,' I say quietly as I think of my plans to meet with Raith for more training.

Mireen tilts her head. 'Right. She's probably wanting to practice some channeling to catch up with Sestra.'

'Right,' I say, suppressing a twinge of guilt because that's not at all what I'm planning.

'Tomorrow, then,' Mireen says. 'Instructor Pilton is off doing gods-know-what with that group of legacies this week. We can use the time we'd normally be in Military Tactics class to practice with Brunhild.'

'Sounds good,' Beck says. 'I'll pass the word on.'

The conversation shifts to more Crucible preparation, but my mind wanders. I can't stop thinking about what Raith and I overheard yesterday at the quarry – Bastian's concern that this year's Crucible would be a bloodbath, his father's dismissal of those concerns, the mention of 'burned-out marks' and a siphon possibly hunting students. The revelation that Bastian, of all people, seemed genuinely worried about our safety.

I can't even remember when the last time Bastian directly spoke with me was. He was there to break up the fight a few days ago, but he hasn't been checking in with me anymore. I wonder if he's conflicted about keeping me a secret from his father. It certainly sounded like his father would have wanted to know he was helping an unbound develop her powers by handing over old secret family books.

But why is he protecting me, too?

'Earth to Nessa,' Beck says, waving his hand in front of my face. 'You still with us?'

'Sorry, just thinking about . . . everything.' I hesitate, torn between wanting to warn my friends and needing to keep Raith's confidence. 'The Crucible is going to be more dangerous than usual this year.'

'How do you know that?' Mireen asks, frowning.

I know I'm already keeping more secrets than I'd like from my friends, but everything new I learn just feels like it would put them in more danger. Still, I can give them the information without admitting where it actually came from. 'Raith heard some older students talking. They said the number of alliances Malakai and Serena are forming is really unusual. And the fact that they're recruiting across affinities isn't normal. They're worried the Crucible is going to be more like a war than a bunch of small skirmishes. Like Malakai's people are going to go hunting for us and only worry about finishing the Crucible after we're all dead.'

'Fuck,' Beck breathes. 'That's grim.' Then he scoops a huge mouthful of soup into his mouth and belches loudly.

'We stick together,' Mireen says. 'As long as we're together, we'll be okay, right?'

'Technically not true,' Ambrose says. 'If we're ambushed by fifty of Malakai's people, it won't really matter if we're together. We'll still be dead. Just . . . dead together.'

I grin. 'I think she was trying to make us feel better, Ambrose. Not speaking literally.'

'Oh,' Ambrose says. 'Right. Together. We can all die together, like Mireen said.'

I think about telling them more of what I've learned – about the siphons or even finally coming clean about what I am. More and more, I think I'll have to tell them before long or I'll burst. I know they'll all understand, too, which only makes it harder to keep the secrets.

Not yet, though. I think I'll know when the time is right. When it feels like it's more dangerous to keep them in the dark than tell them the truth. And I have an intuition that time is coming faster than I realize.

'Raith and I went to the quarry yesterday,' I say instead, immediately regretting the admission when three pairs of eyes snap to me. 'Just . . . reconnaissance. For the Crucible.'

'You left campus?' Mireen asks, eyes wide before she smiles and then whacks my arm. 'You dog. Got tired of fucking in your bed?'

'We were trying to scout,' I say defensively.

'Scouting,' Beck adds with a knowing look. 'What was your scouting report on the contents of his pants? Find any fire serpents?'

'You guys are unbelievable.' I want to be annoyed with them, but find myself laughing a little. Before coming here, I would've thought it was impossible to make jokes and be light when your life was under threat at all times. Now, though? Now I see it's the exact opposite.

If we didn't find ways to occasionally pretend everything was normal, we'd all have lost our minds by now.

'Well,' Ambrose says slowly. 'If nothing else, I think we can say for absolute certain now that Raith isn't planning on killing Nessa any time soon. One could've argued he was worried about being caught if he did it on school grounds. You went outside the walls with him. Alone. And you're still alive. Reckless, but alive.'

Mireen nods. 'I hate to say it, but I agree. I think we can trust him for now.'

I look down at my stew, suddenly fascinated by a floating carrot. 'He's . . . not what everyone thinks.'

'You would know,' Mireen tucks a loose coppery-colored hair that falls from her braid, blue eyes locked on me. 'The two of you spend quite a bit of time "training."'

I shrug, aiming for nonchalance. 'He's good with blades.'

'Oh, yeah,' Beck says with a suggestive wiggle of his eyebrows. 'He shows you how good he is at sheathing his sword a time or two, does he?'

My cheeks burn. 'It's not like that. I've told you all millions of times.'

'Your blush says otherwise,' he teases.

'I do admire him,' I admit, hoping a scrap of truth will throw them off the scent. 'And he's obviously handsome. But he's not remotely interested in me, so it's pointless. Even if I did want there to be more between us, that's never going to happen.'

'Right,' Beck drawls, clearly unconvinced. 'And I'm just friends with Brunhild.'

'That's different,' I protest. 'You two are actually—'

'Screwing like rabbits?' he supplies helpfully. 'Yes, we are. And loving every minute of it.'

'Too much information,' Ambrose mutters, returning to his book. His eyes flick briefly to the next table where Serena's group sits, and I notice Beck's laughter quiets just a bit as his eyes follow Ambrose's.

Sometimes, the constant pulse of danger beating beneath everything seeps through and then I realize it's never really gone. It's like a faint ringing in the ears. You can ignore it for a time. Forget it entirely, even. But once you remember to listen, you realize it was there all along.

'Well,' Beck sighs and starts gathering his things. 'Time for elemental history. Another fascinating lecture on how the Empire saved civilization from chaos and barbarism.'

'Actually,' Ambrose says, 'I'm quite looking forward to it. Some of the things we're taught here are highly exclusive, you know. Things you would have to pay a great deal of money to learn on the outside. Things you'd probably have to know very particular groups of people to know. We should all feel privileged to—'

Beck interrupts Ambrose by chucking a piece of bread at his face. Before it can hit, Arakon materializes in a blue flash and raises his wing, deflecting the bread. The water bird is gone again in an instant, leaving only a misty smear of blue sparks that fade to nothing.

'That's cheating,' Beck says. 'I would've got that straight in your mouth.'

'Well, you didn't,' Ambrose says, standing straighter. 'And you should stop trying so hard to get things in my mouth. People will start to wonder.'

The two of them fall into good-natured bickering and teasing as we gather our things and head for the lecture hall.

The rest of the day passes in a blur of classes and training. Combat theory with Instructor Vail, where we study ancient battle strategies of primal warfare. Physical conditioning, where Beck breaks his previous record lifting a water-enhanced weight system, beaming with pride as the instructor marks his progress in the ledger. Elemental history, which focuses on how there used to be more continents on our world before the elemental civil war completely destroyed them, leaving all of humanity on the single large landmass. There are, of course, outlying islands, but dangerous rogue elementals make traveling that far across the oceans too dangerous for any but the most desperate to make the journey.

Beck found the lesson boring enough to fall asleep, snoring so loudly that Ambrose had to elbow him awake several times.

Through it all, I'm only half-present, my mind constantly returning to the revelations at the quarry and tonight's training session with Raith. I've felt like things between us have been changing lately. But I'm worried he feels it too, and the Raith I know will pull away before anything becomes serious. He'll pull back at the last moment, and if I let myself hope we might become something, I'll be left with a broken heart.

So I do my best to just . . . not think about it. Because I've tried and failed too many times to convince myself I don't want him.

I do, though. Gods, I want him.

The truth of it burns under my skin like fire. It's far too strong to deny, so all I can do is manage periods of time where I force myself to think about other topics.

And maybe, just maybe, if I avoid thinking about him often enough I'll forget how I feel.

'Avoiding the blade at your throat only makes it slice deeper,' Typhon notes.

'Raith isn't a blade at my throat, though.'

'No. A blade at your heart, perhaps.'

Raith's advice about paying attention helps me slip outside the castle walls for a bit of practice with Typhon. I stand in a grassy field with him, mostly shielded by trees if anyone cared to look out from the walls. He waits in front of me, larger now than he was when we returned from Confluence Day by quite a bit. His shoulder is high above my head, and if he extends his long neck and wings, he's simply breathtaking. Absolutely massive.

I put my hands on my hips, staring up at him. *'So . . . Raith thinks I should learn to ride and fight from your back.'*

'You would likely be in more danger on my back than on the ground. I'll have to hold back with you riding me.'

'I still think Raith is right. We should practice fighting together. Who knows when we'll need it?'

'Very well.' Typhon's eyes glow, and I feel a sudden cold against my back. I look over my shoulder and see I'm rising off the ground, lifted by a dragon's paw of pure water. I'm dropped unceremoniously on Typhon's back, soaking and annoyed.

'Really?' I ask him. *'I could've climbed you.'*

'And wounded our collective dignity.'

'You're right. Me looking like a drowned rat on your back is far more dignified.'

Blue magic flares and a saddle appears just below his shoulders. It's the same kind he used on Confluence Day to help me stay on his back. I shimmy into it, feeling as the watery magic grips me tight, holding me in place.

'I would advise you to hold on, but it will not matter. My magic will keep you in place.'

'I can at least—'

Typhon flaps his wings. *Hard.*

My stomach lurches and my vision darkens as we explode upward. I make no sound for several seconds, and then I throw my hands in the air and shout with pure exhilaration and joy. 'Holy fuck!'

I look around, watching the trees grow small and Confluence Academy shift from the huge fortress I know it as to a small, gray dot in a green expanse. Typhon keeps flapping his wings, climbing higher until cool white clouds brush against my skin.

I stare in awe, holding my hand out and letting it slice through the clouds as we soar.

'I always thought they would . . . feel like something. I can't even tell I'm touching clouds.'

There's a faint pulse of amusement and pride from Typhon.

I lean down, hugging his neck and feeling the cool slick of his scales beneath my palms. 'Thank you, Typhon,' I say aloud. 'This is . . . special.'

'It still brings me joy, too. I am glad we could share it.'

I smile, letting the wind whip across my face as he holds his wings wide, opting to glide and drift, banking gently left and right as the winds carry us.

'Next time, I'll do some actual practice. This time . . . I just want to enjoy it.'

'Very well, angry human.'

By the time I return to my room, my cheeks are chafed from wind and cold, but my heart feels full. I'm still smiling as I change into fresh training clothes for my session with Raith, automatically checking my door is still locked – a habit I picked up after hearing about people disappearing from their rooms in broad daylight. I braid my hair tight, telling myself it's only practical, not because I want to look good for him. Wanting things is dangerous here.

Dangerous or not. I know I do want him to notice me – to see me as more than a vulnerability or something to protect.

When I'm not trying to keep him from my mind, I yearn for him to really see me. To see me as a woman. To want me even a fraction as much as I want him. And gods, I know it's in him somewhere. I felt it both times we kissed.

There's no lack of attraction between us, but Raith has done a masterful job of building barriers to keep us apart all the same. And maybe I'm hoping if I look good enough tonight, I can break through a few of them.

I know it's foolish. Our lives are on the line every day. I should only care about training and getting stronger. Wasting time on things like sex is just asking to be killed because I'm not ready when the time comes.

But it's not just sex. It's this feeling, too . . . like he walks around with so much hurt and pain that it's crushing him. And I feel like the only way he'll ever be able to heal is if he lets someone in. And, yeah . . . maybe I hope that someone is me.

'*Your constant wistful thoughts about mating and courtship distract your mind for far longer than a few hours of rutting would. May I offer a suggestion?*'

'*No.*'

'*My suggestion,*' Typhon continues anyway. '*Is to bare your flesh to him. My history with your kind has shown the effectiveness of this strategy. Male humans seem particularly fascinated with the milk glands. You could consider presenting them. It would be a subtle sign of your interest.*'

I grin as I finish fixing my hair in the mirror. '*Typhon . . . lifting my tunic and flashing Raith would hardly be subtle.*'

'*Perhaps you would be wise to take my advice. I am centuries old, angry human. I've navigated more relationships than you could even begin to count.*'

'*You mean you've been through more breakups than I can count? If you're as old as you say and still single, then you're the last one I should be taking relationship advice from.*'

'Damn you.'

I laugh aloud, giving him a sympathetic smile. *'Sorry, Typhon. No offense meant. Well, okay, that's a lie. But I'm sorry if I offended you more than intended.'*

There's a flicker of amusement through the tether as Typhon watches me from the corner of the room.

As I'm about to leave, I notice something on my desk that wasn't there before. My pulse jumps – my room was locked. But somebody had to get in while I was gone.

The thought makes my skin crawl, but I move to the desk and look at the object.

It's a small, curved dagger with a handle wrapped in red leather. Beside it lies a note in elegant, slanting handwriting:

'For protection. Keep this on you at all times. Bring it tonight and I'll show you how to use it.'

Raith snuck into my room? I shouldn't be surprised, but the idea that he could let himself in here any time he likes feels strangely . . . exciting. He even locked my door again behind him, probably making sure he's the only one slipping into my space uninvited.

I put the thought from my mind and pick up the dagger, testing its weight.

It's perfectly balanced, the blade wickedly sharp. This is no training weapon with its dulled edges – this is the real thing, deadly and beautiful. My breath catches as I realize what this means. First-years aren't allowed real weapons; they're restricted to the blunted training versions until second year. Raith must have risked serious punishment to acquire this for me, though I still have no idea how he managed it.

'Quite thoughtful of the fire human,' Typhon observes. *'Perhaps he's not entirely useless after all.'*

'High praise coming from you,' I murmur, turning the blade over in my hand.

I run my fingertip over the finely made weapon and try to ignore the blossoming of warmth and appreciation I feel for Raith. Feeling for him is dangerous, but the damn man keeps making me do it all the same.

And where the hells did he get something like this? I plan to ask him tonight, even though I'm almost certain he's not going to tell me.

Fucking Raith . . .

I slide the dagger into my boot and feel how snugly it fits against my ankle. The weight is comforting as I head toward the room where I'll meet him to train.

The castle is busy as groups of first-years travel around, mostly five in number. It's obvious that everyone is using as much of their time to train for the Crucible as possible, and I feel like I'm watching the preparations for a bloody war. The upper-years look just as preoccupied and tense. Part of me wonders what they're going to face, but most of me doesn't even want to know.

I find the room where I usually meet with Raith and push open the door.

He's standing in the center of the room, eyes heavy as the shadows fall strangely on his face.

'Nessa,' he says, voice slightly flat. *Great.* When we first started training together, his voice had that kind of lifeless quality, as if he was making absolutely sure I knew we were only together for business. Is he trying to push me away again?

'Hey. I got the dagger,' I say as I step inside and close the door behind me. 'Where the hells did you get something like this, anyway?'

'Come closer.'

Of course he won't tell me. Frowning, I approach him.

'Angry human . . . something is wrong.'

'You hid it well,' Raith says. He starts to pace and circle me like we're sparring, but his blade is still sheathed on his back.

'What are you talking about?'

'Not quite well enough, we're afraid. We have had to strike out a few times. Destroy those who suspected.'

We? What the hell is he talking about?

'Raith . . . you're scaring me.'

He smiles, and the unnatural shape of it makes my blood go cold. Raith hardly ever smiles, and when he does . . . it doesn't look like that.

'Show me how well he has trained you, Nessa.' With a whisper of steel, Raith draws his sword from his back and holds it toward me. The metal still vibrates as he levels the blade between my eyes, ringing in my ears.

'How well who has trained me . . .' I ask slowly, mind putting the pieces together, terrifying piece after terrifying piece.

'Raith Hollow,' it says, pulling the sword back, gripping it with both hands, and moving toward me.

Chapter 29

It's a siphon.

Raith's warning comes to me almost immediately. If I see a siphon, I need to run. I can't fight it. I shouldn't even try.

I feel Typhon materializing beside me as I turn and run for the door. But a wave of purple energy flares in front of the door, blasting me back with noxious fumes that stink of sulphur and decay. The force of it slams me against the stone floor, knocking the breath from my lungs.

'We're going to have to try to fight. That's the only way out,' I tell Typhon through the bond.

'Then we fight.'

The slight sense of resolution through the tether worries me. I don't feel confidence. I don't feel excitement. It's more like the feeling one might have before taking a leap of faith. Before rushing toward certain death.

I turn toward the siphon that still looks like Raith, and I draw my rapier. My hand trembles slightly, but I force it steady.

I know it's not him. Not really. It's a siphon and it's taking Raith's form. It's the only explanation.

The real Raith is out there somewhere and likely headed to this very room to meet me for training. And if he wasn't already on his way, I don't have to ask to know Typhon will have called for him through Pyrin. But I can't count on him arriving in time.

I reach into the room around me, pulling in any elemental energy I can manage – fire from the torches, air from the currents coming from high above, water from the moisture in the air, and earth from the dirt packed in between the stones. The energy tingles through my fingertips, making the hairs on my arms stand on end.

Typhon lunges for the siphon, but a lion made of swirling purple and green energy explodes into view at the last second, pouncing and knocking Typhon away. It's huge, even larger than Typhon, even though he's the largest elemental I've seen on campus before now.

I wince as I feel his pain through our connection, the phantom sensation of claws tearing through scales and muscle. But I'm forced to turn my attention away as the massive elementals clash to my left. I have to trust that Typhon can handle himself.

The siphon taking Raith's form rushes me, sword flashing so fast I barely track it. I throw myself to one side with none of the elegance Raith drilled into me. There's no time for elegance.

I fall hard on my side, rapier clattering from my hand. I lunge for it, barely dodging another strike that smashes into the stone. The impact sends vibrations through the floor that rattle my teeth.

Come on, Nessa. You're better than this. You can fucking do this.

I grab the rapier, spin away from another strike and finally get back on my feet. I reach into the earth and lift a stone just as the siphon comes at me again, catching one of its feet. Instead of losing balance, it easily rights itself, turning the stumble into a spinning strike so strong it cracks my rapier in two when I raise it to block.

One broken half of my practice blade spins away, cutting a gash in my arm before clattering to the ground several feet away.

Shit, shit, shit.

Blood runs hot down my arm, the pain sharp and immediate.

Typhon roars, blasting a torrent of water at the void lion, which raises a purple-green shield to deflect most of the magic.

I pluck the dagger Raith gave me from my boot, but I've never trained with a weapon so small and can't possibly use it to block his sword.

Magic. Use your fucking magic.

I twist air and water together, forming a spike of ice the size of my forearm. I keep it behind my back until the siphon swings again at me in a horizontal arc. I lean back and the sword's tip misses me so closely I feel the blade-thin rush of air against my face.

Then I throw the icicle at him. There's a moment of satisfying surprise as the siphon's eyes widen and then the ice spike punches into its forehead, snapping its head back at a ninety degree angle.

I wait for its body to slump and fall lifeless, but it just . . . stands there, head tilted back at that unnatural angle. And then it straightens with the sound of bones cracking, and it is smiling.

Without taking its eyes from me, it grips the icicle and pulls it free from its head. Something thick and black drips from the wound, but it's not blood. Not any kind of blood I've ever seen.

And then the siphon starts to transform, shedding its disguise piece by piece.

The eyes darken to black. The mouth curves at the edges until it's monstrously large. The limbs elongate and its fingertips stretch into claw-like talons. The back hunches and the legs stretch as it lets out a low, inhuman growl.

The thing looks like something straight out of a nightmare, but what scares me more than the sight of it is the feeling passing through the bond from Typhon. It's a kind of resignation. It's a readiness to fight until his last breath, but the knowledge that death is coming for us both.

I look over my shoulder at the door again, thinking again of trying to run or force my way through the barrier, but I see something that gives me pause. The magical barrier of purple and green still guards it, but the door is blackening and turning red. Smoke billows around the edges.

Fire.

I grip my dagger tighter, my survival instincts screaming at me to run while my feet remain rooted in place. There's nowhere to run. All I can do is stand and fight.

The siphon tilts its horrific head, studying me with eyes that seem to drink in light rather than reflect it.

'What do you want?' I ask, desperate to buy time even as I catalog every potential advantage in the room.

'Bait.' The word tears from its throat. 'He comes. He dies.'

Bait? Then it knows Raith is coming. Gods. I'm not buying time for help to come. I'm doing exactly what the siphon wants. I'm luring Raith into a trap.

The door behind the barrier glows brighter, the red now pulsing like a heartbeat. Someone's trying to get in.

Raith. It has to be him.

The siphon charges again, but this time I'm ready. I step into its attack rather than away, ducking under its sword and dragging my dagger across its torso as I pass. The blade – Raith's gift – cuts deeper than I expected, leaving a gash that oozes more black liquid.

The creature howls. It whirls, sword flashing toward my exposed back—

I throw myself forward into a roll, but I'm too slow. The blade catches me across my shoulder, slicing through fabric and flesh. The pain is white-hot and immediate, radiating outward like a brand pressed to my skin.

The siphon laughs, a horrible broken sound.

Typhon roars at the sight of my wound, abandoning his fight with the void lion to surge toward me. The void beast leaps onto his back, claws digging into scales, but Typhon ignores it, positioning himself between me and the siphon.

'You cannot stop this, ancient one,' the siphon hisses. 'You may have cleansed your madness, but you are still tethered to a half-trained child.'

I reach inside, to that place where my power seems to gather when I need it most. The wound on my shoulder burns, but I channel that pain, using it to sharpen my focus. If I can heal myself, maybe I'll have a chance.

I press my hand to my shoulder, willing the flesh to mend. The familiar heat spreads beneath my palm, the tissue knitting together until only a thin, tender line remains. The healing drains me further, but it's worth it to regain full range of motion.

The siphon's eyes widen. 'A healing manifestation . . . Hah! All these years and he'll finally have what he wants.'

He? Does it mean Lorkan Grace?

I don't have time to think as the void lion abandons Typhon's back to charge at me. The ancient water dragon spins with surprising agility, intercepting it mid-leap. The two collide in a tangle of claws and teeth and elemental magic that sends shock waves through the room.

Typhon slams the lion into the ground, his massive claws pinning it as water magic pours from his maw, drowning the beast. For the first time, the void lion seems to be weakening, its struggles growing less coordinated.

My limbs already feel leaden, my lungs burning with each breath. I've channeled more power in the last few minutes than I have in all my previous training sessions combined. And I won't last much longer like this.

The door behind the barrier explodes inward in a shower of splinters and flame.

Raith stands in the doorway, his face contorted with fury, Pyrin a blazing inferno behind him. His sword is already drawn, the blade glowing red-hot.

'Get away from her,' he growls, and the command in his voice is so absolute that even the siphon pauses.

Raith doesn't wait for a response. He charges as a flare of white-hot fire envelops him and burns a path through the purple barrier over the door. Pyrin surges ahead of him in a wave of fire that crashes into the void lion, freeing Typhon from his struggle. The ancient dragon rises, injured but far from defeated, water magic gathering around him once more.

The siphon hisses, backing away from this new threat. Raith presses forward, his sword a blur of motion that forces the creature to defend rather than attack. Each strike of Raith's blade leaves a glowing afterimage in the air, the metal so hot it sears the siphon wherever it connects.

The creature's burning flesh fills the room with the sickening scent of smoke and charred hair.

'Nessa, are you hurt?' Raith demands even as he smoothly side-steps a claw aimed at his stomach and twists, blasting a jet of fire toward the siphon with his left hand.

'I'm okay,' I reply, already moving to flank the siphon.

The creature's attention divides between us, its head swiveling unnaturally to track both threats. It parries one of Raith's strikes, then spins to block my dagger thrust with its forearm. The blade sinks deep, but the siphon barely seems to notice.

'Powerful,' it says as it suffers another gash from Raith's sword. 'You will feed us well.'

Raith says nothing as he parries, dodges, and thrusts. I do my best to stay out of the way, darting inside the siphon's guard to land blows when it's distracted by Raith.

More black blood has splattered across the floor now, making our footing uncertain on the slick substance.

The fight rages, everything happening so fast I can only process bits and pieces. Pyrin and Typhon battling beside us, the horrific monster snarling and suffering dozens of wounds but still fighting, Raith constantly putting his body between me and danger. Protecting me. Always protecting me.

'We need to end this,' Raith mutters, his breathing heavy. 'It's not getting tired, but we are.'

He's right. My vision is already blurring at the edges, my muscles burning with exertion. Even Typhon seems diminished, his move-ments less fluid, his attacks less powerful. The gushing wounds seem to be making him smaller, too, as if his essence is leaking away.

Sensing weakness, the void lion disengages from the elementals and lunges toward us.

Toward Raith.

Everything slows.

I see Raith turning, his sword rising too late to block. I see the lion's claws extended, ready to tear through flesh. I see the siphon watching with those terrible black eyes, satisfaction already apparent in its twisted features.

No. Not him. Not Raith.

I move without conscious thought, throwing myself between Raith and the void lion. My dagger thrusts upward, catching the beast under its jaw as its momentum carries us both to the ground. Void magic washes over me like acid, burning wherever it touches, but I don't let go.

'Nessa!' Raith's voice sounds far away.

The lion hisses and limps to the side of the siphon, joining the other two creatures.

Raith is at my side in an instant, his hand on my shoulder steadying me. 'What were you thinking?'

'You're welcome,' I manage, the room spinning slightly.

The siphon studies us, its head tilted unnaturally. 'How touching. The fire affinity and the unbound, fighting together.'

Raith positions himself in front of me, sword raised. Typhon and Pyrin flank us, both elementals obviously weakened but still defiant.

The siphon and his elementals rush us one last time. It's a chaos of bestial roars, flaring magic, and slashing blades.

We're losing. The realization settles over me with cold clarity. We've held our own longer than I would have thought possible, but the siphon is too strong, and we're only delaying our deaths.

Raith suffers a deep cut to his leg, sags, and then the siphon catches him by the throat.

'Raith!' I shout, trying to charge but the void lion puts itself between us. I try to blast it with more steam, but I've channeled too much. The elements in the room are drained and I have nothing left. Typhon and Pyrin slam into the beast, but the fight is a maelstrom of fire, water, and void magic that I can't get past.

Raith chokes, his face turning purple as black veins begin to spread from where the siphon touches him. The mark on his hand sputters and then dims. Pyrin lets out an inhuman screech, flickering like a candle in a storm.

I struggle to fight past the void lion and reach him, thrashing with my dagger and screaming in outrage as the siphon continues to squeeze Raith's neck, choking him and draining him. The lion slaps Typhon away, sending the water dragon crashing into a wall in a tumble of stones and debris.

I can feel how hurt he is through the tether, and it breaks my heart, but all I can do is keep trying to push past the beast to reach Raith. To save him.

The lion doesn't try to kill me, but it doesn't let me pass.

'I'll fucking kill you!' I shout through clenched teeth as I slash at the lion and try to get to the siphon.

And then the temperature in the room drops dramatically.

'That's quite enough,' a familiar voice says from the doorway.

Rector Voss stands there, his elegant robes billowing around him despite the absence of wind. His silver-streaked hair is immaculate as always, his posture relaxed. There's nothing visibly different about him, yet the siphon recoils as if struck.

Raith falls to the ground, curling in on himself and still gasping like he's choking. I run past the void lion and slide to my knees beside him, cradling his head in my lap.

'*What's wrong with him? Why isn't it stopping?*' I ask Typhon through the tether.

'*He was touched. The void corruption will continue to spread.*' Typhon is getting back to his feet at the edge of the room and shaking off rubble and dust from his wings and back. He's hurt, but okay. Thank gods.

But Raith . . .

'No,' I whisper, a hot tear rolling down my cheek. 'No.' I barely even notice the siphon or void lion as they continue to back away from Voss.

Voss glides into the room, still staring down the siphon. 'You will be leaving now, siphon.'

The siphon takes another faltering step backward.

Why is it afraid of him? Voss isn't even a primal.

Voss smiles, the expression never reaching his eyes.

He makes no recognizable gesture, speaks no words of power. Yet the air around the siphon seems to compress, crushing inward. The creature struggles against some invisible force, its body contorting unnaturally.

'Why . . .' the siphon gasps, its voice strained.

'Tell your master that Confluence remains protected,' Voss says pleasantly.

The siphon shrinks in on itself, its form twisting and diminishing until it resembles a malformed human shadow. The void beast whimpers and fades like mist in sunlight.

With a sound like tearing fabric, the shadow and the remnants of the void lion vanishes. The oppressive energy that had filled the room dissipates, leaving only the smell of ozone, decay, and smoke.

'Raith.' The name breaks in my throat. Black veins are spreading beneath his skin, creeping outward from his throat where the siphon touched him.

Voss approaches, his expression grim as he studies Raith. 'This is void magic. It wasn't allowed to fully take hold, but I fear it will kill him within the hour. His elemental is already failing.' He glances at Pyrin, who has diminished to half his normal size, his flames flickering weakly.

'There must be something we can do,' I say, desperation making my voice crack.

Voss glances around the room, taking in the destruction – toppled columns, shattered stone, scorched walls. 'I would stay, but we're hosting guests, and my absence will soon be noted. Emissaries from Empire here to dig for reasons to bury me, no doubt,' he adds with a sour twist of his lips.

'You're just going to leave us here?' I demand, anger flaring hot and bright. 'How can you—'

'There's nothing that can be done for him. The siphon won't return for now, so you have nothing to fear on that count. Just . . . take your final moments with Raith. And come see me tomorrow. We have much to discuss.' Voss strides out of the room, walking over the remnants of the blown-in door. He regards the open doorway with a faint grimace, then disappears from view.

Typhon moves to my side, exhausted but still alert. *'You will need to try to heal him. It could work. It could cleanse him.'*

'I don't know how,' I reply, panic rising as the black veins continue to spread. *'I've only ever healed myself.'*

'I'm too weak to help you as I did during Confluence Day. If you form a tether with him, it would be easier. The tether carries energy of its own. You could use this energy to fuel the healing. Use it as a pathway to draw out the void.'

I look down at Raith's paling face, the black veins now spreading across his jaw and down his chest. His breathing is shallow, each exhale weaker than the last.

Pyrin whimpers, his form diminishing further as the fire mark on Raith's hand grows fainter.

I can't let him die. Not like this. Not when he came to save me.

'How?' I ask Typhon. *'What do I do?'*

'An oath,' Typhon replies. *'Tether yourself to him as you tethered yourself to me. It will only be a one-way tether, so not nearly as strong or complete. But it could be enough.'*

I take Raith's hand, the one marked with the fire symbol, and press it against my chest over my heart. His skin is cold, the warmth that always seemed to radiate from him nearly gone.

'Raith,' I say, my voice surprisingly steady. 'I don't know if you can hear me, but I swear this oath to you now. I swear I'll do everything I can to help you. To protect you like you've protected me.' The words come from somewhere deep inside me, pulled forth by instinct and desperation. 'Your life is my life. Your fight is my fight.'

For a moment, nothing happens. Then I feel it – a faint vibration between us, like a thread being pulled taut.

The thread grows stronger, more defined, like a slender cord linking us together. It's nowhere near as solid as the tether between

Typhon and me – more like a single thread compared to a woven rope – but it's there, pulsing with potential.

I place my hands on either side of his neck where the siphon touched him, calling forth my healing power. It's harder than healing myself, like trying to pour water uphill, but I push through the resistance.

The black veins resist, clinging to Raith's flesh like parasites. I can feel them fighting me, trying to burrow deeper. But something has changed with our connection. I can sense his life force now, feel how it's intertwined with Pyrin's, see how the void magic is eating away at them both.

I don't just push at the corruption. I reach through our new thread-thin connection, anchoring myself to the core of who Raith is, and then I pull. I pull it from him the same way I draw in his fire when we touch.

The void magic is reluctant at first, clinging stubbornly. Then it begins to flow, sluggishly at first, then in an ever-increasing stream. It pours from Raith into my hands – a thick, oily substance that burns wherever it touches.

I gasp at the pain, but I don't let go. I can't.

'Don't let it linger inside you,' Typhon warns. *'Direct it away. Quickly.'*

I do as he says, channeling the corruption away from both of us and into the stone floor where it hisses and evaporates like dark sludge. But there's so much of it, far more than I expected, and each passing moment drains more of my strength.

The thread between us quivers but holds, growing slightly stronger as more of the corruption flows out of him. I can feel Raith now, sense his essence – all fire and determination and hidden depths.

'Stay with me,' I whisper, as much to him as to myself.

Finally, the last of the corruption leaves him. The veins fade from his skin, and color returns to his face. His breathing deepens, steadies.

To my shock, the scars that have always twisted half of his face grow bright white and begin to dissolve, not completely gone, but far more subtle than the twisted valley of flesh they were before.

'Hmm,' Typhon rumbles. 'You took the time to make cosmetic improvements. Was this for your benefit or his?'

'Shut up, Typhon. I have no idea what I'm doing, but . . .' I run my fingertips down Raith's left cheek, which is now only faintly rippled with scar tissue.

It's almost hard to look at him like this, but I feel a pang of guilt. Those scars were part of him, and I had no right to change them. I can only hope he understands I didn't know what I was doing.

Pyrin's flames grow brighter, his form solidifying as the connection with Raith strengthens once more.

I sit back, suddenly lightheaded. The room tilts alarmingly around me. I've never channeled so much power for so long. And the void magic left some sort of mark inside me that makes my body feel like it weighs a thousand pounds and clouds my thoughts.

'Nessa?' Raith's voice is raspy but strong. He sits up, reaching for me as I sway.

'I'm fine,' I try to say, but the words come out slurred. 'Just . . . tired.'

The last of my strength leaves me. I pitch forward, and the world goes dark.

I feel Raith catching me, his arms strong and warm around my body as consciousness begins to slip away. And somewhere, just at the edge of my awareness, a thin thread pulses between us – delicate but unbroken.

Through it, I feel something warm and foreign, as if it's coming not from my own body but from his.

It's protective. It's warm. It's caring. It's so fierce it nearly takes my breath away, because if I didn't know better, I'd say it feels like love.

Chapter 30

Darkness. Then flashes of light. Voices float around me like wisps of smoke, never quite solid enough to grasp.

I hear Raith's voice, rough with concern, then . . . Bastian? I think I hear them arguing.

I'm vaguely aware of being carried in strong arms – Raith's arms – his heartbeat steady against my cheek as my head lolls against his chest. His scent envelops me, familiar and comforting even in my disoriented state. I hear his sharp voice silencing a few students who ask about me as he carries me somewhere.

'What happened to her?'

'Is that Thorne?'

'Why is Hollow carrying her?'

'Did Raith kill her? I thought they were fucking?'

My thoughts come like fuzzy impressions through a thick fog. I'm unable to tell if minutes or hours are passing. Time stretches and compresses in strange ways. I can sense that the void magic left something inside me, something cold and heavy that pulls me down into darkness whenever I try to surface. It's like being trapped in the depths of a frozen lake, looking up at a world I can't quite reach.

'Stay with me, angry human.' Typhon's voice is distant, as if he's calling to me from across a vast ocean. *'Your body is purging the void corruption, but it will take time. The siphon's touch has lingering effects, even secondhand as you received it.'*

I try to respond, but can't form the words. My tongue feels swollen, my throat raw. Instead, I sink deeper into the darkness that keeps pulling at me, dragging me under.

'*No. Fight it.*' Typhon's voice grows more urgent. '*The void magic seeks to sever our tether. It would leave you vulnerable, and I refuse to lose another human. Not after all the trouble you've been.*'

I want to tell him I'm trying, but the cold is seeping into my bones, making it impossible to resist the pull of unconsciousness. Just before I slip away completely, I feel a surge of warmth from somewhere outside myself – a flicker of fire magic, hot and bright, pushing back against the encroaching void.

Raith. It has to be him.

The last thing I remember is Typhon's voice, closer now: '*Interesting. The fire-touched is lending you strength through the tether, thin as it may be.*'

Then nothing.

I don't know how long it has been before I finally wake with my thoughts more clear, but my body is still diminished.

There's soft linen beneath my fingertips. Warmth enveloping me. I'm in a bed, but not my own.

I force my eyes open, blinking against even the dim light of a single candle burning beside the bed. Everything hurts, my muscles aching as if I've been training for days without rest. My mouth is dry, my lips cracked and bleeding. Even the simple act of breathing sends dull waves of pain through my chest.

'Water,' I croak, the word barely audible even to my own ears.

A figure moves at the edge of my vision, and then Raith is there, his face illuminated by the soft glow of the candle as he holds a cup to my lips. I drink greedily, letting the cool liquid soothe my parched throat. It tastes impossibly sweet.

When I've had enough, he takes the cup away, his movements careful and precise. Now that my vision is clearing, I can see the dark circles under his eyes, the tension in his jaw. He hasn't been sleeping.

'How long?' I manage when I finish, my voice still raspy.

'Two days,' Raith answers, his voice rough with exhaustion. 'You've been drifting in and out.'

Two days. I try to sit up, but my arms tremble beneath me,

refusing to support my weight. Raith's hand at my back steadies me, warm and solid.

Two fucking days? We're not allowed to simply miss classes here. Missing a single day is enough to earn punishment that ranges from extra physical training to remedial lessons, and, of course, marks against our evaluation score. I can tell I'm not in the healer's room, either, so what the hells are they telling our instructors? The panic must show on my face, because Raith's expression softens slightly.

'Voss is handling it,' he says, answering my unspoken question. 'He told the instructors you were injured in a training accident and are recovering under his supervision. No one's going to question him. They aren't counting the missed classes against you.'

I remember dimly that Voss was there when the siphon attacked, though now the memory feels distant, dreamlike.

'Crucible?' I ask, struggling to piece together how much time has passed. I can't even remember if it was more than two days away. 'Have I missed it?'

'Still coming,' Raith says. 'Just a few more days. But you need to rest now,' he says, gently pressing me back down when I try to sit up straighter.

Something about Raith tugs at my awareness until it finally clicks. I remember now. I see his face – his thick tangled scars are little more than a shadow of what they were. He's watching me with an intensity that makes my heart quicken despite my weakness. The ruined left side, the patchwork of scar tissue that had marked him as a survivor of something terrible, I could almost imagine someone missing it now at a glance.

'Your scars,' I whisper, reaching up to touch his cheek before I can stop myself. The skin is smooth beneath my fingertips. 'I'm sorry, I didn't mean to—'

He catches my hand, holding it against his face for a moment before lowering it back to the bed. His touch lingers longer than necessary, a gentle pressure that sends a flutter through my chest. It also sends wisps of his fire essence into my body, warming me from the inside out.

'You saved my life,' he says. 'You have nothing to apologize for. And they were just scars.'

'But they were part of you.' I can't keep the guilt from my voice. I had no right to change him like that, to alter something so fundamental to his identity.

Emotion touches his expression – grief, maybe, or resignation. 'They were a reminder of what I lost. Maybe . . . maybe it's time I stopped living in that moment.'

'*He does not speak all that he feels,*' Typhon observes, his voice clear in my head for the first time since I've woken. '*The fire human harbors deeper thoughts on this matter.*'

'*You've been quiet. Are you all right?*' I ask silently.

'*I have been conserving my strength to aid your recovery. The void energy that sought to consume the fire human infected you as well when you drew it out. It has been . . . taxing to help your body purge it.*'

I look around the room, realizing for the first time that we're in Raith's quarters. I've never been here before. It's sparse, utilitarian, with few personal touches beyond a small table with supplies for cleaning his blade, a few weathered books stacked neatly on a bedside table, and a faded tapestry hanging on one wall. The tapestry catches my eye – a scene of mountains and forests in shades of red and gold. It looks old, and somehow out of place in the otherwise austere room.

Most different of all is the brick making up the walls. Instead of the cool blues of my quarters in the water tower, his are dark gray with glowing veins of orange and red at the seams. The whole place smells faintly of smoke, reminding me of camping trips I used to take with my brothers back in Saltcrest.

'Why am I here?' I ask. 'Why not the healer's?'

Raith's jaw tightens. 'After what happened with the siphon, I didn't trust anyone else to watch over you. And we couldn't exactly explain why you're in your current condition, could we?'

The memory of the siphon sends a shudder through me. The way it had taken Raith's form so perfectly, how it had known exactly where to find me. How it had spoken of using me as bait.

'Voss,' I murmur. 'He saved us, but then he just . . . left.'

'He did,' Raith agrees, his tone neutral but his eyes sharp. 'I've heard the Empire Council is trying to remove him as Rector.'

There's something he's not saying, questions he's holding back. I can sense it in the tension of his shoulders, the careful way he's watching me.

The door opens and Mireen slips into the room, carrying a tray with steaming bowls. Her eyes widen when she sees me awake, her face breaking into a radiant smile that makes my chest ache with affection. Her copper-red hair is braided and pulled back and her blue eyes threaten to water at the sight of me.

'Nessa!' She rushes to the bedside, nearly spilling the soup in her haste. 'Thank the gods! We've been so worried.'

'Hold—' Raith says, lifting his palm and stopping her. 'Password?'

Mireen gives him an annoyed look, but answers. 'Fish slap.'

Raith shifts sideways, letting her move to my bedside.

'Can't be too careful,' she says with a shrug. 'How are you?'

I stare up at her, confusion furrowing my brow. 'Raith . . . told you? And you said "we". Did he tell Beck and Ambrose, too?'

'We didn't give him a choice,' Mireen confirms. 'Beck and Ambrose are outside keeping watch,' she explains, setting down the tray. 'We've been taking shifts with Raith. Making sure no one suspicious gets too close.' She brushes a strand of hair from my face with a gentleness that seems at odds with her usual boisterous nature. 'Even Bastian comes by every so often, though Raith won't let him in.'

My heart swells at the thought of my friends standing guard. 'You didn't have to—'

'Of course we did,' Mireen interrupts, her typical smile replaced by unusual seriousness. 'There's a siphon loose in Confluence, Nessa. One that specifically targeted you and Raith.'

I take her words in stride before realization stabs at me. She knows about the siphon. That means Raith had to have told her . . .

I glance at Raith, who remains expressionless. 'How much did you tell them?'

Raith hesitates. 'I was . . . not myself when I saw the state you were in.'

'He was so worried about you,' Mireen cuts in, a gleam in her eye that I recognize all too well. 'I do feel a little bad for taking advantage of his state. But we may have pressed him for information a little . . . forcefully.'

I frown. 'What the hells does that mean?'

Raith runs a hand through his disheveled hair. 'If there was a chance of telling them saving you, it was one I wanted to take. So I told them what I knew about you. All of it. You can be pissed if you want, but at least you're alive.'

My stomach clenches, a cold dread spreading through me. I look to Mireen, expecting betrayal or anger on her face, but all I see is sympathy and hurt.

'You should have told us, Nessa. We could've been supporting you. Unbound? Siphons hunting you? Private lessons with Voss?' She shakes her head. 'Gods, girl. I don't know how you kept it all to yourself.'

I sink deeper into the bed, guilt washing over me. 'I worried all of it would drag you guys into my mess. I didn't want any of you hurt because of me.'

Mireen finally lowers her eyes and chews a corner of her lip, as if choosing her words carefully. 'It did sting to know how much you hid from us. But only because we're your friends, Nessa. You should have known we'd want to take on that burden if it meant being able to help you more.' She takes my hand, squeezing it gently. 'So don't ever feel like you need to hide things to keep us safe again, okay? We're stronger together.'

Her voice is adorably stern, even though she's stroking my hand reassuringly and leaning over me like a worried mother. Cool, refreshing waves of her water essence flow through the touch. She looks at our hands, eyebrows twitching up. 'So that's what the feeling always is when we touch. You know, I used to get offended that you never would let me hug you and flinched away when I tried to touch you. Now I get it.'

'I'm sorry.' The words feel inadequate compared to the weight of what I've kept from them.

'Good. You should be. So . . . you can even heal scars, it seems?' Mireen wiggles her eyebrows and jerks her head toward Raith, the tension breaking as she returns to her usual teasing self. 'I'm pretty sure he was already the hottest guy on campus. Now it's not even fair.'

Raith looks away, clearly uncomfortable.

'Oh, I didn't want to offend you,' Mireen says quickly, half-reaching for him and then seeming to think better of it. 'It's just . . . you definitely pulled off the scars. Obviously. But they're more subtle, now. You get the badass and rugged vibe without so much of your face being hidden. It's . . . nice.'

Beck slips into the room as Mireen is talking, his large frame filling the doorway before he moves to stand beside her. 'Mireen's right, Nessa. Put his scars back. Give the rest of us a chance.'

He's trying for humor, but I can see the genuine relief in his eyes when he looks at me. He's been worried. They all have.

Raith ignores Beck's comment. 'Bastian has been by three times. He is asking a lot of questions. Questions about the siphons.'

'Raith sends him away with a few harsh words every time.' Beck grins, dropping into a chair beside the bed. 'It's quite impressive, actually. Very dramatic. At one point I thought they were going to fight. Both had their elementals out and everything.'

'And Bastian listened?' I ask, mildly surprised. Legacy students rarely take orders from anyone but instructors and other legacies. And Bastian isn't just any legacy, I've learned. He's heavily favored among them, partly because of his father's status.

Mireen shrugs. 'Reluctantly. I got the impression he was leaving more for your benefit than Raith's.' She shifts her attention to Raith. 'I think Bastian is the only first-year who isn't terrified of you.'

Raith's eyes narrow slightly. 'He should be.'

The suspicion in his voice is clear. I share it, but I'm not ready to voice my concerns about Bastian. Not yet. I may not completely trust him or understand his end goals, but I at least feel confident he's not out to kill me. Here at Confluence, that's saying a lot about a person.

'I need to sit up,' I say, struggling against the heaviness in my limbs. The short conversation has already drained more of my strength than I expected, but I'm itching to be back on my feet again. Moving. Proving to everyone they can stop worrying about me.

This time, Raith helps me, his hand warm against my back as he arranges pillows behind me. The brief contact sends a strange pulse through me – not just the usual heat I feel when we touch, but something deeper, like an echo of his own strength flowing into me.

And with it comes a fleeting impression – a fragment of thought that isn't mine.

Cannot lose her . . .

The thought vanishes as quickly as it appeared, leaving me wondering if I imagined it.

The tether. I'd almost forgotten about what I'd done to save him.

'*It holds,*' Typhon confirms, materializing at the foot of the bed in a smaller form than I've ever seen him take. He's barely the size of a house cat, his scales dulled to a muted blue. '*Though it remains fragile. One-way tethers are not meant to endure long.*'

'*You look terrible,*' I say silently, concern washing through me at his diminished state.

'*Your flattery knows no bounds,*' he replies dryly. '*I have expended significant energy helping your body purge the void contamination. It would have consumed you otherwise, much as it nearly did the fire human.*'

'*You'll get back your normal size?*'

'*Yes. In just a few days. I'm merely lending my essence to you. It's different than the way it disperses when we're wounded or even killed. It won't take me very long to call it back into my core once you've stopped sucking it from me like a babe at her mother's tit.*'

'*Will it fade?*' I ask, meaning the tether. '*The connection to Raith?*'

'Eventually. Unless strengthened by mutual oath. I'll confess this is one area I have limited knowledge. I've never tethered to an unbound before, nor do I know any elementals who have and still retain their sanity.'

I look at Raith, wondering if he can sense the connection between us. If he can feel me the way I'm beginning to feel him – a quiet presence at the edge of my awareness. Can he hear my thoughts? Feel my emotions? The idea is both thrilling and terrifying.

'You should eat,' Mireen says, holding out a bowl of broth. 'You need your strength back.'

I accept the bowl gratefully, realizing how hungry I am. The broth is simple but hearty, warming me from the inside as I sip it slowly. The first spoonful sends a shock of pleasure through my system, my body craving the nourishment after days of nothing.

'The Crucible is in a few days,' I say between spoonfuls, doing the mental calculation. 'I can't afford to be laid up like this.'

'The Crucible should be the least of your concerns right now,' Raith says sharply. 'You nearly died, Nessa.'

'So did you,' I counter, meeting his gaze directly. 'But we survived, and now we need to be ready for whatever comes next. The siphon admitted it was only using me as bait. It was targeting you specifically, Raith. We need to figure out why.'

Mireen looks between us, her gaze calculating. 'I'll let the others know you're awake,' she says finally, standing. 'They'll want to see you. Even Brunhild. And Ambrose has been theorizing non-stop about unbound abilities since he found out. It's driving Beck insane.'

'Truly,' Beck agrees, pushing himself up from the chair. 'He's like a dog with a bone. You'd think he'd discovered a new element the way he's going on about it.'

After they leave, a heavy silence falls between Raith and me. There are too many things unsaid, too many questions neither of us seems ready to ask.

The room feels smaller somehow, more intimate with just the two of us alone again. I'm acutely aware of his presence, of the way the candlelight plays across his features, softening the usually harsh lines of his face. With his scars faded, he looks the same, but different. Though I wouldn't have imagined it possible, he's even more handsome than before, as Mireen so bluntly pointed out.

In a way, it feels like I'm seeing behind the shields he so carefully maintains. It's like I'm seeing who he was before whatever happened that made him so . . . hard.

'Thank you,' he says finally. 'For what you did. For saving my life.'

I meet his gaze. 'You would have done the same for me.'

'Yes,' he agrees without hesitation. 'I would have.'

Something shifts in the air between us, charged with possibility. The tether between us pulses, warm and alive, and for a moment I think he's going to move closer, maybe even . . .

But before either of us can speak again, exhaustion crashes over me like a wave, and I feel myself sinking back toward darkness. I try to fight it, not wanting to break this moment between us, but my body refuses to cooperate.

'Rest,' Raith says, taking the half-empty bowl from my hands. His voice and his touch are heartbreakingly gentle. I can feel a pulse of something, too, like the ghost of an echo through our thin tether.

If it's a hint of how he feels about me, then . . . gods. If that's how Raith feels, he's a fucking master at keeping it hidden.

'I'll be here when you wake,' he says.

It's only moments before I slip back into sleep.

I drift through a dream that feels too solid, too real to be just imagination. I'm looking through someone else's eyes, feeling someone else's emotions.

Marble floors stretch before me. Tapestries hang from high ceilings, depicting battles and coronations. Everything is opulent, rich with history and significance.

I know this place, even though I've never been here. The knowledge sits in my borrowed consciousness with comfortable familiarity.

Home.

I move through grand corridors, my steps light and quick. I'm smaller than I should be, younger. A child's perspective. The adults around me tower like giants, their faces indistinct except for the warmth in their eyes when they look down at me.

'Your Highness,' they murmur as I pass, bowing slightly.

The title feels natural, expected. I acknowledge them with a child's imperious nod, mimicking the grave dignity I've seen in my father but unable to fully suppress the bounce in my step. I'm expected to behave like an adult, but I'm still so young.

I round a corner and enter a sunlit room where a woman sits by a window, her back straight as she embroiders something with long, delicate fingers. She looks up as I enter, her face achingly beautiful, her smile gentle.

'There you are,' she says, setting aside her work. 'I was beginning to think you'd hidden away in the library again.'

Mother. The word echoes with such love that it hurts.

'Father's coming home today,' I say in a voice that isn't mine – a boy's voice, high with youth and excitement.

'Yes, he is.' She stands, smoothing her elaborate gown. The fabric catches the light, so beautifully intricate and well-made it looks like art.

I flicker between feeling like the boy and feeling like myself, watching behind the boy's eyes as the woman – the queen – takes the boy's hand and leads him through more corridors to a grand balcony overlooking a courtyard.

Below, men on horseback are arriving, their armor glinting in the sun. At their head rides a tall figure with a golden crown, his beard streaked with the same auburn as the boy's hair.

The king.

But not just the king. He's my father. The boy's father.

My perspective continues to shift, making my brain hurt with the effort of remembering who is who. Remembering *me* when it feels like I'm overwhelmed with the feelings and thoughts of the boy.

'Father!' I call, waving.

He waves from the courtyard, but I notice something in his

mannerisms that strikes me as odd. A stiffness. An edge to his smile that feels wrong. I push the thought from my mind, writing it off because I know he sometimes comes back from the front lines distant for a few days. The death and constant war takes a toll on him, though he tries not to show it around us.

'Will he come to see you?' I ask my mother.

'Soon. He'll want to say hello to your siblings first. Saving the best for last,' she adds with a wink and a smile.

I smile back, thinking how beautiful she is.

I bounce on my toes as I roam the room with the nervous energy of a small child. I want him to be proud that I waited here with Mother. I want him to see I had the patience not to rush through the castle to greet him first.

So I wait, even as I feel something wrong in the air.

It's a coldness. A kind of nothingness.

It's not long before I hear a scream from down the hallway, high pitched and frantic. It's a scream unlike anything I've ever heard before. In that moment, I know it's my sister's voice, and I know the sound of that scream is going to haunt me for the rest of my life.

I wake with a scream of my own tearing from my throat, my body drenched in sweat. The sheets are tangled around me, restraining like hands trying to drag me back into the nightmare.

Raith is there instantly, his hands on my shoulders, his eyes wide with alarm in the dim light of early dawn. 'Nessa! What is it? What's wrong?'

I can't speak, can't breathe. The phantom pain of burning still courses through me, and beneath it, a grief so profound it threatens to drown me.

'A nightmare,' I gasp finally, trying to control my shaking. 'Just a nightmare.'

But what if it was more? What if it was a memory?

Was that a memory from someone you tethered in the past? I ask Typhon.

Hmm? Was what? I saw nothing.

'*I was in somebody else's mind. Seeing what they saw.*'

'*Ah . . . these things are possible, I suppose. It could have been. I will ask that you don't talk to me about what you saw. The memory of the ones I've lost . . . it's a wound I am not ready to revisit.*'

'*Of course. I understand.*'

I blink away the sleepiness, looking up at Raith's unscarred face. 'I think . . . I think I saw something from Typhon's past.' But even as the words leave my mouth, I wonder . . .

Could those have been Raith's memories?

There's a heavy silence for a moment before Raith's hand drifts to his throat, fingertips brushing the place that's still bruised from where the siphon touched him. 'What exactly did you do to save me?' he asks quietly, an edge to his voice I can't quite place.

'I'm not entirely sure,' I confess, pulling the blanket tighter around me. The predawn chill seeps through my underclothes, making me shiver. And then I realize I'm hardly wearing anything in front of Raith. With a jolt in my stomach, I tug the covers up over myself.

He's just watching me intensely, though. Waiting . . .

I clear my throat. 'I couldn't figure out how to heal you. And Typhon didn't think we had long to mess around. He said if I tethered to you, I'd be able to. So I made an oath to you, and it . . . worked.'

'You tethered to me? How's that even possible? And what kind of oath?' His voice is incredulous.

I look away, suddenly embarrassed. The words had come from somewhere deep inside me in that desperate moment, pulled forth by instinct and desperation. 'Nothing binding. Just a promise to protect you like you've protected me. That your life is my life. That your fight is my fight.'

He's silent for so long that I finally look back at him. His expression is unreadable, his eyes distant, as if seeing something far beyond the walls of this room.

'Raith?'

He blinks, focusing on me again. 'That was dangerous,' he says, his voice tight. 'You don't understand what I'm fighting. You shouldn't have sworn that.'

'You were dying,' I remind him, a flare of annoyance cutting through my exhaustion. 'I didn't have time to think through the implications. I just knew I couldn't . . . well . . . lose you.'

The impression of a smile touches his lips. 'I know the feeling.' He stands, putting distance between us. 'You should rest more. Your body is still recovering.'

'I've rested enough,' I argue, pushing back the covers even though I'm aware that I'm exposing myself again. My limbs feel stronger now, the heaviness lifting. The void corruption is leaving my system, replaced by a restless energy that demands movement. 'I need to move, to train.'

And to put on my actual uniform again. But I admit I like the way Raith's eyes flash with heat as they fall to my chest and my hips. He likes what he sees. I don't just suspect it . . .

I feel it. Through the tether. I can feel his arousal and attraction, the fuzzy impression of thoughts about how fucking perfect I am. How glad he is that I'm still alive. Still here.

'Nessa—'

'The Crucible is coming, Raith. And now we know there's at least one siphon in Confluence targeting us specifically. I can't afford to lie here any longer.'

He looks like he might argue for a moment, but he finally sighs. 'One hour of light training,' he concedes. 'Then you rest again. You're still pale as death.'

'Who took off my clothes?' I ask, arching one eyebrow.

Raith's eyes fall to my chest, and there's a clear hint of hunger in his eyes that sends an unwelcome rush of heat to my face. 'Mireen,' he says. 'You were burning up the first night. I asked her to do it.'

'I see. So am I going to spar with you in my underwear? Or could I borrow something of yours.'

'You'd be swimming in my uniforms.'

'So underwear it is, then?'

'You're going to wear one of my uniforms. There's no way I'm sparring with you looking like that.'

'Like what?'

'Distracting,' he says without turning to face me as he digs through a dresser. He hands me a pair of black pants and a black tunic, both trimmed in silver. They're clean, but the ghost of his scent clings to them.

Raith has his back turned, so I stand and slip into his uniform. Thankfully, the pants have a drawstring, so I'm able to pull them tight and keep them up. I roll up the hem several inches until it reaches my ankles. The shirt hangs off me like a pillow case, so I tuck it into the pants and roll the sleeves up as much as I can.

'Okay, you can look now.'

Raith turns, and another one of those rare smiles touches his lips.

'Still fucking sexy. Of course she is.'

The thoughts hit my mind softly, almost like a whisper.

'Uh . . . Typhon? Was that you?'

'Was what me? If you sensed the rumble in my stomach, I apologize. I was imagining a feast of your enemies.'

'Could I be hearing Raith's thoughts?'

'Perhaps. Your tether is weak, but it still exists.'

'You good?' Raith asks.

I swallow hard, nodding. 'Good.' But I try to take a step forward and the room sways slightly around me. Raith is immediately at my side, his arm around my waist.

'Slowly,' he murmurs, his breath warm against my ear. 'You've been unconscious for two days. Give your body time.'

I nod, leaning into him as I find my balance. The tether between us pulses stronger with the physical contact, and I feel a rush of protectiveness from him that nearly takes my breath away. It's fierce, almost possessive, and tinged with something that feels dangerously like fear.

'He worries he cannot protect you,' Typhon observes, stretching his diminished form. *'The fire human has grown attached. This complicates matters.'*

'*You say that like it's a bad thing,*' I reply silently.

'*It is neither good nor bad. It simply is. But attachments make one vulnerable, and you cannot afford vulnerability. Not with siphons hunting you.*'

'*It felt a lot more like they were hunting him. Not me. Didn't you see how that void lion made no attempt to kill me when I tried to save Raith? It was only blocking my path.*'

'*I would rather they are trying to kill you. The possibility of siphons not wanting to hurt you is . . . troubling.*'

'*You're cute when you're this small, you know. I feel like you should be perching on my shoulder.*'

'*Don't get accustomed to it.*'

Raith is still holding his arm around me, waiting patiently for me to find my balance as I mentally chat with Typhon.

I wonder if he feels anything from me through the tether. Can he sense how my heart races when he's close, how my skin heats where he touches me? How the thought of him dying had driven me to create the tether in the first place?

If he does, he gives no sign of it as he guides me toward the door. His face is composed, neutral, though his hand at my waist is gentle. Even if part of me wishes he'd let that hand slide lower, to touch me the way I know he wants to. The way I want him to.

His hand inches slightly lower, almost as if triggered by my thought. I look up sharply at him and see confusion and . . . something else in his eyes.

A sharp knock interrupts the moment. Raith tenses, moving slightly in front of me as he calls, 'Enter.'

The door opens to reveal Bastian, immaculate as always in his black legacy uniform with silver and gold trim. His pale eyes widen slightly at the sight of me on my feet.

'Thorne,' he says with a polite nod. 'I'm glad to see you're recovering. The password is fish slap,' Bastian says smoothly.

Raith nods. 'As you can see, we're both fine. You can report back to your . . . people that there's no need for concern.'

Bastian's gaze shifts to Raith.

'The Rector specifically requested to see Thorne once she was able. To discuss the incident.'

I feel Raith stiffen beside me. 'She's not ready yet.'

'She's on her feet,' Bastian says, gesturing to me. I see the way his eyes linger on my oversized clothing. I wonder if he's assuming I'm wearing Raith's clothes because we slept together and not for more innocent reasons.

'And she still needs time. I'm not sending her to get interrogated by the Rector. Tell him to fuck off until she tells him she's up for it.'

Bastian's expression doesn't show the slightest reaction. He's just silent for a few seconds, then nods. 'I'll say she's still in bed. Make sure you're not seen when you go wherever it is you two are going.'

'Thank you, Bastian,' I say.

Raith's grip tightens on my waist slightly, pulling me into his side protectively. Possessively. 'Anything else?'

'Thorne's friends asked me to tell you they'll be back this evening. They apparently had some matters to attend to in preparation for the Crucible.'

'Okay, thanks,' I say.

Bastian hesitates. 'There's something I should tell you before the Crucible . . . something I'd rather not say in front of Hollow.'

'Fuck you,' Raith growls.

'It's okay. If you can trust me with it, you can trust Raith.'

Bastian looks between us, his white eyes seeming to see far more than simple appearances. His nod is curt. 'Very well. The legacies have been instructed to stay out of the fight between aspirants during the Crucible. I wanted you to know you can't expect help from me. Our orders are very strict. We'll be standing guard of the objective, forbidden to stray far.'

'Orders from whom?' Raith asks.

'Somebody wants things to play out as they're going to play out this year. They don't want us stepping in and putting a stop to the bloodshed.'

'Like you would have.' Raith's tone is laced with cynicism.

'Actually, we already had plans to do exactly that,' Bastian says. 'Despite what you all think about legacies, we have no interest in seeing potential primals slaughter one another. We may be getting groomed for command, but positions of leadership are rather pointless without anyone to lead. No?'

'Right. So we're your fucking sheep. We're only allowed to die when it's under your command?' Raith asks.

Bastian straightens, looking at me instead of Raith. 'Voss won't wait forever. I suggest you don't put it off for more than another day or two.'

With that, he's gone, closing the door quietly behind him.

Raith and I stand in silence for a moment. Then he says, 'You're not going to see Voss alone.'

It's not a question, but I answer anyway. 'No, I'm not. But I do need to see him. He may know something about the siphon – about why it attacked us. Why it was targeting you specifically.'

'Yes,' Raith agrees, his voice hard. But there's something I feel through the tether. I can feel him holding back. Desperately clinging to yet another secret. I can also feel why he clings to it so desperately. He's still trying to protect me.

I look up at him, studying his perfect, unfamiliar face.

'Let's train,' I say, moving toward the door, determined to rebuild my strength. 'We have a lot to prepare for.'

More than he knows. More than either of us can imagine.

The tether throbs between us like a promise – or a warning. And through it, so faint I almost miss it, comes another fragment.

'Cannot lose her. Not when I've only just found her.'

It's another thought from Raith. I'm starting to feel the difference between his thoughts and Typhon's already. Typhon's voice comes to my mind clear and loud. Raith's are whispers on the wind. So faint and weak I have to strain to hear them. I can't say if it's because he hasn't sworn oaths to me, too, or just because the tether is still so new and fresh.

But gods . . . what the hells have I done? I'm the one who swore oaths to him, so shouldn't he be hearing my thoughts and not the other way around?

'How do you know he's not hearing your thoughts, angry human?'

I glance sidelong at Raith as we leave his quarters. Frowning, I try to form a clear, loud thought and aim it in his direction. For some reason, I don't have any confidence it's going to work, so the thought I send is . . . poorly chosen.

'You're the best thing about this place, Raith.'

Raith's eyes cut to me suddenly and he stops moving. My heart stops as well.

He cups my face with one hand, eyes seeming to devour me. 'I want to hear it from your lips.'

'W-what?'

'Say it out loud.'

I swallow, cheeks burning as his fire flows through the place where he touches me, filling my body with delicious heat. 'You're the best thing about this place, Raith.'

His thumb brushes the line of my jaw and he leans forward. 'Promise me something.'

'Okay,' I breathe.

He hesitates, fingertips still brushing my skin as his molten gold eyes fill with a depth I can't comprehend. 'I've . . . lost people. Before I came here, I swore I wouldn't care like that again. If I let nobody in, they couldn't hurt me. But you didn't care, did you? You barged into my fucking heart uninvited, and now you're here.' He takes my hand and presses my palm to his chest, eyes never leaving mine. 'You're here, and I can't do a single fucking thing to stop it. So you will not let anything happen to yourself. You're going to live. You're going to thrive, or I'll never forgive you.'

His pulse pounds through my palm, racing like he's in the middle of a sparring match. I feel like I can't breathe as I process his words. All I can do is nod, the faintest smile playing at my lips. 'You're going to be mad at me if I die? Isn't that a strange threat?'

'Nessa. I'm serious. When I saw you in my bed these past few days, all I've been able to think about is what I'd do if I lost you. And . . . it's not something I can stand to think about. You have to protect yourself. No matter what. I've already made sure your friends understand.'

'Wait . . . what does that mean?'

'I warned them I'd hold them responsible if anything happened to you.'

'Raith. You can't threaten my friends.'

'I already did.'

I like him,' Typhon rumbles in my mind.

'Not now, Typhon.'

I'm about to continue the argument, but Raith leans in and kisses me.

His lips are firm against mine, nothing hesitant in the way he claims my mouth. Unlike our previous kisses, there's an urgency here, a desperation that makes my knees weak. I press closer, my hands finding his shoulders for balance as liquid heat floods through me.

The kiss deepens, but I can feel the rigid control he's maintaining – holding back, mindful of my weakened state even as his hands frame my face with a possessiveness that makes my pulse race. His heartbeat thunders through the tether between us, matching the frantic pace of my own.

I even feel whispers of desire, arousal, relief, and excitement. I can hardly say which of those are my own emotions and which are his.

'This is all I've thought about since the last time,' he murmurs against my lips, his voice rough with barely contained desire.

'What took you so long?' I breathe, my fingers curling into the fabric of his uniform.

He pulls back just enough to look into my eyes, his thumb tracing the line of my cheekbone. 'You know exactly why.'

And I do. He's been protecting me – from himself, from his secrets, from whatever darkness haunts him. But now that I've tethered myself to him, those barriers are crumbling, piece by piece.

'This doesn't mean I'm not still angry about you threatening my friends,' I say, even as I lean into his touch.

His lips quirk in the ghost of a smile. 'Angry is fine. As long as you're alive.'

'And this doesn't solve anything,' I add, my tone serious now. 'There's still a siphon hunting you. And . . . maybe I don't know what I'd do if something happened to you, either. So you had better make sure you stay alive, too.'

'That's the plan. I can't keep you alive if I'm dead. I can't protect my fires if I'm dead.'

'Forget about that. I don't want anything to happen to you. Not because I'm worried I'll lose a protector. Because I'd be losing you. I'm sure the fires feel the same way.'

I sigh, reluctantly putting a few inches of space between us. My body protests the distance, craving the warmth and strength I felt in his arms, but my mind knows we need to focus.

'One hour of training,' I remind him, steadying myself. 'Then I'll get some more rest.'

Despite my words, rest is the last thing on my mind. Training, too.

I'm thinking about the kiss and the fragments of what I felt through the tether. I want him in bed with me. I want him stripping off my clothes. I want him touching me like I'm not fragile or about to break. Gods. I want him. So. Fucking. Badly.

Raith's lips curve upward. 'You may need to find a way to keep your thoughts quieter if we're going to be tethered . . . I may have picked up on some of that.'

'Oh gods,' I say, covering my face with both hands as my cheeks burn yet again.

Through our tether, I sense his restraint, his desire carefully banked like embers waiting to ignite.

'For the sake of all that is elemental, just mate with the fire human and be done with it,' Typhon grumbles in my mind. *'The tension between you two is giving me a headache.'*

'It's not just about sex, Typhon. Sometimes, sex is just the cherry on top.'

There's a moment of silence, and then, surprisingly: *I've seen many bonds in my time, angry human. Few as . . . intriguing as this one.'* He sounds almost uncomfortable with the admission, quickly adding, *'Not that I care one way or another about your mating habits. Your mortal attachments are fleeting and mostly ridiculous.'*

But I catch it – that rare glimpse of genuine interest beneath his usual arrogance. It's gone as quickly as it appeared, leaving me wondering if I imagined it.

I glance at Raith, at the rigid set of his shoulders and the intensity in his eyes as we walk. Whatever this is between us – whatever it's becoming – it's far more dangerous and far more precious than either of us realized.

'When you're recovered,' Raith says suddenly, his voice low enough that only I can hear. 'When you're back at full strength . . .' He pauses, his eyes meeting mine with a heat that sends electricity down my spine. 'I want you in my bed again, but not for healing.'

The bluntness of his words makes my breath catch, a flush spreading across my cheeks that has nothing to do with the void corruption still leaving my system.

'Is that a promise?' I ask, matching his boldness despite the hammering of my heart.

His answering smile is slow and absolutely delicious.

Chapter 31

I'm running through marble halls toward a scream that freezes my blood and shatters something inside me. It's my sister's voice, warped into something no human throat should produce. A sound of pure terror and agony that rips my heart into shreds.

The hallway seems to stretch on endlessly. Guards lie crumpled against the walls, their armor dented, blood pooling beneath them. The scents of copper and smoke are so strong I start to gag as I keep racing toward that sound.

I should be bigger. Stronger. Faster. More prepared. Maybe then I could do something to stop all of this.

'Mother! Guards! Someone!' I call, but there's no answer. Just another scream from behind a heavy door at the end of the corridor.

As I reach it, tendrils of black smoke curl from beneath. Heat radiates through the wood, the metal handle glowing red. I reach for it anyway, my hand hovering inches away when the door explodes outward in a blast of fire and—

I wake with a gasp, heart hammering against my ribs. For a moment, I'm disoriented, the smell of smoke and blood still so vivid I expect to find the room ablaze and covered in gore. Instead, I'm greeted by cool morning light filtering through a window in the fire affinity tower.

Raith's quarters. I'm still here. Still recovering three days after the siphon attack that nearly killed us both.

I've hardly spent a full day conscious in his room, but it already feels safer than my own. Realizing where I am is a relief, like warm, comfortable sheets wrapping around me in a protective cocoon. I want to curl deeper into his bed and drift back to sleep.

'Another vision?' Typhon asks, his diminished form curled at the foot of the bed. He's still only slightly larger than a housecat, his normally vibrant blue scales dulled to a muted slate.

'I don't know what they are,' I admit, pushing damp hair from my forehead. 'They feel like memories, but not mine.' Deep down, some part of me does know now. Some part of me suspects, but the horror of those dreams makes me not want to believe.

Despite the call of sleep, I sit up in bed and look around the room for Raith. But he's not here.

Without him magnetizing my attention, I notice details about the room I've missed until now. A basin of fresh water by the bedside table. A set of clean clothes and underwear folded neatly at the foot of the bed that look like they've been brought from my own room. A plate with bread and fruit beneath a cloth.

I test my limbs carefully. The bone-deep exhaustion has lifted somewhat, replaced by a dull ache and lingering weakness. Still, it's progress from yesterday. My body is purging the last of the void magic I cleansed from Raith. Other than the occasional flash of cold sweeping across me, I think the worst of it has nearly passed already.

'You heal quickly,' Typhon observes. *'Another benefit of your unbound nature, I suspect. Or perhaps it's because of your unique manifestation.'*

'Or maybe it's just spite,' I mutter, swinging my legs over the edge of the bed. 'Too stubborn to stay down.'

'Spite is an undervalued motivator,' Typhon agrees. *'If not for spite, I may have let the madness fully take me long ago. The call to submit . . . it is deep and terrible. I fear there could be nothing left in the other ancients if you eventually cleanse them.'*

I frown. As much as I want to help them, the idea of facing more gigantic murderous elementals feels like more than I can fit on my plate at the moment. *Problems for another day, maybe.*

I reach for the water, drinking deeply. The cool liquid soothes my throat, washing away the last remnants of the nightmare. Or vision. Or whatever it was. The memory of the scream lingers, raising goosebumps along my arms despite the room's comfortable temperature.

The door opens, and Raith enters, carrying more food and a stack of books under one arm. His eyes immediately find mine, relief flashing across his features before he schools his expression into something more neutral. I see disapproval when he notices the still-full basket of fruit and bread by the bed.

'You should be eating. You need to regain your strength.'

'I just woke up.'

He nods, though he still doesn't seem pleased as he sets down his books on the desk. He sets down the second basket of food beside the first and gestures. 'Eat.'

'I'm not really hungry.'

'I don't remember asking. You need to eat.'

Reluctantly, I pluck a few grapes from the basket and pop one into my mouth, chewing. 'Happy?'

'I'll be happy when you finish everything I brought.' He moves around the room with practiced efficiency, but I notice the way his gaze keeps returning to me, as if he's afraid I might injure myself while reclining in his bed and reaching for occasional bites of food.

His bed.

A question strikes me. 'Where have you been sleeping while I've been hogging your bed?'

He gestures to a blanket on the hard stone floor I hadn't noticed.

'Raith . . . you should've said something. You don't need to be sleeping on the floor.'

'You need every comfort to get better in time for the Crucible. It's not far away.'

'And you think I couldn't have been comfortable sharing a bed with you?'

'I'm a fire. I run hot. You'd sweat through your sheets all night.'

'Maybe I'd like your warmth.'

He's in the middle of reaching for a rag – to polish his sword, I assume – when he pauses a moment. He sets down the rag and approaches the bed to stand over me. I must not be eating fast enough, because he picks up one of the baskets and sets it on my lap.

I give him a sarcastic smile and pick up the bread, taking an oversized bite I immediately regret. I can barely find room for it in my mouth as I try to chew, both cheeks puffing out.

Raith actually smiles a little at that. 'Better.'

He hasn't shaved this morning, so dark stubble coats his strong jaw in a way that I think suits him. I find myself wanting to reach up and run my fingertips down his cheek. Over the fullness of his lips. To touch him like he's mine.

'Other than a stubborn reluctance to eat,' he says. 'How are you feeling?'

'Better.' It's mostly true, at least.

Through our tether, I feel a wave of relief from him, tinged with lingering worry. The connection between us is still tenuous, like a gossamer thread that could snap with too much pressure, but it grows slightly stronger with proximity. When he's close like this, I catch what feels like drifts of his emotions that come and go like scents on a soft breeze.

Fully formed words and thoughts seem highly uncommon. So far, I think they only leak through if he's thinking them with high amounts of emotion. Or, like the case when I sent thoughts his way, if he actually wants me to hear them.

'I spoke with your friends this morning. They'll be by again later. I told them to let you rest when they came last night.'

'Good. You know . . . I've been missing for days now. People must be assuming I'm dead or worse.'

'Most think Malakai's people finally caught up with you. Some say you were injured badly enough to be kept in isolation.' His lips quirk slightly. 'There's even a rumor you challenged Serena to a duel and she burnt you to ash.'

'Well, that's dramatic,' I say, reaching for a piece of fruit. Eating some has woken my appetite, and now I'm worried Raith hasn't brought me enough food after all.

His eyebrows crease. 'I can get you more food.'

I stare. It takes a second for me to realize he picked up on my worry through the tether. Gods. That is going to be hard to get used to. But . . . it's also kind of nice. It's like he can read my mind. Sense my desires. Hopefully not all of them. If he knew about all my desires, I imagine there'd be less calm talking and more ripping off of clothing involved.

'This is fine,' I say.

'I'll get you more when you've finished.' There's no argument with his tone, so I don't bother.

'It might be a good thing if people think I'm dead for a little bit.'

Raith nods. 'I had the same thought. They'll all be planning and scheming for the Crucible, no doubt. If you're out of the picture, you may get left out of plans. All the better when you show up full strength.'

'What about the siphon? You've been careful, right?'

'We're all making a new password each morning. Nobody gets near you without it.'

I grin. 'I saw that yesterday. But couldn't the siphon take the place of someone who shows up to learn it?'

'It's possible. But it's just one way to make it harder to infiltrate our trust. And we have to give the previous day's code to get the next. It's not a perfect system, but it's better than nothing.'

'Okay, but you said to gain access to me. I'm not worried about me. You're the one the siphon was after.'

'There's nothing I can do about that. My fires are with me when I'm not with you. When I'm not with them, I'm with you and your friends. If it wants to come for me, it'll have a fight on its hands.'

I realize he's right. Other than having allies, there's not really much that can be done. We just have to keep moving forward the best way we know how.

'And Voss?' I ask.

Raith's expression darkens. 'He's a question. Yes. If he wanted either of us dead, all he would've had to do was not show up when he did. Makes it hard to consider him the biggest of our worries, at least.'

'Right. Maybe we can rule out him wanting us dead. But what the hell does he actually want?'

'I intend to ask him when we meet with him tomorrow.'

A smile plays at my lips. 'You really think he's going to let you into his office with me?'

'I'm not planning on asking permission.'

A hint of emotions drifts over me. Determination. Distrust. Worry. And rage . . . gods, so much rage.

'I thought we were supposed to meet with him today?'

'Not today.' Raith's voice softens as he finally stops moving around the room and sits beside me on the bed. 'Today is for recovery. If Voss has a problem with that, he can show up at my door and tell me to my face.'

His nearness is . . . nice. It's comfortable and full of unspoken tension at the same time. I'm acutely aware of every point where our bodies almost touch, the scant inches between his hand and mine on the blanket. The memory of our kiss yesterday flashes through my mind, and his eyes darken, suggesting the same thought has occurred to him.

A subtle echo through the tether confirms as much a moment later. He feels it too. The tension. The wanting. The desire.

'I brought books,' he says abruptly, gesturing to the stack on the desk. 'Thought you might be bored.'

'Thank you.' I reach out impulsively, covering his hand with mine. The contact sends a now-familiar surge of fire magic into my body, but alongside it comes something else – clear emotions passing through the tether. Protectiveness so fierce it takes my breath away.

'I'm really okay,' I tell him softly.

He turns his hand beneath mine, intertwining our fingers. 'I know,' he says, but the worry doesn't leave his eyes. 'I just . . . when I saw you collapse after saving me . . .' He trails off, jaw tightening.

'It was my choice,' I remind him. 'And I'd do it again.'

His gaze drops to our joined hands. 'That's what worries me.'

I pull myself to standing, using his strength to steady myself. The room sways slightly but settles as I find my balance. 'I can't stay in bed all day. I need to move, rebuild my strength.'

Raith rises with me, his hand still holding mine, his other arm slipping around my waist to support me. 'Slow,' he murmurs, the word more breath than sound against my temple.

We move together, a careful dance across the room. Each step feels more certain than the last as my body remembers its capabilities. By the time we reach the window, I'm standing mostly on my own, though Raith's arm remains at my waist.

Our 'training' yesterday was an exercise in futility. I mostly stumbled around and needed Raith to keep me upright. Today, with a little time, I think I could actually manage a rough approximation of a sparring match.

Maybe . . .

Outside, Confluence continues its daily rhythms. I can see it all from Raith's window, which faces inward, giving a clear view of nearly the entire campus. Students cross the courtyard, their black uniforms stark against the snow, their colored affinity markings and occasional elemental visible even from this distance. Looking at the castle's majesty from here, it's hard to believe a predator stalks its halls, that in a few days many of those students will be fighting for their lives in the Crucible.

'Can I try something?' I ask, turning to face Raith.

'What?'

'I want to see if I can channel. Just a little.'

His brow furrows. 'You're still recovering.'

'I won't know my limits unless I test them,' I say, offering a smile I hope appears more confident than I feel. 'Just a small exercise. And you'll be right here if anything goes wrong.'

He hesitates, then nods reluctantly. 'Something small,' he concedes.

I release his hand, closing my eyes to center myself. I reach for water, the element that comes most naturally to me despite my unbound status. I can sense it everywhere – in the air, in our bodies, in the basin across the room. I draw it toward me, coaxing rather than commanding, and feel the familiar tingle of magic flowing through my fingertips.

A small sphere of water forms above my palm, wobbling slightly but holding its shape. It's nowhere near what I could do at full strength, but it's something. I open my eyes to find Raith watching with undisguised fascination.

'It's still there,' I say, relief flooding through me. 'My control.'

'Did you doubt it?' he asks.

'After what happened with the siphon . . . yes.' I let the water dissipate, the droplets returning to the air. The small exercise has left me more tired than I'd like to admit, but I count it as progress nonetheless. 'That void magic is drawn to whatever lets us channel. I think if it stayed in our bodies long enough, it could completely cut us off from our abilities. It would—'

I sway slightly, and Raith is there immediately, his arm returning to my waist. The sudden movement brings us chest to chest, his face inches from mine. I can feel his heartbeat accelerating, matching the quickening of my own pulse.

'Nessa . . .' he begins, his voice rough.

Someone knocks at the door, dragging Raith's focus from me. He guides me to sit on the edge of the bed again, taking time to make sure I'm settled before he moves to answer the door.

I hear him stopping each person before they can enter and see them whispering what I assume is the daily passcode in his ear.

Mireen bursts in first, Beck and Ambrose close behind her. Brunhild brings up the rear, her massive frame filling the doorway as she surveys the room with obvious curiosity.

'You're looking better,' Mireen says, assessing me with a critical eye. 'There's actually some color in your face now, though you still look like you could use about three more days of sleep.'

'Thanks for the vote of confidence,' I say dryly, but I can't keep the smile from my face. Despite seeing them just yesterday, the sight of my friends brings comfort. 'I'm getting stronger by the hour.'

'Looks like you could already get on your feet and give us a run for our money,' Beck notes, dropping into Raith's desk chair and immediately putting his feet up on the small writing desk.

'Get your feet off my desk,' Raith says, voice low and deadly.

Beck pops out of the chair like he's been stung by a bee, rubbing the back of his neck. 'Yep. Yes, sir.'

'It's remarkable how quickly you're recovering,' Ambrose says. 'I assume it's a benefit of your healing manifestation?'

'I'm still not sure how to explain it,' I say, conscious of Raith watching from the doorway, his posture alert as if he expects danger to follow my friends into the room.

'Any other perks manifesting?' Ambrose asks, his expression eager behind his glasses. 'After what you did for Raith, I've been theorizing about the possible extent of your healing abilities.'

'Nessa has better things to do, Ambrose,' Mireen cuts in. 'She's probably dying for updates on what's going on while she's stuck in here.'

Brunhild strides forward, assesses me, and nods seriously. 'Good. Power returns,' she says with an approving nod. 'Need strength for Crucible.'

Her presence here and apparent knowledge of my status means she must officially be our fifth member, now. And if we can't trust her . . . well, I suppose the consequences would've already come for me.

'Speaking of the Crucible,' I say. 'What's the latest? I heard you had some kind of important Crucible prep to do last night.'

'We spent the afternoon doing reconnaissance,' Mireen says, settling beside me. 'I think we've identified where Malakai's allies are storing those weapons I mentioned.'

'Where?' Raith asks, suddenly interested.

Nobody mentioned stored weapons to me, but I assume it must have been something I learned while half-conscious. Either that, or they're assuming I won't be recovered in time to help.

'Eastern wing, third floor, behind a false panel in what used to be an old armory storage room,' Beck says. 'And these aren't just practice blades. We're talking actual steel. Daggers, short swords, even a few bows and arrows.'

'How did they get those?' I ask, stunned. 'Weapons like that are locked up until graduation. And I can't imagine upper-years caring enough about their . . . cause to risk their own status here by providing them.'

'That's the interesting part,' Ambrose says, leaning forward. 'Based on the markings I glimpsed, they appear to be Empire-issued weapons. Not the kind made for Confluence primals-in-training. The kind given to rank-and-file soldiers.'

Raith and I exchange looks. 'Someone on the outside is helping them,' Raith concludes, his voice hard.

'Exactly,' Ambrose confirms. 'But I asked around and consulted a few texts. Soldiers can't just ask nicely for replacement weapons. And the blacksmiths under Empire employ get only enough raw materials to make what is ordered.'

'So you're saying someone should know these weapons are missing,' I say. 'Somebody high up. Or somebody with enough power to cover up that number of weapons going missing is helping them?'

Ambrose nods. 'Right. Either way, somebody important with a lot of power is trying to help Malakai and his people slaughter us during the Crucible.'

'Legacies have power and connections,' Mireen says slowly. 'Could it be one of them? Bastian, maybe?'

'No,' I say a little too quickly. I wince when every head in the room turns to me.

A faint throb of jealous anger flashes in my mind. I have no doubt it's from Raith.

'It just doesn't add up,' I continue. 'If Raith told you everything, I assume he told you about the conversation we heard Bastian having with his father.'

Mireen's eyes fall. 'That's right. Bastian wanted him to call off the Crucible entirely. Not exactly logical if you're risking everything to smuggle weapons in to make it more deadly.'

'Unless he planned on you hearing that conversation,' Ambrose suggests. 'Or if the weapons are for something else unrelated to the Crucible.'

'There are more legacies,' Beck says. 'I only know of one that wishes he could get in Nessa's pants. Probably safer to assume it's another one of them. Or somebody completely on the outside. Does it really matter, though? The bad guys are going to have sharp pokey sticks. So fucking what? We've got magic and elementals. Fuck 'em and their weapons.'

'How many weapons are we talking about?' I ask.

'Enough to arm at least forty students,' Mireen says grimly. 'Maybe more.'

'Brunhild has been helping us develop counter-strategies,' Mireen adds. 'She's surprisingly knowledgeable about fighting against armed opponents when you're unarmed. Considering we'll have practice blades, we might as well be against their military-grade steel.'

'Is common where I come from,' Brunhild shrugs. 'Raiders, pirates. Must know how to fight when surprised.'

'She's been showing us some techniques,' Beck says, a note of admiration in his voice. 'You should see her disarm someone. It's . . . impressive.'

'I teach you tomorrow, Nessa,' Brunhild tells me.

'Looking forward to it,' I say, meaning it. 'But why should we let them keep those weapons? We know where they are, right? What's stopping us from stealing them?'

'No,' Raith says. 'You're still too weak.'

'I can manage.'

'We only found out about this because a girl who was with Malakai wanted to join our side,' Beck says. 'Obviously, we didn't trust her. But then she started spilling secrets like the weapons stash.'

'Then we need to ask her how the room is protected,' I say. 'We find a way to steal those weapons or destroy them. That's the plan.'

Beck nods. 'I'll ask her after we're done here. She has channeling class right now. She's an earth. Pretty, too. You should see her—'

Brunhild silences Beck with a hard smack to the back of the head. 'He keeps his eyes to himself and Brunhild, or he loses them.'

Beck's grin is sideways. 'She's some woman, isn't she?'

'There's more,' Mireen says, voice dropping lower. 'Voss cornered me after Military Tactics this morning. He's asking about Nessa.'

The mention of the Rector sobers me immediately. 'What did he want?'

'Questions about your recovery. When you'd be ready to see him. But this time . . .' she hesitates, exchanging glances with Ambrose, 'he specifically asked if your healing abilities had manifested again since the incident with the siphon.'

A chill runs through me. 'How would he know about that? And how does he know you know?'

'Exactly,' Ambrose says. 'We've been careful not to mention your healing around anyone but our immediate circle. The only people who know are in this room. Yet he seemed to know not only that you healed Raith, but that it might be a recurring ability.'

'He was there,' I remind them. 'When the siphon attacked. Maybe he saw more than I realized. Or he could know the effects of void magic exposure? What if the only way Raith could've survived was with some kind of healing magic?'

'Maybe,' Mireen says slowly. 'But something about the way he asked felt . . . calculated. Like he was confirming something he already knew.'

'There's that rumor going around too,' Beck adds. 'The one about the burned-out bodies Bastian mentioned to his father. It's the first I've heard of it, but the rumor is already everywhere. People heard about the fight you guys had with the siphon, too. They just don't know it was you guys and a siphon. All they know is some serious shit went down in the west wing that left a classroom in ruins.'

Mireen folds her arms and shakes her head. 'Voss knows a hell of a lot about this stuff. Are you sure we can trust him?'

'No,' Raith says. 'We don't trust him any more than necessary.'

'He saved me and Raith, though. He gave us an early tip about the Crucible. And all he's done so far when I meet with him is help with my powers. Why do that if he wants to bring us harm?'

'We shouldn't speculate without evidence,' Ambrose cautions, though his expression remains troubled.

'Whatever his interest,' Raith interjects, 'Nessa isn't seeing him until she's at full strength. I don't care what position he holds.'

'Agreed,' Mireen says, surprising me with her easy alliance with Raith on this matter. Their shared concern for my welfare seems to have bridged some of the initial distrust. 'You need to be at your strongest before facing him.'

'Not all news is grim,' Beck says, clearly trying to lighten the mood. 'There was quite the scene in channeling class this afternoon when Sestra found Dain and Kali . . . well, channeling something, but not magic.' He wiggles his eyebrows suggestively.

Despite everything, I find myself laughing. 'In the classroom?'

'Behind the practice dummies,' Beck confirms with a grin. 'Sestra was so angry I thought she might drown them both on the spot.'

'The look on Dain's face,' Mireen adds, dissolving into giggles. 'Like a fish that suddenly realized it was on land.'

Even Raith's lips quirk slightly at the mental image. For a moment, the weight of siphons and Crucibles and secret weapons lifts, replaced by the simple camaraderie of friends sharing gossip. It's a precious moment of normalcy in our increasingly abnormal lives.

'Oh,' Mireen says, as if just remembering. 'The rumors about your absence are getting wilder by the hour, too. There's a version going around that you challenged Serena to a duel and she burnt you to ash.'

'Raith told me that one,' I say, reaching for a piece of fruit from the plate Raith brought earlier.

'My favorite is the one about Nessa's flying fish,' Beck says.

I feel Typhon perk up at the mention.

'They say he fish-slapped Voss and got you both thrown off the highest tower. When we heard that one, we had to make the code "fish slap" in honor of the rumor yesterday.'

We all share some much needed laughs at the increasingly ridiculous rumors. Eventually, though, the conversation turns to more deadly topics. Like our strategy for the Crucible.

Ambrose pulls out a folded parchment from his pocket, spreading it across the foot of the bed. It shows a detailed rendering of what must be the quarry Raith took me to see.

'Where did you get this?' Raith asks, moving closer to examine the map.

'Library archives,' Ambrose says proudly. 'Not the main one – the secondary archive in the west wing basement. You'd be surprised what they keep there if you know where to look.'

Beck rolls his eyes. 'He means he sweet-talked the library assistant. Apparently, she has a thing for guys who can quote tactical theory from memory.'

Ambrose adjusts his glasses, a hint of pink touching his cheeks. 'I can't control if she finds my intellect stimulating.'

'Hey, no need to defend yourself, Ambrose. I'm happy for you. I just didn't know you had it in you. If you want my advice? You show up at her room. Tonight. Wear something sexy. Just walk right in like you own the place. It works every time.'

'Enough,' Mireen cuts in. 'We're here to talk strategy, not Beck's questionable romantic wisdom.'

'It's not questionable when it works,' Beck protests, but subsides when Mireen levels a glare at him.

'So,' I say, leaning forward to examine the map, 'what's the plan?'

For the next hour, we discuss possible scenarios for the Crucible. Ambrose has developed several strategies based on different starting positions, while Mireen and Beck contribute insights on our potential enemies and allies. Brunhild's tactical knowledge proves surprisingly extensive, her understanding of terrain advantages particularly valuable.

Raith remains mostly silent, though he occasionally offers a suggestion when our strategies have obvious flaws. I notice he's careful not to reveal too much about his own plans with the fires, maintaining a certain distance despite being physically present in the room.

Ultimately, there's only so much planning we can do. We won't know our true objective until the day of the Crucible. But knowing where the Crucible is likely to take place has its advantages, which is what we spend most of our time focusing on.

'Don't you all have classes?' I ask once I've realized just how long we've been talking.

'We'll get a slap on the wrist,' Beck says. 'No big deal. We're where we need to be.'

'He's right.' Mireen gives my shoulder a squeeze and I feel wisps of her cool water energy flow into my body. She shivers, but smiles. 'Still think it's incredible how you can draw power from people.'

'She is small, but strong,' Brunhild observes with her muscular arms folded. 'To draw power from enemies is a valuable skill. I will teach her grappling techniques for combat. Ways to get her small, child-like hands on her opponents.'

I raise an eyebrow, then lift one of my hands and give it a look. They aren't that small. 'Thanks, Brunhild.'

Brunhild nods. Her platinum blonde hair is pulled back in a scalp-tight braid that seems as no-nonsense as the woman herself. 'In my home village. Before I come to Empire. We have stories of unbound. Not like stories here. Stories of heroes, not monsters.'

'Where was your village?'

'North islands,' she says. 'Beyond Empire, beyond Red Kingdom. Different . . . perspective.' She taps her temple meaningfully. 'But the elements wished us to leave. Waters rose. My home is now part of the sea.'

'Well, we're glad you're on our team,' Mireen says with a genuine smile.

Brunhild . . . tries to smile. The expression isn't natural on her severe face, though, and it looks more like she's baring her teeth. 'Your team has power. Heart. Good heart makes for good power. We will survive Crucible together.'

There's a simple wisdom in her words that catches me off guard. 'I hope you're right.'

'I am right,' she says confidently. 'I see truth in people. Is why I trust sexy bear.' She nods toward Beck, who preens visibly.

'Nice as this is,' Ambrose interjects, checking the time, 'we should be going. We've got combat training in twenty minutes, and Instructor Vail hates tardiness even more than Sestra. I can handle remedial channeling classes, but Vail will literally make sure we bleed if we're late.'

'It's okay. Go,' I say.

They gather their things, Mireen hugging me tightly before she leaves. 'Take care of yourself,' she whispers. 'And be careful with him.' Her eyes flick meaningfully toward Raith, who is speaking quietly with Beck near the door.

'I will,' I promise.

As they file out, Brunhild stops briefly beside me. 'Tomorrow. Do not forget our training.'

When they're gone, Raith closes the door with a soft click. He stays by the door.

'Your friends are protective of you,' he observes.

'So are you.'

'I only have three days to get you back to full strength. Three days until the Crucible.'

'I'll be ready.'

He turns to me, his expression unreadable in the growing shadows. 'Nessa, I need to tell you something.'

My heart quickens. 'What is it?'

He hesitates, conflict visible in the tense line of his shoulders. 'Do you trust me?' he asks suddenly.

'Yes,' I answer without reservation, surprising myself with the certainty of it. After everything – the secrets, the warnings, the distance he's maintained – I still trust him with my life.

He crosses the room in three long strides, stopping before me. 'Then trust me when I say that during the Crucible, you need to keep your head down. Complete the objective, nothing more. Don't try to fight Malakai, don't try to be a hero, don't reveal your full abilities unless your life depends on it.'

'But my friends—'

'Will be safer if you follow my advice,' he interrupts. 'The less attention you draw, the better. Make sure Typhon knows, too.'

'That's not much of a strategy,' I point out.

'It's the only one I have that keeps you alive,' he says, his voice rough with emotion. 'And that's all that matters to me right now.'

The raw honesty in his voice steals my breath, I feel the truth of his words – the depth of his concern, the fierce protectiveness that borders on desperation. Whatever secrets he's keeping, whatever his true purpose here, his desire to keep me safe is genuine. It matters more to him than anything else.

I reach for him, my fingers finding the collar of his uniform, pulling him closer. 'I'll be careful,' I promise. 'But only if you promise to keep yourself safe, too. That siphon wanted you dead, Raith.'

His hand comes up to cover mine, his skin warm against my fingers. 'I've survived worse,' he says, but doesn't elaborate. Another piece of his past kept in shadow.

'Raith . . .' I begin, uncertain what I even want to ask. There are too many questions, too many mysteries surrounding him. But what comes out isn't even a question. 'Stay with me tonight.'

Surprise flashes across his face, followed by a heat that makes my pulse quicken. Then there's a roguish twist of his lips. 'You are in my room, Nessa. I was planning on staying with you whether you liked it or not.'

'I just . . . don't want to be alone.'

'You won't be.'

'And I want you in the bed. Not on the floor. Only to sleep,' I add.

It's not even dark yet, but Raith shows no sign of caring. He can tell I'm tired and need to sleep again.

We prepare for bed in near silence, the routine oddly domestic despite the extraordinary circumstances that brought us here. I brush my hair out to keep it from tangling after spending so long resting. I change while Raith turns his back, slipping into fresh, clean underwear and throwing a thin academy night shirt over myself. Then I climb into the bed.

The bed is narrow, clearly not meant for two, but we make it work. Raith lies on his back, one arm behind his head, while I curl on my side facing him. There's a careful inch of space between us, a boundary neither of us is quite ready to cross despite everything that's happened.

Just like he warned, the heat radiating from him is like a small furnace. But it's cold, even in the fire tower, and his heat feels absolutely perfect. It makes me desperately want to cling to him and cuddle close.

'The dreams,' I say into the darkness. 'The ones I've been having. They feel like memories, but they're not mine.'

I feel him tense beside me. 'What do you see?' he asks, his voice carefully neutral.

'A castle. A child running. Screams.' I hesitate. 'Fire.'

The silence stretches so long I think he might not answer. Then, 'The tether,' he says finally.

The truth I've suspected and been afraid to acknowledge finally rises up, impossible to ignore any longer. The dreams aren't from Typhon. They're not imaginary. They're memories.

Raith's memories.

Which means . . . gods.

Raith was supposed to be a king. But a king of where?

'Are they your memories?' I ask directly.

Another long pause. 'Yes,' he admits, the word barely audible.

I wait for him to elaborate, to explain the child, the castle, the fire. To explain how the hells a prince in line for a throne could wind up as a volunteer at Confluence and covered in scars. But he remains silent, the weight of unspoken truths heavy between us.

'You don't have to tell me,' I say finally. 'Not until you're ready.' If I hadn't seen what I've seen, I would maybe press him harder. But if those are his memories? The sound of that scream – his sister's scream – comes to my mind so vividly it gives me cold chills. The thought of his brother, Gareth, makes my heart ache. The brother he lost. The brother he cared for so deeply he's trying to take care of all the fire affinities now to make up for what happened.

But none of it was his fault. I want to tell him that. I want to say something, but I can't find the words.

He turns his head toward me, his profile silver in the moonlight streaming through the window. 'And if I'm never ready?'

'Then we'll deal with that when the time comes,' I reply.

His hand finds mine in the darkness, fingers intertwining. 'You should hate me,' he says softly. 'For keeping things from you. For pulling you into . . . this.'

'I don't,' I tell him. 'And I'm here because I choose to be. With you. Whether you like it or not.'

He makes a sound, half laugh, half sigh. 'So fucking stubborn.'

'Says the most stubborn man at Confluence.'

That earns a real laugh, quiet but genuine. The sound warms me more than any fire magic could, chasing away the lingering chill of void corruption.

We fall silent, the rhythm of our breathing synchronizing in the quiet room. Through our tether, I feel his emotions settling – the sharp edges of worry softening into something closer to contentment.

'I'll protect you,' he murmurs, voice heavy with meaning. 'Whatever comes.'

'I know,' I whisper back. 'We'll protect each other.'

As sleep claims me, I wonder which is more dangerous – the secrets Raith keeps, or the feelings growing between us despite them. Both have the power to destroy, to wound beyond healing.

Chapter 32

I wake to warmth – a perfect, comfortable heat that makes me want to burrow deeper into the covers and never emerge. As consciousness gradually returns, I realize the source of that heat is Raith, his body curled protectively around mine, one strong arm draped over my waist. Sometime during the night, the careful inch of space between us had vanished, our bodies finding each other like matching puzzle pieces drifting closer until we clicked into place.

His breathing is deep and steady against the back of my neck, his heart a solid thump against my spine. For a moment, I allow myself to simply exist in this bubble of safety and comfort, memorizing the weight of his arm and the way our bodies fit together as if designed for exactly this.

Too soon, the reality of our situation intrudes on my thoughts – the meeting with Voss, the approaching Crucible, the lingering mystery of the siphon. But I cling to this moment like a talisman, tucking it away to revisit when the world inevitably turns dark again.

'You're awake,' Raith murmurs, his voice rough with sleep.

'Mmm,' I confirm, reluctant to move or speak and break the spell.

He doesn't withdraw his arm as I expected. Instead, his hold tightens slightly, drawing me closer. Through our tether, I catch a whisper of his contentment, a peace that feels foreign and precious to him.

Somehow – whether through the tether or some other intuition – I know touching him all night didn't drain him dry of his fire essence. Instead, we're like two bodies of water that have joined, finding equilibrium as we both hold equal amounts. I think I could draw more from him if I sort of . . . pulled, but it's comforting to know I can touch him as much as I want without making him run completely dry.

'In time, you should be able to stop yourself from draining his energy entirely when you don't wish it,' Typhon says.

That would be nice, even though I've guiltily come to enjoy the feeling of his magical heat swirling and twisting inside my own body.

'Did you sleep?' I ask.

'Some.' His breath stirs my hair. 'Better than usual.'

I smile into the pillow, oddly pleased that my presence has given him even a modicum of peace. 'How long until we need to see Voss?'

'If you're feeling up for it, we could go as soon as you're up and ready,' he says, and I feel a reluctance in him that mirrors my own.

With a sigh, I turn in his arms to face him, our noses almost touching on the narrow bed. This close, I can see the fan of dark lashes, the curve of lips that I've now tasted but still hunger for.

Heat flares in his eyes as they drop to my mouth, and his hand slides from my waist to my hip, fingers splaying possessively. The fire inside me answers his call, curling through my veins with scorching heat.

'Nessa,' he says, my name a warning and a plea.

I lean forward, closing the scant distance between us. Our lips meet with no hesitation. No restraint. This kiss is hunger unleashed – teeth nipping at my lower lip, his tongue sweeping into my mouth when I gasp. I arch against him, my hands finding the hard planes of his chest, the defined muscles of his shoulders.

Emotions flow between us, intensifying each sensation. His desire coils through me, mirroring and amplifying my own until I can't tell where mine ends and his begins.

His hand tangles in my hair, angling my head to deepen the kiss. My fingers find the hem of his shirt, seeking skin, trailing fire up his side. A low groan rumbles in his chest when my nails scrape lightly along his ribs.

'We should stop,' he murmurs against my mouth, even as his hand slides beneath my tunic to trace patterns on the sensitive skin of my lower back.

'Why?' I ask.

'Because I've wanted this for too long. When I finally have you, I don't want to fucking rush. I'm going to take my time.'

The simple statement sends waves of magma beneath my skin. I bite my lip. 'I guess I can't complain about that logic.'

'Good.' His lips trail down my neck, finding a pulse point that makes me gasp. 'Voss,' he reminds us both, his voice strained. 'We need to get it over with.'

I sigh, resting my forehead against his chest. 'I know.'

When he pulls away, the loss of his heat is physical pain. But there's a promise in his eyes that steals my breath – it's a guarantee that what we just started isn't even close to finished, and it won't be long before he has me how he wants.

Focus, angry human, Typhon grumbles in my mind. *Your heat and pheromones are making it impossible to think. And we have much to consider before meeting with the Rector.*

I throw a pillow in Typhon's direction, which he dodges with insulting ease. 'Were you watching the whole time? Creep.'

I was not watching. I was attempting to rest while ignoring the mating display happening in my vicinity. It was most distracting.

'Does Pyrin drive you crazy by constantly talking in your head?' I ask Raith.

He chuckles. 'No. Pyrin doesn't speak much. But he's fiercely protective of me. Always patrolling the area and inspecting situations for danger. He's . . . It's nice having him. I always heard stories, but I didn't realize how much I would appreciate my elemental as an individual.'

I smile softly. 'Yeah. Typhon is . . . interesting. But he's kind of accidentally hilarious, and he does care. He just also loves the sound of his own voice.'

Careful, angry human. I am listening.

'But,' I add with a meaningful look toward the water dragon glaring at me from the corner of the room. He has doubled in size since yesterday, but is still far smaller than normal. 'I know exactly what you mean. Having somebody in your corner no matter what . . . it's a good feeling. Especially for those of us who got used to doing things on our own.'

Raith watches me for a long moment, then nods his head. 'Yeah.' He rises from the bed, stretching. The movement pulls his shirt taut across his shoulders, and I catch myself staring at the strip of skin revealed at his waist.

'I can feel you staring,' he says without turning. 'Keep looking at me like that, and I'm not going to be able to wait until we're done with Voss.'

I let my eyes linger on the muscular, tanned strip of exposed skin a moment longer before dragging them away. 'I don't know what you're talking about. I wasn't looking at anything.'

Raith eyes me over his shoulder, his expression amused. 'Pyrin says you were definitely looking.'

'I thought we were friends, Pyrin,' I say, not knowing where to look to address the fire panther.

I rise too, my muscles complaining only slightly. The void corruption is almost completely gone from my body, along with the strange waves of cold it brings. My strength is returning rapidly, enough that I feel almost like myself again – though I know better than to say as much to Raith, who would insist on more rest regardless.

'How should we play this meeting with Voss?' I ask as we prepare for the day, my voice deliberately casual as if we're discussing the weather rather than a potential confrontation with the most powerful man at Confluence.

Raith pulls on a fresh uniform, his movements precise and efficient. I try and fail not to stare, especially when he strips down completely naked with his back to me.

Gods. Does the man have no shame? Then again, why would he when he has a body like that? It's carved perfection. Beautiful enough that it's impossible not to stare.

'We listen,' he says as he pulls black uniform pants up long, toned and muscular legs. 'We learn what we can. We give away nothing. And we leave at the first sign of trouble.'

'And you're still planning to come with me? He might not let you in.'

'He doesn't have a choice,' Raith says flatly. 'I'm not letting you face him alone. Not after how he abandoned us with the siphon.'

I pull my hair back into a tight braid, thinking as I still sit on the edge of his bed. 'But he did save us first.'

'We don't know what game he's playing, Nessa.'

'If he wanted us dead, why intervene at all? Why not just let the siphon finish what it started?' I shake my head. 'It doesn't make sense.'

Raith tosses me my uniform – not his oversized clothes from yesterday, but my own, freshly laundered along with a pair of academy issue women's underwear. 'That's what worries me. So we stay alert.'

I nod, quickly changing while Raith politely turns away. Part of me almost wants to feel his eyes on me as I slip out of my underwear and gather the fresh pair he supplied. But when I peek over my shoulder, he's standing like a statue with his back to me.

'He has more restraint than you. He's able to keep his eyes from your bared flesh.'

'Yeah, well, I kind of wish he didn't. It's embarrassing how much he . . . gets to me.'

'You could demand he lay his eyes upon your flesh. I have seen this tactic before and it was quite effective.'

Ignoring Typhon, I pull on my underwear and uniform.

When I'm dressed, I move to where my weapons are stored, securing my practice rapier at my hip and checking that Raith's gift – the real dagger – is still safely hidden in my boot.

'I'm ready,' I announce. Whatever Voss wants, whatever he knows, I feel prepared to face it with Raith at my side.

Raith studies me for a moment, then he steps forward, his hand cupping my face with unexpected gentleness. 'The second he says or does anything that makes you uncomfortable, we're leaving. Understood?'

'Yes, sir,' I say, rolling my eyes but not pulling away from his touch.

His thumb brushes my cheekbone. 'I'm serious, Nessa.' He casually adjusts my uniform, fixing the pleats over the collar and giving the hem a tug. The way he fusses with my clothing to get it right feels far more intimate than it should, and I absolutely like it way more than I want to admit.

'I know,' I say, my voice softening. 'But I can handle myself.'

'Yes, you can. You've proved it several times over and saved my ass twice now.' His eyes hold mine. 'But that doesn't mean you have to handle everything alone. And I happen to prefer you alive. So if I think you're in danger, I'm going to be there. You'll need to learn to deal with that.'

My smile is small and I can barely meet his eyes as confusing, pleasant emotions twist inside me. 'Okay,' I say quietly.

I can feel something has shifted between us these past few days, a deepening of whatever this connection is growing into. It's more than attraction, more than the tether that links us. It's trust, hard-won and fragile, but real.

'We should go,' I say, reluctant to break the moment but aware of time slipping away. As much as I want to keep hiding away in his room, I know the Crucible is still rushing toward us. I need to be ready, which means going back to regular life at the academy. And that . . . that starts with this meeting.

Raith nods, his hand falling away. He checks his own clothing in the mirror and scoops up his practice sword before moving to the door.

The walk to Voss's tower is tense, our conversation minimal. Without the distraction of each other's touch, the reality of what awaits us settles heavily on our shoulders. Students part before us in the corridors, their whispers following in our wake. I catch fragments – speculation about my absence, shock at Raith's partially healed face, theories about our obvious proximity to one another.

'What a spectacle they're making,' Typhon observes, swimming through the air in his flying fish form, invisible to all eyes but mine.

'They fear him, but they crave him too. And they wonder about you – the water with a weak elemental who somehow survived when others failed.'

'They have no idea,' I think back, watching as two first-year aspirants scurry out of our path.

'No,' Typhon agrees. *'And let us hope they never do.'*

Voss's tower feels more oppressive than ever as we ascend the winding staircase, past the portraits of former Rectors that seem to watch with knowing eyes. The narrow corridor at the top is empty, the ornate double doors to his office closed. Rather than knock, Raith simply pushes them open, his hand a steady pressure at the small of my back as he guides me inside.

The office is just as I remember – the massive desk, the shelves of books and artifacts, the wall of windows overlooking the grounds. Voss stands with his back to us, silver-streaked hair catching the morning light as he gazes out at Confluence spread below. He wears a tailored black robe, elegant but simple, power in its understatement.

'I see you brought company, Miss Thorne,' he says without turning, his voice mild. 'I admit, I was expecting you to come alone.'

'I expect many things too,' Raith says, his tone just as mild but with an edge beneath it. 'Like the assurance that a siphon won't attack students under your protection. We all have our disappointments.'

I realize something as Raith speaks. Some of the cockiness and cold confidence I've always sensed in him makes more sense now that I know who he was. Who he is.

A prince who never was. Heir to a throne he never claimed. Lone survivor of a royal family. I want to ask him where he's from. It must be one of the outlying islands, or I feel sure I would've heard of him before now. But his past is something I have to approach carefully and cautiously. It's full of pain, and I don't want to cause him any more hurt than he has already suffered.

Voss turns then, his pale eyes taking in Raith without surprise. 'Mr. Hollow. You should be dead.'

'I get that a lot.'

'Yes, I imagine you do. Your survival speaks to the potency of Miss

Thorne's healing abilities. Quite remarkable.' Voss's gaze shifts to me, assessing. On the surface, he looks as calm and collected as ever. And yet . . . I sense something else behind his eyes. Something like desperation. Or maybe impatience? 'How are you recovering, Nessa?'

'Well enough,' I say, matching his careful neutrality. 'Though I was hoping you wanted to talk to us about the siphon. Maybe to assure us we don't need to worry about it happening again.'

'Perhaps you'd both care to sit? This may be a lengthy conversation.'

He gestures to two chairs before his desk, waiting until we're seated before taking his own position opposite us. The deliberate courtesy doesn't escape me, nor does the fact that he's positioned himself with the light behind him, making his expressions harder to read.

'I'll be direct,' Voss says, folding his hands before him. 'I know more about the siphon situation than I've previously shared. I believe there could be more than one siphon within Confluence's walls. How many, though, I can't say for certain.'

'And you're just now telling us this?' Raith's voice is dangerously quiet.

Voss raises an eyebrow. 'I am telling you now, as a courtesy. There was no need for you to know before.'

'No need—' Raith begins, but I place a hand on his arm, stopping him.

'Why tell us at all?' I ask. 'Why not the Empire Council? Or the instructors? Why us specifically?'

Voss studies me, his expression impossible to decipher. 'Whoever else knows is irrelevant. I'm sharing this now because I believe you, Miss Thorne, could be the reason they're here.'

The words land like ice in my veins. 'No. It said it was only using me as bait to get to Raith.'

'I didn't say they wanted you dead. You represent both a threat and an opportunity to them. They serve a master, one who has been hunting unbound for centuries for reasons we can only guess. Perhaps he wishes to gain allies, or perhaps he has other purposes.'

'How the hells would you know what Lorkan Grace is hunting?' Raith asks.

'I make it my business to know things, Mr. Hollow. For instance, I know that Malakai and his allies have acquired weapons they should not possess. I know that there are eyes within Confluence observing all that transpires, eyes belonging to forces that might wish you harm. And I know those eyes will be watching most keenly during the Crucible, representing a very real threat to Nessa's safety if she's forced to demonstrate her . . . abilities.'

'Empire emissaries,' I say. 'We heard they're here to observe the Crucible.'

A flash of surprise crosses Voss's features, so brief I almost miss it. 'You're well-informed. Yes, the Empire Council has sent representatives – ostensibly to evaluate the school's performance and our methods.'

He rises, moving to a cabinet beside his desk. From it, he removes a crystal decanter filled with amber liquid and three small glasses. 'Would either of you care for a drink? Avernium Reserve. Quite rare these days ever since the trade blockade a few years back.'

'No,' Raith says firmly.

'Miss Thorne?'

'I'm fine, thank you.'

Voss pours himself a measure, returning to his seat with the glass in hand. He doesn't drink, merely swirls the liquid, watching the light play through it.

'I have a proposal for you, Miss Thorne,' he says after a moment. 'One I believe will be of mutual benefit.'

'I'm listening,' I say carefully.

'There is a place, not far from Confluence, that I would like you to see. A place of significant historical importance, particularly for someone with your . . . unique heritage. I believe it may help you better understand your abilities, perhaps even enhance them. At this place, you could have the final answers you seek about what you are. No more mysteries. No more questions.'

'And when exactly do you propose this field trip take place?' Raith asks before I can respond, his voice hard.

'Tomorrow,' Voss says. 'It should be before the Crucible, and we've run out of time to delay. I believe what Miss Thorne might learn there could prove invaluable during the trials to come.'

'No,' Raith says immediately. 'Tomorrow is the last day we have to get ready before the Crucible. Nessa needs rest. She needs to prepare. She doesn't need to be traipsing through the woods with you on some mysterious errand.'

Voss's eyes narrow slightly. 'I wasn't aware Miss Thorne required your permission, Mr. Hollow. Just as I wasn't aware I needed the permission of a student to do as I'd like.'

'Then consider yourself informed of this new information.' Raith's voice cuts like a thin blade, sharp and deadly. 'She's not going anywhere when we have a Crucible to prepare for. End of discussion.'

Voss's lip turns up at one corner. 'Bold. I'll give you that much. But I'm afraid I must insist. This matter is quite time sensitive.'

'Raith has a point,' I say, careful to keep my tone measured. Raith may not be acting like it, but I'm keenly aware of who we're talking to. The Rector has the power to dismiss any student, effectively having them killed. I'm not eager to die so pointlessly after everything we've been through to make it this far. 'Is this really the best time for . . . whatever this is? If I spend all day with you tomorrow, I'll be giving up my last chance to prepare, like Raith said.'

Voss sets down his drink, leaning forward. 'Miss Thorne, I have helped you understand and develop your abilities. I have protected you as best I can. I am asking for this one thing in return.' Again, I sense the same impatience in his voice.

'Protected her?' Raith scoffs. 'You left her to die after the siphon attack. How did you know more of those things weren't coming back? And I didn't see you during the elemental trial bailing her out. I didn't see you stopping people who wanted her dead from challenging her. You weren't in the lake when Malakai or that rogue elemental tried to kill her during the water trial.'

'And yet she lives,' he says coldly.

'No thanks to you,' Raith's hand finds mine, squeezing once in silent support. Through our tether, I feel his anger, his protectiveness, but also his restraint – a willingness to ultimately let me handle this how I see fit. 'She's alive because she's a fucking badass who doesn't need your help. So don't try to pretend she owes you this.'

I feel a swell of pride to hear Raith talk about me like that, but I do my best to tamp it down and focus on what matters right now. I know Raith doesn't like the idea, but Voss makes it sound like it could be an opportunity to get stronger.

'What exactly would we be looking for at this . . . place?' I ask, genuinely curious despite my reservations.

Something shifts in Voss's expression – hope? Relief? 'A ruin. One that dates back to the time when unbound were . . . more common. I believe it contains information – perhaps even artifacts – that could help you better understand and control your abilities.'

'And what do you get out of this?' I press.

Voss smiles, the expression not quite reaching his eyes. 'I'll be frank, Miss Thorne. I need you to access these ruins. It's why I would prefer we enter *before* the Crucible. Waiting could risk . . .'

Raith scoffs, shaking his head. 'Un fucking believable. She's just a key to you? So if she dies during the Crucible, you'll be locked out of your precious ruins?'

'Wait . . .' I say. 'Then help me. And I'll help you. Find a way to make sure we survive the Crucible. If we live, I'll go with you.'

A slow smile spreads across Voss's mouth. 'Clever, Miss Thorne. Very clever. There is . . . something I could do to improve the survival rate, perhaps. It will raise suspicions and draw the ire of the council, though. It won't come without cost.'

I force myself to stay strong, voice firm. 'If you want to make sure I'm alive to see those ruins, you'll make sure everybody gets this protection in two days.'

Disappointment flashes across Voss's face before his expression smooths. 'Of course. Though I must emphasize how much less scrutiny there would be if we went tomorrow. What you're asking will make it more difficult for me to travel freely for a time.'

'You have her answer,' Raith says, rising from his seat. His hand finds the small of my back again, a gentle pressure guiding me to stand as well. 'Is there anything else?'

Voss regards us for a long moment. 'I suppose not. You've struck your bargain. There is a protective measure usually only granted to legacies . . . I believe I can extend it to all students this year without too much scrutiny. But remember what you've sworn here. Survive the Crucible, and you'll help me enter the ruins. Yes?'

I nod my head, uneasiness swirling through my body. It feels like a victory, but somehow, I worry I'm not seeing everything.

Voss rises from his chair, moving around the desk to stand before us.

As we turn to leave, he calls after us. 'Oh, and Miss Thorne? I wish you luck during the Crucible. I won't be able to offer you complete safety. Only a slight improvement on your odds. So do prepare with diligence, hm?'

I nod once in acknowledgment before following Raith out, feeling Voss's gaze on my back all the way to the door.

We don't speak until we've descended the tower and found a secluded alcove away from curious ears. Typhon materializes fully, his diminished form hovering between us with evident agitation.

'I do not trust him,' Typhon declares.

Raith's expression is grim. 'I don't like it. There's no way in hell you're going with him to some mysterious ruin in the middle of nowhere.'

'I need to do this. It might mean more information about who or what I am. It might teach me more about how to control my powers.' I push off the wall, pacing the small space. 'If there's even a chance—'

'At what cost?' Raith asks quietly.

The question brings me up short. It makes me feel reckless for even considering this.

'I don't know,' I admit finally. 'But agreeing to go with him might have just saved countless lives. Isn't that worth the risk?'

Raith leans his forehead against mine, eyes closed. He shakes his head slightly. 'It should be. But it doesn't feel worth it. Not to me. I wouldn't trade you for a thousand lives, even if that makes me an asshole.'

'I won't tell anyone if you don't,' I say, biting the corner of my lip. 'But it's not as if Voss is a primal. He doesn't know I have Typhon. If he thinks he can ambush me somehow or coerce me, Typhon will be there to protect me.'

'And so will I,' Raith says. 'I'm following. Wherever he plans to take you.'

'We should talk to Bastian. He seemed to know something about Voss, or at least, his father does. Maybe he could give us an idea about what we're walking into.'

Raith's jaw tightens at the mention of Bastian, but he nods. 'Fine. But not alone.'

'Not alone,' I agree, offering a small smile. 'I'm starting to think you just like being around me, Hollow.'

His expression softens, and he tucks a stray lock of hair behind my ear. 'Maybe I do, Thorne.'

Heat blooms in my chest at the gesture, at the warmth in his eyes. We stand there for a moment, suspended in a sphere of connection that feels increasingly like home.

'If you two are quite finished,' Typhon interrupts, his tone dry, *'perhaps we might consider strategizing for the Crucible? Given that it is rapidly approaching and will likely involve numerous attempts on our lives?'*

I laugh despite myself, the tension of the meeting with Voss dissipating slightly. 'We'll see if Bastian is willing to tell us anything. Then we should find the others, see what they've discovered about those weapons.'

As we leave the alcove, I can't shake the feeling that we're standing on the edge of something momentous, something that will change us all irrevocably. The Crucible, Voss's mysterious ruin, the siphons' interest in us – all threads in a tapestry still with no full picture in sight.

But with Raith's steady presence beside me, with our tether pulsing between us like a promise, I find I'm not afraid. I feel strong. I feel capable. And I feel ready to face whatever is coming.

Chapter 33

The dining hall falls to a hush as I enter with Raith at my side. Hundreds of eyes track our movements across the stone floor, conversations stuttering to silence before erupting into fierce whispers. I can almost feel the speculation rippling through the room like a physical wave, even among the upper-year students who must have caught wind of what was going on.

'Dramatic as always. You would think these humans had never seen someone return from the dead before.'

I smile at Typhon's comment. *'To be fair, I was missing for days. And Raith's face . . .'*

'Yes, yes. You removed most of his scars. Quite vain of you, really.'

'We both know that was an accident.'

Before we can make it halfway across the room, a group of first-year fires approaches us. Cade leads them, his slight frame almost lost among his more muscular companions. When he sees Raith, his face lights up with unmistakable relief.

I know Raith was still keeping in touch with the other fires, but they're probably happy to see me up and moving. It means Raith won't be locked away in his room for hours a day anymore.

'Sir,' Cade says, the title sounding natural despite the fact that they're all supposedly equals as first-years. The others echo the greeting with similar reverence, standing straighter as Raith's attention falls on them.

'Sir?' I mutter under my breath to Raith, but he ignores my comment.

'Report,' Raith says, his voice taking on a tone of quiet authority I've rarely heard.

'No incidents since yesterday,' Cade responds promptly. 'We've maintained the patrol rotations as you instructed. Tifa and Jenner caught a couple of Malakai's waters trying to access the eastern training rooms, but they backed off when confronted.'

Raith nods, his expression giving away nothing, but I can sense his approval. 'Good. Any progress with the earths?'

'Two more joined us this morning,' says a tall girl with intricate burn scars running down her neck – training accidents, most likely. Fire affinities have access to one of the most deadly forms of magic, but also the most dangerous to learn. Almost all the fires bear some small scars by now.

'Keep building those relationships,' Raith instructs. 'We need every ally we can get.'

'Yes, sir,' they respond in near-unison.

Raith's eyes fall on Cade, softening almost imperceptibly. 'How's your neck?'

The boy's hand rises unconsciously to the small cut that has scabbed over and healed from the confrontation a few days back. 'Fine, sir.'

'And you're not going anywhere alone?'

'No, sir. I've been with Tifa or Jenner at all times, just like you said.'

Raith clasps Cade's shoulder briefly. 'Good. Keep it that way.' He glances at the others. 'All of you, be vigilant. Two more days until the Crucible. Stay in groups, stick to the plan, and remember what we've practiced. Anyone who leaves sight of the group for any period of time needs to give the password before they're trusted again.'

They nod, their expressions solemn yet determined. The respect in their eyes isn't just deference to strength – it's something deeper, something earned. These students look at Raith the way soldiers might look at a general they'd willingly follow into battle.

'Dismissed,' Raith says, and they disperse with military precision, though Cade lingers a moment longer.

'The siphon, sir,' he says quietly. 'Is it true it was targeting you specifically?'

Raith's expression hardens. 'Focus on what you can control, Cade. Let me worry about the rest.'

'Yes, sir.' Cade's eyes flick to me, then back to Raith. 'We're ready. Whenever you need us.'

As Cade rejoins his companions, I notice how the other fires watch Raith – with a mixture of awe and absolute trust. These students would die for him without question.

'Was the "sir" thing your idea or theirs?' I ask once we're alone again.

'I've given up trying to get them to stop. They started trying to call me captain and commander, so letting them use "sir" was actually a compromise. But it makes them feel better. Thinking I'm more than I am. Thinking somebody is in control and can lead them.'

'Sounds like a heavy burden.'

He eyes me, almost looking surprised a moment before his expression hardens. 'It's nothing I can't handle. Come on. People are staring.' He gestures and we head to join the waters.

I notice Veeni glaring at me from where she sits in a small group with Serena and Jira. One of Veeni's sleeves is pinned up where her arm should be.

Do not feel guilt, angry human. She delivered you to the wolves. She's lucky I left her head on her shoulders.'

I pull my eyes away from them and head for my usual spot next to Mireen, who is waving frantically as if I might miss her in the crowd. Raith follows me the whole way, not immediately splitting off to join his fires like he normally does. His hand doesn't quite touch my lower back, but he remains close enough that I can feel his heat, a reassuring presence amid the stares.

'I'll come find you after weapons training,' Raith says, voice low enough that only I can hear. His eyes scan the room, assessing threats even in this supposedly safe space. 'I'll find Bastian and tell him we need to talk like you wanted.'

I nod, trying not to think about how his lips looked when he said those words, or how his mouth felt against mine this morning. 'Be careful,' I say instead.

His smile is small and perfectly private. Just for me. 'Always.'

He leaves, the crowd parting before him like water around a stone. There's an unmistakable aura of danger that makes students instinctively clear his path. I notice how the fires watch him go, their postures straightening as if his mere presence reminds them to stay vigilant, to be worthy of the trust he's placed in them.

'Well, well, well,' Beck says as I slide onto the bench beside Mireen. 'Look who's finally rejoined the land of the living.'

'And with quite the escort,' Ambrose adds. 'I've been tracking the rumors about your absence. Would you like to hear the top three theories currently circulating?'

'I would not,' I answer, reaching for a bread roll. My appetite has returned with a vengeance after days of illness, and I pile my plate high with roasted meat and vegetables.

'Too bad,' Beck says with a grin. 'Some of them are really funny.'

'Still not interested,' I say through a mouthful of bread.

Brunhild appears, dropping onto the bench beside Beck with enough force to make the table jump. She slaps a hand on the wooden surface, making our plates rattle.

'You come to training after meal,' she says, her tone brooking no argument. 'I show northern fighting style. Make you strong for Crucible. We focus on unarmed combat and grappling skills.'

'Don't we need to go to weapons training after we eat?' I ask. It has been a few days, and our schedules often shift around, but I'm pretty sure I remember that much.

'Is canceled,' Brunhild says, wiping something slick from her fingertips. 'Someone accidentally spill cooking oil all over classroom floor. Too slippery to fight.'

I stare at her. 'Did you do that just so we had time to train together?'

'Brunhild has no control over where oil spills.'

I glance at her boots and see dark stains on them, then grin. 'Right. Thanks, Brunhild.'

She grunts in acknowledgment before stealing a slice of meat from

Beck's plate. He watches her with puppy-like adoration, not even protesting the theft.

'Any news about Malakai's weapon stash?' I ask in a hushed voice, leaning toward Mireen.

Mireen shakes her head slightly. 'Not here,' she murmurs. 'Too many ears.'

I nod, understanding. Trust is in short supply these days, especially with the Crucible so close. I scan the dining hall, noting Malakai's contingent seated across the room. His one remaining eye meets mine briefly, his face twisted in a glare like usual. Serena has moved to stand beside him and is whispering something in his ear, her eyes never leaving me. The message couldn't be clearer: I'm their target, and they're not bothering to hide it.

Rumors may have swirled about me being dead, but they see I'm not, now, and I'm sure they'll be folding my death back into their plans as soon as possible.

My gaze shifts to the legacies' table, where Bastian sits surrounded by his peers. When he notices me looking, he gives a nearly imperceptible nod.

The conversation spans everything from class assignments, developments in our elemental training, the latest gossip about a rumor that Sestra and Pilton used to sleep together. The idea is about as believable to me as our table growing legs and running off, but the story is at least an amusing distraction.

After we finish eating, Mireen leans close to my ear. 'Meet us in the eastern tower storage room in half an hour. We'll fill you in on everything while Brunhild trains you.'

I nod, rising from the table. 'I'll see you all there.'

'You cannot trust them fully, but they are at least marginally useful,' Typhon observes as I navigate through the dining hall.

'They're my friends, Typhon. Not just tools to be used. And I do trust them fully.'

'Friendship is merely a form of mutual usefulness with emotional attachment complicating matters unnecessarily.'

I smile at his cynicism, even as I feel a whisper of something warmer beneath it – something almost like fondness. The ancient water dragon rarely means what he says, and the tether constantly betrays the softness beneath his cold words.

As I exit the dining hall, I catch sight of Bastian slipping away from his table. He moves with the casual grace of someone accustomed to drawing attention while simultaneously knowing how to vanish when needed. Our eyes meet briefly across the corridor, and I know he wants me to follow.

I hesitate. Raith had been clear that we should approach Bastian together, but this might be my only chance to speak with him alone before the Crucible. After a moment's deliberation, I trail after him, maintaining enough distance to avoid suspicion.

He leads me through a series of corridors and up a narrow stairwell I've never noticed before, eventually emerging onto a small balcony overlooking the northern forests. The view is breathtaking – endless trees stretching to the horizon, their bare branches casting harsh silhouettes.

'We won't have long before someone notices I'm missing,' Bastian says without preamble. 'What did Voss want?'

I lean against the stone railing, considering how much to share. 'Bastian . . . I still don't know if I trust you. Not completely.'

'I gave you the book. I helped you disguise your mark. I haven't told anybody what you are. What more do you want?'

I chew my lip. 'Yes . . . well, I think it's still smart to be safe with my trust. You're practically a stranger to me.'

'That doesn't matter. Being your friend would only make things worse for you. I know what you are, and I am motivated to keep you alive. Distrust me if you want, but all you need to do is look at my behavior to see I'm not lying. A word to my father about what you are and you would've been taken from your bed in the night, Nessa. That is something you can trust. You're here. You're breathing. You're still walking this campus freely. Trust that.'

His pure white eyes hold mine, and I feel a coldness creep into my bones. I believe him.

'So help me help you,' Bastian says softly. 'Tell me what Voss wanted.'

I hesitate for several moments. 'He knows what I am,' I admit finally. 'He's been helping me understand my abilities.'

Bastian's expression doesn't change, but I sense a subtle tension in his shoulders. 'Has he asked you to do anything unusual?'

My heart skips a beat. 'Only this morning . . . he said there's a place he wants to take me. Some sort of ruin that could teach me more about what I am and maybe even improve my abilities.'

'A ruin . . . That sounds dubious, at best.'

'You tell me I can trust you because you could've had me killed, Bastian. I can say the same about Voss.'

'Fair enough. But I can tell you this much: powerful members of the council want Voss removed from his position as Rector of Confluence. They're going to great lengths to discredit him and make his removal possible. They don't trust him, and you likely shouldn't either.'

'I don't know anything about the Council. Them not trusting someone hardly—'

'The Council is the right hand of the tri-emperors, Nessa. Their only purpose is to keep Empire strong. Root out its enemies. Support its allies. Why do you think they're making such a showing with emissaries this year for the Crucible?'

I consider his question a moment. 'They hope to see something that gives them cause to remove Voss?'

'Exactly.' Bastian runs a hand through his golden hair, a rare display of frustration from someone usually so controlled. 'And they're not leaving it up to chance. They've put weights on the scales. Several weights. So I may not know what game Voss is playing with you. All I know is you need to be careful. My advice? Stay away from those ruins.'

I study him, trying to discern his motivations. 'Give me something, Bastian. Something to help me believe I can trust you.'

He's quiet for several beats before he finally answers. There's an earnest intensity in his eyes. 'The history of our world isn't what most would have you believe. When you know the things that have been done. The mistakes that have been made . . .' he shakes his head, as if dismissing something. 'If I play my cards right here, I'll be in a position to change things when I'm a primal. Helping you puts everything I'm trying to become at risk. So if nothing else, ask yourself why I would risk my own future to help you.'

I try to think of a response, but none come. I nod my head, deciding I can at least take his warning to heart. Maybe I'll still go to the ruins after the Crucible, but if I do, I'll go knowing it could be some sort of trap. 'Thank you,' I say. 'For the warning. And for the book.'

His lips curl into something approaching a smile. 'Was it helpful?'

'Very. It's helped me understand . . . certain things.'

'Good.' He glances toward the door. 'We should get back before we're missed. There are eyes everywhere. Be careful, especially with Malakai.'

'I know he's dangerous, but—'

'It's more than that,' Bastian interrupts. 'I believe somebody powerful is involved with him. They're feeding him information and supplies.'

'Why? What would that achieve?'

Bastian's expression darkens. 'Chaos. Disruption. An excuse to question the Academy's leadership. My father and the Council are looking for any reason to remove Voss from power. A disaster during the Crucible would give them exactly what they need.'

The pieces click together with sickening clarity. 'So Malakai's being used as a tool to bring down Voss? But why would he agree to that?'

'Not everyone makes choices freely,' Bastian says, his voice gentler than I've ever heard it. 'Sometimes, the threat to those we care about can be . . . persuasive.'

Before I can ask more questions, the door to the balcony opens. Bastian steps away from me, his expression shifting to one of cool disdain.

'Watch where you're going next time, Thorne,' he says loudly enough for the intruder to hear. 'If you spill water on my uniform again, there will be consequences.'

I play along, keeping my head bowed slightly. 'Sorry. It won't happen again.'

The fourth-year air in the doorway looks between us with mild interest before continuing onto the balcony. Bastian brushes past me, his shoulder barely grazing mine. As he does, he whispers so softly I almost miss it:

'Trust Hollow. Whatever else he might be hiding, he genuinely cares for you.'

Then he's gone, striding down the corridor with the confident gait of someone who has never questioned his place in the world.

I follow more slowly, mulling over everything Bastian has said from the warning about Voss, the revelation about Malakai, and most surprisingly, his endorsement of Raith. None of it makes complete sense, but all of it feels important.

'He withholds much, but what he shares carries the ring of truth,' Typhon observes.

'I thought so, too, even if I wish I believed he was wrong.'

I make my way to the eastern tower storage room, where my friends are waiting. The space is cramped, filled with discontinued training equipment and broken furniture, but empty for now, which is all that matters.

Brunhild is demonstrating some kind of grappling technique on Beck, who appears to be enjoying his predicament far too much despite being bent into an anatomically questionable position.

'Ah, Nessa!' Ambrose exclaims when I enter. 'Perfect timing. We were just about to begin our weapons sabotage briefing.'

'Sabotage?'

Mireen gestures me closer to where she's sketching something on a piece of parchment. 'We've mapped out the location of Malakai's weapon cache. There's a guard rotation, but we've identified a twenty-minute window tonight when the room should be unattended.'

'What then? Steal them?'

'Too obvious,' Beck says, still trapped in Brunhild's hold. 'They'd notice immediately, and we'd just confirm their paranoia about traitors.'

'We're going to sabotage them instead,' Ambrose explains, pushing his glasses up his nose. 'Make subtle alterations that won't be immediately apparent but will render the weapons useless when they're needed most.'

'Ollie can rust the metal from the inside,' Mireen adds. 'Create weak points that will snap under pressure. Typhon could help too, if he's willing.'

All eyes turn to where Typhon hovers in his flying fish form. I can practically feel his disdain radiating through our tether.

They expect the ancient heir to the water throne to engage in petty sabotage?

'They expect you to help keep us alive during the Crucible,' I counter. *'Unless you'd prefer I die a quick, ignoble death at the hands of Malakai and his goons.'*

Typhon huffs a plume of steam. *'Fine. I will assist. But I do so under protest.'*

'He'll help,' I tell the others. 'Assuming we can pull this off without getting caught.'

'That's where I come in,' Beck says, finally extricating himself from Brunhild's grip. 'I'll create a distraction while you, Mireen, and Ambrose handle the weapons.'

'What kind of distraction?'

Beck grins. 'Let's just say the eastern courtyard will experience some unexpected flooding tonight.'

'And me?' Brunhild asks, crossing her muscular arms. 'What is my role?'

'You're our lookout,' Mireen says. 'No one would question you wandering the halls at night, and if anyone gets suspicious, well . . .' She gestures to Brunhild's imposing physique.

Brunhild nods, apparently satisfied. 'Good plan. But first, training. Come, small one,' she says to me. 'I teach you northern fighting style now.'

I look questioningly at the others, who make shooing motions. 'Go ahead,' Mireen says. 'We'll meet in the water tower common room at midnight and head out together. See you then.'

Mireen, Beck, and Ambrose say a quick goodbye, leaving me alone with Brunhild. She stands before me, feet planted wide, a mountain of a woman radiating quiet confidence.

'Northern fighting not like Empire style,' she explains. 'Empire teaches you to be weapon. To channel, to strike, to kill.' She shakes her head disapprovingly. 'Northern style teaches you to be survivor. To use enemy's strength against them. To turn disadvantage to advantage.'

She demonstrates a stance, her massive frame surprisingly fluid as she shifts her weight from one foot to the other. 'You are small. This is good. Small means quick. Means targets on you are small too. Hard to hit.'

For the next hour, she drills me relentlessly in techniques designed to use an opponent's momentum against them. How to break holds, escape grapples, to use leverage, and turn a powerful strike into an opportunity to counterattack. It's exhausting but exhilarating, so different from the rigid forms we're taught in official training.

It reminds me most of the way Raith trained me, and I find I'm already fluent in several techniques she expects to have to drill into me.

'Good,' she says finally, nodding with approval as I successfully evade her grasp for the third time in a row. 'You learn quick. Smart. Your body remembers even when mind forgets.'

I wipe sweat from my brow, breathing hard. 'Thank you for teaching me this.'

She clasps my shoulder, her grip firm but not painful. 'They say unbound saved my ancestors during great flood. Used power to hold back waters, to save children when others had abandoned hope.' She pokes me in the chest with one thick finger. 'You have good heart. Will use power well.'

She dips her chin, eyes suddenly fierce. 'And you will always protect Beck, yes?'

The question feels like a threat, and I find myself nodding.

A familiar voice cuts through the room.

'I've been looking for you.'

Raith approaches, his expression neutral but his eyes alert, scanning Brunhild with barely concealed suspicion.

'Password?' Brunhild asks.

'Sexy bear,' Raith says.

I grin. Sexy Bear? That's really the password they chose for today?

Brunhild nods. 'Training finished anyway. She learns well. Quick. Strong for small one.' She waves to us both before striding away, leaving me alone with Raith.

'Did I interrupt?' he asks, moving closer.

'No, we were done.' I hesitate, then add, 'I spoke with Bastian earlier.'

A muscle ticks in Raith's jaw. 'I thought we agreed to approach him together.'

'He found me after lunch. It wasn't planned.'

Through the thin tether connecting us, I feel jealousy, anger, and a touch of betrayal. His voice is calm and measured despite the feelings I know he's harboring. 'What did he say?'

I relay everything Bastian told me – about Voss, the missing students, Malakai's suspected manipulation. Raith listens in silence, his expression growing darker with each revelation.

'So Bastian's father and the Council want Voss gone,' he summarizes when I finish. 'And Malakai's being used to create chaos that will justify his removal. And Bastian agrees that you should stay the fuck away from those ruins.'

'That about covers it.'

Raith runs a hand through his dark hair, his frustration evident. 'And we're supposed to navigate this minefield while surviving the Crucible and hoping there are no more siphons waiting to come for us. Wonderful.'

Despite everything, I feel a smile tugging at my lips. 'When you put it that way, it sounds almost impossible.'

'Almost,' he agrees, the corner of his mouth lifting slightly. His eyes meet mine, and for a moment, the rest of the world falls away. It's just us, standing together against impossible odds.

Then reality reasserts itself as a group of third-year earths and fires enters the room. 'Oh,' a girl at the front says. She notices we're first-years, then jerks her head. 'Room's ours, now. Out.'

'Come on,' Raith says, his voice dropping lower. 'We should go somewhere private to discuss this further.'

My pulse races at his words, at the memory of his lips on mine this morning, at the promise in his eyes when he spoke of taking his time with me.

'Lead the way,' I say, my voice steadier than I feel.

We brush past the group of earths and fires who barely seem to notice us.

As we walk back toward the castle, I feel a strange mix of dread and anticipation.

Despite everything dangerous coming our way – or perhaps because of it – I find myself drawn to Raith with a ferocity that should frighten me. In a world where each tomorrow feels uncertain, the promise of tonight, of stolen moments with him, burns brighter than any fear.

'*Such longing,*' Typhon observes with a theatrical sigh. '*Is this truly the pinnacle of human existence? Risking all for a few moments of pleasure?*'

'*It's not just pleasure,*' I tell him silently. '*It's connection. It's not being alone.*'

'*You are never alone, angry human. I am always with you.*'

His words, grumpy as they are, bring unexpected comfort. '*I know, Typhon. And I'm grateful for it.*'

'*As you should be,*' he huffs, but I feel a swell of warmth through our tether that belies his tone.

The sun begins to set behind the towers of Confluence, casting long shadows across the grounds. In just over a day, the Crucible will begin, and everything will change. But for now, there's tonight. There's Raith. There's a chance, however small, that we might find a moment of peace before the bloodshed that's coming.

Chapter 34

'I should probably get back soon,' I say reluctantly as Raith walks me through the shadowed corridor toward the water tower. There's a hush through the academy as night falls. Tomorrow is our last day before the Crucible. 'The others wanted to meet at midnight. I might try to catch a little sleep before, since tonight may be a late night.'

I feel his eyes on me. 'Because of the weapons sabotage.'

I nod. 'We only have a small window when Malakai's guards will be away from the cache.'

'And your part in this plan?' he asks, his tone carefully neutral though I can feel his concern seeping through our connection.

'Typhon and I will help Mireen's elemental rust the metal from the inside. Create weak points that will snap under pressure when they try to use them,' I explain. 'Beck's creating a diversion with some flooding in the courtyard while Brunhild stands lookout.'

A muscle in his jaw ticks, and through our tether, I feel his worry for me mingling with admiration. 'It's risky. If Malakai catches any of you—'

'He'll try to kill us. Yeah. But he's going to try to kill us during the Crucible, too. If we do this, we will be protecting others. We'll be giving them a chance of surviving, however small, if Malakai's people come for them. So, no, you're not talking me out of it. Don't even try.'

He studies me for a long moment, then sighs, running a hand through his dark hair. 'Has anyone ever told you you're incredibly stubborn?'

A small smile tugs at my lips. 'You may have mentioned it before.'

Raith's eyes don't leave mine as he seems to come to a decision. 'Midnight. That means we still have a couple hours.'

'A couple hours for what?' I ask, my pulse quickening at the hunger of his gaze.

'Good,' he says, his voice dropping to that low register that makes heat pool low in my belly. 'Because I've been thinking.'

'What about?' I ask, though I suspect I already know the answer.

His fingers brush mine, sending that familiar spark of magic between us. 'We've both been training hard today. I feel pretty filthy.'

'Okay,' I manage, despite the sudden dryness of my throat. It's not what he's saying, it's how he's saying it. It's the way his eyes are practically devouring me.

'Come on. We can get cleaned up together.' His hand finds mine, intertwining our fingers. 'Follow me.'

'Where are we going?'

'Showers. You waters have the best ones. I use them after hours when nobody's there. They'll be empty at this hour.'

My heartbeat races so fast it feels more like one solid, uninterrupted beat by now. Gods, is this really about to happen?

We descend into a dimly lit chamber. Moonlight drifts in through narrow windows, casting silver streaks across the large circular pool in the center. Above it, enchanted clouds hover near the ceiling, permanently drizzling room temperature water into the bathing pools. There are wet footprints on the stone like others were here not long ago, but I see no signs of movement in the pools.

'We're alone,' Raith says, his voice echoing slightly in the empty space. He pulls the latch over the door with a half smile. 'Just in case.'

'If you're about to turn into a siphon, I'm going to be super, super pissed with you.'

Raith shakes his head. 'Sexy bear.'

'Good,' I say, smirking at the silly passcode.

He moves closer, something in his expression making me forget to breathe. There's a vulnerability there I rarely see – a crack in the careful armor he maintains.

'What is it?' I ask softly.

He moves to the edge of the pool and holds his hand out, palm upward. A small flame dances across his fingers, illuminating his face with a golden glow. A miniature reflection of the flames is mirrored in his eyes as he watches the spell.

'I dream about you,' he says suddenly, the flame in his hand flickering higher. 'Not just . . . wanting you. I've been having dreams. Your memories, I think.'

My heart stutters. 'What?'

'The tether, I assume.' He takes a deep breath. 'I saw the storm, Nessa. The one that took your father and brothers.'

Ice fills my veins, and I step back, nearly stumbling on the slick stone floor. 'You saw that?'

Jolts of ugly panic shoot through me.

He knows. He knows what I did. He knows I failed my own family and got them killed. He knows I'm—

'Hey,' Raith's voice is soft as he releases his spell to cup my face and shake his head. 'I can feel what you're thinking. And no. I felt it. The fear. The rain. The waves crashing against the cliffs. The thunder you couldn't control.'

My throat tightens. I feel naked already, more exposed than if I had shed all my clothes.

'You think I'm a monster,' I whisper, the words barely audible even to my own ears. I feel the power inside me churning and reaching out into the room. The normally silent clouds above the bathing pool rumble with the low sound of thunder.

Raith's eyes never leave mine. 'No,' he says, his voice rough with emotion. 'I think you were a child who didn't understand her power.' He reaches for me, fingers brushing my cheek with unexpected tenderness. 'It wasn't your fault, Nessa.'

I try to pull away, but he doesn't let me retreat. 'You don't know—'

'I saw it all,' he insists, his thumb tracing the curve of my cheekbone. 'The storm started before you even realized what was happening. You tried to stop it. You did everything you could.'

'I could've done more.'

'I was in your head, Nessa. I saw it with my own eyes. You swam in those waters for hours. You kept diving for them long after you knew there was no way they were alive. You kept going until you passed out and the waves carried you back to shore. Fuck, Nessa. You did more than most would do. Nobody could blame you.'

'My mom and sister did.'

The thunder above the pool rumbles again, deep and heavy.

He winces, but resolve hardens his features a moment later. 'They didn't see what I saw. *It wasn't. Your. Fault.* Do you hear me, Nessa? It wasn't your fault. They didn't forgive you? That's their failure.'

Something breaks inside me – a dam I've built around my grief and guilt. My eyes burn with tears I've refused to shed for years. 'They died because of me. Because I couldn't control it.'

'They died because of a storm,' he says firmly. 'Because of powers you didn't understand and couldn't control. You were a child. Trust me, I know about blame. About living with ghosts. About carrying that weight – wondering if there was more you could've done. Walking yourself through it countless times searching for the one thing you could've changed about that day.'

Through our tether, I feel the truth of his words – the understanding, the acceptance. It's overwhelming. But beneath it lies something else, something he's not saying aloud.

'Listen to me, Nessa. Running from ghosts is no way to live. Do it long enough, and you become a ghost yourself. All we have is right now. Here. We can't change the past, but we can use it to find strength. So don't run from your past. Use it. Grow from it. Because I need you to be strong. I can't fucking lose you, too. Losing you . . . it would fucking ruin me.'

The admission hangs between us, raw and honest. I reach up, covering his hands with mine where they still cradle my face.

'I don't want to lose you, either,' I whisper, leaning into his touch.

He studies me for a long moment, searching for hesitation, for doubt. Finding none, he nods. His mouth finds mine with unerring accuracy, and the kiss is one without any semblance of control. Just raw need and desperate relief. My arms wrap around his neck as he pulls me flush against him, his body radiating the heat I've come to crave.

We stumble closer to the pool, stepping down into the waters until it soaks our boots and pants up to the calf. The rain drifting down on us is warmer now, drenching our clothes and running down between our hungry kisses.

I feel his power flowing into me, fire essence filling my veins, but it's no longer about siphoning his magic. It's about connection – about giving and taking in equal measure. For the first time, I feel myself giving something back to him, a whisper of my own essence flowing into his body, making him shudder against me.

'Wait,' he murmurs against my lips, pulling back just enough to gesture toward the clouds above the pool. The gentle warm rain droplets still hit the water with soft plinking sounds. But now steam rises immediately.

I feel its perfect heat on my skin. Not so hot that it hurts, but hot enough to soothe away aches and make me want to curl into him forever – just like this.

'Too hot?' he asks.

'No,' I say, looking straight into his eyes until I feel like I'm swimming in their molten heat. 'It's perfect.' I can feel the magic within me shifting as the thunder stops, but the downpour of rain picks up, falling on us in thicker and thicker sheets. I lean in for more kisses, but he presses a fingertip to my chin, making me pause as he stares into my eyes.

'I remember the first time I saw you.' His finger traces the line of my jaw, then drifts back to my lower lip, exploring it slowly as if the world will stand still for us – as if we have all the time we could ever want here. 'I heard you were a volunteer. Assumed that meant you were an Empire fanatic like Serena. I wanted to hate you for it, but I still knew I wanted you, even if I didn't admit it. I was scared to want you, but I couldn't stop thinking about you. Worrying about you. Trying to make sure you didn't get killed, but it turned out you were pretty good at watching your own back.'

I laugh softly. 'I've had a lot of help.'

'People want to help you because they see what you are,' he says, gaze intensifying. 'Your strength. Your determination. Your intelligence.' His hand slides to the back of my neck, fingers tangling in my hair. 'Your stubborn refusal to die when people want you to.'

The words bring unexpected heat to my cheeks. 'Is that what really attracted you to me? My stubborn streak?'

A hint of a smile touches his lips. 'That. And this . . .' He kisses me again, deeper, his tongue sliding against mine. 'And this.' His hand skims down my side, over the curve of my hip to cup my ass greedily, pulling my body up and into his.

I arch into his touch as a moan slips from my lips.

'Let me see you,' he says, his voice rough with desire.

My fingers tremble as I reach for the clasp of my uniform and slip out of my boots, clothing, shoes, socks, and underwear already completely soaked as we stand up to our calves in the pool, rain cascading down on us.

His eyes track every movement, darkening as I slowly undo each fastening of my clothing. The black fabric falls away, leaving me in just my underclothes – simple cotton, nothing fancy, but the way he looks at me makes me feel like I'm wrapped in silk.

Raith's breath catches. 'Nessa.'

Just my name, but the way he says it – like a prayer, like salvation – makes me braver. I remove the rest of my clothing until I stand before him completely bare, the rain drenching me as a slight drift of steam rises from the water around me. Water droplets catch on my eyelashes, slide down my collarbone, trail between my breasts.

His gaze scorches me, traveling from my face to my breasts, down to the curve of my hips, the juncture of my thighs. He swallows hard, adam's apple bobbing.

'Your turn,' I whisper.

He doesn't hesitate. His uniform joins mine on the stone floor, revealing a body sculpted by training and battle, touched with dozens of hidden scars I want to trace with my fingers and ask about in some future, sleepy morning where death isn't breathing down our necks.

I don't breathe as I drink in the sight of him. I *can't* breathe.

Broad shoulders tapering to narrow hips, strong thighs dusted with dark hair, and thick muscle layered beneath tanned skin.

His arousal is evident, thick and hard, and I allow myself to stare, to want without shame. Through the tether, I feel his mix of desire and barely checked restraint – a heady combination that makes my knees weak.

The water is pleasantly warm, growing hotter around him until it's almost like a bath. Rain continues to fall from the enchanted clouds, catching in his dark hair, sliding down his face, trailing over the defined muscles of his chest.

The edges of the bathing pools are shallow enough that the water only reaches waist-height. In the center, it's deep enough to fully submerge yourself.

'Come here,' he says, pulling me through the water until our bodies meet, skin against slick skin.

I gasp at the contact, at the hardness of him pressing against my bare skin. His hands settle on my waist, his grip firm and wonderfully possessive. He touches me like a present he can barely wait to unwrap and enjoy, and *gods* . . . I just want to fall apart in his hands, to ride the wave of his kisses to the perfect bliss I know lies at the end of that path.

'I've thought about this,' he confesses, his lips trailing along my jaw, down my neck. 'About you. Like this. Wet. Wanting me.' His teeth graze my pulse point, drawing a shiver from me. 'Have you thought about it too?'

'Yes,' I admit, my head falling back as his mouth works its way lower. 'More than I should.'

'Tell me,' he urges, his hands sliding up my sides to cup my breasts. His thumbs brush over my nipples, making me gasp. 'What did you imagine?'

Heat blooms in my cheeks that has nothing to do with his fire magic. 'Your hands,' I whisper. 'Your mouth. The way they'd feel on me.'

'Like this?' He bends to take one peaked nipple between his lips, the wet heat of his mouth drawing a moan from deep in my throat. His tongue circles, teases, while his thumb mimics the motion on my other breast.

'Yes,' I breathe, my hands finding his shoulders, nails digging into hard muscle. 'Just like that.'

He takes his time, lavishing attention on my breasts until I'm squirming against him, desperate for more. The water swirls around us, heated by his power until it nearly bubbles, steam rising to mingle with the falling rain.

His mouth travels lower, marking a path of kisses down my stomach. The position forces him to kneel in the pool, water lapping at his chest. He looks up at me, his eyes molten gold in the dim light.

'I want to taste you,' he says, hands sliding to the backs of my thighs.

The request makes my pulse skyrocket. I nod, unable to form words past the desire clogging my throat.

He guides one of my legs over his shoulder, then lifts the other, easily holding me as he guides my back to rest carefully on the edge of the pool.

'You're even more perfect than I'd imagined,' he says, hot breath tickling my inner thighs as he kisses his way up a devastating path toward my waiting heat.

The warm rain trickles down intimately against my most sensitive flesh, but it's nothing compared to the first touch of his tongue. I cry out, hands flying to his hair to anchor myself as pleasure bolts through me.

'Raith,' I gasp, my head falling back and my body digging against the rounded edge of the bathing pool.

He groans as if he's enjoying this more than I am, and the vibration of his voice only adds to the sensation. His hands grip my hips, keeping me steady as he explores with lips and tongue, learning what makes me moan, what makes me tremble. Through our tether, I feel his own arousal building with every sound I make, every shudder he draws from me.

The echo of his emotions is . . . interesting.

I feel hints of what he's feeling. I sense just how deeply he's enjoying this and how much I turn him on. I've never felt so fucking wanted.

The rain falls harder in response to my rising emotions, droplets sluicing down my heated skin. When he finds that perfect spot, circling it with relentless precision, my knees buckle. If he wasn't holding me so tightly, I would sink down and melt beneath the waters.

'I'm close,' I warn, my voice breaking. 'Too close. I want—'

He pulls back, his eyes meeting mine, lips glistening. 'What do you want, Nessa? Tell me.'

'You,' I manage, tugging at his shoulders. 'Inside me. Please.'

His hands slide to my ass, lifting me effortlessly in the water. I wrap my legs around his waist, gasping as the position brings his hardness against my core.

'You're sure?' he asks, searching my face. 'We can wait. Do this properly, after the Crucible, when we have time—'

I silence him with a kiss, pouring everything I feel into it – the want, the need, the fear that there might not be an after. When I pull back, his eyes are blazing.

'I need this,' I tell him. 'I need you. Now.'

His hands shift, one moving to support my lower back, the other positioning himself at my entrance. 'Look at me,' he commands softly.

I open my eyes, meeting his golden gaze. The vulnerability there matches my own – the fear of loss, the desperate need for connection, the knowledge that after tomorrow, everything could change. In this moment, we're just Raith and Nessa, stripped of all pretense, all armor.

'I need you to be sure,' he says, his voice tight with restraint. 'Because once I start, I don't think I'll be able to stop.'

In answer, I reach between us, gripping his thickness in my hand and roll my hips forward, teasing him with my body. 'I've never been more sure of anything.'

Raith nods. 'There's a trick fires can use . . . a little heat in the right place and we're sterile for a day or two.' I feel a flare of his magic in the air and his lips curve slightly.

I chew my lower lip. 'Have you . . . used that trick before?'

'No. You're the only one I've wanted since I stepped foot on this campus.'

His words are like music to me. I thread my fingers behind his neck, urging him closer, breath heavy on my lips. 'Please. Fuck me, Raith.'

He groans at my words, sliding himself into me with agonizing patience. His eyes never leave mine, watching for any sign of discomfort. I can feel his emotions. His desires.

He wants to grip me tight and pound into me, fucking me until I scream. But he wants me to feel safe even more. He wants to make sure I'm comfortable. That I feel protected.

There's a brief stretch and burn as my body accommodates him, but it fades quickly into pleasure so intense it takes my breath away.

'You're so warm in me,' I gasp. 'It feels so good, Raith.'

'Gods,' he breathes, his forehead resting against mine once he's fully seated within me. 'You feel . . . incredible.'

I roll my hips experimentally, drawing a hiss from between his clenched teeth. His hands tighten on my thighs, his fingers digging into my flesh. A devious part of me wants to unleash the beast I feel within him – the beast that wants to fuck me so hard everyone in this wing of the academy will hear my screams.

'Don't move,' he warns, his voice strained. 'Not yet. I need a moment or this will be over embarrassingly fast.'

I smile, oddly pleased by his admission. I press kisses to his jaw, his neck, feeling his pulse racing beneath my lips. 'Been a while?'

'It's never felt like this,' he confesses, his eyes meeting mine again. 'Never this intense.'

The tether between us pulses, growing stronger with our physical connection. I feel echoes of his pleasure mingling with my own, creating a feedback loop of sensation that threatens to overwhelm us both. I can feel his thick heat filling me and stretching my walls, and . . . I can also feel a hint of my own walls squeezing against his heat, as if I'm feeling this from every possible angle.

'I can feel you,' I whisper, awed. 'Not just physically. I can feel your pleasure.'

His eyes widen slightly. 'I feel yours too. It's . . .' He shakes his head, words failing him.

When he finally begins to move, it's with controlled, measured strokes that make the water lap gently against the pool's edge. He watches me carefully and slowly zeroes in on the exact rhythm and spot that drives me absolutely wild with pleasure.

'More,' I urge, my nails digging into his shoulders. 'Faster.'

Thunder rumbles overhead again and the clouds twist, churning with increased speed.

'Patience,' he murmurs against my throat, but he complies, increasing his pace slightly. Each thrust sends water splashing, the gentle sounds mixing with our ragged breathing.

He walks us backward until my spine meets the edge of the pool again. The position gives him better leverage, and he uses it to grind against me, creating delicious friction where I need it most.

'Raith,' I gasp, my head falling back against the stone edge.

I feel his struggle for control, his desire to let go warring with his need to make this last. It's intoxicating, knowing how much he wants me, how hard he's fighting to hold back.

'You're so beautiful like this,' he says, his voice roughened with need. His hand cradles my face, turning it so I meet his gaze. 'Flushed. Breathless. Taking me deeper.'

The words send a fresh wave of heat through me. I tighten my legs around his waist, drawing him impossibly closer. 'I want all of you,' I tell him. 'Don't hold back. Not with me.'

Thunder cracks from the magical clouds and the rain grows thicker, pouring down harder around us until the steam rising from the water blots out everything but his face. His eyes.

Something flares in his eyes – a wild hunger I've only glimpsed before. 'Be careful what you wish for, Nessa.'

The rain falling in heavy sheets that plaster my hair to my face, to my neck. Water in the pool around us begins to move with more purpose, following the rhythm of our bodies, responding to my rising pleasure. I can feel myself drawing water essence unconsciously, making the pool swirl and eddy around us, feeding the clouds above until they swirl and churn, pouring water in a deluge that flickers with white light.

His movements grow deeper, more forceful, each thrust hitting a spot inside me that sends sparks shooting up my spine. I cling to him, hands grasping at his shoulders, his back, anywhere I can reach. The tether between us throbs in time with our bodies, channeling his pleasure to me and mine to him, amplifying everything.

'Tell me what you need,' he pants against my ear, his hands gripping my hips tightly enough to bruise. 'I want to feel you come apart.'

'You. You're all I need,' I manage, my voice breaking as he shifts angles slightly, hitting even deeper.

He maintains the perfect rhythm, the perfect depth. Water splashes around us, steam billowing as his fire essence responds to his passion.

Raith's pace increases, his thrusts deeper, harder, driving me toward a peak I can already feel building. The water around us bubbles with his heat, adding to the dreamlike quality of everything.

'Touch yourself,' he urges, his voice barely recognizable with need. 'Let me see you come undone.'

I slide a hand between us, finding that sensitive bundle of nerves. The first touch makes me cry out, my inner walls clenching around him. Through the tether, I feel his reaction – a surge of pleasure so intense it nearly sends him over the edge.

'That's it,' he encourages, his movements growing more erratic. 'Let go, Nessa. I've got you.'

The dual sensation of his hardness inside me and my fingers against my clit winds the tension higher and higher. Every nerve ending feels electrified, every stroke pushing me closer to the edge. The pressure builds until it's almost unbearable, a coiled spring ready to snap.

'Raith,' I gasp, clinging to him with my free arm. 'I'm going to—'

'Yes,' he hisses, his movements growing more urgent. 'Come for me. Now.'

My release crashes through me like a tidal wave, stealing my breath, my thoughts, leaving only sensation in its wake. My back arches, my head thrown back in abandon as wave after wave of pleasure washes over me. The tether between us magnifies everything, creating a barrage of ecstasy that seems endless.

Dimly, I'm aware of the water responding to my power, creating a vortex around us as if we're in the eye of a storm. But unlike the disaster of my childhood, this power is contained, controlled, never threatening to harm Raith or myself. Never out of control. Not this time.

Raith's rhythm falters as my inner walls pulse around him. With a hoarse shout, he follows me over the edge, his body tensing, his face buried in my neck as his cock throbs and pulses within me, filling me with a fresh wave of subtle warmth. Through the tether, I feel his release as if it were my own, triggering a second, smaller climax that leaves me trembling in his arms.

The water around us has reached near-boiling temperatures, his fire essence completely unchecked in the throes of passion. Steam fills the room, thick enough that I can hardly see anything at all. The rain continues to pour. Compared to the heat Raith is generating, it almost feels cool now.

For long moments, we stay tangled together, our hearts pounding in tandem, our foreheads pressed together. Neither of us speaks – there are no words adequate for what we've just shared. I can feel his wonder, his satisfaction, his lingering desire . . . and beneath it all, something deeper that neither of us is ready to name.

Finally, reluctantly, he eases me off him, keeping me close as we float in the cooling water. My legs feel boneless, my entire body liquid with satisfaction.

'Are you okay?' he asks, his voice rough.

I nod, too overwhelmed for words. I sense his concern, his fear that he might have hurt me or pushed too hard.

'I'm perfect,' I reassure him, pressing a soft kiss to his lips. 'That was . . .' I trail off, unable to find the right words.

'Yeah,' he agrees, understanding completely. 'It was.'

The rain above us slows to a gentle drizzle, then stops entirely. The enchanted clouds disperse, leaving only moonlight to illuminate the room. I study his face in the silvery glow.

'I still feel bad I changed your scars,' I admit, tracing where the scars used to knot and tangle his flesh and now they only cause it to ripple and shine. 'They were part of you. Part of your story.'

His expression softens. 'They're still part of my story. But my story is changing, just like the scars did. Nothing is going to ever give me back what I lost. It hollowed part of me out. Left a void inside me I wasn't sure I'd ever fill. But . . . then you happened.'

I smile. 'I happened, huh?'

'Nessa Thorne. A force of fucking nature,' Raith says with a soft smile. 'I tried not to fall for you, and your stubborn ass wouldn't take "no" for an answer.'

'I'm not sorry,' I say, planting a playful kiss on his neck. 'Not even slightly.'

He considers this, his thumb tracing idle patterns on my shoulder. 'Neither am I.'

The words feel significant, weighted with meaning beyond face value. I lean into him, drawing comfort from his solid presence, from the steady beat of his heart against my cheek.

His fingers trail through my wet hair, combing it away from my face with a tenderness that makes my chest ache. 'When I saw into your memories,' he says softly, 'I felt something else. Something beneath the guilt and fear.'

I tense slightly. 'What?'

'Relief,' he says, his voice careful. 'Not at what happened – never that – but at finally having a reason to leave. To escape a life that felt too small for you.'

The observation strikes so close to a truth I've never admitted, even to myself, that I feel exposed all over again. 'How could you possibly—'

'Because I felt the same way,' he interrupts gently. 'When my world burned down around me, there was grief, rage, horror . . . but underneath it all, a terrible freedom. The freedom to become someone else. Someone new. To break away from the path set for me.'

I swallow hard, remembering what I've glimpsed of his past – the child destined to rule some distant land, the burning castle, the screams of his family.

'I wish there had been another way to make my own path,' I say.

'I know,' he says, pressing his lips to my forehead. 'But sometimes the universe gives us what we need in the cruelest ways possible.'

We fall silent, the only sound the gentle lapping of water against the pool's edge. I think about his words, about the terrible truth in them. Perhaps we are both born of catastrophe, forged in tides and flames we never wanted but learned to harness nonetheless.

'I need you to know something,' he says after a long silence, his voice low and serious.

I pull back slightly to look at him. 'What?'

His hand cradles my face, thumb brushing my lower lip. 'This wasn't just about wanting you. The sex, I mean. It's more than that. It has been for a while.'

My heart clenches. It's not a declaration of love, not exactly, but coming from Raith – guarded, cautious Raith – it's monumental.

'For me too,' I admit softly.

'I meant what I said earlier. I can't lose you too.' His voice drops to a whisper. 'I won't survive it.'

I cover his hand with mine where it rests against my cheek. 'You won't have to.'

'Promise me,' he says, suddenly fierce. 'Promise me you'll be careful in the Crucible. That you won't take unnecessary risks.'

'I promise,' I tell him, though we both know it's a vow that may be impossible to keep. The Crucible is designed to test us to our limits, to push us into situations where death will be around every corner.

He kisses me again, deep and thorough, as if trying to memorize the taste of me. When he pulls away, his expression is serious.

'We should go,' he says reluctantly. 'Your friends will be waiting.'

'There's one thing,' I say. 'Typhon told me our tether will fade over time because I only swore myself to you. At first . . . I thought that was a good thing. But if you wanted—'

'What do I need to do?' He asks the question seriously and so suddenly it warms my heart. The idea of losing this connection scares him as much as it scares me.

'You'd need to swear an oath to me, just like I swore one to you.'

'Tell me what to say.' His voice is fierce, and I can already feel how badly he wants this. 'The tether helps me keep you safe. And now that I've felt this.' He frowns, shaking his head. 'Losing that piece of you. It already feels like a piece of me. I don't want it to go anywhere.'

I nod, understanding completely. 'The oath should come from your heart. Something you mean. Just like when you swore an oath to Pyrin.'

I wait, heart pounding as I watch him think. It's only a moment before he speaks.

'I'll protect you. No matter the cost. No matter the battle. No matter fucking what. I'll be there to keep you safe. Always. Forever. That's my oath.'

His words ignite a warmth in my chest that grows so hot it nearly burns. I feel something snapping into place, like the fragile thread between us is pulsing and growing thicker.

I close my eyes and smile. 'Okay. Yeah. I'm pretty sure that worked.'

'Good.' He runs a fingertip down my cheek. 'I mean it, Nessa. Before you . . . I was fighting for revenge. It was only anger pushing me forward. Grief. Regret. But you've given me something I didn't have. Something that matters. And I'll do anything to protect that. To protect you.'

I kiss him deeply, wishing we never had to leave these waters and this moment. It feels like a perfect bubble of time, a memory I know I'll revisit as long as I live, and yet I know reality is pressing in on us. Time runs on, and our survival might depend on how we spend these next hours before the Crucible.

Neither of us needs to say it. We both know, and we exit the pool, water streaming from our bodies. Raith flares his power briefly, creating a wave of heat that dries us almost instantly. The sensation of warm air rushing over my damp skin makes me shiver.

We dress in comfortable silence, occasionally stealing glances at each other. I feel different somehow – lighter, as if sharing this intimacy has lifted some of the weight I've carried for so long. The guilt over my family's deaths hasn't disappeared, but it's been acknowledged, brought into the light where it can't fester in darkness.

'Our elementals just watched that entire thing . . . didn't they?' I ask suddenly, the thought occurring to me with mortifying clarity.

A rare, full smile breaks across Raith's face. 'I assume so, though Pyrin says he's been trying to give us privacy. In his own way.'

'*I busied myself with other things, angry human,*' Typhon assures me.

As we prepare to leave, Raith catches me by the waist, pulling me against him for one last kiss. It's gentle, sweet, a stark contrast to the desperate passion of before.

'Whatever happens in the Crucible,' he murmurs against my lips, 'remember what you are. What you're capable of. You don't need to hide your power – you need to embrace it.'

'I'm afraid of what happens if I lose control,' I admit.

'You won't,' he says with absolute certainty. 'Not this time. Not ever again.' His forehead rests against mine. 'I believe in you, Nessa. It's time you believed in yourself.'

The words settle into me, a balm for old wounds I've carried too long.

'Survive,' he murmurs, pressing one last kiss to my lips. 'Whatever it takes. And after . . .'

'After,' I agree, understanding the promise in those words.

We slip from the washing chamber, making our way through darkened corridors toward the water common room where my friends await. For the first time since arriving at Confluence, I feel something dangerously close to hope.

Because no matter what tomorrow brings, I have tonight. I have this moment. I have him.

And maybe I'm finally beginning to have myself too – not the broken, guilt-ridden girl who arrived at Confluence expecting to die, but the woman I'm becoming. The woman who might, against all odds, not just survive, but thrive.

Chapter 35

The castle corridors are silent save for our quiet footfalls as we make our way toward the eastern wing. Midnight has come and gone, the torches burning low, casting long shadows that dance across the stone walls. Every creak makes my heart skip, every distant sound has me jumpy.

Beck, Ambrose, and Mireen did most of the planning, and I'm relying heavily on their information. If Malakai or his people realize we know where the weapons are, I have no doubt blood will spill before the Crucible. Maybe worse – if the academy guards catch us near the weapons cache, we'll likely have no way to convince them the weapons aren't ours. We could wind up facing dismissal if caught, which would mean certain execution.

We're walking a tightrope, and my confidence isn't at its highest.

'Ten academy guards,' Ambrose whispers, pushing his glasses up his nose with nervous precision. 'Two in this wing. Beck's diversion should draw them all to the eastern end of the courtyard long enough for us to get inside.'

As odd as it feels, the guards don't pose a physical threat to us. Any one of us could probably handle the whole group using magic and our elementals. But none of us want to hurt innocent guards. That means being caught is a sure path to dismissal and death.

'And if it doesn't?' Mireen asks, her red hair braided tight and her eyes so blue they nearly glow in the dark.

I draw a shaky breath, trying to calm my racing pulse. One mistake, one moment of carelessness, and it could all end tonight.

It's then that I feel it – a sudden surge of anticipation that isn't mine. A ghost of emotion flowing through the tether, bringing with it a familiar warmth. I turn my head instinctively toward the sensation just as a shadow detaches from an alcove, and Raith steps into view.

'You weren't part of the plan,' Mireen says suddenly, tugging at her hair. 'Passcode?' she demands.

'Malakai's crooked cock,' Raith says plainly.

Ambrose mutters under his breath. 'We seriously need to stop letting Beck pick these damn passcodes.'

'I'm helping whether I'm in your plans or not,' Raith says. His gaze sweeps across the corridor before settling on me, his eyes blazing like embers, fierce and protective.

I should be annoyed at his presumption – his automatic assumption we'll be willing to have him along. Instead, I find myself fighting a smile. 'More help is a good thing,' I tell the others, trying to sound practical rather than pleased.

What I don't say is that I knew he'd come before he appeared. Our tether has grown stronger since he swore his oath to me, since the bathing pool, since . . .

Echoes of heat lash at my insides, pleasant and vibrant as the whispers of what we did still curl through my body like smoke.

I can feel his presence now at the edge of my consciousness, his determination and protectiveness flowing into me as surely as his fire magic. And I knew he was coming for us minutes before he arrived. I also didn't need to hear the passcode to know he wasn't a siphon. I could feel it was Raith down to my core.

Brunhild looks between Raith and me, her eyes narrowing slightly as if noticing something different. She gives a curt nod, seemingly unsurprised by Raith's appearance. 'More fighters, good plan. Beck starts water problems soon. We move now.'

As if summoned by her words, the distant sound of rushing water reaches us, followed by shouts of alarm. We hear two pairs of footsteps rushing toward the courtyard. More sounds ring out from deeper in the castle. Guards all heading for the courtyard to investigate.

I hope Beck gets himself out of there before he's caught, though causing an elemental mishap is hardly grounds for expulsion.

'That's our cue,' Mireen says, already moving down the corridor.

I feel Raith's hand brush against mine for the briefest moment. My entire body reacts to the simple touch with tingling heat. Through our tether comes a pulse of reassurance, and beneath it, something deeper that makes my chest tighten. It's still strange to sense emotions that aren't mine, to feel his presence in my mind like an echo of my own thoughts.

Because his emotions are more human, I think I feel them even more clearly than Typhon's.

'You feel his more clearly because he's a barbarian with no ability to mask his thoughts and feelings from you. You will both learn with time,' Typhon notes. *'And then I will not be subject to every whim and fancy that flows through your meat brain.'*

We move quickly through the corridors, our footsteps nearly silent despite our urgent pace. Brunhild takes the lead with her massive frame, moving with surprising stealth for someone her size. She scans each intersection before motioning us forward, her eyes constantly sweeping for any sign of guards.

She splits off to position herself as lookout near the intersection where two hallways meet, her muscular form blending into the shadows with practiced ease. The rest of us continue toward the hidden chamber Mireen discovered earlier – an old storage room behind a false panel in what used to be an armory.

Raith moves with silent grace beside me. I sense flickers of his alertness, his careful assessment of every shadow and corner.

Ambrose signals for silence, pointing ahead. 'This is it,' he whispers, stopping at a seemingly ordinary wall panel adorned with faded Empire insignias.

He presses a specific pattern – left corner, right corner, center – and with a soft click, the panel slides inward to reveal a narrow doorway. The four of us slip inside, and I nearly collide with Raith's back when he stops abruptly.

'We have company,' he says, voice low and dangerous.

The hidden chamber is illuminated by a single lantern, its light glinting off racks of weapons – real steel, sharp and deadly. Daggers, short swords, bows with arrows, and even pieces of full-plate armor. All Empire-issued, just as Beck described.

But what stops us cold is the figure standing among them. A figure whose left hand bears a glowing red flame mark.

Serena.

Her fire-orange eyes reflect the lantern light as she turns to face us, one hand resting casually on the hilt of a sword. Her perfect features betray no surprise at our arrival. Her fire serpent elemental slithers from the shadows beside her, yellow eyes regarding us as its tongue flicks out to taste the air, spraying sparks and smoke.

'If you're here to kill us,' I say, hand already poised to snatch the dagger from my boot, 'you should've brought more help.'

Beside me, I feel Raith shift into a fighting stance. Typhon materializes near my shoulder in his flying fish form, ready to transform if needed.

'Say the word, angry human, and I will show her my true form again. It shall be the last thing she ever sees.'

'Let's try talking first,' I reply silently. *'Save the dramatic reveals for when we need them.'*

Serena studies us, her gaze lingering on each face before settling on mine. Her eyes narrow slightly when they pass over where Typhon hovers. Serena knows better than most what Typhon can become. She knows to be afraid.

'If I wanted you dead, I wouldn't need help,' she says finally, her voice cool and controlled.

'Then what are you doing here?' Mireen demands, water already gathering around her fingertips.

'The same as you, I imagine.' Serena gestures to the weapons. 'Assessing our options for the Crucible.'

'Bullshit,' I say flatly. 'You knew about these weapons all along. You're part of Malakai's little army.'

Serena's perfect lips curve into a smile that doesn't reach her eyes. 'I'm not surprised to see Hollow with your group. He's the biggest traitor of all of you. It's a shame, though. A man like you . . . Empire would be lucky to have you on our side. I could have warmed your bed, too. I'm sure I could've given you more than she ever—'

'That's enough,' Raith snaps. 'What the fuck do you want?'

She sighs, moving away from the weapons rack with casual grace. Her uniform is immaculate even at this late hour, her black hair gleaming in perfect waves that fall over her shoulders. Everything about her radiates deadly perfection.

'How do you think Beck even heard about this place?' she asks. 'Do you really take him for a master of subtlety and deception?' Serena laughs. 'No. I made sure he heard about it. I made sure you knew tonight would be the right time to come. And I waited here so I could send you a message. Something you should know before the Crucible . . .' She pauses, as if weighing her next words carefully. 'There won't be any Empire observers watching.'

Of all the things I expected her to say, this wasn't it. I exchange confused glances with Mireen and Ambrose.

'What are you talking about? Bastian said—'

'Bastian doesn't know everything.' Serena's voice turns sharp, her perfect features hardening with barely suppressed anger. 'There will be magical interference that will make the events completely dark. Empire's people won't know they can't watch until it's too late. The only thing people will learn afterward is how many died and what a failure Voss is as Rector.'

'And you know this . . . how?' Ambrose asks, skepticism clear in his voice.

'Because Malakai told me after a conversation with our . . . bene-factor.' Her perfect composure slips for just a moment, revealing genuine revulsion before she schools her features back into careful neutrality. 'Too many deaths, and Voss will be removed from his position. That's the plan.'

'Why would someone go to such lengths to remove Voss?' Mireen asks, her water magic still swirling at her fingertips. 'There must be simpler ways.'

'This way creates a public spectacle. A failure so magnificent that the Council can justify immediate action without opposition.'

I exchange glances with the others. The parts about Voss line up with what we've already learned. But what does it mean if Bastian is out of the loop, somehow?

I fold my arms. 'So is this where you ask to join our team?'

She smiles without much humor. 'No. Afraid not, Thorne. I still see all of you as traitors-in-waiting. Empire will be better if you all die before graduation. But I won't lower myself to this . . .' she gestures at the weapons. 'I don't need help from the outside to deal with traitors. I don't need to stain my own honor to do things the right way. And I frankly don't give a shit if Voss stays or goes. So I'm here, and I'm telling you what I learned, which is that two members of the Windborne Division will be entering the Crucible. They're waiting on standby in the event that you and your people evade or kill us. Someone wants to make sure the Crucible is a bloodbath, and the windborne are the contingency plan.'

'The windborne?' Ambrose whispers, face paling so quickly I fear he might faint. 'Are you serious?'

Raith's reaction is more controlled, but through our tether, I feel a spike of genuine concern – sharp and cold like a blade of ice sliding between my ribs. 'The Council's assassins,' he murmurs, and there's a knowledge in his voice that feels personal, intimate.

'Who?' I ask.

'Elite air primals trained for elimination missions,' Ambrose says.

'I thought the windborne were just stories,' Mireen says, her water magic faltering slightly. 'Boogeyman tales.'

'They're very real,' Serena replies, her voice dropping lower. 'Just as real as the Earthshakers, Tidewalkers, and Flameheart Divisions. Each element has its special forces. I grew up hearing stories from my father. He served with the Flameheart for fifteen years, just like I will. When they hear what lengths I went to disposing of traitors like you, they'll almost certainly give me an audience after I graduate.'

I feel out of the loop. I've never even heard of these people, though the conversation is making my blood run cold and my throat tighten. Two elite assassins sent into the Crucible? Killers ordered to murder us if it looks like we're going to succeed? 'So they're what, some kind of secret military?'

Raith nods. 'Specialized teams for operations too sensitive or too brutal for regular military. Assassinations. Sabotage. Elimination of undesirable elements.' His eyes meet mine for a fraction of a second. 'The windborne specifically excel at stealth. Whoever is behind this doesn't want anyone to know they were ever here.'

'Empire's invisible hand,' Ambrose adds, his academic tone belied by the tremor in his voice. 'I found references to them in ancient military texts – they specialize in air magic manipulation that allows them to move with unnatural speed and stealth. Methods of killing that leave almost no trace.'

My attention turns back to Serena. 'Why should we believe any of this? You're admitting you want us dead, but we're supposed to just . . . what? Trust you?'

Serena's expression hardens, her eyes flashing with barely contained anger. 'I want to win fairly. That's what Empire stands for – honor in combat, victory through strength and strategy. Not . . . this.' She gestures to the weapons with clear disdain, her perfect features contorted with genuine disgust. 'Sneaking elite killers into a school competition? Magical blackouts to hide evidence? That's not Empire. That's cowardice, and I won't be a part of it. You don't need to trust a thing. But I'll know I gave you enough information to make the fight fair. I'll know my honor isn't stained when I kill you myself.'

Through our tether, I feel Raith's skepticism, but also a grudging respect for Serena's apparent principles. His own code might differ from hers, but he recognizes conviction when he sees it.

I study her face, looking for deception but finding only disgust and what might be genuine concern. The perfect fire affinity with her flawless features and deadly grace, suddenly showing a moral line she won't cross. It's unexpected enough to make me wonder if this is all an elaborate trap.

'Are you expecting us to thank you, now?' I ask. 'Because it's not happening.'

She laughs, the sound sharp and mirthless. 'Hardly. When the Crucible begins, I'll still be hunting you with the others. But I'll do it honorably, with skill against skill, magic against magic. The only thanks I need is for you to be living when I find you.' Her orange eyes meet mine with unflinching intensity.

'What does Malakai think of your pursuit of honor?' Raith asks.

Serena's expression shifts, showing the slightest hint of uncertainty. 'Malakai serves his own agenda. I serve Empire. Sometimes those interests align, sometimes they don't.' She steps away from the weapons, moving toward the door with predatory grace. 'Do what you want with these. They won't help you against me. They certainly won't save you if the windborne find you first.'

And then she's gone, slipping out of the room and disappearing into the darkness beyond, leaving us standing in stunned silence.

'That was . . . unexpected,' Mireen says finally, the water she'd been gathering dissipating into mist.

'Do we trust her?' Ambrose asks, pushing his glasses up nervously.

'No,' Raith says immediately, his hand relaxing its grip on his sword hilt. 'But that doesn't mean she's lying. And we're still here with the weapons, whether we trust her or not about the rest.'

'Her disgust seemed genuine,' Ambrose notes, adjusting his glasses thoughtfully. 'Some people value honor above all else.'

'It's also possible this is an elaborate trap,' Mireen counters, eyes narrowed in thought. 'Maybe she wants to trick Nessa into revealing too much during the Crucible. Maybe giving us the weapons was just bait to make us think we can trust her about the rest?'

I feel Raith's calculated assessment – a cool, analytical part of him that seems to be weighing each possibility with practiced precision. It reminds me again that there's more to him than the fierce protector

I've come to know. There's something methodical, strategic beneath the surface.

'I think I believe her,' I say, moving toward the weapons. 'It all lines up. She just cares about loyalty to Empire and her own ambitions.'

'This magical interference,' Typhon rumbles in my mind. *'I will be able to sense if it exists or not.'*

I grin. 'And Typhon says he'll know if she's telling the truth about the magical interference. If she was, then Typhon could fight beside us in his true form. I could use my unbound powers freely. It would be a huge advantage on our side.'

'Show these insignificant humans what a true ancient looks like. Strike terror into their weak hearts.'

For a moment, the thought is dizzyingly liberating. I may be free during the Crucible. Free to defend myself and the people I care about with every tool I have at my disposal.

And yet . . .

Raith's hand finds my shoulder, his touch grounding me as his concern flows into me. 'That still leaves the problem of the windborne. They're trained killers, not students. If they're in the Crucible, people won't just die – they'll be executed. Ancient or not, I don't even know if Typhon could stop them from getting to you. Not yet. None of us are trained enough.'

His words send an icy chill down my spine, bringing me back to the reality of our situation. Freedom to use my powers, maybe – but only because we're facing a threat so deadly that exposure becomes the lesser danger.

'Then we'd better be prepared,' I say, reaching for a finely crafted rapier among the other weapons. The leather hilt is soft and warm against my palm, the steel edge and tip wickedly sharp. I test its weight, finding it perfectly balanced. 'One real weapon each, and we sabotage the rest?'

Mireen nods, her eyes lighting up with a mixture of determination and grim satisfaction.

Everyone steps forward and claims a sharpened, weighted version of their weapon of choice to replace their blunted and lighter training weapons. Ambrose picks up a weapon for Beck and Brunhild to deliver to them later. Raith collects a few extras for his fires as well.

'Ollie. Do your thing,' Mireen says. The small elemental materializes in a swirl of blue energy.

'Typhon,' I add, glancing at my elemental who hovers nearby in his flying fish disguise.

'*It is beneath my dignity,*' Typhon grumbles in my mind. '*But I suppose I can assist. Though I would rather simply devour all the weapons. And possibly the humans who would wield them against you.*'

'*Subtlety, Typhon. We're going for subtlety.*'

'*Subtlety is overrated,*' he replies, but drifts toward the weapons rack anyway.

Ambrose examines the cache methodically, his eyes widening at the quality of the steel as the elementals get to work.

'Definitely military grade,' Raith says, holding a flat sword in one hand and testing its weight before setting it back down.

'Expensive,' Ambrose agrees, lifting a long knife and checking its balance. 'Someone with resources is backing Malakai. The cost to buy all this? It would fund the construction of a small estate. And that's not mentioning the political power needed to make it happen.'

Typhon and Ollie target the metal's structural integrity, inducing rust that spreads from within like a disease. Typhon, despite his complaints, proves remarkably effective at weakening blades by altering their internal structure without visible signs.

Raith tests their work, lightly swinging a sword against the stone floor, where it shatters into dust upon impact. 'Good,' he says, pursing his lips appreciatively.

'Twenty-eight daggers, fifteen swords, twelve bows with arrows – all compromised,' Ambrose recites with quiet satisfaction. 'Should significantly reduce casualties during the Crucible.'

'No,' Raith says, still inspecting his new sword. 'It just changes who dies.'

'But if we win the fight against Malakai,' Mireen says. 'We'll have the windborne to deal with . . .'

She's right. If Serena's right, then the Crucible is a fight for something bigger than any of us. A fight powerful people don't want us to survive.

Raith speaks, voice quiet but everybody's attention snaps to him. 'We'll fight. It's all we can do. We know the stakes. We know what's coming. The only thing we can do is show up and fucking face it.'

Typhon suddenly goes alert, his small fish form darting in agitated circles. *'Someone approaches,'* he warns, his mental voice sharp with urgency.

'Typhon says someone's coming.'

We all freeze, weapons still in hand, caught red-handed in the midst of our sabotage.

A moment later, Brunhild's signal – three quick taps followed by two slow ones – sounds from the corridor outside.

'Trouble,' Raith translates, already moving toward the door. 'We need to go.'

We quickly slip out of the hidden chamber. Brunhild meets us in the corridor, her body tense with urgency. Even she, normally so stoic, looks concerned.

'Guards find Beck's water trick,' she says, her accent thicker with stress. 'He runs, they chase. Alarm bells soon.'

'Beck?' Mireen whispers urgently. 'Is he okay?'

'Fast runner,' Brunhild replies with a shrug that does little to calm our nerves. 'Maybe okay.'

As if on cue, the distant clang of warning bells begins to echo through the castle, the sound reverberating through the stone walls like a heartbeat. We break into a run, taking a different route back than the one we came by.

'Split up,' Raith orders as we reach a junction where four corridors meet. 'Get back to your rooms and we'll meet tomorrow.'

Mireen and Ambrose nod, each taking a different path without hesitation. Brunhild frowns, looking between us.

'Go,' I tell her. 'Find Beck if you can.'

She nods, relief clear in her blue eyes. 'Will find sexy bear. Keep him safe.' Then she's gone at a full sprint.

I turn to take the eastern path, but before I can move, Raith's hand catches mine, pulling me close for just a moment. His fingers intertwine with mine, squeezing once.

'Be careful,' he murmurs, his breath warm against my ear. His free hand brushes my cheek in a touch so tender it makes my heart stutter. 'I'll find you tomorrow.'

And then we're separating, running in different directions, melting into the shadows of Confluence as the alarm bells finally cease. I clutch my stolen daggers, feeling their weight against my body as I race through the dark corridors.

As I slip into my room and hide my newly acquired weapons beneath my mattress, the weight of everything we've learned tonight settles over me. If Serena's telling the truth?

There will be no observers. Using my unbound ability will reveal what I am to my classmates, but not to Empire's watching eyes. But even Typhon and my powers unleashed likely won't be enough to deal with the trained killers. The windborne.

And behind it all, there may be a hidden, powerful benefactor willing to slaughter half the first-year primals in training just to remove Voss.

But why?

The Crucible won't be what I expected. Not really. Instead of a final test signaling our readiness for second-year status, it'll be a game where we're pawns being sent to the slaughter.

I sit on the edge of my bed, Typhon curled beside me in his fish form, which has nearly returned to its usual size.

Through the window, I can see the first hint of dawn lightening the eastern sky. Another day closer to the Crucible. Another day closer to facing the windborne.

'*They think us weak,*' Typhon says, his words laced with barely checked rage. '*They think us prey.*'

'They don't know what I am,' I reply, running my fingers along the edge of the new rapier. 'What we are.'

Typhon's eyes gleam in the darkness. *'Then perhaps it is time to show them.'*

As I slip beneath my blankets, exhaustion finally claiming me, one thought burns in my mind: our enemies will find we're not such easy targets.

I may be unbound, but I'm no longer afraid of what that means.

And that makes me more dangerous than they can possibly imagine.

Chapter 36

The quiet of the evening seems to amplify each footfall as I walk back toward the dormitory with Beck, Brunhild, Mireen, and Ambrose. We've spent most of the day training until our muscles ached, then refining our strategy for the Crucible. We still don't know what will be asked of us tomorrow, but we did our best to prepare as much as we could. I also slipped out for another private session, working with Typhon on fighting as a team and even riding on his back in an emergency.

Raith had to spend time drilling with his fires and the earths they've recruited. Apparently, they even absorbed a few airs to the cause. He was adamant that we work as a group of five and let him handle the management of other teams. From what I understand, there are four major groups among the first-years. The legacies, those with Malakai, those with us, and the few outliers who haven't declared their allegiance.

I hate admitting that I've already been missing Raith after just one day apart. I know I shouldn't let myself feel so much for him, but I can't stop it. The fact that I can feel pulses of faint emotion and thoughts from him, even halfway across campus, certainly doesn't help. Especially when half of those emotions involve me and how much he wants to see me. How much he's worried about me. How desperately he wants to protect me.

'Get some sleep tonight,' Mireen says, nudging my shoulder. 'We need you sharp.'

'I'll try,' I reply, though I know it won't be easy to calm my mind.

Beck yawns, stretching his arms overhead. 'I'm telling you, there's nothing to worry about. We've trained for this. We're as ready as we'll ever be.'

Brunhild wraps her arm around Beck's broad shoulders, pulling him in for a sideways hug. 'No one will touch my sexy bear. Brunhild and Dora the crab will make sure of it.'

Ambrose wears a grim expression. 'There are too many unknowns for my liking. Will the weapons we sabotaged really break when we need them to? Can we believe Serena that Empire won't be watching? Was the story about windborne true, or just something she told us to make us avoid killing Malakai's people?'

I frown. 'That's all very comforting to hear on the eve of the Crucible, Ambrose.'

He shrugs. 'Akaron and I have gone over the possibilities at length. Wouldn't it make more sense to sacrifice the weapons to buy our trust? A small gesture to ensure we walk into the Crucible with faulty information? Information that all seems to imply we shouldn't fight back if attacked by Malakai's people?'

Mireen chews her lip. 'You're just mentioning this all now?'

'It's okay,' I say. 'I think our safest assumption would be to discredit everything she told us if Typhon finds no magical interference. If it's there, then we should assume the rest was true.'

The conversation continues as we approach the entrance to the water tower, but I find my attention drifting. The Crucible looms like a storm on the horizon, but so does the realization that I'm in way too deep with Raith. Three years ago, a storm of my own making took three people I loved from me. A storm I couldn't control.

I'm not the same person I was back then, and yet I feel just as out of control now. Just as in over my head. I know I shouldn't fall for Raith, but I'm doing it anyway. And I know the Crucible could mean the end of me and all the people I care about, but there's no avoiding it.

The air shifts as we enter the tower, making the fine hairs on my forearms stand on end.

Raith is there, waiting with his strong arms folded across his broad chest.

Mireen startles, hand flying to her chest. 'Gods, Hollow, you need to stop doing that,' she hisses. 'You could just approach with a friendly "hello" like a normal person.'

Raith's gaze is fixed on me. 'Hello.'

'Password?' Ambrose asks.

'Thistlewood,' Raith says, voice completely flat.

Beck sighs to my left. 'You guys pick the most boring passwords. You should really put me back in charge of password creation.'

'Let me guess,' I say, folding my arms across my chest. 'You're here at the water tower because you're going to stand guard outside my door all night like some kind of overly dramatic sentinel?'

The corner of his mouth lifts in what might almost be a smile. 'Something like that.'

Mireen glances between us, eyes narrowing with suspicion. 'You need sleep too, Hollow.'

'I'm fine,' he replies, his tone making it clear the subject isn't up for debate.

Beck clears his throat. 'Right then. We should all probably get some rest. Big day tomorrow and all that.'

'Rest?' Brunhild asks. 'Sexy bear asked me to do thing he likes with tongue and dagger. I even brought the rope.'

Beck's cheeks go red. 'Uh. I'm not even going to try to make something up. Yeah. We're gonna go do some weird shit.' He takes Brunhild's hand, leading her up the stairs.

'See you in the morning,' Ambrose says, offering a mock salute before heading up the stairs as well.

Mireen gives me a lewd wiggle of her eyebrows, then leaves me alone in the corridor with Raith.

'Come on. You need to get to bed.' Raith starts ahead of me, taking the stairs by two as if he's determined to travel in front in case some danger is waiting.

He waits at the landing for me to catch up, hand resting on the hilt of his newly stolen military-grade sword that he wears across his back. He gives a jerk of his head, indicating he has deemed the empty hallway safe.

I roll my eyes but grin as I follow him toward my room. 'You're not seriously planning to stand guard all night, are you?'

He shrugs. 'I've gone longer without sleep.'

'Don't be ridiculous.' I grab his wrist and tug him toward my door. 'You need rest as much as I do. Come inside.'

'If I come in there, I'm pretty sure both of us are going to get a lot less sleep, Nessa.'

The dark promise of his words lights a thrill in my chest. I bite the corner of my lower lip, softly lifting my shoulders. 'Is that a threat, Mr. Hollow?'

He steps closer, invading my space in the most delicious of ways. 'Staying apart from you today was the hardest fucking thing I've ever done. All I want to do is touch you. Feel you again.' His voice drops several registers, nearly becoming a growl. 'Be inside you.'

I swallow, suddenly unsteady on my feet. 'Okay. I hear you, and I'm still insisting that you come in.'

For a moment, I think he might resist, but then he follows, closing the door quietly behind him. Neither of us speaks as I move to light a candle on my desk, the small flame casting soft shadows across the walls.

'So,' I say finally, turning to face him. Part of me is curious if he's planning to strip my clothes off and fuck me right away, or if he's going to continue trying to fight it. Just to tease him, I casually pop a few buttons over my chest, eyes lingering on his. 'You came to stand guard over my room. Was there something specific I should worry about? Or were you just feeling overprotective?'

His eyes linger on the place where my breasts meet and he pulls his lower lip between his teeth, eyes finally lifting to mine after a few long seconds. 'Whispers,' he says. 'Some have worries Malakai may strike against priority targets tonight. Remove threats before the Crucible to improve their odds.'

I frown as my thoughts immediately turn to my friends. 'Did you tell Beck, Ambrose, and Mireen this? Are they safe?'

'Their names weren't mentioned as priority targets. Yours was. So I'm going to be here with you all night.'

'Who else was a priority target besides me?'

Raith hesitates. 'Me.'

I can't help smiling, even though the idea of students plotting to kill me tonight shouldn't be something to smile about. 'Anyone else?'

He shakes his head. 'It was just us.'

'So you're protecting me by making sure they can find both the people they want to kill in the same room? I thought you were supposed to be a military strategist, Raith.'

I sense his frustration. 'I'm not leaving you alone tonight. End of discussion.'

'I wasn't asking you to. I just like hearing you try to justify it.' I step toward the bed, turn my back, and then casually strip out of my clothes, making sure to bend very low and very long to unstrap my shoes. I can feel the heat of his gaze on my ass – the barely controlled temptation throbbing through him and the desire to put his hands on me, to take me.

To fuck me.

I finally steal a look over my shoulder. 'Well? Are you going to come to bed with me, or stand in the corner like a gargoyle while I sleep?' I sit on the edge of the bed, crossing my thighs and patting the bed beside me.

He hesitates, then moves to sit, the mattress dipping under his weight. We sit in silence for a moment, the space between us charged with everything we aren't saying.

'I keep thinking about what Serena told us,' I admit finally as I work on taking my hair from its braids. 'About the magical blackout during the Crucible that'll keep the emissaries from watching. About the windborne. If she's telling the truth, I just don't understand it. Why would Empire sacrifice potential primals just to get rid of Voss?'

'It's not our concern.'

'How can you say that? If Empire is sending assassins into a training exercise—'

'Empire does what Empire needs to do,' he cuts in, his voice low and controlled. 'Our job is to survive. Nothing more.'

I turn to face him, frustration building. 'Is that really all you care about? Surviving?'

'Tomorrow, all I care about is *you* surviving.'

The simplicity of his answer steals my breath. I shake my head. 'That's not true. You care about Cade. The fires. They look up to you like a big brother.'

'That's true. But . . .' He rakes a hand through his hair, jaw ticking with his barely controlled emotions. 'Losing you? I . . . can't. I just fucking can't.' Before I can respond, he stands and moves to the window, gazing out at the darkened campus.

'You should sleep,' he says, his back to me. 'I'll wake you if anything happens.'

I would feel offended that he's not currently taking my very obvious offer for sex, but I can feel what he's feeling – shadows of it, at least. Desire. Temptation. Arousal. Yes, that's all there as clear as day. But he also feels frustration with himself.

He's frustrated that he let himself feel so much for me. That he opened himself to weakness. Nothing I say or do right now can change that. All I can do is resolve to be strong tomorrow. For myself. For my friends. For Raith. Because his words aren't empty. He really doesn't think he would survive if something happened to me.

I find myself lying down, pulling the blanket over my shoulders as I watch him silently standing vigil.

'You need rest too,' I murmur, my eyes growing heavy despite my racing thoughts.

He turns slightly, his profile outlined against the moonlight. 'I'll be fine.'

'Raith,' I whisper, 'just come lie down. Please. It will help me sleep if you're here with me.'

For a long moment, he doesn't move. Then, with a sigh that seems to carry the weight of worlds, he crosses the room and carefully stretches out beside me on the narrow bed. He remains above the blankets, rigid and tense as he stares at the ceiling.

'I won't break if you touch me, you know,' I say, the words little more than a breath between us. 'You certainly didn't worry about that the other night in the showers.'

His eyes find mine in the darkness, a flicker of heat passing through them at the memory. 'That was different.'

'How so?' I challenge softly.

'It just . . . was,' he says, but his arm slides beneath my shoulders all the same, drawing me against his side. I rest my head on his chest, listening to the steady rhythm of his heart.

'Tonight could be our last chance for a repeat,' I murmur, my fingers tracing idle patterns on his chest.

I feel his temptation like a slumbering beast trying to roar to life. Somehow, he manages to control it before he speaks. 'I'm not going to be the reason you didn't get rest tonight, Nessa. Sleep.'

I smile up at him, mischief playing across my face. 'And if I sleep well, will you reward me in the morning?'

The slumbering beast of his desire flares bright. Raith's grip tightens on my bare shoulder. 'Only one way to find out.'

I can feel the careful restraint in his touch, the way he's holding himself back. With the warmth of his body seeping into mine and the comforting weight of his arm around me, sleep claims me more quickly than I expected, pulling me down into darkness.

Darkness. Then flashes of light. I'm seeing through eyes that aren't mine again, feeling emotions that belong to someone else.

The castle is burning. I can smell smoke, hear screams echoing through marble halls. I'm running, my breath ragged in my throat, desperation driving each step.

'Keira!' The name tears from my lips – no, from Raith's lips. This is his memory again, bleeding through our tether as we sleep.

I round a corner and skid to a halt. The door ahead is half-open, firelight spilling through the gap. Something is wrong. The quality of the light is strange, tinged with an oily darkness that seems to absorb rather than reflect.

Fear grips me, but I push forward, shouldering through the door. What I see inside sears itself into my mind.

A young woman in her early twenties stands in the center of the room, her arms outstretched. She looks like Raith – the same golden eyes, the same proud bearing, though her hair is a deep auburn rather than black.

She's breathtakingly beautiful, and I can feel Raith's admiration and respect for her. His heartbreak and fear at what he sees.

Fire spirals around her in intricate patterns, but it's fighting against something else – a darkness that seems to move with purpose, with malice.

Across from her is a figure that shifts and changes, its form unstable, like smoke given flesh. The energy clears and I see it fully, familiarity prickling through my own memories into the vision.

The tall, pale and twisted flesh hunched over with limbs that are too long. The gaping mouth like a smile and the sightless eyes.

A siphon.

The air around it ripples with void energy, purple, green, and consuming. Somehow, this one seems even more powerful than the one I faced in Confluence. More deadly.

'Keira, stop!' I scream, lunging forward.

Her head turns, and for a single moment, her eyes lock with mine. Recognition flashes, followed by a depth of regret that cuts like a blade.

'I'm sorry, little brother,' she whispers. 'Run. Run now.'

She draws deeper, pulling forth more fire essence than any human body should be able to channel. I can see it happening – the magic rushing through her, brightening her from within until her skin seems translucent, until the veins beneath glow bright orange.

I can see the outline of her skeleton through flesh and watch as the bone flakes away to ash, consumed by impossible heat.

The siphon shrieks, a sound no human throat could make, and lunges forward.

'No!' I scream, but it's too late.

Keira detonates.

There's a moment of perfect silence, a breath suspended in time. Then fire explodes outward in a blinding wave. The wall of heat slams into me, searing the left side of my body, throwing me backward through the doorway. The siphon is enveloped entirely, its form disintegrating in the inferno.

The last thing I see is the ceiling collapsing, massive stones falling toward me as pain consumes everything.

I wake with a gasp, bolting upright in bed. My heart pounds against my ribs, and I can still feel the phantom pain of burns across my skin, the echo of Raith's anguish. The pain of those burns . . . I only felt it for an instant, and it breaks my heart. I can't even imagine suffering that. Being marked by that. Knowing the source was the death of my own sister trying to protect me.

Beside me, Raith is already sitting up, his eyes wide in the darkness and touched by a distance and sadness that tears at my insides. I wasn't just seeing his memory. I was having the dream he was having. Reliving the same memory he must be haunted by night after night.

'Nessa?'

'I saw—' My voice breaks. 'I saw what happened to your sister.'

His entire body goes rigid. In the dim light filtering through the window, I can see the muscle jumping in his jaw. 'I'm sorry you had to see that.'

I swallow hard, tears pricking at the corners of my eyes. 'I'm sorry, Raith. I'm so sorry. I don't know how you go on when you have to keep reliving that. Nobody should've had to see that once. To be haunted by it in your dreams . . . it's—' I trail off, unable to find the words.

He doesn't speak, just stares ahead at nothing, lost in memories I've now witnessed firsthand. Tentatively, I reach out, placing my hand over his where it rests on the blanket.

'She tried to save you,' I whisper. 'She must have been so powerful.'

His head turns slowly, eyes finding mine in the darkness. 'She was. The strongest fire affinity in generations.' His voice is tight, controlled, but I can feel the grief pulsing through our connection.

'The siphon,' I say, the image of that shifting, formless creature burned into my mind. 'It was there for you, wasn't it? Just like the one at Confluence.'

His laugh is bitter, hollow. 'It wasn't just one. Every member of my family died that night. My father. My mother. Gareth. Kiera. All dead. I didn't understand why until later. I had to hear it from a stranger's lips spreading gossip in a tavern miles from home.'

I move closer, drawn by the pain I can feel radiating from him. 'Tell me.'

For a long moment, I think he won't answer. Then his hand turns beneath mine, fingers interlacing. 'Not tonight,' he says softly. 'Not before the Crucible.'

The haunted look in his eyes stops me from asking more. Instead, I lean forward, pressing my forehead against his. 'Then let me help you forget, just for tonight.'

His breath catches. 'Nessa . . .'

'Please,' I whisper, my lips brushing against his. 'I need this. I need you.'

The kiss starts soft, almost hesitant, but that restraint lasts only seconds before deepening into something hungry, desperate. His hands come up to cradle my face, fingers threading into my hair with a tenderness that contradicts the heat of his mouth. I can feel him holding back, that iron control he maintains at all times still firmly in place.

I don't want his control. I want all of him, broken edges and all.

I slip off my bra so I'm only wearing the thin panties, sliding into his space and pressing my body flush against his. My bare breasts and hardened nipples against his chest. My legs spreading over his thick, muscular thigh. I feel the exact moment he surrenders. A tremor runs through him, and with a groan that's half need and half resignation, he pulls me fully onto his lap.

'This doesn't change anything,' he murmurs against my neck, his teeth grazing the sensitive spot beneath my ear that makes my entire body shiver. 'This is just—'

'Release. A distraction,' I finish for him, already working at the buttons of his shirt with unsteady fingers. 'I know.'

But I can sense the lie in his words and my own, feel the emotions he's trying so desperately to conceal. A tangled knot of desire, protection, possession, and something deeper, something he refuses to name even to himself. This isn't just physical for him, no matter how much he wants it to be.

I run my hands over the sculpted planes of his chest, the hard muscle beneath tanned skin. Moonlight spills through the window, painting his body in silver and shadow. I trace the lines of his torso with reverent fingers, following the dips and ridges of muscle, marveling at the perfection of him.

His hands slide down my sides, calloused palms rough against the sensitive skin of my waist, trailing warmth in their wake. The cool night air kisses my bare breasts, but I barely notice, too consumed by the heat of his gaze as it sweeps over me.

'Fuck,' he breathes, the word whispered like a profane prayer. 'You're perfect.'

His hands move upward, thumbs brushing the undersides of my breasts with a touch so light it's almost torturous. I arch into him, seeking more, but he holds back, those golden eyes watching me intently, gauging my every reaction.

'I won't break,' I breathe, frustration edging into my voice. 'I'm not made of glass, Raith. I want you to use me however you need tonight. Let me help you forget. Let me make you feel something good for a change, because you deserve it.'

In answer, he lifts me effortlessly, turning to lay me back against the pillows before covering my body with his own. The weight of him is perfect, grounding me, making me feel simultaneously protected and utterly at his mercy. His mouth claims mine again, more demanding this time, and I respond with equal fervor.

The kiss deepens, turns volcanic, his tongue sliding against mine in a rhythm that makes heat pool low in my belly. One of his hands drifts down my side, tracing the curve of my hip before slipping beneath the waistband of my panties. I lift my hips in silent invitation, and he hooks his fingers into the fabric, dragging it slowly down my legs until I'm completely bared to him.

He pulls back just enough to look at me, his eyes darkening to a brassy depth. 'How do you look more fucking sexy every day?' His words are rough with desire and awe.

As his gaze traverses my body, I feel magic rising between us, a physical presence in the small space that separates us. My power responds to his, essence flowing between us in a bond that transcends the physical. It's intoxicating, this sharing of something so intrinsic to who we are.

I reach for him, pulling him back down to me, craving the feel of his skin against mine. His mouth finds my throat, trailing hot, open-mouthed kisses down to my collarbone. When his lips close around my nipple, I arch off the bed with a gasp, one hand flying to the back of his head to hold him there.

He lavishes attention on me, alternating between gentle suction and the light scrape of teeth that sends fire cascading through my veins. All the while, his hand traces maddening patterns along my inner thigh, drawing ever closer to where I need him most, but never quite giving me the relief I crave.

'Raith,' I moan, frustration mounting as he continues to tease. 'Please.'

He lifts his head, those eyes meeting mine with a wicked gleam. 'Tell me what you want. I want to hear it,' he bites his lip, fingertip tracing my lips, which are already swollen and tingling from his kisses.

I love how turned on it makes him to hear me speak my desires. How much my own pleasure is his favorite part of being together like this.

'Touch me,' I demand, beyond caring about pride or patience. 'I need you to touch me. Everywhere.'

His smile is pure sin as he slides down my body, pressing kisses to my ribs, my stomach, my nipple, the sensitive mound of flesh between my legs. He tortures me, kissing a circle around my clit, so close I can feel his heat washing over me, but taking his time. Kiss by agonizing kiss.

When he finally pries my thighs apart and settles his face between my legs and meets my eyes, my breath catches. I grip his hair, tangling my fingers in it and squeezing in anticipation.

The first touch of his mouth against me is stunning. My back bows, a cry escaping my lips as pleasure surges through my body like a current. His hands grip my hips, holding me in place as his tongue traces patterns that make coherent thought impossible.

I'm dimly aware of the candles around the room burning brighter, their flames stretching higher as they respond to the fire essence flaring in both our bodies. Shadows shift and dance across the walls as Raith continues his delicious torment, bringing me to the edge only to back away, again and again until I'm writhing beneath him, desperate for release.

'Damn it, Raith,' I gasp, my nails digging into his shoulders. 'Stop teasing. I want to come. I want it so badly. Make me come, Raith.'

His chuckle vibrates between my legs, deep, dark, and absolutely delicious. 'Patience,' he murmurs, but finally, mercifully, he focuses his attention on the spot that makes stars burst behind my eyelids.

Pressure builds within me, a coiling tension that grows tighter and tighter until it feels like I might shatter. When he slides one finger inside me, then a second, curling them to hit a spot that makes me cry out, it's too much. The tension breaks, release washing over me in a tidal wave of sensation.

I come with his name on my lips, my body arching off the bed as pleasure consumes me. His emotions cascade into mine, his desire amplifying my sensation, intensifying my climax until it seems endless, unbearable in its sweetness.

Before I've fully recovered, he's moving back up my body, his mouth claiming mine in a searing kiss. I can taste myself on his tongue, and it sends a fresh surge of arousal through me despite my recent release.

'I need to feel you,' I whisper against his lips, my hands moving to the waistband of his pants. 'All of you. Inside me. Filling me. *Now.*'

He helps me, shoving the fabric down his hips and kicking it away. When he settles back between my thighs, I can feel the hard length of him pressing against me, hot and insistent.

His mouth trails down my neck, and I feel more than hear his words against my skin. 'We shouldn't do this.'

'Why not?' I ask, already knowing his answer.

He raises his head, eyes burning into mine. 'You can't fall for me. It's too fucking dangerous.'

'What if it's too late for that?' I whisper.

Something shifts in his expression, a softening that makes my heart clench. He lowers his head, resting his forehead against mine. 'What am I going to do with you, Nessa Thorne?'

'Love me,' I whisper before I can stop myself. 'Like I love you.'

His entire body goes still, and for a moment I think I've ruined everything. Then I feel it – a pulse of emotion between us, raw and undeniable. Shock, wonder, and beneath it all, something that mirrors what I feel for him, something he's been desperately trying to deny.

'You can't love me,' he says, but there's no conviction in his voice.

'I can feel it, Raith,' I tell him, hands sliding into his hair. 'You can lie to me with words, but not through the tether.' I guide his hand to my chest, placing it over my heart. 'What you feel, I feel. You love me too.'

He closes his eyes, a tremor running through him. 'You don't know what you're asking for,' he says, his voice rough. 'You don't know who I really am.'

'Then tell me,' I challenge. 'Show me who you are, Raith Hollow. All of you.'

For answer, he kisses me again, deep and searching, as if trying to pour everything he can't say into the connection of our bodies. I meet him halfway, giving back just as desperately.

He positions himself at my entrance, his eyes locked with mine, waiting for confirmation. I nod, lifting my hips in silent invitation.

I feel the brief flare of magic again – the trick fires can use to sterilize themselves.

Then he's pushing into me, inch by exquisite inch, giving me time to adjust to the stretch, to the fullness.

When buried in me all the way, the sensation is even more overwhelming than that first time. I already know the feel of him, the perfect way our bodies fit together, but there's something about this moment – maybe the knowledge that tomorrow could be our last – that makes everything more intense, more significant.

'You feel like you were fucking made for me,' he murmurs, his voice strained with the effort of remaining still.

'Move,' I urge, my hands sliding down to grip his hips. 'Please, Raith.'

He begins to thrust, slowly at first, watching my face with fascination and hunger.

'Let go,' I urge, wrapping my legs around his waist to draw him deeper. 'Just let go, Raith. I can take it. I can take you. All of you,' my words blur into moans as each sentence pushes him farther over the edge. 'Fuck me the way you want, Raith. As hard as you want.'

With a groan that sounds almost pained, he surrenders, abandoning that careful control. His movements grow more urgent, more primal, and I match him thrust for thrust, my nails digging into the solid muscle of his back as pleasure builds within me once more, hips rising to meet him as our bodies collide.

I hear my own desperate moans as if they're coming from someone else. It feels like I'm hardly in control anymore, like desire slid its velvety fingers around the controls of my body and has taken me over.

Our connection pulses stronger with our physical intimacy. Magic surges through us both, his fire essence mingling with my unbound power in a dance as ancient as the elements themselves. The candles around the room transform, their flames stretching into ribbons that curl and twist through the air like living things. Clouds gather above us, curling and twisting across the ceiling as a fine mist begins to fall, soaking everything in my room.

Maybe in the morning I'll care, but right now, I don't.

I see and hear steam hissing as the cold water falls on his fire-hot skin. I can feel his approaching climax mirrored in my own body, his rhythm growing more erratic as he nears the edge. One of his hands slides between us, finding the sensitive bundle of nerves at the apex of my thighs, circling in tight, precise motions that have me gasping.

'Come for me again,' he demands, his voice rough with need. 'Break apart for me. With me.'

His words push me over the edge. I explode beneath him, crying out his name as pleasure radiates outward from my core in waves of mounting intensity. My inner walls clench around him, drawing him deeper, and I feel the moment he follows me into oblivion.

Fire essence rushes through me, hot and wild and exhilarating, as his climax triggers currents of even greater pleasure through my body. His ecstasy becomes mine, mine becomes his, transforming both into something transcendent, a perfect unity of sensation.

The rainclouds conjured by my wild magic thicken and the mist turns to a small downpour, absolutely soaking us, my bed, the sheets, and what little furniture I have in my room. The candle flames sputter in the falling water, spraying magical golden sparks as they extinguish – globes of light that hang suspended in the air for breathtaking seconds before fading to darkness.

As the aftershocks of our pleasure fade, the magic dims and passes, too. Raith collapses beside me, careful not to crush me with his weight. His arms wrap around me, drawing me against his chest as we both struggle to catch our breath. I can feel his heart pounding in time with mine, his skin slick with sweat against my own.

For long moments, we lie in silence, the only sounds our gradually slowing breaths and beating hearts.

His fingers trace idle patterns on my bare shoulder, and I find myself melting into his touch, boneless with satisfaction. 'Did we just cause a rainstorm to nearly flood my room?' I ask, a note of wonder in my voice.

He huffs a quiet laugh, the sound vibrating through his chest beneath my ear. 'I think we might have,' he admits. 'Your power is something else.'

'It wasn't just me,' I point out, my fingertips tracing the lines of muscle across his abdomen. 'You're pretty formidable yourself.'

'Together, then,' he says, and there's something in his voice – a weight, a significance – that makes me lift my head to look at him.

His eyes meet mine in the darkness, golden as a sunrise even in the dim morning light. There's an openness there that I've never seen before, the careful mask he usually wears completely gone.

'Together,' I agree softly.

In the aftermath, we lie tangled together, his warmth both drying and heating the soaked blankets and sheets. He keeps me close, one arm curled protectively around my waist. Eventually, I feel his magic flare and the room grows hotter. Steam rises as he magically dries the water on the floor, my bed, and even our bodies. The warm magic feels like him. Like his hands all over my body again, lovingly wiping away every drop of water and making sure I'm perfectly dry.

'Thank you,' I whisper.

'Are you alright?' he asks, brushing the now dry hair from my forehead with gentle fingers.

I smile, stretching languidly beneath him. 'More than alright.'

He shifts, rolling to his side and drawing me against his chest. For several minutes, we simply exist together in comfortable silence. Content. Safe. *Happy.*

'When are you going to tell me?' I ask finally, tilting my head to look up at him.

His hand stills. 'Tell you what?'

'Who you really are.' I prop myself up on one elbow, studying his face in the moonlight. 'I know you're not just some random fire affinity prince from some outlying island. That's what I thought at first. But . . . it doesn't feel right.'

His expression closes off, that careful mask slipping back into place. 'Why do you say that?'

'The castle in your memories,' I say. 'The way you carry yourself. The way the other fire affinities look to you like you're . . .' I pause, the truth suddenly dawning on me. 'Like you're their rightful leader.'

He sits up, the blanket pooling around his waist as he runs a hand through his tousled hair. 'I can't control how they look at me.

None of them know who I am, either. And fuck. If they knew, they'd probably hate me, not bow to me.'

I sit up beside him. 'No more secrets, Raith. Not between us. We both swore oaths to each other. I swore that your fight was my fight, and I don't even know what that fight is.'

He looks at me for a long moment, conflicted emotions battling in his eyes. Finally, he sighs, resignation settling over his features.

'I was born Raith Aurenciel,' he says. 'Crown Prince of the Red Kingdom.'

The revelation hits me like a physical blow.

The Red Kingdom – Empire's greatest rival, the vast nation that has been at war with us for generations. My mind races, trying to reconcile the man I've come to love with this new information.

'That's impossible,' I breathe. 'The royal family of the Red Kingdom was killed in an accident eleven years ago. There were no . . .' I trail off, because I already know. Don't I? I saw it happen through his eyes. Through his memories.

There weren't supposed to be any survivors. But . . .

'I was found half-dead in the rubble, burns covering the left side of my body. A loyal servant of my family was the one who found me. They knew it was an assassination attempt. They knew I'd be killed if my identity ever became known. Within an hour, I was hidden away and sent toward Empire. It was the last place they'd look for me. And the scars helped keep anyone from recognizing me.'

'Assassins?' I echo, my mind struggling to keep up.

His laugh is bitter. 'The official story is that my sister lost control of her powers, causing an explosion that destroyed the royal wing of the castle. A tragic accident that killed the king, queen, and both heirs to the throne.' His jaw tightens. 'Leaving my father's cousin, Darian, as the only remaining claimant to the throne.'

I feel the sickening picture forming. 'You think this Darian arranged for it to happen? For the siphons to kill your family?'

'I know he did,' Raith says, his voice hard. 'And when I graduate, I'm going to return to Red Kingdom to make sure he regrets it.'

My hand rises to cover my mouth. 'If anyone discovers you're alive . . .'

'His claim to the throne would be forfeit,' Raith finishes. 'And he would stop at nothing to silence me permanently. He's the king of Red Kingdom. He could have an entire contingent of Red Kingdom primals hunting me at a moment's notice. Tens of thousands of armed men and women searching for me. For anyone who dared call themselves an ally or friend. Especially someone I care about. *Someone I love*,' he adds, eyes heavy on me with significance.

I swallow. I can see now why he was so afraid to let me in. So afraid to let anyone in. He's worried they'll be casualties of his uncle's wrath if he's ever discovered.

'It's okay,' I say. 'I'm willing to take the risk for you, Raith. I'll fight by your side if they come for you. You have to know I would.'

'An exiled prince . . . Interesting. Let him know I will fight to protect him as well, if needed,' Typhon adds.

'Thank you, Typhon.'

Raith's expression darkens. He shakes his head. 'You don't understand, Nessa. I'm not just planning to hide and survive, to live my life out in obscurity as a tool for Empire. I'm going to take back what was mine. I'm going to fucking kill "king" Darian myself. I'm going to retake my throne, whatever it takes.'

The words land like stones in my stomach. 'You want to become king of Red Kingdom?'

'It's my birthright,' he says simply. 'And Darian is a tyrant who has brought nothing but suffering to my people.'

A chill runs down my spine as I finally understand. The man I've fallen in love with doesn't just want to survive – he wants to become the ruler of Empire's greatest enemy.

'The war,' I say, the question I can't not ask. 'If you took the throne, would you continue the war with Empire?'

'The war is not what you've been taught, Nessa. The history your scribes record is carefully curated to support Empire's narrative.'

'What does that mean?'

'It means I've seen atrocities committed by Empire that rival anything the Red Kingdom has done,' he says carefully. 'I've seen it from both sides now. Neither is innocent.'

'But would you end it?' I press, needing to know.

Before he can answer, the deep toll of a bell cuts through the slowly brightening morning air – a single, solemn note that makes my blood run cold.

The Crucible is beginning. Earlier than planned. Much earlier. It's the middle of the night, not morning like we were told.

Raith is already moving, gathering his clothes with swift efficiency. 'It's starting early,' he says, pulling on his pants.

'The sun hasn't even risen,' I protest, even as I scramble for my own clothes. 'They can't possibly expect—'

'They can expect whatever they want,' he cuts in, his voice hard again, all traces of tenderness gone. 'They want us caught off guard. Sleepy. It's all part of the trial.'

Our conversation is left hanging as we dress hurriedly in the darkness. I want to ask him more, to finish what we've started, but I know what he'll say. He'll want my mind on the Crucible, not on the complicated mess of whatever just happened between us. Love. Betrayal. Confusion. Conflicting loyalties.

'Raith,' I say, catching his arm as he moves toward the door. 'Promise me we'll finish talking about this after.'

His eyes meet mine, and for a moment, I see the conflict there – the man who loves me warring with the prince who has a kingdom to reclaim.

'Later,' he promises, though whether he'll actually tell me the truth remains to be seen. 'For now, all that matters is getting you through today alive.'

He presses a swift, hard kiss to my lips, then helps me fix a place where I've missed a button on my tunic. The rushed, tender moment threatens to break me as the bell continues to ring, signaling we're all about to fight for our lives in the Crucible.

Chapter 37

The bell's deep toll is persistent and impatient. I give myself one last look in the mirror while Raith checks the edge of his sword with a calloused thumb. Satisfied, he sheathes it with a click.

The door to my room bursts open. Two upper-year legacies stride in, their expressions cold and impassive.

'Time to go,' the tallest says, his air elemental – an eagle twice the size of Ambrose's water hawk – hovering above his shoulder. 'With us.'

Raith moves instinctively, positioning himself in front of me. 'She's not going anywhere with you.'

'You'll both follow us, or you'll both be disqualified before the Crucible even starts.' His eyes narrow. 'Your choice.'

'What's happening?' I ask, grabbing my rapier and strapping it to my hip.

'We're going to the courtyard. That's all you need to know,' the other legacy says, this one a water affinity with a serpent elemental – similar to Serena's but somehow more refined, more controlled.

Raith and I exchange glances. I feel his suspicion, his anger, and beneath it all, a cold determination that matches my own.

My mind is a war of emotions. Fear for the coming Crucible, but there's also hurt. I understand his reasons for keeping secrets from me, but I still can't believe he's Raith Aurenciel. He's the heir to the entire fucking Red Kingdom. The man I've sworn an oath to and tethered with wants to reclaim his throne and presumably continue fighting against Empire and everyone I've ever known or cared about.

But there's no time to talk. No time to process everything properly. I'm escorted out of my room and led through a hallway where the same scene is playing out everywhere I look. Raith is dragged ahead of me, led down the stairs and out of view.

Upper-year students are everywhere we go. They're hauling more first-years from their rooms, confusion and fear etched on the faces of my peers. Most are half-dressed, fumbling with uniforms and boots as they stumble into the predawn darkness.

A masked figure wearing Empire black and gold moves through the crowd, pressing small discs into trembling hands. When they reach me, they place one in my palm – cold metal carved with pulsing blue runes.

'Stasis token,' they explain tersely. 'Activates if you're about to die . . . usually. Don't lose it.'

I study the token with awe. If it really does what they say, maybe there's a chance we'll make it through this thing alive. I'm reminded of my bargain with Voss. He agreed to help tip the scales in favor of survival, but not without cost.

He's going to still expect me to go with him to the ruins when this is all over.

Typhon materializes beside me, still in his flying fish disguise but clearly agitated. *I do not like this, angry human.*

'That makes two of us.'

I'm led from the water tower to the courtyard, where I scan the crowds of students for my friends. Instead, I see Malakai's people gathered in the corner – not confused or disoriented like the rest of us, but organized in perfect formation. They're already wearing full gear, weapons strapped to their sides, faces set with grim purpose.

They look like a fucking army, and the only thing that eases my mind is knowing the weapons they wear are all sabotaged. It'll only be a slight edge with magic and elementals involved, but it's something.

Seeing the way they're all ready, dressed, and even look well-rested makes me certain they knew. They knew we'd be roused early and they were prepared. So what other unknown advantages have they been given?

Malakai sees me glaring and has the audacity to wink at me.

A horn blasts from high on the walls, vibrating through my chest. We're all shoved and pushed toward the center of the courtyard.

Voss waits for us there, silver hair gleaming in the moonlight. Behind him, Empire emissaries watch with cold eyes. I try again to spot my friends and Raith in the chaos, but the darkness and confusion make it impossible. Around me, others are moving around frantically searching for their teams of five. A few pair up but most are still looking.

'The Crucible begins now,' Voss announces, his voice carrying over the frightened murmurs. 'Your objective is to reach the quarry, retrieve the ceremonial blade, and return. The winning team will earn legacy status.'

'What about—' someone begins, but a second horn blasts, and the world twists inside out. Magic rushes through me, pulling me apart and reassembling me somewhere else entirely. My insides lurch as my vision clears, revealing dense forest bathed in the first pale light of dawn.

I double over, vomit from sudden nausea, and wipe my mouth with a grimace as I take in my surroundings. I'm not in the courtyard anymore. I'm not surrounded by the chaos of hundreds of bodies.

I'm alone. Alone in a fucking forest somewhere outside the castle. Thick wisps of early morning mist curl around me, shrouding everything from my knees and below in white.

Was I just teleported? I didn't even know teleportation was possible, but I suppose I don't know much about the power of a true primal. Maybe it's some form of air magic?

'*Typhon?*' I whisper, trying to get my bearings.

He materializes instantly, his small fish form darting anxiously through the air. '*I'm here. The others were transported elsewhere. Deliberately separated and disoriented, it seems. I should note I sense the magical interference Serena spoke of. This area is shielded. Invisible to any but those who are here in this forest.*'

Before I can respond, a cry echoes through the trees – pain and terror cut suddenly short. I press myself against a massive trunk, breathing hard as I try to locate the sound.

But I remember the stasis tokens. With any luck, I didn't just hear someone die. They were only put into stasis. Taken out of the challenge. I creep closer to the sound of the scream and spot a downed pair of water affinities in a small rocky clearing.

Corpus, one of Malakai's elites, looms over the downed girl.

The girl is frozen stiff, surrounded by a shimmering blue kind of shield.

The stasis worked, then. Thank the gods.

But Corpus kneels down and presses his hand against the shield. Blue energy flares at first, repelling him. He tries again, more slowly this time. His hand slips inside the barrier, letting him rifle through the clothing of the frozen girl. He jerks his hand back, clutching the stasis token.

Her shield snaps out of view and she gasps, eyes fuzzy with confusion, as if she just woke from deep sleep. Before she can get her bearings, Corpus grips her hair, jerks her head back, and drags a blade across her throat.

The world lurches beneath my feet as I watch red blood flow in the moonlight, spilling down her uniform and disappearing into the swirling white mist. Corpus clutches the hem of her shirt, wipes his dagger, and stalks off into the darkness.

Gods. It's as if he knew exactly how to bypass the stasis. How to make sure they could still murder fellow students, even with the protections Voss put in place. I think I might be sick again as the implications settle, but I don't have time.

Someone else is coming toward me. Fast and loud.

Footsteps crash through the underbrush and someone gasps for breath between pained whimpers. A girl with an air affinity mark on her left hand bursts into view, terror etched across her face. Her elemental, a small water fox, streaks alongside her.

Behind her comes another student I recognize as one of Malakai's elite. It's Titus, the huge water affinity who tried to kill me in weapons training. His water turtle elemental glides silently through the air beside him. The girl doesn't see him raise his hand, doesn't see the blade of compressed water forming between his fingers.

I don't think. I just move.

I use a thread of earth essence to fling dirt into the air and a burst of wind essence to blast it into his face. Titus flinches back, nearly stabbing himself with his own water blade as he reaches to wipe his eyes.

He never sees me coming.

I'm on him in a heartbeat, rapier flashing and catching him below the arm. The empire steel bites deep, punching into his flesh and drawing blood.

Titus howls in pain, losing his water blade as his concentration is broken. He spins to face me, teeth bared in rage. His elemental abandons the pursuit of the girl, turning black eyes toward me instead and opening a beak that looks sharp enough to sever limbs. But Typhon darts in, distracting the turtle with powerful jets of magical water sprayed from his mouth.

'Thorne,' Titus snarls, recognition dawning on his face. 'Malakai will reward me well for your head.'

He lunges, summoning another water blade. I parry, my rapier singing through the air. It's different fighting with real steel – heavier, deadlier, an extension of my arm rather than the flimsy training weapon I'm used to.

Titus slashes wildly, but I can see the patterns Raith has drilled into me.

I side step a slash, left palm opening as I spray a jet of water against his inner thigh. The pressure of the blast makes him slide back, costing him balance as I spin inside his guard, flicking away another strike with my rapier. I use my momentum, pulling my elbow up and forward to slam beneath his chin.

Titus' teeth clatter and he makes a pained sound.

I don't give him time to recover. I stab upward, rapier finding the soft spot beneath his ribs. He gasps, eyes wide with shock, but the token at his neck flashes blue, and he freezes mid-fall, suspended in stasis. To my surprise, his elemental freezes too.

For a moment, he's completely still, and then his body falls back with a heavy thump to disappear into the thick mist. Only his curled, frozen fingers stick up above the fog.

The fleeing girl has stopped, watching us with wide eyes.

'Go,' I tell her. 'Find somewhere to hide. Malakai's people aren't worrying about the objective. They're just trying to take out anyone who isn't with them. Tell anyone you find to hide their token well. They're taking it once stasis triggers and executing people while they're dazed.'

'Thanks, Nessa,' she says shakily, nodding before disappearing into the trees.

'That was unwise,' Typhon notes. *'He could have bested you.'*

'I couldn't just let her die.'

'Your compassion may get us killed.'

'And there's no point surviving if I can't live with myself.'

I have no way to know where the quarry is from here. I doubt I could even find my way back to the academy if I wanted to. There are sounds of struggle and fighting all around me. I hear magic flaring and see the bright lights of elemental attacks.

I press my back to a tree, eyes wildly scanning as I try to think of something resembling a plan. I can distantly feel Raith's presence through the tether, and it seems like he's slowly getting closer. Of course he is. He's coming for me. And knowing him, he's not letting anything slow him down.

If I wasn't worried about Mireen, Beck, Ambrose, and Brunhild, I would lie low and wait. But I need to find them. I can't risk them getting caught out alone.

With a hard swallow, I slowly move deeper into the trees. Bright green flashes to my right and someone screams. There's harsh laughter a moment later, then an explosion of blue light followed by cursing and shouts. I hear the clatter of weapons clashing, more shouting, someone cursing in frustration.

I look down and see my hand is shaking.

'Calm, angry human. We need to stay calm. Be ready for anything.'

I take a shaky breath and nod my head. 'Doing my best.'

I freeze as movement catches my eye to the right. It is a blue shark's fin cutting through the mist a little ways ahead. My blood goes cold and I duck behind a tree, peeking out to make sure it's not coming closer.

The shark slices through the mist without a sound, and then I see it . . . Two waters hiding behind a large rock. They don't realize—

I open my mouth to warn them but it's already too late. One of them is yanked under the mist with a strangled scream that is cut off instantly. The other makes it a few steps before the shark leaps above the mist and bites the back of their head, triggering their stasis immediately.

Malakai . . . the shark means he's close. That, or he simply told it to go out and hunt down anyone it could. The only saving grace is that he may not find their frozen forms beneath the mist. The shark may have just saved their lives.

It swims through the mist, curling around the rock to disappear in the distance, searching for more prey.

It takes all my willpower to start moving again, but I do it. I remind myself that I've trained as hard as anyone here. Maybe harder. I'm unbound. I'm tethered to a fucking ancient water dragon. I can do this. I need to do this, because my friends might need me.

The sounds of struggle are already becoming less frequent. I stop twice when I see organized groups of five or more jogging through the trees like patrolling soldiers. Everyone else seems to be scattered in small groups.

'Perhaps Malakai's groups were teleported in together?' Typhon guesses as we watch another group pass far ahead in the distance, trailed by a team of deadly elementals.

'I wouldn't doubt it. The corruption goes all the way to the fucking top, apparently. Titus and Corpus may have just split from their groups to hunt down more people before they could find their groups.'

I get back to searching. I have no idea how I'm going to find anyone like this, so I start taking the risk of whisper yelling for my friends when I think there aren't any enemy groups nearby. 'Mireen? Beck?' I whisper.

A branch cracks to my left, seemingly in response.

'Ambrose?'

But no response comes, and cold starts to drift up my spine.

An earth elemental erupts from the ground – a massive boar of living stone, tusks sharp enough to gore. A tall student with a green earth mark steps into view behind it.

'Found one,' he calls to someone unseen, voice chillingly casual. 'It's Thorne.'

Two more students emerge from the trees – a water and an air, elementals at their sides. The air's falcon circles overhead, its wings leaving magical contrails of mist. The water's jellyfish pulses with menacing light.

'Three against one,' the earth says, smiling. 'Malakai said to bring you back alive if possible. Dead if necessary.'

Fear bites at me, and I feel the first pang of worry through the tether. It's not from Typhon. It's Raith.

He's feeling my fear, and I can sense his desperation to reach me no matter the cost. I try to calm my fear so I don't worry him or force him to be reckless in getting to me, but it's no use.

I reach for every element around me – moisture from the air, heat from the plants and trees around me, earth beneath my feet, the breeze rustling through the leaves. Power flows, waiting to be shaped.

'I don't want to fight you,' I say, buying time, stretching my senses through the forest. Raith's concern for me joins my heartbeat as a frantic, pulsing awareness.

The earth laughs. 'No shit. I wouldn't want to fight three on one either. Hurry up. Get her.'

They attack in unison – the boar charging, the falcon diving, the jellyfish sending tendrils of water whipping toward me. I jump back, acting on pure instinct. I know their tokens will stop my attacks from being lethal, so I don't hold back.

Typhon darts between me and the three elementals, skillfully zipping through the air as he uses powerful water jets to distract and enrage the creatures, leaving me to focus on the people.

I press both palms together, forming water and making it spin outward before I harden it into a razor-sharp disc. I fling it at the earth affinity, who jumps out of the way just before it hammers past him, slicing a tree at the base.

Before the tree has even begun to tip over, I've summoned a spear of water and hurled it at the air affinity, but her falcon disengages from Typhon, diving in front and taking the spear in the wing with a shriek of pain.

I'm already almost empty of water essence, though, and the three students are slowly advancing on me, eyes full of murder.

An idea forms, and I don't hesitate.

I use all my air essence to form a disc of air beside a tree several feet to my right. It's difficult shaping and controlling it at such a distance, but I manage to fling it toward the group.

It misses horribly, but it does the job. All three pause, staring toward the trees. 'Who's there?' the earth asks.

I reach out to the other side and form a magical ball of fire and fling it at them. By pure luck, it nearly hits the earth, who dodges at the last second.

'You thought I was alone?' I try. If this goes my way, I'll only be triggering stasis. These three will live to tell what they saw. But I can use my unbound powers to make them think they're surrounded by more students.

The earth takes a step back, head swiveling. 'Come out. Cowards. Come out and fucking face us.'

'Cowards?' I ask. 'You're the ones who started a fight three against one. Or so you thought.'

The earth forms a spike of rock in his hand and then throws it at me. Once it's in the air, it fragments into a swarm of small, piercing shards all screaming toward me.

I try to raise a shield of solid water, but I don't have enough essence left to make it solid. It only slows the projectiles. They punch through, one cutting across my arm like a hot blade as others bite into me, drawing blood.

I hiss in pain, falling to one knee as I clutch the worst wound on my arm. Blood squeezes free, dripping to disappear into the mist.

'*Enough,*' Typhon growls in my mind.

'Not yet,' I warn. 'Just keep the elementals from surprising me.'

Reluctantly, Typhon continues to dart in and out of his fight with the elementals.

I feel myself automatically beginning to heal. But the power doesn't come for free. I'm already low on water, air, and fire essence. Already almost unable to perform more magic after just a few displays of power.

Unless . . .

'Try me one on one and I'll tell my friends to stay out of it,' I shout to the earth. 'You and me. Unless you think you can't take me?'

He hesitates. 'Fine.' With a gesture, he signals for his two friends to back off.

I pretend to motion to hidden allies in the trees.

'Clever,' Typhon notes. *'He is a fool for believing you, but it's clever nonetheless.'*

'Shocker. Malakai's people aren't exactly known for their intelligence.'

And then I rush him. He fires more shards of rock my way, but I dive to the side and roll. It hurts like hell landing on tangled roots I can't see through the mist, but it's better than the alternative.

I sense Typhon battling the boar elemental through the tether, but can feel that he's toying with it and in no danger, so I put it from my mind.

I use the mist for cover, crawling on my belly toward the earth who shouts in annoyance, firing more magic blindly all around me. Dirt sprays and rock punches into the soil, but none of it finds me as I get closer.

Finally, I jump up from the mist, rapier blurring as I slip inside his guard. I could've put him in stasis, but that wasn't my goal. I just wanted to get closer. To . . .

I hook my arm around his neck, pressing my entire body to his back and urging as much of his earth essence to flow into me as possible. He was burning through it as he sprayed magic, but I feel power rushing into me anyway.

'What the . . . fuck are . . . you doing?' he gasps, barely able to get the words out around the crush of my arm on his neck.

'Winning.' I give a hard jerk, wrenching his head to the side. Thankfully, I feel him go completely stiff and cold before any real damage can be done.

Stasis.

His body falls to the ground as I turn to face his two allies. They exchange a look, and then I point to the trees. 'My friends are impatient. You two can run if you want. It would be the smart thing to do.'

'Get her!' the air shouts.

I don't give them time. I use the stolen earth essence to lift a huge spike of earth from the ground and aim the point at the water affinity. He's knocked aside, blue stasis flaring to life around his body instantly.

And then the air is on me with his short sword.

Behind it all, I can feel Raith's worry for me warring with his confidence in my abilities. He's terrified I'll get hurt, but he also believes in me, and he's using that belief to keep as calm as he can.

I dodge the first two slashes of the air's sword as Typhon handles the elemental. I raise my rapier to block the third attack and the air's weapon clatters against my steel, crumbling to pieces.

The air stares at his broken weapon in shock, giving me the perfect opening to stab at his throat. There's a flash of blue magic and then he's locked into stasis with his elemental.

And then it's over. Three down. I fall to one knee, gasping for breath as I look around, making sure there aren't more enemies coming.

'Gods . . . This is fucking brutal.'

I am enjoying it, Typhon says.

The sound of footsteps makes me groan and raise my rapier again. That spike used almost all the earth essence I managed to steal, and healing my wounds has drained the rest of my magic. If it's another fight, I'm going to have to hope I can steal more essence or handle it with my rapier.

My throat goes dry when I see the size of the figure stepping out of the shadows. They're huge, and I know it's not Raith. I can still sense he's trying to reach me, but he's not this close.

'Ah! I find you,' a familiar voice says.

I lower my rapier a few inches, squinting into the shadows. 'Brunhild?'

She comes closer and I finally make out her face.

I let out a heavy breath, relief washing through me.

The northerner doesn't smile, but her eyes show recognition. Dora clicks her massive claws as it scuttles behind her.

'Sexy bear and others waiting. Not safe here.'

With a nod, I follow her through the forest. I can't decide if it's a good or bad thing that I hear almost nothing now. The forest is eerily still, and I don't know if we've already lost all chances of winning this thing. For all I know, Malakai's people could have hunted down everyone but our group already. Well, everyone but us and Raith. I can sense he's still alive and coming my way.

'How did you find me?' I ask as we run.

'Ambrose's bird.'

The sounds of another battle reach us before we see them – the crack of elemental magic, shouts of pain and fury. We emerge from the trees into a small clearing where Beck, Mireen, and Ambrose stand back-to-back, surrounded by Malakai's people.

Beck's water bear, Uther, smashes into a group of attackers, sending them flying as blue flashes and tokens trigger mid-air. Mireen and Ollie have created a swirling vortex of water that keeps another group at bay.

But they're outnumbered. At least eight students circle them, elemental magic building for a coordinated strike.

'There!' one of them shouts, pointing at me. 'It's Thorne!'

Several break off from the main group, turning toward us. Brunhild steps forward, her crab growing to twice its original size.

'I crush,' she says matter-of-factly.

She charges into the fray, her crab scuttling beside her as she draws her huge, two-handed hammer. I follow, too drained of essence to do much.

Allow me to show them what I'm capable of. It's time they knew. Typhon's voice is quiet, but insistent.

I lick my lips, taking in the situation. 'Not yet. It's a last resort, okay? Only if there's no other choice.'

He doesn't complain. He just flies into battle, slashing and spraying magic at elementals, quickly drawing the attention of most of them.

'Nessa!' Beck calls, relief evident in his voice. 'Took you long enough!'

'Been a little busy,' I reply, parrying a strike from one of Malakai's waters who rushes me with a spear. I sidestep the attack, rapier sliding inside his guard with a blue flash as his stasis token triggers.

Typhon weaves through the battle, seemingly small and harmless, but the fierce power of his magical blasts of water are doing serious damage. The other elementals already realize he's the biggest threat and are converging on him.

'You okay?'

'I'm toying with them. Keep yourself alive, angry human. If your token triggers, it freezes me, too.'

Brunhild and Beck fight well together, isolating attackers and overwhelming them with strength. Ambrose works with Akaron, occasionally reaching into the air and grabbing one of its legs to lift himself out of harm's way, where he can fire magical attacks from above. Mireen's channeling dispatches enemies with ease as she slides daggers of water around their defenses with deadly accuracy.

I hardly need to do anything before stasis tokens have flared, immobilizing every last attacker. It's all over in a matter of seconds, and we're all still on our feet. Every last attacker is shrouded in blue and lying in the mist.

'Everyone okay?' I ask between ragged breaths. It can't have been more than half an hour since we were teleported here, and I already feel as though I've run a marathon.

'They're slaughtering anyone they catch,' Beck says, his usual lighthearted demeanor replaced by grim determination. 'Activating stasis tokens then killing people while they're defenseless.'

Mireen nods. 'We saw Serena's group shortly after we arrived. They triggered stasis, then pulled the tokens from their victims and cut their throats. They're executing people.'

'I know. I saw Corpus kill someone already. I was hoping the others didn't know . . . but I suspected they did.'

'Someone clearly put them up to it,' Ambrose says. 'And they were given every possible advantage. Malakai's people knew exactly where they'd be transported. They were ready, and they came in with their groups while the rest of us were scattered and disoriented.'

'Someone wanted this to be a bloodbath, but they wanted to make sure they got to pick which side survived it,' I say, lips twisting in disgust.

Through our tether, I can feel Raith growing closer. His determination pulses through our connection, along with flashes of what he's seen – bodies lying where they fell, students hunting students, blood soaking into the forest floor.

A warning cry from Akaron makes us all tense. Ambrose's eyes widen as he interprets his elemental's message. 'Someone's coming.'

We form a defensive circle, weapons ready. I can hear them now – footsteps approaching rapidly from multiple directions.

'Get ready,' Mireen whispers, water gathering at her fingertips.

But through our tether, I feel a surge of relief from Raith – not fear or preparation for battle. He's close. Very close.

The trees part and figures emerge from the mist – fires, at least ten of them, their elementals blazing like beacons in the morning light. There are a few earths, airs, and waters, too. At their center, I see Raith, his eyes immediately finding mine across the clearing.

'Nessa,' he breathes, eyes reflecting the slowly rising sun staining the sky a deep, bloody red. Above, clouds are thickening, too, growing darker as the air fills with the unmistakable scent of an approaching storm.

The fires spread out in a protective formation around us, their elementals making a perimeter that pulses with heat. I recognize Cade among them, his slight frame half-hidden behind two larger students. The other students fill in, eyes wary as they scan the distant trees.

'Raith's gathered an army,' Ambrose murmurs, adjusting his glasses as he takes in the newcomers. 'Impressive.'

Raith strides toward me, radiating purpose. I feel his relief at finding me unharmed warring with the horror of what he's witnessed in the forest.

'Malakai's people—' I begin.

'I know,' he cuts me off, his expression hardening. 'They're executing people.'

'We need a plan,' Mireen says. 'We can't just wander the forest hoping to evade them.'

Raith nods. 'The quarry. That's where the blade is. The legacies are guarding it.'

'We're not seriously still trying to win this thing, are we?' Beck asks incredulously. 'People are dying out there.'

'That's exactly why we need to end it,' I say slowly, understanding dawning on me. 'He wants to get the blade because that will signal the end of the Crucible.'

Raith's expression is approving. 'Exactly. If we hide, the Crucible keeps playing out. They'll have all the time they want to hunt us to the last person. We either wait to be hunted, or we go on the offensive. Push through the legacies guarding the blade, take it, and win. We end this before more have to die.'

I see the logic in his plan, though it means walking straight into what could be a trap. 'Do you think Malakai will guess our plan?'

'Almost certainly,' Raith says. 'We'll likely have to fight our way to the quarry. But if we go soon, we may catch them before they've fully gathered. They might still be scattered and hunting for stragglers.'

'So we fight our way to the quarry.'

Raith's eyes meet mine, and I feel his fierce determination through our tether. 'Together.'

A dark shape cuts through the mist behind him – a fin, dark blue against the white. The shark. Malakai's shark.

'Look out!' I shout, but it's already too late.

The massive elemental erupts from the mist, jaws wide and coming straight for Raith's exposed back.

Chapter 38

I scream a warning, already lunging forward though I know I won't make it in time. Typhon rockets past me, abandoning his flying fish disguise for something sleeker, faster — a blue-scaled serpent that slams into the shark's side, knocking it off course.

Pyrin is there a moment later, pouncing on the downed shark and biting viciously at its side. Water magic explodes from the wound like blue blood, steam hissing from between Pyrin's fiery teeth.

Raith spins, sword drawn as the shark slips free of Typhon and Pyrin, already turning to attack again. This time, he's ready. His blade is a blur, catching the elemental across its flank. The shark shrieks, a sound no natural creature would make, as more blue energy spills from the wound.

'Everyone,' Raith shouts, his fires immediately moving into defensive formation. 'Get ready!'

I search the fading mist for threats, feeling magically drained and vulnerable. The rising sun and gathering clouds cast everything in eerie, deep red light, turning the forest into a scene straight out of a nightmare.

Without essence, I'm limited to my rapier and whatever Typhon can do while maintaining his cover. But I won't let fear paralyze me. Not now, not when we're all depending on each other.

They emerge from the trees like ghosts — Malakai and his elite guard, at least thirty students with grim faces and drawn weapons. Various colored affinity marks glow in the shadows. I even see Veeni among Malakai's people, sleeve pinned up over her missing arm.

Serena walks slightly apart from the rest, her perfect features set in cold determination, her fire serpent slithering behind her. Elements of various forms drift behind the group, some flying, some crawling, others lumbering between the trees.

It's fucking terrifying, but my hand remains steady as I grip my rapier and watch them approach.

'Thorne,' Malakai calls, his single eye gleaming with malice. 'And Hollow. How convenient to find you both in one place.'

His shark circles back to him, bleeding elemental energy but still somehow looking eager to attack again. It hovers beside him, teeth bared in a permanent snarl. Malakai pats its head like it's a gods-damned dog, smiling and saying something so quiet I can't hear.

Raith steps forward, placing himself at the front of our combined forces. 'Call off your people, Malakai. Last chance.'

Malakai laughs, the sound hollow and cruel. 'This is a competition, Hollow. Not my fault if the weak can't survive it.'

'Executing defenseless students isn't a competition,' I spit. 'It's murder.'

Serena steps forward, her orange eyes finding mine. 'This isn't just about winning anymore, Thorne. It's about proving who belongs here and who doesn't.' Her gaze shifts to Raith. 'Empire has no place for traitors and sympathizers.'

I feel Raith's cold rage ignite at her words. His hand tightens on his sword, but he maintains his control. 'We're going to the quarry. Stand aside or face the consequences.'

They're at least equal to our numbers now, maybe even outnumbering us slightly. But many in our group are injured or exhausted.

Malakai tilts his head, considering. His smile is a knife-edge. 'On your way to the quarry, huh? Sure. It's that way,' he hooks a thumb over his shoulder. 'Just gotta go through us to get there. And then the pair of legacies you'll face if you make it.'

'I'm tired of talking,' Serena says, face twisted with hatred. 'I want to watch them burn.' She claps her hands together, fire magic flaring brightly. A moment later, she has gathered a fireball and launched it toward us.

The magic streaks through the sky, headed directly for the center of our group. But Mireen conjures an even larger sphere of water and flings it high into the air. The spells collide with a splash and sizzle, canceling one another out.

The sound and sight is breathtaking, but the stillness only lasts one heartbeat.

Two . . .

Three . . .

Someone shouts and then the sound is picked up by students on both sides. More magic explodes through the trees, shaking the air itself and making flashes of light that are blinding. Shadows stretch long as students clash, weapons swinging and sabotaged blades exploding into dust, providing a small advantage for our side.

'Stay to the back,' Raith says, one hand held protectively in front of me as he uses fire to blast away a small vortex of air someone threw at us.

'I can help,' I whisper, nodding toward Malakai's closest ally – a muscular earth whose elemental resembles a bull made of living stone. Together, they're both smashing away students, triggering stasis tokens left and right. 'I'll need to get my hands on one of them.'

Understanding dawns in Raith's eyes. I feel his concern and worry, but strongest of all is his confidence in me. He believes in my ability to handle myself. To be useful.

Raith gives me the slightest nod. 'Be fucking careful, Nessa. I'll be close.'

We fight our way into the chaos as elementals clash overhead in dizzying displays of power. I see Malakai's shark swim just past me, biting a girl in the leg and triggering her stasis token.

Raith cuts a line with his sword toward Malakai and the earth. Nobody can touch him. Nobody even gets close. I follow in his wake, rapier ready.

Blue flashes bright and steady like lightning through the chaos. Stasis tokens trigger rapidly at first as the first waves fall and the pace of spells and sounds slows significantly.

Elementals fall from the sky or tip sideways, suddenly frozen as their humans are locked in stasis.

I clench my teeth, trying not to think about what will happen if the last of us falls. Malakai's people will go through us one by one, executing us. We have to win this.

Distantly, I sense Typhon whirling among the elementals like a demon, his serpent form not as deadly as his dragon form but doing more than enough damage. He's single-handedly turning the tide of the elemental battle.

The earth with the stone bull charges me, clearly hoping to overwhelm me with brute strength. I sidestep his initial rush, my blade slicing across his arm. It's not enough to trigger stasis, but it slows him. When he turns for another charge, I don't try to dodge – I step into it, letting him barrel into me just like Brunhild taught me.

Raith senses my intention at the last second, and I feel his sudden alarm and desire to reach me.

But it happens too fast.

The earth charges me, body slamming me as I do everything I can to hold on, hands squeezing as I suck his essence in as hard and fast as I can. Power floods into me, raw and vibrant, filling the emptiness inside. He realizes too late what's happening, tries to pull away, but I've already taken enough.

Using his power, I flick my wrist, raising a chunk of stone from the ground and flinging it for his head at high speeds.

His eyes widen in shock as the stasis triggers, freezing him mid-gasp.

Around me, the battle rages. Beck and Brunhild fight together, their elementals creating a perimeter of raw destruction that keeps attackers at bay. Mireen weaves water into deadly blades that flash in the morning light. Ambrose lingers near the back, seeming to call out targets for Akaron to surprise attack from above.

Raith cuts into the enemies with brutal efficiency. His sword moves like an extension of his body, each strike calculated and precise. Nearly every time he slashes that blade, there's a flash of blue as yet another of Malakai's people is cast into stasis. I feel his absolute focus, his mind working like a commander on a battlefield rather than a student in a competition.

I use my stolen earth essence to raise last-second shields of earth, saving students on our side from being put into stasis.

'They're trying to surround us,' I warn Raith through our connection.

He nods, shouting orders that his fires follow with brutal efficiency. They fan out, making it harder for Malakai's people to pinch in around us.

'Nessa!' Beck shouts, his voice tight with warning.

I turn to see Malakai himself bearing down on me, shark elemental launching ahead of him. Its jaws open wide, teeth gleaming in the pale light.

Typhon abandons his serpent disguise in a flash of brilliant blue. Wings sprout from his back and his jaw lengthens, filling with sharp teeth. He grows larger until he's easily twice the size of the next largest elemental. He flaps his powerful wings and explodes through the air, putting himself between me and the shark. They collide with such force the ground beneath us shakes, water magic exploding outward in a concussive wave.

Malakai is coming for me, water blade forming in his hand as his single remaining eye glows with deadly purpose.

My stolen earth essence is nearly gone, my body aching from the impact. I reach for any magic I can find – a trickle of air from the breeze, a hint of water from the mist – but it's not enough. But I don't have much left. Scraps of earth left and little more.

And Raith is locked in a fight with three students, trying to find an opening to get to me but being held back.

Around us, the battle has shifted. We're losing ground, our forces pushed back toward the treeline. Brunhild is bleeding from a gash on her arm, her crab elemental missing a claw. Beck is surrounded, fighting desperately to keep three attackers at bay.

Typhon continues to battle Malakai's shark, along with Serena's fire serpent and several other elementals at once. His blue scales gleam, wings unfurling, his form expanding beyond any elemental anyone has ever seen at Confluence.

Students stumble all around, eyes wide as they stare up in horror at Typhon. He's putting on such a display that it's impossible not to see him. Not to notice what he is. Malakai, Serena, and some of their people saw his dragon form on Confluence Day. But he was diminished then. He's twice as large now. His foreleg is as tall as Malakai from toe to shoulder. His long, elegant neck and head tower high above everything, dwarfing the battle as he stands nearly thirty feet high. His wings spread three times as wide, casting shadows over all of us.

Mireen uses the moment of distraction to create a wave that knocks down several enemies at once, slamming some so hard into trees that their tokens flash blue, locking them in stasis.

Smoke, steam, and mist churn around the battle until it's impossible to make out detail. I feel the air displace as Typhon streaks past, a smaller elemental clenched between his teeth as it leaks green essence.

Malakai steps forward, water sword raised. 'You're done, Thorne.' He's grinning, as if he's already certain of his victory, circling me. 'I stasis you and your dragon is done. Easy.'

I'm coming,' Typhon growls.

'I can handle this. Keep everyone safe.'

To my surprise, Typhon obeys, continuing to dart through the maelstrom high overhead.

Malakai rushes in, swinging overhead. I dodge to the side, then send a trickle of heat straight into his water blade. Steam hisses from it in a rush, blinding him for a moment, but he recovers before I can land a strike. He uses his free hand to blast my chest with water, knocking me aside and nearly catching me in the neck with his sword a split second later.

We fight viciously for several seconds that stretch like ages. Dodge. Block. Parry. Feint. Counterattack.

I use everything I've learned from Raith and some of my own improvisation and it still doesn't feel like enough. Malakai is bigger than me. Stronger. He's almost as good as Raith.

I'm losing ground, falling back with every blocked strike as my limbs grow heavier by the minute.

He keeps coming, seeming to get stronger as I grow weaker. I can feel Raith trying to fight his way back to us, but there are too many students and elementals blocking his path.

Typhon roars in victory as he splits a reptilian water elemental in two between his jaws. Malakai glances toward the sound, and I let instinct take over.

I pluck the stasis token from my clothes and toss it to the ground before he can notice.

When he rushes me, sword leveled low for a piercing strike, I don't dodge.

I let the blade sink straight into me.

The pain is blinding. It's cold and biting, threatening to wash away all coherent thought as I let out a strained gasp, body curling around the sudden ice in my stomach.

'Nessa!' Raith roars.

I sense Typhon's rage at the same moment and feel him tearing through the air toward me. Raith's emotions spike through the tether, urgent, terrified, and heartbroken all at once.

But I raise my head, straining against the agony as I reach for Malakai's wrist and grip it. He frowns at my hands, lips curling into a smile. 'You were pretty good, Thorne. I'll give you that.'

'I'm not . . . done . . .' I manage.

He frowns, even as I see Raith from the corner of my eye sending students into stasis as he cleaves his way toward us, rage burning in his eyes like twin flames.

Malakai feels it too late. His essence flowing into me. Filling me. I summon a sharp disc of water in my left hand and sling it toward his neck at point-blank range. His eye goes wide a split second before the stasis shield flashes blue, sending him thumping to the ground.

I fall to my knees once he's down and the blade is out of my stomach. I use the last of his essence to try to heal the worst of it.

Typhon crashes down to the earth beside me, wings flared as he lets out a deep, bone-rattling roar and blasts magical blue energy from his mouth, warning away anyone from getting too close.

Raith rushes to catch me, arms tight and protective. 'You're going to be okay. It's okay.' His voice is calm, but I feel the sheer panic in his heart. The rage. And I feel the certainty that if I don't survive, he's going to take Malakai's token and finish him once and for all.

But Raith's touch sends more essence into me and I can feel it all flowing to the wound, healing me.

Pyrin sits beside him, wounded in several places, but his orange eyes watch me with what I think is worry as Raith continues to run his hands through my hair.

I grin. 'I can heal myself. Remember?'

He frowns. 'You let him stab you on purpose?'

I scoop up my stasis token from the ground and smile as the pain starts to finally subside. I can feel the magic doing its work quickly. 'All part of the plan.'

'Gods damn you,' he hisses between his teeth.

I'm about to say something very clever when I see Serena stalking through Typhon's blue flames toward us. Her sword drags in the dirt at her side and one of her eyes is crusted shut with blood. Behind her, a fire serpent slithers, tongue flicking the air.

A bone-deep weariness threatens to take me. It's too much. I can't fight anymore. I need time to recover. To process. To—

'This ends now,' Serena says through her teeth, sword dragging in the dirt as she stalks toward me.

'*Yes, it does,*' Typhon whispers in my mind.

He roars, firing a jet of water so thick that Serena just seems to vanish. I think I see the blue flare of her stasis triggering, but can't be sure. When the jet of water stops, she's simply gone.

'That was . . . effective,' Raith says.

'Thank you, Typhon.' I reach up to pat his foreleg, then use it to help me stand on wobbly legs.

It feels like there isn't a scrap of magical essence left in my body, but my wound is little more than a dull ache now. 'I think Serena is going to hold that against you,' I note.

Typhon's only response is a low rumble.

Around us, I realize the fight is nearly over. There are a few stragglers being put into stasis, but it's clear we've won. We've actually done it.

Mireen limps to my side with a grin. 'Ambrose and Beck got put into stasis, but Brunhild and I made it.'

I see Brunhild standing guard over their motionless forms. 'Brunhild will guard the frozen ones.' Her crab raises its remaining claw, clicking it loudly.

'How many are left?' Raith demands. The magical clouds of smoke and steam are still fading, making it hard to see the entire battle. Cade comes into view with a dark red cut across his face from forehead to chin. 'Six left, sir. Including you two. But all of his people are in stasis. Orders?'

'Good,' Raith says. 'Gather all the people in stasis in one place. Malakai's people, too. We need to guard them. Make sure Malakai doesn't have other teams out there planning to come finish us off. And make sure nobody wakes up Malakai's people and gives them a second chance to come for us.'

'How far are we from the quarry?' I ask.

Raith eyes me. 'Not far. But going for the blade means leaving the students in stasis more exposed.'

'Look how many there are,' I say, gesturing as the survivors already work to drag blue-shielded people toward a thick patch of trees. 'There can't be many left. We don't need to buy time or stand guard. We need to finish this. Someone has to claim the blade and end the Crucible. It should be you, Raith. You're the only one who stands a chance at beating the legacies guarding it.'

'I'd rather give you the blade.'

I shake my head. 'Becoming a legacy would just mean more scrutiny. I'm safer as an aspirant, and you know it. You're the one who needs to do it. And if you really want to protect me, you'll have more resources to do it as a legacy.'

'Damn it.' Raith looks back toward the large group of students in stasis.

I frown, head tilted. Something feels . . . wrong.

Raith draws his sword and grips it tightly, head slowly swiveling to take in our surroundings. He feels it too.

The air grows still, electric with tension.

Two figures drift slowly down from the sky, landing with no sound in front of us. One male and one female, both lean, muscular, and practically radiating violence. There's an unnatural grace about both of them, and they wear stylized white leather armor with cloud-like patterns and masks that completely cover their faces.

'Windborne,' Raith whispers.

Chapter 39

The windborne advance, their movements synchronized and predatory. They say nothing. Give no warnings or dramatic speeches. Their intent is clear, and it's deadly.

The taller windborne raises a hand, and the air ripples with power. An elemental materializes beside her – not an eagle or falcon, but a creature of pure air, its form constantly shifting, eyes glowing with ancient intelligence. It doesn't look like any elemental I've ever seen.

The female summons a similar elemental.

Both pause for only a heartbeat and I think they're looking at Typhon – probably wondering how the hell any of us tethered something so massive. But Typhon only gives them a moment of hesitation.

And then they're attacking, movements so fast my eyes can't begin to track them. The air around me compresses, squeezing my lungs, lifting me off my feet. I can't breathe, can't move, can't reach my rapier.

My legs kick uselessly as I float a few inches above the ground, invisible hands squeezing in around me from all sides.

I hear the electric sound of stasis tokens triggering behind me even though the windborne hardly even seem to be paying the others attention.

They're wiping us out like we're nothing. No games. No speeches. Just pure violence and efficiency.

Raith charges the woman who is squeezing the air around my head, sword flashing, but the male windborne intercepts him, his elemental blocking Raith's path. I feel Raith's desperate need to protect me, but the male windborne is impossibly fast, dodging his every strike and preventing him from interrupting the woman.

My vision darkens as the air compresses further.

Small, pin-like daggers of air form and try to slide into my body. I use the last scraps of essence I have to hold them back, just barely, but it's a losing battle.

Typhon roars, a sound so deep and terrible I can feel it through my entire body. He launches himself upward, flips, and then begins a death spiral straight for the woman as he tucks his wings tight and gains speed like a projectile.

The woman's focus falters as she lifts her face toward him and has to float backward, invisible winds lifting and yanking her away as if she's being pulled by strings.

I collapse as the distraction breaks her spell, gasping for breath. Typhon's jaws snap at her, but her elemental moves to intercept, the two creatures clashing in a maelstrom of water and air magic.

I look behind me and see there's nobody left. The windborne have already sent every last survivor into stasis.

It's only Raith and me. And if we fall, nothing will stop the windborne from collecting our tokens and finishing us for good.

The windborne facing Raith moves like smoke, her strikes too fast to track. Raith's skill keeps him alive, but just barely. Through our tether, I feel him drawing on every technique he knows, his mind calculating each move seconds ahead. Pyrin battles beside him, snapping at the windborne when Raith's guard falters or he's in danger.

There's a sudden rush of wind as Bastian appears on his steed made of pure air. It leaps for the man fighting Raith as Bastian jumps from its back and joins the fray, long spear stabbing fiercely.

I stare in disbelief as the blonde legacy throws himself into battle. If I had any doubts about his loyalty, they fade quickly. He's fighting side by side with Raith, trying desperately to save us when he must know his chances of making it out of here alive are slim.

Together, they're barely managing to buy time, but it's clear they're outmatched. Even Bastian and Raith together are outskilled. The windborne combines two short blades with rapid magical attacks that Raith barely burns up or deflects. Bastian has an easier time, using some kind of heavy wall of wind to disperse the worst of it.

But I can tell they won't last much longer.

Typhon is struggling against the combined might of both windborne elementals and the female windborne.

I feel useless as I stumble to my feet, searching for any source of elemental power. There's nothing left to draw from – I've burned through everything I had. Every last shred of power is gone and my body is completely exhausted. My only hope is to reach someone, to make physical contact.

The female windborne battling Typhon seems to be the greater threat. Her elemental is pushing him back, its form constantly shifting to counter his attacks. No matter how much power Typhon unleashes, the creature adapts. It fades from existence to dodge his power and reappears, making it impossible for him to land a single blow. All he's doing is keeping it busy.

I need to help him. I need to stop her.

With a deep breath, I charge toward the woman.

'Nessa, no!' Bastian shouts, but the male windborne takes his momentary distraction and uses it. He suffers a deep cut to his leg and is blasted away by a torrent of wind, flipping through the air like a ragdoll.

Bastian lands hard in the mud, motionless, even though the blue of his stasis token hasn't flashed.

Gods. I hope he's okay, but there's no time to worry.

The female windborne senses me coming, whirling to face me with inhuman speed. Her elemental turns from Typhon, rushing to protect its primal.

I throw my rapier toward her as a distraction, then dive.

The only thing that saves me is how pathetic she must think the attempted attack is. Instead of dodging, she only stands there, head tilted as if puzzled.

But I manage to land with one hand clasped around her ankle, drawing out her essence. Power floods into me. More than I've ever felt. So much I think I might burst from the rush of it.

The windborne screams, a sound of genuine pain and surprise that buckles her knees and makes her fall to the ground. Her elemental hisses as Typhon catches it, pinning it to the ground before it can reach me.

I claw my way up the windborne's body, mounting her as I grip her tighter, urging her power into myself in a mind-numbing rush.

'What are you doing to me?' she gasps, struggling against my grip. 'Stop!'

I don't stop. I can't. The power flowing into me is intoxicating, filling me with strength I've never known. I pull harder, drawing more and more of her essence into myself.

Above us, the sky darkens rapidly, clouds gathering and swirling in an unnatural pattern. A deep rumble of thunder vibrates through the air, followed by the sharp crack of lightning that illuminates the battlefield in stark white.

I feel her reaching for a hidden blade in her armor. By instinct, I know I need to act now or I'll die. The power flooding me reacts before I can form a coherent thought. The air around the woman's head responds to my fear and alarm, pressing inward.

With so much air essence in my body, it feels like nothing more than a magical flinch – a reflexive tensing of the muscles. But I've never wielded so much power before, and the air essence gushes from me, enhancing the attack.

Warm liquid splatters my face, hands, and arms.

I flinch from the sudden splash, eyes blinking as I struggle to understand what I'm looking at.

Her head . . . it's a red ruin.

Dead. No stasis token. Just . . . dead.

'Oh, gods,' I breathe as I stumble back, face and hands covered in droplets of blood. Horror washes over me as I realize what I've done. I've killed her. Actually killed her.

Lightning cracks again, followed immediately by a thunderous boom that seems to echo my shock. The sky opens up, releasing a torrential downpour that washes over the battlefield, mixing with the blood at my feet.

A scream of rage tears through the air. The second windborne has seen his partner fall. He abandons his fight with Raith, rushing toward me with murder in his eyes.

I can't move. I can't process what's just happened. The dead windborne lies at my feet. Her blood covers me, staining me with the visceral knowledge of what I've just done.

Rain sluices over me, somehow failing to clean the blood from my hands as I stare at what I've done. My hands tremble, my vision blurring at the edges. Too much power. I've drawn in too much.

'You'll pay for that with your life,' the male windborne hisses, his voice cutting through the storm.

I only have moments left.

Before he can reach me, Typhon's roar shatters the air – not the sound of a mere elemental but the primal scream of an ancient being whose patience has finally snapped.

The ancient water dragon abandons all pretense of restraint. His form swells, blue magic drifting from his body like steam as his scales gleam brighter with blue-white intensity. His wings extend to their full span, casting shadows even through the downpour.

'ENOUGH!' Typhon's voice thunders aloud for all to hear. *'YOU WILL NOT TOUCH HER.'*

Lightning splits the sky as Typhon launches himself at the windborne's elemental. Not the careful, measured combat of before, but an unleashing of raw, ancient power. Water magic explodes from his jaws in a torrent that would put a hurricane to shame, cutting through the air elemental like a blade through mist.

The attack makes the windborne turn and take notice, forgetting me as his elemental fights for survival.

The elemental tries to reform, but Typhon doesn't give it a chance. He gathers his massive body, then slams down with such force that the ground shudders. Water essence radiates outward in concentric rings, disrupting the very magic that holds the elemental together.

The windborne falters, clearly shocked at facing the unrestrained might of an ancient. His elemental dissolves completely under Typhon's assault, wisps of air magic scattering in the wind.

'Impossible,' the windborne breathes, backing away.

Typhon's answer is another devastating attack, his claws slashing through air and rain to pin the windborne to the mud. The assassin uses some kind of air magic to free himself, barely dragging himself out of Typhon's grip. But Typhon is prowling toward him, deadly and terrible.

As Typhon holds the windborne's attention, I see Raith's form materializing through the rain. His eyes catch the lightning as he moves with predator's silence behind the distracted windborne. In one smooth motion, he draws his blade across the assassin's throat.

Blood mingles with the rain as the windborne's body goes limp. Again, no stasis. Just death.

I feel relief, but it's only temporary.

The power I've drawn is too much, burning through me like wildfire. My legs give way beneath me as my vision narrows to pinpricks.

'Nessa!' Raith's voice reaches me as if from underwater.

I sense Raith rushing toward me.

Typhon's massive form curls protectively above me, sheltering me from the rain.

Lightning flashes once more, illuminating the battlefield in stark relief. Thunder crashes so loudly it seems to shake the world itself.

Then darkness swallows me whole as I collapse into the mud.

Through the tether, I feel Raith's panic as my consciousness fades.

'Nessa!' His voice sounds so far away, drowned out by the pounding rain and rumbling thunder. And then nothing.

Chapter 40

Raith

'Nessa!'

I watch her collapse into the mud, her body crumpling like a marionette with cut strings. Through our tether, I feel her consciousness slip away – not the sudden flash of stasis, but something deeper, more dangerous. A void where her vibrant presence should be.

The windborne's body lies motionless beside her, throat cut clean through, his blood mixing with the rain and mud. A necessary death. One I don't regret.

Typhon shudders, his massive form retracting slightly as the strain of unleashing his true power takes its toll. Blue essence still leaks from wounds across his scales, but the ancient water dragon curls protectively around Nessa's unconscious form, wings forming a canopy against the relentless downpour. His teeth are bared and sapphire magic seeps from between them, as if warning off any who would dare get close.

'*She draws too deep,*' Typhon's voice resonates directly in my mind, surprising me. We've never communicated directly before. '*The essence she took from the windborne . . . it overwhelms her.*'

I drop to my knees beside her, pressing my fingers to her throat. Her pulse flutters erratically beneath my touch, too fast and too weak. 'What can I do?' I demand, looking up at the ancient dragon.

'*End the Crucible,*' Typhon replies, his massive head lowering until one blue eye is level with mine. '*The ceremonial blade. If you claim it, this ends. She will be weak for a time. Vulnerable. End this, Raith Hollow. It's the only way to protect her.*'

I hesitate, torn between staying at her side and the knowledge that Typhon is right. Every second the Crucible continues puts her at greater risk. *'Do you have the strength to guard her while I'm gone?'*

Typhon's head draws back slightly, a flash of indignation crossing his ancient features. *'With my last breath,'* he rumbles. *'She is my tethered. Mine to protect. But if this Crucible continues for too long, I fear more of the windborne will come. You must end it. Now.'*

I nod, trusting the ancient's word despite everything. 'Keep her safe.'

Movement makes me draw my sword in an instant, fire flaring in my free hand. I lower my weapon when I realize who it is.

Bastian is struggling to his feet, pristine uniform now filthy and covered in a combination of blood and mud. He is dragging himself toward us, face contorted in pain. 'You have to go,' he says through his teeth.

'And leave you alone with her? Not a fucking chance.'

'Then trigger my stasis. But go, Hollow. And know this. The other legacies aren't following orders. You won't only face a pair of two down there. They're working together, guarding the quarry from all sides. You'll have to fight your way through quickly and reach the blade before the others get to you. The blade is enchanted. Touch it and you'll be teleported back to Confluence along with everyone else who lives. Touch it, and this all ends.'

I nod my head, considering if I want to stab him and trigger his stasis token, removing the possibility of a threat to Nessa. Behind him, his air elemental stands in the rain, leaking white mist from numerous wounds. Wounds it suffered trying to save us from the windborne.

'Dammit,' I say, reaching a hand out to help him to his feet.

Bastian takes it, stands, and winces as fresh blood oozes from a deep wound on his thigh. 'Hollow. There's one more thing. The ceremonial blade has a reputation. The one who claims it never survives to graduation.'

'Thanks for the warning,' I say, walking past him into the pouring rain as thunder booms overhead. 'If anything happens to Nessa while I'm gone, I'm holding you personally responsible.'

I look back toward the group of fallen allies and enemies once before heading deeper into the forest. Bodies coated in blue litter the area like fallen leaves. It'll be up to Typhon and Bastian to keep all of them safe if any stragglers from Malakai's group arrive. But Typhon was right. The real threat is letting this thing go on – risking the arrival of more windborne.

A flash of lightning illuminates Typhon's massive form as he mantles his wings over Nessa, sheltering her from the storm. His eyes meet mine across the clearing and he gives a deep nod.

I turn and head for the quarry, sprinting through the forest. The layout of the Crucible grounds is etched into my memory from hours of scouting the area over the last several weeks. Even through the darkness and downpour, I navigate with precision, aware that every second counts.

The lightning seems to intensify as I approach the quarry, each flash burning afterimages into my eyes. Thunder rolls continuously overhead, as if the sky itself reflects the chaos below.

Through our tether, I can still feel Nessa, though her presence is faint, flickering like a candle in a windstorm. *Hold on,* I think desperately, hoping some part of her can hear me. *I'm coming. I'm ending this.*

The quarry appears ahead, a massive gash in the earth illuminated by braziers that somehow remain lit despite the storm. Stone steps descend into the pit where, on a central dais, glints the ceremonial blade.

Lightning splits the sky overhead, giving me a momentary glimpse of the legacy defenders. Two groups. The larger of the two is at the northern entrance to the quarry. It's the easiest way in. The most likely point of attack.

But a smaller group of three stands directly in front of the dais, guarding it in case anyone is brave or stupid enough to attempt to climb down the sheer cliff face. I'll face the three, then. I notice

Kienna at their head, a tall air affinity with a reputation for vicious-ness. Her wind wolf prowls the grounds, lurking with predatory intent.

I don't have time to hesitate or think of a better way. Every second this goes on is another chance for more windborne to be summoned.

I kick one leg over the cliff face and begin climbing down, stone and mud slick against my fingers. I squeeze tight, digging my toes into anything I can find for purchase as I descend at a reckless pace. Once I'm ten feet from the bottom, I let go, landing with a splash in the mud, forearms burning from exertion.

'Hollow,' Kienna calls when she spots me, voice carrying over the storm. 'We were wondering if anyone would make it this far.' Her eyes narrow. 'Where's the rest of your team?'

'Get the fuck out of my way or get ready to fight,' I call, drawing my sword as I take long strides toward the group of three.

She laughs, the sound brittle against the thunder. 'Alone? Against the three of us?' She gestures to her companions – an earth, and a water – all legacies, all more well-trained and powerful than any students I've faced yet. But compared to the windborne, they're nothing.

'Last chance.' I climb the steps toward the dais, feeling Pyrin's heat intensify beside me. 'Step aside, or I go through you.'

'The arrogance of a fire,' Kienna sneers. 'Come then, if you're in such a hurry to die.'

I don't wait for her to finish. I launch forward, channeling fire essence into my blade until it glows white-hot. Rain hisses into steam as it touches the metal.

The first legacy – the water – barely has time to raise his weapon before my sword cleaves through his guard. He crumples as his stasis token flares blue.

Kienna's eyes widen slightly, recalculating. She signals to the earth and they move to flank me, Kienna on one side and the earth on the other.

Under normal circumstances, I might appreciate their coordination and calm performance under pressure. But with Nessa's life hanging in the balance, I see only obstacles to be removed.

The earth legacy strikes first, summoning a spike of stone from the ground beneath my feet. I sidestep, only to meet Kienna's blade as it arcs toward my throat. I parry, the impact sending ripples of pain through my already overtaxed muscles.

Pyrin roars, engaging the legacies' elementals to keep them from overwhelming me. Through our connection, I can feel his strain, his essence depleting with each passing second.

'You're good,' Kienna admits as she closes in, her air magic swirling around her in visible currents. 'But you're also exhausted. How long can you last?'

Not long, if I'm honest. The Crucible has already pushed me to my limits, and I can feel my reserves of both physical and magical strength waning. But I don't need to last long. I just need to reach that blade.

I feint toward the earth legacy, then pivot at the last second, driving my shoulder into his chest. He stumbles back, momentarily breaking their formation. I capitalize on the opening, sliding between them toward the dais.

I know touching the blade will end this. All I need to do is get my hands on it.

Kienna reacts instantly, conjuring a wall of compressed air that slams into me like a battering ram. I fly backward, crashing into the stone steps with enough force to drive the breath from my lungs.

Pain lances through my ribs – broken, probably – but I push to my feet, ignoring it. Through our tether, I can feel Nessa's presence growing dimmer. She's slipping away.

No. Not like this. Not after everything.

Something shifts inside me, like a dam breaking. I've spent years controlling my power, leashing it, hiding what I'm truly capable of. But there's no point in restraint anymore. Not when Nessa's life hangs in the balance.

I draw on my fire essence, all of it, letting it flood through my veins like liquid heat. Fire erupts across my skin, dancing over my arms and chest despite the downpour. The rain evaporates before it can touch me, creating a cocoon of steam.

The legacies take an instinctive step back, eyes widening at the display.

Kienna scoffs. 'You think a light show intimidates us, Hollow? We're legacies. We've trained our entire lives for this.'

'So have I,' I reply simply.

What follows isn't a fight so much as a calculated destruction. I move with singular purpose, each strike precise, each step bringing me closer to the dais. The earth tries to circle me, but I rush him, flames exploding from me like wings that extend and wrap in behind him, forcing him closer into the blaze of my power.

He flinches, trying to raise earth to protect himself, but my sword is faster. It cuts through the stone and his guard in a single blow, triggering his stasis and leaving me alone with Kienna.

She catches me with a blade to the back of my thigh, but I barely feel it as I whirl to face her. Through the tether, Nessa's presence has grown so faint it's like trying to hear a whisper in a hurricane.

Pyrin bellows in rage, his form swelling with my unleashed power, flames consuming Kienna's air elemental in a rush of hissing steam.

Kienna backs up the steps, her eyes hard but not without a flicker of fear. A hint of desperation touches her words. 'You know it's cursed, don't you? Take that blade, and you'll die before graduation. It's how it always goes.'

'I've been cursed my whole fucking life,' I reply, advancing on her.

Her air magic condenses around her blade, extending its reach to twice its normal length. It slices toward me in a glittering arc, faster than most eyes could track.

But I see it. I've been training for this moment since I was old enough to hold a weapon. I sidestep, pivoting inside her guard, and drive my elbow into her sternum with enough force to lift her off her feet. My free hand sprays an inferno of fire across her body. I see the blue light flash through the flames and cut off the spell.

The quarry falls silent except for the relentless drumming of rain and the distant rumble of thunder. Magical flames still burn in several areas, hissing and refusing to dim despite the rain.

I turn to the dais where the ceremonial blade awaits – a simple thing, really, for all the blood spilled over it. A length of polished steel with an Empire crest on the hilt.

I climb the steps, each movement a fresh agony for my battered body. My hand closes around the hilt, and I feel a pulse of ancient magic respond to my touch.

The moment I lift it from its resting place, the world around me erupts in blinding light. Magic surges, disorienting and powerful. When my vision clears, I'm standing in the central courtyard of Confluence Academy, the ceremonial blade still clutched in my hand.

One by one, I see the air distort and twist as other students appear around me. The stasis has lifted, and they're all disoriented, straining to get back to their feet or staring wide-eyed at the courtyard in confusion.

The Crucible is over.

Instructors move among the students, cataloging survivors, treating the wounded. There will be questions about the dead windborne, about what happened in the forest, but those can wait.

Only one thing matters.

'Nessa,' I rasp, desperately scanning the courtyard for her. 'Where is she?'

I push through the crowd, ignoring the thick-voiced congratulations, the hands that reach for me, the voices calling my name. Through our tether, I can still feel her, but it's weak, dangerously so.

And then I see her.

She's lying on her side and Typhon hovers over her in his flying fish form. The disguise is probably useless, though, as I'm fairly sure half the school saw him raging as a massive dragon during the Crucible.

I drop to my knees beside her, reaching for her hand. It's cold, too cold.

I gather her into my arms, cradling her against my chest. 'Nessa,' I whisper, pressing my forehead to hers. 'Come back to me. Please.'

Our tether pulses faintly, a fragile thread connecting us. I pour everything I have into it – my strength, my heat, my essence. If I could trade places with her, I would do it in a heartbeat.

'Take what you need,' I tell her, knowing that somewhere, somehow, she can hear me. 'Take all of it.'

For a terrifying moment, nothing happens. Then I feel it – a subtle shift, a drawing sensation as her unbound nature responds to my offering. Fire essence flows from me into her, guided by our connection. Before going for the blade, she was too weak to take anything. Now she's at least taking scraps – magical sips of my power that begin slowly and grow more desperate with each passing second.

I give and give until I'm lightheaded, until Pyrin whines in alarm.

Her eyelids flutter, a soft sigh escaping her lips. The tether between us strengthens, vibrating with renewed life.

'Raith?' she murmurs, eyes still closed.

'I'm here,' I tell her, relief making my voice crack. 'I've got you.'

'So much power,' she whispers. 'Too much.'

'I know. But you're stronger than it is. You control it, remember? Not the other way around. Focus on me,' I say, guiding her face toward mine. 'Just me.'

Her eyes finally open, finding mine with effort. 'Did you . . . get the blade?'

A laugh escapes me, half relief and half disbelief. 'Yes. The Crucible is over. We won.'

'We won,' she echoes, a ghost of a smile touching her lips before her eyes close again, this time in simple exhaustion rather than dangerous unconsciousness.

I lift her carefully, mindful of her injuries and the strain her body has undergone. 'I'm taking her to the healer,' I tell Cade, who found me and waited silently with the other fires.

As I carry her through the parting crowd, I hear the whispers and see the stares. Most will know about Typhon now. They'll know Nessa

Thorne is tethered to the most powerful elemental on campus. Some may even suspect she's no simple water affinity. They'll talk about how she took on Malakai and Serena and won.

I see Beck, Mireen, Ambrose, and Brunhild all gathered. They give me a nod of thanks and acknowledgment as I carry Nessa away. Brunhild and Beck even help move some gawking students out of our path.

Whatever comes next, I think Nessa's days of being underestimated are over. But none of it matters right now.

The only thing that matters is the woman in my arms and the quiet miracle of her survival.

Rector Voss watches from the edge of the courtyard. Waiting.

I think of the stasis tokens and the lives they saved. The countless students who survived because of the deal Nessa struck. The fucking deal that means Voss is still expecting to take her to those ruins.

But not tonight. Tonight, she needs to rest.

I press a kiss to her forehead, feeling her unconsciously lean into my touch. 'You're safe now,' I murmur, not caring who hears. 'I've got you, Nessa. I've got you.'

Chapter 41

I wake to sunlight filtering through familiar windows. *My windows.*

The sun means the Crucible must be over. The storm has passed. But how?

The room is cool and quiet, the scent of healing herbs lingering in the air. My body feels distant, as if I'm floating slightly above it – the aftermath of drawing too much essence, of pushing my unbound nature beyond what it could safely contain.

Memories flood back in disjointed fragments. The Crucible. The storm. Killing the windborne. Collapsing as Typhon roared his defiance. Raith . . .

'Raith,' I whisper, my throat raw. I reach for our tether, finding it present but strangely muted, like a voice heard through thick glass.

'Nessa!' Mireen's face appears above me, her copper-red hair falling loose around her shoulders. Relief floods her features. 'Thank the elements. You've been out for days. Good thing we already had practice with the whole routine of keeping an eye on you while unconscious.'

I try to sit up, wincing as my muscles protest. 'Days?'

'Easy,' she says, placing a gentle hand on my shoulder. 'The healers said you nearly burned yourself out. Whatever you did in the forest . . . it was too much. But on the bright side, I had a lot of fun practicing a eulogy for you. And no, I won't tell you what was in it. I'm still saving it in case you decide to croak in the near future.'

Typhon materializes beside the bed, his flying fish form diminished to nearly half its usual size. *'The angry human lives,'* he says in my mind, but there's no hiding his relief. *'I told them you would survive, but they insisted on fussing anyway.'*

'Where are the others?' I ask, scanning the room.

'Beck and Ambrose are fine,' Mireen says. 'Brunhild too. They've been taking shifts watching over you. *Again,*' she adds with a grin. 'You're quite the celebrity now, you know. Everyone saw Typhon in his true form. They're calling you the Dragon Tamer.'

I groan, letting my head fall back against the pillow. 'Wonderful.'

'It's not all bad,' she continues, pouring water from a crystal pitcher. 'I think people are going to think twice before crossing you now. Malakai's alliance has completely fractured – most of them are distancing themselves from him and Serena as fast as they can.'

I take the offered water, drinking deeply. 'What about Raith? Where is he?'

Mireen's expression falls, and my heart drops along with it. 'He . . .' she hesitates. 'He got you back safely, but he was pretty badly injured. Collapsed right after getting you to the healers.'

Ice floods my veins as I bolt upright, ignoring the pain. 'What? Where is he now?'

'The healers are taking care of him,' she says, but there's uncertainty in her voice. 'They wouldn't let any of us see him, not even the fires. Voss was personally looking over him apparently and keeping people away for Raith's safety.'

I throw back the covers, swinging my legs over the edge of the bed. 'I need to see him.'

'Nessa, wait – you're still weak.'

'I don't care.' The tether between us pulses, but it's so faint, so distant. Fear claws at my throat. 'Something's wrong, Mireen. I can feel it.'

The door opens before Mireen can respond. Rector Voss enters, silver hair immaculate as always, his face a careful mask of concern.

'Miss Thorne,' he says, inclining his head. 'It's good to see you awake. How are you feeling?'

'Where's Raith?' I demand, ignoring his question.

Voss's expression softens. 'Mr. Hollow's condition is . . . complex. His injuries were severe.'

'I want to see him.'

'Of course,' Voss says, surprising me with his easy acquiescence. 'That's why I'm here. I thought you might want to see him as soon as you woke up.'

'Rector,' Mireen begins, 'the healers said she shouldn't—'

'It will be fine,' Voss interrupts gently. 'I'll personally ensure Miss Thorne's safety.'

I do not trust him, angry human, Typhon warns in my mind.

I glance at him, noting the tension in his small form, but my concern for Raith overrides all else.

'Let's go,' I say, pushing myself to my feet.

Mireen looks unhappy but doesn't argue further. 'I'll tell the others you're awake,' she says, squeezing my hand before stepping back.

Voss guides me from the room, his pace slow to accommodate my still-weak legs. Even this small exertion leaves me breathless, but I push on, focusing on the faint pulse of our tether.

'Raith was quite the hero,' Voss remarks as we walk. 'Claiming the ceremonial blade, ending the Crucible. He and the others in his team have been granted legacy status, as promised.'

I barely hear him. My fear for Raith pounds in my head like a deafening heartbeat. Raith Aurenciel. Heir to the Red Kingdom throne. The man I foolishly gave my heart and my oath to. But gods. If anything happens to him . . .

'The Empire Council was most displeased,' Voss continues. 'They had . . . other plans for the Crucible this year. I'm afraid they won't be able to remove me as easily as they hoped. But I imagine they'll be quite surprised by how events play out. Perhaps even happy.'

We reach a door I've never seen before, tucked away in a rarely-used corridor of the academy. Voss produces a key, ornate and clearly ancient, and unlocks it.

'Mr. Hollow is just through here,' he says, gesturing for me to enter.

The room beyond is small and circular, with no windows. As soon as we enter, I feel the same jarring sensation I've come to know as teleportation. The world condenses, spins, and then there's a *snap* sound.

Voss is still beside me as I appear in a damp and dark cave, his hands on my shoulders, steadying me.

The cave is lined with bookshelves and desks full of ancient texts and scattered papers.

'Wh-what?' I breathe, alarm pulsing in my mind.

'As I said,' Voss gestures smoothly to a blue column of light at the center of the cave. In its center, Raith floats, suspended with motes of dust and rotating slowly. There's a gash across his stomach and it's frozen in time, drops of blood suspended mid-air. 'I brought you to Raith.'

'Raith!' I rush forward, heart pounding.

I reach for him but the column feels like glass, stopping me from getting close. I pound on it, palms sliding down the magical barrier. 'Let me help him. I can heal him.'

'Yes,' Voss says, moving to stand beside me. 'That was why I brought him here. Without your healing, he would have certainly died.'

I stare at Raith. His eyes are closed and his expression is peaceful. He's shirtless, revealing numerous half-healed wounds across his chest and arms. The stasis has preserved him exactly as he was, frozen in time.

Through our tether, I sense him – distant but present, as if sleeping deeply.

'Why does he feel so far away?' I whisper.

'Feel?' Voss asks.

I shake my head. 'It's nothing. It just . . . feels wrong.'

'No, Nessa. This is exactly what you are meant for. Saving the ones you love, just like you told me.'

I study Raith's face, memorizing every line, every curve. Even in stasis, he radiates strength, determination. The man who fought his way through legacies, who claimed the blade, who carried me to safety despite his own wounds.

'What do I do?' I ask, not taking my eyes off him.

'I'll release the stasis,' Voss says. 'But you must act quickly. His injuries will resume their damage the moment he's free.'

Typhon materializes at my shoulder, his form tense with watchfulness. *Something here is wrong,* he warns in my mind.

It's Raith, I reply silently. *What choice do I have? Even if it's some sort of trick. I need to help him.*

Typhon's unease radiates through our tether, but he doesn't argue further.

'I'm ready,' I tell Voss, gathering what little essence I've managed to recover.

Voss waves his hand and the blue light flickers, then fades. Raith begins to fall forward as gravity reclaims him, and I rush to catch him, staggering under his weight. But he feels lighter than I expected, as if he's already lost so much blood that I can feel its absence.

Gods . . . Raith . . .

I lower him gently to the floor, cradling his head in my lap. Blood seeps from his wounds, his breathing shallow and labored.

'Hurry,' Voss urges, standing back.

I place my hands on Raith's chest, calling forth my healing power. It comes sluggishly, still depleted from my overextension during the Crucible, but I push harder, drawing on reserves I didn't know I had.

Warmth flows from my palms into his body. I focus on the worst injuries first – a punctured lung, internal bleeding, fractured ribs – letting my instincts guide me through the healing process.

Raith's breathing eases, color returning to his face.

'It's working,' I murmur, watching as the smaller wounds begin to close.

But something strange happens as the healing progresses. Raith's form seems to shimmer, like heat rising from summer stone. At first, I think it's my exhaustion playing tricks on my vision, but the effect intensifies.

'What's happening?' I ask, alarm rising as Raith's features begin to blur.

Voss doesn't answer, his eyes fixed on Raith with an intensity that sends chills down my spine.

Beneath my hands, Raith's body continues to shift. His shoulders narrow, his jawline softens, his hair lengthens and darkens from black to deep auburn. The scars on his face fade completely, replaced by smooth, flawless skin.

I try to pull away, but some force holds my hands in place, drawing more and more of my essence into the transformation.

When it's complete, it's no longer Raith lying in my lap, but a woman. She's breathtakingly beautiful, with high cheekbones and full lips. Her military uniform is of an unfamiliar design, its style ancient yet somehow timeless. Silver swirls mark the uniform that look nearly identical to my mark when I'm not holding the disguise.

Her eyes flutter open – silver, eyes. Older than her face, somehow.

She looks up at me with momentary confusion, then turns her head toward Voss. Recognition dawns on her face, followed by a smile of such devotion it makes my heart ache.

'Lorkan, my love,' she whispers, voice rich and melodious. 'Is that really you?'

'Milena.' He kneels beside her, taking her hand and pressing it to his lips with reverence. 'At last. It's finally time we take back what is ours.'

I scramble backward, horror and confusion warring within me. 'What . . . who . . .' I stammer, unable to form coherent thoughts. 'Where is Raith?'

Through the tether, I search desperately for him, for any trace of the connection we'd forged. But instead of the void I feared, I find him – distant but strong, his essence pulsing with life. Not weakened or diminished, but simply far away.

Lorkan turns to me, his expression almost kind. 'Raith Hollow is perfectly safe, Nessa. He never left Confluence. My unbound power is transformation. It's how the siphons take so many forms. It's how I made Milena look like Raith. She was wounded and nearly killed over a thousand years ago. But now that she's back, she can create more siphons. We can control them again. Finally.'

'You used me,' I whisper, the full weight of his deception crashing down. 'You tricked me into healing her. To helping . . . you're—'

Milena rises gracefully to her feet, her movements fluid despite centuries of stasis. 'You are unbound,' she says, studying me with open curiosity. 'Like me.' Her gaze drops to my marked hand. 'Though you hide it. Why?'

Before I can answer, the floor beneath us begins to glow, patterns of ancient runes illuminating one by one in concentric circles.

'What's happening?' I demand, feeling magic building around us.

'A necessary departure,' Lorkan says, helping Milena to steady herself. 'The ruin will collapse once the stasis chamber is fully deactivated. A failsafe I installed long ago.'

The walls tremble, dust and small stones raining down as the runes glow brighter.

'You're just leaving me here?' I back away, looking for an exit.

Lorkan regards me with what seems like genuine sympathy. 'I know this is confusing. But it's not what you imagine, Nessa.'

'Why?' I ask. 'Why all of this?'

'Because the world is broken,' Milena answers, her silver eyes burning with conviction. 'It has been since the Empire and the Red Kingdom tore it apart. Since they hunted our kind to the edge of extinction.'

'We're going to fix it,' Lorkan adds. 'And when we do, there will be a place for you among us. Among your own kind. You may think us your enemy, but know the deception was a necessary one. We are not your enemies, Nessa.'

'You certainly look like fucking enemies from where I'm standing,' I say between clenched teeth. My confusion is slowly turning to rage. Anger. Hurt.

'There are others like you, you know,' Lorkan says softly. 'I've been monitoring the various primal academies for centuries now. Both here and in the Red Kingdom. There have been several others, but none quite like you. I could take you to meet them, if you like. They are all quite eager to meet you.'

I shake my head, still feeling dazed. Confused. 'I don't want to go anywhere with you.'

His smile is sad, but he doesn't seem surprised. 'Yes. I imagined you would say that. It's because of young Aurenciel, no?'

My chest goes tight. *He knows who Raith is. How the hell does he know?*

'It's quite alright,' Lorkan continues. 'You've done me a favor I cannot begin to repay. For this, I'll allow you to see for yourself that the Aurenciels cannot be trusted – that their hatred of our kind runs through their very blood. So you may return to Confluence. You may go back to Raith. And when you've seen him for who he truly is, we will be waiting for you. Ready for you to join us.'

'Find us when you're ready,' Milena says. 'When you've seen the truth of what they are. What they've done. Find that you're not as alone as you think. We can be a family for you, Nessa. A family of those who truly understand you. Who won't fear you. Won't try to cage or use you.'

Lorkan gestures and I sense magic gathering in the air around me like prickles across my skin. I brace myself for destruction. For oblivion. When I think about what I just helped Lorkan do, part of me almost welcomes it. Part of me almost hopes I'm about to be destroyed.

The last thought in my mind before the magic hits is of Raith, of wishing we'd had more time together before it all came crashing down around us.

Chapter 42

Raith

I can't even feel the fucking tether anymore. The absence is a black void in the center of my chest, an aching awareness of what was there. *What was lost.*

He got to her. I don't know how I know it, but I do.

Voss.

I can feel it in my fucking bones.

I drag myself from the bed in the private healer's area I've been confined to. I ready myself to challenge the guards at the door, to demand release.

But I try the handle and find it's open.

Three days of confinement to this fucking room and the door is just . . . open?

I limp into the hallway, shirtless and bandaged, but knowing nothing is going to stand in my way until I find Nessa. I can feel fear, confusion, hurt, and betrayal through the tether. But it's all so faint and distant. One moment, she was resting like she has been since we returned, and the next there was so much emotion.

The thought of her being in danger and not being able to help is unbearable, a knife twisting in my gut. If anything happens, I'll tear this entire fucking academy to the ground. I'll hunt whoever took her to the ends of the earth.

Students roam the halls, all smiles and relaxed laughter as they enjoy the brief weeks off before next year's classes begin in earnest. They slow and stare as I pass, glaring at anyone who gets in my way.

Pyrin follows me, his concern mirroring my own.

She feels so godsdamned far away. But I'll find her. I don't know how. I don't know where she is. I just know I won't stop until I've found her.

I keep replaying those final moments together in her room before the Crucible. Seeing the look of hurt on her face when she learned who I really was. Feeling the slight withdrawal and the questions running through her mind. Did she really know me at all? Could she really trust me?

I tear down the stairs, ignoring the aches in my ribs, legs, and the rest of my body as the emotions Nessa feels through the tether intensify. She feels like she's in danger. Like she might be killed any moment.

I'm breathing hard, moving through the busy courtyard of Confluence when something changes.

I pause mid-step, sensing Nessa's closeness like the sun finally appearing from behind thick clouds.

I turn and see her. She's on her knees in the courtyard and students are staring. Her eyes are distant, fixed on the ground. 'Lorkan and Milena Grace are back,' she whispers.

Nearby students grin and mutter among themselves, but she says it again.

'They're back. Lorkan and Milena Grace are alive. And they're back.'

A ripple of whispers sweeps through the courtyard. Heads turn, bodies shift.

It takes a few moments before my brain processes what I'm seeing.

She's alive. She's here. Relief floods through me, so intense I nearly stumble.

I'm running toward Nessa, wanting nothing more than to pull her into my arms where I can protect her. Where I can put my hands on her and make sure she's real.

I sense her confusion, her fear. And something else – a darkness, a horror that wasn't there before. *What happened to her? Where has she been?*

Nessa's voice is faint, but clear enough that there's no mistaking the words.

'Lorkan Grace is alive.' She keeps saying it, and the words finally register.

The name hits me like a physical blow, and I feel my body go cold. Lorkan Grace. Milena Grace. The monsters responsible for siphons. The man responsible for the death of my entire family. The name whispered like a curse by those with the misfortune to know his sins.

The siphons were proof enough of his survival, but the way Nessa says it. The fear and twisted bundle of emotions in her mind when she speaks his name . . . she doesn't just know he's alive because she saw his creatures. She knows because she saw him.

I shove my way through the rest of the crowd, my hands finding Nessa's shoulders as I take her into my arms. I steady her as she sways on her feet. Up close, I can see the exhaustion in her eyes, the way her body trembles with fatigue.

'Where were you?' I demand, fighting to keep my voice level. 'I thought—' I cut myself off, eyes scanning her blood-covered form. 'Are you hurt?'

She shakes her head, her eyes never leaving mine. 'Voss,' she whispers. 'Voss is Lorkan Grace.'

The world stops spinning. Everything freezes.

Voss. The Rector of Confluence Academy. The greatest monster in our history has been here all along.

Rage rips through me, hot and violent.

I let her be alone with him in his office. I ignored my instincts and let her trust him.

The urge to find him, to kill him, is nearly overwhelming. I grip Nessa's shoulders tighter, trying to anchor myself to her rather than the murderous fury burning through my veins.

'He took you,' I say, the realization dawning. 'Come on. Not here,' I take her hand and lead her from the courtyard and the gathering crowd watching us.

There's an explosion of whispered gossip and glances our way, but none are foolish enough to try to follow.

I take Nessa carefully and lead her from the courtyard, eyes alert as I scan every shadow for danger. Through our tether, I send her every ounce of reassurance I can muster. I'll protect you. Whatever Lorkan and Milena Grace are planning, they'll have to go through me to get to you.

But beneath these thoughts, a subtle doubt takes root. Nessa was with him. She came back unharmed. What did he tell her? What did he show her?

I know our family history. I know what my ancestors did to the unbound, but it's part of why I tried so hard to protect Nessa once I found out what she was. To break the cycle. To change things.

But what if he poisoned her against me? Implied I was just like them? Could I even blame her if those words sank deep, shaking her ability to trust me?

We don't speak as I bring her back to her room and lay her in bed. She's covered in blood, but none of it seems to be hers. She doesn't need healing. She needs sleep.

I brush the hair from her forehead as her eyes flutter closed. She's completely exhausted. Drained beyond all reason.

And maybe that's why her final thought slips through the tether to me. But the words I hear aren't her voice. They're from Rector Voss.

'You've done me a favor I cannot begin to repay. For this, I'll allow you to see for yourself that the Aurenciels cannot be trusted – that their hatred of our kind runs through their very blood. So you may return to Confluence. You may go back to Raith. And when you've seen him for who he truly is, we will be waiting for you. Ready for you to join us.'

The blood drains from my face as I study her sleeping form.

I didn't understand how she survived an encounter with Lorkan and Milena Grace. Now I do. I know exactly why.

They've shaped Nessa into a dagger and aimed her directly for my fucking heart.

Unbound Exclusive
Bonus Chapter

The following chapter takes place during Confluence Day, giving a glimpse of Raith's perspective while Nessa was fleeing the fire wolf and meeting Typhon for the first time.

Confluence Day

Raith

Somewhere close, another student's scream is cut off in a gurgle. I don't look toward the sound. I don't even stop walking.

We tether or we die today, and I have no intentions of dying. And yet . . .

Some stupid, *stupid* part of me is wondering about her. *Worrying* about her.

It's exactly the kind of shit I should be avoiding. Attachments. Weakness. Feelings.

They're all liabilities I can't afford, not with everything I need to accomplish.

Thoughts swirl in my mind as I continue walking, boots crunching scorched grass that shifts before my eyes. Everything here moves without moving, as if the entire place is breathing. I remember my sister talking about it.

In Red Kingdom, primals are trained in three major schools, and the portal from my sister's school took her to some kind of ancient ruin within the elemental plane. But she talked about the colors. About the way the whole world seemed to shift when you weren't looking.

I'm jerked back to reality when I see a flash of orange ahead.

Fire.

I pause mid-stride, eyes locked on the spot. I have my training sword, but I let it hang limp at my side. It won't do me any good against an elemental. They aren't looking to see if we can best them in a fight.

A small hill blocks my view, but whatever I saw is moving just out of sight – the orange glow of its flames flickering and shifting across the trees.

Part of me itches to walk away. Memories of fire – the white-hot agony of burning, the smell of my own flesh and hair cooking – bubble up, unwelcome and vivid.

But I don't run. I can't. I need to fucking do this.

I clench my teeth tighter and slowly lower myself to my knees. I set my sword down beside me and place my palms on my thighs, waiting.

And then I see it rise up from behind a small hill ahead. Two yellow-orange eyes in a head of rolling flames. I see the ears, then the muscular shoulders and arms, all crafted of pure fire.

Gods. It's a panther.

Even regular panthers in our world are deadly enough, but an elemental taking a panther form would be an incredibly strong ally. My father once told me that elementals don't choose their forms. Instead, the form is a natural expression of the beast's nature.

I feel my breath coming faster, but I'm oddly calm. The whole left side of my body burns in phantom agony as I watch it stalk closer, its paws leaving prints of flame that hiss and sizzle in its wake. The beast draws closer, flames shifting in hypnotic patterns.

My heart pounds in my ears, but I stay motionless, waiting.

The elemental comes close enough that I feel the heat rolling from its body, baking my skin until the memory of my scars is almost too much to bear. But I still don't move. I don't even fucking flinch. I stare back at it as sweat rolls between my shoulder blades and down the small of my back.

It regards me with blazing eyes, each brighter than the hottest coals. I sense the intelligence in those eyes. If the flames aren't enough to show that this is no ordinary creature, the eyes are. There's knowing in them. Judgment.

Even as my body itches for distance, I don't move a muscle. Not submissive, but open. Unafraid. The elemental pauses, head tilting as if surprised to see I'm not trying to flee or even fight.

'*Speak your heart, human.*' The voice comes in my mind, fuzzy and difficult to hear, but unmistakable.

It's speaking to me. It's a start.

'Revenge,' I say simply, surprising myself with the single word response. But I can feel so much emotion filling the word that I think maybe he understands.

The panther's head lifts, fiery nostrils flaring as if it's sniffing me. '*You burn, Human. From the inside out. You burn for more than just revenge, though. You wish to protect. To find justice.*'

'I want them to pay,' I say through clenched teeth.

The panther pauses, then continues to circle me. It moves around my back, that unbearable heat following it every step of the way. When it reaches my face again, it brings its muzzle inches from my face. So close that I can see myself reflected in those burning eyes, scarred and grim.

There's a small, tired part of me that would welcome the oblivion of death. But I've been driven by promises I made to ghosts and ash for so many years. Death would mean failing them. It would mean stepping into the afterlife and having to explain why I didn't avenge them.

No. Surrender isn't an option. *Death* isn't an option.

So I stare straight into the beast's eyes without any fear. I don't move when I smell the scent of burning hair and see smoke starting to rise from my uniform.

The elemental makes a chuffing sound, filling the air with the smell of cinders. It opens its mouth, tilting its head back as it roars, giving me a glimpse of raw, open flame where a tongue and throat should be.

And I know my fate rests in the next moments. Live or die. Tether or burn.

'*You seek revenge, Human. Justice. You are a guardian who sees himself as an executioner. There is honor in this, even if you do not see it. Speak your name. Your heritage. Your past.*'

'I'm Raith Hol—' I stop myself. No. Not that name. Not for him.

'I'm Raith Aurenciel, betrayed heir to Red Kingdom. Rightful ruler of the North.' I speak the words slowly, confidently. 'Everything that has ever mattered to me is ash. Everything except my throne. My family. My home. They're gone. But there's one thing they took that I can still take back. And I fucking plan to.' My voice roughens, but I push through. 'Choose me, and we'll make them burn for what they did. Choose me and we'll fight together, or not at all.'

The panther takes a step back, but the sweat is already dripping from me in rivulets, his heat nearly unbearable. I hear a voice in my mind. It's getting clearer. Louder, but still soft as a whisper but with a raspy edge. Deep and slow.

'Protection and justice. These are causes that strengthen your kind and mine. Noble causes. They are the fuel we can burn for energy. Revenge burns those who seek it for fuel. It's a pursuit that ends where you started – a circular mission that will only bring you more ash and ruin, human.'

Some deeper part of my mind recognizes the wisdom in his words, but I'm not able to hear it. Not really. 'They're going to pay. That's all that matters.'

The beast sits on its haunches, almost as if it's mirroring my own posture. Several moments pass, and then its voice comes again in my mind.

'Then I will be your flame, Raith Aurenciel. Your weapon when justice demands it. Your shield when the innocent need protecting.' The panther's eyes bore into mine, unblinking. *'But your oath to me is this. You will seek to let the fire go. It has already burned you, and if you fail to let this rage go, it will take all you have left. I will risk my tether to you because I believe you can learn. And I believe together, we can do great things. So swear my oath, and we will take this journey as one, Raith Aurenciel.'*

The words land in my mind with more power than I would expect.

I know the cost to an elemental when its bond is broken or its human dies. This panther is taking an immense risk, and he knows it.

And yet . . . I don't see the side of me he hopes to find. I lift my eyes to his. '*There's too much rage,*' I say softly. '*I can't tell you I'll change. I can't imagine it ever calming. Every day . . . it just grows hotter.*'

'*Honesty. Honor. Bravery. I see all these things in you. I only ask you to swear you understand the cost of seeking revenge and nothing else. The cost of letting it consume you. Swear this, and it will be my risk to take.*'

I close my eyes. I do understand. And that's the problem. I want to burn it all down, and once I've done my dark work, I want to burn down with it. Once everyone has paid, I'll happily let the flames take me.

But I nod my head, feeling the wisdom of his oath even as the darkest parts of me want to rage against it. 'I swear it,' I say, the words heavy with finality. 'I know the cost of the path I'm on.'

The connection snaps into place like a key turning in a lock. Heat snakes through my veins like liquid fire, but there's no pain. Even the heat radiating from the elemental snaps off like a torch being extinguished and my sweaty skin begins to cool.

Something new blossoms deep inside me. An awareness. A knowing.

It's a sense that feels as if it was always meant to be there, and through it I feel him.

'*Pyrin,*' he says in my mind. '*I'm called Pyrin.*'

I can feel his nature through the tether. His patience but also his fierce temper when those he values are threatened or mistreated. His loyalty, but also his keen awareness and intellect. And beneath it there's something stranger still, almost like a childish curiosity. It feels innocent, despite the deep and surprising wisdom of his words.

'Pyrin,' I repeat aloud, and the elemental's tail lashes once in acknowledgment before he pads to my side, our tether hanging beyond sight like a thread of fire.

I rise to my feet, scanning the forest around me. I still hear screams in the far distance. Shouts of triumph. The terrible chaos of beasts prowling just beyond sight.

And then I see her.

It's only a glimpse as she darts between the stony trees to my left.

I see the flash of her white offering's uniform and her dark hair in its usual braids. She's running at a dead sprint as if death itself is chasing her, but I can't see what's pursuing her until . . .

Human shapes move between the thick trees like shadows. Shadows drifting in Nessa's direction.

They're following her.

I break into a jog, closing the distance quickly as Pyrin lopes beside me, easily keeping pace.

When I get closer, I recognize the leaders of the group instantly.

It's Malakai and Serena, and they're flanked by more students. Serena's newly tethered fire serpent coils at her feet while Malakai's water shark circles overhead like it is swimming through air. The others don't seem to have tethered yet, but they're all clutching weapons and looking after Nessa with murder in their eyes.

I don't need to think. I hold my sword the way my weapons masters taught me, tight but not too tightly. Loose enough that my strikes can flow and snap like whips and I can use my whole body for every attack.

And part of me revels in the opportunity. The chance to release even a small fraction of my rage on them. To vent some of the flames that burn so fucking hot.

'Are your skills in counting underdeveloped, Forgotten King of the Red Kingdom? I count seven of them and one of you.'

'They're following her,' I say through clenched teeth.

'I see. And the man who cares about nothing but revenge is going to risk his life to stop them from doing this?'

'Shut up, Pyrin.'

Pyrin sighs in my mind, but I feel his resolution, too. Even if he thinks we're about to die, he's willing to stand by my side. And beneath it all, I feel his respect and approval. The damn cat *wants* me to do things like this.

'Malakai,' I say, projecting my voice.

All seven students and their elementals whirl to face me as I step into a clearing surrounded by trees.

'Going somewhere?' I ask.

'Nowhere that concerns you, Hollow.' Malakai says, his good eye narrowing as he looks to either side of me. 'Did you forget to bring your little followers? All I see is you and a house cat.'

Serena moves to his side. 'We could have done great things together, Raith. This was your choice.'

I look past them to the space where Nessa disappeared. Even though it makes no fucking sense, I feel overwhelming relief to know they're worrying about me now. Not her.

And maybe while they waste their breath fighting me, she will get the time she needs.

Gods willing, she'll use it to tether and get the hells out of this place before Malakai and his people find her.

I let my sword hang low with one hand and call fire with my other. One of the water affinities seems eager to prove himself, rushing to meet me with a two-handed axe raised high.

He runs in yelling like an idiot, so I step to the side, wrist flicking as I catch him in the stomach with my sword. Training blade or not, his momentum and my speed do the job, bringing him down as his shout cuts off abruptly.

His body lands hard, skidding a few feet before coming to a stop.

'Next?' I say.

Pyrin prowls in front of me, and through the tether, I feel his resolution to die fighting by my side here in this clearing.

'You're not so bad, cat,' I say quietly.

'*I'm happy to have the approval of a dead man, human,*' Pyrin replies.

And then they charge us.

Read on for a sneak peak . . . .

Unveiled
CONFLUENCE ACADEMY BOOK TWO

Chapter 1

'How many people did you kill in your first year?'

The question hangs in the air, spoken by a first-year water aspirant whose name I've already forgotten. Twenty pairs of wide eyes fix on me, waiting. These students survived their elemental trial just hours ago, still wearing the stunned expressions of those who've faced death and somehow stumbled away alive.

The question sparks a vivid image in my mind.

Kneeling over the windborne woman with her power flooding me. Watching her head explode and feeling the warm spatter of her blood mingling with the rain on my face. The crack of thunder overhead and the terror beating in my chest.

I blink, reminding myself where I am to wash away the memory.

I breathe in the summer air on the wind that carries a faint scent of flowers and the distant pines beyond the walls of Confluence. I look over the high wall we're standing on at the fields outside campus – fields that are already filling with hundreds upon hundreds of Empire carriages.

Each of those carriages carries an offering. I watch them emerge, dirty, confused, and scared. I see them being herded into groups. A year ago, I was down there, feeling what they feel.

A year ago, I had no fucking idea what was in store for me. I grin to myself. I suppose I could say the same right now.

'Well?' the boy presses, reminding me of his idiotic question.

A flame of rage lights in my stomach. I turn my gaze to him. 'How many people did I kill?' I repeat. 'As many as it took to protect the people I cared about. No more, and no less.' I let my words linger, scanning my eyes across the group. Maybe some part of me wants to reassure them, but I can't bring myself to. They're about to face a nightmare, and there's no point lying to them about it. 'This place wants to strip away your humanity. Turn you into a weapon for someone else to wield. The question you should be asking is how to stay sane. How to stay who you are.'

These aspirants I'm guiding now were part of the morning batch, the first to survive the trial. They've been issued uniforms and are being assigned quarters while the next group faces the elementals. Just as it happened when I arrived a year ago – an efficient machine designed to process and test hundreds in a single day. The only difference is that I arrived after the legacies and aspirants were processed last year. This year, we're all given jobs to help lead them to the right places.

'*Evasive response,*' Typhon observes, materializing beside me in his flying fish disguise. He hovers at my shoulder, scales gleaming with iridescent blue in the morning light. '*But clever. Better to let them think you massacred scores of fellow students than admit you only truly killed one windborne.*'

'We both know that wasn't my intention.'

Amusement passes to me through our tether. Typhon is, in the most respectful terms possible, a bit of a bitch. He loves nothing more than pushing my buttons.

'*A bit of a bitch . . .*' he muses. '*Others would call me first of my name. Lord of the tides. Rightful heir to the water throne. And yet you—*'

'Is it true you tethered an ancient elemental? A water dragon?' a girl asks as we continue toward the water tower.

Typhon continues raging on in my mind, but I've become pretty good at tuning him out when I want to.

When I ignore her, the students begin talking among themselves.

'I heard she faced an entire squadron of windborne and lived.'

'I heard Lorkan and Milena Grace were with the windborne. Her dragon fought all of them off.'

'That's bullshit. No first-year is going to survive facing a windborne.

My uncle trained with one of them. Said the woman was a fucking demon.'

'Yeah, well—'

I try to ignore their gossip. Try not to let more images come back to my mind, bitter and unwelcome. But the memory of healing Milena Grace comes anyway. The damp ruin where Lorkan tricked me. Where I stupidly helped the most dangerous unbound in our world's history revive his greatest ally.

'*It was a clever deception,*' Typhon says in my mind. '*You can be forgiven for falling for it, even if I saw through it the entire time.*'

'*You did no such thing.*'

'*I prefer to let my humans make their own mistakes. A learning experience, as your kind call it.*'

I grin to myself, then turn to face the aspirants, expression suddenly stern. They all seem so young already. So foolish. So . . .

'*Screwed?*' Typhon asks.

'*Yeah, kind of.*'

'You should all focus on what matters,' I say, silencing them as we pause in front of the water tower. 'Surviving. It's going to take everything you have just to live through this coming year. Worrying about stupid rumors is only going to distract you.'

A girl raises her hand – actually raises her hand.

I suppress a sigh, pointing at her. 'Yes?'

'Are we allowed to . . . well . . . sleep with other students?'

There are some smiles among the group at her question.

'You're allowed to do whatever the hells you want here. The only rule is you can't leave. You're students of Confluence, now, and you either leave in a body bag or as graduates of your fifth year. As primals.'

I see a few students swallowing visibly and looking around. It's not new information, but maybe my delivery was a bit . . .

'*Intense,*' Typhon suggests. '*It's good. Let them fear you. Nessa Thorne. Tamer of dragons. Resurrector of ancient enemies of human-kind. Lover of the fire-touched, who currently—*'

'*Typhon?*'

'*Yes, angry human?*'

'*Shut up.*'

I finish leading the latest group of aspirants to their rooms. They, at least, aren't offerings. They get to room alone, and they'll have at least some semblance of protection from instructors. Instead of being not-so-subtly encouraged to kill one another, they'll be led to believe the academy would rather they don't.

Small victories.

I stop in front of a mirror in the hallway once I've dropped off the last new student. I check my uniform, fixing a place where the fabric folded over from the wind on top of the walls. The black fabric is otherwise immaculate, silver trim gleaming at the cuffs and collar. No longer an offering or even a simple aspirant. Now I'm a second-year, a survivor of the Crucible, and my status is marked by two gold bars on my collar. Second year.

Survivor.

Something I never expected to be.

My dark hair is pulled into a tight braid because wearing your hair loose is a liability. I wear it so there's nothing for my enemies to grab. Nothing to give them an edge. My posture is upright and my shoulders are back naturally, a benefit of hard training day after day for an entire year. And my eyes . . . they were once blue, but they're drifting toward silver now. Not the white of an air affinity and not the deep, ocean blue of water affinities. Something else.

When people ask, I tell them it's because I bound Typhon. Mostly, though, people are too afraid to ask me or talk to me. Stories from the Crucible have circulated heavily in the months since. Months . . . it's hard to believe it has been that long since I've seen Raith or any of the other second-year legacies, too. They were taken on a secret legacy-only mission by the new Rector as soon as he arrived.

All I have of Raith are those tangled, messy moments together after the Crucible and the ever-present pulse of the tether assuring me he's alive. Alive, but so, so far away. Physically and emotionally.

Everything that happened in those final days drove a wedge

between us, and the time apart only seems to be letting it sink deeper and deeper with every passing day.

'*You're scheduled to meet the new water aspirants in thirty minutes,*' Typhon reminds me, drifting around my head in his least impressive flying fish form. As an ancient, he can take several forms, and the smallest form was his first. It was also the form we agreed he should take in public to avoid drawing suspicion. Now everybody knows he's a dragon, and I think he likes using the smaller form ironically. '*Better hurry if you want to see Mireen's latest . . . project before your duties begin.*'

I suppress a groan. '*What has she done now?*'

'*You'll see.*' His tone carries a hint of mischief that makes me instantly suspicious.

The water tower is quieter than usual this morning. Most second-years, like me, have been assigned to help with the integration of new students. Those who haven't are trying to enjoy their final day of relaxation before second-year classes begin in earnest.

I make my way down the curved staircase, nodding to the few waters I pass. Some nod back with respect. Others avert their eyes, still unsure how to interact with the girl who commands an ancient water dragon.

I don't have that problem with my core group. They know exactly who I am, what I am. And against all odds, they've chosen to stand with me anyway.

I find Mireen's door slightly ajar, muffled curses, and the sound of flapping wings spilling into the hallway. I push it open to find absolute chaos.

At least a dozen small birds dart about the ceiling of her room, chirping frantically as Ollie, her water otter elemental, leaps from furniture attempting to catch them. Mireen stands in the center of the mayhem, copper-red hair falling from its braid as she waves her arms, trying to direct the birds back toward the open window.

'Just a little more to the left – no, you idiots, the *other* left!'

'What,' I say, leaning against the doorframe, 'the actual hells?'

Mireen whirls to face me, her blue eyes lighting up. 'Nessa! Perfect timing. Help me get these little bastards back out the window.'

'You know, most people would be satisfied with just one pet,' I observe, stepping fully into the room and closing the door to prevent any escapes into the hallway. 'Why do you need an entire flock?'

Last year, she started with one pet rat and ended up flooding her room with the things. Eventually, she decided the smart thing to do was slip them under doors of random legacies. The resulting panic and anger was legendary, and nobody ever traced the source back to Mireen. A few weeks ago, she mentioned she was thinking about trying to lure a bird into her room.

Now this . . .

'They're messengers,' she explains, making a whistling sound that causes half the birds to swoop toward her extended arm. They land in a fluttering line, their tiny heads tilting as they eye her expectantly. 'I've started training them. Watch.'

She whispers something to the smallest bird, a brown sparrow with white speckles on its wings, then tosses it toward the window. It shoots outside like an arrow, wings beating furiously as it vanishes into the distance.

'Messenger birds? You do realize we're not supposed to communicate with the outside world. Under punishment of death, right?'

Mireen grins, the old crescent-shaped scar at the corner of her eye crinkling. 'Sure, but it's not like I'm going to *actually* send messages. They just like having jobs. Makes them feel special. Besides, it's not against the rules for me to use them to send messages to a certain well-endowed earth affinity to arrange clandestine meetings.'

I roll my eyes, fighting a smile. After a year at Confluence, Mireen has lost none of her irreverent spirit. If anything, surviving the Crucible has only made her more determined to find moments of joy amidst the danger. It's one of the things I love most about her.

'So you and Jorvan are old news, then?' I ask.

She shrugs, sending another bird out the window with a whispered message. 'Jorvan couldn't handle me. Anyway, Ambrose thinks the

birds are a genius idea. Says if we ever need to coordinate outside the
academy walls, these little friends could be invaluable.'

I help her coax the remaining birds back to the window ledge,
my thoughts turning to the rest of our group. 'Any news from the
outside?' I ask.

Mireen wiggles her eyebrows. She has a way of getting people to
say things they shouldn't, and has been pestering the Empire guards
posted around campus for updates all summer. We'll likely get our
fill soon when classes resume, but we've been starved for updates
about what's going on.

'The guard with that silly little mustache did give me a nugget
this morning. I think he was in a good mood at the idea of pushing
around some offerings. You know the guards love us most when we
first arrive. We're not scary. *Yet*,' she adds with a wiggle of her red
brows.

'Okay,' I say, making a circular gesture to get her to the point.
'And the nugget of information?'

'Right. He said there are rumors Krusk fell a few weeks back.'
She sees the look of confusion on my face. 'A city along the border.
Years ago, it was Red Kingdom territory, but Empire took it and
has been holding it. The thing is . . . they say it didn't fall to Red
Kingdom. My little guard friend said silver flags are flying. Flags
showing a silver spiral.'

I unconsciously touch the mark on the back of my left hand. We're
all marked to show our affinity when we first arrive, and the mark
I was given was a silver spiral. Unbound. Different, deadly, feared,
and once hunted to near extinction.

I was able to disguise the mark so it looks like a water affinity
mark, though, and aside from the silver threads running through my
mark, it's a perfect disguise.

'Lorkan and Milena,' I murmur, the names sending a chill down
my spine despite the warm summer air drifting through the open
window.

Mireen nods, suddenly solemn. 'Makes sense. Right? But it sounds like they had a small army. They'd have to if they wanted to take Krusk. The place is a fortress, and there would've been primals stationed there along with soldiers.'

My insides twist.

'What do you think they're planning?' she asks. 'Conquer everything? Gods. Can you imagine?'

I shake my head, but I have a small idea of at least one of their plans. They want me. It's why I'm still breathing. They think if they leave me alive, I'll see the 'truth' about Raith eventually. That Aurenciels can't be trusted because their history is filled with atrocities committed against unbound.

I just wish Raith was here. Here so I could talk to him about all the things that have been hanging unsaid between us. And I wish part of me wasn't afraid Lorkan and Milena were right – that letting me come back here on my own would slowly poison me.

Because that same part of me understands something more clearly than I'd like: Empire and Red Kingdom will never accept someone like me. I'm a threat to them. Dangerous. Too dangerous to be allowed to live unchained, at least.

The best I can hope for if I stay here is to grow my power until I can break any chains they may try to put on me. But what then? Would I simply exist as a rogue force in Empire's army, too strong to cage but too powerful to trust?

Lorkan and Milena might offer me the only place I could ever just . . . be.

But every time I think of them, I remember the siphon that nearly killed Raith and me last year. The people responsible for making a creature as terrible as that can't possibly be people I should join. Right?

'Hey.' Mireen touches my arm, bringing me back to the present. 'You okay?'

'Fine,' I lie. I can't confide in anyone about my doubts. Raith is the only one I could even imagine talking to about them, and he's not here. He hasn't been all fucking summer. 'Just thinking about the new aspirants. I should probably get going.'

She eyes me skeptically but doesn't press. Another thing I love about her – she knows when to push and when to let things be. 'I'll see you at dinner, then? Beck wants to get everyone together, catch up before classes actually start.'

'I'll be there.' I move toward the door, pausing with my hand on the latch. 'And Mireen? Try not to adopt any more wildlife before then.'

Her laughter follows me into the hallway, bright and genuine. For a moment, I almost feel normal – just another student preparing for a new academic year. Almost.

But then I pass a group of second-years who fall silent at the sight of me, their eyes tracking my movement with a mixture of fear and fascination. The illusion shatters.

I am not normal. Maybe I never was.

The next group of aspirants are waiting in the central courtyard when I arrive, a group of twenty waters fresh from the elemental trial. They huddle together beneath the shadow of the water tower, eyes wide as they take in the massive structure with its perpetual waterfall cascading up its sides, defying gravity and common sense.

'Waters,' I call, my voice carrying across the stone courtyard with the authority that seems to come naturally, even after just one year here. 'Form a line.'

They scramble to obey, arranging themselves in a ragged formation as I approach. Their uniforms are new and pristine, not yet marked by training or battle. Some bear visible signs of the trial – minor burns, scrapes, haunted eyes that have seen death up close for the first time.

'My name is Nessa Thorne,' I tell them, pacing slowly before their line. 'I'll be showing you to your quarters and explaining the basic protocols of the water tower. You'll receive your training schedules tomorrow morning.'

A ripple of whispers passes through their ranks as they recognize my name. I ignore it, continuing my instructions about meal times and curfews, until a tall boy with sandy hair interrupts.

'Is it true?' he blurts out, immediately flushing when all eyes turn to him. 'About your elemental? That it's an ancient dragon?'

I keep my expression neutral even as Typhon's amusement bubbles through our tether. We've been going through this routine all day, and it was already old the first time. 'What's your name, aspirant?'

'Tavish,' he says, straightening his shoulders in an attempt to look confident. 'Tavish Melwood.'

'Well, Tavish Melwood,' I say, stepping closer until he has to tilt his head back slightly to maintain eye contact, 'at Confluence, it's generally considered poor form to interrupt your superiors. As for Typhon . . .' I allow a small smile. 'Usually, the only people who get to see his true form are about to get eaten. So he could show you, but it would be the last thing you ever see.'

I resume my pacing, but another voice breaks the silence.

'We made it through the trial,' a petite girl with dark braids says, her tone a bit too smug for my liking. 'That means we're safe, right? Until Confluence Day, at least.'

My laugh is sharp and without humor. 'Safe?' I stop directly in front of her, noting how she shrinks back slightly. 'Nobody at Confluence is ever safe. Nobody. The sooner you understand that, the better your chances of surviving until Confluence Day.'

Her face pales, and I almost feel bad for the harshness of my response. Almost.

'Follow me,' I say, turning toward the water tower's entrance.

Inside the water tower, the temperature drops noticeably, a perpetual cool mist hanging in the air. The new aspirants gasp as they enter the central atrium with its spiraling staircases that seem to float without support. Water flows up the walls and across the ceiling in complex patterns, forming and re-forming into beautiful shapes.

'Second-years and above occupy the fourth through sixth floors,' I explain, directing them toward the third level. 'You'll be on the third floor for your first year. Males on the east side, females on the west.

After settling the final group of aspirants into their quarters, I have an hour before I'm expected at my next assignment. I make my way back to my own room on the fifth floor, looking forward to a moment of peace before dinner.

The moment I open my door, I know something is wrong.

My room appears untouched – bed made, books stacked neatly on my desk, the small potted plant Mireen gave me still thriving on the windowsill. But the air feels disturbed, as if someone has recently been here.

Typhon materializes in his dragon form. He can't expand to his full size in the cramped room, but he still towers impressively, blue wings half raised as his long, serpentine neck extends, head swiveling and nostrils huffing with quick inhales. '*Someone was here,*' he confirms. '*Recently.*'

Adrenaline spiking, I move deeper into my room with caution, following his gaze to a small object placed at the center of my pillow. A pendant on a silver chain, the metal worked into a spiral pattern that exactly matches my hidden mark.

Beside it lies a folded piece of parchment. With trembling fingers, I unfold it to reveal an elegant script:

When you're ready to understand your true nature and potential, wear this. We will find you. -L&M

'Impossible,' I breathe, even as my pulse races. 'They can't have been here. Not inside Confluence.'

Instinctively, I pull fire from the heat in the air and incinerate the parchment in a quick rush of flame. If anyone saw this in my room . . .

'*They have allies within these walls,*' Typhon says grimly. '*We've always suspected as much.*'

I pick up the pendant, and the moment my fingers touch the metal, my disguised water mark flickers, revealing the silver spiral beneath for one terrifying second before the illusion reasserts itself. The pendant pulses with a subtle magic that calls to something deep inside me.

'What should I do with it?' I ask, fighting the peculiar urge to slip the chain around my neck.

Typhon's eyes narrow. '*Destroy it. Or at the very least, hide it where even you cannot easily reach it.*'

I know he's right. The pendant is dangerous – a direct link to Lorkan and Milena Grace. A reminder that they're watching, waiting for me to come to them. And yet . . .

I tuck it into the small box where I keep my most private possessions, unable to bring myself to destroy it. Not yet. Not when it might be the only clue to understanding what I truly am. Not when there's still doubts swirling in my mind about where my allegiances should lie.

'This changes nothing,' I tell Typhon, trying to convince myself as much as him. 'I made my choice. I'm staying here.'

He doesn't answer, but his silence speaks volumes. He can feel my own doubt and how hollow the words ring to my own ears.

I see movement from my window. A group of second-year legacies is striding into the courtyard, parting the sea of offerings still being gathered and prepared to face their elemental trial.

My heart leaps before I can stop it – a reflexive response to what I already sense through our tether.

Raith is back.

After months of nothing but ghostly emotional impressions, he's close enough that I can feel the pull of his essence, warm and vital through our connection. With it comes a tangle of emotions so complex I can't begin to unravel them.

Relief. Wariness. Longing. And beneath it all, a current of doubt that wasn't there before.

'*You'll see for yourself that the Aurenciels cannot be trusted – that their hatred of our kind runs through their very blood.*' Lorkan's words echo in my memory, unwelcome but impossible to ignore.

I lift my window for a better view, using a touch of essence to shift the water always running down the exterior of our tower out of the way. Their legacy uniforms gleam silver and gold in the afternoon sun.

And there he is.

Even from this distance, Raith is unmistakable – tallest of the group, his powerful frame moving with fluid grace despite obvious exhaustion. His dark hair is longer now, tied back from his face. The scarring on the left side of his face, once so prominent, has faded to a subtle pattern of lighter skin since I healed him after the siphon attack that nearly killed him.

Students part before him, some ducking their heads in deference, others watching with undisguised curiosity. The Aurenciel heir. The last prince of the Red Kingdom, hidden in plain sight within Empire's most elite academy. It's a secret only he and I share. A secret that still threatens to destroy the beautiful connection we formed before I knew who he really was.

As if sensing my gaze, he pauses, head tilting back to look directly up at my window. Our eyes meet across the distance, the tether between us humming with recognition.

For one breathless moment, I feel everything he feels – the weight of secrets too heavy to carry alone, the desperate need to explain, to be understood. To be trusted.

Neither of us moves. The distance between us feels both infinite and meaningless, physical space nothing compared to the gulf created by revelation and doubt.

Beneath my bed, hidden in its box, I think of the pendant from Lorkan and Milena, along with its promise to let them find me when I'm ready.

If I'm ready.

Two paths. Two possible futures. And I'm standing at the crossroads, uncertain which way to turn.

Raith's hand twitches at his side, as if he might raise it in acknowledgment. Instead, he turns away, following the other legacies into the main hall.

I should feel relieved. I'm not ready to face him – to demand explanations about his family's history with the unbound, to ask him directly if Lorkan's accusations hold any truth. But instead, watching him walk away sends a pang of loss so sharp it feels like physical pain.

I turn from the window, my hand falling to my side. Behind me, Typhon watches with ancient eyes that have seen civilizations rise and fall, hearts break and mend.

'*Whatever you decide,*' he says quietly, '*know that I am with you.*'

A small comfort, but one I cling to as I prepare to face the second year at Confluence Academy – a year that promises to be no less dangerous than the first, perhaps even more so.

Because now the threats come not just from outside, but from within. And the most dangerous enemy may be the one I've tethered to my own heart.

Stay in touch . . .

Sign up to the Penelope Bloom newsletter now
www.authorpenelopebloom.com

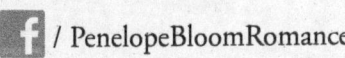 / PenelopeBloomRomance

/ @authorpenelopebloom

TikTok: @penelopebloomauthor

Enjoyed this book?
Don't forget to leave an online review!

RAISING READERS
Books Build Bright Futures

Dear Reader,

We'd love your attention for one more page to tell you about the crisis in children's reading, and what we can all do.

Studies have shown that reading for fun is the **single biggest predictor of a child's future life chances** – more than family circumstance, parents' educational background or income. It improves academic results, mental health, wealth, communication skills, ambition and happiness.[1]

The number of children reading for fun is in rapid decline. Young people have a lot of competition for their time. In 2024, 1 in 10 children and young people in the UK aged 5 to 18 did not own a single book at home.[2]

Hachette works extensively with schools, libraries and literacy charities, but here are some ways we can all raise more readers:

- Reading to children for just 10 minutes a day makes a difference
- Don't give up if children aren't regular readers – there will be books for them!
- Visit bookshops and libraries to get recommendations
- Encourage them to listen to audiobooks
- Support school libraries
- Give books as gifts

There's a lot more information about how to encourage children to read on our website: **www.RaisingReaders.co.uk**

Thank you for reading.

hachette UK

---

[1] OECD, '21st-Century Readers: Developing Literacy Skills in a Digital World', 2021, https://www.oecd.org/en/publications/21st-century-readers_a83d84cb-en.html

[2] National Literacy Trust, 'Book Ownership in 2024', November 2024, https://literacytrust.org.uk/research-services/research-reports/book-ownership-in-2024